Praise for Kevin Baker's *Dreamland*

A *New York Times* Notable Book

"One of the Best Books of the Year."

—*Los Angeles Times*

"One of the 10 Best Books of the Year."

—*Christian Science Monitor*

"One of the Best Books of the Year."

—*Virginian-Pilot and Ledger-Star*

"A wild amusement park ride. . . . Historical fiction at its most entertaining." —*New York Times Book Review*

"[One] of America's best new writers." —*Boston Herald*

"Brilliantly imagined and assiduously researched. . . . An outrageous celebration of a crueler, more innocent America . . . still holding out for Horatio Alger's impossible American dream." —*San Francisco Chronicle*

"Remarkable. . . . Original. . . . [It] mingles real and fictional characters in an American fin-de-siècle swirl."

—*Wall Street Journal*

"Pitched somewhere between the magical Brooklyn of Paul Auster and the sinister Manhattan of Caleb Carr's *The Alienist* (with a dash of Luc Sante's *Low Life* for good measure). . . . This is heady, marvelous writing . . . with a m⬛⬛⬛⬛⬛⬛⬛⬛⬛⬛⬛⬛⬛⬛⬛⬛⬛characters."

⬛⬛⬛⬛*shire Post* (UK)

"A sprawling, vigorous novel . . . with a fast-paced plot.
. . . . [Its] charm lies in its energy, its humor, and the
panoramic portrait it offers of turn-of-the-century
America. Baker has a lively social conscience and a
keen sense of the way the strong make life miserable for
the weak. . . . This novel entertains us, and it also
makes us think." —*Chicago Tribune*

"A searing and . . . magical chronicle of life in turn-of-
the-century America." —*Houston Chronicle*

"Mr. Baker's rich work provides a keen sense of historical detail, and a lively and engaging storytelling style
that makes for a thoroughly enjoyable read. A swirling,
magnificent Tilt-a-Whirl® ride. . . . An exuberant chorus of characters scrambling pell-mell to survive."
—*Dallas Morning News*

"Rich with sensual imagery, rife with well-imagined characters, and elegantly written. You never know what's
going to happen next. And the end comes too soon."
—*Seattle Weekly*

"Epic and atmospheric. . . . A distinct and fascinating
chapter in the history of America. While Baker's . . .
research and eye for detail make *Dreamland* a captivat-
ing story, it's his talent as a writer that will keep readers
enthralled. It's a literary gem, polished on all facets."
—*Denver Post*

"An engrossing odyssey. . . . As dazzling as the amusements on Coney Island. A rich tale of lost souls making their way in a confusing world."   —*Hartford Courant*

"Compelling. . . . A rich tapestry. . . . Fluid, like a dream. Baker . . . imagines us back to the days of the Triangle and the Dreamland fires, and sees possibilities in the past as well as in the future."

—*New Orleans Times-Picayune*

"Masterful and moving, this novel can transform a reader's relationship with our history."

—*Booklist* (starred review)

"A fabulous novel. . . . Vivid, roiling, and passionate. . . . [A] delirious play of fact and fiction. . . . Alive with unexpected magic, moments of grace that send shivers down the spine."   —*National Post* (Canada)

DREAMLAND

Books by Kevin Baker

DREAMLAND

KEVIN BAKER

HARPER ⬤ PERENNIAL

NEW YORK • LONDON • TORONTO • SYDNEY

HARPER ● PERENNIAL

A hardcover edition of this book was published in 1999 by HarperCollins
Publishers.

P.S.™ is a trademark of HarperCollins Publishers.

First Perennial edition published 2002.

First Harper Perennial edition published 2006.

Library of Congress Cataloging-in-Publication Data is available.

ISBN-10: 0-06-085272-0 (pbk.)
ISBN-13: 978-0-06-085272-6 (pbk.)

16 RRD 10 9

With love to Ellen—
and the rest of the *fabrente maydlakh*

DRAMATIS PERSONAE

Esther "Esse" Abramowitz, a sewing machine operator from the Lower East Side of New York City.

Moshe and Sarah Abramowitz, her parents, a rabbi and his wife.

Lazar Abramowitz, a.k.a. Gyp the Blood, a gangster.

Josef Kolyika, a.k.a. Kid Twist, a rival gangster to Gyp.

Sadie Mendelssohn, Gyp's whore.

Clara Lemlich, a seamstress and union activist.

Patrick Mahoney, Jr., a.k.a. Trick the Dwarf, a carnival performer.

The Mad Carlotta, his consort; Queen of the Little City.

Mr. Charles Murphy, the Grand Sachem of Tammany Hall.

Big Tim "Dry Dollar" Sullivan, an entrepreneur, politician, and the number two man at Tammany.

George B. McClellan, the Little Little Napoleon, figurehead mayor of New York.

Paddy Sullivan
Flat-Nose Dinny Sullivan
Florrie Sullivan
Little Tim Sullivan
Christy Sullivan
Larry Mulligan
Photo Dave Altman
Sarsaparilla Reilly

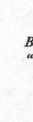

Big Tim Sullivan's "Wise Ones"

Dr. Sigmund Freud, the father of modern psychology.
Dr. Carl Jung, his protegé.

Dr. Sandor Ferenczi, their friend and colleague.

Dr. Abraham A. Brill, their American host.

Lieutenant Charles Becker, commander of one of the City's most active police strong-arm squads.

Herman "Beansy" Rosenthal, a talkative gambler.

Frances Perkins, a social worker.

Mary Dreier, a society lady.

Matthew Brinckerhoff, a genius and architect.

Elijah Poole, an electrical wizard.

Thomas Alva Edison, an inventor.

Samuel Bernstein, a garment factory general manager.

Wenke, a garment industry subcontractor.

Arnold Rothstein, a rising sportsman and gangster.

Monk Eastman, head of the Eastmans' mob.

Paul Kelly, head of the Eastmans' main rivals, the Five Pointers.

Dago Frank
Louie the Lump } *members of Gyp the Blood's*
Whitey Lewis   *Lenox Avenue Gang*

Spanish Louie, a gangster.

The Grabber, a gangster.

BOOK ONE

New York is a nine-day town.

——BIG TIM SULLIVAN

1

I know a story.

"I know a story," said Trick the Dwarf, and the rest of them leaned in close: Nanook the Esquimau, and Ota Benga the Pygmy, and Yolanda the Wild Queen of the Amazon.

"What kind of story?"

Yolanda's eyes bulged suspiciously, and it occurred to him again how she alone might actually be as advertised: tiny, leather-skinned woman with a mock feather headdress, betel nut juice dribbling out through the stumps of her teeth. A mulatto from Caracas, or a Negro Seminole woman from deep in the Okefenokee, at least.

"What kind of a story?"

He swiped at the last swathes of greasepaint around his neck and ears, and looked down the pier of the ruined park to the west before replying. *All gone now, even the brilliant white tower festooned with eagles, its beacon reaching twenty miles out to sea. Gone, gone.*

It was evening, and the lights were just going up along Surf Avenue: a million electric bulbs spinning a soft, yellow gauze over the beach and parks. The night crowd was already arriving, pouring off the New York & Sea Beach line in white trousers and dresses, white jackets and skirts and straw hats—all quickly absorbed by the glowing lights.

The City of Fire was coming to life.

He could hear the muffled fart of a tuba from the German oompah band warming up in Feltman's beer garden.

3

Beyond the garden was the Ziz coaster, hissing and undulating through the trees with the peculiar sound that gave it its name. Beyond that was the high glass trellises of Steeplechase Park, with its ubiquitous idiot's face and slogan, repeated over and over—STEEPLECHASE—FUNNY PLACE—STEEPLECHASE—FUNNY PLACE—. Beyond *that* the ocean, where a single, low-slung freighter was making for Seagate ahead of the night.

He could see even further. He could see into the past—where Piet Cronje's little Boer cottage had stood, or the Rough Riders coaster, before some fool sailed it right off the rails, sixty feet into the air over Surf Avenue. Where a whole city had stood, back beyond the ruined pier—

> Meet me tonight in Dreamland
> Under the silvery moon

Soon, he knew, the soft yellow lights would be honed by the darkness into something sharper. They would become hard and clear: fierce little pearls of fire, obliterating everything else with their brightness.

None of them now on the pier would see it, not Yolanda or Ota Benga or Nanook the Esquimau. They would be working by then, in their booths and sideshows. They would not see the lights again until they were on their way home, in the early morning; would see them only as they shut down, already faded to a fraudulent, rosy hue by the sun rising over the ocean.

> Meet me tonight in Dreamland
> Where love's sweet roses bloom
> Come with the lovelight gleaming
> In your dear eyes of blue

Meet me in Dreamland
Sweet dreamy Dreamland
There let my dreams come true

They liked to sit out on the ruined pier during the dinner hour, between the heavy action of the day and the night shows. They slumped on the rotted pilings, where once a hundred excursion boats a day had tied up, to smoke and eat, and spit and smoke and tell their stories: Ota Benga, spindly and humpbacked, no real pygmy but a tubercular piano player from Kansas City, exotic moniker lifted from an old carny sensation of the past—

In the City everything was passed down, even the names of the freaks and the gangsters—

—Nanook the Massive, Nanook the Implacable, slit-eyed hero of the north—who was in fact a woman from some extinguished Plains tribe, signed on after her old man had tried to force her into whoring at the Tin Elephant hotel along Brighton Beach.

And then there was Yolanda. Immense frog eyes still staring up at him, curved beak of a nose, skin the color and texture of a well-used saddle—

"It's a love story," Trick told her. "It's a story about love, and jealousy, and betrayal. A story about a young man, the young woman who loved him, and a terrible villain—a story about death, and destruction, and fire. It is a story about thieves and cutthroats, and one man's vision, and the poor man's burden, and the rich man's condescension.

"It is a story about Kid Twist, the gangster, and Gyp the Blood, who was a killer, and Big Tim the politician, and poor Beansy Rosenthal, who couldn't keep his mouth shut. It is a story about Sadie the whore, and the brave Esther, and the mad Carlotta, and the last summer they all came together in the great park.

"It is a story about the Great Head Doctors from Vienna,

and the rampages of beasts, and the wonders of the Modern Age. It is a story about a great city, and a little city, and a land of dreams. And always, above all, it is a story about fire."

"Ah," said Yolanda, satisfied now, leaning back and lighting up her pipe. "Ah. The usual."

2

TRICK THE DWARF

This is how you kill an elephant.

They tried the carrots first. Buckets of carrots. Whole bushelfuls of carrots, and each one loaded with enough strychnine to kill a man but only intended to make her stand still.

She ate them. She ladled them into her great, pointed maw by the dozen, and after an hour of carrots she was still standing—still looking as mad and dangerous as ever, and the big holiday crowd was growing restless.

Next they tried sending in the trainers—one-armed Captain Jack, and Herman Weedom, and even Mademoiselle Aurora, to smooth her huge, rough shoulders with their hands, and whisper into her enormous ears. She only stomped her feet and waved her trunk around their heads until they turned and ran for cover. After that they tried the police, wading in with their new blue coats and their nightsticks to clap the chains around her legs like they would slap cuffs on a pickpocket. She knocked them down like ninepins, slapped and tumbled them around the ring like vaudeville mayhem players.

Finally they sent in the pygmies—figuring, hell, that even if they weren't in the same weight class, at least it was their game. No one was sure if they had ever seen an elephant before, but they were troupers: racing around the beast, hooting and gesticulating, yelling at it in their strange heathen tongues until she was so distracted the roustabouts could slip in and knot a chain around one of her great legs.

She broke it off like a thread, but there was another one. Then another, and another, until the thick black coils of iron held each of her legs in place. Another one weighing down that deadly trunk and even her tail, until she was as completely immobilized as her tin image, the hotel down the beach. They soaked her with fire hoses, and wrapped the cables around her hide—smooth black rubber lines, bright copper wires sticking out of the ends like a bagful of eels.

Then they stepped back to see the show.

She must have known it was coming: the crowd gone still with anticipation, the workmen stepping back as quickly and gingerly as cats. For all they denied it later—claiming she was just a dumb beast, that she never knew what hit her—we could see it in her look, in those great, unblinking eyes, yellow with hatred and bile. Knowing all the while. Knowing, and hating, and staring out at me as the moving picture cameras began to roll, and the Wizard's hand went up, and I pranced out in front of the crowd.

3

TRICK THE DWARF

Call me a dreamer.

I was drinking down at the Grand Duke's Theatre that night. This was a habit of mine. It was a way I had of leaving myself behind. Whenever I found myself unable to live without beer laced with chloral hydrate, or whiskey sucked through a rubber hose; whenever I found myself unbearably lonesome for trimmers and knockout artists and dancing transvestites; for blind pigs, and block-and-fall joints; for the Hell Hole, and the Cripples' Home, and the Inferno and the Flea Bag and the Dump——then I found my way up to the watery world of the Bowery. This was my substitute for the razor, and the rope. If they but knew it, all men, some time or other, cherish the same feelings toward the abyss with me.

I was looking for a boys' bar that night. It was easy enough to find them in the City: there was at least one on Worth Street, another on Mulberry, another on Mott. I knew, from times when the urge came on me too strongly and repeatedly, and I had to change bars to keep from being found out.

I had seen what happened when others of my kind were caught trying to pass. They were not tolerant, these rough boys, for all their own misery and deprivation. I had seen them strip and beat others like me—seen them tarred, some-

9

times even mutilated, then driven into the street and exposed in all their shame, while the street boys danced gleefully around them. Sometimes I had even joined in, dancing around the howling, weeping victim. You can imagine how much that cost me, but I assure you it was necessary—if I were to stay a boy.

Besides, I had no sympathy to share with them. They must have wanted to be found out: some secret shame, some masochistic wish, as the German head doctors would say, screaming out despite everything, *I am a man in this body!*

It was easy enough *not* to get caught. All it required was a close shave, some soot to cover the lines in an aged face. Loose canvas pants belted high above the waist. An oversized jacket to hide stunted arms and legs, a big cap for the oversized head. *Voila!*—a ready-made boy.

A newsboy, a match boy. A chimney sweep, perhaps, with a dirty face. All I had to do was grab a mop from the janitor's closet, or a pile of dirty old *Daily Mirrors*, and I was the same as the rest of them: a make-believe innocent in a city of monstrous children.

You think I am to be pitied. But I ask you: what normal man ever had the opportunity I did? With a little makeup, I could not only hide my misshapen body, I could be young again. And what, after all, is the greater deformity—size or age?

All dressed up, there were plenty of places in the City where a boy could go to get a drink, and buy a woman, and get his head smashed in. My favorite was the Grand Duke's, which was run by the Baxter Street Dudes, a gang of cutpurses and cutthroats and knockout-drop artists, ages five to fourteen.

In a town that specialized in minimalist saloons, the boys' dives were the barest of all: A plank across a few crates for a bar. A couple more crates and boxes for furniture, and a dirt floor. Homemade whiskey served in an old tomato can. The Grand Duke's—typical, wishful boys' name!—was something more.

The Dudes had built themselves an actual theatre, constructed from leavings filched or salvaged off the street. There were a half-dozen oil lamps ranged across the front of the stage for footlights. Rows of plain benches served as the stalls, and on either wing of the audience there were even a pair of dilapidated, red velvet couches, elevated on slats: reserved boxes for the top boys and their ladies.

It was ten cents to sit in the stalls, just a nickel for the gallery, a high, wobbly pile of crates in the back. The Grand Duke's had a regular company of players: boy actors and boy playwrights, boy stagehands and boy set designers, and officious boy directors. I don't doubt that they would have had their own, pretentious boy critic—save for the fact they would have cut his goddamned throat.

They performed the standard fare: the goriest bits from *Lear*, or *Macbeth*, or *Richard III*. Free adaptations of the most terrible murders and sex crimes of the day, bits of song and jokes cadged from the grown-ups' vaudeville and burlesque—all of it played and received far more fervently, more avidly than anything in the regular theatres up on Fourteenth Street and Times Square.

Their favorite was *The Immigrant's Peril, or Paddy in a Poke*—that old chestnut of a stranger in a strange land. The nationality would change, but the story was always the same: our hero might be a Paddy, or an I-tie, a Jew, a German, but always a greenie, just off the boat, who goes into a bar thinking he is among friends.

Instead, they get him drunk, and drug him, while everybody there connives in how best to rob him and take his life. They all join in—the whores and the bartender, the regulars at the rail and the cop on the beat, mugging and joking outrageously with the audience. The little boys around me reeling and giggling with the suspense, gripping tightly to their tottering crates—yellow, consumptive faces peering eagerly up at the stage.

The deed would be nearly done: the Paddy or the Jew or the *Deutscher* lying facedown on the bar. A fraudulent insurance policy drawn up by the barkeep, signed by a whore, witnessed by a policeman. All that remained was to give the poor yok a little more chloral hydrate and slip him down a trapdoor chute, into the river—

That was the cue for Mose, the Bowery Boy. Nobody knew where he came from, exactly. He was as old as the Bowery itself, a stage perennial, but always, unmistakably, *one of them:* the biggest boy they could find—dressed in their clothes, speaking their language, blunt and gigantic and omnipotent, cutting through all lies and hypocrisy.

He would plunge into the murderous bar from the wings, laying about himself. Smashing up the chintzy sets, the tables and chairs and the bar, smashing the heads of the barkeep and the trimmers and the foresworn cop. Thrashing all about him until the whole audience of fellow wanting, wishing, dreaming Bowery boys was reduced to wild, frenzied cheering. Shaking the sodden immigrant awake—*rescuing* him, the way they had always wished, deep in their most murderous street-boy hearts, to be rescued, and never had been, and never would be.

I know. Many was the evening, clutching desperately to my seat on top of my own, tottering pile of crates, that I cheered right along with them, and I could not put it down only to the bad whiskey, or the need to pass.

This night's entertainment was different from other nights. The boys had opened up a rat pit down in the basement. Once you could find a rat-baiting on every other corner in the Bowery, but that was before the goo-goos had put across another wave of Reform, and the Society for the Prevention of Cruelty to Animals and Children had driven them out of the City.

Not that there still wasn't cruelty to children, of course—that was a matter of business—but they *had* put a stop to the torture of rats. Or more exactly, had driven it underground—for no vice ever really disappears in the City. The Dudes had rooted out a few old men who still trained the fox terriers, and rats were never hard to find.

It was a bloody sport. What can you expect, after all, when you bring dogs and rats and men together in a dimly lit basement room? Besides, I wasn't playing. I lost nothing, I put nothing down. It was enough just to see these things—to stand shoulder-to-thigh in the company of men, undetected, and watch them drink their whiskey, and breathe in the smoke of their cigars with them.

I could slip inconspicuously enough among them. A kick there, a slap here—they barely noticed me. No one detected the Mayor of the Little City, moving among them. Only boys noticed me, they were the only ones on my level, and they seemed to sense that I was different, somehow, and gave me wide berth. Good as my disguise was, I moved differently from a boy, kept more quiet than a boy, existed somewhere in that slim space between their consciousnesses, Big and Little.

There was one exception: not a sparrow fell without *his* considering the play on it. He had a killing look, cold, calculating face weighing us all in the balance. A natural leader of men, with all the horror that implies.

I felt his eyes on me before I saw him, and then I was afraid. I should have gone right then, I should have run, but I was too arrogant in my game: the King, out for his *incognito* among the people. Nothing could happen to *me*—I was just the observer.

4

KID TWIST

It all started that night at the rat pit when he hit Gyp the Blood over the head with a shovel. Not that he planned it that way, in fact he was never really sure how it happened at all. Gyp had been doing his old trick from the Eastmans gang, breaking men over his knee on a two-dollar bet for the entertainment of the yoks and the rubes, and he had already snapped the back of a slumming department store clerk in three places, leaving him to flop around on the dirt floor of the basement like a hooked fish. Then he reached out for the newsboy, and the next thing Kid knew he was bringing the shovel down—*bang!*—right along the part line on Gyp's big, handsome head. And then there was really hell to pay.

The boy, watching from the side with his eyes big as moons, rooted there, like a mouse before a snake. Huge, quick hands flicking out to seize him by the neck, dragging him over his lap, the other clerks and the sporting gents yelling and waving their money in the air. Kid reaching for the coal shovel, before he even had time to think about it—

Of course, Kid wouldn't have been there at all if it hadn't been for Spanish Louie, he didn't have any plans at all that night other than to hang around the New Brighton rolling the flats and the rabbit suckers or maybe to slide over to Mock Duck's for a quick trip to Hopland with the high-

14

binders. He certainly had no intention of going out and hitting a citizen like Gyp the Blood over the head with a coal shovel, and *certainly* not for the sake of some half-pint newsboy who turned out to be a crazy little carny dwarf out on a bender.

But then Louie rolled in, all decked out in his gold chaps and the bandeleros and the huge black sombrero with gold piping that made the *girlchiks* swoon, and worried to death the Grabber was after him over the proceeds from a fake charity ball the two of them had run.

"You gotta help me, Kid," he told him. "He thinks I cheated him. You gotta settle for me."

—which Kid didn't doubt for a minute, Spanish Louie being just the sort of *nayfish* who would try and bunco the Grabber. Louie liked to put it about that he was some kind of Apache, or fallen Spanish royalty who had killed twelve men down in Mexico, or was it Texas, but frankly, Kid didn't think so.

"You know there's no help for the Grabber," he told him—but then Louie told him the Grabber was going to be at a rat-baiting down at the Grand Duke's and it had been a long time since he'd seen a good rat-baiting, ever since they'd closed up Kit Burns's once and for all.

"All right, let's go," he had decided, but it was only then, typically, that Spanish Louie had told him another piece of vital information.

"Course, you know Gyp's gonna be there—"

Which, of course, he *didn't* know, that was a whole different story, particularly now that the whole business of Beansy Rosenthal was still unresolved between them. Of course there was always something unresolved, that was the nature of business and you had to think twice anyway before getting too close to Gyp the Blood, particularly in a basement pit where the blood was flowing, and money was at stake, and the light was none too good in the first place.

15

But the matter of Beansy was something else: one more squawky gambler, who was blabbing to the D.A. about a police lieutenant shaking down his place in Times Square. It all looked on the up-and-up. Gyp wanted Kid to help knock him off, and it had been cleared uptown with Big Tim, and even Mr. Murphy himself, but Kid still didn't like the play. It was police business, after all, and he didn't see what it had to do with him. He didn't like the fact that the Gyp was involved, and he couldn't help but think he was getting himself set up.

He'd put Gyp off, but Gyp the Blood was a hard man to stay put, and consequently he was not the person Kid wanted to see at the present time. But he'd told Louie he would go and the *last* thing he wanted was it to get around that he, Kid Twist, was frightened of Gyp the Blood, even though he was in fact scared to death.

"Let's go," he told Spanish Louie. "After all, he couldn't be any worse than the Grabber."

A little broken tail of men stood in the dark street, looking suspiciously about themselves. Before them sagged a five-story tenement, the only building left on the block, leaning like a single tooth in an old mouth. A long, rending sound came from inside, and a door swung open, revealing nothing but darkness. They all filed down into the basement, bummies and gangsters, shopkeepers and family men, and a few drunken sports out on a tear.

The rat pit was lit by a single, dim lightbulb, swaying over the center of the ring. It was a dirt oval, wooden walls five feet high, a trap door on either end, a set of high, rickety bleachers mounted all around it.

"It's the best kind of action there is," the clerk ahead of them said excitedly, his breath sour with whiskey in the Kid's face. "It's the only sport where you can't fix the game!"

Such talk was offensive to his ears, but the Kid didn't bother to enlighten him. There was always a way, there was no action on this earth that couldn't be fixed. You could always dope the dogs. You could tenderize their paws with mustard seed, or salt their food, or best of all you could poison the rats so they'd be all the easier to kill at first—but slowly, almost imperceptibly, the dog would begin to tire as it soaked up the poison itself. There was always a way.

"How many? How many? What's the setup?"

—an anxious little man was asking, jumping back and forth among them, pulling at their coats. They all crowded in around the pit, bumping into each other in the dark, giddy with the anticipation men always had when they gathered together to do something they knew was wrong. Kid had seen it many times before: in a brothel or a lynch mob, it was always the same.

"If Mary knew what we was up to——"

"How many? How many?"

"I'm gonna get me a whiskey!"

"Be polluted here."

"If she only knew——"

Kid felt uneasy, sensing something beyond the low stench of corruption from the dead rats and dogs, buried under the basement dirt where they fell. Something else besides the darkness in the cellar, so dense you could barely see your hand in front of your face.

A boy climbed into the pit, one of the Baxter Street Dudes, in a tattered red hunting coat he had somehow managed to scavenge, and began announcing the first dog. Kid looked up—and there, staring back at him across the pit, rapacious, intelligent face just visible through the grainy yellow light, was Gyp the Blood.

He could have been the Kid's double, in the bad light: same starched white shirt and collar, red checkered vest under his coat, gold horseshoe pin in his lapel. Derby

17

pulled down so low Kid could barely see his eyes. Kid nodded, and touched the brim of his own hat—and after a long moment the Gyp nodded almost imperceptibly back.

"First up," the ringmaster in his borrowed coat hollered, "Shadrach, from Harry Weisberg of Greenpoint."

"Bets! Bets! Place your markers!"

The bookies circulated through the crowd, men in long undertaker's coats, scribbling with pencils in their tiny black books. The bet was how long it would take the dog to kill its century—one hundred struggling, squealing rats, and Kid only laid down a finiff at first. He didn't like to bet on what he didn't fix himself, and besides he wanted to see the dog before he was going to lay any real cash on it.

One of the little trapdoors opened at the far end of the oval pit, and out trotted a proud, trim-looking fox terrier, white with rust-colored patches and a long, broken scar across its nose.

"It's a bitch!" one of the bettors crowed behind him.

"Lookit her prance! Oh, she's a killer!"

"How many?"

At the other end of the oval a boy slid up a smaller gate—and out came the rats. They were little more than shadows in the grainy light, eyes gleaming redly as they scuttled around the ring. One of them sprinted right at the terrier in its terror, halfway up its leg before it realized its mistake. The dog seized it with one quick stab, gave it a short, professional shake to break its neck, and tossed its lifeless body to the side.

"Thirty! Thirty minutes!"

"Twenty-five!"

The terrier took its time, waiting to get the rats it could grab in one bite. They let them out ten at a time, every few minutes, and the dog broke them all with the same sure, efficient shake—*So like a cat*, Kid marveled—or it ripped their throats out, or bit their heads off, whatever was quickest. It had been well trained.

"How many? How many?"

The dog paused, seeing everything dead in the ring around it, and gave its paw a short, satisfied lick. The next ten rats ran out, swift and furtive as a fog, and the killing began again.

"That's fifteen! No—nineteen!"

The rats careened around the sides of the ring, they tried to scramble up the five-foot walls. Some of them hoisted themselves, somehow, all the way over the top—only to be flung back into the pit by the roaring, jeering crowd.

"That's thirty! At least thirty!"

Kid could see the dog was starting to tire, but he kept up a champion's steady, killing pace. It was harder to maneuver, the pit floor slippery with rat blood and rat pieces now, the long, gray creatures burrowing and gnawing under the carcasses of their own to get away from the pitiless, snapping jaws.

"Clean the pit! Clean the pit! It's not fair!" the same drunken clerk who had assured Kid you couldn't fix the game cried out—as brokenhearted as if he'd lost his only sweetheart. His friends took up the call.

"Clean the pit!"

"Hazard of the game, hazard of the game!" the short-bettors yelled back at them.

It didn't matter; Shadrach the dog had a second wind. She spotted the live ones by the twitches of their long, scaly tails, dragged them back and ripped their life out. Kid put more finiffs up high and low, to cover himself, then tried to gauge the action and hit the middle.

He glanced over at Gyp the Blood, across the pit—who was not trying to lay any more wagers at all. He stared evenly down at the ring instead, black eyes patient and luminous. The Kid had a bad feeling.

"How many?"

The rat door slid up again, and another ten rodents tumbled into the pit. Seeing so many of their own already heaped up around the ring they went for the dog now, out of sheer terror and desperation.

This was where a rat-baiting always got interesting. They ran right at the terrier, leaping at her legs and face and throat. She was able to bat the first couple down with her paws but then one got past her, tearing at one of her forelegs near the shoulder. Then another, and another, until they were hanging from her snout and ruff and legs, clutching on by their awful little jaws.

The dog gave a low, plaintive howl. She managed to shake some of them off, leaving ragged red tears through her wiry fur. They rolled over and jumped right back on, clinging to her with all their strength.

The small boy invisible behind the ring wall slid open the door for the next ten rats. These were bigger rats than the others, a black, greasy color, leaner and longer. Kid smelled a fix. He beckoned to the closest bookkeep to cover himself.

"No bets! No more bets!" the man declared, snapping shut his little black book——but under Kid's steady gaze he came over and took his wager anyway. Looking across the ring, Kid saw that Gyp was still gazing down imperturbably at the action; the faces of the boys around him gleamed with excitement.

"Cover me on a wash," Kid told the bookkeep.

Sure enough, the dog was tiring fast now; it had lost some blood. The big, bold new rats ran right for her throat. The proud little fox terrier stood her ground, knocking them aside, ripping the snout right off one, which went tumbling away with a horrible, wounded squealing. But she was losing blood, and the rats kept coming. One of them leapt up and got itself wedged halfway down her throat, so the dog couldn't use her jaws. She fell back on her haunches, flailing away—then on her side, still fighting, the slick black rats scratching and scrambling over each other to get at her.

"No more! That's enough, she's had *enough!*"

Weisberg the trainer leaped over into the pit to rescue his dog, stomping at the rats. When he came in the ring, some of the rodents were still so frenzied they leapt at *him*, hanging from his pants and sleeves. He brushed them off without a second glance, grinding their heads under his boot heels. He had eyes only for his dog, trembling on the ground, her ruff and throat steeped in blood. He cradled her head in his arms, wrapped her up in his coat and carried her from the ring.

"My poor girl," he crooned to her, the dog's alert little eyes still shining up at him. "My poor girl, what've they done for you?"

"There's no throwin' in the towel here!" one of the boys near Gyp called out, disappointed not to see the finish—any finish.

"Water rats! Water rats!" the clerk and his friends chanted now, looking around them for the bookies.

"Fix, fix!"

A few of the Baxter Street Dudes had hurried down into the pit, pushing Weisberg away from the rats and rushing to corral them back into their cages. Gyp and his entourage still sat gloating quietly by the ring, the bookies hovering around them defensively.

The crowd surged sullenly out toward the makeshift bar in the back, planks set up over trash barrels, while the older boys kept trying to round up the rats, yelping and clutching at their fingers as they skittered around the ring. The younger boys doled out the whiskey and took the dough, lanks of hair hanging down in their eyes, scrambling up on crates to reach over the bar.

A few trimmers moved around the crowd, trying to find

the smiling winners. Most of them were no older than the Dudes themselves, Kid noticed, hoisting up their paper-thin dresses to hide their tubercular chests and necks. They found their marks, and slid their arms around their necks, settled into them as confidently as another girl their age might be sliding into her daddy's lap.

Kid would just as soon have taken off then: he had broken even, more or less, maybe even a few dollars ahead on the night, and he would just as soon not have talked to Gyp the Blood. Spanish Louie was ready to go: the Grabber hadn't showed after all and there were no mollies on hand to impress with his twirling moustachios and matching, inlaid-pearl-handled Mexican revolvers.

The trouble was how to get past Gyp at the bar. Kid had a pop in each coat pocket, and a good blade in his vest watch pocket, and a razor in his shoe, and as a last resort there was a blackjack in a back pocket, but he still didn't like the odds. Gyp had his boys with him, Lefty Louie and Dago Frank and Whitey Lewis, and he had only Spanish Louie, who made a very good killer if this was a nickelodeon show.

There was no hope for it, though; the current of prostitutes and boy gangsters and sporting swells forced them up toward the bar, and by the time they got there Gyp was already holding court like the King of Siam, seated in a huge rattan chair the ever-resourceful Dudes had acquired somehow. He peeled a few bills off the enormous wad he had won, handed it to Dago Frank for the boy behind the bar.

"This round's on me," he called, and the crowd around him cheered and bellowed, and pressed in closer.

"Hullo, Kid," he said when Kid came up, face to face with him, with Whitey Lewis and Lefty leaning eagerly over their boss's shoulders, smiling evilly as a couple of watchdogs on a long leash—while at the same time Kid could sense the less-than-reassuring efforts of Spanish Louie to hide behind his back.

"Hiya, Lazar," he said, trying to use his real name to throw him off. The Gyp's eyes never wavered—except to flick over to a newsie and some clerks who had moved too close to his right shoulder, a boy carrying a shovelful of dead rats over to the trash barrel. He picked up everything, and he was goddamned quick, Kid knew.

"You had the run of 'em tonight—"

"You thought anymore about what I said you oughta think about?" Gyp cut him off, picking his nails with a stiletto sharp as glass and concealable as a toothpick. The papers made out that Gyp read philosophy in his spare time, and that his favorite authors were Voltaire and Darwin, and Huxley and Herbert Spencer, but somehow Kid really didn't think philosophy was the man's major preoccupation.

"Leave it alone, Gyp, that's cop business. Let 'em take care of it their own selves, we don't gotta do their dirty work for 'em."

"'Gyp'? You're Gyp the Blood?" It was the drunken clerk he had heard talking so ignorantly outside the Grand Duke's.

"Sure," said Gyp, keeping a cold, speculative eye on Kid.

"Is it true what they say? Is it true you can break a man over your knee on a bet?"

"You wanna find out?"

When he said that the Kid began to back away, right hand reaching as surreptitiously as possible into his coat pocket. He saw that Lefty Louie and Whitey Lewis were reaching into their own pockets—though Gyp himself never moved.

"Hell, yes!" the clerk snorted greedily. "I'd pay to see that!"

Gyp's terrible eye stayed on Kid.

"It's gonna happen," he said. "The question is whether you're on that train or not."

"Well? Is it true?" the clerk demanded.

Gyp looked at the man for the first time while the Kid kept moving back, circling around a little to Gyp's right.

"You wanna know? Then make the play."

"How's that?" the clerk asked, a little unsteadily now.

"Two dollars. Make the play."

"All right, sure," the clerk laughed nervously, figuring he was being put on, and he pulled a couple of silver dollars from his vest pocket and dropped them in Gyp's lap.

"I'll bite. Who's it gonna be?"

Without another word, Gyp grabbed the clerk by his tie and yanked him down, smashing his knee into the man's face. His legs buckled, and Gyp tossed him over his lap, face up, and held him tight by the neck and legs.

"All right, you wanna see?"

The whole room was suddenly quiet, everyone pressing in to stare, the newsie, the trimmers, the Baxter Street Dudes. Only Kid kept moving, working his way slowly around until he was just behind the Gyp's right shoulder. He noticed that Whitey Lewis's and Dago Frank's eyes were off him, fixed on the clerk themselves. The boy who had been scooping up rats stood beside him, shovel lowered to his side.

"Two dollars."

The clerk's eyes were dazed and round, he was too terrified even to beg, choking up little yellow spurts of vomit over his mouth and face. He was a slight man, Kid could see, pathetically small and helpless over Gyp's legs in his rumpled suit, worn bowler wobbling around on the floor.

Gyp looked up at the rest of them. Then, without further warning, he lifted the clerk up and pressed him down— bringing his knees up as he did.

"One, two, *three!*"

24

—right, left, and right again; three distinct cracks louder than pistol shots reverberated through the room. The clerk screamed like a woman, and Gyp pocketed his coins.

"Two dollars."

He tossed the wreckage of the clerk onto the floor, beside his hat, where he still flopped about, no longer a man, arms and legs paralyzed, unable even to scream anymore or do anything other than make short, terrible, gasping noises.

"Any more action?"

A low, impressed murmur ran through his audience and then everyone was talking at once. Men were pushing forward, waving their money in the air, ignoring the clerk still gasping in the dirt. Gyp's watchdogs were pounding him enthusiastically on the back; they had forgotten all about Kid now.

"Who's next?" Gyp cried out, and the crowd surged forward.

"Do it again! Do it again!"

"I wanna see it this time!"

"Who's it gonna be?"

They stopped short as Gyp turned his fierce eyes on them all, waiting for his selection. Then his great hands reached out and grabbed the newsboy, before anything could stop him, before even the newsie himself realized they were upon him.

That was when Kid felt the rat collector's shovel in his hands, the boy himself oblivious that he had taken it, his attention riveted on the action. Gyp the Blood laid the newsboy out across his knees, gauging his height and weight, one hand rubbing contemplatively over his throat.

"This one'll take a short shot," he grinned, and the crowd laughed appreciatively.

He turned back to his prey, preparing to break the boy's back with one thrust of his knee—and it was then that Kid lifted the shovel up over his head and brought it down as hard as he could right along the part line of Gyp's fine, jet-black shock of hair. He didn't know why he did it, he never would know why, but it was done and what was done could not be undone, particularly not Gyp the Blood's fractured scalp. The next thing he knew all the bummies and the Dudes and the slumming shipping clerks were shouting, and the mabs and goohs were screaming, and everyone was going for the stairs—

Kid brushed a couple of the trimmers out of the way and leapt up on the first step. Some sporting gent in a top hat loomed ahead of him, coming down the steps, his mouth agape, hands still buttoning his fly, just coming down from God only knew what for still more fun. The Kid kicked him in the balls and flung him aside, still making for the door, Spanish Louie and the little newsie glued to his side. A couple of the Baxter Street Dudes tried to stop him at the top of the stairs and it was too close even to get a pop out but he ploughed the flat of his hand into the first one's nose until it was halfway back in his head and backhanded the second one away and then they were free—up on the ground floor, and out the front door.

Behind him, he could hear more screams as Gyp's boys started to blam away, cutting a path through the crowd, but he didn't look back, he didn't look back until they were out the door and long gone down Baxter Street and all the way over to the Bowery—a couple of wild, hopeless long shots clanging off the lampposts behind them like hail on a tin roof, a few distant curses and cries rising up from the dark streets, and then they were back among civilization (if that's what you could ever call the Bowery) leaving only the question of what the hell did he do now that he had mortally offended the most dangerous lunatic in New York?

At least the newsie had got out with him—at least the boy was safe. Breathless, Kid leaned down to the child with his big wondering eyes, huge flat cap pulled down over his head, and clapped a hand on his shoulder.

"All right, kid, you're safe now."

The little newsie looked back up at him, his blue beard starting to show through his soot-covered face.

"Who's a kid?" he said, in a voice like pounded gravel.

5

TRICK THE DWARF

I hid them out at Coney, in the Tin Elephant's arse. Louie—the one who looked like an evening of Spanish passion dances—flagged down a hansom cab and I told the driver to head for Brooklyn. He peered down closely at us from the box—a tall, wraithlike figure under the Bowery el—and tapped his whip respectfully against his hat.

There was no doubt he would sell us as soon as he got back. We ditched the cab in Brooklyn Heights; the driver's mouth turned down in dismay even though we tipped him handsomely. We walked a few blocks, past McCooey's grand, futile city hall, then swung over on Joralemon and down the handsome, brownstoned streets, quiet as a country village.

Behind us, somewhere, we could hear the single, muffled clip-clop of the cab—trying to follow, looking for us. We dodged down an alley, then took another hansom back past Prospect Park and the Parade Grounds. Then we walked again: down a new avenue they had named after Coney, even though it seemed as far away as one of the islands of the Malays.

There was nothing around us. They had razed all the Irish shantytowns, and the old Negro villages that used to spring up along the flatlands like spring mushrooms after a rain. Now there was nothing but the rubbled ground—the blocks-to-be already carved out into tidy squares, neat little signs announcing the pretentious English names of the neighborhoods: Kensington and Borough Park, Bensonhurst and Gravesend, and on past them, trudging all the way out over that barren, optimistic landscape until we reached Coney Island.

I took them straight out to the old Tin Elephant. I could have put them up in my town—after all, I had a palace!—but they would have stood out like, well, like two sore thumbs.

Fortunately, even Coney Island has never been short on places where you could hang yourself in complete solitude and anonymity. It was easy to get a room in the Elephant's arse at that hour. It was almost dawn by the time we got there, and the last tricks of the night were just stumbling out, hats pulled down over their eyes, reeking of sausage, and gin, and bed sweat.

The whores were still up, washing themselves in their room basins. We could hear them calling, each to each, as we climbed the winding, spiral staircase; lovely, bright voices, twittering like songbirds, happy to be at the end of the night. Though it was at this hour, too, that they tended to kill themselves, when all the sensation of the early evening—the promise of the brightly lit parlor, and the piano music downstairs and the smell of a first, freshly poured beer—had metamorphosed into nothing more than one more grunting, sweaty, two-hundred-fifty-pound brush salesman. One of the songbirds' voices would be missing, and they would find her in her room, hung with her own kimono sash or doused with opium.

I took my new friends back to the last room—the one

where I used to live, before I persuaded Matty Brinckerhoff to build The Little City for me and mine. Some mad predecessor to Brinckerhoff had put it up thirty years before, back when that sort of thing was the rage: an entire hotel constructed in the image of an elephant. Complete with tusks and a trunk, an observation deck up in its howdah, shops and penny arcades and entire shows and dance halls jammed into its immense legs. At night its yellow eyes shined out over the boardwalk and the ocean, some rough beast lurking amidst the more respectable hotels.

It had been slowly chipped away over the years, like everything else at Coney: a wonder surpassed by many other wonders, its rooms filled up with whores and other human flotsam. I had lived in my little room with only the bed, a basin, a table and chair I sawed off myself—the management didn't care much what you did, so long as you paid every week—and the black steamer trunk I had hauled through thirty seasons of grand expositions and international spectaculars and other such degradations.

It was too noisy to actually sleep at night, with the mabs and their customers. The tin roof broiled when the sun was out, and it rang like hammers on an anvil when it rained. Fortunately, I had work: barker for a Son of Ham act among the Luna Park sideshows:

"*Hit the nigger Hit the nigger in the head Three balls for the price of five Three balls and a big prize if you can hit the nigger in the head!*"

Luke, the poor, addled Negro they had for the act, would stick his head through a crude yellow drawing of the moon, and grin a great, toothless grin at the crowd. It was a terrifying sight: his old prizefighter's head, gnarled as an apple branch, odd lumps and contusions sticking up on all sides. Let's face it, you could never get a man to do such work if he wasn't more than a little punch-drunk already.

It wasn't hard work—for me, anyway. I didn't have to do

30

very much, and how quickly and viciously the baseballs would start to fly! Real, hard-cored baseballs, too, tight as the ones Christy Mathewson threw up at the Polo Grounds. The rubes so excited to score a hit that half the time they didn't even remember their prizes, and every hour or so I had to take old Luke back behind the stand and wash him down so the whole thing didn't get too gory for the family crowd. Well, let's just say that it was a less than edifying profession.

There were worse jobs on Coney Island, believe it or not—at least, worse jobs for me. Over at Steeplechase Park, where the paying customers came off the mechanical horses, there was another one of my kind: a smirking, demonic caricature of a dwarf, done up in a harlequin's suit and hat and painted face.

I had watched him, chasing all the flushed-faced clerks, and the day laborers, and the factory girls, with a cattle prod, driving them back across the blowholes that sent the women's skirts billowing up around their ears—and all for the benefit of their fellow patrons, sitting up in the bleachers of the Laughing Gallery. He made them howl: the men high-stepping through the air, holding their hands on their backsides like Mack Sennett's Keystones—the women running and squeaking in fear, holding their hands over their sexes.

He leapt and skipped across his stage after them, pumping his tiny fists. Leering and winking back at the gallery, and all of them roaring back at him—all the the lady's maids and the hod carriers, the streetcar conductors and waitresses and peanut politicians, rubbing their own damaged behinds.

Sometimes a big man would try to catch him, but the little demon was too quick. He scuttled around him, back and forth between his pursuer's legs, harlequin's pointed hat sliding back and forth over his greased white head—flogging away at the man's genitals until he screamed for mercy.

31

As I watched, a once-innocent young girl tried to get by. She looked unsettled already by the shenanigans on the Steeplechase, plump, greasy fingerstains visible on the bosom of her white shirtwaist. The crowd screamed as he advanced on her, oversized clown's head lolling grotesquely. He drove her backwards, terrified, the girl clutching her hands to her chest—her fellow passengers scurrying by, just glad to be unnoticed. Once outside, they exhaled in relief—and took their own seats among the screaming faces in the Laughing Gallery.

I had to turn away. That was my greatest fear, before the construction of The Little City, that I could be compelled by necessity to take such a situation. That is always the thing with depravity: just when you think you've plumbed the very depths, there's always someplace lower to fall.

By night, I made my nocturnal rambles around the Bowery. It was there that I saw her—on an earlier, more successful visit to the Dudes, and the Grand Duke's Theatre. The love of my life, my queen and empress of The Little City. The Mad Carlotta.

I was at the bar when he brought her in, just dipping into a whiskey sweetened with hot rum and camphor and benzene, and a few loose sweepings of cocaine and sawdust. You couldn't get drinks like that just anywhere, or maybe you could.

He was calling himself Marconi, Master of the Invisible Airwaves, after the famous wop, all done up with waxed moustaches and greased-down hair. He even had a cape. He brought her in slung under one arm, like a salesman's valise. Swung her right up on the bar, like a real doll, no more than three feet tall as she was, and announced himself to the denizens of the Grand Duke's in his thunderous, idiot's voice:

"La-dies and gen-tel-men! Intro-ducing a small sample of

the even-ing's enter-tain-ment: The Incredible—
Mechanical—Thum-be-lina!"

She sat up there perfectly still, among the glasses and the
puddles of needled beer, in her tattered black mantilla, and
for just a moment I thought maybe she *was* a doll. I had
never seen one of us who looked so perfect. Her hair was
dressed in dolly curls, and her cheeks were painted with red
dolly circles, but there was no obscuring the fine, porcelain
skin, her blue china eyes staring rapturously out into space.
Everything was there, in exquisite miniature, limbs and head
and bosom—a perfect, little *woman's* body.

I was in love.

"The latest in mechanical genius which I, the great
Marconi, have invested with life through the invisible
Kingdom of the Air!"

He flung his hands up, in a cheap, dramatic flourish—just
the sort of thing the boy toughs loved—and she began to
move. First her head, shifting haughtily, slowly, a few inches
from one side to the other, like a doll's head would move. It
seemed to take forever, and by the time her perfect, porcelain profile was turned to us, we were mesmerized.

"It's a miracle!"

"He's another Edison!"

Yet she was not done yet. Slowly, slowly, with incredible,
doll-like restraint, she began to move her right arm. The
tiny, white, perfect thumb and fingers extended rigidly.
They began to move up and down, up and down, in a steady,
slicing motion—looking to me like nothing so much as the
expressed desire to cut off all our heads.

"Look! It's a blessing!"

"She's blessing us! It's luck, it's luck!"

"That's all for now! Showtime in one hour!" the ersatz Marconi cried, scooping her off the bar and shoving her back under
his cape—limbs still extended in perfect, rigid, dolly fashion.

"Fraud! White slaver! He's no more Marconi than macaroni!" I shouted from my stool, in vain falsetto. I was pushed aside, swept away by the real boys, crowding up around the stage, eagerly awaiting her reappearance.

"Could she *be* real?"

"What else can she do? *Every*thing?"

I had to stay and watch then. I don't know if it was the whiskey—or the sawdust sweepings—but I knew I had to save her. It was my destiny.

The Grand Duke's was packed for the show, word racing through the street like it always did. The boys could barely contain themselves for the opening acts, even through another appearance by their beloved Bowery Boy. Before he had finished smashing up the stage furniture, they were calling for her:

"Thum-bel-ina! Thum-bel-ina!"

"Bring on the doll! Bring on the doll!"

Next up was a barbershop quartet of boys, dressed like whores—the sort of act that never failed to get a good reception at the Grand Duke's, especially when the baritone sung. But they had no patience for it tonight.

"Bring on the beee-yooo-tee-ful dooooolllllll!"

Rotten fruit and eggs began to fly—something I had never actually seen in a theatre before. God knows where they got them; it was probably their night's meal. The curtains closed on the barbershop quartet, setting off more cheers, and curses, and whistles—then opened again on "Marconi"—sitting with his "doll" balanced perfectly, uncannily still on one caped arm. The boys went wild.

"Gen-tel-men, gen-tel-men!" he announced—finally having realized, apparently, that there were no ladies in the house unless you counted the Water Street whores in the corners, giving prepubescent newsies blow jobs for the price of their day's wages.

34

"Wel-come to the Won-der of the Age! The As-*tound*-ing-Mechanical-*Thum*-bel-ina! She can perform any act—— *any* act *at all*——that a normal, human woman can!"

The response from the boys was predictable.

"Strip 'er! Strip 'er!"

"Have 'er pull up her skirts an' let's see her quim!" somebody yelled, and the rest shouted with laughter and approval. Marconi faced them down, waving a grand, reproachful hand at them.

"Do I hear a le-*git*-imate request?"

There was another outburst, and the idea of stripping her and then seeing what was what still commanded considerable support. But then a more innocent voice made itself heard above the din.

"Make her walk!"

"What?"

The crowd was disappointed at first——but then they seemed to warm to the sheer simplicity of the test.

"Yeah! If she ain't just a wind-up doll, let's see her walk!"

The Marconi nodded gravely, in his best cheap carny style, as if he were summoning up all his powers from the vasty deep.

"Very well. Behold! The *Amazing*——Me-*chan*-ical—— *Thumbelina*——walks!"

He lowered her gently to the floor, and she did even this perfectly. She was an amazing actress, sliding off his arm just the way a real mechanical doll might: head still bowed, limbs paralyzed. Her knees bent so far to the floor that the whole crowd, myself included, made a spontaneous stooping motion, trying to catch her as she fell.

Marconi thrust out his arms just as she sagged——and instantly——perfectly——without even seeing him, she sprung rigidly to life. Eyes alert, legs stiff——but still not moving, not even seeming to breathe.

He lifted his left arm—and slowly, excruciatingly, her left leg lifted up. He raised his right arm—and just as excruciatingly, her right leg jutted out, and she completed one small stride across the stage.

"Walk!" he bellowed—and she walked. Straight-legged as a goose, yet somehow elegant, an unworldly, mechanical, sleepwalker's step.

She kept moving her small legs forward, walking right toward us, eyes fixed over our heads until we thought she would walk right off the stage. She reached the edge, dangled one foot over—

"Return!"

Instantly, she executed a perfect, mechanical ballet turn, and began to march back toward her master—Marconi drawing her back with cheesy, pantomine motions that looked like he was hauling in a dinghy.

"Stop!" he commanded, pressing his hand out flat like a traffic cop's—and she stopped in midstride, her left leg still raised but *motionless*.

The crowd was in an uproar. They must have known in their hearts by now that she was really a person—those cynical, streetwise boys—but they cheered anyway.

"Now—dance!"

She made another perfect, balletic turn to face the crowd, and then dipped the raised left leg to the ground, bending awkwardly at the knee. Now she began to move her arms—very mechanically again, thrusting them up in the air like a marionette.

Then it changed—quickly, seamlessly, right before our eyes. The arms moved up over her head, her feet touched the stage more rapidly. She spun, and bent at the waist, and pivoted as gracefully as any dancer from the Ballets Russes. Her arms swayed like willows, the curls of her hair sweeping out; her face still fixed and expressionless. She was dancing something from an epic now, this small, immaculate woman, like a Trojan princess, or a captive Hebrew maiden.

She waited until we were dazzled into silence—until we believed it all—and then she slowed. Rather, she *wound down*—just like a mechanical doll again. Slowly, slowly, folding up on herself until, in the very last movement, she seemed to give out entirely. Her head lolled, hands fell to her sides. Finally, she dropped lifeless to her knees—with an authentic, wooden knock ringing out when she hit the stage.

There was a gaping silence—then the boys in the Grand Duke's Theatre went wild. They mobbed the stage, and it took all the magic Marconi could muster to preserve any of his doll's illusions. He hustled her away under his cloak again; fighting them off with his free arm.

"There will be an-other show in *one* hour! One hour!" he shouted above the mob—tossing her into the closet that served as a backstage dressing room and barring the door with his body.

"Please! Time is required to restore the magno-electro waves!"

They kept shouting and stamping and whistling for her. The stage managers tried to start up the next production: excerpts from *Richard III*. Clarence drowned in his barrel, Hastings's head delivered to Richard at dinner, the princes smothered in the Tower—all the good parts. They would have none of it. They kept yelling for Thumbelina, pelting the poor actors with foodstuffs.

Marconi kept guard over her dressing room for a while, but I knew he would not stay. I noticed before he had a drinker's eye, darting greedily back and forth between all the lovely, amber glasses. I knew he would get thirsty, and I bided my time until he put a padlock on the door, turned it with a key he shoved down somewhere deep beneath that mysterious cape, and went off to join the youth of New York at the bar.

37

I could pick any lock made—one of the lowly, useful skills one picks up over a lifetime in show business. I opened his in seconds, with a hairpin. The door swung open and there she was—beautiful and human and animated now, curling her hair up before a warped old vanity some of the Dudes had managed to pinch off the back of a furniture wagon traveling down Broadway at midday.

She didn't look at me when I came in, for which I was grateful. She didn't look around at all, until she realized that I wasn't blocking the light behind her and therefore could not be the Big Person in her life. When she did, she turned around slowly, regally—no doubt assuming I was some real boy.

"It is five dollars," she said, haughtily as a queen.

"My God, does he make you do that, too?"

She heard my voice then, undisguised, but she only turned back to her curls, in the mirror, answering me with the lofty candor of royalty *in extremis*—Charles I asking for an extra shirt, Louis XVI picking up the revolutionary cockade.

"No—not what *you* mean. I . . . show. That is usually enough for them."

"And when it isn't?"

She said nothing, letting me stew in that indiscretion.

"Do you *like* this life?" I asked her.

"One indignity or another—what difference does it make, after the crowned heads of Europe abandoned our husband to his fate? We are condemned to suffer everything."

I didn't know what she was talking about. Was she having me on—or had her life driven her truly mad?

"Have you been sent by the Holy Father?" she asked casually, turning back to me as she powdered her face.

"The *Pope*?"

"He often sends emissaries to us. *Incognito,* you understand; to see if we are truly mad. It is all the same to us. We would have the *world* see the grief of Carlotta, to let them know what foul betrayals have been perpetrated against us, and our beloved Maximilian."

I should have walked out then and there. The Mad Carlotta!—that creaky old number. One impersonator or another holding court behind the midway for nearly fifty years, in every carny show around the country. The Empress of Mexico, gone mad in the Pope's chambers trying to save her dim-witted husband from a firing squad—and who was, by all accounts, more than three feet high.

It was the most pathetic of stage disguises to get lost in, and I should have told her I had to hotfoot it back to the Vatican.

But I didn't. Maybe it was because she was so beautiful, or I was so needy, or the sawdust and camphor had rotted my brain. I think, though, it was because of what she did next: she leaned over as calmly as ever, lifted up the bottom of her mantilla, and tied two curved wooden slats around her legs, like a baseball catcher lacing on his shin guards.

I should have anticipated something like this. It was the slats, of course, that made the wooden *knock* when she bowed to the floor at the end of her dance. Yet it was such a strange, such a touchingly pathetic gesture that I could not help but stay.

"What if I could make you queen again?" I asked impulsively, trying to think of anything that might interest her.

She looked up at me for the first time with genuine interest, crystal-blue eyes spinning speculatively.

"*Could* you?"

"Yes—yes, I think I could."

I must have been mad already—as mad as she. I was employed at the time egging people on to hit their fellow human beings with baseballs. But the best ideas are born on the tongue and only then proceed to the mind. I had a plan percolating even then.

"How?" she asked directly, all business now.

She finished adjusting her shin guards and sat up, staring directly at me—and I thought I would do anything to have that perfect face before me, it didn't matter what the price. I started to answer her, to say anything—and then the door swung open behind me. The Great Marconi was back.

"Show ain't back here, sonny," he said, shoving me halfway across the room with one large, hairy hand—the great Italian's accent now somehow akin to that of the Border South. "'Less you got more money than it looks like you do."

"You are a common panderer," I told him in my real, adult voice—words right from a dime novel, words I could hardly believe I was uttering. "And if you put your hands upon me again, I will cut your tongue out!"

—ridiculous words, foolhardy words, and just the heroic language for her. At thirty-eight inches, I would have had to get up on a chair just to reach his throat. But I could see her eyes shining.

Marconi just laughed—a sudden, unpleasant fart of sound—and sat himself down on a barrel across the little room.

"You best get outta heah now."

"Come with me," I said to her, holding out my hand. Like any good performer, I knew who my real audience was.

"Come with me, and I will make you a queen," I said, trying to look as cool and masterful as anyone can be with six-inch forearms.

"You're not very funny anymo'," the Dixie Neapolitan said now, getting up off his barrel.

He was quicker than he looked. He stamped his foot, and I broke to my left, and before I could dodge back he had me. He hauled me up to his face by my lapels, my feet dangling ridiculously in the air.

"Let's see what we got heah."

He held me out at arm's length, both hands around my throat. I flailed and kicked at him, but mostly I choked: a futile, silly dwarf, hung up in the air for her to see.

"Yes, suh," he chuckled, and licked one big thumb and ran it through the soot on my face, exposing a whole matrix of lines and craters. I could see it myself, in the vanity mirror: the stubbled skin, the blue shadow. The face of a man: a twisted, little man.

I pounded on his arm with both fists, but he just let me drop to the floor where I lay, scrambling for breath.

"You people," he said disgustedly. "You people. You always find each other, don'tch you?"

He stepped back, grinning like a wolf, and put an arm around her shoulders. Her face was completely frozen, the perfect little doll again.

"'Thumbelina, won'tch you marry me?'" he mocked in a high, tinny voice. "'Thumbelina, won'tch you leave that big awful man an' run away with me?'"

She didn't move, didn't say anything, and he advanced on me again.

"Run away with you to *what*? The *circus*?"

He laughed, and leaned over me, where I had managed to sit up on the floor.

"You don't understand. You're all *freaks*—dwarves, hunchbacks. Warped little sideshow attractions. She—she's *fine*."

He stood up, and the smile left his face.

"Now *get out*!"

He reached for me again, but I pitched forward and rolled through his legs, kicking at his shins as I passed. He nearly fell right on me, and before he could get up I was out the door—pausing only to blow a kiss back to her, and promise like some addled cavalier:

41

"I will return for you!"

I went running back out through the Grand Duke's—his great, carny barker's voice booming after me soon:

"Tha's no boy! He's no boy, he's a goddamned *freak*!"

—but all they did was mob him on stage, chanting *her* name, thinking his appearance meant that *she* would be back out soon. I ran crouching through the rows of crates, holding up my jacket to conceal my ruined boy's face.

I got outside and kept running, down Water Street, as fast as my stubby legs would carry me, then ducked around a warehouse on Maiden Lane, where I could at last get my breath back, and resoot my face with whatever bile presented itself. There was nobody else around but an ancient woman, gathering coal in the vacant lot.

She turned to me when I ran up, white hair shining in the moonlight, and asked, "Wet yer whistle in a mouth sweet an' soft as yer old mother's, sonny?"

TRICK THE DWARF

I sat behind the left ear of Satan, and watched the sun come up over Sheepshead Bay, and dreamed of an empire of little men and little women, ruled by a mad queen.

"Hell is very badly done," that snotty Russian anarchist Gorky had sniffed, after his visit, but I thought it was perfect. From where I sat I could see all the weary banalities of damnation: the fake, piled brick, as dismal and forbidding as the Tombs prison. Old Nick himself leaning speculatively over the front gate, one heavily muscled arm and his enormous, hooked wings resting on the entrance. Up close you could see that Satan's nose was chipped, and the red plaster head could use a new paint job. The eyes glaring down in perpetuity at the sign strung over the front— H-E-L-L-G-A-T-E—10¢. Just ten cents to go to hell—though I knew places in this city where you could do it even cheaper.

Inside was a red, papier-mâché Underworld, a prancing, grimacing Devil in red tights, a gorgeous angel, a bunch of tubercular imps wandering about. There were several hilarious tableaux of sin: a young man was dispatched to eternal torment for a drink of whiskey, another for smoking a cigar, others for making sport on a Sunday.

The most popular, though, was a young woman trying on

a new hat. She preened and primped in front of her mirror—too vain to notice the grinning devils that rose up from the floor around her. They spun the mirror around, turning it into a casket. The young lady was pushed into it, screaming impressively, then pitched down a trap door billowing smoke and fire. Only the hat, and a new mirror, were left behind.

This never failed to get a real scream from the working girls. How they howled to see that!—rows of them doubled up with laughter at the Sunday matinee, a few dreamily contemplating what it might be like to once be tempted to damnation by something so grand as a hat.

Most of the others, the workmen and the animal trainers and my fellow freaks, liked to go up to the Shoot-the-Chutes at night, from where they could look down on the lake, and the picture-postcard view of Dreamland, and the Tower, and the Fall of Pompeii. They went there to drink and make love and dream, after Dreamland closed for the night.

Only I preferred Hell Gate, and Old Scratch. The whole park sleeping before me like some lost Mayan city. The scraps of newspaper, and hot dog wrappers, and half-eaten candy apples still blowing about from the day's action, but the whole place nearly silent for once—the hissing lights shut off, and the calliopes, and the shooting galleries and the rumbling roller coasters. The only sounds the steady sweep of the ocean and the closer, quieter sweep of a hundred brooms, already preparing for the next day. Here I would figure out how to win her, my queen.

How that cheap wop charlatan had got hold of her in the first place I could only guess. He might have bought her from a brothel, or one of the moldering freak museums

44

along the real Bowery, back in Manhattan. These were the depths to which any of our kind could easily descend. The more we reflected some larger beauty, the higher the price we brought.

My father had thought he would escape this marketplace. He had been an educated man, at Harvard, or so he said— after a lifetime in a carnival, you understand the whole world is just a story. He must have been quite a curiosity there, if he did go: a tiny, fastidious man, bustling earnestly about in his miniature suits, and cap and gown, gloriously oblivious to the sniggering behind his back.

He had studied law, thinking he could make his claim on the world. He didn't understand; *his* parents had been normal, a dry-goods merchant and his wife from Utica—no doubt frightened by a geek during her time. It never occurred to him that knowledge of the law, good manners, a serious intention would not be enough. He had even married a big person, a dull, flaxen-haired farmer's daughter from outside Braintree—the one girl he could convince that he had a future in society.

By the time I grew up, his greatest ambition was to make Barnum's. Instead, we lived in a single room above one of the lesser Bowery dime museums. There was a surfeit of dwarves—always has been, always will be—and all my father could do was recite on request any line from Shakespeare, Homer, Dickens, or Blackstone's Law, and we didn't get many requests for that sort of thing on the Bowery.

The farmer's daughter had left as soon as I was born. She must have known right away: by my twisted body, the grotesque shape of the head that tore her. *Good-bye, mother, good-bye! I'm only glad I hurt you while I still could.*

At night, he would read to me from his books. Every few days he pulled a new one out of the traveling trunks he had stacked around the room: wonderful books, magnificent books! The whole literature of the world, jumbled together in the bottom of his trunks: Herodotus and Hawthorne, Poe and Plutarch, Milton and Mark Twain.

It didn't matter to me what he read, as long as it was a good story. Washington Irving's tales, or Melville, or Crane—I didn't care. The whole world swam before me, and I loved it. I wriggled down in the little bed we shared, staring into the fire; listening to his tinny, passionate voice reading from *The World's Great Narrative Poems*—"How They Brought the Good News from Aix to Ghent," and "The Wonderful One-Hoss Shay," and "The Highwayman"—

> The road was a ribbon of moonlight
> over the purple moor,
> And the highwayman came riding—
> Riding—riding—
> The highwayman came riding,
> up to the old inn-door.

Whether or not he had ever been to Harvard, he read his stories beautifully, carefully, pausing every now and then to sip from his glass of brandy, or spoon some of the oatmeal he kept heating in a brass steamer over the fire. Stealing a look back to see my reaction before he set himself, he read as carefully as he would presenting a case to a jury—a real jury, a rapt jury, one not distracted into bouts of uncontrollable giggling by his very appearance.

During the day, I wandered through the dusty corridors of our museum—much to the displeasure of the proprietor, who resented the idea of anyone getting a look at the abnormal for free. I scuttled unobtrusively around the legs of the sailors and drummers, and the trolling whores, watching all the people I knew displayed in glass booths: the dog-faced boy and the Dahomean giant, the glass-chewers and the crayon-sketch artists and the armless wonders and the egg cranks——

Nearly everything was copied from Barnum, right down to the "Feejee Mermaid," a dead manatee sewn into a giant fish tail, floating serenely in a sea of chloroform. The famous sign, "This Way to the Egress!!"——which seemed so clever until the day a bunch of Boston sailors nearly wrecked the place on finding themselves out in the alley.

One late afternoon I happened into a dark room where someone was showing magic lantern slides against a stretched white sheet. At once, I realized there was something different about this exhibit——something *authentic* to it. The rubes and the sailors stood rigidly, backs against the wall, their eyes glued to the pictures on the sheet.

I couldn't make out what the pictures were at first: wondrous details of flowers, perhaps, or billowing clouds of smoke. Only after I had stared at them for a long time, again and again, did their true nature begin to emerge. They were case studies of venereal disease, doubtless filched from some doctor's office: enormous black whorls, blooming like mushrooms, in perfect, miniature rings.

Most of the pictures were taken close up, or at least the subjects were turning their heads away, still modestly holding up a sheet, a bit of shirt over the rest of their body. But sometimes, too, the whole person was captured, staring listlessly back at the camera, faces as pitted and lifeless as their sexual organs.

I saw those faces——and those intricate, beautiful whorls and flowers——and I knew what I was. I ran out of the room, knowing then that there could be no escape for me, or the old man. We were life, too, just like those beautiful, terrible tumors, churned out by the same, offhanded perfection of the universe. We were just life, and there was no helping it.

My plan to win Carlotta came to me while contemplating the Dreamland imitation of Venice, catercorner from Hell: a perfect likeness of the Doge's palace on the outside, as banally innocent as Hell itself inside. Here was no labyrinth of corridors, no watery, forgotten little cells—no Bridge of Sighs. Instead, there was a ludicrous imitation of the canals, winding their way around restaurant stands, and serenading quartets from Little Italy. The sky above painted the color of midnight, to hide the ceiling just above the waiters' heads.

It was perfect: a trite, hermetic little city of our own. A new nation, of the mad and the misshapen, conceived on top of Hell, and dedicated to the proposition that all men can live in any world they please.

Do I contradict myself? Very well then, I contradict myself. I am small, I contain microcosms.

Matty Brinckerhoff was the one to take it to, I knew. Big Tim Sullivan was the money man, he and his partners would like it well enough once the dollars began to roll in. Brinckerhoff was the genius to sell it to them.

I knew where I would find him, even at this hour. I had sat up with him before, sweltering summer nights when I was too tired to get up my disguise for the boys' bars, but too sleepless to lie in the arse of the Tin Elephant, listening to the whores and their customers.

He would be up there now. Up at the very top of the highest spot on Coney, the glowing white tower of Dreamland, just beneath its crowning ball, where his eagles were gathered—staring back across Surf Avenue at his lost paradise. The stunning, gold electric elevators were shut down for the night; I had to climb the whole seven flights to his office, insufficient legs trembling with the effort. I arrived panting, open-mouthed, in the incredible New York heat. Not yet dawn, and already like an oven.

"It is nearly perfect," he said when I came in, without bothering to turn around.

He was just where I thought he would be: tilted back in his chair, legs propped up on the windowsill. His back to Dreamland, gazing out at his beloved Luna Park.

"Of course, it is not perfect. Nothing can be, that is why there is always the need to build another. But it is a great consolation to me."

"Yes."

Beside him was a bottle of good gin, a glass, a pitcher of iced lemon water, perspiring freely over his latest blueprints. When he was like this I knew he could go on babbling all night.

"They say I am not a serious architect, but visitors to an amusement park are not in a serious mood and they do not want to encounter seriousness. A *serious* arch is no more welcome at an amusement park than a clown at a funeral."

"Yes."

Was it frivolous? Silly? Amusing? Oh, yes—all that, and so much more. Even then, slumbering blissfully in the early morning gloom, with all its million lights extinguished, Luna Park looked like nothing else in this world.

It was still new then, uncorroded by time or fresher miracles. A vast ramble of trellises and hanging gardens, lagoons and turrets, flowered colonnades glowing orange and white and gold. Minarets and onion domes, roller coasters and loop-the-loops, fairy-tale castles and flying buttresses and miniature railways and huge mocking clown heads. All the world, rolled into a ball. Arab bazaars and Alpine peaks, and all the great floods and volcanic explosions and the latest wars.

And in the evening, in the electric glowing evening, it came into its own. It humbled Nebuchadnezzar and his hanging gardens, and made Kublai Khan a piker. When the lights went on it was all spinning wheels and rivers and pearls of frozen fire. Burning, burning along the sands of Long Island, burning but was not consumed.

"I had to throw all my books and plans into the ash heap, I stuck to no school, I departed from all known rules of architecture. It is no one style at all, really, but all the license in the world."

"Yes."

He turned to me for the first time then, but his eyes didn't see me. His thick, dark, receding hair was frazzled by the heat, long moustaches drooping past the sides of his mouth. He dressed like a dandy but in the tropical, early-morning heat even his vanilla-ice-cream suit and green silk bowtie drooped, matching green carnation wilting in the lapel.

He pointed out toward his masterpiece.

"Everything here must be different from our ordinary experience—*everything*. We must manufacture the carnival spirit, in this manufacturing age, with all the will and ingenuity we are capable of. Whatever we see must have: life, action, motion, sensation, surprise, shock, speed—or at least, comedy.

"We must create a different world—a dream world. A nightmare world, if that's what it takes!"

He paused, recovering himself, swaying a little from the effect of the gin. He ran a hand back through his ruffled hair, and drew himself up straight.

"And of course, we build for the ninety-five percent of the American public that is pure and good."

He stopped then, his face twisting distastefully. For that was not what Dreamland had become, and we both knew it. He had realized his dream in Luna Park, all right, it was indeed like nothing else, ever—but not in Dreamland. How could he? How could it possibly have matched what he had already created—and anyway, Big Tim Sullivan's syndicate, the money men, had insisted on something more conventional. Something solid, recognizable, relying on sheer electrical power to outshine Luna Park, and Tilyou's Steeplechase down the street. The central tower we were standing in was immense and straightforward, a standard ball and eagle perched on top, gilded eagles running all up and down the sides—yet only one more wonder in an age that was rotten with them. Dreamland was bigger, its million bulbs glowed even brighter—but it was not fantastic.

Brinckerhoff had never gotten over it.

"I was betrayed, you know."

"Yes," I interrupted, before he could get started again. "Yes, I know. But I have an idea."

He cocked his head, indicating his brief desire to listen. Matty Brinckerhoff scooped up ideas the way other men grabbed loose change off the street.

"For something that's never been done before—"

I had his attention.

"An Empire of the Small," I continued. "A Midget Metropolis. Just for us."

The disappointment was visible in his face.

"Another dwarf circus?"

"No—something more. Not just some cardboard facades to knock down. A real town. A whole, permanent, year-round *city*. Everything built for us. *Scaled* for us."

The droopy moustache and big, sad, hound-dog eyes showed signs of life.

"The real deal. No more Little Big Man Revue. A bunch of dwarves parading around—it's been done. You can see that at any carny show in the sticks."

He nodded slowly, and I poured it on.

"I'm talking about something more. A whole fairy city."

"You would need everything."

He was already pulling paper, drawing pencils, a t-square out of his desk.

"Everything—absolutely everything——"

"A miniature town hall. A precinct house. A tiny fire station with real, tiny hook-and-ladders——"

"Why not, why not?"

"A rail station. A post office. A church——no, a midget *cathedral*——"

"A real palace," I snuck in, "for a real king and queen."

"*There has never been such a thing!* A city——a real, livable city——built to your scale. The architecture of the small, and the low. Doorknobs two feet off the ground. Windows and doors that open with a child's touch; fine and delicate as a Japanese pagoda. A masterpiece in miniature! Why not, why not——when all the world is getting *bigger*?"

He was already mapping out the parameters of the town, bushy hair curling up demonically in the oven heat.

"Yes, a palace," he murmured.

". . . Perhaps the Palacio Nationale. From Mexico City . . ." I suggested.

"But who would we find for such a thing? What king and queen?"

It wasn't something he really concerned himself with. The buildings were what he loved; everything else was just props, to be filled in later.

"Don't worry about it," I told him. "I have somebody in mind."

The rest of it was easy.

All it took was another trip up to the Bowery in my newsboy disguise. I waited for an appropriate moment, until after her first show was over and the Dudes were absorbed in a new production of *The Jew of Malta,* featuring added scenes in which Mose the Bowery Boy bounds onto the set and unmasks Barabas before he can have Abigail poisoned.

I made my way around the back, among the lascivious props of the Grand Duke's: a particularly bulbous, blood-stained set of woman's breasts. A bloody, papier-mâché head, with tear-away scalp; a horse's head, bleeding from both eyes. Wading through the stage gore, I found what I was looking for: a wooden pistol, nearly as big as my arm. I picked up an enormous stage saber for good measure; this was my heroic hour. Armed with only these props, I stormed her dressing room. In one quick motion, I picked the lock and slammed the door open, prepared for whatever might come.

He wasn't there. *She* was, though——still regal as a queen, sitting at her makeshift vanity. Even with the door crashing in, she did not hurry her royal, deliberate turn. I could swear, though, that I actually saw a hint of admiration in her eyes——something that sent chills through me.

"Quickly——there's not much time!" I told her, dramatic as any romance hero. "Get your things together."

"Are we going somewhere?" she asked, still perfectly self-possessed.

"To your palace——where else? It is being built even as we speak——*Your Majesty*."

The salutation did it. Her mad blue eyes glistened with the thought. A palace! It's one of the advantages of dealing with the truly insane; they wish for the moon but are completely satisfied with cheese.

"I must pack," she insisted——still testing me.

She hopped down from her chair, wooden shinguards knocking together, and opened up a traveling trunk stuffed with the most exquisite, miniature dresses and gowns——a living doll's wardrobe.

"Please hurry——*Majesty*!" I begged her, trying to keep the panic out of my voice. She ignored me, of course, neatly folding and packing away her ensembles as if she were going on tour.

I ducked around the corner, and peered out through the wings: I could see him at the bar still, towering above the boys. Even as I watched, he finished the last swig of his whiskey, dashed coins absently out on the bar and began to make his way toward me, through the merry crowd cheering the thrashing of the Jew.

"Now!" I screamed at her, bolting back into the dressing room.

She was working carefully through her yards of fine, silken underwear, sorting through mounds of credible paste diamonds and pearls and tiaras—humming "The Blue Danube" to herself as contentedly as if she were awaiting her lady's maid.

"We *must*, uh, *fly*, Your Majesty. Before he comes back!"

She gazed coolly up at me, pausing from her work.

"If he does come," she said as imperiously as Queen Victoria herself, "you must deal with him."

I rushed over to help her, rudely shoving her things down into her trunk. She frowned at me, but finally pulled down the lid and locked it shut.

"All right. It is ready."

"It can't be done!" I gasped, staring at the enormous trunk. I lifted at one end, but all the heroic gestures in the world wouldn't budge it. I could hear his steps in the hall outside.

"Eugénie, my love, it's almost time!" I heard his comfortable Bourbon drawl—employing both a name and a loving tone that astonished me. Eugénie, the old, exiled empress of France: Could she be *doubly* mad?

I didn't have time to reflect upon it. I secreted myself behind the door and swung my wooden saber down at his knees with all my might when he came through. He screamed and fell to the ground, clutching at his legs.

"For the love a God, don' murder me!" he begged——suddenly cut down to my size.

I was a man of action now. I shoved the sham pistol into his lowered gut, then banged it up hard beneath his chin. Marconi swooned on the floor.

"Let us fly," I said bravely to my queen, whose eyes shone with adoration.

Somehow, I managed to pick up the trunk, haul and shove it out the backstage door, and down an alley to Pearl Street. I was ready to drag it all the way out to Coney Island by myself, even if it tore my arms out of their sockets. Yet a block away, she placed a surprisingly soft, tentative hand upon my shoulder.

"There's a cab," she said——and I was in no mood to argue, even though I knew it would take my last five dollars to get us out to Coney.

"Where can I take you kiddies?" the coachman grinned down at us.

I flipped a silver dollar up to him, ordered him to boost our trunk. He did as he was told, still smirking——though I fancied he shot an appraising glance over my Carlotta, or Eugénie, or whoever this strange, immaculate little doll was. I helped her up into the cab, her little hand small and cool and smooth in my palm.

We took off, clopping at the usual lumber truck's pace through the streets of lower Manhattan. I knew the cabbie would squeal——they always did——but I figured her Marconi would be reluctant to come out to my territory for her, and if he did I could handle him there.

"Lower the curtains," she commanded, inside the warm, leathered coach, and when I did she moved against me, put her arm through mine, lowered her head to that soft spot where the neck meets the shoulder.

I sat there rigidly, stunned by what she had done. It was everything I had ever wanted, in that one, simple gesture of affection. I was afraid to move, afraid to hold her—afraid to do anything that might end the moment.

Slowly, slowly, I laid my head against hers, crept my arm around her shoulders until I was actually holding her, like some strong and protective man, her body soft and pliant and trusting against my chest.

"Are you all right?"

"Yes. Is it really a palace?"

"Yes. Or it will be. I promise."

The cab began to rise steadily, as we pulled onto the bridge over to Brooklyn. She sat up, and I pulled aside the curtain a little, to show her the traffic careening madly around us, even at this hour, automobiles and trucks and bicycles, all lunging avidly ahead.

Far below, we could see the slips along South Street pier to our left, the harbor to our right—the ships with their running lights like lily pads in a shimmering night pond.

"Will it be like this?" she asked, her eyes like pinwheels inside the cab, and for once she didn't seem like a queen at all but a young girl, dreaming of married life and her own first home.

"Better," I told her, willing now to say absolutely anything she wanted to hear. "*Better.*"

I was afraid that she might bolt once she saw the Tin Elephant. I kept telling her it was only temporary the whole way up the spiral stairs, the coachman bumping her trunk carelessly along behind, grinning and quipping with the whores. There was no disguising the place—but to my surprise she took it all in stride.

"To true royalty there are no indignities," she said with regal equanimity.

Somehow, she didn't mind it—not even the moldy, salt-etched walls and the hookers, the deliberately leering, suggestive signs in the halls: BATHERS WITHOUT FULL SUITS POSITIVELY PROHIBITED BY LAW.

That first night, she sat on my bed in a dark blue evening gown she put on especially for the occasion. I know it was silly, it was silly as young love and honeymoon nights, but I loved it.

The whores stood out in the hall and sang us a drunken shivaree. A blind girl they called the Yellow Kid led them. She wasn't much to look at, a stringy, jaundiced street whore, but the johns all loved her because she played the zither and sang sad, homesick songs from Kiev to Dublin in a sweet, clear voice:

> She's as white as any lily
> As gentle as a dove
> She threw her arms around me
> Saying Johnny I love you still
> She is Nell the farmer's daughter
> The pride of Spancil Hill . . .

"You may undress me," my empress said, her voice calm and self-assured as ever.

"I never—I mean, I didn't *plan*—"

"Go ahead," she commanded, and I began to undo the stays on her dress.

"You will have your palace. I swear it."

"I know."

I undressed her the way I might have undressed a child, or indeed a doll—my sweet, pretty bride, how many things were you? Mad queen; mechanical wonder; lost, wandering freak. Reverently, carefully, I pulled the midnight blue dress down over her perfect, white shoulders; it made a gorgeous rustling sound.

She sat comfortably through it, moving just enough to accommodate me here, help my thick, clumsy fingers with a catch or a stay there. I took off her clothes layer by layer, first the dress, then the outer petticoats, then her slips and stockings, until she sat small and naked and even more beautiful on my rough bed—still as regal as ever.

> I dreamt I held and kissed her
> as in the days of old
> Saying Johnny you're only joking
> As many's the time before
> But the cock he crew in the morning
> He crew both loud and shrill
> I awoke in California many miles
> from Spancil Hill

I touched her all over, unable to help myself in the face of such unmitigated beauty. And she sat there, and let me, and then she was holding me, kissing me back, her arms around me, soft and giving.

It wasn't simply the lust. The popular imagination has it that we are all freakishly lusty creatures, diddling away like little demons. It couldn't be further from the truth; after all, the only partners usually available to us are other freaks— the bearded lady, the fat woman, the alligator man—or prostitutes, or thrill-seekers—or those like ourselves. It becomes a degraded act, filled with self-loathing, in which the best one can hope for is an all-too-accurate mirror of one's own, despised self.

But this was different. She was beautiful, and she offered herself up to me freely, and unabashedly. Afterwards, I bathed her in my wash basin, kneeling before her, until her skin shone. She put on a fine, white, embroidered night-gown—where she obtained such things I could only imag-ine—and then she rolled over and fell asleep in my bed, trusting as a child. I sat up for a long time, and watched her, stroking her hair.

After my revelation in the anatomical museum, I had run back home to my poor, deluded father—his already feeble act beginning to falter as he forgot his lines, his brain mari-nated in brandy by now.

I kissed him good-bye, took one trunkful of books for my own, and hooked on with Proctor's, then the old Sunday School Circuit, doing anything I could. I learned a little tumbling and how to tell jokes, and how to juggle. I turned magic tricks on a bill between Evelyn Nesbit and Convict 6630, The Man Who Sang Himself out of the Penitentiary. I played the old ten-twenty-thirties, in the stock shows *The Earl of Pawtucket* and *Are You My Father?* and *What's the Matter with Susan?* and I sang in the chorus of *Beautiful Edna May, Salvation Army Girl*—

—I tell them to follow, follow Jesus,
but they always follow, follow me—

In short, I did anything, no matter what the degradation. For what was I, but life?

Above all, I kept moving—back and forth, every season, from Lake Quinsigamond to the old German Sharpshooter Park in Chicago; from Euclid Beach to the White City to Paragon Park. For a time, I would stop back on the Bowery and see how the old man was doing, got him a new room when he couldn't do the act at all anymore.

One season I stopped going back—just stopped. Until, three years later, when I finally mustered the courage to go

59

back and see him one more time, he was gone. Whether he had died or not I could never determine, but his books kept popping up, in raggedy little notion shops and ragpicker alleys all around the Bowery. I always recognized them, even before I saw his name, and the date he had bought them, penciled neatly in on the title page: "Patrick J. Mahoney, *Sr.*"—that last, conscience-plaguing acknowledgment of my existence. I bought them up whenever I could, but I never found any other trace of him.

And after it all, after all the coon songs and the Carrie Nation lectures, after all the freak shows and the midways, the Chautauquas and the rube towns, after all the endless nights picking up rude bits of knowledge in parlor cars and fleabag hotels and blind pigs—after all that, I had been tossed up on the shore of the Atlantic Ocean, on Coney Island, like so much flotsam and jetsam myself.

Was I home now? Outside, the whores slowly drifted away, off to the next batch of customers. I stayed chastely beside my beloved the rest of the night, one arm draped around her so that no hand could take her from me in my sleep. Was I home? I watched her for a long time before I nodded off, dreaming fitfully of us both in a great palace.

BOOK TWO

*I have no trust, and fear the prudery
of the new continent.*

——SIGMUND FREUD

7

THE GREAT HEAD DOCTORS FROM VIENNA

Freud wasn't sure that he had really seen the man at first. It seemed impossible, like a waking nightmare, or one of Jung's apparitions.

He had just finished a long stretch of work, writing up the Rat Man case, and he was sitting contentedly on the terrace of the Cafe Landtman with the rest of the Vienna bourgeoisie. Reveling in his cigars and his *einen kleinen Braunen,* like a pleasure-loving philistine, swapping his favorite old Yiddish jokes with the *maskilim.* When this vision appeared—

He was both more and less than a man. A monolith, really, something primitive and huge, standing out there on the Ringstrasse. One more refugee from the East, come from a land past all human memory and knowledge, and more than likely having walked all the way. Face swathed in a ragged, aimless beard, tattered skullcap on his head. Plodding open-mouthed up the Ring in his beggar's rags, past the fairy-tale buildings, the long file of lifeless statues.

Even as Freud watched, some of Mayor Lueger's bully-boys caught up to him in front of the Landtman. They taunted him for awhile, and he obviously did not understand, staring back at the students in their close-cut hair, their uniform brown suits and black ties. Clutching his little pile of rags closer to his chest. They began to push him about, jostling him more and more seriously until his package fell into the street. They kicked it apart—revealing just more rags, some old vegetables, a few leaves of a book he had got somewhere.

Freud stood up at his table. Everyone else was looking away, all the *sheyne yidn,* and the contented, gentile burghers, too, staring into their coffee grounds. There was not a policeman in sight—just more shopkeepers and bureaucrats strolling imperturbably by. The man reached out blindly for his possessions—but they kept kicking them away from his grasp, knocking the skullcap off his head as he leaned over.

Freud started to step around the table—still with no good idea of what he would do but convinced that he had to do *something*—when the municipal police appeared. They shooed the youths away, took the young beggar into custody. It was safe for the Landtman's patrons, Jew and gentile alike, to look up again. The strolling crowds quickly covered over the whole scene, like a corpse dropped into an ocean.

It was a strange scene, a disturbing augury on the eve of his great voyage, and Freud could not help mulling it over. Not that he believed in auguries, that was Jung's department. He believed in science, even the science of the mind, and his trip would be an unprecedented opportunity to advance that Cause.

The invitation from America had been so deferential, even flattering: a generous stipend and an honorary degree from Clark University, in return for a chance to give five lectures before the greatest minds of science: Dewey, Wundt, Boas, Ebbinghaus, Metchnikoff—an incredible, waking daydream.

He had even managed to secure three lectures and another degree for Jung, his crown prince. They would travel over together, along with good old Ferenczi—his leading acolyte, aide, and errand boy of the moment. They would go through New York, take some time to tour the country—though he had joked to Ferenczi that all he really wanted was to see a porcupine.

To Jung, he had written:

"We are certainly getting ahead. If I am Moses, then you are Joshua and will take possession of the promised land of psychiatry, which I shall only be able to glimpse from afar."

That evening, the Vienna Psycho-Analytical Society gave him a grand send-off in the Prater, the huge city park by the Danube. By day it was a crowded, roiling place, with a midway and a beer garden, but by night the park was transformed, its gracious trees wild and brooding as a Wagnerian forest.

The assembled psycho-analysts had tromped solemnly up a hill under boughs of jasmine and hyacinth, and glowing Chinese lanterns. At the top, a banquet table had been laid out, and there they sat, and feasted, and drank toast after toast of *Gewürztraminer* to their master. They presented him with a carved African idol, some kind of gaping fertility god, and Freud held this totem solemnly beside him at the head of the table, accepting their toasts and tributes under the swaying lanterns with royal equanimity.

The previous spring he had descended on the first psycho-analytical congress like Moses indeed come down from the mountain, striding into their meeting unannounced and uninvited. He had got word that there was consternation in the ranks over Jung, the son, the heir.

"Most of you are Jews, and therefore you are incompetent to win friends for our new science," he had told them. "Jews must be content with the modest role of preparing the ground. It is absolutely essential that I should form ties in the world of general science. I am getting old, and worn out with always being attacked."

Dramatically, he had grabbed his own coat by its lapels, as if to rend it.

"Don't you see? We are all in great danger. This cannot be known as the 'Jewish science'—they won't even leave me with a coat on my back. Jung and the other Swiss will save us—will save me, and all the rest of you!"

Overawed, they had done as he demanded. Jung had thanked him profusely for it and sworn again his fealty to the Cause, to the new science of psychology.

Yet almost as soon as he had anointed his crown prince, he had had . . . *misgivings*. Jung had come to visit, and talked all kinds of mystical foolishness about *Nirdvanda*, and the *numinosum* of sense and nonsense.

Freud had been stunned, telling himself this was simply Jung's age, his restless, searching intellect. But then, when they were alone in his study, a sudden, loud noise had burst from his bookcase. Freud thought one of the supports had broken, burdened as it was by his massive works of science. Everything stood undisturbed, precisely as it had been, but Jung had jumped up, breathless with excitement.

"There! I knew that would happen!" he proclaimed, pointing at the offending bookcase. "My chest felt like it was made of molten iron—and then, *voila!* A perfect example of a catalytic exteriorization phenomenon! There is a poltergeist in your bookcase."

"Come now," Freud had blurted out. "You must know that is sheer bosh."

"It is not. You are mistaken, *Herr Professor*," Jung had huffed. "In fact, I predict there will be another such noise in a moment!"

66

As luck would have it, of course, there *was* another such noise—Freud leaping to his feet this time, though more out of fear that the whole bookcase was about to come tumbling down on their heads than of any poltergeist. Jung looked at him triumphantly—and after that there had been no convincing him the noises were not somehow linked to their relationship.

To his extreme annoyance, Freud found himself listening to his bookcases over the next few weeks. The noises recurred, randomly, the result of the books or the house settling. He had written about it to Jung, gently chiding his "dear son" and attributing it all to the cooperation of chance.

"Whatever you do, don't let them drag my theories down into the black mud of occultism," he had begged him, but there was no reply.

Alcohol never agreed with him, and the grand reception in the Prater was no different. On the night train up to Bremen he tried a little more beer to settle himself but it had only made things worse. He was up half the night, padding back and forth to a filthy public toilet. There he clung for dear life to a side handle, while the train rocked and whistled through the Bavarian countryside.

Finally, he sank into a restless dream. It was part of an old dream, a dream he'd had before under similar circumstances; the primary dream of his greatest work, the *Traumdeutung*—

In the dream he was in the Aula, the great ceremonial hall of the university, in Vienna. It was filled, now, with all the great scientists who would be at Clark. He felt nervous but prepared, stepping up to the lectern with his notes in hand.

But then, just as he got there, he realized that he had an over-

67

whelming need to urinate. He muttered an excuse and stepped away, trying the doors behind the lectern, looking for a toilet. Behind him he could hear a growing murmur from the assembled scientists, a sound of indignation, but he couldn't help it, he knew that if he waited any longer he would wet his pants right in front of them.

He found a door, and went through it. It led through a long series of rooms, all of them beautifully appointed apartments, or majestic offices of the imperial ministries——but not one of them, a toilet.

Then the scene changed, and he was out of the Aula altogether. He was standing on a platform of the Stadtbahn, the suburban railway, and holding a glass urinal——a sort of glass bedpan, with a long, penile stem in his hand——but he no longer had to pee. He was holding the urinal, instead, for an old, sick man, blind in one eye, whom he was accompanying.

It felt better, being out in the open air, but he still had a great feeling of anxiety. A conductor was moving down the platform, he realized, and neither he nor his charge, the old, half-blind man, had a ticket. Hastily, he handed the one-eyed man the urinal——then put up a disguise, a mask in front of the man's face, to fool the conductor. A mask that was the face of the idol, the African totem he had been given the night before——

After that, the old dream faded, but he still did not sleep well. He was happier than usual to see Ferenczi's boyish, homey face when the train pulled into Bremen the next morning. The man had already made all the arrangements and now he stood waiting on the platform, smiling cheerfully, red Baedeker guide in hand. He had everything well in hand, and they met up with Jung on schedule at the ship's luggage depot, where he was exulting openly over their trip:

"Just think of the women we shall meet! The wealthy American females to analyze!"

"*Jah,*" Freud had agreed more guardedly. "America should at least bring money, not cost money."

The money itself, when they did exchange it, was a disappointment. It was appallingly ugly, Freud thought, a thick, dull roll of notes, all the same size, black on the front, a picture of some exotic animal he took to be an American buffalo printed in green ink on the back.

"Ah, there you are, there is no reason to go now," he had joked with Ferenczi, still feeling relieved to be off the train. "I was only going so I could see a buffalo—or better yet, a *porcupine!*"

Jung had been to Bremen before, which meant that he insisted on showing the way around the sites, the usual churches and picturesque stairs. At the cathedral there was a *Bleikeller,* a lead cellar, where they could stare down at the preserved body of a workman. He had fallen from the cathedral roof four hundred years before, and the lead had mummified his body—his skin tanned like fine leather, mouth stretched into a final scream by the contraction of the tendons in his neck, arms still clutching scraps of his medieval guild's shift up around his neck. Looking inconceivably ancient—

Freud found the whole thing morbid, but at lunch that afternoon Jung could not stop talking about it.

"Perfectly preserved like that! A window into the past!"

"Yes, but why wasn't he taken out of there and buried?"

"What does it matter?" Jung shrugged, knifing aggressively through his fish. "He serves our purposes."

"But why?" Freud pondered. "Did they just go on working, with his corpse in the cellar?"

"Why not? Is a cemetery burial any less barbaric?"

They were dining at a fish restaurant, the *Essinghaus,* which had a fine menu of Rhone wines. It was a glorious summer day, bright and warm, but not too hot yet. Their dining room was full of light and flowers, and everyone was talking about the air show in Berlin, and whether Orville Wright would bring his new machine over from America.

Jung would not stop dwelling on the man in the lead cellar. Freud tried to distract him by urging him to drink some of the delicious wine. He could barely drink it himself after his night on the train but he knew that Jung had not had a drop since the start of Forel's abstinence campaign at the Burgholzli, nine years before. He resisted for a moment, contemplating both the wine and Freud—then poured himself a full glass.

"*Jah*, I am renouncing my abstinence," Jung said with sudden decisiveness, his eyes shining. "You must encourage me in this endeavor."

"We will make a Viennese libertine out of you yet!" Freud exulted—but Jung only resumed talking about that wretched man in the lead cellar. He began to speak of other preserved men as well, recently unearthed from the peat bogs in Denmark—all the while methodically cutting his fish to pieces.

"The acid in the peat tanned and cured the skin. The bodies were flattened by the weight of the earth, and the bones had disintegrated. But the hair, and teeth! The whole face and form of the body, the jewelry on their arms! All, perfectly preserved!"

"Why are you so concerned with these corpses?" Freud cut in peevishly.

"Think of the implications. The bodies in the bogs were even older than our friend in the lead cellar. Prehistoric, perhaps. Preserved complete with remnants of their clothing, their totemic burial charms."

"*Jah, jah*—what of it?"

"Think of what we could learn! Imagine if their brains were as well preserved as their bodies."

70

Freud took a deep draught from his glass of wine to hide his exasperation, but when he put it down he only felt more irritable, and a little woozy.

"*What* would we learn? We learn from the couch, from *talking* to patients. My dear doctor, a well-preserved physical specimen is no more relevant to our work than a mounted butterfly!"

"How do you know?" Jung persisted. "Who knows how the mind has evolved? Maybe they *are* different. Maybe we can find a window, deep into the primitive soul——"

"What are you talking about?" Freud snapped, his voice rising. "*Every* living person contains the *whole history* of the human race!"

He took another sip of the wine to steady himself, but the room was lurching around him. He stood up abruptly at his place, his vision narrowing to Jung's face across the table—inquisitive as a terrier's, the squashed circles of his pince-nez magnifying his eager, greedy eyes.

"My dear friend!"

"*What?* What is your obsession with this poor man, deserted by his friends and fellow workers? Left to be a sideshow exhibit—a *freak*—on display for the gawking public!"

"It was just an observation, in the spirit of scientific inquiry."

"*Jah!*" Freud shot back sarcastically. "Are you sure, *Herr Doktor,* that what you are not really after is my death? My crown prince!"

That was when he swooned. He tried to move away from the table, but his legs were suddenly as heavy as bags of sand, and he slid down to the carpeted restaurant floor. Fainted away, just like some little virgin—the last thing he remembered being the not unpleasurable sight of their worried and astonished faces.

•   •   •

Sigmund Freud awoke to find himself staring into the face of Carl Jung. He closed his eyes again.

"How sweet it must be to die," he murmured.

"How's that?"

Freud's eyes snapped back open. Jung's balding, bullet-shaped head was still hovering over him.

"Never mind."

He sat up on the sofa where they had carried him and where Jung had laid him out like a schoolboy, feet crossed over each other on the soft red cushions.

"It must have been the wine," he said weakly. "I hardly slept last night, I had the most extraordinary dream."

Jung smiled patronizingly, his eyes skeptical behind the flattened orbs of the pince-nez.

"Naturally, we will not let Papa pay for us anymore," he said to Ferenczi.

Freud got quickly to his feet, buttoning his coat and smoothing his hair to mask his agitation. Jung offered his arm, but he shook his head, leading the way back to the table, ignoring the other, whispering diners—already analyzing his own behavior.

"There was, perhaps, an element of guilt involved," he conceded, once he had regained his seat. "Over getting you to break your abstinence, I mean."

Jung contemplated him for a long moment—then resumed his dissection of the fish.

"Perhaps," the crown prince said—and Freud had the sudden, irrational desire to snatch off the pince-nez and grind it under his heel until he heard the glass snap. Instead, he smiled inquisitively.

"What, then?"

"Well, it's just that you fear me as a usurping son," Jung said. "Taking your place."

"Really? You deduced all that, just from one fainting spell?"

"It's just a hypothesis, of course," Jung said calmly,

springing his trap: "If I could psycho-analyze you, perhaps on our voyage over."

"Perhaps," Freud said darkly.

"There may be an element of truth in what both of you were saying," Ferenczi intervened sweetly, always the precocious child, mediating between his quarreling parents.

"The two greatest psycho-analytical minds in the world, searching for a solution! Think of it!"

"We shall see," Freud told him. "We shall see."

After lunch, Jung hired an automobile to take them around town. Another patronizing commentary on his age, Freud thought, but he was secretly grateful not to have to walk, after his experience at the *Essinghaus*.

They drove toward a Viennese cafe Jung knew, on the banks of the Weser, but they had to stop to let a regiment of German artillery pass, on their way back from field maneuvers. Jung had insisted on climbing down from the car, peering closely at the long gray line of men and cannons as they swung past.

"Of course, the captain of the Swiss army reserves must inspect the kaiser's troops," Freud had joked with Ferenczi, but he soon found himself staring as well.

The Germans moved quickly, serious and deadly as the guns they towed. By the time they had passed he realized he was holding his breath, and looking around he saw that Ferenczi was staring, too—mesmerized by the murderous living machine moving past them.

This was nothing like the Imperial Austrian army of Freud's own military reserve experience. Then he had crouched in a trench, the generals parading above him in their sky-blue and yellow uniforms like so many parakeets. A major approached, his tunic the color of a baboon's ass, and handed Freud the list of wounds he could expect as company medical officer.

"Large intestine and stomach wall repeatedly perforated," he had read. "Spine severed at the second vertebrae. Lower jaw and tongue shot away, upper palate severely mutilated——"

The troops lay all around in great, grotesque piles, faking slaughter.

"Prepare!" the officer snapped at him.

"Prepare? But how am I to prepare for such wounds? What could I possibly do?"

"Prepare!"

That night he slept restlessly, despite his exhaustion, but with no dreams he could remember. The next day they took the ship train on up to Bremerhaven, and boarded the *George Washington,* a large, elegant ship of the North German Lloyd line. Their cabins were exquisite, and a wealthy woman patient who lived in Nassau had surprised them with a splendid bouquet of orchids.

Freud was pleased, and he tipped the steward to put them in a vase on their table in the dining room, where he could share them every night with Jung and Ferenczi. Already his mood was improving, and he was sure now that all he needed was the sea air to be back in fighting trim again, ready for his triumph.

The weather changed that afternoon, though, before they were even out of port. It began to rain in sheets, driving them all off the deck and back into the dining room, where everyone was wondering if the weather would keep Captain Spelterini from flying his hydrogen balloon over the Alps, and ruin the air show.

Freud retreated to his stateroom, to watch the tugs churn through the purple water of Bremerhaven harbor, and ruminate with his cigars over his nagging doubts. He was never afraid to examine and reexamine everything; that was his great strength, even if he did not always admit it to others.

"I have the spirit of a conquistador—a Cortés, or Pizarro," he had written about himself, and he was pleased with the analogy, despite its ruthlessness.

He had no fear of the voyage itself. He loved the ocean, was never seasick in even the roughest weather. He did have some doubts about the lectures: he was worried the Americans would be too prudish, too easily shocked. There would be the usual outcry when they heard his ideas first-hand, perhaps even some more Jew-baiting.

"We could soon be up shit creek the minute they come upon the sexual underpinnings of our psychology," he had confided to Ferenczi, but he had been through all that before. Here, for the first time, was an audience ready to honor him—before they had even heard his lectures.

It was something more that was making him uneasy. Something hidden, and primal, he sensed, like the enormous painting of the white horse with frenzied eyes and flaring nostrils that dominated his study on the Berggasse. His literal nightmare, rearing its head from the darkness.

He could not shake, for one thing, his memories of the military training camp, and the officer with his terrible list. Jung's image also stayed with him: the expressionless, bespectacled face, hovering over him, peering in so intently at the awful gray German guns as they passed.

Then there was the joke about the porcupine he felt compelled to keep making. It was something from Schopenhauer, he realized—a line about how porcupines had to be the most solitary of animals, for their barbs kept them even from huddling together against the elements. Yet what that had to do with his own situation he could not yet imagine.

He mulled it over until well after they were under way, then he risked a brandy and climbed into his bunk. Lying there, he remembered a favorite saying of Napoleon's mother:

Ça va bien pourvu que ça dure—
It goes well as long as it lasts.

He couldn't help adding the next line to himself:

Said the roofer as he began to fall.

8

ON THE BOARDWALK

They met on the beach at Coney. He was making his way through the Sunday crowd, looking out for his opportunities, and when he happened to glance down there she was: buried up to her thighs in the sand like a child, wearing a shiny green mermaid's bathing suit, still wet from the sea, and brushing out her hair with a silver brush.

Esther felt him over her, blocking the sun. She looked up and smiled to see him there—looking so solemn, in his flashy suit the color of peach ice cream and a brilliant blue bow tie. He tipped his hat to her, and held out his arm, and without even thinking about it she reached up and took it, and let him guide her back toward the parks.

Anyplace else, she would never have done such a thing. Anyplace else but on the beach on Coney Island, on a beautiful Sunday morning. She put the cheap, silver-painted brush she had bought at Wanamaker's away, and took his arm, and let him lift her up, watching him watch the skirt of her costume slip slowly down over her bare, white legs.

"Let me treat you," Kid told her.

Esther laughed at him, but there was something very serious in his face.

"Treat me?"

"Anything you want," he told her impulsively. "The best piece of goods there is!"

"My Rockefeller prince!"

She laughed again, and let him take her back up the beach, toward the pavilions of fun, trying discreetly to brush the last of the sand off her legs, the green-gold imitation scales of her suit glistening in the sunlight.

Up on the boardwalk, up on the breezeway at Feltman's they ate lobster and clams and corn on the cob, until their tiny white-tableclothed table was drenched in melted butter and warm sea brine. A band in lederhosen was playing Viennese waltzes, and everyone was laughing. Esther even let him give her some of his beer; she thought it tasted awful, but she wanted to know what the goyim went padding down into the German saloon beneath their tenement for.

"You like it?" Kid asked, nudging her. "Beer agrees with you, moon?"

She shook her head, and smiled secretly to herself.

"*Hertzalle meine,*" he beseeched her. The usual seducer's words, but he said them flatly, as if he were trying to convince himself more than her. A hand lay on her knee under the little table, the fingers trembling slightly. Esther pushed it casually aside, used to much more from the factory foremen, and there was no resistance.

"How can you be here with me?" he asked her——trying to smile, but actually very serious again. "How do you know what kind of man I am?"

"I like you," Esther shrugged, trying to sound bold, and brazen, groping for reasons. "I like how you laugh. And you have kind eyes."

Why was she there?

"But I could be the worst *yentzer* in the whole world!"

"I can take care of myself."

"But you don't know what I am." Completely serious again, his eyes large dark circles. *He did have nice eyes—*

"What does it matter?" she said, as bluff as she could manage. *What a strange seducer, warning her to look out.* "What does it matter, here and now?"

"I guess you're right there," he laughed uncertainly, and went back to tearing up his lobster.

After lunch, they walked hand-in-hand to the Steeplechase, past the chop suey joints and the shooting galleries. Past the player pianos and the beef dripping from a spit and wash-boilers full of green corn, and the men taunting them from the quick-lunch stands:

"Who's your sweetie?"

"Where're you two goin'? Off to see the elephant?"

He only glowered at them and pulled her on, through the shuffling, indifferent crowds.

A million encounters, she thought. *A million encounters every day, all meaning nothing—*

He towed her through the Gates of Mirth, into the glassed-in Pavilion of Fun, with its sheared-off, manic head, grinning from ear to ear:

STEEPLECHASE—FUNNY PLACE

The track wound around the entire park, long and undulant, and lined with American flags. He paid her quarter fare, and a grinning youth in blackface and tattered jockey's silks stepped forward, to help her mount the mechanical horse.

"Up you go—"

"No, you don't!"

He pushed the attendant away and helped her on himself—staring at the white flash of her ankles again, as she swung her leg over. He climbed on behind her, and she didn't protest. All around them other men were bowing and smiling, helping other women they had just met onto their mounts.

A million encounters, meaning nothing

"Better hold on, little dove."

She could feel his warm breath on her cheek, murmuring into her ear.

"It gets going."

But it didn't. The horses didn't go very fast at all, that was the attraction. Another youth in checkerboard silks and painted darkie face blew a trumpet, and bells clanged, and the horses shot off—just fast enough to send the women squealing into their escorts' arms. They moved so slowly the men didn't even need a hand to hang onto their hats. They could devote both arms to the work, hands sliding and grabbing and caressing.

The horse soared effortlessly up and the whole expanse of the parks spread out beneath her, inexpressibly beautiful. It was the smoothest ride she had ever felt—as smooth as air, smooth as pudding under her feet. She had gone fast before. She had felt the speed in one of her brother's new automobiles, or when some idiot of a conductor took the el, fast as he could hold her, around the Dead Man's Curve on 110th Street. But she had never known anything like this—fast enough but smooth, too, as smooth as fine lawn—

They glided back down, the rest of the park beneath her, all the rides and attractions shining beneath its glass trellis like jewels through ice. The Mixer, and the Barrel of Fun, and the Bounding Billows, and the Golden Stairs, and the Razzle Dazzle and the Cave of the Winds. And around them, all the distended men and women, still shuffling relentlessly forward—

A million encounters, all useless

He slid his arms around her waist, and leaned them expertly into the curves. Soon they were out ahead of the rest, a small breeze blowing pleasantly across her face. At her waist, she could feel his hands beginning to move on her: still hesitant, awkward but gentle now, caressing her through the mermaid costume.

"You're all soft silk and fine velvet," he murmured in her ear, and she wanted to laugh to hear him say it.

He moved his hands slowly up her waist, her belly, to places where she had never felt a man's hands before, and she let him——glad that he had pushed them ahead of the other, groping men, away from their leering eyes. They rose again, and she could see the ocean turning toward them, and the mobs along the beach: the pleasure boats, graceful as swans, with their huge white decks and romantic names— the *Pegasus* and the *Prometheus* and *Anacreon in Heaven*.

They encompassed half the earth in a matter of seconds—then they were down again: the other riders chortling and cursing on their own horses, the women screaming. His hands, his hands slid up almost to her breasts, stopping when she flinched, sliding, stroking down her again, and she let him. They were moving too quickly, too high up for anyone else to see, alone among the millions.

"You're finer than silk and velvet, I'll give you only dove's milk to drink——" The seducer's voice gone now. Only his own words remaining, eager, and uncertain, and a little desperate.

They made the final turn, past the pier, heading in toward the land, the streets and the slouching summer houses on Brighton Beach. Houses of easy virtue, she remembered— like going to see the elephant. He was lowering his face to the open collar of her mermaid's bathing costume, nuzzling his lips down her neck.

Like a horse, Esther thought, ludicrously, his lips wet and soft as a horse's.

He kissed her ear, stroked his hand along her neck, and she let him. They were going a little faster now, coming into the finish, and she knew that she ought to stop him but she was not sure that she could push him away and hang on. She did not want to fall off, plummeting out on the mechanical track on her bottom. She could get electrocuted, she could get run down like that poor woman she had seen in the nickelodeon at Union Square, running out before the King's horse at the Derby for women's rights——

Run down by a horse

She leaned her head back into him at the home stretch, looked at him there. His eyes were closed, to her surprise, his face boyish and sweet. She leaned back, and held onto his arms, let him hold her as they swooped down past the last American flags, over the finish line, to another, mocking jockey in black-face who pinned a blue ribbon on both their chests.

Esther struggled off the horse, her legs weak, bare white ankles flashing in front of him again. Kid struggled to get off himself, the burnt-cork jockey jeering:

"Whatsa matta? Too many legs?"

"Wait for me!"

It was too late. She was already wandering out past the finish line. She stopped to find herself on a stage——row after row of bleachers in front of her, every seat filled with laughing men and women, pointing at *her*.

A terrible little man in a clown suit rushed up to her waving some kind of club in his hands, mongoloid face grinning hideously. He swung it at her, and she backed away, holding out her hands. He only kept advancing on her, swinging the cattle prod like a baseball bat.

"Piece of wretch!" she shrieked, barely dodging away in time. "Wild animal!"

He laughed, yelling her words back at her in his ridiculous, high, dwarf's voice while he jabbed at her legs:

"Piece of wretch! Wild animal!"

She felt a terrible shock run through her body, as if a hand had wrapped itself around her heart. She fell back——and cold air rushed mortifyingly up her backside, blowing up the skirt of her mermaid bathing suit and making her jump in the air before the laughing crowd.

"Filth! Get away!"

Kid came running out on the stage, shooing away the dwarf. The mongoloid clown smirked, and scooted around him—but there was something in his face that made him go on to torture the other riders. Kid wrapped his arms protectively around her, guided her out past the Laughing Gallery and its barker:

"Come on in! Only a penny! *You* be the one laughing this time!"

"Little dove, are you all right?"

"Sure, sure," she said, smiling to reassure him—enjoying how he looked at her so solicitously, so sweetly now.

It was fun, Esther told herself, feeling her heart pounding wildly. It was terrifying, she had beat it, she had got past the awful little man, had gone through it all and survived.

It was fun, and I liked it

That night Kid took her to Stauch's for a steak, and they sat in the balcony and watched the dancers shuffling around the huge ballroom under a giant, electrified American flag. Afterwards he wanted her to go to a moving picture at the Sunken Gardens or a show at Henderson's but it was late, she should have left for home already. The park was already beginning to take on a spectral look, as the music lowered, and the crowds wandered out. Little clumps of debris swirled around their feet like tumbleweeds: used paper napkins, and wax paper, and half-eaten hot-dog buns.

She could *hear* the lights now, the million bulbs, hissing loud as snakes. Couples hurried past, and in the darkness she could see a man's straw hat bent furtively over a dress, both faces hidden in the darkness.

He walked her over to the train platform, pleading good-naturedly, not really expecting her to stay, but wanting her to—wanting her to, she could *tell,* underneath it all.

"Just a little longer, bridie mine."

"No. It's late, I got to get back."

Fiery geysers of light shot up into the night—the closing fireworks, raining down in sizzling streams of red, white and blue. The bands struck up a patriotic air.

Distracted, just for a moment, Kid turned back to look for her—and she was gone. Only at the last moment did he spot her again, waving from the train window, holding her shoes in one hand. She had taken them off for speed and run onto the train barefoot.

"My little dove!" he yelled to her, half smiling, his face falling flatteringly. "My little dove. Next Sunday—over at Dreamland!" he hollered, running along the platform, smiling and frowning, unsure if she could even hear him.

"Next Sunday—by the archangel—"

But she only waved at him, smiling, until the packed train pulled out of the station, its passengers smashed right up against the windows, waving frantically to their own Sunday lovers; and the next train pulled in.

9

ESTHER

It was hotter than ever by the time she got back to Orchard Street, and the whole block was still up. Kids ran back and forth, screaming along the sidewalk as if it were midday, and old people slumped over their windowsills. Mothers walked back and forth under the streetlight, comforting their babies, they turned blue and convulsed in the heat, too exhausted to sleep.

They would still be up, she knew. Waiting for her.

She walked up the high stoop, passing under the archway with its Star of David superimposed over the old relief of a grinning satyr's head. It was the star that had convinced her father this was a place where people lived—a kosher building, somehow, as if there were any such thing. Another one of his idiotic, greenhorn mistakes: no man had ever been less equipped to deal with the traps and snares of the New World, but there was no telling him, he was a great scholar.

Inside, Esse felt like she was like climbing up through a giant, human hive. From every apartment, she could hear the squeak of water pumps, the little buzz of conversations, could smell the reek of sausages and cabbage and potato. The voices, in a dozen different tongues, fell away as she approached. There were footsteps on the loose floor-boards—doors cracking open to see who it was, shutting again as she passed.

Outside her apartment, up on the fifth floor, she put her fingers to her lips and nearly touched the *meζuζah* next to the door before she realized what she was doing. At the last moment she jerked her hand back as if it had been burned, smiling to herself in secret defiance before she went in.

"The *Amerikanerin* is home," he announced—to the air or to her mother—as soon as she stepped through the door.

Her parents were sitting at a small table by the windows of their bedroom, her mother hunched over what looked like a little pile of thorns. Her father holding the *Jewish Daily Forward* up to the open, white cheesecloth curtains like a sacrifice, trying to read by the refracted light from outside.

"Why she should come home at all, I don' know. For her, the dancing never stops. For her, life is a feast."

This was his way of addressing her, and had been for many months—always indirectly, or through her mother, except for when he lost his temper completely, and called down all sorts of curses and insults upon her head. Or in her own, private conversations—but that was another matter.

"Don'tch you like it, so lump it," she called back into their bedroom, not bothering to budge from where she was in the kitchen.

The apartment was three small rooms, running away from two back windows that looked out over a tiny, squalid courtyard, then another tenement, then beyond that the looming, black bar of the Allen Street elevated. The room with the windows was her parents' bedroom. The room where she stood was the kitchen, piled high with trunks and dressers and chests, and then to her right was the *roomerkehs'* tiny room.

Three little rooms, all in a row, moving in that order away from the outside windows. Both the interior walls in the apartment had windows cut right through them—the only way at all that any natural light got into the kitchen or the *roomerkehs'* room.

One of the *roomerkehs,* a salesman named Kapsch, was sitting at the kitchen table now, a slight, balding man, with a permanently quizzical expression on his face. Esse knew he was a little bit in love with her. He gave a respectful little bow from where he sat when she came in, mumbled something she couldn't make out.

"That I should live to hear such a thing! From my own daughter——" her father was still going on, standing up now and rattling the newspaper at her, advancing on her from the bedroom.

"Don' bother, don' fuss," her mother said, shuffling in nervously around him and rubbing her hands together. Her fingers were pricked and swollen from making the *tzatzkes* all day—beautiful wire roses and lilies and forsythia. They had points as sharp as razors and the dyes, the gorgeous red and purple and yellow colors, got into the cuts and made them ooze and fester.

She might make twenty-five cents worth, winding them together all day. Before that she had worked parting threads of silks to make tassels and before that, of course, they had been able to almost make a living together, sewing the secret garters. But this was the best her mother could do at home, now that her fingers had stiffened up.

"You got anythink to eat? You want somethink?" she asked anxiously, hobbling in to Esther and taking her hands.

"No, Mama. I'm fine, Mama."

She looked down into her mother's face, and was filled with pity and disgust. Her cheeks were sunken and sallow, eyes still darting about apprehensively.

"How are your hands, Mama? How are you feeling today?"

"Oh, my hands," she said absently, evasively, her eyes moving all around the room. "All right. Pushink along, pushink along."

Still trying to keep the peace. To please her husband

"How you have done for us," she muttered, looking up at her father. "How you have done for us all."

He advanced casually upon her, a white-haired old man, his beard full of crumbs from the midday meal she knew her mother had brought him at his desk. The skin around his eyes and cheekbones still surprisingly pink and young, the eyes dark and vibrant with cheerful hate.

"Must I empty my bitter heart upon you?" he said, almost casually, addressing Esther directly for the first time in weeks. "What right do you have to say anything? Coming in here as full of sins yourself as a watermelon is full of seeds!"

"Go to the devil!" she answered, and smiled despite herself at the *roomerkeh,* to remember such sins. Kapsch looked away in confusion.

The old reb started to cough——a low, phlegmatic, indulgent cough——and sat down heavily in one of the kitchen chairs. There was a noise, and her mother shuffled quickly in between them, waving her bruised hands.

"Ssh! Sshh! Now you got the *downstairsikehs* up with your yellink!"

But it wasn't the downstairs neighbors: just Abady, who took the four-to-twelve shift in the rented room. He was a swarthy, brutish-looking man with a long, drooping moustache, a Syrian Jew who worked on construction crews. He came out in his undershirt and single pair of pants, barefoot and scratching himself, and went on to the hall bathroom without so much as looking at the four of them.

Kapsch quickly excused himself to take his turn in the warm bed. He had the prime, twelve-to-eight shift, while Cuti, the third *roomerkeh*——a fastidious little Italian plasterer——got the eight-to-four. Esther's mother bustled around the kitchen, coaxing the old man back into the bedroom, putting together her litter for the night.

"Esse, you sure you ain't hungry?"

88

"No, Mama."

"You sure? I can fix you somet'ing . . ."

"*No,* Mama, I got no appetite for this living," she snapped, suddenly feeling deeply tired and sorry for herself. The Triangle would be open again tomorrow, after the two-week summer layoff, and she would be up at dawn. Back at her machine.

"*Gottenyu,* why do you always have to tear up the world like a crazy?"

"Oh, Mama!"

"I don' know. It just seems like you'd be happier."

She pushed aside the little kitchen table and the trunks, put together the couple of chairs that served as her bed. She placed a pillow and blankets down on them, turned over the edge of the blankets as carefully as if it had been a real bed.

"You sure there's nothink more I can do for you?"

"No, Mama. You done enough already."

Sarcasm was lost on her mother, as was despair. She shuffled over to give her a kiss and a quick, tremulous hug around the waist.

"Sweet dreams, Esse."

"Sweet dreams, Mama."

She hurried back to the bedroom. Esther waited until Abady had dressed and left, then she got out one of the little towels her mother had laid out for her. They were nearly threadbare, but in her few spare moments around the *tzatzkes,* she had painstakingly embroidered them with bright sunsets and rainbows, and sayings in Yiddish like "A life into your eyes!" and "Peace upon you!"

Esther pumped herself a sink full of water and unpinned her hair. She lowered the top of her bathing costume, then the white slip under it, the green and gold scales painted on it shimmering away beneath the water, where she would wash it along with her hair. Before she did, she paused for a long moment again, before the tub, thinking about the day just past.

Outside, the elevated sped by, rattling the dishes and shaking everything else in the apartment. She gathered up her long dark hair and dipped it down into the water. It was lukewarm, almost cool, a relief on a night like this. She lowered her hair all the way into the water, and began to wash.

The *roomerkehs'* room was more a cave than a real room, with a long curtain instead of a door, little blue curtains that Esther's mother had sewn and hung over the interior window, and a single bed that took up nearly the whole space inside. Her mother didn't let Esse go in to clean, but she had glimpsed a small shaving mirror nailed to the wall inside, a single shelf—with three small towels, three collars, and three straight razors laid out along the shelf. The very thought of it—those bare possessions, laid out so simply—always filled her with despair.

But now, though she could not see, Kapsch peeked out through the little blue window curtains, watching intently as she washed herself. She stood solemnly before the wooden sink, her white skin radiant in the darkened room. She swung her long hair down into the water, emerged again with her eyes closed.

He took in every part of her: Her bare calves, and ankles. The long, gracious sweep of her neck as she bent over; her round, white, dimpled shoulders; the gentle curve of her body under the slip. He watched ecstatically from the window as she dipped her hair down again, ducking back into the lovely and enveloping darkness, dipping it down again, white and black, white and black in the dim light.

10

ESTHER

This life is too much for me

Esther lay in the dark on her crude litter, all her exhilaration from the day and the night—all her satisfaction over her own daring—seeping away from her now. She ran a hand searchingly over her nightgown: her breasts, her legs, her stomach, her sex—every place he had touched her today. What did it mean? What was any of it for?

She never even saw herself—outside of her nightgown, at least. A glimpse of thigh, of pale white flesh, glowing in the mirrorless darkness of the hall toilet. She was only a head that walked around, filled with worry, trying not to think about how tired she was all the time.

This life is too much for me. There is no place in it for me

You know what your place is

Her father's voice. Ever since he had stopped talking to her—speaking to her only when she had goaded him beyond endurance, like tonight—she had made up her own conversations with him.

She had thought of these make-believe conversations originally as a test, a way to win him over with the logic of her arguments, and at first the made-up father in her mind had been everything she wanted him to be: wise and rational, merciful and abiding.

But somehow, as time had gone by, the father in her mind had become just as angry and obstinate, just as cynical and caustic as the one snoring now in the next room:

The first thing you must learn is what you are.

I'm no donkey for you to ride, that's for sure!

But what are you? A woman without a family is not a woman. A woman alone is nothing, she will never enter into the Kingdom of God—

And how should I have a family—working all the time, with you on my back?

If only you knew how deep is your ignorance, then you would be truly ashamed.

I only know what you let me learn!

—reduced once more, even in her own mind, to a ranting child. Lying on her pallet of chairs, she felt herself miserably small and insignificant. Wrapped up in her sheets, in this tiny apartment, like her mother before her.

How he had betrayed her:

"She shall be brought before the king in raiment of needle-work . . ."

She had been thirteen—late for work outside the house, though she had not become a woman yet. At the Triangle Shirtwaist Company off Washington Square, where she worked now, there was a corner on the tenth floor they called the kindergarten. Girls of eight and nine worked thirteen hours a day—fifteen, at the height of the season—pulling loose threads off the finished waists. When the factory inspectors came around Mr. Bernstein told them, "Quick, girls! Into the boxes!"—and they made a game out of it, diving into the big cardboard boxes, giggling and pulling the shirtwaists over their heads.

Of course, she had already been working on the secret garters for years, at home with her mother. Her father had no idea what they were doing; he could not have imagined anything so immoral as a garter belt even in America or he would never have let them under his roof, and so they conspired to conceal the work they did to earn his daily bread.

It was good work, as those things went. They could make five hundred in a day, depending on the season and how long her mother could hold up. She sewed on the lace, and Esther added the tiny hooks and eyes around the fringe, and wondered how anyone could wear such a flimsy, frilly thing.

Once she tried one on, when her mother went out to buy dinner and her father was still at the synagogue. She pulled it hurriedly up under her dress—but no matter how she tugged and twisted it hung limply on her girl's waist, and fell down around her ankles, and she quickly stepped out of it and flung it back on the table, feeling vaguely humiliated.

She almost never left the apartment in those days. She only got out to use the library, or maybe, during the slow seasons, to go to the public school—a big, drafty classroom with fifty other kids, reciting the impossible admonitions on the blackboard by rote:

> I must keep my skin clean
> Wear clean clothes,
> Breathe pure air,
> And live in the sunlight—

At home, her mother brought her tea, and bread with maybe a little quince jam, smiling at her over her needle and thread as they worked through the endless piles of silly underwear. And when she was tired, and her hands were cramped, her mother let her go and hop around the apartment a few times. And when she was bored, her mother would tell her stories

93

from her own childhood, and sometimes Esther thought it wouldn't be the worst thing to do—sewing next to her mother for the rest of her life. And other times she thought it would be like the story she had read in the Seward Park library, about a man who was walled up alive.

While they sewed, her father sat by the window, chanting and rocking back and forth over his books, paying no attention to them.

"Your father has no acquaintance with the face of a coin," her mother told her when she asked what he did for a living.

"He is a *luftmensch*—a higher man," she tried to explain to her.

Esse did her best to figure this out. At supper, she watched her mother put aside the best cut of meat, the biggest portions for him, eating her own food very slowly, so there would always be some left over for him. Breaking away from her work to bring him cheese and cucumber sandwiches in the afternoons.

He accepted it all, unquestioningly. He did not even seem to notice when it was brought to him—reaching for the sandwiches as if they had been provided by God. His eyes never strayed from the words in front of him.

"To give wine to a Talmud scholar is like pouring it out on an altar," her mother would say. And when she was older and asked why, all her mother could do was talk about when they had first met, back in her village, her eyes dreamy with the recollection.

"Oh, but he was so beautiful! A beautiful boy. Not even a beard yet; a *yeshiva bocher*, with his cheeks like peach fuzz, hurrying off to class every day. I remember the first time— I thought I was very bold—I touched his cheek. Oh, I knew then he was made for somethink *fine!*"

Sometimes, when he was in the mood, he might read with her for a little while. He preferred trying to teach her brother Lazar, no matter how little he wanted to hear. But sometimes, usually at the start of *Shabbos*, he might sit her up on his lap and read to her from the *Gemara*, or the Bible. He never went over the great conundrums of the *Mishnah*—those were reserved for Lazar, as much as he resisted—but it was all right. She loved simply tracing the Hebrew words with him. Their favorite verse together was a psalm, which she was soon able to pick out every time:

"She shall be brought before the king in raiment of needlework."

From over at the kitchen table her mother would smile to see her, there on her father's lap. She would not listen to her recitation but would turn away to light the *Shabbos* candles, wearing her wedding dress, the shawl over her head, holding her hands firmly over her eyes while she recited the prayer.

The same year that Lazar left, her father had been thrown out by his congregation, in the great controversy over the Grand Rabbi from Cracow. Her mother's tiredness and her hands made it impossible for her to sew all day. She had to switch to threading the tassels, and then the sharp, colorful *tzatzkes*, and someone had to make up the money.

The night before her mother took her to the shop, she was almost too nervous to sleep. She got her up while it was still dark out, and they made tea as silently as they could in the kitchen, so as not to awaken him. She noticed that her mother made it thicker than usual, and made Esther drink two cups, and eat a thick chunk of challah. She pulled off another big chunk of the bread for her, wrapped it in wax paper along with a thimble and a pair of scissors, and three extra needles. Then she led her out into the dark.

It was a freezing morning, and there was still snow on the sidewalks. All the way over her mother held her close to her, Esther walking half-dazed, leaning into the warmth of her thin, sheltering body.

As they walked, she rehearsed her:

"Remember—whatever you do, don't twist the linink. And take your time. He wants you to rush, but take as long as you need. Do it right, and he can't take the money out."

Esther nodded. They had practiced it the previous Sunday, over and over, on an old coat of her mother's, but she had trouble thinking straight now, and it was impossible for her to believe that her hands could do any such thing. She wanted nothing so much as to bury her head into her mother's coat, and go back home.

The shop was on Division Street, a narrow, lightless block under the blue steel tiers of the Manhattan Bridge. It was lined with rotting wooden tenements, doors and windows all boarded up. She trailed behind her mother as she searched for the number, their breath billowing up in the darkness.

Finally, she found the door she was looking for—another tenement, a small puddle of light leaking out from under the door.

"All right now, don't be scared, *bubbeleh*. My big girl. It's nothink you can't do. Remember: *Don't twist.*"

She nodded mechanically, her mind blank as the snow.

"You work to seven, that's the contract. Keep track of how many you do. All right?"

Esther nodded again, and her mother hugged her and kissed her cheeks. She hustled away, turning to wave from the end of the dark street.

"Good-bye!" she called back. "Good-bye! Oh, my good girl! Good-bye!"

96

She waved until her mother had turned the corner, then turned back to the dilapidated tenement. A knob hung from the front door like a distended eyeball. She pushed it back, shook and twisted at it until the door swung grudgingly open.

Already, she could hear the hum and whir of the machines. She followed the sound up two listing staircases and down a hallway, with no real idea of what to expect. There was another battered door, and when she pushed it open she found herself in a world of coats.

Brown coats, black coats, ladies' and gentlemen's coats. They lined the walls, hung from the doorjambs, the water pipes, the window frames. They piled up chest-high all around the room, up to the ceiling in places. A baby in diapers, its face and chest covered with red splotches, crawled and teetered along their crest like it was riding the waves out at Coney Island.

It was not yet seven o'clock in the morning, but there was already a full team of men and women hard at work around a narrow table—three young women and an older one doing needlework, two men with gray beards on the machines, stitching collars. They barely lifted their heads when she came in, and went quickly back to their work.

Esther stood where she was, not sure what to do or how to talk to them. Finally, a tall, stooped man in another long gray beard and a yarmulke stepped in from a back room, through a curtain of still more fine, finished coats.

"What," he demanded, already gesturing impatiently with his hand.

"I—to fell sleeves. From Mrs. Abramowitz," she stammered out.

"*You're* the new feller hand?" the man ejaculated. "Look, her mother's milk is still fresh on her lips! *Schmuel!*"

He shouted back through the forest of coats, and another, shorter man came from the back room.

"She one of your lost sheep?" The man with the beard jerked a thumb at her. "The one the mama sent?"

The shorter man looked her over, twisting up his face. "What's your name?"

"Esse. Esse Abramowitz," she told him——hoping suddenly that it was all a mistake, that she was at the wrong address, or the position had fallen through, and she could go home to her mother. But she would have no such luck. The shorter man stared at her for a little longer, then shrugged his shoulders.

"I guess," he said finally.

"*This* can fell sleeve lining?" the bearded man still asked incredulously. "You be lucky she can pull strings."

"Her mama paid me," the short man shrugged again. "What's it my trouble?"

"It's a black year on you if she ruins one of my coats, that's what it is," the taller boss snorted. He looked at her again.

"So thin and small, like a dried-out herring," he sighed. She heard one of the women sewers give a short, hard laugh.

"All right, *feller*. Over there—let's see your work."

Esther squeezed onto the only open stool around the table, between the two men on the machine. She started to squirm out of her coat but the taller man seized it by the collar and shoved it roughly up around her ears.

"Don't get so comfortable, *pitsel*. Let's see what you can do first."

He plopped another coat down on the pile on the table. It was a good coat, too, she recognized, thicker and better cut than anything she or anyone she knew had ever worn, and her hands were shaking as she picked it up.

"C'mon, still yourself a little!"

Much later, she understood that he was hoping she *would*

98

damage the coat—at least a little. Then he could squeeze her first weeks' wages as a string puller out of her for nothing. What they would have done then for money, how it would all have worked out, she did not like to think about. But she had always had a way with a needle. Not so fast as some girls, not so adroit as the fine ladies' seamstresses but agile enough, delicate enough. With her coat still on, she pulled one of the needles out of the wax paper, threaded it up, and started to sew.

Don't twist! Small, false stitches at first—

The tall boss paced and tsked and tapped his foot impatiently, but she took her time, just like her mother had said. The machines on either side of her made her head ring; the men smelled heavily of onions, and themselves. They glanced contemptuously at her but she kept sewing carefully, deliberately, smoothing the silky lining and stitching, stitching and smoothing.

"You finished already?"

She held the heavy coat up to the boss. He tore it from her hands, flung it back down on the table and went over every stitch with his own needle—probing and testing, craning his head right down to the lining. Finally he stood up, an enigmatic, almost pleased expression on his face, and she was afraid he had found some secret flaw, some beginner's bit of ignorance.

"All right," he said, and brought a whole armful of coats over from the corner, threw them down in front of her without another word. Beyond them she could see the lips of the other sewing women twisting dourly.

She dropped her eyes to the work in front of her—pausing only, this time, to shrug out of her coat in the stultifying room. She was sewing before it landed at the foot of her stool.

● ● ●

They worked for hours, without any break. Once, one of the younger women—after squirming in noticeable discomfort for half an hour—tried to get up to use the toilet across the hall but the boss, Mr. Himmelfarb, waved her back onto her stool.

"Oh, no!" he told her. "You *pish* on your own time, not mine!"

The girl sat glumly back down and Esther, whose own bladder felt close to bursting from the tea her mama had made her that morning, pulled her legs together under the table until she thought her knees would pop.

They didn't break until a man came in selling more tea, and hard rolls. Esther didn't know what time it was, but she was sure it was well into the afternoon. The others all bought the rolls, but she just had a cup of the weak, flavorless tea, and nibbled at the chunk of challah her mother had torn off for her. The women across the table stared and gestured openly at her—particularly the older one—but she couldn't follow what they were saying in the rapid amalgamation of English and Yiddish and Italian they used, and she kept her head down.

They went back to work as soon as they were finished eating, without another break for the rest of the afternoon or evening. From time to time the boss, Himmelfarb, would stalk in and sort quickly through their coats. When he found a mistake he would curse and scream at them, waving his arms around. Then he would tear out their flawed work, however miniscule and undetectable the mistake, flinging it back on the table for them to do over again.

Esther worked more carefully than ever—afraid she might break down and cry if he yelled at her like that, afraid that her hands might betray her under the constant repetition of the job. At first, she had enjoyed the challenge of the coats: their size, the fineness of the linings—so much more intricate and difficult than the secret garter belts. When she finished one, she could not help holding it up to look at her work——even when she heard the snorts of derision from the older woman across the table, the giggles of the other sewers.

Yet as the afternoon wore on, she began to feel dizzy from her hunger and the close air of the shop, the musty cloth and the odor of the men. The unchanged baby crawled its way back and forth, back and forth across the coats, bawling and coughing. The work became even more numbing and endless than the garters, and there was no mama to make her a cup of tea or talk to her, not even the lulling chant of her father reading the Talmud. She stopped holding up her coats to look at them.

She had no idea what time it was, or if it was still light outside. There were no windows in their room. She learned to listen for the sound of the church bells, to distinguish the tingling of the quarters from the solid gong of the hours. These sounds were the only remaining tie she had to the world——the only indication that something existed outside this cave of coats——and once she learned to decipher them she carefully counted off the hours: four, then five, then six. Picturing the streets outside, imagining the sidewalks filling up with men and women, coming off the elevateds. What her mother was doing at home.

Finally——she counted out seven chimes of the church bell, and rose to go. No one else moved. Unnerved, she made as if she had only stood to stretch her back and knees, the way the others did, then sat back down.

She finished the coat she was working on, and looked up again. Still——nobody moved. The boss only hurried over with another coat, then another one after that.

The bells counted out eight, then nine. Still, they sewed. The other women worked with their heads almost to the coats, too exhausted even to make fun of her now. Esther's arms had begun to tremble with fatigue, she was petrified that she would tear a lining, or miss a stitch. She forced herself to work carefully, slowly, until she did not think she would be able to finish another coat.

Finally——finally, finally——the rest of them stood up as one. They were out the door, down the long, dark hallway and the slanting stairs and gone——even the poxy baby, gone——before she could get her coat on.

"Twenty-seven," she reported shyly to Himmelfarb as he went about the room, piling up more coats wherever he could find room, labeling them for the expressmen to take to the factories.

"What, what?"

"Twenty-seven coats."

"You think that's somet'ink to brag about? You're a beginner, you get paid by the week."

"But *they* work by the piece!"

"They have experience!" he yelled in her face. "They are grown-ups, with families to support! You're still a child, from a greedy mother."

She stumbled back down the pitch dark street, gnawing at the little bread she had saved. She was certain, on her way home, that she could never do this again. She would plead with her mother to let her work with her again at home, and if she couldn't she would go someplace else——run away out West, do something, *anything,* but this.

When she got home, though, it was not her mother, her smiling, nervous face that greeted her, but her father, scowling through the door. Mama sat behind him on a chair, face suffused with worry, rubbing her tortured hands together.

"What do you mean, coming home at an hour like this!"

He pulled her roughly inside by her elbow.

"*Amerikanerin!* What kind of unclean things have you been up to?"

"I was working!" she shouted back——shocked at herself.

It was the first time in her life she had ever raised her voice to her father.

"You work until seven!"

"Nobody moved!"

"Liar! Do you think I believe a dog because it barks?"

"Nobody moved, and they kept giving me coats, and I did them!"

"Liar!" he said again—but already she could see that the anxiety and the rage were fading. He was contented—as long as she was actually sewing coats.

"That's how you work!" she screamed at him, infuriated now not by his suspicion, but by his indifference. "You— you *angel*!"

He slapped her face then—not too hard, she noticed, but even this was an insult. It was not anything like the way he had hit Lazar, the night he left.

"Wild-head," he told her, almost affectionately.

He sat down calmly at the tiny dinner table while her mother bustled around the kitchen, hoping the worst of the storm was over. Esther stood where she was, amazed that there was no more to be said.

"Well?" she finally blurted.

"Well, three extra hours," he said, beginning to eat. "That's not so bad."

"Not so bad for you!"

"You have better things to do?"

She sat numbly at the table, realizing for the first time in her life how little he thought of her.

"It's not what was contracted. He's paying me by the week, not the piece."

"So? You do it for now," he said reasonably, his mouth full. "You learn the trade. Then you see."

Her mother had made her favorite meal, pierogis covered in butter, and a kasha knish on the side, but when she laid the plate before her Esther could barely eat any of it. In the room of coats, the last couple of hours, she had been so hungry she thought she might pitch headfirst into the pile on the table and sleep until the next morning. But now she pulled away from the table and began to sob in the corner, shouting at them as they sat at their meal:

"Nobody cares! Nobody cares!"

Her mother started to rise and go to her, but her father stopped her.

"Let her blow from herself for a while, if that's what she wants," he said, so of course her mother sat down, shooting worried looks over at Esther for the rest of the meal.

She cried to herself for the rest of the evening, ignoring her dinner and her mother's attempts to console her again.

"There is no place for me in this world!" she sobbed to herself in the corner, hoping they would hear her, but they didn't—at least they made no sign of it.

Later, she lay dry-eyed in the darkness, staring at the ceiling—and from where she was, she could hear them talking in their bedroom:

"Be reasonable," he was telling her. "What do you want from me? To walk the streets like those other great scholars? Giving advice on chickens?"

"No, *gold meine*——"

"She is a child, she would only fill her head with ice cream soda, and *Amerikaner* books!"

"She is still young——"

"Do I ask her to walk the streets for me? It is a decent trade, sewing. Remember: '*She shall be brought before the king in raiment of needlework.*'"

She lay in the dark, on her two chairs, and listened to him say that. She listened to him use her words against her, and she never forgave him. She concluded then and there that he was indeed some kind of angel—one of those that were always hovering just above the concerns of men and women, holy enough, pure enough, but essentially *indifferent*. It was up to her to go out and work eighty hours a week in a sweatshop on Division Street.

11

ESTHER

That night—the night of that first, unendurable day—Esther was sure that she could not possibly go out to the suffocating little sweatshop on Division Street again. And yet, when her mother came shuffling into the kitchen before dawn to start the fire, she got up, and combed her hair, and drank her tea.

This time she made sure to tear off two large chunks of the challah, refusing to notice her mother's consternation over how she was feeling. She went out to the filthy hall bathroom to change, barging in before anyone else on the floor could. She had to get to work.

That second morning she reached the shop on Division Street before seven, but the others were still already in their places, and Himmelfarb the boss scowled at her.

"Like a born Mrs. Vanderbilt, she comes an' goes when she chooses!"

He plopped a full new load of coats into her arms. Esse nearly bent under the weight, but she took them without saying anything, and sat down on her stool between the two machine operators.

By midmorning it seemed to Esther that she had never known a world beyond the pushing of a needle through felt and cloth. She had thought her anger would carry her through the day, but even it dissipated into mindless fatigue. She tried counting the bells again, but now that only made the hours drag by interminably. She tried not to think at all——but the realization wormed its way up into her head, unbidden and unavoidable, that she would have to do this not only for the rest of the day but again the next day, and the day after that, again and again, for the rest of her life.

When the lunch break finally came, she tried moving her stool quietly over to the other women, but they kept talking about her and laughing, in between their gulps of tea and bread. Leah, who was the older woman, seemed to hate her the worst of all. It was her baby crawling endlessly through the waves of coats, and Esther realized that she must be at least twenty years younger than she looked.

The baby didn't look so good itself——she never knew what it was, boy or girl——Leah only referred to it as *it*, barking instructions to whoever was closest when her child seemed most bent on self-destruction:

"Stop it. Get it down from there. Move that plug away from it."

Whatever it was, the child was still covered with red spots. It had an amazingly deep, hacking cough, and it sneezed and drooled constantly as it crawled over the coats. Himmelfarb yelled and screamed when he saw it.

"What if the inspectors was to come in now? They're always worryin' about gettink the cholera from the coats!"

Leah would take the baby off and put it on the floor. Within a few seconds it would be back on top of the piles, wheezing and hacking its way along. She paid more attention to how many coats Esther was felling, and Esther could hear her, whispering loudly to the others:

"Look at her, the bundle-eater! A little piece of wretch like that, takink the money from our pocket. And with a whole family at home she can eat off!"

Esther blushed and kept her head to her work, face burning with resentment. *What person was there in the world who didn't have to work?* she wanted to tell her—aside from her own father, the angel. *Who was she to add to her troubles?*

Yet when the week turned, and Esther came back to work after the Sabbath, Leah was not on her stool. She got up the courage to ask the other women about it, she was so surprised, but they only shrugged, and looked uncomfortable. When she got up the courage to ask Himmelfarb, he shrugged, too—as if a flood, or some other act of nature had taken Leah away:

"What do you want from me?" he asked her, accusingly. "I don't have room in my shop for every beggar on the street."

She never did find out what happened to her. Leah had disappeared as suddenly and completely as if the floor had opened up and swallowed her. Esther took her place—the other girls letting her in now, on their side of the table. The laughter stopped, and much to her surprise she seemed to be the leading feller in the shop now. At the end of the day, Himmelfarb the cockroach boss always had one more coat he brought over to her. Even after nine o'clock, when all the others were slowly unbending from their places, finally ready to go home, he would still drop one more in front of her.

"A special order," he would say. Or: "We need this one for the morning."

"He's sweatink you because you're young," her mother fretted when she came in later than ever.

Yet Esther would always sit back down and do it without a word—convinced that it must count for something, somehow. She was proud of her new status, her position as number one girl in the shop. Yet when the week was up and she went to Himmelfarb for her pay, he only sniffed at her.

"How many coats did you do?"

"One hundred an' sixty-two."

"And you think that is a week? I'll tell you what a week is, *knaydl*. A week is two hunerd an' fifty coats! You do two hunerd an' fifty, you get paid for a week."

Esther stood before him speechless over the blatant unfairness of it all. Yet she knew there was no alternative. There was no one to stand up for her: not the others at the shop table, certainly not her family. She realized then, for the first time, how fully alone she was.

She had to work right through *Shabbos* and into the following Tuesday to get the pay that was rightfully hers. She didn't even bother trying to explain it to her father when she walked in the house after sunset on Friday, and worked all day Saturday—but then she noticed that he did not press her for an explanation, either.

"Un' wie soll es gut gehen in Amerika?" was all he uttered, the standard refrain of the neighborhood—*How can anything possibly go well in America?*

It was the same lament he had made when he had lost his rabbi's position, or when Lazar had left them, or when he could not get decent sour cream in the morning. And she resolved, then and there, to violate the Sabbath every week for the rest of her life.

When she did finally finish the week she dropped the last of the two hundred and fifty immaculately lined coats into the lap of Himmelfarb himself. He dropped three small stacks of quarters into her hand.

"Three dollars?" she said, counting it at a glance. "That's all?"

"American children always want things over their head. I'm doink a favor keeping you on, a girl your age."

She stayed where she was, trying to keep from crying—or letting her fury overwhelm her.

"Don'ch you like it, lump it," he shrugged. "You think I can't get a dozen like you?"

"He will hurry me to my death in there," she told her mother that night, but she just rubbed her hands together nervously.

"Go along until you get to the rush," she told Esse. "Vait 'til he needs you too much."

"Ah, America the thief," her father sighed reflexively, and went back to his paper.

Soon she was not only doing the best work, she was felling far more coats than anyone else around the table. The other girls looked on her with open jealousy, but they had no time to do anything about it. Himmelfarb, on the other hand, was ecstatic: the faster they worked, the more he increased the load, spending all day leaning over them at the table, screaming for them to go faster still.

The fatigue pressed down on her all the time now. She learned to work with it, finding her way to what energy was left in her like a swimmer trapped under the ice, fighting her way to the air pockets. At home, she insisted on eating heavily despite her father's moaning that she would blow up like an Irisher cow. She grew broader, sturdier, more resilient.

She began to almost enjoy the extra work, at the end of the evening, alone with Himmelfarb in the shop. At least then the day was nearly over—and she tried not to think about how she was waiting for her whole life to be over, one day at a time.

She was a little nervous to be alone with Himmelfarb, but all he did was pray. She could hear him in the next room, once the machines were quiet, the only other sound the faint rustle of vermin under the coat piles.

Himmelfarb was what they called a double-harness

Jew—phylacteries wrapped around both arms, carefully tied in seven knots. She had seen him once, when she peeked through the curtain of coats into the cavelike back room. He was on his knees, rocking feverishly back and forth the way her father did at prayer, shawl over his shoulders, eyes shut tightly against the surrounding mountains of cloth.

One Friday night, no less, when she was alone in the front room, working on coat number two hundred and thirty-four, he kissed her. He walked out of the back as if he were in a trance, and kissed her on the mouth.

Esther was so surprised that she didn't move at first. She had never been kissed before, never experienced anything like it. She began to stand up—arms flailing out to each side, feeling like some ludicrous heroine in the motion pictures calling for help. Himmelfarb clutched her fervently at the waist, kissing her all over her face, stroking one hand across her cheek.

How ridiculous, was all she could think, even then. *My first real kiss, in a subcontractor's shop.*

And yet, somehow, for all that she almost welcomed his touch. The hot, sour breath on her lips, his hand on her cheek—the touch of any other person, breaking the isolation in which she lived.

"Esse, Esse," he was gasping, sinking down to his knees among the coats.

"Esse—you are my best feller hand."

She started to laugh convulsively.

"Your best feller hand?"

It was all she could do to push him away; she was nearly out of breath with laughing. He groped for her, the phylacteries still tied to his sleeve.

"No. *No,*" she said with sudden contempt, standing over him.

She felt no fear, despite the fact that she was still a child then. She felt immeasurably superior to the man—now

111

kneeling on the floor, arms still stretched out toward her. She put her coat on and strode to the door, barely pausing on her way out:

"And from now on, I want to be paid by the piece!"

Himmelfarb was afraid of her after that. He no longer screamed at her, or insisted that she stay late. It placed her all the more above the others and she reveled in her superiority—but there was nobody now for her to talk to, in the shop, or anywhere else.

It was then that a new woman had come in, and everything had changed. Her name was Clara Lemlich, and nobody in the shop had seen anything like her. It was the height of the season, and Himmelfarb had been forced to hire her, but right from the start she made him regret it.

"Hey, Himmelbum—you lump of horse!" she would yell at him, giddy, almost unbalanced in her defiance, fierce, dark eyes spinning with indignation.

"All right with you we take a few minutes to eat like decent people?"

She stuck her tongue out at him when his back was turned, insulted him to his face. She was a little thing, barely five feet, with a thick tangle of hair, pretty bow mouth in a square face. Only a girl, really, not much older than Esther herself. Himmelfarb loathed her, but she was a skilled draper, and all he did was mutter that he had hired himself a real *kochleffl*.

"Ah, you should have seen me back in Russia. Then, I had fire in my mouth!" she scoffed.

She talked constantly while they all worked—ladling out advice on work, cooking, life. Mostly she told them the epic story of herself, and her struggle to get to America.

"My mother and father wouldn't even let me speak Russian in the house because we couldn't go to the public school, but at the same time I wasn't allowed to read the Talmud in Hebrew——just that little *shprekl* of a holy book in Yiddish.

"I did anything I could to get money for real books: sewed buttonholes, wrote letters for mothers to America. I bought all the Russian classics. Hid them underneath the meat pan, in the kitchen. Tolstoy! Gorky! Turgenev!"

She banged out the names on the table with her forefingers——so loud that Himmelfarb turned around, but said nothing.

"What better place to hide books from a man than under a cooking pan? He found them anyway——my mother must have given it away. He burned every one, right in front of me, in the kitchen stove. *Every* one!"

She paused in her sewing again, and they all paused with her——even the men on their machines. But when she spoke again, Clara's voice was sure and matter-of-fact.

"It took me a long time to build my little library up again. It was much harder. This time, I hid them in the attic, where there were all kinds of things. When everyone was sleeping, late at night, or on the afternoon of the Sabbath, I would sneak upstairs and read. Then, one day, when I was ten years old, our neighbor saw me."

"What happened?" Esther whispered. She could see all of them, even Himmelfarb, listening tensely, their hands forgetting their work completely.

"Well, I was lucky, kiddo, I can tell you."

She chuckled at her good fortune.

"He was a very kind man. He was a saint! He never told my parents. Instead, he got me more things to read: pamphlets from the Socialists, the Zionists. The Anarchists, the underground. It was a very dangerous thing. My mother and father could have gone to prison if the police found out I had such things. But what of them——they burned books! I didn't care. It was the beginning of my political education.

113

By the time I was a woman, I was a revolutionary myself!"

"Were you? Were you a revolutionary?"

"Well, you know, I was still young," she chuckled, holding up a coat to examine her work.

"I wasn't so crazy about the Zionists, I got to admit. Go live in the desert with the Arabs? I liked the idea of blowing up the Czar!

"But then, one day, there was the pogrom in Kishinev. All my old comrades were speaking against the Jews—all in one day! My neighbor, that kindest of all men, he was in town on business. Somehow, he didn't get himself killed but they bloodied his face for him. I can never forget it: watching him coming up the road, pulling his pony cart himself. His coat in rags, his goods all burned."

Her voice was choked with emotion now, and they were all silent, imagining the terrible scene. Only years later, after watching Clara speak from the street corners, did Esther wonder at how she could make her audiences well up with the same emotions—make herself well up—time after time.

"And I knew then, there was no revolution coming in Russia—no revolution more than killing the Jews, anyway. I knew I had to come to America."

"And you think there is a revolution here?" one of the men at the machines scoffed.

"You wait, *bubbeleh*," she told him, dark eyes spinning. "*You—wait.*"

Esther followed her around like a moon calf. It was Clara who helped her when she first became a woman. She was lining her fourteenth coat of the day when she felt a warm flush run through her abdomen, and then something rushed out of her and began to form a dark stain across the shapeless brown shift. It was nothing her mother had ever told her about. She sat there, watching the stain spread with only the vaguest idea what it was about, while the other girls sneered and held their noses, and Himmelfarb looked away with obvious disgust.

"It's only your monthlies," Clara had said, smiling, and insisted on taking her out to the dirty hall bathroom and getting her cleaned up despite Himmelfarb's bleating about the rush.

"You're a woman now," she said almost tenderly, smiling at Esther in the close, noisome toilet. Then she slapped her twice, quickly, first one cheek and then the other, before Esther could raise a hand.

"That's good luck," she said soothingly, to the girl's stunned face. "That's congratulations. It's what my mother did for me."

"It hurt," was all Esther could say.

"Ah, *mamaleh*—life is all about pain."

That night, she had sat down and written out to Clara the first love letter of her life:

"I understand you to the depths of my being, as only one who has long suffered can," she wrote. "From the bottom of my soul, I promise you: we shall be friends forever, in joy and sorrow! What is sweeter in life than the sympathy between woman and woman? What is purer than the gratitude of hearts? What greater than the harmony of minds?"

She had signed it, "Yours, in friendship and socialist comradeship," and when she had finished her whole body was shaking. She had been as shy about slipping it to her as a schoolgirl—but finally she had managed to push it into Clara's coat pocket when no one else was watching. The next day, Clara had stopped her in the hall, out by the bathroom, and stroked her cheek with her hand this time.

"Such a nice letter. You are certainly a person among people," she'd told her, and after that Esther was sure that she would do anything in the world for her, follow her anywhere.

It was Clara who first took her to the union, over at the hall on Clinton Street. It was late, after work one night, but the place was still full of people bustling impressively about, and nearly all of them women—some of them girls no older than Esther herself. Clara put up the few cents for her first dues, taught her how to hide her union card in her hat, and they went to the meetings together after that.

Esther liked them at once, even though they were always jammed into drowsy, overheated halls, endless successions of speakers gabbling away at them in Yiddish, Italian, Portuguese, German. She liked that there was advice on how to get on in this life, liked looking over all the choices of classes and lectures on hygiene, child-rearing, literature, the social graces. She liked the sound of the word "International" in the union title, how it implied that there was a whole world of girls just like herself out there, all somehow banded together. Even when she was bone-tired, during the height of the rush—when she felt she could no longer lift another stitch—she went to the meetings, or one of the lectures at the settlement houses, to let herself be sustained and comforted by them. She liked that it would make her father wonder where she was, so late at night.

On her own, she might have been content just to keep going to the meetings. It was Clara who insisted they had to bring the union home, right into their little shop.

"Look at how he pays us," she sighed. "America the thief!"

"But what can we do?" Esther asked. "The union is supposed to help *us*."

"We can build the union right here in this shop!"

They decided first to clean up the abominable bathroom in the hall, and keep it clean. It was their little project at first, but soon Clara had rallied the rest of them around it. It was a small thing, just a clean bathroom, but it was the first time Esther had ever been able to go to the toilet where it wasn't loathsome and dank and foul. It was the one place she could be alone and Clara encouraged her to take breaks, even bought her cigarettes she could smoke while she sat in there, thinking and resting—the one, tiny space she had carved out of the world for herself.

The others spoke of the union furtively at first, whispering to them when Himmelfarb was in the back. But soon they were talking of it openly, even the men. Himmelfarb gave them a black look whenever he heard them, but there was nothing he could do.

"It's the height of the season, he needs all his hands," Clara reminded them again and again.

"But what about when the season's over? Then what?" one of the other women wanted to know.

"Then he'll throw you out anyway like a lump of cholera, won't he? Better you should at least get what you can now."

The shop was busier than ever. Himmelfarb sweated them routinely until midnight now, yelling and screaming, frantically counting and recounting his coats. They worked all *Shabbos* day, until Esther daydreamed about seeing her mother again in her wedding dress, covering her eyes after she lit the candle. She knew the others were looking to the two of them to do something.

"But to risk that money, now, at the rush!"

"It *is* the rush. *Tochises afn tish*—this is it!"

The next day, Clara demanded a raise in the rate. She took a vote at lunch, while Himmelfarb was out at the factories. They all went along, even the men at the machines, slowly raising their hands like shy white water plants, reaching for the light. When Himmelfarb came back in, they all stood before him in the front room, Clara and Esther a little out in front—and eyes blazing, Clara told him they wanted a nickel more for each piece.

"You should go and put a knife in my children's throat, askink a rate like that," he sneered at them.

"We know you got it," Clara said right back to him. "I know what you get from the factories."

"Yap! Go bluff a dead rooster, not me. My head is still on my shoulders."

"All we want is what we got coming," Esther spoke up, not sure where she got the courage, gratified by the radiant smile Clara shot her.

"We don't get it, you can sew your own coats."

"My shirt has turned to linen from fright."

He stomped out the front door—locking it behind him.

They stood where they were, frightened and exhilarated, and completely at a loss for what to do next. Some of them thought he would refuse, and others thought he would give in, and all of them thought he would be back in a few minutes—that he had locked them in just to frighten them.

Half an hour dragged by, and there was still no sign of Himmelfarb. They felt almost drunk with their freedom—to be standing and talking as free as they pleased, in this tiny, suffocating room, where they had always worked so hard! An hour went by, though, and then another one, and they began to feel a little nervous. One by one, they drifted back to their tasks.

"The higher the rate, the more coats we want to get done, after all," one of the men rationalized, whirring the engine on his little machine.

"Mebbe it's some kind of trap—"

"We should just walk out, right now," Clara said, tapping a thimble against the table. "We made an offer, he turned it down."

"We don't want to wreck his contracts," Esther reasoned.

"After all, he has to pay us out of *something*."

"That's right," another one of the men spoke up. "He's only doin' what he has to do to stay in business."

"A disease he is," Clara snorted. "Besides, we're not dogs, we just want what's coming to us."

They worked on through the afternoon as usual, without a break. For a while still, they were very jolly, trading jokes and insults about Himmelfarb as they worked, but then one of the women killed that.

"What if he's on the other side?" she said, nodding toward the scarred wooden door of the shop. "What if he's list'nin' to everythink we say?"

"What if he is?" Clara challenged. "We got a right to talk."

After that, though, they lapsed into silence, concentrating on the coats before them—wondering when Himmelfarb was going to return. Esther picked up the bells, slowly tolling away the hours. When they reached seven o'clock they began to talk among themselves again, trying to figure out what there was to do.

"Do you think he's coming back with some gangsters?" the phlegmatic little underboss who had been Esther's *shadchen* wondered. The others looked up, alarmed.

"America is not Russia," Clara insisted.

"America!" The presser snorted. "A land where the lice make money, and good men starve!"

They fell silent again for a while.

"Mebbe he's tryink to starve us."

"No—he's just bluffing. Wait him out!" Clara commanded.

They worked on—past eight o'clock, nine o'clock, before they decided that someone should try the door. The presser and the men who worked the machines put their shoulders into it, but it was heavy; reinforced with metal bands and hinges against thieves and factory inspectors, and they couldn't get it to budge. They all tried it together then, but there wasn't enough room to make their collective weight felt.

They retreated to their stools and benches, sweating and panting and nearly distraught—and went back to work.

"We'll do the same work we always do."

"Dat'll show him."

"It'll show him we are bargaininink in good faith."

"You can have all the good faith you want, it still don't impress the devil."

"Say, do you think he forgot about us?"

They worked furiously again for a while, but soon they began to tail off, slowed by worry and exhaustion. Finally, when the church bells chimed midnight they all stopped and tried the door again. It still would not budge. The men went into the forbidden back room then and pushed aside the *mizrach*, the view of the temple wall that was the sole ornament Himmelfarb had in the entire shop, hung over a boarded-up window on the east wall. They knocked out the slats that covered it, and leaned out into the cool, dank air of the alley.

"Help! Help!" they cried together. "We are locked in here! Do something! We will starve to death."

From the front room the women could hear them yelling, over and over again, until some of the girls began to laugh, it all seemed so ridiculous. But the whole street was made up of sweatshops, and illegal tenements, and there was no response—no sign that anyone heard them at all.

"Help! We want to go home to our wives and children!"

Finally Clara strode to the back, and pushed the ineffectual men away from their space at the window.

"Fire! Oh, God, *fire!*" she shouted at the top of her lungs, in a voice that seemed to make the foundations shiver.

"Fire, *fire! My God, it will kill us all!*"

There was another long silence. Then, at last, they could

hear the sound of the fire bells approaching, the roar of the local hook-and-ladder company pulling up to the curb below. The men came trotting around the back: hulking young Irishers with huge moustaches, who grinned to see them waving desperately from the shop window.

"Halllooo! Jews up a tree!" they jeered.

"Lookit—twelve of 'em! Whatsa matter? Did Jesus get away this time?"

"Help! Help us!"

"Oh, yeah? Where's the fire?"

"Please—help us!"

The firemen finally condescended to run the long, wobbly ladder up to the window. One by one, they came down: a straggly line of men and women, hunched over, groping their way slowly down the ladder in the cold moonlight.

"Lookit this—like rats desertin' the ship," the Irishers continued to taunt them.

"Did you ever see such a thing? Jews on the highwire."

Clara had thought they should bring all the coats they could carry with them, just to make sure they had something over Himmelfarb. But the rest of them were worried he would have them arrested for stealing and anyway they needed both hands and feet on the rubbery ladder. They stumbled down to the bottom, with the Irish firemen still laughing all around them, then walked home to their beds freezing and exhausted.

But when they came back the next morning, there was nothing there. The shop had moved. Somehow, Himmelfarb had had everything carted away during the night, after they had gone. The little rooms were now completely bare, stripped of all the coats they had once held as completely as if no sweatshop had ever existed there. Even the *mizrach* was gone.

They asked all around for Himmelfarb for weeks after that, but nobody had heard anything. He had changed his name, or moved to another city, or thrown himself in the river, for all they knew. Esther and Clara were able to scramble around and get work for the rest of the season. The others went off to different shops, and she never saw anything of them again, either, in the vast, changeable sea that was the garment industry.

She worked with Clara at one small shop or another for years after that. Clara was more and more in demand as a speaker for the union, going into shops all over the City for the union, but they still kept in touch, still told each other whenever they found a position.

In the slow season, they went to the settlement house, or to improvement lectures together, or Clara took her to the library. Not only the Seward Park branch, with its endless line of Jewish children waiting patiently outside, but also the great central library uptown, where Clara instructed her in all the great authors to read: Hardy, and George Eliot, and Dickens and Tennyson and Keats.

The next fall Esther had made a connection in women's cloaks, with a nice Italian girl named Gina she knew from the shop after the one on Division Street. Putting up everything they had saved, they were able to open up a subcontracting shop of their own. Esther asked Clara in, but she turned them down. She had bigger plans than that, she was saving up her money to go to medical school—once she had finished making the revolution.

"God bless, go make a million dollars, but no," she told them. "I'm a worker, that's who I am. Never a boss."

They hired on four other girls—teenagers like themselves—and they did everything they had always wanted, everything she and Clara had always talked about. They let them take toilet breaks, and a real lunch hour, and share in the profits. They all worked hard, and they even made money for a while.

Then the season ended, and they were swept away like all the other small operators. By the time the next season came around they didn't have the money to open again, and then there was another Wall Street panic, and there was no work at all, no work to be had anywhere, and Clara got the idea they should go and camp out in the open air, so their families could at least make some money letting out the extra rooms. They had got Gina, and Clara's friends Pauline and Fannia, and Clara Rukus, and Martha Holman, who was a bookkeeper, and Alma Nitzchka, who brought her little boy with her. They had taken bedrolls and cooking pots, a big canvas tent they had stitched themselves, and books—piles and piles of books—and gone up to take the Edgewater Ferry over to the Palisades.

It had been bliss. Pure bliss—like sleeping out on the roof, only much better. They scrounged work wherever they could get it, taking in sewing from the little New Jersey villages, or picking vegetables, and they shared whatever they had between them. More friends had come to visit on Sundays, and brought along fruit and bread, and dried fish, a bit of cake, and most especially beans—sack after sack of baked beans. They had eaten beans that summer until they couldn't stand the sight of them, cooked in a big pot over an open fire, like they were cowboys.

The locals would come and spy until they got used to them: hard-faced farmers, carrying shotguns, or girls in blousy flannel uniforms from a nearby convent, peering through the foliage at them as if they were carny freaks, or dangerous animals.

They didn't care. After a few weeks, their clothes began

to turn ragged around the edges. They grew thinner, and browner, and began to take on the look of the hills around them. They went bathing naked in an abandoned quarry, and climbed the sheerest cliffs, and Esther learned to identify birds, and to play poker, to set up a tent and chop wood and start a fire—all of the great, frivolous things she would never need to know again.

They spent whole blissful hours, too, reading out in the sunlight, all their Dickens, and Hardy, and George Eliot, Shakespeare, and Byron and Keats and Alfred Lord Tennyson. They were more impatient with *Madame Bovary* and *Anna Karenina,* they didn't understand why such women didn't use their considerable free time to better their minds—though Esther was moved by the hot tears they shed.

But most of all they talked—talked about everything under the sun: about the theories of Marx, and the science of psychology, and the philosophies of Pragmatism and Social Darwinism, and above all the Revolution. Esther was the youngest, and she was afraid she wouldn't be able to keep up, but instead she found it exhilarating. It was like the tea-houses, only better, even better.

As the days went by, and the summer wore through their shoes, they began to wonder why their idyll could not last forever. Pauline and Clara plotted rent strikes, and shop walkouts back in the City, and they dreamed of the One Big Strike—but they all hated the idea of their extended camp-out ending. Esther was aware that more than a few of them were falling in love, and she felt that she loved them all herself, more than she had ever loved anyone else.

The nights began to turn colder, the trees along the great grey cliffs slowly dulling and thinning out. The night before they were to go back they sat around the fire one last time, and sang the old songs from home, from everybody's home:

Rumania, Rumania, Rumania, Rumania
Geven amol a land a ʒisse, a sheyne——

—and then Pauline read them a lecture she had copied down at the Henry Street Settlement, from a Professor Davidson whose ideas were currently setting the ghetto on fire:

"All great world movements begin with a little knot of people who, in their individual lives, and in their relations to each other, realize the ideal that is to be," she read—and the women seated on the logs they had cut around the generous fire smiled shyly at each other.

"To live truth is better than to utter it. Isaiah would have prophesied in vain, had he not gathered round him a little band of disciples who lived according to his ideal," Pauline continued, her teenaged voice rising a little unsteadily, but determinedly, into the crisp, autumn night.

"Again, what would the teachings of Jesus have amounted to had he not collected a body of disciples who made it their life-aim to put his teachings into practice?

"You will perhaps think I am laying out a mighty task for you, a task far above your powers and aspirations. It is not so. Every great change in individual and social conditions begins small, among simple, earnest people, face to face with the facts of life. Ask yourselves seriously, 'Why should not the coming change begin with us?'

"You will find that there is no reason why the new world, the world of righteousness, kindliness, and enlightenment for which we are all longing and toiling, may not date from us as well as from anybody. A little knot of earnest Jews has turned the world upside down before now. Why may not the same thing—nay, a far *better* thing!—happen in your day, and among you? Have you forgotten the old promise made to Abraham, 'In thy seed shall all the nations of the earth be blessed'?"

125

All of them were weeping silently, joyously by this time, even Pauline, as she read the last words of the lecture. Esther felt shivers from the cold night, from all the emotions running through her, and she thought something that she had never thought consciously before, which was that she was glad she was alive. Without another word, they embraced each other and went back to their tents, to fold up the few possessions they had, and strap up their precious piles of books.

Fannia had brought along a camera, and in the morning, before they left, they all posed for a photograph in their best clothes to commemorate the summer. Esther was chosen to take the picture, for she had the best eye, and the steadiest hand. She stood at the bottom of the Palisades, peering up at them through the camera on its tripod as they made their way down the cliffs—city girls, edging their way myopically, determinedly down the dizzying heights in their long, white summer skirts, strung out along the cliff ledges like so many mountain goats.

And after that, and after that Clara found Esse a place at the new Triangle factory, working on a machine. It was a little better in the big, new factories. There was more air, and the work was much steadier. Otherwise it was the same grind, day in and day out, working for somebody else. It was where she worked right up to this day—rising from her rough half-sleep, covered in sweat, troubled by all the restless, shifting images from her first day.

It was the Monday after her trip to Coney Island. Time to get up—time for the first day of the new season, down at the factory. Nothing changed, she thought, in all these years, since that first day on Division Street, nothing at all—she had been sleeping on a couple of chairs, then, too.

She corrected herself: nothing had changed, but everything had changed, because she had learned how to do it.

The household was already up around her: her mother, cooking at the little iron stove where a fireplace had once been. Kapsch replaced at the table by Cuti, the plasterer, neat as a pin, eating his breakfast, waiting placidly for his turn in the warm bed; her father still sleeping in the bedroom, his snores reverberating around the little apartment.

This world is too much for me—

They were the words she used to cry herself to sleep with, back when she was just starting. And now, she knew, it wasn't true—something which filled her both with immeasurable pride and sadness at the same time.

"Esse, you want you should eat?" her mother asked, shuffling over with a small bowl of porridge and a cup of tea.

"Yes, Mama."

Esther moved quickly about the room with a practiced economy, folding up the bed litter, moving the chairs back. The flannel nightgown hung heavy and wet on her—much too heavy for the late summer heat, but there was no other privacy, with the *roomerkeh* already up. She crumbled a lump of brown sugar over the porridge, ate it down in neat, rapid mouthfuls, then grabbed a skirt and a shirtwaist, some underwear, and slipped out to the hall bathroom.

It wasn't really a bathroom at all, the room no bigger than a closet. There was barely space to stand up in beside the tiny sink, the indescribably filthy toilet. Her father liked to rail against the neighbors and their Irisher daughters—big, dirty, cowlike creatures—for not keeping it clean—

"A curse upon the goyim, they have made a misery of the world with their filthy ways!"

—though the fact was anyone who wanted to could get in from the street, or from the whole other world up on the roof. There were always stories of unspeakable things happening in the toilets, and she made sure to turn on the light

127

and check behind the door before she went all the way inside.

When she was done she came back into the apartment and checked herself in the mirror: a dark striped skirt, faded and washed almost purple; dark stockings; an old white shirt-waist. She twisted up her thick, wavy brown hair, and pinned it firmly to her head. The factory wasn't as bad as a mill, where a girl with long hair could easily be scalped by the machines, but there were risks just the same. She looked, for just another moment, before her father might catch her, at the rest of her image in the mirror:

The face too plain, she thought, the nose too long, her teeth too crooked, the only redeeming feature her large brown eyes. She fiddled with her hair, tugged at the dress over the body she was also dissatisfied with.

He seemed satisfied enough with it—the sudden, unbidden thought making her smile. *He seemed to like what there was. My dybbuk, out on Coney Island*—

It was late, she knew, without even looking at a clock. She moved toward the door, picking up her old *shmatte* of a hat.

"Good-bye, Mama."

"Esse——"

"I don' know what time I'll be home. Maybe a meeting, I don' know."

She brushed aside her mother's concerns, entreating arms literally extended, still rubbing her hands fearfully together.

Better you should have worried more back then, when I needed you.

Down on the street, it was the best time of day in the summer—the only time when it wasn't too hot. She hated going out so early in the winter, when it was still cold and dark, and in the clear, smoldering autumn she only regretted all the more bitterly that she would be cooped up the rest of the day.

But in the summer the sun was shining, the heat only beginning to shimmer up from the paving stones. The sidewalks were already teeming with people, the streets jammed with pushcarts, wagons and trucks and automobiles, all creeping forward.

She walked rapidly, dodging up and down off the sidewalks, through and around the crowds. She prided herself on her ability to maneuver through any streets—on walking like a human being, a real New Yorker, instead of one more greenie. In the bad weather she might take the horse car, then the trolley to Greene Street, but in the summer she was just as glad to walk, enjoying the last few minutes before she had to be inside.

With every block she walked the buildings grew: bigger, wider, starker, blackened stone and brick and steel, rising up from the sidewalks like cathedrals. Soon, the streets began to widen—new, planned, industrial blocks. She turned down a short, broad street with an alluring swath of green at the end of it: the park at Washington Square, bright with flower beds and trees, a glimmering fountain in the middle, and on the other side a graceful, Florentine bell tower.

But everyone was streaming toward the newest and tallest building on Washington Place, where the Triangle factory waited, up on the eighth and ninth and tenth floors. They were pulled in like flotsam to a whirlpool: young women, some only girls, dressed in the same long, dull skirts and shirtwaists. Scores of men in white shirts and black vests and yarmulkes.

In the lobby there were two thin elevators, with the company's credo posted prominently above them: IF YOU DON'T COME IN ON SUNDAY YOU NEEDN'T COME IN ON MONDAY. The lifts hissed like jackhammers, scooping up a dozen men and women with each trip. The rest shuffled in place, edging slowly forward toward the next load.

Esther pushed past them, joining a thinner stream of people at the stairs. It was a long climb up to the ninth floor but she always felt trapped in the elevators, and if you were more than five minutes late the floor supervisors sent you home for a half-day without pay like a recalcitrant schoolgirl.

She climbed steadily among the crowd, cheek to heel, saving her breath, feeling the strength in her legs, in her back. She liked to pretend, sometimes, that she was climbing up a mountain somewhere, making her way up one of the Alps, above a little Swiss resort and a clear blue lake—though this morning thoughts of the Steeplechase began to fill up her head again. Such a thing it had been, she had never done anything like that before in her life. But she wasn't sorry; she wasn't sorry even if she never saw him again. He was hers now, that boy—her dybbuk.

On the eighth floor some of the women and the cutters peeled off—those men who could make a dress or a shirt with one long, elegant sweep of their shears. Going all the way up to the tenth floor were the boy clerks, and the women on the switchboards, and the pressers, biceps bulging from their work on the heavy, steaming machines.

She got off on the ninth, squeezing through the one small, unlocked door with the other machine operators. As soon as she opened the door her spirit ebbed. She didn't know what she could expect, exactly, but there it was—the same shop floor; the open, reeking barrel of machine oil that sat by the door; the long rows of benches where the operators, nearly two hundred and fifty of them, at the height of the season, would be packed in, hip-to-hip. Already she could feel what it would be like by midday, her body crammed into that unnatural, numbing position over the machine, like she was stuffed into a little box.

She hung the shapeless nub of cloth that was her hat on a wall peg—where all the outside clothes were hung, like children's coats in the back of a classroom. Then she made her way over to her place on the benches with the peculiar hop-skip they all used to navigate between the rotating axles and the baskets of cloth on the floor, seating herself finally behind the machine that she knew like one of her own limbs by now, and could use with even more agility.

The door to the shop opened, and another gaggle of women came in: Italian girls, who walked the few blocks over from the West Village and Little Italy together, laughing and singing. They were singing even now: the latest show tune that had drifted down to the dancing academies, and the wine gardens:

> Every little movement has a meaning
>   all its own
> Every thought and feeling by some posture
>   can be shown

—a strange little song, all words, like American songs always were—nothing like the doleful songs from Russia, packed with sheer emotion. They made you tap your feet and snap your fingers whether you wanted to or not, and now the other girls began to pick it up, in a tremulous range of accents and pitches, humming or adding words they made up themselves:

> And every love thought that comes a-stealing
> Over your being must be revealing
> All its sweetness in some appealing
> Little gesture all its own

It didn't seem quite so bad, then—with the sun streaming through the windows, and that foolish little song stuck in her head. It seemed possible, even tolerable, then. She knew that would change, of course: the supervisors would hush the women to keep them from singing or talking, and the dust would billow up so thick it obscured the sunlight, and they would have to keep the gas jets open, day and night, just to see the cloth in front of them.

She knew it would change, she was at this too long not to know it. Yet still it was early enough that she could tell herself with a certain pride along with a sustaining and inveterate weariness:

Well, this is what I am I am a worker not an angel

BOOK THREE

*That cabbages thrive in dung
was something I had always
taken for granted.*

—CARL JUNG

12

BIG TIM

Big Tim Sullivan sipped his coffee and watched the lawyers filing into the Tombs, the words running through his head:

Land of the people Land of the people Land of the people

They moved in a long, shuffling row, battered leather satchels in hand, disappearing behind the forbidding, gray walls of the prison. The new Tombs jail wasn't ten years old but it was already sinking, much to the embarrassment of the organization. Like its predecessor, it had been built on top of the old Collect Pond in lower Manhattan, and it leaked like a sieve. The water kept seeping slowly, inexorably up through the cells, the walls dripping with moisture, the bottom cells often ankle-deep in water and muck.

"Look at 'em," Cousin Florrie sneered at the lawyers from where they sat in Big Tim's saloon across Centre Street, interrupting his reverie. "Leeches workin' over the carcass."

"An imprecise analogy," Big Tim corrected him. "A vulture, say, or some other scavenger might pick over a *carcass*. A leech battens off living things."

"Same t'ing."

"No—no, it ain't the same t'ing at all. Words matter, you know."

Did they? *Land of the people Land of the people*

He snapped out his pocket watch, and a small notebook and pencil from some inner pocket, and the men around the table sat up—his brothers, Paddy and Flat-Nose Dinny, and his half brother Larry Mulligan; Florrie, and the other cousins, Christy and Little Tim; and Big Tim's own, self-appointed valets, Photo Dave Altman and Sarsaparilla Reilly.

The Wise Ones, they were called in the neighborhood, or simply The Sullivans, and they were nearly indistinguishable in their somber black suits and derbies. Stern as judges, inscrutable as bankers. Nothing stronger than coffee, or sarsaparilla, or soda water before them.

"You oughtn't to blame the poor lawyers, Florrie," Big Tim said, turning back to his cousin. "They're joost out after the early worm, just like us, and if we are a bit more beneficent, perhaps it is because we have the more to give."

"Can't stand the lousy skinners," Florrie insisted, arms folded grimly across his chest.

He had marked this obstinacy before in his cousin. Florrie had grown inexplicably darker, more unappeasable over the course of the last year or two—just like the other one, Little Tim. Sullivan felt the first sharp twinge of the day in his own groin.

Perhaps we are all cursed

"Personally, I still miss the Great White Hunter, meself," he said, trying to turn the conversation to a lighter subject. News of the Honorable Ex-Prez Teddy Roosevelt's exploits were plastered all over the morning papers.

"You could set your watch by the man, back when he was police commissioner. Marchin' down through the Mulberry Bend, gabbin' away to his Swede."

"Sure, and a big hoss pistol in his pocket," Photo Dave gloated. "Like it woulda done 'im any good, goin' t'rough the Bend, if some plug chose to do him."

"Oh, you mustn't underestimate the Honorable Ex. I've

no doubt Teddy wasn't *dyin'* to use it. Pot hisself a Yid, or a dago. Put 'em up wit' the elephants and the Ben-gal tigers around his parlor."

Big Tim had seen the parlor, some ten years ago, when he'd snuck out to Oyster Bay to get the great man's help in his war with old Boss Croker. The whole place had been covered, wall to wall, with skins and horns and tusks. There was even a badger-skin rug, the creature's tiny jaws set ferociously as a lion's. Still, the man had understood the situation readily enough. His own great white teeth slashing away murderously, while Big Tim tried to recruit him in Tammany Hall's civil war. A natural-born killer.

Now the Ex-Prez, Ex—Police Commish was away in darkest Africa, finding more things to shoot—slicing his way through that strange and wondrous land like a man in an abattoir. Big Tim remembered a passage from Teddy's memoir of San Juan Hill, about shooting a Spanish soldier with the same huge pistol: *He doubled up like a jackrabbit.* Beware the muckraker, indeed.

"I remember that Swede of Teddy's," Sarsaparilla Reilly was saying. "He tried to take a picture of me cousin's attic down the Dirty Spoon, in Blind Man's Alley. Nearly burned down the place with the flash, then he goes out an' tells a cop about the unfit conditions. Unfit! Sure it is, once you set it on fire!"

"Reform, there's nothin' to it!"

A fresh ripple of indignation ran around the table.

"Anybody ever see a nickel from it?"

"I ask you, anybody ever see a *penny* from reform? When did Teddy Roosevelt ever get anyone a job?"

Big Tim let them talk. He knew the Swede: a stern, self-righteous man named Riis, a Dane actually—though more a Yankee than the Yankees themselves. Sullivan had even read his book—*How the Other Half Lives*—and thought it naive right down to the title.

If it were only *the half, we would have no problems. "How the World* Is*" would be more like it.*

Yet the pictures had been compelling, staged and calculated as they were: Street boys huddled in alleys. Soot-covered immigrants staring blankly back at the camera in their basement hovels. Young women and children, numbed and listless, the look of death already in their face. In between were yards of damning statistics. Pictures and social statistics—what couldn't you sell with those?

"Now, boys, let us go easy on the Ex," he told the Wise Ones, starting to wrap it up. "Even Teddy has his uses."

"Like what?"

"Teddy is a splitter," Big Tim said, using the worst epithet anyone at the table could imagine. "He is a splitter in the caucus, and he will be a splitter at the polls. He is a young man, still in the full bloom of health, an' when he is done slaughterin' the poor, defenseless craytures of Africa, an' done beatin' up on the poor crowned heads of Europe, he'll come back an' split his party right down the middle over Mr. Taft. You see if he don't."

The table broke up in laughter—a hard, vindictive sound—and Big Tim called the board to order.

"All right, let's get this aggregation under way. Now—how're we comin' along for the chowder?"

Every midsummer, the Timothy D. Sullivan Association hosted an enormous picnic for its constituents up on College Point. There would be a parade, and an excursion boat, and hogsheads of beer, and all the chicken and clams and ice cream they could eat. There would be gambling, and baseball, and they would sing all the old Tammany songs.

And at the pinnacle of it all—when the crowd was at just that perfect, glowing pitch of early tipsiness—Big Tim would rise and give them his speech:

"Boys, I'm a Democrat." (Cheers.)

"I've been a Democrat all my life." (More cheers.)

"I have voted the Democratic ticket straight all my life."
(Uproarious cheers.)

"I never scratched a ticket since I cast my first vote when
I was seventeen, and I never will." (Pandemonium.)

This year he was trying to work on something a little
more, since he was leaving Congress to go back to his far
more influential seat in the state senate. So far, though, all he
had was that one, bothersome line:

Land of the people Land of the people

"How's Charlie Solomon over in the Tenth comin'?" he
asked. "I don't want him thinkin' he's his own man just yet.
An' get on Tom Foley, he owes us forever—"

Everyone who owed him was expected to ante up, in
money or goods. This meant damned well every politician
and proprietor and public employee in what had become Big
Tim's kingdom, below the Line at Fourteenth Street.

"How's the boat?" he asked, getting to the main question.

"Comin' along," Dinny said soberly.

The very mention of the subject cast a pall over the table.
A few years before, another summer excursion from old
Kleindeutschland had gone up the East River, on the paddle
wheeler *General Slocum*. Somehow, a fire had started in the
rough water at the Hell Gate rapids. Like a bad dream, the
fire hoses and the life preservers were all rotten, and fell
apart in the hands of the crew. Before the boat could be
beached over a thousand Deutschers had drowned in the
swift current or burned on the boat, most of them women
and children. The procession to the German Lutheran
Cemetery in Queens had stretched out for more than a mile.

At least, thank God, it had been a church outing, but the
disaster had put a chill through every district leader in the
city. *Kleindeutschland* had been completely wiped out and
replaced by Jews, the church turned into a synagogue—an
entire constituency wiped out overnight.

"You're checkin' her over?"

"Sure thing."

Big Tim would not be appeased.

"I mean yourself—don't leave it to anybody."

"Sure thing, Big Tim."

He turned to the daily business: the rents and evictions, the jobs and jails. He would take care of most of this himself, later on, down in the Poor People's Court, where the magistrates picked the pockets of the poor. Then there was the ice to take care of, it being the summer, and the funerals, which went on at a steady clip all year.

"All in order, lads," Big Tim said finally, snapping his book shut and putting away his watch. "This district can just about run itself. I have half a mind to retire to Ireland with Mr. Croker."

"One t'ing," Dinny interjected, flattened boxer's nose turning up objectionably.

"What's that?"

"That old black crow's been comin' around again, raisin' a can racket about the next legislature session."

"Ah, the iridescent Mrs. Perkins," Big Tim needled his brother. He rather liked the woman himself. She was a queer duck, but she had none of the airs the other Yankee social work ladies possessed. She even wore a dowdy, tricornered black hat, just like the one his own mother used to wear.

"Goin' on about the work hours bill again, is she?"

"The goo-goos are set on it," Florrie said gloomily.

Officially, Tammany Hall was always on the side of the working man, and the working woman. The reality, of course, was that the money—the money that greased the wheels, and kept the whole world turning—came from the garment factories, and the sweatshops, and the cigar companies, and all the other noble concerns of American business that kept their employees sweltering twelve to sixteen hours a day in conditions unfit for a horse.

It was a terrible thing, but there it was. Sullivan had no

illusions about it: business would be served. The trick was how to give up just enough to keep the voters out of the hands of the Socialists.

"Well they might be set on it," Big Tim said expansively. "And what of it? Might not be the end of the world, you know, lettin' babes an' wimmin work a mere fifty-four hours a week. But we'll see. Anyt'ing else?"

"Just that Mister Murphy sent his greetings. To remind you about a certain matter," Little Tim hemmed and hawed, with impeccable Irish discretion.

"Ah, yes. Ah, that."

The rest of the Wise Ones maintained a judicious silence. All of them knew what Little Tim was talking about, of course; there was only one police matter that he could possibly mean, and that was Herman Rosenthal.

"Ah, yes. Poor old Beansy."

Whatever you say, Big Tim. Whatever you think I should do.

Big Tim had always had a soft spot for Beansy Rosenthal. He had started out as a newsie, just like Sullivan, even hawking his papers in front of the same Park Row beanery he had worked himself when he was seven years old.

"Stick with gambling. Gambling takes brains, and you're one smart Jewboy," Sullivan had told him, and Beansy had listened.

Herman had become a racetrack tout, then a proprietor. Big Tim had made him one of his favorites—one of his Jewboys, as he called them affectionately. From the start, he had helped him with loans, with protection, and for a time Beansy had done well—opening up gambling houses from Far Rockaway to Harlem, covering himself in the mono-grammed gold jewelry he loved.

I'm just trying to stand up for myself, I'm just trying to make a buck—

Yet everywhere that Beansy went, a problem was sure to

follow. He was always getting into messy feuds with other gamblers, and when things didn't go his way he had the amazing habit of filing his hollers against the cops through the daily newspapers.

This was not at all regular. There was something, Big Tim had come to realize, that wasn't quite right about Herman. No amount of punitive police raids seemed able to cure him of the habit: he actually seemed to like publicity. There was something childlike and disarming about the short, fleshy man in his dapper suits and flashy jewelry, yet it was a wonder that he hadn't got himself killed. Big Tim had taken pity on him, given him one last chance—a sweet setup in Times Square, no less. He had squared it with Lieutenant Charlie Becker and his Strong-Arm Squad; even loaned Beansy a couple thousand for start-up money.

But then Herman had queered it again. Becker had raided his joint—not a real raid, just one of the annoying, showy assaults Handsome Charlie had taken to arranging for the newspapers, as part of his never-ending campaign to become police commissioner. The strong-arm squad hadn't even smashed up the roulette wheel or the stuss table, and instead of breaking down the front door with the customary axe, they had politely rung the doorbell.

The idea was just to shut Herman down for a day or two, win Becker a headline. Handsome Charlie had even brought along his press agent, a ridiculous little man named Plitt, for the purpose. Yet somehow, it had all come apart, the way it always seemed to happen with anything involving Herman. Beansy had put up a stink, everything got out of hand—and before it was all over Plitt the press agent had managed to kill the house janitor with a revolver.

Sweet Jesus, but it was foolish enough already! Only in New York would a vice squad lieutenant have a press agent, and a murderous one at that. But there it was . . .

Big Tim had tried to quash it all, but of course it had only

142

got worse. Furious, Becker had kept Herman shut down until he handed over five hundred dollars for a lawyer for Plitt. Herman had refused to pay, and gone to the newspapers again—and this time, before Big Tim could fix it, dear Beansy had sworn out an affidavit for the new Reform idjit of a district attorney. The details of which had been immediately leaked to the D.A.'s pet reporter over at the *World:*

> There is only one man in the world can call me off, that is the big fellow, Big Tim Sullivan, and he is as honest as the day is long, and I know he is in sympathy with me. If I need money I can go to him for it and he will give it to me or get it for me. It is purely a matter of friendship, and he never expects to make a nickel profit out of it. He is the only man that could call me off, and he has told me that he believes I am doing right in trying to protect myself and my home.

No doubt Herman was making some typically misguided effort to exonerate him. Instead, he had only queered it further. There was no way that Big Tim could back him against every other power in New York—no one but a gambler could be so relentlessly optimistic. Well, there was no other way around it. Beansy would have to be settled, once and for all.

"Send a reminder through our friends, if you don't mind," Sullivan said, turning to Sarsaparilla Reilly. "That's a boil we have to lance."

"Gentlemen."

Big Tim rose ponderously to his feet.

"Photo Dave, you come with me today. Sarsaparilla can meet us at City Hall after he sees to his errand. I have to go see the Little Little Napoleon, an' I'll want to be properly attended."

The men were already heading out the door, Sarsaparilla Reilly and Photo Dave snickering obligingly at his little jest about the mayor, George B. McClellan, son of the famous Civil War flop by the same name. Big Tim paused by the bar before he went out. Feeley the barkeep had his towel ready for him, and a mirror in which he could fix his hat and tighten the knot of his tie.

A hard, florid slab of a face looked back at him: intelligent, skeptical eyes, ironic mouth. The face of Tammany Hall? Or what? The words tumbled together in his mind until they had no meaning: the same insults, flatteries, and tributes. A political thug? A shield against the vagaries of a hard, new world? A *father*?

He felt the stirrings within him again——a small, sticking pain in his groin now. Nothing much——but nothing quite like anything he had felt before.

It was all chaos outside the Organization, he knew. There was only the clubhouse, the neighborhood, the home, the church——the same eternal verities, like the Celtic snakes of life, coiling over and over on themselves.

But for what? *For what?*

Land of the people——

He looked up from himself, confused and frightened in the moment, but he saw no alarm registered on the faces of Feeley the bartender or Photo Dave. He could still keep up a politician's face, at least. Thank God for that.

"Thank you, Richard," he said, placing a shiny silver dollar quietly on the bar, same as he did each morning.

"Don't let those lawyers skin you on the draughts today"——their standard morning joke.

"Aye, I'll keep on me toes." The bartender grinned.

He looked around the place one more time. He owned three more saloons officially, and had a sporting interest in countless others across town. They were all placed strategically: this one by the Tombs, another right across from City Hall, another next to the newspapers down Park Row, the fourth one by the new police headquarters up at Centre and Grand. Then there were the vaudeville theatres and the racetracks, the nickelodeons and the movie houses—and the three vast amusement parks out at Coney, Steeplechase, and Luna Park, and Dreamland.

He had at least a controlling interest in them all—and then there were his kickbacks from the trolley line, and the electric power, and the water concessions, the cuts from every prizefight and every gambling house and every rat pit throughout the City. A good living he made, and he knew he would have made it one way or another, and damn what the newspapers said.

"Dave, me boy," he said, turning to his self-appointed bodyguard, perennial clubhouse nominator, and bearer of the sacred grease that made the wheels turn:

"Load me up."

"Certainly, Dry Dollar," Dave grinned, using Sullivan's old, childhood nickname that only the Wise Ones called him by.

Photo Dave pulled fistfuls of jinglers from his coat, carefully stuffing them into the many pockets of Big Tim's custom-tailored, his coat, his pants. Sullivan stood patiently in front of him, arms extended like a scarecrow, not unamused by the spectacle he knew he presented.

"Ah, me God, Dave," he said when the man had finished. "If the Gold-Plated Holies had it in mind to finish me, all they'd have to do is t'row me in the East River right now."

Another standard joke, delivered in the exaggerated brogue from the variety houses, the old Joe Millers that he knew Photo Dave loved. The man roared with laughter on cue, and Big Tim was settled by the ritual.

"Now some greenbacks for the booly dogs, and all the Little Little Napoleon's little needs."

With due solemnity now, Photo Dave produced great rolls of currency, clipped together thicker than a man's fist, for his inner pockets. How the Reform papers would howl if they could see it! The public's money—spent to bail felons out of jail! Secure employment and housing for the indolent!

Of course, neither Big Tim nor anyone else could tell the goo-goos, the Simon Pures, how much money there was, or whether it was really the public's money at all. Did the weekly shakedown from the gangs and the whorehouses count as the public's? How about the money extorted from honest merchants, or Chinatown dope dens, or semi-legitimate-to-thoroughly-incorrigible saloonkeepers?

It was a different world *they* lived in, the good government types—a place where everything was carefully marked down and accounted for, in great, separate ledger books. Commerce in this hand, corruption in the other. Progressive reforms here, and the buying of votes or gangsters there. It was a world which had nothing to do with the inside of a police station, or a polling booth, or a tenement house.

But you can decide—that mocking, inner voice again. *You know what's best.*

He shook off the cobwebs, smiled up at his valet and the bartender again.

None of that matters None of us picks our position in this life

"All right, Dave," he said. "Let us be on our unappointed rounds."

They were surrounded by children as soon as they stepped out on the street. He smiled to see them, they looked so delighted, so determinedly grown-up. The boys wore overalls and big caps, the girls, dresses cut from old sacks or horse blankets, nearly all of them barefoot on the granite-cobbled city street.

Once, a few months before, in the fetid alley that ran behind the Dirty Spoon, he had come upon a little girl of at least seven who was completely naked. Not a stitch of clothes on her, and none that she owned—and even though it was no surprise to him, even though he knew well that such things and much worse went on, he had not been able to stop crying.

"Hey, Big Tim! Big Tim!"

"Hey, Mr. Sully-van! Whattaya got for me?"

His groin kicked, and he almost broke his stride. The pain was spreading, burning. He had had a case before, back when Nell, the wife, was still with him, but it was nothing like this. The grinning, dirty faces swirled around him, little hands groping at him, and he made himself smile back.

"Hey, Big Tim!"

They pushed their fingers into his outer pockets, pulled up shiny new quarters and dimes and nickels, marveling at the prizes. They laughed and skipped, leaped around him like any other children—though if you looked closely enough, he knew, you could see how thin they were, how quickly they tired.

The newspapers liked to romanticize them. They called them Street Arabs, and wrote about the city as if it were one big playground for them. He knew the truth: how they fought to sleep over a warm grate in the winter; in an out-house, or maybe an abandoned boiler in the summer. They were at the mercy of older cutthroats and panderers. The wagons and the streetcars cut them down in droves, and now, too, the big new auto cars, swooping and careening recklessly through the crowded city streets.

Yet they were the pictures he had liked best in the Swede's book, he had to admit. Not the worked-out adults—vacant, staring eyes, the last spark snuffed out—but the children, still so fiercely proud, so independent. They scared the tourists; when the sightseeing omnibuses came by they would throw rocks at the guide with his megaphone, yelling, "Here are the monkeys!" but he loved their spirit.

You could see it in the faces of the boys, if you looked closely enough—pretending to sleep at the photographer's behest, barely able to fight back the laughter, their smiles over this make-believe already curling around the edge of their lips. Or a girl in an apartment sweatshop on Ludlow Street, already condemned to a life of cutting and sewing knee pants in an endless series of suffocating little shops but *smiling,* smiling back at the camera anyway. Smiling through a pair of scissors, of all things, holding it up flirtatiously to her lips like she was one of Goya's senoritas with a fan—

"Gimme! Gimme there!"

He scanned their faces as they thrust their hands in, looking for some semblance of his own. Of course he had set aside something for *them*—all the ones he knew were his, anyway: the girls down in Jersey, the boy out West, where there was air, and room. They were all well provided for. He took care of his own—

Unless there were others. Ones he didn't know about— *his* children, living out on the street. When, irony of ironies, Nell could never give him one—

His groin kicked again, making him bend down to the children.

"That's all, that's all now, kiddies, you milked the man dry," Photo Dave was shooing them away.

With a great effort he straightened up, moved on up Broadway as jauntily as he could, trying to ignore Photo Dave's quizzical looks. Behind him the children scampered off, waving and hollering.

"Good-bye, Big Tim!"

"Big Tim, Big Tim!"

"I love you!"

He turned at that last cry. It seemed to him it came from a girl with curly black hair, who looked almost familiar. But then she was gone—then all the children were gone, disappearing down their holes and alleys, back to their unending game on the streets of New York.

He turned at that last cry. It seemed to him it came from a girl with curly black hair, who looked almost familiar. But then she was gone—then all the children were gone, disappearing down their holes and alleys, back to their unending game on the streets of New York.

13

ON THE BOARDWALK

Esther met him at the main gate of Dreamland by the Angel of Creation—its great wings spanning the whole width of the entrance arch, perfectly formed breasts pointing the way to the future. He was waiting for her at its foot, in a white summer suit with a kelly-green vest that looked as cool and elegant as an ice cream sherbet—gazing up at the angel's exquisite teats.

Kid Twist grinned, and squeezed her hand when she came up, and she couldn't help but grin back at him.

"I'm glad you came."

"Didn't you think I would?" she mocked him.

Inside, the park was just gearing up for the day, looking almost wholesome in the morning light. The pavement was pristine, the coasters making their first tentative whooshes around the tracks. A long line of the Dreamland cash girls filed by in their immaculate white academic caps and gowns, marching like so many novitiates to their registers.

"We have the whole day," he said, and pulled her along.

They rode on the Alpine railway, past tiny Swiss chalets and frozen waterfalls, and pink snowy peaks. The little open cars shaped like sleighs, with bells that tinkled as they careened

150

around the curves, climbed laboriously up the Starn-bergersee. They plunged over—and a long, delighted cry rose from the women and children filling the cars ahead.

They rode in the back, the only couple on the train, squeezed into the childlike seats of their car. His hand was around her waist, dangling over her hip, brushing her waist and thighs.

They sped into a tunnel with a sign inscribed gratuitous-ly NO KISSING ALLOWED IN THIS TUNNEL. As soon as they were in the dark she felt his hands on her, pulling her to him. He smelled like fine bay rum, and peppermints, and she wanted to laugh to think of her first kiss with the cockroach boss, grappling in his room of coats. She shut her eyes and kissed him back, ignoring the women and children shifting and giggling all around them.

They pulled out of the tunnel, the other passengers laughing and pointing at them, but to her surprise she found she didn't care at all. She turned her head away, smiling, staring dreamily down at the matrix of toy trains below her, whizzing in and out of their snowy little tunnels and caves.

In the Streets of Cairo, men in turbans and caftans led their camels and elephants along the midway. A raven-haired woman undulated before a plaster mosque—its dome chip-ping sky-blue paint.

"The warmest spectacle on earth! See her dance the Hootchy-Kootchy! The *danse du ventre*—if ya know whatta mean!"

She danced out on the boards in stars and bangles: one forelock slicked down in the shape of a crescent moon, eyes painted into mysterious slits above her veil, a paste sapphire mounted in her navel. Her bare, rounded belly wriggled like nothing Esther had ever seen, suggesting whole new worlds.

"*Any*where else but in the ocean breezes of Coney Island

she would be consumed by her own fire!"

She jiggled and shook slowly around, back toward the sky-blue mosque. A small knot of men, grinning sheepishly, shambled after her into the plaster mosque.

Later, when it got dark, he took her dancing out at the end of the Old Iron Pier. They shuffled slowly around, listening to the waves below them and singing along softly with the old favorites:

> My evening star
> I wonder who you are
> Set up so high like a diamond
> in the sky
> No matter what I do
> I can't go up to you
> So come down from there
> my evening star—

She had him request "After the Ball Is Over," which you could barely go a quarter of an hour at Coney without hearing, but none of the other dancers seemed to mind:

> After the ball is over
> After the break of morn

It was late, and everyone was tired. The dancers slumped around the floor together, smelling each other's rank, pleasurable scents of salt water, and sun, and fried food—

> After the ball is over
> After the break of morn
> After the dancers' leaving
> After the stars are gone

> Many a heart is aching
> If you could read them all
> Many the hopes that have vanished
> After the ball

It was late by the time he walked her to the train station. The fireworks were already going off, the last trains pulling out.

"Stay with me," he told her—meaning it this time, really trying to convince her this time.

"No. I got work."

She looked up at him and smiled, to show him how much she wanted to stay.

"My little dove. Stay."

"No."

He helped her push through the crowds to her train. On board, everyone was exhausted, the children already asleep in their mothers' laps. She threaded her way into the car, and stood looking back at him through the open door.

"My sweet. My little crown."

"No——"

The warning bell sounded—and he stepped across the threshold, into the train. Her eyes widened, not sure of what he could be doing.

No one else noticed. Everyone was dozing, or standing stupidly, clutching onto the handrails. No one else cared—but he held her in his arms by the door, as if they were married. Both of them staring at themselves in the darkened windows as they sped back through the ash pits and the coal yards.

They moved up through the sleeping neighborhoods of Park Slope, and Boerum Hill, and over the bridge into Manhattan, the train stopping more frequently now. Everyone exhausted, everyone too tired even to make any noise, the dozing families somehow intuiting when it was their stop, trudging off the train. Half the car cleared off when they reached Delancey and it was her stop, too, but she didn't budge.

She stayed by the door with him, holding him. They could have had a seat now, but they stayed by the door, holding each other and looking gravely back at their own reflections. Soon the car was all but empty, just two or three single men who had missed their stops snoozing in the corners. They rushed up along the elevated tracks, tenements and new, block-long apartment houses sweeping by. So close they could peer right into their windows and homes and lives—men and women reading or eating, comforting babies or making love, or just sitting under a dim light, having a smoke.

They sped uptown, all the flickering, inscrutable little dramas running together, and he held his arms around her waist and began to kiss her. He kissed her neck, as he had on the Steeplechase, and she leaned her head back, and kissed him full on the mouth, and held her arms around his head. She broke it off, then kissed him again for a long time, and leaned back against him—both of them staring out the window at all the houses going by, the men and women leaning on their windowsills in the hot, still night, staring dully back at the train rushing past them.

14

KID TWIST

When the train would go no farther they rode back to her stop, and then he walked her back home. At the end of her block she pulled away from him, but he held on to her hand—toward what end he did not know. They stood mutely at arm's length for a moment—then he released her, into the dark of Orchard Street, watching her go through the smears of street-light.

He walked back toward the elevated in the sweaty post-midnight, along streets that were far from deserted. It had always amazed him the most about New York—how many people there were still up, and out, well after midnight. Whores and peddlers, a few working women of a different trade, trailing back from factory shifts, the exhaustion over-coming the fear on their faces.

But mostly it was men—men of all sorts and shapes, but the same furtive demeanor. They hurried past him on the street—trying to seem bold and confident, trying to straighten their weaving drunk walks. Heads buried in their jackets and collars, straws and bowlers pulled down tight over their heads, looking straight ahead.

What was he doing here among them? It was madness for him to come back to the City, Kid knew. Any one of the wraithlike figures scuttling up the elevated stairs could be a snitch or an assassin, happy to get in good with Gyp by putting the finger on him—or worse.

What was he doing? Why hadn't he got out already—and all the way out, not just to the whore's hotel where that crazy little dwarf had stashed him? He had a little money— why wasn't he already on a New Orleans steamer, or a Pullman car to St. Louis? Somewhere, anywhere, he had a good chance of staying out of the eye of Gyp the Blood forever?

Was it the girl? But there had been girls before, albeit mostly mabs and goohs, and lonely green factory girls, just off the boat. This one was different—but was she worth his life?

He was not unaware of the bigger question, too: *why had he done it in the first place?* Why in the world should it have mattered to him what Gyp the Blood did? What was it his place, to run around saving people?

That was not what he had come here for, he told himself, as he boarded the train for the long trip back to Brooklyn and Coney Island and the Elephant's Arse. That was not what he was doing here, in New York—not why he had come all that way. Though what he *was* doing, he did not know anymore.

He shaved his face the day they buried his father. As soon as he came back from the funeral, with its straggling line of mourners, he pulled out the slab of mottled glass, and the straight razor he had bought from the goy in Kovno. First he cut the coarse, tangled hair of his beard, already graying, with a knife. Then he splashed his face with a little water, and went to work on the remaining nub.

What a massacre it was. His poor skin had never been shaved. Neither had anyone else's in all of Old Zagare, or even New Zagare, where they were all sinners. Except when the Cossacks had come, and held them down and shaved them off with a cavalry saber, and most of those had not survived very much longer.

He wiped his cheeks and chin with a rag, and looked into the glass again. A pale, serious face stared back, suddenly youthful. His large, jagged nose and dark hollowed eyes loomed large, and innocent, and ungainly.

He placed the glass and the razor in the meager pack he had prepared, along with a picture he had of his father and another of his mother, from their wedding day and, for reasons he did not quite understand, one that an itinerant photographer had taken of Old Zagare itself: a ridiculous picture, really, featuring the wagon-rutted roads at the height of its spring mud season, the bare trees and huts, a pathetic fence trailing off to nothing.

He stuffed it in his pack anyway, and slung the bundle over his shoulder. No more than these possessions: the photographs, his father's Bible with the family tree written in the first pages, a couple of rolls, the few vegetables that had come up this year. He slapped a worker's cap on his head, bought at Kovno the same day he got the razor, and set out— not bothering to so much as close the door or even look back at the two-room log cabin, covered with mud and straw.

He walked out through the rest of Old Zagare, past the synagogue and the school, the slaughterhouse and the *mikvah,* and the long line of *luftmenschen* waiting patiently outside the almshouse for their daily soup and bread. He walked right down the center of the main dirt road, its mud already whipped to clouds of dust by the first winds of the summer, smelling the herring and potatoes from the midday meal.

He walked through the cemetery, where he had just been that morning, past the freshly turned earth of his father's grave. There the schoolboys from New Zagare liked to come and hide themselves behind the gravestones, hoping to glimpse the corpses from Old Zagare their parents told them about. He laughed to see them stare and run off when they saw him, knowing he was a greater shock than any hundred-year-dead rabbi risen from the dead.

He crossed over the bridge into New Zagare itself—its own collection of log and mud and straw huts, with its own *shoichetin* and *mikvah;* its own schools and synagogues and town hall and *luftmenschen,* all bitterly opposed to anything having to do with Old Zagare. He was through it in minutes, a meaningless speck in the middle of nowhere, and he paused only for a moment to look back at the twin villages where he had lived his whole life, before walking into the enveloping dust of the open road:

Oh, that I should only bury you all in one day!

He kept walking. He walked until he was too tired to walk anymore, and then he lay down and slept by the side of the road and when he woke up, he started walking again. He walked for weeks and months, he walked until he had no idea how long he had been walking—until he had walked out of the flat, treeless land, stretching out to the horizon.

He walked west, always west, albeit getting lost time and time again, drifting north and south. When the few vegetables and rolls he had brought were exhausted, he lived by his wits. He begged work where he could get it, cadged food from the carts in town markets, ate with strangers on the road. Sometimes he got a lift in a wagon for a few miles, a ride on the back of some peddler's donkey—but almost always, he walked.

He walked through all the double eagles emblazoned on the border gates. The splendidly uniformed border guards, Habsburg or Hohenzollern, caressing their moustaches with immaculate yellow gloves while they pored over his papers: JOSEF KOLYIKA—his old face, now barely remembered by himself, creased and stained and covered with more eagle

158

stamps. Invariably, they refused to let him cross over, whatever the border. They weren't sure what new subterfuge this was——a man who shaved his beard to reveal his face!——but they didn't trust it.

He began to stay away from the border posts, feeling his way at night down the ambiguous edge of empire——looking for a place to cross over. He was spat upon in some estaminet of Warsaw, beaten by the police in Budapest, set upon by gypsies in Prague.

Still, he kept walking. He came at last to a great and leisurely city, emerging slowly from a pleasant woods, opening up to him in ever wider streets and boulevards. The avenues were full of students in uniforms; fat, contented people in good coats; thick clouds of dust rising from the soft, red paving blocks.

He staggered among them in his heavy, ill-shapen clothing, gawking at the palaces and mansions. He was somewhere German, he knew, by the harsh, guttural language. The windows groaning with meats and breads and fantastic pastries; the endless file of statues standing stonily along the main boulevard. The streams of pedestrians opened and closed around him like he was some derelict tree trunk in their course, their faces filled with distaste.

Of course, he could not be allowed to remain out in public, looking like he was. The police removed him from the streets as quickly and efficiently as the municipal sanitation service snatched up any droppings from the carriage horses. They marched him to a station house, ran him through a booking——but his papers were so pawed by then they had finally become illegible. In the little German he had, he told them he was from Ruthenia——a province so geographically and intellectually removed from the capital that its very existence had never been confirmed.

They were suspicious, but it was clear he wasn't an anarchist, or some assassin snuck in from the Balkans. They dropped him off at a flophouse around the corner, gave him a coin for a meal and a night's lodging. That evening he sat at the big communal table in the kitchen, gratefully wolfing down the bowl of hot potato soup and bread.

It was a clean, well-lighted place, run with Germanic tidiness—more a dormitory for transients than a true flophouse. Beside him at table were men speaking in all the dialects of the immense, ramshackle empire. On his right was a man with wild, dark eyes and a short sweep of hair, dressed like a street artist and obviously a lunatic. He tried to speak to him kindly at first, but when the man discovered he was from the East he turned away abruptly, declaiming something about the Jews at the top of his voice.

The others ignored him, more interested in the soup with its large dollops of fat swimming in the broth, its generous chunks of potato. He turned to the man on his other side—dressed like a day laborer, with a mouth that crinkled merrily when he smiled, but eyes like a wolf. He had some Russian, at least, they could talk a little, though there was something evasive about him. He noticed that one of the man's arms was not right—that it was crippled, or withered, though one barely noticed at first the way he held it.

"They don't like the Jews here," the man confirmed, looking over at the lunatic artist.

"Where do they?" Josef asked, and the laborer seemed to think that was very funny, his mouth crinkling up again like the pictures of Father Christmas he had seen in Kovno.

"Besides, I don't want to be a Jew anymore. I'm through with it."

The laborer thought this was funny, too—though he noticed that the man never really laughed.

"I mean it," he said. "I'm going over to the *goldineh medina*."

"You had best go," the man agreed, cheerful as ever. "This is a charnel house, over here."

He leaned in confidentially.

"At least, some of us are doing our best to make it that," he added.

He wasn't sure if the man was joking, or if he, too, were mad, but the laborer only smiled his enigmatic, merry smile again, and Josef smiled back, not wanting to offend him.

All things considered, it was still better than Old Zagare, and he slept that night in a good bed, the first one without bugs and off the ground he could remember. The next day he was even issued a pair of pants, a shirt, a jacket, and some shoes. They fit as badly as his old clothes but they were lighter, softer at least, and free of the old, familiar reek of himself.

He washed in the dormitory baths—in warm water, no less!—then dressed in his pleasurable new things and started to walk again. He walked north; he had some idea where he was and where he was going now. Sneaking up through more empires, more imperial eagles, until at last he stood at the great, bustling docks to America.

That was when he realized that he had absolutely no idea of how to proceed. He had thought only of walking, and when he had set out even the horizon had seemed so far away that it was useless to consider anything more. Yet here he was now, and he had no ticket, no money to buy one— no skills anyone here would value, and a language that would only get him deported.

Before him, gangs of dockworkers in overalls and blue work shirts were busy filling the maw of a great ocean liner, tumbling in the trunks of the first-class and steerage passengers alike. He looked down and saw one of the blue shirts, lying along the dock. Emblazoned over one of the pockets was "Jos. K.," and seeing it was more or less his own name he put it on almost without thinking.

"Hey, you! Kalikeh! Get over here!" one of the workmen called to him. He wasn't sure what the man was saying but he went over to him anyway.

"What are you doing? Idiot!"

He just shrugged, unsure of any other reply, of what he was supposed to be, and the man waved him on over to a huge, mysterious wooden box. The only markings on the box were FRAGILE! and DELICATE! and NAT. THEATRE OF OKLAHOMA, but it took a whole team of workmen, using all their might, to tug and push it into the ship's hold.

When they were through, the other longshoremen leaned over, resting for a moment, then went back to moving cargo, and Joseph realized that he was now aboard the ship. No one was paying the slightest attention to him, and he wandered slowly back into the hold, deeper and deeper into the vast boxes and carriages and auto cars, piled up for their voyage to America.

He kept expecting that someone would call him out—that surely it could not be so easy to get into the vast ocean liner, and he would be apprehended, and perhaps even taken off to jail again. But no one called, and soon he could hear the whistles screaming, and the ship's horn blaring. He wandered up onto one of the lower decks, a narrow walkway for the passengers in steerage class. People were cheering on the docks, and cheering along the first-class decks, and somewhere a band was playing. The ship's great smokestacks belched to life, and two guns barked a salute from the great fortress across the harbor. Down below, the brightly-pennanted tugs were beginning to pull the liner irresistibly away from the docks.

They were under way—a single ship, casting off a continent.

He burrowed down deep into the ship, into cubbyholes below even the steerage compartments. There was a whole community of stowaways there, beneath the great, throbbing city of the boat—their numbers constantly rising or falling, more strays picked up at Antwerp, or Bristol, as patched and starved and secret as himself.

It was rough for days, and then it was calm—both ways throwing them around deep in the unbolted hold, making them retch up what little food they could scrounge. They were never sure what the weather was like in any case, the only news was in old copies of the ship's paper, which they used over and over again. They read what they could make out from it, then used it to wipe their ass, throwing it down the bilge holes to be quickly devoured by the sharks that followed the great liner all the way across the North Atlantic.

Deep down in his hole in the wall by the hull, he studied English from a dog-eared book given to him by one of the stokers who knew of their existence, trading them food and a blanket in exchange for what little money they had left, or sex, or the opportunity for cruelty.

The stories, he slowly, gradually discerned, were all part of a series, an endlessly repeated tale called things like *Luck and Pluck,* or *Sink and Swim,* or *Fame and Fortune,* about a young boy with incredible luck. Sometimes the boy was called Ragged Dick, or sometimes he was Tattered Tom, or sometimes Mark the Match Boy, but his story was always the same, it was always about getting rich. As sure as bread, the boy in question would *rise.*

He read them doggedly, over and over again, with the help of a particularly friendly ship's engineer named Schubal, America unfolding for him a few words at a time. The one he loved the most, the one he first understood the meaning of, was *savory.* It was something that Mark the Match Boy (or Ragged Dick) was always eating: *savory* stew.

He was not sure just what it was, he could not be sure if he had ever had anything like it himself, but he could not imagine why anyone would even bother to rise—if he could eat *savory*, and live in that world of cigars, and oysters, and roasting corn, the shady characters, and the women of bad reputation, and the elevated trains, and the raucous balconies of the Old Bowery Theatre—

The stories always ended the same way, with the boy making his fortune through the device of saving a rich man's son or halting a terrible crime, or recovering the money of a poor widow. The boy in question, the Ragged Dick or the simpering match boy, was then carted off to some distant and much less interesting place—to Milwaukee, or Boston, or New Jersey—so that Joseph was never altogether sure what the point was of rising at all.

Before he could find out, he was told by Schubal the engineer they would be docking that very night, and after it was dark he risked sneaking back up to the steerage deck, to see if he could catch his first glimpse of the new continent.

The whole ship was alive and excited around him. Up on the first-class decks, he could hear Americans in the ship's bars, singing happy choruses of "Auld Lang Syne"— though the Jews on their deck, clustered around their few possessions, sang a mournful Russian song:

> By the little brook
> By the little bridge
> Grass was growing . . .

"Fire! Fire!"

Someone was yelling from the deck above. The Jews in their little circles paid no attention, but Joseph looked around anxiously, wondering if the ship could be on fire.

"Fire, fire! A terrible conflagration!"

People on all the different decks were crowding along the rails now, staring out into the darkness. Far ahead, along the rim of the world, he could indeed make out a fire, white-hot flames roiling along the whole length of the horizon.

"What could *make* a fire like that?"

"These American cities are put-up jobs. Look at Chicago——"

"Throw 'em up one day, tear 'em down the next——"

The passengers chattered away in half a dozen tongues, excited by the remote catastrophe. It was truly an incredible fire, limning their faces along the rail, looming high and white above the shore. The whole land was ablaze——the flames turning over and over on themselves like a tormented animal.

"How *can* it keep burning like that?"

Only as they rocked slowly closer through the swells could they see that there was something strange about this fire. It was an unnatural, constant blaze, burning but not consuming. Never increasing or diminishing, falling back in on itself again and again——

Soon, they could see, it split into distinct patterns and shapes——spinning globes, and obelisks and castles, and swooping wheels of fire. They shivered to watch it now, no longer quite so pleased by the disaster. What could make such a fire, they did not know.

"It's the steel itself burning!"

"The skyscrapers!"

But already they could make out the wheels within the wheels. The roller coasters and miniature trains, the whirligigs and giant merry-go-rounds, and the great tower of fire, trimmed with golden eagles. As they rocked even closer they could make out the safety lines staked far out into the water, the bronzed heads and chests of the electric bathers bobbing out under the spotlights. Soon they could hear the wild calliope chords, could smell the frying clams and beef and roasting corn.

"It's an amusement——all an amusement!"

He stood riveted by the rail—even more astonished than when he had thought it was a fire, and despite the chance that he could still be spotted as a stowaway, and hauled right back to Rotterdam on the next boat. He kept watching, as the great ocean liner hove slowly about and passed down the whole length of the parks, stretching for miles and miles, past the last leering, electrified idiot's face, and the blinking sign: STEEPLECHASE—FUNNY PLACE—STEEPLECHASE—FUNNY PLACE.

Two hours later they tied up for the night at South Street, before heading over to Ellis Island the next morning, and he crept back out on the steerage deck. A few belongings clutched to his chest, wrapped in oilskin and tied with his belt: some biscuits and tins of meat, his shoes, and the Book, which Schubal had let him have. He paused there, crouching down, until he was sure it was clear, and then he scuttled quickly and silently over to the bow.

The City lay glowing before him. The ship's prow pointed straight up one avenue, flowing out toward the west like a river of gold. Grids within grids of flickering yellow and white light. He stood, and leaned toward it.

There was a noise behind him. He ducked back down, heaved his oilskin package over the side—and after a very long time, heard it splash into the dark water below. Then he pulled himself up over the rail, and jumped in after it.

He fell . . . .

He tore through the water and sank quickly through the incredible filth and offal of the harbor. He could see, floating past him in the oily yellow light as he sank: chicken guts and horse bones, loose turds, the severed paw of a dog. Giant gray, drowned rats, floating peacefully, their heads bent over.

He closed his eyes against it and struggled. He had no

idea how to swim, but he struggled, writhing and flailing his arms toward the dim light above. He began to rise back up, the gritty, corrupted water fluming into his mouth and nostrils. He spat it out, and struck for the surface.

Something large and soft and rubbery bumped against his face. He opened his eyes, thinking it might be his oilskin.

A huge pink head grinned back at him. A hideous face—slanted, vicious eyes and ears, enormous, pushed-up nostrils. Coarse black hairs waving in the current—

He struck out at it, and the face fell away—then bobbed back toward him. Only then did he realize that it wasn't human but a gigantic pig's head, swollen and distorted in the water. He kicked it to one side, but it hung there before him for another long moment, grinning mindlessly until the current carried it away.

He broke the water a few yards away from the boat, choking and gasping. He saw his oilskin floating nearby, trapped by the mooring lines, and he hauled it in and rested on it, then pushed his way over to the wharf.

He scraped and clambered up the rock wall, over the rats and the slippery scum, and crouched there for a moment, covered in the oily black muck of the harbor. The ship loomed silently above him, seemingly deserted. There was no one else on the pier—only the distant sound of laughter and piano music coming from the bars and the bawdy houses down the wharf.

He unbelted the oilskin, and used it to wipe himself off as best he could before he tossed it back into the water. He sat down on a piling and put on his shoes and cap, slipped the tinned meats and apples into his pockets. Then he stood up and walked quickly down the broad, golden avenue, into the new city.

● ● ●

167

Not that he had any idea where he was going.

He just wanted to walk for awhile, until he got the lay of the land—the way he had done in the Ukraine, walking around entire *goyishe* villages when he didn't like the look of them.

He had already got the idea from the *Ragged Dick* that it wouldn't be so easy here, and his glimpse of the myriad, glowing squares confirmed it. Instead he just walked—past all the waterfront saloons, lit up out front but dark places inside, where he could just make out the shapes of men and women shoving up against the bar, still wearing their hats and coats. Outside men with hard faces stood watching him pass, hands in their pockets, their soft words calling after him down the street.

He stayed clear, walking down the middle of the road. Soon, though, he was pushed to the side by all the traffic: hansom cabs, and automobiles, and wagons, thick as mid-day. He was astonished, for the first time, to see how many people there were and how fast they were moving. Straddling each avenue were high steel girders, pylons holding up the trains that raced madly through the night, sometimes two at a time, in opposite directions, until they made the whole street shake. It was a frantic, crowded, nightmare world that he could not wait to join.

Still, he held back, unsure of himself. Just to get across the street required a mad dash, taken largely on faith, sprinting across the paving stones with as big a group of people as possible—hoping they would discourage or at least absorb the blow from the autos and wagons that kept careening toward them at top speed.

He began to cut up and down different streets almost at random, moving vaguely toward the north and west. He kept away from people still, skittish as a small dog. Once, when he stopped under one of the huge steel girders, a woman's face peered out from the other side, covered with a white veil—scaring him almost as badly as the pig's head in the harbor.

"Lookin' for me?" she snapped, lifting the veil to reveal a rouged, gap-toothed grin, eyes painted into broad, black circles. He wasn't sure what she meant but he kept walking, leaving her to call plaintively after him:

"It ain't much, you know, but you can do me while you're walkin'!"

His legs had begun to ache from the now unfamiliar resistance of the land when he came out on an avenue grander and cleaner than any he had seen so far. A mountain range of houses ran up and down the street: one solid mass of carved gables and spires and stained glass, trellises and wrought-iron balustrades and balconies and ballrooms, rising up to heaven.

He had never seen anything like this before, not even in the great cities on the Continent he had walked through: houses vaulted and large and solid as churches. Each one a formidable chocolate-brown or slate-gray color in the streetlight, forbidding iron fence out front, a fat policeman pacing back and forth every few feet along the immaculate sidewalk.

He could make out nothing inside: thick drapes and curtains were pulled forbiddingly across every window. He had to sprint across the road to get a better look—running like a madman, the way he had learned, head turning in every direction at once. The traffic was more ordered and elegant here, but swifter than ever, the sleek private carriages with matched teams bobbing in and out of the stream like dolphins. He dodged past them, finally put his head down and just flat out ran, until he stood tentatively on the spotless slate sidewalk, staring up at the precipices of the great houses.

A policeman started toward him at once, and he turned and began to walk down the avenue—already cognizant that you had to have a direction, a sense of purpose in this city. He walked with his head down, clutching importantly at the Book and his other meager possessions, sneaking glances at the great houses, as if he were looking for a certain address. He looked up, cautiously, wondering if the cop were still there—and it was then that he saw them: his destiny.

There were three of them: the parents, both plump as pigeons, and the little boy, wandering toward disaster. All of it laid out before him like some perfect Coney Island tableau: *The Negligent Family, or The Poor Boy's Opportunity*—

He never discovered why they were there, out for a Sunday stroll after midnight. He never found out why the coachman hadn't brought them right up to their doorstep, or why they paid so little attention when the boy began to wander, or why the child was with them in the first place. All he knew was that the boy was walking right into traffic, and that this was his chance.

He began to run hard, lest he was too late—who knew what happened to those Ragged Dicks who missed their chances? The couple looked up at him as he flashed by: the man with a long, waxed moustache and carrying a silver-knobbed walking stick, the woman in a fathomless purple cape. Ruddy, plump faces registering surprise, suspicion.

There was no time to explain. He ran past them, watching the whole scene unfold before him. The child was already in the street, paying no attention to the carts and the automobiles hurtling past him. *Could he be deaf—or a little slow, perhaps?* He tried to yell out to him but the words came out all garbled: "Walk—the car—no!"—not even sure what he *could* say that would alert the boy.

It didn't matter—he was pretty sure that a shouted warning didn't merit rising up. The child kept walking on out into traffic, in his Little Lord Fauntleroy get-up, all knee stockings and bows and puffy cap. Joseph bolted right out into the street after him, a cab narrowly swerving past, the horse screaming and bumping his shoulder. He stumbled, and nearly fell, but he kept his eye on the boy.

The child was out in the middle of the street now, trapped between the streams of traffic pouring up- and downtown. It was only a matter of time before they converged on him, ran him down without even knowing, nearly invisible as the child was in his brown, fancy duds.

An open automobile swept past him, horn harooging impatiently, the hot, oily exhaust filling Joseph's mouth and nose. They were coming too fast, and he felt as if he were drowning. The boy was just a couple feet ahead, standing perfectly still now, petrified. He had no idea how he would grab him and drag him back safely but he went for him anyway, scooping up the child in both arms and yelling exultantly in his face:

"Hey, boy! Hey, boy!"

He felt pity for the child when he saw his white, staring face, quivering under his grasp. He tucked him under his arm, turned to find the way back.

There was a terrible, heavy rumbling—a huge brewery wagon bearing down on them, racing its cargo downtown in time for the morning rush. He started forward, then stopped, the horses so close he could smell their sour breath. There was no turning back—a cab whipping its way uptown toward him—and so he closed his eyes and jumped recklessly ahead, aware that he had given himself too little space in front of the brewery wagon.

He made it, somehow. He opened his eys, and there they were, only a few feet from the curb. He pirouetted around a newspaper truck like a matador and fell toward the sidewalk, putting the boy down safe and secure on the pavement like a footballer sneaking his way across the goal line.

They were safe—the boy shaking and crying now. He got to his knees and put his arms around him, shaking himself—the boy's chest throbbing against him like a frightened bird's. This was *real*, he thought. He was an actual hero—a complete stranger, who had come all the way across the ocean in time to rescue the boy by blind chance—

He heard shouting, and people running toward them, and he stood up solemnly, ready to receive his reward and fighting down the glee that raced through him. He smiled faintly, gravely; one arm around the boy's shoulders as the well-dressed, round-faced couple ran shrieking over to them. Pulling himself up, trying to look like a hero should, oblivious to the black harbor muck encrusted on his body.

The woman ignored him, of course, rushing to clutch her son to her bosom. That was as it should be—but to his surprise the father looked distinctly unprepared to discuss a reward, glowering and holding his silver-knobbed stick in the air until he saw the policeman hurrying toward him.

"Officer, this man has my son," he said, in a surprisingly high and mellifluous voice, before Joseph could even quite decipher what the words meant.

"Aye, sir, I saw the whole t'ing," the cop replied in a calming, reassuring voice—surprising Joseph even more when he looped the nightstick from his belt and hit him so hard on the back of his head that he fell face forward on the spotless sidewalk.

He tried to get out what had happened then, to explain the story of Ragged Dick, but his tongue would not form the words. He tried to rise, to push himself up—but the policeman only gazed down at him sympathetically and gave him another tremendous whack on his head.

"Ah, will you stay down now, there's a good fella," he said in the same calm and reassuring voice.

15

GYP THE BLOOD

The trick to poisoning a horse was a good oatmeal cookie.
Gyp had learned it from Monk, and Monk had learned it
from no less than Yoshki Nigger, the King of the Horse
Poisoners, who had learned from long practice and experience that they liked something sweet, something they didn't
get every day, and besides the oatmeal hid the taste of
strychnine.

It was a fine horse he was going to poison now——a proud,
handsome bay, with high white leggings. She all but pranced
up Hester Street, hauling her cart of dresses and fine ladies'
things. She was something lustrous and new on a street full
of the faded and the secondhand. Not yet stoop-shouldered
and big-ribbed from a diet of spoiled lettuce and apples like
all the other peddlers' nags, not yet glazey-eyed and
rheumatic, the way they all became eventually.

Gyp strolled after her, cradling the sack of cookies under
his coat, running his hand unconsciously along the still
throbbing wound just beneath his hat. He didn't know from
horses, but he was just glad it was a new one he was going
to poison: all the better to make his point with the dress peddler. The little *pisher* walked protectively by his horse's
mouth now, keeping one hand on its bridle all the time,
glancing behind himself every few feet. He was a careful

man, Gyp could see—but he would have done better to be afraid.

It wasn't hard to stay out of the peddler's sight. His wagon was piled high with dresses and shirtwaists, skirts and petticoats. All dirt cheap, made by one family or another trying to work independently in their claustral apartments. The peddler had to sweat them, he knew, to undersell the department stores—and it was his living to sweat the peddler.

Gyp stayed back until he saw Sadie step out from the push-carts along the curb. She looked at him, and he nodded, and she walked out in the street to the vendor and pointed at his dresses. The man began to stray from his horse at once, making excited little genuflections, peeling back the layers of lawn in his wagon for her to see.

"Yes, la-dy, how can I interest you? The finest dresses, just like in the store—at half the price! *Less* than half—"

Gyp the Blood stepped casually around the other side of the cart, pulling out the small linen sack of oatmeal cookies. He ran a hand soothingly along the animal's long, chestnut neck—then pushed the bag up into its nose and teeth.

The horse snuffled at the sack of cookies, intrigued. Gyp held it there while he kept his eyes on Sadie and the dress seller. Her face was covered with paint, he saw to his displeasure. She was supposed to look like a Hester Street housewife, not the Bowery streetwalker she was. She was getting less and less confident about her looks—and not without reason, he thought. Soon she would not even be good enough for the Bowery.

Gyp had to admit she was a natural-born actress. As he watched, she widened her eyes coquettishly at the vendor, let her hands linger on the fine lingerie. She had coaxed out the two best dresses the peddler had, and now she shifted

174

from foot to foot like a schoolgirl, and bit her knuckle.

"Maybe I should just take the both," she wondered.

The little peddler was nearly beside himself at the prospect of selling his best lawn, before it got too folded and begrimed in the wagon.

"Look at this *dresske*—a piece of gold! It's a *nebach* if such as you can't have at least a taste of life, missus. I don't know, but they say when she goes to face the Almighty a person must account for all the pleasures she never had—"

"Do you really think they enhance my figure?" she said, holding one of the dresses up against herself.

The peddler ogled her with eyes lascivious for the sale.

"Oh, la-dy. *Your* figure? In these it will be finer than silk and velvet!"

Gyp looked back to see how the bay was doing. The horse was still sniffing at the cookies, thick, elastic lips moving back and forth—but she was not eating. He lost his patience, and tried to thrust the bag right up into its mouth, *forcing* the horse to eat. Instead, it took a step backwards, swaying the cart, and the next thing he heard was a sharp click behind his right ear. He turned slowly around, not altogether surprised to find a cocked derringer inches from his face.

"My horse don' wanna eat today," the dress peddler told him, arm trembling a little to see what he had caught. "An' I told you I don' want no insurance."

"So what're you gonna do? Shoot me here in the street?"

Gyp stayed where he was, keeping the bag shoved up in the bay's face. He was certain the man wouldn't pull the trigger, at least so long as he didn't move. Behind him Sadie stood waiting for his signal. All he had to do was nod and she would cause some distraction. He would have the ridiculous little gun out of the dress seller's hand, and his knife at the man's throat before he knew what hit him.

"Shoot him! Shoot him now!" a voice cried urgently.

"Sol, don't do something so stupid—"

A little circle had opened around them in the packed street, the other pushcart vendors flocking round to see the diversion, kibitzing on the action. Best to just cut the horse, Gyp calculated, with this many witnesses. He fingered the knife handle in the right outside pocket of his vest. A nod to Sadie, then one quick thrust and he could just walk away.

"Shoot him *now*! Before the police come!"

A sleek, white cap was already cruising through the crowd toward their little clearing—one of the new, Reform police hats. Gyp let his grip on the knife relax. Now, he knew, everything would be all right.

"All right, what're ye thieves up to in the temple?"

The short, squat cop pushed his way through to them, and immediately shoved down the peddler's extended arm with its gun. Sadie had already faded back into the sidewalk crowd, but Gyp stayed where he was. He knew the cop, a corrupt old bull named Buckley. Even better, Buckley seemed to know the dress peddler.

"Ain't you the Hebe bastahd who wouldn't gimme a shift for the missus last Christmas?" he demanded, hands on his hips, the thick wattle in his neck quivering back and forth. "Isn't you the same louser?"

"Excuse me, it could not have been me," the dress man said, gesturing nervously toward his wagon. "Take what you want—only the finest goods! For your wife an' daughter—no charge!"

"Sure, an' how does that help me last Christmas?"

There were a few guffaws from the watching vendors. Like them, Gyp knew the cop was making his case as dramatic as possible. More likely the dress peddler had once refused to pay the twenty-five-cent weekly shakedown Buckley imposed.

"Get on wit'chas!" The cop frowned at the watching men and women. "Get back to yer own thievin'!"

Seeing his witnesses leaving, the dress seller gestured wildly toward Gyp.

"*He's* the *momzer*!" he cried. "The yellow-faced murderer—tryink to poison my horse right out on the street!"

Buckley looked fully at Gyp for the first time, and Gyp met his gaze. The cop lowered his eyes deferentially.

"Here! He'p yourself. Like Christmas twice over!"

The dress peddler was loading dresses over the officer's arm.

"Just give me justice——"

Buckley stared stonily back at the dress man——though he made no move to remove the lawn from his arm.

"That's a mighty bold accusation yer makin' against the gentleman."

"*Gentleman,*" the dress seller repeated, looking stunned.

"You want me to run you in for libel, do ya?"

"Libel," the peddler repeated again, his voice now bewildered and sick with anticipation.

"Yer callin' the gentleman here a horse poisoner, when all he's doon is to feed yer poor animal a cookie, am I right?"

The fat cop turned to look at Gyp, and gave him a knowing smirk. Gyp did not deign to respond, and Buckley turned back to his prey.

"That's right," he answered himself. "Just feedin' him a cookie. Do ya see that now?"

The dress seller looked fearfully back and forth between the two of them, still hoping he could salvage something.

"I—yes. Maybe that was."

He looked away, as if he were afraid of what more he might say. But the cop wasn't finished.

"I take it, then, you wit'draw the accusation?"

"Yes."

"So you agree—he was just feedin' the horse a cookie—"
Buckley drew the bag obsequiously out of Gyp's hand.

"Yes."

177

"—like I'm doin' now."

The cop pushed the bag of poison-laced cookies up to the horse's mouth himself, and the dress peddler looked stricken.

"Take anudder dress! Take three! Anythink you like!"

Yet the horse still did not eat from the bag. It snuffled inquisitively at the cookies again—then took another, reluctant step back. Buckley stood holding the sack for a moment, contemplating the animal.

"Or maybe *yer* gonna feed the t'ing yerself."

He thrust the cookies at the dress seller, who stepped back much faster than his horse, waving the bag away.

"That's all right, she's *fed*! She had enough—"

Buckley held the sack up in the man's face now.

"What're you implyin'? There's somethin' the matter with these? What're ya sayin' about the gentleman here?"

"No! No, nothink like that!"

"*Take 'em,* then. Or I run you in right now."

To suffer such a fate, the peddler had to know, would be to forfeit all his stock—and the horse as well. By the time he was released, after a day or two in jail, the fine bay would be nothing more than a few hair rings around children's fingers, and all his dresses would have disappeared into the street.

Slowly—as reluctantly as if he were being forced to eat them himself—the dress seller reached out and took the sack of oatmeal cookies. He hesitated still, looking at the cop and at Gyp, saying half-imploringly, half-defiantly:

"I am a person among people—"

"*Feed it!*" Buckley bellowed at him.

The peddler slowly swung the bag of poisoned cookies back under his own horse's nose, his face suffused with grief and bitterness. This time, the magnificent bay stuck its head right in, crunching contentedly through the cookies.

"There's a good girl—"

Buckley's pudgy, short-fingered cop's hand stroked the doomed horse's chestnut nose.

"Eat up now."

So that's how it was, Gyp realized. The dress seller had taught the bay to eat only from his own hand—a wise precaution on these streets. That was one he was going to have to remember.

"There you go."

The bay finished the last cookie, thick horse tongue avidly licking up the last crumbs from the bottom of the sack. The dress peddler kept it there in front of her, letting the horse have all of its last meal, staring hatefully at the cop.

"It is a crime," he said. "It is a dirty crime."

"What crime?" Buckley asked drolly, walking away with the dresses still on his arm. "You fed the t'ing yerself. Maybe next time you'll do better in observin' the spirit of Christmas."

For a long moment the cookies seemed to have had no effect: the horse stood as tall as ever in the crowded street, licking its lips. Then the big, proud bay dropped suddenly to one knee. The cart listed behind her, the mountain of dresses and ladies' underwear spilling into the street. There was a low exclamation up and down the block, but no one moved. The horse trembled all over for a few more moments, trying to support herself on three legs. Then she dropped to her other front knee, then fell all the way over to the ground.

"*Gottenyu!*" the dress seller cried out in his grief, bending over the dying animal.

The horse's head shivered behind her blinders, but she never made a sound. A burst of black bile spewed suddenly out of her mouth and down the beautiful, brown breast. Then she lay still on her side.

Gyp the Blood stepped gingerly over the dead animal, and stood next to the peddler.

"Next time—remember. You can't *be* careful enough."

179

The dress man looked up at him, tears running down his face. He obviously wanted to say something, but he held back. Gyp smiled down at him, inches from his face, and started to walk away.

"You were a thief already in your mother's belly!" the man called after him, unable to contain himself any longer. He stood in the street, arms shaking with rage, and the endless streams of vendors and shoppers pushed slowly past him, their eyes averted.

"You're a *shande*!" he cried. "A *shande* for the goyim!"

Gyp chuckled, and turned to show him his teeth.

"The goyim!"

He pointed at Buckley the cop, waddling before him down the street with his boodle.

"The goy is my hand servant!"

He walked away, leaving the dress peddler standing by his horse and his piles of finery. Little hands crept in, snatching at the dresses and petticoats that lay in the street. The peddler only watched—unable, now, to summon the wherewithal to stop them.

Gyp strolled back down the *Hazzer Mark,* stopping to buy some *bubkes* from an old lady selling them out of a pot on the sidewalk. She measured them out in a paper sheaf, and he walked contentedly on, popping handfuls of the warm black-eyed peas into his mouth.

Buckley was waiting for him at the end of the block, down at the corner of Mott Street, the fine, gold-and-purple dresses still hanging off his arm.

"How 'bout that, a trained horse? I knew it, I seen that once before—" he prattled on triumphantly, offering the clothes up to Gyp.

"Do me a favor, will ya, an' take these around to the missus? Won't do for me to be seen walkin' around with the spoils, will it?"

He laughed as he said it, but Gyp only stared icily at him.

"So now I'm your valet? *A goy bleibt a goy.* You did what you get paid for, that's all."

Gyp finished his *bubkes,* crumpling up the paper sheaf in a ball and tossing it away, then licking up the grease from his fingers.

"All right, Gyp, if that's yer feelin'," the fat cop said good-naturedly. "Yer a cute one, all right. God help ya if Big Tim ever puts the mark a Cain on yer back."

"Bite the feather bed," Gyp told him absently, gingerly taking off his bowler and attending to his damaged head as best he could with his fingers, making sure the large, ugly, white bandage was still in place.

"Jesus, but that's a piece a work," Buckley said with professional approval. "How'd ja get that?"

"None of your goddamned business!"

"All right, be like that."

Buckley started to walk away, giving him a sarcastic little salute with his thumb and forefinger, but then he stopped.

"Say, there was a *bhoy* by earlier, wanted me to pass on a message to you. Says you oughta get movin' on that matter they talked about."

"Uh-huh."

Gyp smoothed his hair around the bandage, carefully replacing his hat.

"What's it about?" Buckley leaned in, porcine eyes glittering avidly in his pink, puffy face. "He was from uptown, too. You can tell me—"

Gyp shot out his right arm, catching Buckley by the shoulder and spinning him around before he knew what had happened.

"I *said,* it's none of your business. But tell that person for

181

me, I'll take care of his job soon as I settle a little debt of my own. You got that?"

"Sure, Gyp, sure," the cop said, wincing under his grip. "But I dunno, they're serious about this, whatever it is."

"*Tell 'em.* Tell 'em exactly what I said. Soon as I settle this, I'll take care of it."

He fished a few coins out of his pocket and placed them in Buckley's hand, grinning mirthlessly as he watched the cop's face light up.

"'Preciate it."

"'Show a *treyfe* cop a kosher coin and he will shiver with the ague,'" Gyp quoted to the man's face, and let him go. Buckley strolled off cheerfully, the fancy dresses trailing from his arm like so many pennants, shaking his head back at Gyp:

"You think you're quite the boy now, but you better listen, it won't last forever!"

Sadie was waiting for him at the corner, and he walked her back up to her stand under the Bowery elevated.

"You know I hate jobs like that," she told him in a trembling voice, sneaking him reproachful little glances.

"Uh-huh."

"How can you *do* something like that?"

"I dunno—how *can* you do something like that?"

He considered slapping her for her insolence, but he was too disgusted by how she looked to do even that much. Now that he saw her up close he could tell that her makeup was on crooked and her hair wasn't even combed. It lay graying and tangled under her shapeless black hat. She was really letting herself go.

"*Gevalt,* how do you expect to get a fare like that? Use a mirror sometime, why don'cha."

To his surprise, her eyes filled instantly with tears. Somehow, she could still be shocked and hurt by him, he realized—to his further disgust, and a certain arousal. There was something infinitely punishable about her, and it made him want to hurt her worse than he ever had before.

"You said you wanted me down here on time—"

He snapped his fingers in her face.

"Shut it. What're you, a child who can't comb her own hair? You think I wanted you out there lookin' like any *kurveh*? You're workin' for me, you gotta look right. Got it?"

She nodded, and he pushed her aggressively back against the pillar of the elevated train where she stood all day, looking for trade. She bounced off it, and he gave her another sharp push back.

"You got it?"

"Yes, I got it."

"All right."

He stood before her with his hands in his pockets, balancing back and forth on the balls of his feet.

"You make any money last night?"

She nodded submissively.

"How, I don' know. Give it. And yesterday? The day before?"

He made her hand over every cent, and when she had he still poked and prodded at her. He pushed his hands up roughly through the flimsy, red-and-black layers of her dresses, to where he knew she hid her secret purse, and she cried out but she let him do it, let him pull it off her garter. He nosed through it—pleased to find that it was completely empty.

"Here, take care a yourself," he said, magnanimously counting out five dollars of his own money and handing it back to her. He pushed up against her, still running his hands over her, his voice stern and paternal now.

"You all right? Everything all right?"

She nodded, eyes lowered.

"Yes, Lazar."

"You feel sick? Coughin' or nothin'?"

"No, Lazar."

"No rash or nothin'?"

Her face reddened——*How ridiculously modest she still is,
after all these years on the street*

"No."

"Mmm, you still feel so good, I could do you right here."
He rubbed his groin up into her, in the midday darkness
under the el. He nuzzled into her neck, whispering in her
ear.

"My fat little pigeon!"

He stopped abruptly and yanked her chin around with his
hand, her eyes still submissively shut.

"Anyone been *hokking* your *chainik*? Anyone falling in
love?"

"No, Lazar."

"You sure? You sure you don't got a fancy boyfriend,
some *shaygets* uptown?"

"No, Lazar."

"You sure? It's all right if there is, you know, you just
gotta tell me. All I want is f'you to be honest."

"There's nobody."

"Really? 'Cause I heard from McGlory there was, you
know."

"He's lying!"

She looked up at him.

"No—body—is—in—love—with—me," she said firmly,
looking into his eyes.

Nervously, she fingered the red ribbon she wore around
her neck for protection against the evil eye, but he could see
she was telling him the truth. It was not in her to hold anything back from him.

"Sure, why would they be? Lookin' like that, can't even comb your hair—"

He reached out and grabbed one breast, holding it absently in his hand, like a vendor weighing a melon.

"You used to be such choice goods, Sadie Mendelssohn," he said—then smiled at her.

"Here, here. Take another dollar."

She was crying now, but he gave her the dollar and folded her hand up over it.

"It'll be all right. I'll take care of everything. You take that dollar, getcha self somethin' nice. Somethin' to fix yourself up. Okay, now."

He smiled his benediction at her, running his fingers through her hair. She'd had such nice hair once, too; thick and brown and shiny, with a streak of red.

It was the first thing he had noticed when he saw her, the long, brown-red hair framing her face, pale as the moon, when she reached out for him under the Bowery el. Her hand on his coat, gentle and timid:

Give me a penny, mister?

—that ancient solicitation of the old hot corn girls. He'd wanted to laugh, wondering what her next line could possibly be. Then he'd looked closely at that pretty white face. The fine blue veins visible even in the poor light under the tracks. He'd had no trouble deciding to take her in hand.

Now he could barely stand her. Those rooms over McGlory's saloon—the last time she had undressed for him, he could actually see the fleas, jumping off her body. How disgusting she was, how dirty and corrupted, especially compared to his pure Esse—

"There's something else," she said hesitantly.

"See? I thought there was," he covered, feeling the sweet, red rage building up inside him. "I knew there was. *Tell* it."

"Your father sent someone by. He wants to meet with you."

"My father?"

He could not have been more surprised if she had said she really did have a lover.

"I don't have a father!"

"That's all he said," she said quickly. "Your father wants to meet with you. You want to know where?"

"I know where to find him. You piece of earth—when was this? Last night? Last year?"

"Today, just. Before I came over."

"*Loch in kop*, whattaya waitin' to tell me for?"

But he was distracted now, wondering what the old man could possibly want.

"All right. I'll be around maybe tomorrow, maybe the next day."

"Ah, Lazar!"

He smirked at her.

"You don' like it, you can maybe go work in the factories. With my Esse, huh? You'd like that, wouldn't you, little Sarah? No whiskey, no float. Just twelve hours wit' the sewing machine, an' then maybe citizenship classes on your day off? Huh?"

He kept taunting her until she bowed her head, then he pulled her to him and kissed her roughly on the mouth—and after a few, reluctant moments, sure enough, she responded, her body trembling slightly against him, hand shyly clutching his coat the way she had that first time.

Gimme a penny, mister?

He thought of all the other mouths that had kissed her since. All the mouths just since that morning, lips greasy with eggs and beefsteak, bits of it caught in their moustaches—

"You be good," he told her, breaking off the kiss as abruptly as he had started it, and walking away from her—a joke, she knew, and a warning.

186

She watched him go: a small, compact man, in a neat suit and bowler, walking into the shadows under the el. A train rumbled in, and a whole new crowd of men in dark suits and bowlers spilled down the steps, and he was lost among them.

Yet from where she stood, she could see her whole future. He was right about her hair; it was getting gray no matter how many times she combed it. She could dye it but soon, she knew, she would not even be pulling in enough for McGlory's. Then it would be the rough trade down on Cherry Street, then down by the waterside, humping sailors one-legged against a wall.

It would only be a matter of time then before she had a case. She had seen the women down there, offering themselves behind the Water Street bars for the price of a whiskey, or a draught of opium—anything to kill the pain. Women she had worked with under the el not six months before, screaming in agony, their minds already rotted away.

The crowds of men streamed past her, looking for a fresher face. She watched them pass, looking to be sure that he was really gone. He was a clever one; she never underestimated him, but after a long time she was confident that he wasn't coming back, and she took off her limp black hat, and unpinned a small patch on the inside lining.

She counted out the dollars she had concealed from him there. She had actually managed to hold back money from him, to lie to him successfully, and now she weighed the money in her hand, and wondered what she was going to do about this development.

16

GYP THE BLOOD

Gyp walked back over to the Lodz synagogue on Hester Street, where he knew he was most likely to find his father at this hour, attending a funeral or a *mincha*. It was a red-brick, hunchbacked old church, once the home of some forgotten Protestant sect that had long ago moved uptown. Milling around out front was an aggregation of old men, the wealthiest among them in new brown derbies, the rest covering their heads with velvet yarmulkes. They wore leather shoes soft as house slippers, with no laces or buttons, and striped shirts and baggy trousers cinched halfway up their bellies.

The younger men sat slouched on the front steps, defiantly smoking and wearing American suits. Wandering around between them were beggars even more ragged than the old men. Most of these were former rabbis, Gyp knew, who had lost their congregations and their families. They subsisted on apples and cheese, bits of herring or chicken that mourners and pious pushcart peddlers would put on their begging boards. They kept up a pretense of collecting for charity, always sure to make an appearance at any funeral, rattling their little collection boxes and calling out: "*Isodoh tatzel mimovess!* Charity saves from death!"

• • •

Inside the synagogue it was dark and cool, the old church sanctuary lit only by the *Ner Tamid* oil lamp and *yahrzeit* candles. The Torah ark loomed dimly up between the windows of the east wall, signs of the zodiac painted along the upper galleries. It was a close, musty place, filled with the smell of old books and sweat and candle wax, and for a moment it overwhelmed him with memories, as only a smell can—taking him back to his days in the *bes midrash,* when his father had had the old synagogue on Forsythe Street.

There was a steady murmur of prayer. More old men were swaying back and forth up front, in the slanting, crudely painted pine benches: a funeral service, or a memorial for one of their steadily declining number. One by one, they stood, hobbling back through the room, pausing at the aisle for the *shammes* to make the small, ritual cuts in their coat lapels with a straight razor. As they shifted slowly past him, Gyp could see how many times the lapels on their suits had been cut, and stitched up, and cut again.

The last man out had a face like a stone. He walked steadily, without the aid of a cane, a surprising hint of color in his cheeks and a brisk, lively glint of hatred in his eyes. His father.

"So—what make you?" he asked conversationally when he spotted Gyp, as if it had been hours instead of years since the last time he had seen him. As if Gyp did not know that the oldest incisions on his coat had been made for him.

"How goes the life of the *beggerin*?"

"I thought I was dead," Gyp said, and his father looked up at him, supremely cheerful in his hatred.

"So you are. So you are. Mebbe, then, you are my golem. My own monster."

"Did you want something?" Gyp said, gesturing at the others. "Or did you just want me to hang around with the rest of the *lomdim* an' the *loaferin*?"

The old man laughed crudely, and wiped the spittle away from his beard.

"No, no. I have somet'ink in mind for you, my golem," he said, rubbing his hands together thoughtfully. "That's why I brought you to life."

"Cut it out with that golem stuff——" Gyp started to say, but his father was distracted. Some of the other old men hailed him as they talked, lingering in the door of the synagogue, but he did not deign to reply.

"What a feast of corpses!" he hissed merrily to Gyp, unconcerned that they could hear him.

He still considered himself vastly superior to the rest of them, Gyp knew, even though he had been going to the Lodz synagogue every day for over ten years—even though it was practically the only synagogue on the Lower East Side that would tolerate him, since the rift over the Grand Rabbi from Cracow.

Chrystie Street had never seen anything like it, the day the Grand Rebe had arrived. He was carried along in a chair with velvet cushions: a short, round young man with a placid white face, dressed in a frock coat and silk top hat, and held high above the clamoring crowd, so everyone could see him.

All the elders of the synagogues had walked on ahead, carrying torches and the Torah scrolls, their congregations and anyone else who wanted to following behind, holding up banners and blowing on shofars, banging on pots and pans from their kitchens and anything else that would make a great noise. Thousands more had shouted and clapped and gaped from the sidewalks, and even the Irisher cops had craned their necks that day, to get a look at the great man.

Afterwards there had been celebrations throughout the Lower East Side: great feasts of blintzes and knishes, and latkes smothered in sour cream, and whitefish, and sponge cake; and the men and the older boys had drunk their fill of slivovitz and plum brandy.

Even his father had indulged. He had only the small congregation over on Forsythe Street, but he had argued more fiercely than anyone else for bringing the *rov* over from the old country, and as he walked ahead carrying his torch, his son saw for the first time in his life that his face was wreathed in happiness.

Yet right from the start, Gyp had sensed trouble in the pale, stupefied face of the Grand Rebe, lurching along in his chair. Probably it was doomed to begin with, there were far too many little congregations burrowed into abandoned churches and former storefronts and old stables throughout the East Side for their rabbis to surrender power to some medieval potentate from Poland. There had been arguments over everything, and eventually the Grand Rabbi had accepted a better offer: presiding over the sanctity of the large kosher meat businesses. But even then, the old man had argued that they should all bend their necks to him.

"After all, he is from the old country, who is to say he does not know best?" he had argued. "Is not everything else more pure there? Maybe his turning away is a judgment on us—maybe we should offer him more!"

"Why should we submit ourselves to this Grand Butcher? This authenticator of sausages?" the elders had scoffed.

They had driven his father out, in the vituperative struggle that followed, and for a time there had been a small sliver of the congregation that had gone with him, and set up another synagogue in the front of another old grocery store. For there was never any argument in any synagogue that didn't end without at least a few Jews splitting away to form their own congregation.

But eventually these, too, had drifted away from his father. He was too stiff-necked, and he dreamed too much of the old country, and besides he insisted they revere a man who spent all his days seeing to it that the necks of chickens had been properly cut.

"I wan'ch you to do sometink for me, *oytser*," his father continued to mock him in the synagogue now, his eyes positively beaming.

"What?"

"It's your sister, Esse. She's on wit' somethink."

"You mean with her Socialists and *appokoros?*" Gyp snorted. "I tell you what, I don' care if she eats pork at noon, right in the middle of Delancey Street——"

"No, not that, you plague upon my head!"

He leaned in closer, the scent of onion rankling on his breath.

"Somethink else. She got a boyfriend somewheres. Maybe a *shaygets*."

Gyp made himself laugh, despite the cold feeling deep in his stomach.

"A *shaygets*, is it? Well, whaddaya know. Afraid she won't work herself to death so you can lay about gabbin' with the rest of the *gaonim?*"

"Listen, golem! Can't you see I'm black with worry?" he said, grabbing the lapels of Gyp's fine suit. "Do this for me, and mebbe I'll bring you back to life for good. Hmm? Your family restored to you. Eh? *Mein ben yochid*. You could come over for dinner on *Shabbos* and everything. Lazar."

Gyp carefully peeled his father's dirty fingers from his suit, bending them, hurting them a little as he did it, letting him feel his superior strength. Careful not to let the old man see how much the mere mention of his real name had surprised him——just as he must have figured it would.

"I would rather *be* dead than to ever sit down to another meal with you," Gyp told him. "You understand me?"

"Lump of stench—have you no heart? I know you are determined to kill your mother an' me, but don't you have a care for your sister?"

"A care? I hope for your sake she's with the rottenest pimp she can find."

Yet even as he said it he could imagine throwing that possibility in his father's face. And even as he said it, he could feel the possibility clutching coldly around his vitals. It was Esse who had cried for him when he left and still dreamed of shaping him into something—

And before that—that time up in the apartment when both their parents had been out. He had had to tell her then. He had walked right up to her, and put one hand on her hip, and she had not turned her face away

Esse, with some *shaygets*.

"All right, I'll see what she's up to," he told the old man, grinning sardonically despite himself. "But whatever it is, I'll tell you."

"Yes, yes!" the reb said, squeezing his shoulder excitedly. "Promise me!"

"Oh, it's a promise. It's a promise I will hold you to."

BOOK FOUR

*It is that we are never so
defenseless against suffering
as when we love, never so helplessly
unhappy as when we have lost
our loved object or its love.*

—SIGMUND FREUD

17

TRICK THE DWARF

Each of the great parks on Coney——Dreamland, and Luna Park, and Steeplechase——generated their own electricity, enough to light a large town, out in the dark fields of the republic. Dreamland's powerhouse lay just west of the central lagoon, next to the Fall of Pompeii Building. It was shaped like the rolling, white armature of a dynamo, monumental and ornate. An attraction unto itself with its glowing, egg-white enamel engines, and gold-plated tools, and a mosaic table to hold the oil cups. There was a series of grand murals along the walls and ceiling, depicting the whole history of electricity——Edison and his bulbs, Sam Morse and his telegraph, Franklin and his kite, all the way back to God Almighty Himself, touching Adam and jump-starting the world with the same juice we had bottled up for your entertainment pleasure.

The attendants wore spotless white duck jackets with brass buttons, and white gloves——all emphasizing the cleanliness, the purity, the immaculate, magical divinity of electrical power. All except the chief engineer——a small, courteous, bitterly droll little Negro named Elijah Poole, who had worked with the Wizard of Menlo Park, Edison himself. He wore a sort of necromancer's hat——a little fez, covered with hoary gold stars, and suns, and crescent moons——and

Brinckerhoff had put it about that once Poole had actually been white, before an accident with the humming wires had left him charred his present, purple-black color.

That was all the usual nonsense, of course. Before Dreamland, Poole had worked on the Wizard's ceaseless campaign to prove how deadly alternating current was. Together, with the other assistants, he paid local schoolboys to bring in subjects, two bits for each cat or each dog, until the town of West Orange, New Jersey, was nearly devoid of pets. They pushed the animals onto a wired tin sheet and pumped in a thousand volts—the schoolboys jumping up and down outside the windows, to watch their beloved pets get the chair.

After that they went state to state, bidding for the new electric chair contracts against Westinghouse's men. Each one trying to prove how much more dangerous the other one's power was—using the other side's apparatus to elec-trocute a dog, a pig, a cow, for the commissioners and con-cerned clergy, and prison officials. The State of New York announced that it would test the new method on a live, human subject, a murderer named William Kemmler, and Dr. Poole and his team had rushed up to Sing Sing on the flyer, carting along their latest chair and a Westinghouse dynamo in the baggage car.

"We used a low charge—to show just how dangerous it really was," Dr. Poole recalled, in his soft, bitter, wondering voice. "But of course it wasn't—it wasn't dangerous at all. That was the whole problem."

The execution was a bloody mess, even worse than a hanging, Kemmler screaming like a banshee, breaking his wrists and his ankles as he convulsed. The smell of slow-roasting flesh filling the room until all the prison officials were all bent over puking—and then a visible, crackling bolt of electricity burst right out of the man's temple.

The State of New York was altogether satisfied. It ordered

up three chairs, but Poole quit and came down to Coney, where he was another attraction, along with the dynamos and the gilded oil cups. Now, every evening, as the sun began to fade, he pulled the levers and flicked the switches that brought up the new, garish light of a million individual bulbs. Dreamland going up most dramatically of all three parks, ride by ride, attraction by attraction. Until finally he lit the luminous white central tower, and it went on story by story, blazing window by window, right up to its crowning ball and eagle, the highest structure on the island, holding sway over all the rest of Coney.

18

ON THE BOARDWALK

The great green ship lay before them like a sleeping dragon, its wings slowly stirring to life as they filed into its belly.

"All aboard for the trip to the moon! The great Luna excursion! Journey to the unknown! All aboard!"

The eerie, disembodied voice repeated itself exactly, over and over again.

"It's recorded," Kid whispered to her.

Inside, they were strapped down into seats as if they were on a roller coaster, the shop girls and shipping clerks tittering at the pretense. But soon they could actually feel the power of the engines increasing, the ship tilting as if it were indeed lifting right off the ground.

"Ladies and gentlemen, this is your captain!"

On the bridge were men in sporty blue uniforms and elaborate gold braid, and an admiral with a white beard.

"Soon we will be skimming the cream from the Milky Way!"

"Do you feel us soaring, moon?" Kid teased her, sneaking a hand around Esther's waist until she giggled.

But not even he could find anything to joke about as the rush of the wings began to accelerate madly, the airship rocking and swaying as if it would burst apart. The blackness outside the portholes swept past them, and there was a clap of thunder—so sudden and terrible that she shrieked out loud, along with half the other women on the ship; the men shouting in surprise.

Another clap of thunder, then another, and soon long cracks of lightning were piercing the sky outside, some so close they lit up the ship. Rain pounded on the great green canvas wings, and they began to roll furiously, the storm getting louder and closer, all the more terrifying for its recorded sights and sounds—the projected lightning, the staticky bursts of thunder from some strange God.

"Ladies and gentlemen, we are just passing through a storm!" the captain's voice boomed out. "We are quite safe!"

The thunder began to roll away, the lightning faded. Soon, a tranquil black sky flowed past the portholes—now filled with stars, more stars than Esse had ever seen before from the street stoops, or the roof of their tenement. The levered green shade around the ship's bridge peeled back to reveal a pink, glowing orb in the distance.

"Behold, ladies and gentlemen: the moon! At morning light!"—though it looked more like the color of stomach medicine to Esther.

Still, as they approached the moon grew impressively. Its pink gauze slowly receded, the planet becoming steadily whiter, then a sort of wavy green, expanding until it filled up the whole view from the bridge, and every porthole on the ship.

"Come on! Come out and see the moon!" the captain cried merrily, waving his arm—and as if in a daze they began to stumble forward, out onto the bow of the ship, where a spotlight swept over the strange ground before them.

"Go ahead! Go on out and take a stroll! We won't go without you!" the captain winked—and one by one they climbed over the rail and staggered about the barren, pockmarked surface of the moon.

They went only a few feet, and stopped—though they all knew that if they walked much farther they would reach the wall of the aerodome. The moon was obviously made out of plaster of paris, the green paint chipped in places, the lunar surface hollow under their footsteps but no less alien for all that—the spotlight swinging slowly back and forth over the desolate, cratered landscape.

Just then a horde of little moon men and moon women began to swarm up from the craters, and from behind the enormous square boulders. They wore green tights and smocks, with more green paint smeared roughly over their faces and hands, and they converged on the flabbergasted passengers, shrieking and pressing chunks of moldy green cheese into their palms. Then they joined hands, swaying back and forth, and in that strange, alien, celestial atmosphere, began to sing in unbearably high and shrill voices:

If the man in the moon were a
  coon, coon, coon
What would you do?
He would fade with his shade
The silver moon, moon, moon
Away from you
No roaming around the park at night
No spooning in the bright moonlight
If the man in the moon were a
  coon, coon, coon—

19

ESTHER

She sat out on the stoop, watching the neighborhood change into evening and reading the Gallery of Disappearing Men in the *Jewish Daily Forward*.

HAVE YOU SEEN THESE MEN? ran the headline, like the post office wanted posters. Underneath were their pictures, and a short history of each man who had absconded with his family's happiness:

". . . Solomon Feuerstein, late a tailor. More recently a day laborer of 17 Hester Street. Husband and father to three daughters. Last seen the night of Sunday, May the fifth, in the company of his *landsman's* club . . .

". . . Morris Berlant, a dress cutter, of 33 Eldridge Street. Widower, and sole support of seven children. Last seen at the Grand Central train station, May the fourteenth, in the company of a certain female person in a red velvet dress . . ."

—each indictment ending in the stern imprecation, "If you have any information regarding these irresponsible individuals, it is your duty to contact the editors of the *Forward*."

These were the men who had got away. The husbands and fathers who had finally given up, and taken off one day for parts unknown: Philadelphia or Chicago, St. Louis or Cleveland—all those distant, exotic destinations. Even back to the old, damned country. They were the objects of Abe Cahan's avenging fury, no less unremitting than that of God Himself, as the *Forward*'s editor tried to shame his people into models of citizenship, socialism, Judaism.

He shall be like a tree planted beside the streams of water, read the psalm quoted just under the damning headline— though Esther suspected that the whole column might be self-defeating. The little pictures of each man were almost invariably taken at a wedding, a bar mitzvah—some joyous occasion when there was a photographer around. They grinned into the camera, decked out in their best clothes, looking delighted to have made their escape.

She put the paper down on her knee and gazed dully out on the street. It was another humid evening, the air already so heavy that the ubiquitous white paper badges of mourning barely fluttered from each tenement doorway. Despite the heat, boys ran about in the gutter, screaming, "Shame, shame! Everybody knows your name!" Some of them playing base-ball, their heads shaved for the summer against lice, waving a broom stick at socks rolled up in a tight ball and yelling *"Aus! Aus!"* A Russian girl sat on the steps below her, reading the *Blue Fairy Tale Book* to her sister, both of them wearing penny bows in their hair, staring intently into the large picture pages.

It turned seven and all around her, up and down the block, Esther could hear the small whoosh of pilot lights being lit. She could hear the murmur of a hundred conver-sations—in Yiddish, but also in Russian, Polish, German, Armenian; even the soft, steady thread of Chinese, like the whir of her sewing machine. A bit of *Aïda,* the favorite opera of the ghetto, playing on a wobbly phonograph. The scissor grinders pushing their big wheels down the street, ringing bells and crying for the housewives to bring their knives down before they cut the chickens' bellies.

The children ran off, the street filling up now with men and women walking home from work, coming in waves from the el on Allen Street. They walked slowly in the humid, heavy air. Even Muller, the goat that was the mascot of the German saloon under the stairs, lay on the sidewalk—forgoing, for once, his eternal quest to butt down the lamppost to which he was chained.

Esther looked up and down the murmuring old street: the little girls reading, the goat with its gold-painted horns, the little white paper badges—and wished it would all go away.

She could imagine: a big, wide avenue, with no elevated out back on Allen Street to billow soot in through the windows. The sidewalks scrubbed clean, and clear of peddlers; children and their parents walking out each day, well-rested, to eight hours of school, and meaningful work. The words stuck with her from one of the inspirational lectures at the settlement house:

The world must be made gracious for the poor.

She stood up, and stretched her hands high over her head, ignoring the men trotting down to the German saloon as they whistled and called to her. She cracked first her knuckles, then her back, and then her entire neck, making a sound like a pistol shot. The men blanched, and hurried on down to their beer, and she laughed.

It was her way of breaking out of the box into which she was forced during the day. Working the machine was better than felling coats, but her back still throbbed from leaning over the needle, and her knees ached from pushing the pedals, and her hands were stiff from feeding the monotonous yards of cloth into the machine all day long.

She told herself she was returning now to the person she had been before work: well, and whole, and untired. There was a world of possibilities open to her. She could go to the opera house, where for twenty-five cents she could climb to the upper gallery, and see Caruso or Pavlova or Kreisler.

She could go out to a philosophy lecture or one of the dancing academies or the Yiddish theatres along the Bowery, where the audience threw cabbages at the stage, and stomped their feet and shouted "Shame, shame!" if an actor lit up a cigar on the Sabbath.

Best of all, she could go to the Automatic Vaudeville, in Union Square. There she could drop her penny into one of the gilded nickelodeons in the long, marble-floored parlor, and see—*anything*, from all over the world: a love story or a pogrom. Colonel Dreyfus on Devil's Island or Teddy Roosevelt on safari in Africa or the Czar and his court—the long files of generals and priests swaying majestically along, scattering clouds of incense, carrying their magnificent, plumed hats under their arms—

The movie she loved most of all, though, was set much closer to home. It was simply a moving picture made from the back of a truck, driving through the streets of lower Manhattan.

She never had any trouble getting that machine. It had been around for months now, and most people were bored by it, but she could never get enough. It was all there: the pushcarts and the stores, and the cops and the peddlers and the housewives, all moving in sped-up, jerky movements across the street. The trolleys and automobiles whizzing past them all like meteors. The same streets she walked every day, down past the Flatiron Building, and over to Union Square, through the crowds on Delancey, and Hester Street, and back over to Chinatown, and Little Italy. The grinning boys, chasing after the truck, and the daughters of the *maskilim*, trying to stride with utmost dignity under their parasols, and the peddlers squinting up suspiciously from their vegetable carts. Her whole world, swarming by in front of her like one gigantic play, so fast she could barely keep up with it—

●   ●   ●

206

Esther stretched again on the stoop—and caught sight of her own hands. They were so large now, the knuckles huge, and swollen and calloused. *Mr. Singer's fiancée*, they liked to call it. How they grew with each year, how her skin yellowed from the shop—

She shall be brought before the king in raiment of needlework

She stared out into the crowds still pouring off the trains, wanting to look anywhere, to see anything but her own hands. It was then, amidst the blank, strange faces of the crowd, that she saw her brother.

He stood out from the rest of the crowd, as always, dressed in a snappy cutaway the color of the sky, a bowler, and a silky white four-in-hand fastened at his neck by a diamond stickpin. Where the rest of them shuffled along, he seemed to move on the balls of his feet, barely touching the ground—the way only a man who didn't work for a living could walk at the end of the day.

When he saw Esse there he couldn't help but walk up to her. He had thought to just nose around, see what he could, but there she was: standing on the stoop in some old *shmatte* of a dress. Looking tired and gaunt, and just as beautiful and immaculate as ever. He bared his teeth, and went up to her.

"The big *macher*," she said, not unaffectionately, and he could tell she could barely contain her excitement at seeing him again.

"Hello, Esse," he saluted her from the bottom of the stairs, the two Russian girls with their fairy tale book sidling away from them.

"What make you?" he asked formally—but she only continued to taunt him:

"What is it they call you now? Billy the Kid? Or something with blood?"

"Ya, ya," he said, waving her words away. "So how are they?"

How beautiful she still was How good

"Better than you, *chachem*," she said, noticing the bandage on the back of his head, and coming down the stairs toward him. She reached out a hand toward it, but he swatted it away.

"Just some business."

"*Nu,* how is pimping these days?"

"You shouldn't use words like that," he told her, really annoyed now. He hated to hear such things come out of *her* mouth, to have to think of Sadie in the same breath—

"A pimp is a pimp."

"And a whore is a whore, all right? I never made anybody walk the streets."

"No—and I suppose they made *you* a pimp. And the peddlers made you a horse poisoner, and the cards made you a gambler."

"What about you? Working yourself to death. Letting them eat the head off your bones. Is that better?" he burst out—not wanting to, knowing he had let her get to him, but unable to contain himself any longer. "Look at you! You couldn't take the place of my oldest girl, the way you look now!"

It was not true. She was still beautiful—still as immaculate as the first day he had really seen her, and he had put his hand on her hip, and she had not turned away

"Stop it!"

He expected her to slap him, and he was ready for it—the hard, flat feel of her hand on his cheek—but all she did was hold out a hand, appealing to him, until his face burned not with the slap but with shame.

"How can you talk to me like that?" she asked, her voice horribly understanding and calm.

She was still so exasperating so righteous. But he had gone up to her and she did not turn away

"I am your sister. You have blood, you know."

"Yes," he said, dropping his eyes. Hating her for such restraint.

She ran her hand through his deep shock of black hair, feeling carefully around his wound.

"Ah, *bulvon*——what are we ever going to do with you? When will you remember you are a person?"

She had not turned away from him, and when he had dropped his trembling hand in shame all she had said was Don't feel bad It's nothing bad Don't feel bad——when in fact he knew it was evil

She was the only one he regretted.

It was back when they were still living on Forsythe Street, where the whores used to sit right out on the sidewalk, naked under their flimsy wraps. Papa raved at them when he passed, but they just laughed, and spat at his shoes, bulbuous white thighs spreading out over the pavement. They whistled at Lazar when *he* walked by, lifting up their skirts, calling to him:

Boychik, come have one on the house! Oy, that face! Softer than my tochis!

They tangled up his feet in their legs, grabbed at his crotch. He was such a sweet-faced boy then, they took him for a blushing *yeshiva bocher,* though he knew the poison was already working within him.

He walked about carefully in those days, aware of the invisible boundaries all around him. There were Poles and Ukrainians just to the east, and Italians a few blocks to the south of them, and if he wanted to venture over to the West Side docks he had to look out for the Hudson Dusters, and the Five Pointers, and the other Irish gangs.

The Irishers were just thugs, big, musclebound bruisers he could evade easily enough. The Italians he found more intriguing. They set up blazing shrines of candles at the end of their narrow alleys, and paraded with bands, and statues of saints pinned with pink roses and dollar bills. If they caught you, though, they would take your money, force you to your knees to recite the Lord's Prayer, the Hail Mary—

"*Say* it, yid! We *know* you can say it!"

—all the strange, terrifying *goyishe* rituals. Spit on a crust of bread from the gutter and press it into your mouth, laughing: *This is my body. Take, eat*—

"Now you're a convert!"

He broke away, raced back home, spitting out the awful bread, their harsh laughter chasing him down the street. Gentile bread, he came to think of it, something they would really eat. Monk had been right:

Never get on your knees to a Christian

Better to let them kick and stomp you insensible. He knew what he would do the next time.

Not that he ever had much time to leave the street, the immediate neighborhood. There was his job sweeping out the pharmacy on Great Jones Street after school. Waiting to get into the public library at Seward Park, where the lines of *yiddishe* children stretched around the block. More hours reading over the Talmud with his father, listening to all the endless, arcane arguments of the older men. Droning through his lessons in the dark, smothering *bes midrash* behind the synagogue, amidst the sweet, decrepit smells of old books and candle wax, the damp and musty odor of his fellow students, sweating in their heavy coats and pants—

It bored him nearly to death. He was restless, and nervous, looking for something—anything—else. He knew he was supposed to like it, to prepare for the life of a great scholar like his father, but he thought that if he stayed in this life he would blow apart from sheer frustration.

That was when he had noticed her. Esse was always

around, of course—his younger sister, working hour after hour with his mother around the kitchen table. Doing whatever they did with a needle and thread until it was time to clear it off for the scholars' supper. They were far enough apart in age to be casual allies in the household, joking behind their backs about the old people and their *haimishe* ways, keeping each other's little secrets. But he never really noticed her until one day—just one day for no real reason at all, when he saw how good she really was.

After that he was mesmerized. He followed her with his eyes everywhere she went around the tiny apartment— helping their mother with supper, putting the bedding away, hauling the washing up to the roof. He couldn't keep his eyes off her, he couldn't help from bumping into her—how could he not?—in the little space they inhabited: brushing against her, smelling her neck, her hair, watching the curve of her dress as it hung down her girlish legs. He couldn't help noticing her, he was suffocating in the little home with her. It was wrong, he knew, but then he was evil, and the fact that it excited him only proved how bad he was.

And then, one day, their *mamaleh* had been so sick the old reb had actually been prevailed upon to take her to a doctor. Usually, when she was ill, he preferred to let her lie in bed and give her wide berth, the way he did when it was her monthlies, but this time she was too sick to be ignored, actually vomiting up green bile, and he was persuaded to at least take her to, if not a real-life doctor, at least a *baba* over on Ludlow Street.

They had been left alone in the apartment, and he had gone up to her. She was supposed to keep sewing the frilly little women's things she was always doing with her mother, she was supposed to keep sewing but she got bored and left her post at the table to go and hop up and down the living room, turn spins and cartwheels in the shafts of sunlight. Singing to herself—absorbed in what she was doing like a little girl.

He had gone up to her then. He had gone up to her and put his hand on her hip—just one hand, light as a feather, trembling on the jut of her right hip. Just a *touch*, for she was the most beautiful, the most pure thing he had ever seen, and he was afraid to go any further.

She had turned to him. She had turned to face him, out of her game now, and she had not looked away. Her face filled with damnable compassion for him. She did not turn away but looked right at him, and he was certain he could have done anything he wanted then—that she knew just what he was about but he still could have done anything, anything at all, and she would have followed.

He turned away. Instead he turned away, full of loathing for himself, and that was when she had said it:

Don't feel bad It's nothing bad Don't feel bad

—but he knew she was lying.

It was that very *Shabbos* he had left home. Not that he had meant to; it was just something, like a bad dream, that had spun out of control.

Every Friday evening his mother gave him the family *cholent* to take over to the *goyishe* baker on Delancey Street—the *Shabbos* dinner, beef and beans and barley, in a stew she made so rich and thick they would have no power to do anything for the rest of the Sabbath anyway but lie around the room in a torpor.

It took her three days to make it. She would put the dish together on Wednesday, cook it lightly, then leave it to sit in the kitchen, wending its aroma throughout their home until the Sabbath eve. Then he would lug the heavy, black pot over, along with dozens of other boys his age—a scattered parade of first sons, in caps and short pants. Mothers would smile to see them, and old men would dance on the street corners, giddy with the holiday atmosphere:

212

"The *Shabbos*! The *Shabbos* bride comes!"

His mother gave him a nickel for the baker, a harried, beetle-browed man, to let the *cholent* simmer in his oven for the next twelve hours along with every other Sabbath supper in the neighborhood. The next day, after synagogue, he would retrieve it. This was a much harder haul, rushing the steaming black pot back home before it went cold, but he was always proud to do it—his stomach gurgling just at the smell of it, the faces of his family—even his father's—radiant with joy when he carried it in.

But that particular Friday on his way to the baker, he saw the dice players. They had always been there, insolently rolling their dice right out in the open, against the brick wall of Pinsky's Market on Attorney Street—but this Sabbath he looked at them with new eyes: a group of sharp-looking young men sitting in their center, coats turned up to their chins, kneeling around a sidewalk littered with money: pennies, nickels, even dimes and quarters.

"Come, baby, come. Be nice to papa."

As he watched, more young men and boys shoved past him, and knelt down to try their luck, pushing out a penny or two. The dice rolled, and a quick, hatchet-faced young man stepped nimbly around the bettors and the shooter, flicking up the money before it could be retrieved, shoving an occasional coin to a winner like a man pushing a bad apple back into a fruit cart.

It was those coins that Lazar found himself the most fascinated with—money for nothing but the risk. He stepped forward, barely aware of the heavy pot still balanced on his arm, and with no further thought flipped down the nickel he had been given for the *goyishe* baker. The hatchet-faced young man's eyes flickered briefly over it—then he scooped up the dice and passed them along to a smaller, angelic looking boy, no more than a child, who had thoughtfully pressed a penny down on the sidewalk.

*"Them dice know who's fadin' ya an' they'll never, never
come to ya——"*

The small boy hurled them artlessly off the wall. They
flopped back down on the cement: a single white dot showing on each black face. Before Lazar could give it so much
as a last look, the nimble young man had grabbed up his
nickel, the shooter's penny, and every other coin along the
pavement.

"Yiddishe mazel," he muttered in formal condolence——
then grabbed the dice back from the child, who looked positively agonized.

New players shoved in, pushing Lazar back from the
game——not that he had anything more to play with, anyway.
He stood for a long time on the curb, the pot of stew in his
hands, trying to think of what to do next. The nickel was
gone, and he had no more money and no way to get any, and
the baker, he knew, was not about to give credit to some little *yiddishe pisher.*

He wandered back along the darkening streets with the
cholent, still teased by the ignorant, smiling passersby: *Better
move your tochis, kinderle.*

He walked very slowly, thinking that something had to
intervene. A nickel found in the street, an uncommonly generous stranger——he kept his eyes on the gutter the whole
way home, looking for lost money. Maybe he could even
save somebody from a runaway horse, like all those ridiculous stories about match boys and newsies on the rise he had
once thumbed through at the Seward Park branch——

There was nothing. No runaway horse, no money lining
the streets. He turned into Forsythe Street, the sidewalk barren of whores now in the late fall weather. Esse was just
coming down the steps of their tenement and she stared at
him, so concerned, so instantly aware that something was

wrong, the way she always knew. He almost choked to see her, but he carried the *cholent* pot on past, unable to say anything. He walked on up the three flights to their rooms, where he put the pot down on the kitchen table, under the stunned gaze of his mother.

"What's this?"

She looked toward the window, where she could see nothing of the day.

"You will be late! *Shabbos*——"

He sat in his father's chair at the table, staring at his hands.

"I can't. I lost the five cents."

"What was it? The *goyim*?"

She knelt before him and stared into his face, her eyes so frantic that he could not even tell her the story he had planned.

Better she should see his true nature

"No. *I* lost the nickel. I lost it gambling on the street."

Better that they knew

She let him alone then. She let him sit silently at the table, looking at the floor until his father came home, and she had to repeat what he had told her in her tremulous, teary voice. Somehow, some part of him enjoyed listening to her tell it, right there in the same room, her voice full of awe at the terrible thing he had done.

"Thickneck! Piece of wretch!"

His father had raged predictably at him, struck his face, torn his own shirt dramatically.

"You wild beast! I do declare you sin!"

It was the worst of all their terrible times in the little apartment on Forsythe Street. It was the same month that the battle over the Grand Rabbi from Cracow had come to a head, and his father's congregation had kicked him out.

"The worst thing that ever happened to us was making it to America!" the old man lamented, banging his fist over and over again on the table, stalking back and forth like a madman, raving until they could no longer understand him and beating at Lazar with his belt.

That Friday night it had been as if they were sitting *shivas*. They had nothing to eat for Saturday now. It was against God's law for his mother to cook the *cholent* herself, of course, and it had been too late to round up some *Shabbos goy* and send him off to the baker in Lazar's place. When they got back from synagogue there was only the cold, half-cooked pot of stew, congealing in the kitchen. Yet his father had sat down at table anyway.

"It is time to eat, let us eat," he said.

His mother and Esse looked at each other, obviously wondering if the reb were in his right mind by then. He had been all but shunned that day at their synagogue. Some of his oldest friends—men he had known from back in Lodz—had refused to speak with him anymore, sick of his hectoring over the Grand Rebe and their new country. But he insisted they all sit down for dinner.

"This is what we have been given through this *boy*. It is what the Uppermost means for me to have."

His wife pleaded with him with her eyes but he ignored her, gazing fixedly out across the table as if they were about to receive their usual feast. She lifted the cover of the *cholent* pot—and stopped when she saw it sitting there, coagulating in its own grease.

"I will not serve food like this to my family," she said—but he jumped up almost gaily, and grabbed the ladle from her hand.

"All right, if you won't, I will," he told her. "The son does not obey, and the mother does not serve. If nobody in this family will take their rightful place, I will do all of it."

He spooned out a heaping portion of the mess onto his own plate first, as usual; waxy orange lumps of fat oozing over onto the table.

"Who wants next?"

216

No one said anything. The reb snatched up first his wife's plate, then Esse's, clopping down more cold, congealed lumps of the stew on each.

"There! There! And now for the little *momzer*."

Lazar thrust his own plate out at his father, holding it as steadily as he could. The old man's eyes widened, delirious with anger now.

"Oh, hungry for the fruit of your labors, my little plague? Well, then, you will have all that you can eat!"

He slopped a huge ladleful onto Lazar's plate, much bigger than the ones on Esse's or his mother's—then another, and another. Still, Lazar kept his plate extended, until his father finally let the *kochleffel* fall back into the pot.

"Go on! Eat up!" the old man cried.

Lazar began to eat—leisurely at first, knowing they were all watching him and despising most of all the pity from his mother and his sister. Soon he began to eat faster—stuffing the soggy chunks of beef, the hard, uncooked little pellets of barley and beans down his throat. It was all putrid, the thorough corruption of his mother's dish. Yet he kept eating, gagging on the spongy mush once but still forcing it down, one heaping forkful after another.

"Go on! Eat, eat!" his father cried, incensed. "Look at him, this great lump of hog! He can't get enough of his handiwork!"

Lazar stared at his father, mouth forced into a smirk around the cold and greasy meat. The reb pointed to the open window, through which they could hear the usual depravities of the *goyishe* Saturday night down on the street—the whores laughing, the men singing and jeering drunkenly.

"He should be down *there*, with the rest of the swill! *That* is what he is good for!"

Lazar finished his last bite, leaving only the orange grease stain on his plate, then got up and walked stiffly over to where his hat and coat hung from a peg on the wall.

"Lazar!" his mother shrieked, while Esse watched silently from the table.

"Where are you going, now you can't stand your shame?" his father bellowed, jumping to his feet.

"Tell me, please," Lazar said, looking straight at him again. "What are we mourning—me, or the *cholent*?"

"Listen to him! Go to the devil with your gangster friends! Leavink the house on a Sabbath. You are *dead* to me, do you hear that? I no longer have a son!"

Lazar put on his hat, managing despite his trembling fingers to flip it up and on his head in one, impudent motion—something he had practiced with the other boys at school. He struggled to keep his voice level, his face expressionless.

"I would rather *be* dead than to stay in this house."

He turned and walked casually out the door then—even as he wondered where he would go, how he would eat. His mother held out her arms to him; her calls followed him out into the hallway—*Lazar! Lazar!*—so plaintive and heart-broken that had she come after him he thought he might have walked right back in, and knelt at his father's knee, and asked his forgiveness. And even then, he knew that he *would* have been forgiven. His father would have relished it like some scene from Torah, the errant son returning.

But his mother did not come out, obedient as always to his father's will. He kept walking, down the winding flights of stairs. Only Esse had come after him. He heard the door open again, his father's mad taunts echoing out into the hall:

"Let him go, let them *all* go! *Gornisht mit gornisht!*"

Esse called after him, watching him descend the stairwell, a dark figure dropping down a dark hall.

"But Lazar, where will you go?"

He waved a hand back over his head, not trusting himself to look at her. It was better that way, better that she had stayed—though he had often thought differently since.

"Something. Anything."

But he knew now: he was no good.

Esse ran down the stairs after him, but he was already gone. She turned and walked slowly back up, staring at her father now leaning over the banister on their floor.

"Gottenyu," he sighed most piteously for himself. "America has made a mountain of ashes out of me."

He spent that night in an alley that reeked of cat piss and rotting vegetables, and the next morning he walked back over to the dice game on Attorney Street. This time he waited, and watched, until all became clear to him.

There was always the banker: the hatchet-faced young man who ran the games, and handed out the dice, and stepped nimbly about picking up the money. There were at least two other shills, hovering around the edge of the crowd. And then there was the child: the baby-faced boy who had rolled his losing snake eyes and seemed so disconsolate.

Whenever they needed more marks, he saw, the angelic little boy would be called upon to come forward and toss the dice, like he was any other rube off the street. He might even win two, three times in a row—the banker glaring elaborately at him—until enough new players had decided the game was worth a try. Then the hatchet-faced boy would slip him a pair of new dice from an inner vest pocket—a pair that came up snake eyes every time.

When he had learned what he needed to learn, Lazar spent the rest of the morning hunting for the lucky nickel that had evaded him on his long walk home with the *cholent*. It was still not easy to find, five cents did not linger long on the street. He had nothing but time now, though, and he searched the gutters head down until he had managed to collect five pennies that had somehow slipped through the fingers of the yentas and the *goniff* peddlers.

He went back to the game then, and waited until the baby-faced shill came forward again. When the dice were in his hands, Lazar stepped in and plunked his pennies down on the pavement. The boy made his point—and Lazar scooped up his money as quickly as he had put it down, not hazarding another toss.

The hatchet-faced banker glared at him but he had no choice: he either had to pay off or alert the marks. One of the shills started toward him as he backed off through the crowd—a tall, broad-shouldered boy—but Lazar was not about to be stopped by anything now and he stared the *shtarkeh* down until he moved sullenly back toward the game.

That day was the start of his fortune. He moved up and down Attorney Street, then Delancey, and all over the Lower East Side, repeating his play. He never milked it, never made anyone mad enough to try to cut him—just moved in when he had figured out the score and made his nickel or dime, then moved on.

By the end of his first day on his own he had two dollars, and by the next day he had ten more, and after that the possibilities were endless. He never went back to his father's house, not even the day he saw his own picture in the Gallery of Disappearing Men, and wept alone in his hotel room.

And she was still with them, after all this time. She stood before him now, a princess in the street

"Esse, why are you still here?" he asked—forgetting his mission, forgetting even his father's promise. "Why don'ch you come away?"

—and he knew even then he would have gone with her anywhere she asked, he would have lived with her anyway she wanted.

"You have to stay together," she told him, though he thought he could detect the doubt in her voice.

"Leave them to their own misery. I got enough for us both."

"It's blood money."

He would make her see

"All money is blood money," he scoffed. "Come with me."

She looked at him, her face so horribly compassionate again.

"And do what? A man without anything—without family, or friends, or anything to believe in—what can he be but a beast?"

"You sound like papa," he said bitterly. "They're the beasts. Get out now, before they devour you."

"And be kept by you? Like your other ladies?"

"You think they won't? You think they won't eat you up 'til there's nothing left?"

"Lazar—"

She held out her arms to him, in that same gesture—the same insufferable, helpless pity. He went down the stoop, away from her, and began walking back up Orchard Street. The wound along his scalp throbbing, and hating her, hating himself, most of all hating the old man—

He would make her see Even though she would never forgive him for it

"Okay. You think so? You just wait an' see."

He waved to her as he walked away, his open hand folding into a fist as he went.

"I'll prove it to you. Just wait an' see I don't."

20

BIG TIM

"'Girls in Their Nightgowns'! 'French High Kickers'! 'The Soubrettes' Picnic'!"

The Little Little Napoleon stared down uncomprehendingly at the piece of paper before him.

"A flirt," Sullivan said helpfully. "A coquette."

"I know what a soubrette is!" thundered the mayor. "It's filth, is what it is! Undermining the moral character of our city!"

Big Tim settled back into the sofa between Photo Dave and Sarsaparilla Reilly. It was beginning to look like another one of those days when the mayor pretended he had never heard of politics.

"Look at these!" McClellan commanded, holding up a sheaf of photographs—and to Big Tim's amusement both Sarsaparilla and Photo Dave craned their heads forward, hoping to catch a glimpse of some naughty soubrettes in action. To their infinite disappointment the photos were only the front of moving picture parlors, and the Automatic Vaudeville nickelodeon on Fourteenth Street.

"Do you see? Do you *see?*"

"Yes, I see," Big Tim said calmly.

"Next to everyone of these establishments is a *saloon.* Most of them with a *common entrance,* no less!"

"Sure dogs will have fleas, yer honor."

And men would not know how to get a drink, or find a whore, unless they dropped in a nickel to watch the tiny, flickering image of a girl in her nightgown and bare feet.

"We must crush them, then. *We must give this dog a proper bath, sir!*"

Big Tim sighed. The man had an unnatural obsession with the moving pictures. Big Tim had his own reservations about the movies and the nickelodeons but it hadn't stopped him from investing in a whole chain of them with Fox and Loew. They were inevitable, the movies, and he never believed in trying to stop anything that was inevitable. Man was born to trouble, and it was not the part of politics to keep the sparks from flying upward.

He had to admit that the movies were the best way to lie yet invented. Newspapers lied, but nobody took them very seriously. Photographs lied much better. His own mother, to the day she died, had kept at her bedside some spiritualist photo of his father's shade, hovering protectively above her.

Yet even photographs lacked the vital element of animation. The movies were *real*—as real as life. What couldn't you sell people with such a device? Out in the Sunken Gardens at Feltman's, he had watched the audiences flinch when a gun was fired, or a train came hurtling at them on the screen. No wonder Hearst was already reaching for this new marvel—you could create any reality you wanted with it.

"Do you hear me? We must close these vice pits, once and for all!" the Little Little Napoleon was still expounding, dark eyes flashing fiercely.

Leave it to Tammany to choose the scion of a well-known bust for mayor

Well, the Democracy was a forgiving institution. Its heroes included all the spectacular failures: Stuart and Emmet, Tone and Parnell, Kossuth and Mazzini. Only the most tragic exiles, and the greatest uncrowned kings, and the men who said the most beautiful things from the gallows.

McClellan, at least, was even more handsome than his dashing father, and just as formidable in appearance: square-jawed, clean-shaven face; cold, aristocratic eyes. He *looked* like the very model of a mayor, which was all that Tammany required and not a drop more.

There was no controlling him sometimes—like the day they opened the new subway system. The mayor was only supposed to start up the first train, but he had insisted on keeping the helm and driving it all the way to Grand Central himself. The train bucking and jerking wildly, pitching the notables about in their cars until all the politicians, and the society ladies, and the ambassadors and the generals and the great money men were puking in the aisles.

"The nickelodeons were bad enough, but *parlors*? Young people of both sexes, sitting together in the dark? Where will it end?"

Sullivan felt suddenly weary.

"Do you want us to give up the boodle from the movies then? Not to mention the saloons. Shall we give it all up? Hand it over to Mr. Hearst, along with a whole new subject to git up on his high horse about? Or wasn't the last race close enough for you?"

He meant to hit home with that. McClellan had only just beaten the newspaper prince last time out, and that was with the boys tossing entire ballot boxes into the East River. Yet now the mayor put on his finest airs, literally turning his face away from Big Tim.

"I should like to think that my office rests on firmer ground than that," he said loftily, gazing out the delicate Georgian windows at what appeared to be a squirrel's nest high in the trees of City Hall Park.

"Ah, so it's like that, is it? Planning to run against *us* again, are you, George? Well, it worked a treat last time."

• • •

It was Mr. Murphy who had come up with the idea. The man was a genius, even if he did look like a country parson, and not a very bright one at that. He and Big Tim and all the other Tammany sachems had ensconced themselves conspicuously on the second floor of Delmonico's. There they sat each day lunching in a blood-red room, on a magnificent table with four carved tigers' paws, summoning the rest of the City's pols and money men before them.

THE COLOSSUS OF GRAFT! Hearst's headlines had screamed: WHAT GOES ON IN THE SCARLET ROOM OF MYSTERY???!! LOOK OUT MURPHY! IT'S A SHORT STEP FROM DELMONICO'S TO SING SING!

McClellan's role had been to run *against* the Colossus of Graft. It was the ultimate trick: Tammany running against Tammany. The mayor had hired on a Reform police commissioner, and stuck the cops in sharp new uniforms, and fired a few decrepit old clerks. Meanwhile Mr. Murphy had released anguished statements about Benedict Arnolds, and the unkindest cut of all, and the sharpness of serpents' teeth. And the day after the votes were in, it had been business as usual.

"I am the mayor of the city!" McClellan harrumphed to Sullivan now, with all the indignation he could muster. "You will address me properly."

"You're *our* mayor, and *we* have a real problem on our hands," Big Tim snapped. "Not the fact that grown men like to look at pretty girls in their underwear. We need you to squash this t'ing, an' squash it right now, before it gets even more out of hand."

"You mean Rosenthal?"

McClellan cocked his handsome head at him, like a curious terrier.

"It would be improper for me to interfere in any way. That's the district attorney's responsibility now!"

"George, George. Do ya really think anyone's gonna go quietly? Just to git you another term?"

"Then they must be ripped out, root and vine!" the mayor declaimed, slapping his desk for emphasis. "Let the chips fall where they may! We must wipe the slate clean!"

"Ah, George. It's more of a mandrake root, this one—a root in the shape of a man, and one that screams when you pull it out. Face facts: if Beansy Rosenthal keeps hollerin' to the D.A., there's bound to be an investigation—an' I don't mean the usual, blue-ribbon panel of distinguished citizens wit' well-trimmed beards, revealin' to a stunned public that policemen take bribes an' bars stay open after hours. It'll go deep this time—there's no tellin' where it'll end if we don't put a stop to it now."

"I cannot risk the integrity of my office. That's all there is to it!"

Big Tim stood and moved over to the mayor, suddenly hovering over him.

"It never does to play the same hand a second time around, you know," he said softly.

"I'm the mayor of this city!"

"Uh-huh," said Big Tim, gesturing to Dave and Reilly that it was time to go.

"That you are. And as such you're made of clay, and another can be fashioned in your image. G'day."

He gave a little tip of his straw boater as he left the room, leaving the Little Little Napoleon still blustering in his wake.

"Jay-sus, didja ever see anyt'ing like that?"

Big Tim smiled as they cantered down the front steps of the City Hall.

"Oh, but you told him, Tim!"

"You showed him his duty, Dry Dollar."

"Oh, but he's a pip! Didja ever see him at his rallies?"

Of course they had, but they wanted him to tell it, their faces grinning and eager around him.

We are a people enchanted by stories

"—he'd always make sure to have a plant in the crowd. And at just the right moment, the man would flog hizzoner like a real heckler:

"'Speak to us in our own language!' the plant would yell out. An' people would boo, an' McClellan would look uncertain, like he didn't know if he could do it.

"'Speak to us in our own language!' the cull would yell out again, an' pretty soon more people would take it up—in Italian, or German, or French, whatever they was: 'Speak to us in our own language!'

"And then he would straighten up an' launch right into the most beautiful speech you ever heard. Oh, marvelous, marvelous! Like he was makin' it up right there. Italian, or German, or goddamned Mandarin Chinee. The most gorgeous, elegant stuff you ever heard in your whole life, whatever the hell it was. He'd memorized every word the night before, but oh! Sweet Jesus, it was a piece of work!"

The three men stopped to shake with laughter. They had come around the City Hall now, and stood at the center of all the world that was worth knowing. Behind them were the towering, red-brick buildings of newspaper row, Hearst's and Pulitzer's kingdoms. Over to the east was the white new Municipal Building, and the great bridge rising across the

227

river. And directly in front of them, squatting behind the elegant City Hall like a beggar woman behind a lady, was the Tweed Courthouse—The Building They Never Stopped Building.

Tweed had dreamed it up after the Civil War, and it represented the apotheosis of his genius. He had contracted the work out to his usual cronies, for the usual kickbacks. When the goo-goos had squawked about what a shoddy job it was, Tweed had simply handed out new contracts, to more cronies, for more kickbacks—the circles of corruption and mutual benefit spreading ever wider.

By the time they finally locked him away in the Tombs they had ordered up enough theoretical carpet to circumnavigate the globe, and enough brooms to sweep it clean, and enough paint to give it two good coats. And there still wasn't a roof on the thing.

There was brilliance, he couldn't help admiring; thinking with admiration. *Standing before it like Aristotle contemplating a bust of Homer—*

"How 'bout we go in, shake a stick with old G.W.?" Photo Dave suggested hopefully, but Big Tim just grunted. The mere mention of the man brought on the twinge in his groin again.

"No, I think today I can spare meself the story of how George Plunkitt created the moon, an' the stahrs, an' the seven planets in three days, paddin' it all out to six wit' honest graft," he told them.

"You go on if you want, though—the both a ya. I'll find me own way home."

"Thanks, Dry Dollar."

"See you back there."

They moved off apologetically but quickly, anxious to be inside, swapping more stories.

We are a people enchanted by stories

Down on the first floor of the courthouse, placed strategically next to the men's washroom, George Washington Plunkitt sat like a king on his bootblack stand. A canopy of American flags and framed Tammany chieftains on the wall behind him, puffing on his cigars and telling one story after another about Croker and his race horses, and Black Pete Sweeney, and Honest John Kelly.

Plunkitt didn't actually own the stand, though he might as well have, for all the hours he spent there since The McManus had ousted him. He was an old Tammany district leader from up in the Fifteenth, cannier than most, and richer than Midas. At one point he had managed to get himself made magistrate, alderman, supervisor, and state senator, all at the same time, and raked in the money.

The trouble was George Plunkitt had never been able to resist showing off, and he had got some newspaperman to write up his windy monologues on practical politics in a book. Just more hot air, most of it, but it had attracted plenty of attention, and Big Tim didn't think it was wise.

In the men's room behind G.W., he knew, in back of the last urinal, lived a gigantic cockroach. Sullivan had seen its antennae for years, whenever he went in to take a leak——the two stalks, maybe six inches long, wavering just above the porcelain; as chary as any good district leader.

That was all he ever saw of it: Just the two antennae—and many a time he had been seized with the urge to grab those two wavering stalks, drag the giant roach out, and crush it on the cold, tiled floor.

But in all those years he never had. No doubt it was many different roaches by now, whole generations of roaches carrying on at their post, but he would never know for sure. Some things were better left unseen.

21

THE GREAT HEAD DOCTORS FROM VIENNA

The funny little man flickered across the glasses of Sigmund Freud. Running, falling, eating, waddling forward with his odd little walk, dabbing at the black smudge of moustache just below his nose. He seemed to exist in a state of constant, frenetic turmoil: his black bowler hat bobbing along on the tide of humanity that engulfed him whenever he stepped out the door——the same tide they had taken refuge from up on the roof garden.

Before the little tramp, up on the screen, there had been another frantic comedy about a gang of incompetent policemen who went charging around after a fire engine, wrecking everything. Before that some sort of kitchen drama from the ghetto with everyone, right down to the humble mother in her apron, throwing their arms about with the gestures of grand opera stars——

It was the first time any of them had seen a moving picture. Freud had to admit they were innately engrossing, creating a world of their own on a two-dimensional screen. What kind of psyche would it create in the future, he wondered, once they perfected the process, and people were sure that they could *see* all of life?

Ferenczi especially seemed to love it, laughing out loud and clapping his hands like a little boy. Freud himself only smiled quietly, content to sip his beer and puff on his cigars—while Jung, to his annoyance, was even more enigmatic, peering out at the screen through his large pince-nez like a biologist examining a rare bug.

"*Herr Doktor,* the clinic is closed," Freud called over to him, still smiling, noting to his further displeasure that Jung had returned to his abstemious ways. Since they had been in America he drank nothing but seltzer water, or a bilious tonic called celery soda, which the Americans claimed aided the digestion but which tasted to Freud like old socks.

"In our profession, the clinic is never closed," Jung smiled back at him. "That's the joy of it—we never have to stop working."

"Yes, I *know,*" Freud said quickly, but Jung cut him off, waving an arm to indicate the roof garden all around them.

"Take this place, for instance. Think of how much is hidden here, in between the palms."

Freud gritted his teeth, and turned back to the movie. In fact, to his further chagrin, Jung was right. The roof garden seemed very strange to him indeed—another thoroughly disconcerting American place. It was up in one of the newer districts of the city, on a street brimming with theatres—yet just a couple blocks from a slum; where everyone gleefully, even proudly, warned them not to walk.

The theatre itself was another mass of contradictions, a spectacular art nouveau palace called the New Amsterdam. Up on the roof garden, next to the whole louche scene—the tuxedoed businessmen, fat as pigeons; the glittering, jaded women; hungry young gigolos prowling through the potted palms—was a homey little recreation of the *old* New Amsterdam: complete with miniature windmills, and gabled Dutch houses, a real cow and a buxom set of milkmaids who sashayed around the tables, selling buckets of their warm, fresh milk to the customers.

"They are like children, these Americans, with their insistence on innocence," Freud sniffed, faintly annoyed by Ferenczi still giggling like a schoolboy next to him.

There had been dinner, and dancing to a small orchestra, everyone around them laughing and talking so loudly they could barely hear each other. Then, out of nowhere, the great blank, white screen had been put up. The droning, clattering projector was pulled out, overruling everything else; everyone turning their full attention to the screen.

The whole trip had been just as strange and unsettling, from the moment they pulled out of Bremerhaven. He had grown close again with Jung on the boat over. He had been Carl the crown prince, the good student, once more—even proposing to give his own lecture about childhood sexuality first, to break the ice for Freud by citing the case of his daughter, Agathli, and her anxiety over his wife's pregnancy.

Freud had been grateful. He thought it was a sacrifice worthy of the Torah, for Jung to offer up his own daughter. Agathli would indeed serve as an ideal battering ram, as it were, softening up their audience at Clark for the shocking idea that sexuality began before puberty.

Yet there was a price: Jung, he was aware, still wanted to psychoanalyze the Master. Freud had put him off. He had no intention of being stuck on the *George Washington* with a triumphant Jung, smugly confident that he had uncovered some part of Freud he had not previously suspected in himself. Perhaps not even telling him what it was—

There had been a disturbing incident, as well, a small thing, but one that had bothered him all the way over. On their second day out, they had run into another of the ship's company after breakfast, a certain Professor Stern, from Breslau, on his way over to Clark himself to give a lecture on the psychology of court testimony.

This Stern had had the temerity to question *The Interpretation of Dreams* in a review a few years ago, and Freud had neither forgotten nor forgiven. He prided himself on being able to endure any and all attacks on his person, but he would tolerate nothing against the Cause. He cut the professor himself, but Stern had succeeded in cornering Jung. While Freud waited a few feet away, impatiently tapping his walking stick, the little *ekel* had gone on and on, discussing theories of word association. He had finally felt obliged to call out to Jung:

"Now, *Herr Doktor,* when are you going to bring that conversation to an end?"

Stern had blushed then, and excused himself. Freud reclaimed his crown prince, hooking their arms together and guiding him off down the deck.

"Look at the shabby little Jew go," Freud said with satisfaction, glaring back over his shoulder at the retreating Stern.

In New York Harbor he had stood by the rail, staring at the famous green statue of Liberty, standing like a colossus over her brood. It was modeled on the sculptor's mother, he recalled from Ferenczi's Baedeker.

What a thing for the Land of Rebellious Sons: a stern mother figure, wielding a phallic symbol! But was its real purpose to substitute for the mothers they had left behind—or to warn off more bad boys?

He left the question for later as their ship was towed through the bustling harbor, and over to the Hoboken docks. Contemplating the heroic statue, the soaring, vertical city awaiting him, he felt like a conquistador again, invincible and roguish, capable of anything.

• • •

233

The mood lasted until the men from the American press came aboard.

"Isn't this all about sex, *Herr Professor?*" one of them shouted out, and the others had all laughed while he fumed and stammered, unable to get out a quick answer in their promiscuous, careless language.

"What are your lecture fees?"

"Do you expect to get many society clients?"

"Are any of you married, doctors?"

—this last query bringing another great laugh, as Ferenczi and even Jung blushed red as schoolgirls. They scribbled in their notebooks and popped their flash pictures until the doctors were quite blind—still obviously convinced their whole trip was no more than some kind of traveling con game, the latest sensation for their front pages. Even worse, he noticed the next day that his name had been universally misspelled as *Freund*.

"Professor, whattaya think of America so far?"

"Well, we have only just got in the harbor," he hemmed, fighting down the impulse to point out what an astonishingly stupid question it was. Yet it was all the reporters really wanted to know.

"Professors, are ya gonna take in a baseball game?"

"Are you gonna visit the Grand Canyon?"

"Are you gonna go up to the Statue of Liberty? How 'bout the subway?"

"Well, whattaya think of the harbor *so far?*"

Dr. Brill, from Columbia's Psychiatric Clinic, had finally succeeded in shooing the reporters away. Brill was an old friend; he had done his practicum at the Burgholzli, and been analyzed for a time by Freud, and he took them in hand—leading them off the boat, down through endless tunnels to a taxi, then a train in the subway—a deafening, terrifying experience—and then finally back up more tunnels and through the kitchen of their hotel.

"It is a great world city now, New York," Brill informed them. "I will take you everywhere—everywhere! You won't want to miss a bit!"

"I will be perfectly satisfied if I can just get to see a porcupine," Freud tried his standard joke again, but actually, as it happened, he would have been satisfied if he had been able to keep anything down. The American cooking had proved unbearable, and since landing they had all taken turns being laid up with stomach maladies. At least it had given him a further excuse to avoid Jung's demands to analyze him.

Jung himself had recovered first, and thrown himself enthusiastically into American culture: jumping up on the rushing, clanging streetcars that swooped down like birds of prey on anyone trying to cross the street. Running out to buy the newspapers everyday. He was avidly following an inquiry over which man, Peary or Cook, had made it to the North Pole first.

"Can you think of anything more crazily American?" Freud scoffed. "Two men, risking their lives on such a race? And to where? Not even a continent, but a drifting ice floe! How can anyone determine a winner?"

"But what finer example of the hero myth in action?" Jung had chided him. "America is full of heroes—or at least, people who think they are. That's why it's the country for us!"

"A whole country full of *ubermenschen*," Freud said darkly. "But tell me, please, what do such marvelous creatures need with us?"

"Surely, *Doktor*, there is always a need for analysis, even of the healthiest ego. When are you going to let me have a go at you?" Jung had baited him.

"Soon, soon," he had muttered, flustered and annoyed again.

Since their arrival, he had analyzed Jung's and Ferenczi's dreams, but it had been a one-way street; he was not prepared yet to let his crown prince at his.

In the dream, he leapt off the ocean liner and pulled it ashore after him, Jung and Ferenczi struggling to keep up. In one hand, he carried a great, green torch, and as they watched he lowered it to the boat, setting it aflame.

"There will be no turning back now," he told them gleefully.

But when he turned around again, the shore was littered with soldiers. The general in his absurd, parakeet uniform leaned in at him, eyes furious behind his pince-nez. In one hand he still held up the list of terrible wounds.

"Prepare!" he bellowed. "Prepare!"

The little man, the tramp, was not nearly so frantic as he was clever, Freud decided, outwitting the larger, angrier characters for all his clownish bumbling. Beside him, he watched Ferenczi laugh again. Jung snapped out his notebook, making a quick, furtive note before shoving it back into his dinner jacket, pushing his pince-nez back up on his nose as he returned to the movie.

The Rat Man had worn a pince-nez, Freud realized—the sweet, neurotic young doctor who had come to him in such despair.

Freud had taken him into his own household, shared meals with the man—like Jung before him. He had been sure he was going mad, but Freud had saved him, tracing his neurosis to a story the Rat Man's superior officer—the figure Freud had labeled the Cruel Captain—had told the man during military training.

It was all about some legendary Oriental punishment—a cage of starving rats strapped to the buttocks of a convict.

Something so cruel and sadistic that Freud even questioned whether someone could really have told his patient such a story.

But no, the young man had insisted: the Cruel Captain had described it all to him with great relish—leaving no doubt that he would like to carry out such a punishment on the young doctor himself.

Later, the young doctor had lost his pince-nez during maneuvers, and had to send for a new pair from Vienna. He had entrusted the Cruel Captain, of all people, with the postage due—an incredibly masochistic move! Of course, somehow the money had never been paid, the glasses never delivered. There had been accusations, and charges of insubordination. The Cruel Captain had haughtily denied that he had ever been entrusted with any money. He threatened to lock the young doctor up in the guard house—to come to him at night with his cage of rats—

The pince-nez, then, had been the token at the center of it all. But what did it mean for Freud? Was Jung *his* Rat Man—the sweet, young doctor he had taken in, somehow turned on him? Or could he be the Cruel Captain?

Slowly, methodically, he did the *Traumdeutung*—the dreamwork—in his head. On one level it was easy enough, as it always was: the Aula, the great ceremonial hall in Vienna, filled with the best minds of science, stood for the upcoming lectures at Clark. His need to use the toilet demonstrated his nervousness over this great opportunity. Burning the ship came from his identification with the great conquistadors, with Cortés, who had burned his boats before conquering Mexico.

The dream of waiting in the train station with the old, one-eyed man he had had before. The man was his father, he had already concluded. The urinal referred to the time, when he was seven or eight, that Freud had peed on his parents' floor, and his father had railed at him: *The boy will come to nothing!* Yet now, obviously, he had come to something, even holding up before the old man's face the totem that was the symbol of his success.

That was the surface. But what lay beneath it all—all his recent anxiety? That was always more difficult. Dreams, he found, slept in layers. They were like the ruins of Troy, one city buried beneath another.

What were the beautiful rooms that he had passed through in the Aula? What did the officer, and the dead soldiers mean—the detritus of his military experience? And why was it necessary in the first place to disguise his father with the totem, the savage mask?

Freud sat contemplating the face of Jung while he tried to piece the puzzle together. Up on the screen, there was a rare close-up of the tramp's face, poignant and child-like and slightly mad, all at the same time, the large, seal-like eyes pleading into the camera, the little smudge of a moustache twitching compulsively just below his nose.

BOOK FIVE

*Dreams do not consist
solely of illusions.*

——S. STRICKER

22

ON THE BOARDWALK

Their next afternoon, Kid took her on all the wild, spooning rides. They rode on the Cannon Coaster——WILL SHE THROW HER ARMS AROUND YOUR NECK AND YELL? WELL, I GUESS, YES!——and the Barrel of Love——TALK ABOUT LOVE IN A COTTAGE! THIS HAS IT BEAT A MILE!——and on the Mixer and the Barrel of Fun, and the Bounding Billows and the Golden Stairs. They went on the Razzle Dazzle and the Human Roulette, and the Cave of the Winds and the Human Pool Table and the Down and Out——all the numbing, bone-jarring rides that were guaranteed to throw you together with your honey until they were banged black-and-blue by a pen salesman from Poughkeepsie, a scullery maid from Murray Hill, a collection of farmers from Flushing.

When it was over they were left just as frustrated as when they had begun——more so, thinking of the promises that had been made, of love in a cottage and all the rest. Kid had walked her way down Brighton Beach, and they found a spot in the dunes, and necked and ran their hands over each other until they had ached.

It felt delicious; it felt better than anything Esther had ever done. Smelling him, holding him as much as she wanted to, the taste of his skin, of his face and neck and shoulders. But it was still no good; it was too public, there was too much detritus from other summer romances here: a busted rum bottle and bits of bathing suit, a broken parasol and used condoms, discarded on the sand like little white, broken-necked birds. They brushed themselves off, and walked back to the train.

That night he got off with her at the Canal Street stop, and walked her all the way back to her door. Esther didn't think she should let him—surely somebody would see them together—but it was the hottest night yet that summer, and by the time they reached her stoop all of Orchard Street was sleeping as if they'd been drugged. All the landings of the fire escape were covered with blankets and pillows, and there were children out on mattresses right on the sidewalk.

He walked up to the front door with her. He walked right up to the front, and came in. They went up the narrow hall stairs together, up into the giant hive, the sounds the building made even when it was asleep surrounding them, its boards and beams creaking and settling like a ship.

"Welcome to the *goldineh medina*," Esther joked as she ushered him in, tapping the gas lamp to make it give off what little light it was capable of, revealing the dirty, blood-red, painted *lincrusta* that lined the hallway.

Many of the doors were yawning open as they walked up, the apartments deserted as if a plague had swept through. She remembered what her mother liked to say: *Poor people can leave their doors wide open, because nobody will come to steal poverty*. But Esther knew it wasn't true. People would steal anything they could get their hands on, even other people's misery. The open, abandoned apartments only marked the surrender of people too suffocated to care anymore.

"Where are they?" Kid asked.

"On the roof."

"Ah. Of course."

Their door was open, too. Esther had him wait outside, vaguely embarrassed to have him see how she lived, though she didn't know why. She peered into the darkened apartment, cautiously calling out:

"Momma? Papa?"

"They went up."

Kapsch the *roomerkeh* sat on the kitchen chair that was half her bed, his hands trying modestly to cover the long underwear he was wearing. He craned his neck, trying to peer out into the hallway at whoever was there.

"You should too," she said affectionately, and crept into the kitchen, gathering up her bedding.

"Eh. It's cooler down here alone."

"Suit yourself," she smiled at him.

She gathered the sheets and pillow in her arms, and led Kid to the roof door. They went up a small staircase reeking of cat piss—and there was the whole tenement camped out before them, white bundles of sleepers encamped on the black tar roof. Along all the roofs and fire escapes of the buildings around them, as far as the eye could see, there were more white bundles, more sleepers pried out of their apartments like soft white oysters.

She picked her way carefully among the sleepers, Kid following at a safe distance. Each apartment slept in its own little encampment, boarders and family together, a perfunctory gap between each group, like on the beach at Coney. They lay snoring head-to-head, tenants and subtenants alike, on the bedding and the cushions they had brought up from chairs and sofas.

Somewhere up here, she knew, her mother and father were sleeping

They made their way to the only space left, in the corner near the pigeon coops. The birds were cooing softly under their wings, huddled together, their smell dank and earthy.

243

She made up their pallet on the rough tar paper, spreading out a blanket, then a couple sheets over it, and one pillow for her head—all the bedding she used herself, alone in the kitchen on her chairs every night. She slid underneath, fully dressed, and turned down the other side of the sheets, waiting for him.

He stood above her for a moment, watching—then climbed under, carefully removing his bowler first, and she had to giggle.

"A gentleman always removes his hat before coming to bed!"

He laughed, too, and they moved in close together. They lay on their backs, holding hands, unbearably warm in all their clothes beneath the sheets.

"I'd like to study the stars," she said, in the same wistful voice with which she was always hoping for things.

"Oh? Where?"

They laughed softly again. There wasn't a star in sight above them. Instead, the night sky was a cataclysmic orange color, as if there were some terrible conflagration just below the line of rooftops and the water tanks.

They lay there, and listened to the other voices whispering around them—young, excited voices like their own, before they were hushed by families and neighbors, or faded into sleep. Through the darkness, too, she could see other eyes staring at them, hard and covetous. The red flicker of a cigarette—

Somewhere, among the silent bundles, her mother and father were sleeping, maybe just inches away

He began to move, under the sheets—and to his surprise, she helped him, helped him work his way through all the catches and stays, all the yards of undergarments.

"My moon—my tiny dove," he began to chant distractedly.

"Wait," she told him.

244

She wanted to stop, and smell his sweet breath, the sweaty, musty smell of sleeping bodies all around them. She kissed him on the mouth again and again, and then placed his hand on her breast herself.

"Okay. Go on."

She helped him some more then, fumbling under the sheets, her hands feeling curiously around. He was mortified at first by how his body smelled, the shabbiness of his clothes. He wasn't used to taking off all his clothes for the act, for the whores he usually slept with, but he let her undress him. She went on until he had absolutely nothing on, not even the socks on his feet, and they were both completely naked beneath the sheet. He began to kiss her again, running his hands quickly and roughly over her beautiful breasts, her thighs, but she made him slow down.

"It's all right, my sweetness, my birdie boy——"

He moved onto her, and began to make love to her, up on the tar roof, with the pigeons cooing over their heads, and the sleepers turning and groaning in their sleep, all around them. She smiled up at him, her brown eyes large and luminous in the reflected orange light.

"My wealth——my little crown——my golden heart," he panted quietly, trying not to use her name——though there was no indication that anyone heard, no sound from her sleeping family and neighbors save for their restless sighings and turnings.

He moved slowly over her body——surprised to find that she was still a virgin, and then trying to go even slower, desperate not to hurt her——and at the height of their awkward lovemaking, he put his hand up to cushion her head against the rough surface of the tar paper.

She took him in, held him to her by his skinny thighs, and kept kissing his mouth as they did it. It hurt, and when he was finished she lay there, a little sore, and curious, but so pleased with herself that she had done this thing.

"You have to go soon," she told him, holding his head in her hands, rubbing his hair, kissing him on both cheeks.

"It will be morning."

"Yes."

Oh, what a thing she had done!

She lay back running a hand along his thigh, happy at the reluctance in his voice.

If she could do this on the same roof with her mother and father all the neighbors all around what could she not do? What could she not do?

"My dybbuk."

"Huh?"

"Nothing."

They slid into sleep for awhile. She awoke with a start, the brooding sky still reassuringly in place above them, billowing orange clouds drifting slowly past.

"You have to go."

"Yes."

He sat up, and began to pull on his shirt.

Kapsch the *roomerkeh* saw him rise, and began to back toward the stairs. He crept swiftly down into the apartment, careful to make as little noise as possible on the uneven floorboards. When he was inside he listened for the man to go past, thinking over the dim view of bodies he had seen across the rooftop, wondering if it really could have been what he thought it was.

23

KID TWIST

He loitered ecstatically in the night.

After he left her, he walked out under the Bowery el and the crowds there. It was after midnight, but the street was busier than ever, the dime museums and the barber colleges, the tattoo parlors and the shooting galleries and the mission halls all glowing like little coals dropped from the roaring trains above.

Kid liked to catch the face of a stranger hove up suddenly before him—surprised in the streetlamp light, walking purposefully, somewhere, at this hour of night. The drunken young gentleman, staggering along the sidewalk, money all but falling out of his pocket. The soiled dove, who stared boldly back at him, just outside the ring of light from the theatre lobby.

Sated and magnanimous, he knew the City was his. He could go anywhere, do anything. He knew whorehouses, and bars, cockfights and gambling joints that were just getting warmed up. He knew where he could go to get fresh bread on Hester Street, or a quart of strawberries for five cents on Essex Street, or a man on Pitt Street who would write a letter to his love for a dime, so beautiful it would make her cry. Now that he had a love—if he had a love—

Pushcarts full of food still lined the gutter, each one lit by its own blue gas jet, glowing faintly in the night. He bought some oysters, and potatoes in sour cream, wandered aimlessly on down the street.

Anything was possible at night. Once he had seen a long string of llamas on the Bowery at four in the morning, being guided up from the docks to the Madison Square circus by Peruvian peasants. Another time he had seen a delegation of Sioux Indians, another time a string of elephants, linked trunk-to-tail.

It was dangerous, he knew—but then it always was, and not just because of Gyp the Blood. His checkered suit, his scent and hair pomade marked him as a man with money. Even the most consumptive Bowery wretch could lie in wait until the next express train thundered overhead—drowning out all other sensation—then dump a pail of ashes over his head, and club him with a slung shot, take his watch and money and slit him gizzard to navel like an upended turtle.

He could not worry about it. Somehow, he could not even worry about Gyp, who might be waiting around the next corner. At worst he would be broken down to his particulars, his useful parts. Tumbled back down into the East River, among the drowned rats, and the wretched refuse from whence he had come.

After he had saved the boy, after he had spent his first night in the City in jail, a man came down from Tammany to bail him out. He only figured that out later, of course, he had no idea why he was free, or what the man was doing—staggering along the street after him still dizzy and nauseous from his clubbing the night before, fearful of what new trap this might be. But the man—a simple peanut politician who looked mighty important, then, to Josef's untrained greenie eyes, in a new coat with a pocket watch and a brown derby cocked on his head—the man merely bought him a two-dollar suit, and a cap, and gave him fifty cents for a flop-house. Then he shook his hand, told him he was a citizen, and walked away. And from that moment on, Josef had roamed through the streets, looking for his opportunities, looking for the money that was everywhere, *everywhere,* just waiting to fall into his hands.

In the winter he got work shoveling snow, following the horse carts through the deep slush tracks in the streets of Jewtown and Little Italy. He hoisted it up into the back of a wagon, heavy with frozen garbage and gravel, where two men with more seniority stood waiting to pack it down. When the wagon was full, they trudged over to the East River and shoveled it out again in the late winter afternoon: the snow turning over white blue and silver and white again as they dropped it through the ice, into the dark river that ran below them like a half-remembered dream.

On a clear day, he could see the ruddy-faced women from the House of Refuge, over on Welfare Island. They sat out-side on their break, smoking cigarettes against the work-house wall, in their shapeless, gray-striped smocks and ker-chiefs. And once there had been a houseboat lodged in the glinting ice, a thin trail of smoke curling up from its smoke-stack. A lone woman had come out on the deck, hanging clothes on a line there—a thin, dark figure, pausing in her task to stare back at them, the diggers, shoveling snow into a river.

When there was no snow he worked as a jury-checker; he worked as a puller-in, yanking passersby off the sidewalk into the low-tin-ceilinged haberdasheries along Baxter Street. He worked for bucket shops sponging the beer dregs off bar tops; he rummaged through ash cans for unburned bits of wood and coal; he ran through the back courtyards of tenements with the other bummers, screaming "Line! Line!" for clothesline to hang——when they would just as soon have hanged themselves.

He didn't require much. For a penny he could get a hard roll, and for another penny he could get a coffee over at the charity stand on the Mulberry Bend. He could sleep on barroom floors, or on half a bed in a dank, flooded basement. In the summer he bathed in the public saltwater baths on the North River, and in the winter he went dirty.

In the *Chasir Mark* on Hester Street, the men and women lined up every day with the tools of their trade, sorting themselves out in an unspoken hierarchy: carpenters with their hammers and T squares, then masons with their trowels, washerwomen with their basins. On down through the nurses and bakers, the chimney sweeps and the thread-pullers, down to the greenest day laborers.

He stood there all day, with no tools at all to show for his toil. Watching the mad bustle of the *Chasir Mark,* the Pig Market, where it was said one could buy everything in the world except a pig: the children selling shoestrings, and matches, and penny notebooks; women selling little paper packets of horseradish they ground in the street; men peddling old peaches for a penny a quart, cracked cups for a penny apiece, cracked eggs for a penny a dozen; until he marveled that there was any such thing as trash in the ghetto.

One morning, instead of buying a hard roll, he used his penny to get a paper and answered an ad for a cutter at the Triangle factory. He wasn't sure exactly what a cutter was, though he reasoned from the salary offered that it was some sort of skilled labor.

"How hard can anything in America be?" he told himself. "After all, I can already shovel shit."

At the factory he waited all day outside the office of Mr. Bernstein, the general manager. Finally, when his stomach was all but rolling over from hunger and he thought he could stand it no longer, the man had flung open his door, asked without any further formalities:

"Name?"

"Joseph Kay."

"Uh-huh. If he was Garlic in the old country, here he's Mr. Onions."

Bernstein grabbed his right hand, turning it over, probing his callouses, wiggling the fingers.

"I don' know," he shrugged. "Tough enough, but flexible? And the fingers? It's a *goyishe* hand."

"Mr. Bernstein," he interrupted, thinking about *Luck and Pluck*, and *Ragged Dick*, and summoning up all his courage. "Mr. Bernstein, I can *do* this job. I *know* I can."

The general manager shrugged again.

"Well, sure you can try. All right—let's see if you're a cutter."

He took him down to the eighth floor, where the pressers' irons sizzled against the back wall, the cutters peering down suspiciously at them from their high tables.

"Now this one is a cutter?"

"He'll eat the head from our bones. Bringing in children!"

Yet they left off from their work, craning their necks to see past the patterns that hung over their desks on a thin wire clothesline.

"Benny—bring me some old *shmatte*," Bernstein commanded, and at once a boy in knee breeches and high socks scuttled forward, handing him a long, thin scrap of green cloth. He thought Mr. Bernstein might be displeased, since there was a wide blotch of oil right in the middle of the material, but instead he nodded with satisfaction.

"Good—this won't miss much."

He pointed to the nearest cutter's table, its slanted top nearly level to Joseph's chin.

"As soon as Morris is finished with this job—you do."

He watched the man intensely, knowing this was his only chance to even see how the job was done. Morris was a gaunt, balding man with enormous ears who looked too short to so much as reach the cutting table—but before Joseph knew it he had hopped up on a soapbox, already covering his table with layer after layer of fine material.

Next he plucked four patterns off the thin metal wire that ran the length of the cutting tables, laying them out over the fine lawn before him—four perfect outlines of a woman's shirtwaist. His hands flew over them again, moving faster than a street monte dealer, arranging and rearranging the patterns until he had left as little extra cloth as possible.

When he was satisfied, Morris the cutter picked up a short, stubby knife, pressed his left hand down on the patterns, and sliced through the fabric with one long, fluid motion. He sheared through the longerine as if it were paper, one pattern after another, producing four perfect shirtwaists in a matter of seconds. Then he flipped the finished waists up over the wire and pushed the remaining scraps through a slot into the bin below—his table already swept clean, and ready for the next batch of lawn.

"Now you," Bernstein told him.

"All right," he said, his mouth already dry.

Another cutter protested from down the line—"What does a chicken know about these things?"—but the rest of them were quiet, restlessly arranging their lawn, stealing glances down at Joseph.

Bernstein piled up a couple more layers of the spoiled cloth, threw a pattern over them, then pressed the knife down into his palm. It felt like an oysterman's blade, thick and round, and Joseph grasped it firmly. He took a deep breath, thought of what Ragged Dick or Mark the Match Boy might have done, and plunged right in.

He placed his left hand firmly on the cloth, then ploughed around the shirtwaist pattern just as he had seen the cutter do it. The knife caught, but he kept going. The fine, papery material balked and bunched, shredding around the fine metal borders of the pattern, but he forced it back in line.

"Lookit that!" someone breathed, in a tone of wonder.

He could feel Mr. Bernstein and the cutters moving in around him, watching in silent fascination. But he didn't let it distract him, he didn't stop until he had brought the knife around the entire pattern in one, continuous motion, just like he had seen Morris do, then shoved the scraps down into the bin and left the finished waist. Only then did he look up, triumphant, into their astonished faces.

"*Gottenyu!*"

"Now *there's* a natural-born cutter!" someone exclaimed. Then they all dissolved into laughter.

The room revolved around him. Joseph looked down at the table and saw a tortured blob of material—a jagged, child's copy of a pattern. One of the cutters snatched up the first layer and began to parade it around the room.

"That's murder on a piece of cloth!"

"A horse couldn't do better, *maybe*!"

They went writhing about the room with laughter and relief, dancing with the hideous cutout until the pressers and the women at their machines looked up and started to laugh, too.

"Oh, miss, miss, what a fabulous dancing partner you are! Only—I must say—you are looking a little bit *shredded*!"

Even Bernstein was smiling, around the unlit stub of cigar in his mouth.

"All right. So you're not a cutter," he said. But he had provided them with such a laugh that Bernstein gave him a job as a floor boy right there, sticking a broom in his hands.

"Here, this is the only piece of equipment in the shop I trust you with!"

He spent his days sweeping up the great piles of scrap and lint that fell like rain between the rows of operators. He hauled oil to the machines from the big barrel on the ninth floor; scuttled underneath the benches to replace the greasy, black leather belts that tied the machines to the central axle—

He loved sliding himself under the benches, deep down among the machine girls, among their skirts and petticoats. He loved how they smelled, even amidst the machine oil and the clouds of lint and dust. He had never been around so many girls before: sloe-eyed Italians with olive skin, milky-white Jewish girls with their thick, curly nests of hair. He loved just watching them come in to work in the morning, laughing and singing, mothers coming in with daughters, sisters with sisters.

His favorite task of all was at closing time, when they had to be searched. At five minutes to nine, every night, Mr. Bernstein would go around making sure the fire doors on all three stories of the factory were closed and padlocked. Then he and the foremen and the floor supervisors and the errand boys would station themselves at the elevators, and the stair doors, and everyone in the factory would have to go by them, and hold out their bags and pockets for inspection.

It soon became Joseph's greatest, secret pleasure. Many of the girls preferred him—knowing at least he wouldn't leer or pinch at them, or make some remark. They always complained, but he was convinced they liked it, at least with him. They held open their handbags—and he would stick his face right down into their lovely, velvet depths, turning over the little clues he found—a scented handkerchief, lipsticks and powders, the photograph of a man. Gently, curiously handling and sniffing at their most intimate possessions.

"What are we looking for, anyway?" he asked Mr. Bernstein after a few weeks on the job.

"Dolt! Don'ch you know already? Any piece of cloth you find. Anything that belongs to the company," he told him, clouting him lightly over one ear.

"Anything at all?"

"It's all the company's. You'll see."

A week later the felt dealer came by, and Joseph had to help him cart away the tons of leftover cloth under the cutters' tables. When the cutters finished each stack of lawn there were always at least a few useless corners left, like leftover pie crust, no matter how carefully they had plotted their patterns.

These leftover bits were all swept into the enormous wooden bins beneath their tables—along with everything the boys swept up from the shop floor, and every piece of lawn ruined beyond repair. It didn't look like much by itself, but at the height of the season it took the felt dealer's two burly sons to help him push and yank each bin over to the elevator, then out to the curb and the scrap wagon and then, with one last, great heave, dump them over into the open cart. Dozens of bright little triangles of cloth escaping, flitting off down the street in the afternoon breeze . . .

"Everything has a value," Mr. Bernstein explained to him, as solemnly as if he were disclosing the secrets of the pyramids. "That is the key to mass production—*everything* is worth something."

—and in that instant it was clear to Joseph how things worked. It fit in perfectly with the philosophy of the *Chasir Mark*. Everything—the factory, the tenements, they themselves—*everything* was made up of such little pieces, and it was only a matter of rearranging, *redistributing* them for profit.

●　　●　　●

Soon afterwards, he was promoted to expressman, carting goods and running errands all over town. He liked being out on his own, even though it meant he had to spend more time away from the girls. He would pad down into the cool, dark subway station like a thief, and stand in the middle of the platform, between the express and the local trains as they came in. He would wait until they pounded into the station together, letting the whoosh of the stagnant tunnel air sweep over him. Ecstatically sounding out the words on their windows:

INTER-BOROUGH RAP-ID TRANSIT—

The promotion enabled him to rent a single, first-floor room, looking out into an airshaft: a bed, and a chair, and a bathroom in the hall. He bought a new two-dollar suit in the *Chasir Mark*, and a black bowler hat to go with it, and went to eat every Sunday at the cafeteria the society ladies had set up on Grand Street, where you could get a full dinner with a schooner of beer and an after-dinner smoke for fifteen cents.

How the taste of the fat melted in every limb! A bit of brisket, some corned beef. A lump of sugar, held under the tongue. White bread, and cinnamon rolls, and poppyseed rolls—

The place had flowers on each table, and white table-cloths, and its respectability attracted many of the single factory girls. He would eye them from his table, hoping to talk one of them into coming back to his room—hoping they would at least meet his eye. They almost never did, but that was all right, too. Mostly he was just happy to watch them, sitting and eating in their best Sunday clothes, he in his suit, feeling more and more *oyshgreen*—more un-green—every day.

24

KID TWIST

In the factory Joseph followed Mr. Bernstein everywhere, paying attention to every word he said, for he was certain that it was through him he would make his rise.

But then the season shut down and he was laid off, just like the others, with not so much as a note from Bernstein in his final pay envelope, and Podhoretz and Kristol searched him at the door just like the machine girls to make sure he hadn't tried to smuggle out any of the factory's invaluable lint. He had to give up the room after that, and carry around all his possessions, and go back to sleeping in slung hammocks, or on the barroom floors, and the warm grates behind bakeries.

That was when he saw the felt wagon again.

He was just crossing Broome Street, and there it was—all but identical to the one that called every couple weeks at the Triangle. It was deserted, too—the carter and his assistants no doubt inside the factory, wrestling the scrap bins around—and in that instant he saw the golden opportunity he had always been sure was his.

Sure and steady as Ragged Dick himself, Joseph got up into the driver's seat and flicked the reins. He didn't give it a second thought, sliding into his life of crime as easily as he would bite into a white roll. It went slowly at first, for he had no idea of how to drive a horse and wagon——the wagon bucking and jerking down the street, little felt triangles spewing out into the gutter——but eventually, through luck or pluck, he was able to get them trudging through the densely packed, cobbled streets, guiding them to the headquarters of a felt dealer he knew on Great Jones Street.

"Where the hell'ja get this?"

The dealer, a huge, gotch-eyed slab of a man, stared up at him, suspicious as a cyclops.

"Heist it, didja? I should call the bulls right now—— "

——but when Joseph offered him a price he knew was half the going rate for the cartful the man shrugged, and sent his own burly sons to unload it more quickly than they had ever loaded up the carts at the Triangle.

"Just make sure you dump the horse an' wagon, an' keep your mouth shut," he grumbled, counting out the money.

That was the beginning. He left the emptied cart three blocks away, in front of a station house——the cops out front watching without the faintest curiosity while he stepped down and walked away into the crowds, leaving a perfectly good horse and wagon unhitched and unattended.

After that he took any wagon he could get his hands on. It wasn't hard. They were all over the city, sitting there in the street unprotected, practically begging to be taken while their drivers hauled carpets down winding cellar stairs, teetered twenty-foot glass plates into barrooms, pausing on the fifth story to wipe their brows before carting a piano the rest of the way up a back fire escape.

He preferred felt carts because he knew the dealers, but he would take anything——redistributing, *rearranging* all the little pieces of the city. All it required was a moment to reconnoiter the situation, and an actor's instinct to move into the driver's seat with the weary aplomb of the regularly employed.

It was while hijacking a wagon that he first met Monk Eastman. He was driving a cartful of stolen celery up the Bowery near Chatham Square, early in the morning, when he spotted the crowd of cats and pigeons, peaceably fluttering and pacing about together. He stopped to look down— and saw the ugliest man he had ever seen in his life.

His nose was flattened, and his ears were chewed half off, and there was a neat pool of blood congealed around his head like a halo. He would have thought the man was dead if it had not been that his eyes were open, and his mouth puckered sardonically—as if he were not lying in a Bowery gutter but home in bed, measuring all the regrets of his life along the ceiling.

"You all right?" he asked.

"*Eh,*" the man shrugged, his gaze still turned up to the sky. He was profoundly, awesomely ugly, short and thick, with no neck and veiny, pancake jowls, his hair sticking straight up off the point of his bullet head.

"You want a ride?"

"All right," the man said, raising himself up on one elbow. "But da kits an' da boids got to come, too."

"All right," Joseph shrugged back—since after all it wasn't his wagon to begin with.

The man hopped up with surprising agility and started gathering up the animals around him, tucking the cats under his arms, the pigeons alighting on his shoulders as if he were Saint Francis of Assisi. Joseph leaned down to help him.

"Easy wit' dem," the man warned. "I take care a anybody what gets gay wit' a kit or a boid."

He straightened up, and Joseph noticed then there was blood still seeping through the white undershirt that was all he wore under his jacket. He casually covered the wound with his fingers.

"I t'ink maybe we should go to de Gouverneur Hospital," he suggested, once he had deposited the birds and yowling

259

cats in the back of the wagon and taken his place in the seat.

"Uh-huh."

"*Farshtinkener* Five Pointers. Dey caught me wit'out me irons. I got t'ree of 'em, but the last one had a pistol."

"You're shot?" Joseph gaped.

"Well, kid," the man grinned. "He didn't kiss me."

Joseph flicked up the reins, starting the horses trotting toward the hospital, trying hard not to look at the oozing wound. Monk continued to grin at him, with his horrible, stubby brown teeth.

"Don' worry, kid. Dis was a real *mitzvah* you done me."

It was through Monk, in turn, that he met Gyp the Blood a week later, in the middle of the night. There was a knock on the door of the one-room, air shaft apartment he had been able to reclaim, and dazed with sleep he had opened it, not stopping to think who might be on the other side. Standing in the dingy hall before him was a man in an immaculate sky-blue suit, reeking of bay rum and hair pomade, and looking more immediately, palpably lethal than anyone he had ever seen before.

"Monk wants you t'come wit' me," he said.

Joseph hurried into his clothes and went with him unquestioningly through the milling nighttime crowds. At Lafayette Street the man swung onto a downtown trolley and Joseph followed him—still without a word passing between them about where they were going, or what they were doing.

He clung to the railing, ahead of him the trucks and wagons whizzing past on all sides, people walking quickly across the street with little jerky motions. He stared into the car—full of leering, swaying sports and drummers. Fat, ringed fingers squeezing the knees of women with fixed and spectral faces

They reached Park Row, and the man in the sky-blue suit jumped off, Joseph doggedly following right behind. They hurried past the towering brick piles of the newspaper offices, the air thick with ink, windows blazing with light. The underground presses shaking the sidewalk beneath their feet; newsies and printer's devils sleeping curled up, oblivious, on the grates.

They walked around a corner, then down a little alley off Ann Street, where the man pushed him through a dilapidated double door with the name DOCTOR'S etched above it. Joseph staggered across the threshold into a barroom darker than the street outside, and tripped over something. A leg.

It went spinning woodenly across the floor, sock and shoe still attached. A beggar jumped down from the bar and ran over nimbly to shake a fist at him.

"Watch dat leg! *Watch dat leg!*"

His guide shoved the beggar out of the way—and peering down through the grainy light of the bar Joseph could see that the floor was scattered with false legs and arms, crutches and slings, all closely watched by the fake cripples hunched around the room. They lay their good right arms on the bar like gross white worms; jabbing them back to life with needles, rubbing knee joints numb as real amputations after a long day bound up under their coats.

Above the bar he could make out a bit of crude, sanctimonious verse, carved onto a cruder plank, as much a threat as an entreaty:

HELP A POOR BLIND MAN AND DON'T TURN HIM AWAY
JUST GIVE HIM A DIME FOR YOU HE WILL PRAY
YOU MAY GET AFFLICTED THE SAME WAY SOME DAY
HELP A POOR BLIND MAN AND DON'T TURN HIM AWAY

His guide looked over significantly at the man behind the bar, and the man nodded back and pulled up a metal pail.

"What is it now?" he asked the bartender.

"Twen'y-six, Gyp," the bartender told him, very respectfully. "Right now, anyways."

"All right."

The barman passed the pail over to Gyp. One of the fake crip beggars trying to grab it when he did, and spilling a swath of beer he could lick up from the counter in exchange for his beating. The bartender pushed him back.

"Get off! That ain't the growler!"

The barman handed the bucket on over to Gyp, who immediately passed it over to Joseph.

"Here. Take this in back," he told him—pointing to the dim outline of a door on the other side of the room.

Joseph peered down into the bucket. There was no beer, but something that sloshed like water, and smelled sharp and medicinal.

"What's it about?" he asked.

"Do like I told ya! Give it to the corner of the man in the black trunks. You got that?"

"The black trunks."

"That's what I said. *Now!*"

Gyp gave him a rough push toward the door, and Joseph stepped into an unlit hallway, painted black. It was darker even than the hold of the boat he had come over on, darker than anything he could have imagined and then he was afraid, but he groped his way down it, and finally through a door at the far end.

He came out at the top of a short stairs, where he looked down on a silent mob of men, writhing together like snakes. In the middle of the room was a ring laid out with sagging hemp ropes under a single, swaying lantern. Inside it the boxers wrestled and flailed away, one in red trunks, one in black, bodies sheathed in sweat and leaning into each other for support.

There was only the dimmest murmur from the men crowded in around them. They swayed and gestured, pumping their own fists furiously with each punch—gamblers and beggars, newspapermen and slummers in their evening clothes, all of them almost completely silent lest some chance honest cop hear the noise and break it up. An elegant gentleman in his shirtsleeves sat sketching the scene, sitting up in a high chair—the whole room so strangely quiet Joseph could hear the sound of his pencils against the pad.

"That's it!"

A man in a vest in a neutral corner stepped forward, reading his pocket watch while a boy with him banged a padded spoon against the bottom of a frying pan. The referee moved between the fighters, and then the crowd broke apart, too, into little congregations, slapping down more money with the bookies.

Joseph came down the stairs and made his way through the crowd, unheeded. Only a weighty, dignified-looking man in the black-trunked boxer's corner seemed to notice him at all, his eyes trained on Joseph as if he had been waiting for him the whole night.

Up close he could see the small wet smears of blood on the cornerman's suit, as he kept working on his fighter. Massaging his arms and legs and sponging water over his head with the steady, continuous motions of a cat cleaning itself. Joseph put the bucket down—and the cornerman grabbed him by his shirt and pulled him up close.

"*Tell* him," he whispered fiercely. "Tell him next time he waits this long, he won't have anyt'ing left to fix."

He let go of his shirt and Joseph started to walk away, but the man grabbed him again, by his arm, his grip strong as iron.

"Not *yet*," he hissed.

He stayed, unsure of what he was waiting for, while the cornerman kept watering down his fighter. He covered him over and over again with the sponge from his own pail of water—identical to the one Joseph had lugged in. Dipping the big gray sponge into the water, then over the fighter's face, and back down in the water. Then, on his next pass, he dipped the sponge into the pail Joseph had brought—almost too fast for the eye to follow—and passed it this time not over his fighter's face or chest, but the front of his gloves.

Then the sponge was back in his bucket, the cornerman tipping the whole pail over with his foot. For that instant it was exposed in the low, lurching light, and Joseph saw what he had brought: a green, brackish, evil-looking liquid. Then it was lost in the sawdust-matted floor, already soaked with sweat and blood.

"Look whach yer doin', boy!" the cornerman snapped— a few eyes from the crowd already scrutinizing the spill suspiciously, more money silently changing hands.

Nothing went unobserved

"Now go get me some more water for the next round. Go—*now*. Up to the bar!"

He backed toward the stairs with the empty bucket, the silent crowd closing in around him. The boy banged the frying pan again, and the referee, a potbellied man in a bowler and a bow tie, stepped nimbly into the center of the ring and waved the fighters forward. Joseph turned and made for the stairs, looking back for a moment when he was at the top.

The two boxers staggered forward again, each man's face a mass of welts and cuts, the bleeding only barely contained. The man in the red trunks ducked in, jabbing. All the man in black could do was flick a long, ineffectual blow to his face as he was moving backward—but suddenly his opponent stopped, his hands up around his eyes, stock still in the middle

264

of the ring. The fighter in black moved in on him, looking suddenly renewed——

Joseph turned away and pushed through the door. In the blackness of the hall he heard the cheer go up that had been so long contained, savage and vicarious, a short, vicious bark of triumph.

He trotted back down the sightless hall, pushed open the door to the barroom and nodded to the handsome, deadly little man who stood by the bar, sipping a short beer. He held up the empty pail and Gyp nodded, listening to the distant cheer.

"All right," he said. "All right."

——and they were flying along the sidewalk again, around the corner back to Ann Street. Gyp shoved him into a cab, drew the shades after them, and said nothing all the way back to Monk's place——sitting knee-to-knee across from him, cold, intelligent eyes level with his own through the darkness.

Gangsters in bright checkered suits shuttled their women back and forth across the dance floor like streetcars. A small aggregation of musicians sawed away at their instruments up on the dilapidated stage——a piano, a harp, a bass fiddle.

Monk patrolled his realm benignly, with a smile and a glad hand for everyone. He tapped a huge club in one hand, a pair of brass knuckles prominent on the other.

"Drink up, drink up! Before de booze gets too old!"

Joseph sat up front, eagerly, shyly taking in everything around him. He had already been made one of the Eastmans by then, rechristened again as Kid Twist, after some long departed champion of the Dead Rabbits, or the Plug Uglies. Basking in the glow of a good cigar, a glass of whiskey infinitely smoother than anything he'd ever had at a block-and-fall joint.

On each table in the hall was bread and a stone: a thick red brick clapped between two pieces of moldering bread, so that the establishment could claim to be a restaurant, serving sandwiches—instead of the clip joint battening off the theft of whores and the blood of tourists that it was.

"You can't eat this!" a salesman, seated between two hookers at the next table, howled—and in his drunken despair bit down on it so hard that his molars cracked, and the blood ran out of his mouth.

"See? That ain't no goddamned sandwich!"

Monk was on him at once, signaling for Whitey and Spanish Louie. He lifted the taller drummer up by the collar with one hand, spinning him around toward the wall.

"All right, dat's it. You broke de rules of de house," Monk told him, pointing him toward the endless, nonsense list of regulations mounted there:

NO LOUD TALKING

NO PROFANITY

NO OBSCENITY OR INDECENT EXPRESSIONS

NO ONE DRUNKEN

NO ONE VIOLATING DECENCY
WILL BE PERMITTED TO REMAIN

NO MAN WILL SIT AND ALLOW A WOMAN TO STAND

ALL MEN MUST CALL FOR REFRESHMENTS
AS SOON AS THEY ARRIVE AND THE CALL MUST BE
REPEATED AFTER EACH DANCE

IF A MAN DOES NOT DANCE HE MUST LEAVE

"Which one? Which one did I break?" the bleeding salesman demanded.

"Oh, believe me, you broke 'em all. Da drunkenness an'

de profanity I could overlook, but you know, if a man don't dance, he *must* leave!"

Whitey and Spanish Louie rushed him on out through the throngs of dancers on the floor, the drummer still clutching his sample case to his chest—going slowly at first, then faster and faster, like the tiny Mack Sennett characters Kid watched racing through the nickelodeon at Union Square. They strolled back in presently, whistling and carrying all that remained of the drunken salesman—his suit, his bowler, his sample case, even his underwear, as if the rest of him had just evaporated into thin air.

"That was our play!" one of the trimmers who had been at the drummer's table protested, but Monk struck her suddenly with his bare fist—hard enough so that it raised an instant welt, closing one eye and sending the woman stumbling, crying from her seat, the other prostitute sitting stock still where she was.

"Don't worry, kid, I never hits da ladies wit' me club," he smiled reassuringly at Kid. "If dey gets out of line, I just gives 'em a little poke to raise a shanty on de glimmer. An' I always takes me knucks off first."

He turned back toward the stage—and a woman in a red velvet hussar's jacket and silken harem pants walked over to his table and slid right into Kid's lap.

"You got a girl, mister?" she asked, her voice low and tender, and all he could do was shake his head. She laughed at him, and he realized he must have looked terrified.

He had had girls before—young ignorant girls, barely teenagers, in the whorehouses on Elizabeth Street. Lonely Portagee girls from the factory he could barely speak a word to, in his single-room apartment. But she was different. She had beautiful grey eyes and smelled of lilacs, and she was so close to him—

She was also one of Gyp's girls, he knew, and he wondered dully if he were being set up for something. He looked across the room, to where Gyp sat apart, with the rest of his women, all of them dressed in black, like a covey of nuns. His cold, deadly eyes swept back and forth across the dance floor, but he was not looking at them, and right at that moment Kid didn't care what happened. All he wanted was for her to stay where she was on his lap, smelling like flowers, with her soft hand against his neck. She leaned down and wriggled her bottom against his cock, her laugh low and throaty.

"Don't worry, it's on the house," she assured him. "How 'bout gettin' us a bottle?"

"All right," he croaked, and hailed weakly for a waiter, who was on them instantly, setting up two glasses and a bottle of cheap champagne, the house specialty.

"Whatcher name?" she asked, looking down at him, stroking his hair back from his brow.

"Joseph."

"Joseph. That's a nice name. It's from the Bible. My name is Sarah," she told him. "That's from the Bible, too."

"Sarah," he repeated foolishly—while she expertly poured herself a glass of champagne with one hand, drank it off in one gulp, and poured another. He knew it was standard john's patter, but she was smiling at him, and she smelled so good, she felt so good against him—

A hatchet-faced waiter stood up on the stage, a towel slung ceremonially over one arm, and began to sing. He had a high, tinny voice, and he hurried through the song as if he were afraid he was going to miss a streetcar. But to Kid's surprise the dancers stopped and the whole room hushed while he sped through the maudlin ballad:

> The ballroom was filled with
> fashion's throng
> It shone with a thousand lights
> And there was a woman who
> passed along

The fairest of all the sights
A girl to her lover then softly sighed,
"There's riches at her command."
"But she married for wealth,
  not for love," he cried,
"Though she lives in a
  mansion grand."

Slowly he realized, to his amazement, that everyone in the great hall was beginning to cry: Dago Frank, and Louie the Lump, and Whitey, and Spanish Louie—even Monk, his great, ugly face twisting grotesquely as he mumbled the words to himself. The whore whose eye he had blackened was crying, too—and so were all the gents, and their goohs and mabs in the private boxes, and the gangsters out on the floor in their gaudy suits and their molls hiding their pistols for them in their high Mikado tuck-ups.

So was Gyp the Blood—still taking in everything with his cold gaze from across the floor, but a tear running down his cheek. So was Sarah, seated so confidently in Kid's lap, the tears streaming through her mascara and rouge, little sobs shaking her chest as she sang along:

She's only a bird in a gilded cage
A beautiful sight to see
You may think she's happy
  and free from care
She's not, though she seems to be
'Tis sad when you think of
  her wasted life
For youth cannot mate with age
And her beauty was sold
For an old man's gold

—the whole hall full of pimps and ponces, killers and thieves, pickpockets and knockout-drop artists sobbing openly now, as the waiter reached the final line of the chorus——

She's a bird in a gilded cage——

When it finally came to an end, after many more maudlin verses and encores, the hall was filled with the sound of sniffling and nose-blowing. The gangsters and their women trailed back to their seats; a string of whores dancing the cancan took the waiter's place on the stage.

"That was a sad song," Sarah said to him, very close, in a small voice. He noticed that nearly half the bottle of champagne was gone already. Her face was a clownish mask now, where the black streaks of mascara had run through her powder, but he was aroused by her sadness, her vulnerability, gripping his hand more tightly around her waist.

"I like it when you hold me," she whispered.

The can-can whores kicked up enthusiastically on the stage. They did not move even vaguely in time with each other, but they threw their skirts up higher and higher, whooping and laughing, the crowd starting to stamp along. Until, all at once, they threw the skirts right up over their heads and ripped down their tights in one motion: A whole line of their pale white legs, and hairy sexes, standing suddenly headless along the stage—before they sank into their splits, and the lights went out, and they scrambled giggling off the stage.

Afterwards there was more dancing, and the singing waiter, cranking out another tune that brought them all to tears again:

There a name that's never spoken
And a mother's heart half broken
There is just another missing from
the old home, that's all;
There is still a mem'ry living,
There's a father unforgiving,
And a picture that is turn'd
toward the wall——

——and there was more champagne, and whiskey, and half a dozen drunken brawls, Monk wading in each time to cheerfully club the troublemakers.

Sarah clung to him for a long time, her head resting on his chest, one small hand around his neck. Finally she stirred, her small, blurred face floating up in front of him.

"Do you want to come upstairs?"

"What?"

"Do you want to come upstairs?" she asked again, and slid down from his lap, reaching out a hand to help pull him up.

He stumbled toward the stairs to the private booths, leaning on her shoulder. Down on the floor, he was aware, there was some kind of new commotion going on. Gyp had a man over his lap for some reason, gripping him firmly by the neck and knees, while a small crowd had gathered, taking bets over something.

"Come on, that's not very nice," she told him, towing him away by his arm.

"What?" He moved groggily up the stairs.

"You don't wanna see that. Come on."

She ran, laughing, on up the stairs ahead of him, into a darkened hallway with little curtained boxes on either side, muffled cries and groans coming from behind the red velvet curtains.

"Come find me!"

• • •

He lay on his back, on an enormous, zebra-striped pillow, the private box revolving around him. It was a cheap Bowery dream of a bagnio: a square little room, painted the color of blood. A table with something on it that looked like a samovar with a hose. A print of a naked young woman reclining on a bed, with a ribbon around her neck and a black lady's maid behind her——

She slunk in through the curtains, doing a little dance for him along the far wall. Her face was somehow washed clean now, and surprisingly young and vulnerable. She shimmied out of her silk harem pants, unclasped the red velvet hussar's jacket so that it revealed the plump, white sides of her breasts, just shy of her nipples. He dived for her, but she pulled effortlessly away from him, laughing again—then began to slowly swivel down over him, her hips swaying, pushing him back into the pillow.

"Say you love me," she laughed. "Do you? Do you love me?"

He looked up at her, pale white body glowing in the gas light. Her face smiling but serious, as if she really wanted him to say it, and this was more than just some whore's talk. Outside, he could hear the piano breaking into another maudlin melody, the waiter bawling through another tune like a runaway freight wagon:

> She is more to be pitied
> than censured
> She is more to be
> helped than despised
> She is only a lassie
> who ventured
> On life's stormy path
> ill-advised——

"I do. I do love you," he told her, as seriously as he could manage in his drunkenness because, of course, at this point he would say anything at all to be with her.

"Yes, I love you."

—and she laughed as if it had all been a joke, which he knew it hadn't, and pulled him to her on the bagnio cushions where they made love, and he sunk peaceably down to unconsciousness, wondering dully what he had done.

Yet when he awoke, with a splitting head, she was gone. There was no trace of her at all, even though most of his money was still intact—just enough deducted for the going rate—and he didn't see her again for months, not until late that September when Big Tim Sullivan took him and Monk and some of the other Eastmans up to Washington Heights to watch the Highlanders and the Boston Pilgrims play for the pennant.

It was the last game of the year, and across the Hudson the Palisades were ablaze in reds and yellows. In the stands everyone was talking about whether they would get to play the great Christy Mathewson in the Series, and how Big Tim had one of the Boston infielders in his pocket.

Sullivan had some action going on the game with Bill Devery, one of the gamblers and pols who owned the Highlanders and who made his grand entrance into the park in a touring car, with a brass band striking up his campaign song: *Oh, I'm for Mr. Devery/Ev-ery, ev-ery time!* Devery had paid off his own first baseman, though—an ugly character with a pockmarked face—who would race in to snatch up some squib or bunt before unhurriedly straightening up and hurling the ball off into right field.

Kid sat in the stands, drinking beer and munching red-hots and watching it all unfold, enjoying the quick, serious action, though he didn't understand any of it. Sarah arrived in the third inning with Gyp—wearing the same red velvet hussar's jacket, a little the worse for wear by now. He turned around and tried to catch her eye, and hoisted his beer to her, but she didn't seem to see him. He noticed now that everyone called her Sadie and on a nod from Gyp she went off, arm-in-arm, with one after another of the pols and gamblers hovering obsequiously around Big Tim. He kept looking out for her, but just as soon as she had returned, she was off with another of Big Tim's pals, then another one after that.

The game stayed even, in an endless series of nullifying corruptions, until the Highlanders' pitcher——a relentlessly lachrymose character everyone called Happy Jack—— whipped a truly accidental wild pitch past his catcher in the last inning, and Big Tim roared with laughter at his lost bet:

"Well, well!" He pounded Mr. Devery on the back. "We could just've well have let them play it for real!"

Kid didn't care. Late in the day, as the shadows began to lengthen over the park, he had gone down onto the field. The crowd had long overflowed the grandstand, and men stood and sat behind a flimsy rope in the outfield, watching Happy Jack put down the side, another hulking, sardonic character doing the same for the Pilgrims——the ball getting smaller, and grayer, and more invisible with each inning, until it seemed like they were playing a pantomime game.

Kid sat under the rope, with his knees tucked up, listening to the fans agonizing over each play, and bantering back and forth with the Highlanders' fine little center fielder——a man who looked almost small enough to be a midget but who seemed able to run down anything hit beyond the infield. From where Kid was sitting, he could see everything: the whole grandstand, and the brilliant, fiery Palisades, and the pols and gamblers coming back down to Big Tim's box every half-inning or so, joking and clapping each other's backs like the players coming back from the plate——Sadie following behind, pinning her hair up under her hat again.

He sat watching the shadows lengthen over the infield, over the plywood outfield fences plastered with advertisements for tooth powder and bunion ointment. Watching the stately, mysterious procession of the fixed game: the players running off the field in their baggy, gray wool uniforms, spitting and tugging at their caps, and flipping their gloves out by their positions as they went down into the dugout. Watching the whole, lovely, inscrutable ritual until he was sure that he loved it, that he loved it all even if he couldn't understand it, that he loved baseball.

TRICK THE DWARF

Our city went up on a back lot of Dreamland, a treeless, rubbled flat, where the flotsam of the world floated through. It was there that Brinckerhoff had housed his exotic tribes— his Pygmies, and his Esquimaus, his Boers and his Bantocs, and his Dog-eating Igorrotes—all the funny little peoples, with colorful costumes and odd facial hair, who the world had passed by.

Once upon a time there had even been a fairy tale Dutch cottage. There, in the old days, you could find General Piet Cronje sitting out on his porch in the evening, smoking his pipe and stroking his long white muttonchops, contemplating the bygone glories of the veldt, or the day's receipts.

Each afternoon at precisely three-fifteen, Oom Piet rode out straight and true as an acacia tree to surrender his sword to the British again. Brinckerhoff gave out that this was the exact time the Boer War had ended——though in fact it was merely post time over at Big Tim Sullivan's racetrack over at Brighton Beach, and Big Tim didn't care to have any of the fake guns spook his prize horseflesh.

Yet the silence when the old Boer rode out each afternoon was so sudden and startling, he played his role with such immense and impregnable gravity, that his audience was truly awed. A hush fell over the whole grandstand, the only sounds the muted cries from the roller coasters over by the sea and the pounding of the horses' hooves from the track—like some distant echo of the real war, still galloping over the grassy hills of South Africa.

It didn't draw, though, even with real veterans from both sides, and cannons and enormous painted canvases and an ingenious, glistening tin waterfall. Maybe it was the participants—after all, between the Boers and the British, how much of a rooting interest could you take?—but in any case the veterans began to drift off to Central America to find work as mercenaries, until there weren't enough left to contest the issue.

For awhile they tried pitting the remaining white men against an imported tribe of Bantus—black against white always being a surefire draw at the box office. They figured they wouldn't have to pay the Bantus *anything,* just drive a mangy Jersey cow or two into their kraal for them to slaughter and eat right there—an added attraction that drew more paying spectators than the battle itself.

Yet the Bantus surprised them and went on strike; as the *World*'s editorials tsked, it seemed they had been corrupted by the modern world after all. One afternoon, instead of falling in murderous ambush upon the Brits and Boers from behind the potted palm trees Brinckerhoff had dragged in from every ten-cent restaurant in Manhattan, they simply marched out and, with tremendous dignity, laid down their stage spears and sat on the ground.

Naturally, this being America, they were treated like any other strikers. A load of toughs was driven in one night to break their heads and smash up their sham palm huts. Even General Cronje and his mercenaries agreed that this was the only way to deal with the black bastards. But a few nights later, after the parks had shut down, they shucked off their spectacular, sky-blue headdresses, and slipped the plaster chicken bones from their noses, and snuck silently off into

277

the greater city, disguised in the uniforms of pantomime policemen they had found in a storage locker. Of course, no one noticed them—a long line of barefoot black policemen, male and female, without a word of English between them, creeping through the streets of New York together in a long line. They had gone for good, disappeared into the impenetrable vastnesses of San Juan Hill, or Harlem, irrevocably Americanized.

By the time we got there they were long gone—every last remnant of their existence bulldozed to make way for The Little City—their *kraals,* and their grass huts, and even Oom Piet's nostalgic little cottage, all wiped away. Brinckerhoff laid out the plan of the town over their bones, plotting the broad avenues and squares himself with the surveyors. At night he worked ceaselessly in his tower, designing every house, every public building, every stick of furniture.

"Everything has to fit," he commanded. "No slums, no tenements, no delinquency. It must be a model of city planning!"

They went up with breathtaking speed: no flowering Aztec city, but a modern, progressive village behind a gingerbread facade, planned after Nuremberg—for in those days anything clean and orderly had to be modeled after the Germans. There was a lovely little public square, and a clock tower, and livery stables, and even an exquisite miniature railway to draw passengers around and around our town. There was a powerhouse, and a gas works, and a fire station with a real working fire wagon, drawn by a team of Shetland ponies.

It seemed impossible. I had instigated the whole thing, I know. I had set the wheels spinning in Brinckerhoff's head out of my desperation, but nonetheless it was incredible to see it actually taking shape. It emerged like a half-remembered dream the next day—impossible, fantastic, but somehow familiar.

My queen took it all in her royal stride. She liked to saunter out each afternoon and inspect the construction—obviously crazy as a loon, with her royal purple gowns and fake ermine furs flowing behind her. The workers would patronize her, sweeping their hats off in low bows when she approached, barely hiding their grins. They answered whatever lordly question she asked them with elaborate courtesy—"Oh, *yes*, Your Majesty!" "*Certainly*, Your Majesty!" "However you desire it, Your Majesty!" At Coney Island, every day was All Fool's Day, and they were used to mock royalty: African kings, Gypsy princesses, roller coaster attendants dressed up like Teddy Roosevelt.

I scowled back at their sniggering, their insolent, smirking faces. She simply swept on, imperious and impervious, through her incredible new domain.

Which of us was more crazy?

"It's built to last," Brinckerhoff confided, in his quiet, confident way. "Inhabitable all year round. When all the rest of Dreamland—when Luna Park, and Steeplechase, and all the rest of Coney is gone—*this* will still be here."

It *was* perfect, a miniature superior to the original—to the squalid, sprawling behemoth that lay just west of Coney. And with every day Brinckerhoff invented something to make it even more perfect, more complete: a police station, complete with jail cells, and fingerprint pads, and a tiny, windowless third-degree room. A town hall, and a church, and library, with miniature special editions that fit smoothly, easily in our hands. All of it so ingenious, so meticulous and perfect and unique, until only one, final addition remained.

"Don't worry, I haven't forgotten your contribution," Brinckerhoff confided. "You will be the mayor, and live in the palace with your queen."

For that's what we were to be, strange combination: mayor and queen of The Little City. And there was a palace: not so grand as what I had promised her—for when has man not disappointed woman?—but still by far the biggest building in the whole miniature town, three reduced stories high, with red gables and turrets, and a splendid little garden.

Inside was an exquisite little jewel box, just for us. There was a working fireplace, and a library, and a billiards room; the walls hung with old swords and muskets and trophies and even portraits of fabulous, important-looking ancestors. All of it still *reduced;* even the stuffed rhinoceros head, and the moose, and the elephant-foot umbrella stand by the front door—one final, none-too-subtle joke from Matty Brinckerhoff.

"Come, come now," he chided. "You must have the whole world, cut down to size. What is an elephant, compared to a dream?"

He couldn't fool me. The miniature elephant's foot clinched it. The palace, the town, even my poor, mad consort—all this was one more terrific joke. Mockery more terrible than any snickering workman's—mockery worse than anything my father had endured, in his academic gown.

And yet I was seduced. I was seduced the way men usually are seduced, which is not by love, or lovely flesh—but by leather upholstered chairs, and fine thick carpets. By wainscoting, and oak panels, and a liquor cabinet full of the best Madeira. By substantial curtains, and real silver, and a quiet, soothing place to think and rest, and cut the pages of my books.

And for her—for my queen—there was a dressing room, and a bath tiled with leaping, Minosian dolphins. A bedroom that was an exact replica of the old queen's—the real queen, the only real queen there ever would be, ever again, Vicky herself—drawn from a Sunday rotogravure. Perfect right down to the patterns on the wallpaper and the hairbrushes on the dressing table. Save that cut into all of it—into the corners of the mantelpieces, and the frame of the dressing mirror and the bedposts, and the carpets—was an imperial "CR." *Carlotta Regina.*

I saw her then. I saw her go up the stairs the first day we were in the finished palace, while I walked around gaping at the fixings. I saw her walk into what must have been far and away the most luxurious room she had ever seen, and sit herself at the dressing table without a second glance—as if she had been doing it all her life. And if that wasn't the true embodiment of royalty, then I don't know what is.

It was all ready before the season was even half over—all the fine, gingerbread buildings, and the broad, tree-lined streets. Only one thing was missing: the last, living props.

How do you advertise for a freak show? We needed so many, all at once, not just the usual trickle of the outcast and the disinherited. I suggested something in the Help Wanted, a call for your wretched refuse, perhaps, yearning to be tall. Brinckerhoff only smiled his sated, crocodile grin.

"Oh, they'll come, sure enough," he said. "They'll find out, believe me, and when they do we'll have to beat 'em off with sticks."

He was right, as always. As soon as word got around they poured in. Dwarves and midgets. Hunchbacks and freaks, and acrobats and clowns, and jockeys disgraced for doping horses—and children. Real children pulling my disguise in reverse, pasting on false whiskers and trying to lower their voices—posing as little people just in the prospect of steady meals and a warm place to sleep.

My people swarmed in from around the country, and even the Continent, from vaudeville houses, and ten-twenty-thirties, and circuses and bawdy houses and Son-of-Ham shows. They came from the medical schools, where they were trotted out every hour on the hour, as examples of perverted physiology. They came from the attics in their isolated upstate homes, where they'd been stored since the day their parents first understood they were more than just short for their age. They came from working their pickpocket scams or crawling in among the gear wheels of gigantic machinery or serving some particularly delicate inclination in the most exclusive of brothels—in short, from anyplace where a fine hand was needed.

There were thousands of them. They came in by the trainloads, piling off at the New York & Sea Beach terminal. Blinking in the harsh Coney sunlight, sniffing the salt air, wondering if they could make it in the big-little town. They came in all shapes and sizes: there were the big heads and the Pekinese faces, the Chinless Wonders and the Ape Men and the cripples, the almond heads and the pinheads and the mongoloids. And those few, perfectly proportioned midgets, like my Carlotta, who merely had the misfortune to be short—if misfortune is what you could call such beauty in exquisite miniature.

We winnowed them down to four hundred, sorting them day after day through the endless, winding lines. Brinckerhoff had a doctor and a professor of anatomy on hand, to prod and poke at them. Their disqualifications were chalked on the back of their coats: "H" for a hunchback, "F" for freakishness, "T" for talentless, "U" for excessive moles, or hair, or simply overwhelming, repulsive ugliness. The losers were trucked back to the station without so much as a farewell handshake or the train fare—to discover their defects only later, when they happened to take their coats off.

The four hundred chosen ones stood screaming before our palace. The good citizens of our model town—drinking and brawling, frolicking and fondling each other in the town square, where they'd been ordered to assemble. Slobbering obscene ditties up at our palace—

"God save the runt! God save the cunt!"

—giddy with relief, I knew, at having survived another test of their humanity. Goaded by the very idea of a queen, a superior being who was still *one of us*. Taking full advantage of that fool's license which is all we are ever granted.

"Don't go out there," I warned her. "Leave it to tomorrow, at least, when they've sobered up!"

"But We are their queen," she said, beaming as serenely, radiantly as any real monarch, so that even I was overawed. I still thought it was a mistake. Just as she was about to step out onto the balcony a brown blob of some unknown pedigree came flying up from the street, plopping on the balcony like a fish out of water.

"God save the runt——"

She didn't even seem to notice it. She walked right on out—the whole insolent mob of them falling quiet the moment she appeared.

"My good people," she said. "My *good people*——"

—though it wasn't so much what she said, some inane speech, no more or less mad than the palaver of all royals everywhere in the real, big world. It didn't matter what she said, even mad as she obviously was. Standing there on the balcony of our palace in her widow's mantilla, head straight and regal as any European monarch's, and much more beautiful, she had made us a *people* with their own, magnificent queen. Simply by believing in it, all the way, by being the regal creature she was.

"My good people," she said——

—and they were good. And when she finished they burst spontaneously into applause. And when she made that peculiar, chopping, guillotinelike motion that passed for the sign of the cross, they actually knelt, and bowed their heads to receive her blessing.

Then they wandered off to find their wonderful new homes. To live, for once, like real people, in a real place—even if it was wrapped up in a greater flight of fancy. They could ignore all that, for the sake of happiness.

Except for the Big Tent.

The tent was what gave the lie to it all. It was set up just off the main square, painted with clowns, and lions and tigers snarling in their cages. It was here that we all ended up. For in The Little City, everyone—the police and the firemen, the priest and the mayor and the Queen herself—*everyone* worked the Big Tent.

They took a spin or two around town in our miniature train, then they filed inside—all the usual drummers, and the cigar rollers, and the draymen. The hair weighers and the cloth cutters and the soda bottlers, plopping down their nickels to watch us perform.

There were the bona fide circus acts, of course, the jugglers and the clowns and the tiny women who twirled by their teeth from a rope. Real animal trainers who faced down cats able to devour them in a single gulp.

But mostly what they saw was the rest of us—whose everyday existence had become another act, no matter what we did or how well we did it. Every matinee and evening, the alarums would ring out, and The Little City Fire Department would come galloping to the rescue: bells clanging, men clutching stoutly to the back of their cart—a fire department that never answered anything but false alarms. Every day, some midget would swipe a purse from a

284

plant in the crowd—and police whistles would shriek, and The Little City mounted police would come riding in on their ponies to clap the malefactor off to jail.

In The Little City, we could hear God hiccough—and laugh and jeer and spit, every day. A whole gallery full of gods, who changed with each performance.

After each show the spectators were free to wander through our town and peer into our windows. Pushing their way through our doors, stumbling through our walls—leering at every perfect, miniaturized inch, so much superior to anything *they* lived in. We would parade down Main Street, leading them back to the big tent, where the whole town assembled to sing a maudlin farewell song—voices pitched as high as we could make them, until a baritone stepped forward at the very end, dipped to one knee, and sang the chorus again in a voice as deep as the bottom of the sea. It never failed to get a big laugh.

My Carlotta presided over all this with her usual mad aplomb. She made a short welcoming speech at the beginning and the end of every show, never varying so much as a word of it. During the grand tour she would receive guests at tea in our living room, glowering impressively at them if they sat before she did, favoring them with a smile or two if they were particularly obsequious. They ate it up, shaking with laughter behind their hands. She couldn't seem to get enough of it.

I thought she didn't understand: no matter how good our manners, no matter how fine our conversation or how accomplished we were, no matter how much we tried to be like *them*—it didn't matter. It only amused them that we could do such things, like a horse that does arithmetic or a bird that tells your fortune. But she was not bothered by it.

"Royalty does not lie in what other people think," was all she would say. "Otherwise, it could never exist. The point is that they come to see Us. They acknowledge We are queen."

I hated it. Can you comprehend what it was like—living in a world where parades were a numbing, daily grind? Where everything you do, no matter how well and how honestly, is the same endless, running joke?

All those tea parties, day after day, with a bunch of snickering shopgirls, and brick masons. Watching them squeeze themselves down onto our miniature chairs and couches, gaping at the size of our tea service. Giggling as they broke the handles of the perfect, tiny china cups off on their pinky fingers. Asking me, again and again, without fail, if I had shot a *baby* elephant to make our umbrella stand—

Not that there was anything else for me to do: I had no real duties; The Little City ran itself. The rest of my subjects didn't mind the intrusions, it sure beat how they had lived before. They even began to take their roles seriously—the firemen working real shifts, maintaining their equipment, their fine garden hoses and three-foot ladders and adorable ponies. The cops walking regular beats, even at night, after the tourists had all gone home. The newsies hawking their papers, despite the fact that there was no news at all in The Little City.

Soon, there were even marriages. They had to be performed in public, by our own Reverend Cherubim, at the delighted Brinckerhoff's insistence. Nobody on the circuit had ever cared whether we were married or not. We were assumed to be like the African slaves, living in a state of nature. But now, matrimonial bliss was the order of the day. Matty Brink even reminded me of our own situation.

"She thinks she's still married to the Emperor Maximilian," I told him.

"So tell her it's a morganatic marriage," he shrugged. "After all, isn't The Little City worth a mass?"

She took to the idea like a trouper, of course. She was a great actress, and there are no actors so mad they can't recognize a great part. In the end we were dragged out beneath the big tent like all the rest, shriven and wed before an overflow Sunday matinee crowd.

Brinckerhoff spared no expense. It was held on the all-important opening weekend of the season. The tent was covered with boughs of lilac and myrtle—my queen in a pure white dress of lace and bows, myself in the general's uniform of an operatic country, sky blue and canary yellow. There were twenty-four bridesmaids to carry her endless white train, a twenty-four-man honor guard to walk beside them up the aisle, toy sabres rattling at their hips.

My poor subjects: they stood around looking as dazed and thrilled as if they were at the coronation of the Czar. The firemen and the police force standing at attention in full uniform, buttons and shoes shining. The ladies-in-waiting hurling white rose petals before us.

We strode majestically up the red-carpeted aisle to Mendelssohn's march, stride by tiny stride—the gallery gods leering and calling out all sorts of predictably lascivious remarks. Up at the altar waited the Reverend Cherubim, standing on a stack of Bibles—a chubby little fool, with rosy cheeks and twinkling eyes, who had played this part for years. He wandered through a leering, pun-strewn ceremony before pronouncing us "half-man and *all* wife"—with a great, burlesque wink at the audience.

This drew a huge laugh, as did each of the wedding presents, also opened before the crowd: a gargantuan rolling pin, right out of Maggie and Jiggs, and nearly as tall as Carlotta herself. A pint-sized bed that was really a trampoline. A tiny touring car, out of which climbed dwarf after dwarf after dwarf.

The crowd loved them all, roaring as each one was unwrapped. But the greatest joke of all was us.

I stood at the altar, dressed in my general's uniform, and lifted the veil of my beautiful beloved. Her eyes closed as she awaited my kiss, while thousands of guests looked on breathlessly—everyone of them ready to roar with derisive laughter.

Can you imagine it? Your silliest, grandest, childhood daydreams—anyone's grandest dreams—transformed into a great public joke. In that moment, while my mad bride stood waiting blindly to receive my kiss, I realized I had been wrong to despise my father. That there was no way, no way after all, to outstrip their mockery.

The grand reception that followed was filled with celebrities, starting with everyone who walked in off the midway and plunked down their two bits. The proprietor, Big Tim Sullivan, was there, broad, fixer's face betraying nothing, congratulating us as warmly and sincerely as if we had been any other two, normal citizens. Even Mayor McClellan came, well-welling and smirking down at us, cruel, aristocratic smile running across his lips, fingering my golden, tinsel epaulettes—

—"If my father had had you on his staff, perhaps he would have swept the field at Antietam!"—

"Yes, then all he would have needed was a spine," I told him, but he was already moving on down the receiving line, my small voice lost among the bigger people. A hand clamped down on my shoulder.

"Very droll, I am sure."

Brinckerhoff swayed sardonically above me, reeking of gin. He staggered, bumping a miniature plaster head of Caligula off a coffee table, to smash on the Persian carpet. He steadied himself on my shoulder, and patted me knowingly:

"You are such a funny fellow. Well, now you can get busy on the issue," he slurred.

"Whatta you mean?"

"Oh, you were right," he nodded. "She's a real queen. Now it's time for you to be fruitful and multiply—or can't you manage that?"

I flung his hand off my shoulder, left him stumbling over his damned elephant foot—but I suppose I should have anticipated it: the royal wedding would draw only one day's play, two at the most, in the dailies. There were too many other rough miracles in this town.

So there would be children, skipping and singing on the sidewalks of The Little City—if not our royal progeny, then someone else's. But what would happen if they turned out to be Big? Would they be banished from our magic kingdom, along with their dwarf parents? Or would they become one more addition to the act—the tiny parents spanking the recalcitrant schoolboy who towered over them? The schoolboy turning around and spanking the parents? Oh, the possibilities were limitless!

And what would happen when there were too many children, big or small? For our model city was a contained place, circumscribed by its toy railway. There was no room to expand, and the excess would have to be pushed out into the carny streets, and the unplanned world, and how would such decisions be made?

None of my constituents seemed to care. Theirs had always been a hand-to-mouth existence; they weren't about to start worrying now. They went on personalizing their model homes, adding on rooms, planting trees and flowers and bushes, acting like regular people. Looking forward to the winter, when the winds would rake the beach, and the breakers would roll huge and gray out beyond the piers.

When all the visitors would leave, and the parks would shut down, and it would be just us, alone in our own world at the spit end of a continent.

I couldn't stand it. That was when I started sneaking back up to the watery world of the Bowery again, after hours. Not that anyone would miss me. Carlotta was the attraction; out-and-out madness always sells better than the more subtle kind. Brinckerhoff kept harping on my failure to come up with some kind of act to match her: another tiny general's uniform, perhaps, or maybe a stovepipe hat so I could be a pint-sized Abe Lincoln.

"If you're not goin' to be a proper consort, why then you'd better consort," he warned again.

But I was tired of Carlotta's act myself. There is no aphrodisiac like madness, but it wears off quickly. Not that she ever reneged on our unspoken bargain: I had complete access to all that perfectly proportioned beauty. Soon, though, it had no more appeal to me than the matching oak pistols or the miniature Velázquez copy above our fireplace.

She could feel her allure diminishing: like all great actors, she was sensitive to the slightest fluctuation in how she was adored.

"Do you want Us to dance for you?" she volunteered one night, surprising me, dragging her costume, wooden knee clogs and all, into the study where I was sipping brandy in my smoking jacket and pyjamas, cutting my way through Roosevelt's latest tome about slaughtering gazelles on the Serengeti.

"We have not danced for you for a long time," she said, and I was so touched by her offer that I let her.

It was the same, strangely mesmerizing dance she had performed for the Baxter Street Dudes that night in the Grand Duke's Theatre. The magical transformation from mechanical doll to living beauty, back to doll again, performed as perfectly as ever, without music, and an audience of one. So moving that when she had finished, falling woodenly to her knees, I leapt out of my chair and went to her, lifting her up by her hand.

"Doesn't it . . . don't you feel . . . it *humbles* you?" I asked her, mortified now that she would do such a thing for me.

"Nothing humbles a queen," she informed me. "Haven't you learned that by now?"

I picked her up, fragile china package that she was, and carried her right back to her imperial bed in her royal bedroom, and ravished her thoroughly. But it was never the same: the queen in exile, the queen in chains, dancing for a gang of orphaned toughs was one thing. The queen at her duties, presiding over our sequestered, sideshow world was another, and I no longer wanted any part of it.

I returned to my Bowery dives, hunting for—what? Another such fantasy? It was foolish, I knew: a mindless debauch of drinking and voyeurism. I didn't care. I went too far, was far too careless—which was how I came to be dangled on that monster's knee at the dog pit, my back nearly cracked open like a lobster's.

The thing was, I still preferred the old dream, the old pretense, to this new, fantastic existence: the one where I pretended to be a boy. Nobody else wanted to see that act. I could walk, invisible, through the nighttime streets, and I would be the only witness to my depravation. That was how it had to be.

I had decided: There would be no issue. No fruitful marriage, no happy, make-believe existence in our gingerbread city. The joke had gone on long enough, and it was an iron law of vaudeville—every gag must have its end.

26

BIG TIM

He walked uptown as the long, summer dusk painted the evening sky, strolling toward his saloon across from the police headquarters. Soon he was away from the official buildings, and the newspapers, and walking among the tenements.

He was in a Bohemian neighborhood, he knew, from all the ash barrels stuffed with stripped tobacco leaves. The Bohemians rolled cigars piecework; they hung the tobacco to dry in long strips hung all over their tiny rooms, even blocking up the windows. He reminded himself to learn a little bit of their gab, start getting acquainted. Downtown was filling up with them now—along with the Italians, and the Poles, and even the heathen Chinee.

What a place to be a politician, where the leaders stay the same but the people always change

Big Tim's specialty had always been Jews, which was how he had made his way in Tammany. He liked them as a people; they liked to read a book, and keep themselves clean, and they stayed away from the drink.

He cultivated their gang leaders and peanut politicians. *My Jewboys*, he called them affectionately. They were an infinite source of help at the polls, though you had to watch them all the time. They were idealists at heart—born splitters, and purblind, pigheadedly stubborn when they got a wind up. Their own book put it best, in Exodus, if he recalled correctly:

"*And the Lord said unto Moses, 'I have seen thy people, and behold, they are a stiff-necked people . . .'*"

Like Beansy. His wide, trusting face swam up before Big Tim again, unbidden. Like a child, he'd always been—like a wayward, simpleton son.

By God, he didn't like this business. His job was to help such people. He was used to making the hard deals, to doing what had to be done—but this, *Jay-sus*—

When he reached the saloon, his eyes watered in the weak yellow light, and the cigar smoke, and the ready love that it offered.

"Hey, Big Tim, Big Tim!"

They all hailed him when he came through the door: Jake the night bartender, and the elbow lifters at the bar, and the cops from the police headquarters across the street, working over their free steaks and chops.

"Heard ya saw the mayor today, Tim——"

"Hey ya, Big Tim!"

Over in the corner, the piano player had launched into a sloppy, sentimental new number:

> Now is the hour
> When we must say goodbye
> Soon you'll be sailing far
> across the sea——

• • •

It was a standard pol's saloon, much like the one down by the Tombs: Starched white tablecloths, fresh from the Chinee laundry. Pickled eggs on the bar. The ubiquitous painting of that ass Custer—Irish, of course, somewhere on his mother's side—making his last stand against the savage Sioux. Many saloons, he knew—even good, loyal organization ones—were supplanting that barroom staple with monochromes of the Great Man's charge up San Juan Hill, but Big Tim felt it safer to stick with poor old Custer. Better another historic flop than a very lively success.

He could have thrown in all the fashionable trimmings, like Mr. Murphy's joint up in the Tenderloin: potted palms and pink lights, waiters in military uniforms, and a string orchestra on the balcony. A maudlin tenor in tails, and a waxed moustache. But he liked it better this way. It made his constituents feel more at home. Even now, he knew without looking that there was a small group of nervous men standing at the bar, shifting uneasily from one foot to another, fixed smiles on their faces. They were always there, every night, at all of his saloons. They were, he knew—from their faces, from their nervousness—men who had never asked him for anything in their lives before.

"Come, have a drink on me, my friend, and tell me how it is wit' you this day," he would call them over, one at a time.

It was the preeminent politician's trick, and the one he had taken the most care to learn: the art of making a favor to *them* seem like a favor to *him*.

Grudgingly, they would come over, and he would talk to them—no matter what their race—as if they were no more than old townsmen, reunited in the new world. He talked to them about their families, and their neighbors, and their work. He remarked upon the beauty of their children, and the modesty of their wives, and the rectitude of their forebears. And then—only *then*—did he extract what they wanted. So delicately, so painlessly, that it did not seem like they had asked for anything at all.

Once it was determined what they needed, the transaction could be completed effortlessly. A few dollars, a note with a name and an address on it——

How little they want from us——

A job with the street cleaners. Money to buy the kiddies shoes. Admittance for the wife to the consumptives' hospital on Blackwell Island. He provided it all, any request within in reason, executed with speed and grace. After all, he was a boss.

They were grateful enough. He knew, to his embarrassment, that there were tinted lithographs of another live politician going up on the walls of saloons and even private homes, all over the Fourth Ward: a man with a florid, Irish slab of a face.

And yet he wondered if——an hour or two later, well into his third beer, smiling gratefully at how here, that hadn't been so hard after all——the man did not feel the pickpocket's touch on his soul.

> While you're away
> O, then remember me
> When you return you'll find me
> waiting here——

"Give that racket a rest, why don'cha," he called over to the piano player, as good-naturedly as he could. "Play something from home."

Immediately, the piano player swung into an old tune from County Kerry, and Big Tim waded through his saloon, gladhanding his way to the back room where there was a poker game that had been going on continuously, night and day, for over five years.

"Boys——how are ya settin' tonight? Boys——"

All along the walls were murals of voluptuous blond

nudes, romping before some token classical ruins. They reclined under grapes, or fled laughing from red-eyed satyrs. Just below all their grand, pink pulchritude lay a sideboard groaning with turkeys, and hams, and carved roast beef. Waiters in white smocks padded diligently back and forth, keeping the beer and whiskey circulating. Half a dozen men clustered around the big table where the game went on; at least two or three times as many loitered around the room, making deals or looking for handouts, filling themselves from his table.

Here were all the full-time jobbers and the grafters, men with connections, or an angle. Most of them were pols, now that the legislature wasn't in session—Al and Bob and Jimmy, and the rest of the boys, down from Albany—but there were also firemen and police captains, contractors, and reporters and union delegates, even actors off the kerosene circuit.

"Big Tim!"

"Dry Dollar!"

"Boys."

He threw himself back in the great, padded chair that was always kept open for him, with a fresh seltzer water kept by one arm like Elijah's glass. He grabbed up a fistful of chips, threw them absently down on the table before him. When he wanted to, he could play cards with any man in the City, but that wasn't the purpose of this game. Here he was content to dribble away a few small pots, and attend to more important business.

"Say, do you remember that dinner Big Tim gave over at the Occidental, for Johnny Hitt, the elevator boy?"

They started to tell the old stories, the bald-faced flatteries as soon as he had sat down.

"God, that was a feast—"

"Now, boys, why not? He was a good man, was he not? Well-liked by all?"

He had sunk into the soothing bath of their chatter, the endless card game before him—when Cousin Florrie came up and whispered in his ear. Big Tim's poker face broke in his surprise.

"He's here? Now?" he whispered back.

Florrie nodded grimly.

"Jesus jumped-up Christ!"

He threw in his cards and stood up, his expression amiably blank again. No one really seemed to notice.

"Now boys, I can't hear no more a this or you'll be causin' me to blush——"

They all laughed, and went on telling stories about him as he left the table. They didn't need the real Tim Sullivan, he knew, to honor his generous shade. Florrie led him down a hallway to the back entrance, where the man was waiting— menacing, bloodhound's face jutting out from under one of Commissioner McAdoo's new gleaming white caps.

"Jaysus, Charlie. Why di'n'tcha wear yer sash from the Policemen's Benevolent Association while you was at it."

"I need to talk to you," Handsome Charlie Becker said, direct and to the point as ever.

"Uh-huh. And I guess no brass bands were available for hire. Come into me office, before every reporter in town gets here."

He ushered Becker into a windowless anteroom, only slightly bigger than a broom closet. There was nothing inside save an empty desk with a telephone on it, a couple of hard-backed chairs. When they were seated Becker looked directly at him, with his same unwavering, bloodhound stare.

"I want him dead," he said simply.

"Jesus, man! No wonder yer head of the Strong-Arm Squad. Could you maybe repeat that a little louder for the payin' customers?"

Becker just sat there staring at him. There was a general air of belligerence about the man. He had a sharp, sardonic mouth, a granite chin—and an incongruous, boyish dimple in his left cheek that was responsible for his nickname. He was a huge man, bigger even than Big Tim, a towering, broad-shouldered Hessian from some hick farm town upstate.

Big Tim could see at once why he was such a favorite target of the newspapers, and the Holies, in their latest crusade to root out corruption in the police force. He had great, hairy hands, and it was said he could kill a man with one punch. Not that he didn't seem to be trying. A few years before he had got into trouble for slugging a housewife who asked him the way to the subway, and then there was the teenager he had beaten up before a lobby full of theatergoers, and the suspicious shooting of an alleged burglar. Misunderstandings seemed to follow Charlie Becker around like a Pinkerton detective.

Once a goo-goo D.A. had been elected, and the Little Little Napoleon had appointed McAdoo commissioner, most of the force had got the message and soft-pedaled the boodle for the time being. Not Charlie Becker.

Instead of toeing the line, he had come up with a little game of his own. He had kept collecting his payoffs from the gambling houses scattered all over the new Tenderloin, up in Times Square. Only now, he took protection money *and* raided the houses as well.

Not badly, mind you—not in classic strong-arm style, breaking down doors, and busting up the furniture. Just a little—the way he had done with Herman's joint—so the gamblers would have to close down for a day or two, but could then open up again, more or less intact, and with their payoff money ready.

Jay-sus, but everybody had a racket goin' in this town

It was a cute game—too cute by half. The gamblers didn't

298

like being shut down, even for a day or two at a time, and especially when they were already shelling out for protection. It ate into profits, and it scared the respectable trade away. But Handsome Charlie didn't seem to care.

"I paid my dues," he insisted now, resting his fine white lieutenant's hat on one knee. "I been the bottom dog long enough, workin' my way up from roundsman. I done what everybody asked of me, and now I want what I got comin'."

"What you deserve."

"What I deserve," he nodded.

Handsome Charlie was not a man for irony. But what the hell was he doing here, done up in his Sunday best uniform and his shiny new white hat like a goddamned commodore?

"All right, Charlie," he sighed. "You got a case. Just whattaya want us to do with Herman?"

"I dunno," shrugged Handsome Charlie Becker. "Murder 'im."

"Ah. You said it."

"I don' care," the cop went on, oblivious. "Run him outta town, if you want. I don' care what ya do with the lyin' Jew bastard, just so long as you shut him up."

"All right, Charlie," Sullivan soothed him. "Whatever you want, Charlie."

Becker picked up his hat and stood to go.

"Tell 'em to hurry it up, too," he said, the belligerent policeman even here, in the back of Big Tim's own saloon. "That indictment's comin' down any day. Tell 'em to hurry or I'll do it myself."

"Oh, that you will, Charlie, that you will, I have no doubt of it," Sullivan told him, by now thoroughly sick of the man. "Now git yourself home—an' don't be leavin' by the front door, neither."

He waited while Charlie Becker put on his big lieutenant's cap and left, cocksure as ever—then still sat awhile in the tiny, windowless room, pondering the situation. He didn't like it, that was for sure. He didn't like it so much that he had already broached as discreetly as possible with Mr. Murphy the idea of ridding themselves of this troublesome cop:

"If, say, we was to excise the complainant, we would excise the complaint."

"It's a solution with the immense benefit of simplicity," Murphy had conceded in his blandest, country parsonage voice, putting down the teacup he held as delicately as an egg in two fingers.

"The trouble is, keeping it quiet."

"Oh, certainly, we would be very quiet."

"Somethin' always comes out. It always does, you know that as well as I do."

Mr. Murphy had brooded over his teacup.

"The, uh, *absence* of a police lieutenant could not be overlooked. Unless there were a *reason* for it."

"Such as? Hypothetically speakin'?"

"Well, it seems to me as if you have two problems on your hands." Mr. Murphy blinked, as if he were explaining transubstantiation to a particularly dim Sunday school student.

"One is Herman, raising such a ruckus in the papers, hurting business all around. The other is Lieutenant Becker, with his overzealousness. It seems to me that one problem could take care of the other."

His meaning began to come clear to Sullivan.

"That would take care of things, all right," he conceded. "But I don't know as how Charlie could ever be induced to perform such a rash act himself."

"He wouldn't have to be," Mr. Murphy blinked. "It just needs to get done—now that Herman has so helpfully fingered the lieutenant in the papers."

"I see—but wouldn't that give the Holies all kinds of fodder? Corruption permeating New York's finest, all that kind of thing?"

"Oh, I think it would make for a nice diversion. By the

300

time they're done running after their police lieutenant everyone will be thoroughly sick of Reform."

Mr. Murphy's political logic was unassailable, as always. If Beansy Rosenthal were to be knocked off now, the good government types would go for Lieutenant Charlie Becker hook, line, and sinker. Big Tim could sit back and let Becker take the splash—secure in the knowledge that Beansy had already got him off the hook with his newspaper statement.

It was brilliant—*but Jay-sus, what a thing it was!*

Knocking off two men—one of them a police lieutenant? Politics was a rough game, Big Tim had always known that. He had played it with Boss Croker himself, who had once shot a man dead at the polling booth. He kept, on salary, at least two dozen seasoned cutthroats to take care of various matters. But it was one thing to tolerate murder, another thing to plot it.

He thought of the big, blunt, ignorant cop, so oblivious to the grave he had dug for himself. And he thought of Herman's trusting face.

Whatever you *say, Big Tim*

He had already sent a reminder down to Gyp the Blood, through a fat, odious little cop named Buckley, that there was a chore waiting to get done. It was so tempting to just walk back into his poker room. To go back to his easy chair, and the overburdened sideboard, and his whiskey and cigars. To let that little monster do the job he had given him, and go back and sit around the fire, and the light, and listen to them tell all the old stories.

Instead, he stood up and followed Charlie Becker out into the dark. He couldn't just let it go at that. The whole key to the thing was Beansy: with him out of the way, everything else would be taken care of. He had to warn him, he decided—one more time. He owed him that much, at least, though he wasn't sure why. He limped blindly out into the dark alley, his groin beginning to ache again, trying to think where he might find that fool Herman this time of night.

27

By the middle of the morning there was a pile of shirtwaists rising inexorably from the bench next to her station. A cloud of lint rose too from the shop floor, and the gas jets had been lit so they could see the cloth before their faces. Esther thought of nothing but her *dybbuk* on the roller coaster, against the constant drone and whine of the machines.

The thread jammed, and the needle pulsed through her fingers as she held the fine cloth in line—tiny drops of blood trailing along the excellent cloth. She was not sure if it was because she was thinking of him, or because she was not fully back in the rhythm of her work yet, but at least dreaming of the boy helped to kill the time. Usually she looked forward only to her next little respite: her allotted bathroom break, a stolen cigarette, lunch. She refused to consider anything more, such as when the day would end, or the week, or the next season—or when everything might finish, once and for all.

But now—she had her *dybbuk* to think about. Not that it was really thinking, so much as mooning: *Him* on the Iron Pier with her. *Him*, on the Steeplechase, up on the roof. . . She should, she supposed, be considering how to ease him into marriage, or banish him from her thoughts altogether, but she didn't want to do either one. Mostly,

302

she just wanted to be with him all the time, to be around him.

How foolish it all was! How like her father—dreaming of the impossible. Wanting to live like nobody had ever lived before. There were real things to take care of, besides all this useless wanting. She had work, and her parents, and after she got off tonight she would go to collect dues for the union, and then meet Clara over at the Clinton Street Hall.

Was that all there was, though? Just one thing after another?

She dreamed of him kissing her on the Alpine Sleigh Ride until the floor at the Triangle revolved, and the needle bit into her finger again.

Just before noon, and the lunch whistle, there was an unscheduled interruption—a small disturbance that spread in ripples across the floor from the back of the shop, near the stairs. A long file of women, most of them very young, straggled into the room, holding their heavy black sewing machines in their arms.

"This way, this way!"

It was the daily visit of Wenke, the *shadchen*—the labor subcontractor, a bony, excitable man with pop eyes and waxy white hair. Nearly every day, during the peak of the season, he hauled a new string of girls into the factories. He would leave them standing behind the last, back bench, the heavy machines still in their arms, while he went up to Mr. Bernstein's office on ten to dicker over the rate. The other women refused to make room for them on the benches, spat through their fingers at the newcomers the way they did when they passed a church. Their very presence was a reminder to the regular operators of how precarious their existence was, and the women knew it, and hated them the more for it.

"Look at them, these *bummerkehs*. They will starve us yet!"

Most of the day girls were younger than the youngest operators in the shop—though Esther spotted a few older, gray-haired women among them, no doubt widows desperate to get back into the trade. The day girls were the poorest and the most desperate, the newest and the clumsiest of them all. They hired out from firm to firm at the height of the season, renting their machines from Wenke and handing over half of what they made to him. In return, he walked back and forth behind them on the shop floor, helping and chastising them, replacing needles and thread, straightening the lawn and yelling at them relentlessly.

"There! You call that workmanship—a *miesse meshina* to you!" he would point out, thrusting a finger at a missed stitch or a tiny tear.

"That will cost me—I will never hear the end from Bernstein about *that*!"

He would mark the girl's mistake down with a little pencil, in the tattered black notebook he carried in his vest pocket.

"That's a penny off for you, *metsieh* that you are!"

Esther had seen him go through a girl's whole pay that way—until after ten hours work and hundreds of perfectly good shirtwaists she had nothing to show for her stint, nothing at all, and was reduced to crying over her machine. Then Wenke the *shadchen* might hand her a nickel back:

"Here, here—at least so you don't starve on my head."

The contract girls were the *shadchen*'s responsibility—though the women supervisors walked constantly around them in their silent, rubber-heeled shoes, searching for any mistake that could be deducted from their pay. The foremen, Podhoretz and Kristol, would lay their hands heavily on the women's shoulders, kneading and pulling fiercely at them, pinching and prodding and taking liberties the regulars wouldn't let them get away with.

"You are starving the marrow from my head!" Wenke

came down from the office, screaming and gesturing at Bernstein, who walked imperturbably beside him. It was the same old story.

"No one can work at this rate. Better you should be *dead* than work for this!"

"You don't got to take it," Bernstein calmly pointed out.

For a moment, Wenke looked like he actually might entertain the offer, his eyes wilder than ever. Finally, he threw up his hands.

"All right. I don' know what game this is, but you want corpses on your head, so be it! Girls!"

The new girls were put immediately to work, at whatever empty spaces could be found, the other women moving as far away from them as possible. They worked with their heads down, not daring to so much as sneak a glance around themselves—though after a few minutes they had been all but forgotten.

At noon, when the whistle blew, the machines all shut down together, and there was a sudden, ringing hush throughout the big room. The women sat at their work places to eat, or on the windowsills, or the boxes of waists—anywhere they could get a seat. They sipped their tea out of saucers, ate chunks of thick black bread and little tins of sardines, talking eagerly, rapidly even as they chewed.

Esther eased her bum down gratifyingly on the biggest, softest bundle of longerine she could find, staring idly over at the *shadchen*'s girls where they half stood, half sat along the wall in the back like birds on a wire, nibbling at their own bits of bread or fish—their heads still down, not even talking much to each other.

It occurred to her that she should go over and chat with them, make them feel at least a little at home—but she knew her friends would not understand. The *shadchen*'s girls were driving down the rate, and if there was another strike they would be the first ones called as scabs. Their only hope for acceptance was to get a regular position somewhere, somehow—and that depended on replacing one of them.

When the Triangle had opened the papers had been full of what a bold new model of rationalized industry it was. They had raved about the smart new benches, the airy, well-lit work spaces—the new, shiny black electrical outlets hanging down from the ceiling like so many snakes. A whole shop, just devoted to making waists!

The waists—the shirtwaists—were the light, shapely blouses the Gibson girls wore: the wasp-waisted, sleek young society women—and the department store clerks and ladies' maids who tried to imitate them. They *all* wore them now, every woman on the street, every woman in the shop, save for the greenest greenies, just off the boat. The factory was supposed to put them out—more quickly, safely, efficiently, than ever before.

Yet once they had set to work it was much the same. They were packed in like herrings, and Mr. Bernstein and his supervisors drove them just as hard as any sweatshop. There were still layoffs in the slack seasons, and during the rush they simply hired the *shadchen*'s girls to keep down the rates. It was still work, much as it had ever been.

The whistle blew again, and Esther had to leave her throne of lawn. The *shadchen*'s girls trudged back to work with the rest of them.

They would not have another break until they got off, just at the end of the long, late-summer dusk. The shirts kept coming—the shop boys bringing up more and more heaps of lawn from the cutters on the eighth floor below, floppy, enigmatic cuts of clothing for them to sew, within a matter of minutes, into another perfect shirtwaist.

They wasted almost nothing—and at the end of the day, before they could leave, they would all be searched to make sure no one was stealing so much as a scrap. Podhoretz and Kristol would stand by the single shop door, and the elevator; and the other door, the fire door, was closed and padlocked, lest anyone get away with even a few pennies' worth of the fine cloth.

Their big, meaty hands rummaging blind as a dog through her well-ordered bag, their odious, smirking faces only inches away from her own—making some nasty remark, before she could snatch the bag back, and run all the way downstairs to the street—where she could dream her ice-cream-soda daydreams again, kissing her boy on the roller coaster.

28

ESTHER

Delancey Street was melting in the heat, the carters' horses suctioning up tar with every step they took. Winos lay in the street, dousing their stomachs with buttermilk, and everyone moving up and down the avenue dabbed at their faces with little white handkerchiefs, until the whole street was a sea of fluttering white flags.

The deep, soggy heat of the day had not relented, even in the last light of the evening. Esther pushed her way past the window shoppers, and the vendors peddling pink paper roses and Italian ices and slices of coconut swimming in water, until she stood before the little shop at Essex Street. She had told herself she was not going to stop. She had told herself she was not even going to look, but there it was.

There was a new hat in the window.

It seemed to float there, beneath the fanciful legend etched into the glass, PARISIENNE CREATIONS. It was a broad straw, with a delicate, white organdy band, and bunches of blood-red felt grapes, just in time for the last weeks of the summer. The organdy finer than lace, the grapes darker and rounder and more tempting than any picked off a fruit cart.

The creations, she happened to know, came not so much from Paris as a scab walk-up off Rivington Street, but for this hat she didn't care. She feared that if she'd had the ten dollars, nothing in this world would have prevented her from buying it—not the class struggle, nor the union, nor even the knowledge of the half-dozen or so girls, just like herself, sewing fourteen hours a day in an unlit, sweltering room.

She was already late for the union offices over on Clinton Street, and she would have pulled herself away and gone onto the hall if the saleswoman hadn't come into the window. She was the *tokhter* of the shop, Esther knew, tall and plump, decked out in the finest striped-silk maroon waist. She stepped out into the window to fetch the straw—and as she did, she spotted Esther out on the sidewalk and gave her a long, appraising look.

It was the worst look Esther had ever had—worse than any she had ever received from her father, or the floor supervisors at the Triangle. It was a look filled with such contempt, with such pity, that Esther had to go in then, pushing her way through the shop door before she knew what she was doing.

"Ex-cuse me! Ex-*cuse* me! *That hat!*"

The saleswoman stared at her. At that moment the mother of the shop poked her head from behind the counter—their plump, matching faces filled with surprise and suspicion. But it was too late; Esther had to go through with it.

"That straw——" she insisted.

"What do you want with it?" the younger woman asked. She held it up casually in one hand, the dazzling red grapes and fine organdy mesmerizing Esther so close.

"Yes, mmm, well, maybe to *buy* it."

"We have somebody who's interested in this one. Somebody to pay real cash——"

"Was there somethink else you wanted to luke at, *mam'zelle?*" The older woman pushed forward, her accent from Paris by way of Kiev.

"Somethink in a different *price* range, *purr-ted?*"

Esther stood her ground.

"No! *That* one!"

She pointed to the hat in the daughter's hand, suddenly as imperious as any of the *sheyne yidn,* the beautiful Jews who usually frequented the shop—wives and daughters of the most prominent rabbis, and landlords, and the executives of the Pants Pressers Bank.

"It's new—"

"*Ouay, madame.* It's fresh from our *I'lltellaya.*"

"Are you thinking of trying it on?" the daughter asked incredulously.

Esther opened her bag, and deliberately pulled out her mirror. She let the pocketbook dangle in front of them while she pretended to look over her nose—enough so they could clearly see the roll of two hundred dollars, union dues fresh from the bank. When she put the mirror away and shut her bag, both mother and daughter were beaming at her.

"I would like to see it!" she commanded.

"Of course, *m'ambadam!*"

The mother ushered Esther into one of the plush clients' chairs, and clapped her hands. Another young woman came out of the back of the shop, with a conveniently long, thick roll of hair that could be parted or bunched to fit almost any head size. The proprietor of the shop sat her down by the window and worked the beautiful hat back and forth over her head, Esther cringing with each fold she made in it.

"This should give you some *edie-yay, mammon,*" she cooed, marching the girl back to Esther.

"Of courze, her head shape does not have the mature *butay* of a lady sooch as yerzelf . . ."

The girl took short, dainty steps back and forth in front of Esther, trying to walk like the most elegant uptown mannequins until she was trembling in her high heels. Esther let her do it for as long as she could, trying to gaze indifferently upon the immaculate hat. Finally, she gave another, imperious wave of her hand.

"All right. I will try it!"

The mother nearly ripped the straw off the girl's scalp. She and the daughter were all over her, hands flying above her head.

"If *m'azam* will allow . . ."

She settled back luxuriously into the soft felt cushions of the chair, letting them gently unpin and lift off her own frayed, shapeless hat. They didn't question it: there were always people showing up with money made overnight, and as long as they had actually seen the cash they would believe her. Lovingly now, they gathered up and smoothed out her hair, settled the new hat on her as delicately as a feather and fastened it in place with one long, thin pin under a bough of the perfect grapes.

"And—*walla!*"

They held a mirror up in front of her. It was even better than she had imagined: the straw gleaming palely in contrast, the grapes and the organdy rich and vivid as a painting. Under the hat, her face no longer looked too round, the way she hated it, but long and elegant. She stared yearningly at herself in the glass.

"If you will allowze me, *mamdam*—"

She let them fuss over her again, the older woman pinning it up first to one side, then the other, carefully bending the brim, setting it back and forth over her head until she looked like a different portrait each time.

"I don't know. It could be amusing," she finally forced herself to say.

The mother and daughter of the shop stayed where they were. She felt a little surge of panic when they didn't move to unpin the hat. She stood up and waved the mirror around her head, as if she were examining herself carefully.

"It *is* late in the season," she tried to hedge. "Maybe it isn't quite right—"

The two women stayed rooted above her, and Esther thought she saw the first hint of suspicion in their faces.

311

"All right!" she said desperately. "Please—wrap it up, while I write out my address for you. I want it delivered."

The women were instantly wreathed in smiles again. They pulled out the pins, finally lifting off the hat that now sat like lead upon her. The mother handed her a fountain pen and an exquisite little address card, with the name and address of the shop in raised lettering.

"*Merzey, magnum!*"

She turned away to help her daughter with the wrapping, fussing over a confetti of light blue and white ribbons. Esther doodled distractedly on the perfect little card, fingering the thick roll of bills that was not hers at all, but the collection from some three hundred and seventy-seven women in the union—wondering how she would get out of this without completely humiliating herself.

Just then two statuesque actresses from the Thalia breezed in, laughing and exclaiming. The mother and daughter looked around—and Esther squeezed between them, pretending to recognize someone out on the street.

"Oh, my goodness, that's Rachel," she exclaimed. "What *is* that girl doing?"

The daughter of the shop tried to go over to her, but the actresses were *kvelling* over something, and she could not get past them.

"Do be a dear and finish wrapping, I just have to see what the girl is doing with my son!"

Esther glided on out the door, the fine note card and fountain pen still in her hand, and raced down Delancey as fast as the crowds and her long skirts would let her. She did not stop until she had reached the settlement house on Clinton—and only then did she realize that her bag was still open, the collected dues of nearly four hundred women exposed to any vagary of the street. Miraculously, they were untouched—through no fault of her own.

312

Maybe he's right, she thought, of her father. *Maybe there is no limit to the evil I can do.*

The settlement house where the union had its offices was a scrubbed, determinedly cheerful red-brick building, six stories high, pigeonholed with rooms for all the countless causes and preoccupations of the Lower East Side: for all the landsman's clubs and English classes, the Socialist reading societies and women's health clubs, the numismatic societies and trade unions and amateur theatricals. Up on the roof there was an outdoor gymnasium, entirely enclosed in wire-mesh fence, where women in baggy sailor's suits pushed medicine balls at each other, and huffed around and around a tiny running track.

Esther had never been interested in the track. Instead, when Clara first brought her to the settlement house she had signed up for a citizenship course. There she sat in a windowless classroom with sixty other students, learning the Bill of Rights and the Declaration of Independence. Rising at the end of each class with her fellow students, housewives and little girls and men in gray beards, all to recite the poem to the flag together:

> I love the name of Washington
> I love my country, too
> I love the flag, the dear old flag
> The red, white and blue

She had liked it all right, at least the parts about the Constitution, but the course was at night, and her fellow students fell asleep at their desks after working their fourteen hours. They snored right through the teacher's droning, uninspired presentation, and there were many times in that crowded, over-heated room when she, too, felt very close to sleep.

What she longed for was a real education. That would be something, she was sure, that would transform her—draw her up past all her fear and self-loathing. Clara, she knew, had been offered a full college scholarship by a wealthy couple who had been impressed by her fiery speeches. She had turned them down, insisting she could take no such privilege as long as it was not available to all the girls. Esther admired her terribly for it—though she was sure that if she had ever had such a chance she would have taken it, and all the other girls be damned.

"The paper said, *'Buona paga, Lunga stagione'*—union shop."

"Then he tol' me to go home——"

Inside the hall, a long queue of women stretched down a staircase from the office. A longer line than usual, mostly Italians today, arms stained halfway up to their elbows, red or tan or black, from the color of the cloth they had worked on. Quietly telling each other their grievances while they waited to tell them to the union.

Not one of them wore a hat like the one she had come so close to buying today. Why would they? She had never seen a hat anything like it at the Triangle, or any other shop she had worked. The thing would be dreck before the day was out—from the lint and filth alone, if Podhoretz didn't bash it in on purpose when no one was looking. That she could even have considered doing such a thing made her deeply and irrevocably ashamed of herself. And yet—in all her wickedness—her greatest regret was that she did not have the hat.

"Say hire for piece—now for week——"

"Oh! How he grabs!"

Esther moved past them, up the stairs to the front desk, where Clara was sitting among the women—patiently writing, translating, noting their complaints. Grievances over rate and wage cuts. Grievances over unsafe conditions.

314

Grievances over being docked for using too much thread, or fired because you wouldn't let the foreman squeeze your breasts or because you didn't like being screamed at like an animal all day long.

"And ten cents less!"

Every day, the lines on the stairs grew longer. More grievances, carefully written out in longhand, typed in duplicate, filed in their crowded, metal drawers. Why they bothered to collect them all, Esther never knew. They might as well be piling them up for God to read, for all the attention paid.

"Don't put up with their dog's tricks! You're worth what you work for!" Clara was proclaiming to a young thread puller, holding her arms out like the Christian missionaries who came down to the neighborhood to convert them. The girl, who looked like she had just stepped out of a convent, took a step back, her face full of doubt and confusion.

"Ah, Italians, we need Italians!" Clara complained, turning aside to Esther. "They don't understand this *mama-gab*—"

"I know, I know—"

It was Clara's constant complaint: more Italians. More Poles. More Russians, more Bohemians, Ukrainians, Portuguese, to spread the word of the union. Yet from what Esther had seen, most of the other women were just as glad to hear the Jews like Clara. They were the *fabrente maydlakh*, the fiery girls, and they spoke to the other women through more than words. She had seen such a glow of righteousness before only in the faces of the Hasid rabbis and their followers, dancing down Norfolk Street in their ecstasy, oblivious to the hail of insults and spit from the nonbelievers.

"America for a country, and 'Dod'll do' for a language," Clara repeated her old plaint, then turned her full attention on Esther.

"What have you got for me?" she asked—and then exulted when she saw the money Esther had changed into bills at the bank, from the endless pennies and nickels and dimes she had collected and meticulously recorded—and then nearly cast away in a moment.

"Good, good! More than I expected!"

Clara pulled her back into the inner offices, locked the dues away in the safe. Already, Esther was feeling a little better. It made her heart jump just to see her old friend, and Esther always felt a jolt of exhilaration when she visited these crowded little rooms, pungent with the smell of ink and blotters, luminous yellow balls of light hanging from the ceiling. And everywhere were women—all women, most of them no older than herself—bustling around the metal file cabinets and battered wooden desks. Men were supposedly in charge of the union, they sat in committee somewhere uptown, but here, in the office, it was almost solely women. Some of them even wearing tweed jackets and ties, or bobbed hair, writing, arguing, conferring. *This* was where something important got done. Something urgent and manly and *real,* beyond the endless assemblage of shirts.

This evening, there was something else in the air—an extra edge, a barely contained excitement you could see in everyone's faces, hear in their voices: there was a strike coming on.

A strike, it seemed to Esther, was indeed like a natural phenomenon—like the thunderstorms she sometimes saw, slowly building across the Hudson. The union tried to organize everything, to strike at the optimum moment, but there was really no directing it. It came on when the anger and the frustration in the shops had built up to the boiling point, and then there was no stopping it, or predicting where it would end.

This one had been building ever since the start of the new season, two weeks before. The operators had been shaking out early, despite all the supposed advantages from the new, rationalized factories. They had been driving everybody down—cutting the prices for piecework, cutting wages for the regular operators—even shaking down the pressers and the cutters, the indispensable princes of the business.

The office was more crowded than ever now, everyone trying to see what they could find out, or put their two cents in, or just drawn by the general excitement in the air. There was supposed to be a meeting later, over at the Talkers' Cafe, and little Rose Schneiderman, and Leonora O'Reilly, who always spoke like she had a tear in her voice, were coming over, along with the society ladies, Miss Marot and Miss Dreier from Brooklyn, and Mrs. Perkins the social worker. There were even rumors that men from the union's executive board would be there.

"We're nearly ready, *bubbeleh*! Two years of building, two years of planning," Clara breathed, her eyes dancing. "*Now* we make our move. *Now* we make the big strike, we get the *momzers* to recognize us!"

"Really? But how?"

"You'll see," she said. "Come with us tonight."

"All right," Esther agreed, even though it was another sweltering evening, and she was so tired. She had so wanted to go home and maybe read a little, then climb into her bed of chairs to dream of her *dybbuk*.

"All right," she repeated, this time more enthusiastically. After all, Clara said it was the big strike, the one they had always hoped and prayed for, making wishes in a New Jersey hay field the summer they had all camped out on the Palisades—making wishes for anything, anything in the world they might want on the clouds drifting by, pregnant with rain in the orange evening sky.

•   •   •

Yet out on the hot, crowded street, her enthusiasm wilted as quickly as the real flowers the barefoot little girls tried to sell her.

The false ones were better, the bright metal flowers that pricked her mother's skin and made her hands fester Blood-red grapes on a shop window hat

What good would it do?

She had to ask herself: they could strike all they wanted, the biggest bosses were happy to see them walk out—just long enough to squeeze the smaller operators. Even if they won something—a few more cents in the rate, slightly better conditions—it only made it easier to clear out the little shops, which couldn't afford the better rates. Then, when they had eliminated the competition, the big factories would cut their wages again.

Against such people, how could they do anything?

She worried it as she moved back down Delancey Street. Past the winos with their buttermilk. Past the mothers nursing their babes in the shadow of the elevated, and the pink paper roses, and the slices of coconut swimming in their dirty water. Past all the blank, ignorant faces, rushing somewhere, blindly, into the night.

29

ESTHER

The Talkers' Cafe was no more than a large storefront on East Broadway, in the shadow of the high clock tower of the *Forward* building. Two rows of little tables and cane chairs, each of them filled with journalists and cloakmakers, anarchists and socialists, single-taxers and Zionists, Zwangwillites and assimilationists and all-purpose kibitzers. All arguing and declaiming furiously under the low tin ceiling of this Babel.

"Look at these *loaferim!*" Clara said loudly as they walked in the door, gesturing at the men in their shabby coats and ties, who peered up, dazed as moles, through the clouds of their cigarette smoke.

"All day long they blow from themselves, and still not one of them with enough sense to tie a cat's tail!"

Esther made sympathetic noises but secretly she loved the teahouses: these parliaments of tailors and pants pressers, hunched over their samovars and their chessboards. It was here that she had first learned to think, and to listen, and to talk.

So many Sundays past, she had spent the whole day in one such cafe or another. She went early in the morning to stake out a good table and sit for hours, slowly sipping lemon-flavored tea through a lump of sugar held under her tongue. She ordered white bread, or maybe a poppy-seed roll, and smoked cigarettes and read the newspapers, in half a dozen languages, that hung from sticks along the wall. The whole day was hers, to read, or dream, or watch the other idlers.

Up front, there was always a table full of the *Forward*'s staff. From time to time, a grim-faced delegate from the *Arbeiter Zeitung,* the *Forward*'s great rival, would march in and deliver a long, esoteric harangue in Yiddish—until at last the *Forward* staff rose as one and pushed him physically back out the door. Then they would put their heads together, and a few minutes later send their own emissary across the street to the *Arbeiter*'s cafe and fling it back in their faces.

They argued, gloriously, all day, over everything from religion to the medicinal attributes of celery tonic to the inevitable triumph of socialism. Such a noise—such a raging symphony it was: of sarcasm, and cigarette smoke, and bitter, heartfelt passion over the size of a poppy seed. All to reach a perfect, theoretical conclusion, tottering there somewhere in the sky, above their heads. Above this tawdry world, where they sat dragging out cups of cold tea and bits of kaiser roll.

Sometimes she wished she had the nerve to join them in their harsh, slashing men's debates. They would be disdainful of her at first—a little *fifer* of a machine operator like herself. Soon, though, she could imagine them won over by her careful logic, her calm, insistent voice, the lack of casuistry or personal insults in her arguments. Just like her father would be won over.

She never did join in—though she was just as happy to spend the day by herself, reading or trying to think. She tried to savor each moment in the close, overheated room, but of course the more she tried to appreciate them the heavier they weighed. As the hours slouched by she started to think about the next day, and work. When evening came, she ordered a slice of lemon pie, perhaps, or chocolate raspberry cake—a final treat to herself. But it always turned sour on her tongue. Buried in its sweetness lay the end of the day, the end of Sunday, and the end of what little time she could call her own.

Tonight the women pressed in together, in the dim back room, knees bumping politely under the table: Esther next to Clara, and then Clara's friend Pauline Newman, the formidable Leonora O'Reilly, little Rose Schneiderman, the society lady Miss Dreier, and Mrs. Perkins, the social worker. A couple more she didn't know, and whose names she was too shy to ask again. They sat debating the strike over and over again, fervent in their argument, yet cool and calculated as any group of Tammany politicians. Always, they returned to the same impasse:

"Don't you see? They're forcing us out anyhow. We have to do it *now*," Clara insisted, rattling a sugar cube behind her teeth.

"We have to do it?" shrugged Leonora O'Reilly. "We don't have to do anything, much less on their timetable."

"But they're going too far. They're driving down the rate every day. Even the *shadchens* are getting mad."

"If they're cutting the rate now, they *want* us to go out, so they can have the excuse to crush us."

"But if the rate's too low even for the *shadchens*, who are they going to get?" Clara asked triumphantly. "Who will scab for them then? We got more girls than we ever did before, we got a strike fund—"

"How far does that get us? We want recognition for the union, not just another nickel on the rate. They'll fight us to the death for that. You know they will."

They all fell silent, considering such a prospect. Everyone

at the table knew what a strike would be like.

"They will bring in the gangsters, and their whores, and the police will let them do what they want," Leonora continued. "You know that. They don't care if it's women and children out on the line, and if you think your sex will save you from anything, think again. It will only make them worse."

She was right, they knew: going out on strike meant giving up the last vestige of their respectability. It meant leaving themselves exposed—to the cops, and the company thugs, and the crowds of jeering, smirking men. A major strike like this meant being treated like whores, with whores. It meant they would be fair game for whatever anyone wanted to do to them, and a small but palpable current of fear ran around the table.

"At least we have the society women. They can help us," Clara said weakly.

"Them!" Leonora O'Reilly snorted. "Listen, there's one thing I've learned: if you ever let anyone do for you they will do you!"

She caught herself then, and they all shot glances over at Miss Dreier and at Mrs. Perkins, who sat perfectly composed as ever in her tricornered hat.

Mrs. Perkins, she knew, was a professional social worker. A woman from some old Yankee family up in Massachusetts, who had a college education but who had for some reason decided to come down to work in the City's slums. She held a niche all her own in the settlement house, and no one was quite sure of what to make of her—not as rich as the real society ladies, but certainly different from the rest. She never said very much, but Esther had noticed that she listened to everything very intently, eyes glistening determinedly in her sharp, Yankee face, as if she were trying to memorize everything that was said.

They all deferred to her, and to the other ladies. Often

they found the society women unbearably smug and condescending, but their power was undeniable. A few years before they had organized a boycott against those department stores that didn't let their women clerks sit down or go to the bathroom on their shifts. The response had been stunning, the owners forced to back down within weeks.

No one knew if they could do the same thing to the factories—if they would have the interest or the staying power for a big fight. If their concern extended beyond the counter girls, right in front of them every day.

"I think," Mrs. Perkins said in quiet, measured tones, "that you would have support among society—as far as that goes. I know you would have it from me."

—and the rest of the table visibly relaxed, glad despite themselves to hear it. A little rustle of hope went through the working women.

"*There*. We *have* to do it now!" Clara jumped in.

The argument went on for hours, finally winding down after midnight, still unresolved. The women unbent themselves slowly from their little cane chairs, wearily contemplating the fourteen-hour day ahead. The majority was leaning to a strike, but no one wanted to go out just now. The new season was starting and some money was coming in, and anyway the men who ran the union executive board hadn't bothered to come down after all.

But if not now, when? When would it ever change?

—though secretly, Esther had to admit she was just as glad no decision had been made. She was sure she was a coward, but she was still glad she didn't have to think about it just yet: the gangsters and their jeering whores, the policemen's heavy wooden billy clubs. She should be braver, she knew, but what misery this life was.

"Good night, sweetest," Clara told her when they reached

the street corner. She hugged her, then kissed her once on each cheek.

"Wait—I have something for you."

Esther pulled a small package out of her purse. She had almost forgotten, after all the nonsense about the hat, and everything else. It was not wrapped as nicely as Clara herself would do it, she knew—but she had done it up in her favorite, red paper, and tied it round with a bright yellow bow.

"Here you are," she told her. "They're the sonnets. I found them in the *Freie Bibliothek*."

Clara carefully opened the package. Inside was a small packet of notepaper, folded over, on which Esther had written out some of Shakespeare's sonnets that Clara had first introduced her to. She had written them out in her best hand, going over them painstakingly, late at night—though now she blushed to see her own writing:

> . . . How would (I say) mine eyes be
> blessed made
> By looking on thee in the living day,
> When in dead night thy fair
> imperfect shade
> Through heavy sleep on sightless eyes
> doth stay?
> All days are nights to see, till I see thee,
> And nights, bright days, when dreams do
> show thee me.

"Oh, but it's *fine!*" Clara said, looking up at her and smiling warmly.

"I'm so glad," she said, looking down at the pavement, grateful when, for her sake, Clara changed the subject:

"Tell me—did you get through much last night?"

Their Socialist Literary Society was working its way

through *Great Expectations,* all of them now trying to puzzle out who Pip's mysterious benefactor was as he rose through London society.

"A little. I had to get ready for the meeting. Who do *you* think it is?" Esther asked.

"I don't know—but I think it's someone else," Clara said confidentially. "I don't trust that Miss Havisham!"

"Really?"

She leaned in closer to Esther.

"Guess what? I'm a walking delegate if there's a strike. And if that goes well—maybe even a traveling delegate."

"*Really?*"

Such a job—

It meant organizing all the other women out there, spreading the Cause to their sisters in all the other factories, out in the intriguing vastness of the country. It meant going from city to strange new city by train. Racing along the rails through the night, sitting up in the parlor car while it hurtled across whole new lands. It was far beyond anything she thought she could do herself, but Esther ached to go with her.

"Keep it under your hat."

Clara winked, and hugged her tight. Pauline and Miss Dreier and Mrs. Perkins stood waiting, a little ways off, to walk home with her and talk over the strike some more, and it only reminded Esther of how little she was, even in the union. She couldn't help but look down, filled with envy—wanting to tell Clara everything about Coney Island and her *dybbuk* there, just to have something to cut through her good news.

Clara noticed her expression, peering in at her closely—filled with such obvious concern that Esther felt ashamed.

"Everything all right, *mamaleh?*"

"Yes, yes, it's nothing. Just a little tired." She smiled weakly.

"Well, see you get some rest then. Even if it don' mean reading tonight."

"Sure."

"All right then. Sleep tight, dear heart!"

"All right, dear heart."

They each kissed their knuckles and pressed them together, in one of the secret, affectionate little signs the girls at the factories all had, and she watched Clara walk away with her new friends.

Esther turned and walked back toward Orchard Street, following the course of a garbage wagon home—the iron ash cans ringing and sparking along the sidewalk in the dark as the garbagemen wrestled them up and over, into the cart.

She had thought about the society women many times since she had started coming to the union office. Where she was too shy to say hello to them, Clara had been invited on vacations to a cottage Miss Dreier had at Gravesend, and to a house Mrs. Perkins's family owned in the Berkshires.

"They're just like anybody else," Clara had laughed at her when she asked what it was like, but she did not believe it.

Like most of the others, Esther tiptoed around the society ladies and the social workers in the office. She didn't quite trust them. She could not figure out why they were there, and she feared that if *she* had been a wealthy woman, living in Brooklyn or Massachusetts, she would never have come out to the union hall at all.

A sudden gust of wind broke the still August night, and there was a terrible fluttering sound above her. Esther started, and jumped into a shop door—but it was only a dentist's shingle, a huge, gold tooth, swung loose and flapping like a demented angel over her head.

I'm scared of a cat and I'm scared of a mouse

She hurried on home past vacant lots strewn with dilapidated baby carriages and broken suitcases, old shirts and worn-out shoes. Up on the fifth floor, she nearly stepped on a cat and its litter, lying right out on the landing. The mother's slit green eyes peered up weakly, her kittens prodding her body for what little it could provide. The cats were everywhere; they yowled all night in the summer with their lovemaking and in the winter they clutched at the door whenever you opened it, desperate to be in someplace warm. Sometimes she would find whole litters frozen to death together in the corners, their eyes not yet open.

She crept on into the apartment, where everyone else was asleep, her pallet lying already prepared for her in the kitchen. She did not lie down, though, but pulled out her battered copy of the Dickens—bought secondhand from a pushcart peddler for ten cents—and tried to read for at least a little while by the oily glow of the kerosene lamp.

She was dead tired, but she always tried to do something—anything—before she went to bed. Something every night, so that it would not be one more day with nothing accomplished, nothing earned except for someone else.

There were some Sundays when she never got to the Talkers' Cafe. Some Sundays when the weight of the world lay unbearably upon her, and it seemed pointless to go out at all. She hid from the *roomerkehs* in her parents' room while the old man walked around the neighborhood, eagerly peering into each new storefront synagogue and scoffing at its impertinence.

Those afternoons she would sit and stare out into the desolate back courtyard. The yard was her constant star. In the summer, it was littered with broken flags and fish heads, gutted mattresses and dead cats—whatever anybody from the tenements might throw down. There was a sign reading ALL BOYS CAUGHT IN THIS YARD WILL BE DELT WIT ACCORDEN TO LAW—though she knew in the winter it would be thick with boys, and girls, and older street bums, trying to soak up the heat from the building furnace.

Sometimes, through all the junk, she could make out the old slate stones the yard was paved with, scavenged from one of the city's countless uprooted cemeteries: winged death's-heads and crossbones, above a mysterious antique lettering, slowly eroding away. *What kind of people would put such things on their gravestones?* she wondered. Nothing like the simple Jewish stones, with a name, a date, to mark where a person lay.

She would sit and stare at the strange winged skulls, and think about how little she knew, and how little she was likely to do in her life. A feeling of gnawing, inexplicable dread enveloped her, until she was close to weeping. Sometimes she actually did cry—hot, bitter tears that she knew were silly. Over nothing, really—nothing but the fear of being afraid, and the future, and what would become of her. But that just made her cry all the harder, ashamed all over again of her fear, and her hopelessness.

And then for a few hours only, at the right times of the year, direct sunlight flowed into the courtyard. On those afternoons, she might pry open the old, encrusted windows and bask in the sun, with her eyes closed. On those Sundays, she might dry her tears, and decide that maybe she felt well enough to go out for a walk after all. Maybe even to the cafes.

She had only wished that her father could see her in such places. He would never deign to set foot in them himself, of course, but she had hoped one of his old congregation would tell him, out of spite.

Why do you insist on pouring ashes on my head? You have

come to love talk more than you love the Almighty.

And how should I love Him? What have you ever taught me of Him? All I know is a needle and a thread.

Can you fathom the sea? Then neither can you fathom the depths of Talmud.

She would kneel before him, put her hands in his and look up seriously into his face.

Then teach me.

I cannot. You are not my son.

Who is your son? Your son is not your son.

All right, I have no son. I have a son in Talmud. That is my fruit, my offspring—my learning.

Arrogance! And me? And me?

You are not my son.

The Dickens swam and wavered before her, in the tiny kitchen. In such moments, such bleak flashes of truth just before sleep, she was not sure that he wasn't right. Looking deep into her heart, she didn't know that she even wanted a strike, or that she would be content to hide here forever, dreaming of new hats and secret benefactors. But that didn't make her feel any better.

BOOK
SIX

There's always a certain number of
suckers and a certain number of men
lookin' for a chance
to take them in, and the suckers are
sure to be took one way
or another. It's the everlastin'
law of demand and supply.

——GEORGE WASHINGTON PLUNKITT

30

THE GREAT HEAD DOCTORS FROM VIENNA

"Look out, you idiot!"

The big yellow touring car wheeled around the corner too fast, and just managed to avoid the little boy standing in the crowded street. Looking back, clutching onto his hat, Freud saw a slab-faced man in a straw boater, clutching the boy's hand and shaking his fist after them. He shuddered to think what might have happened had they hit him.

"Slow down! You're driving like the characters in those idiotic movies."

"*Ja,* it just takes a little getting used to," Ferenczi muttered nervously, trying to work the gearshift. "You have to swim with the current."

"We will lie with the worms if you aren't more careful!"

Instead, Ferenczi accelerated, and Freud felt his stomach turn over. It was not just the speed of the car. Everything was proceeding much too rapidly, too haphazardly.

He didn't know where they would be without Brill, their old colleague, so insistent on giving them his grand tour of the city that he still had not taken them up to his clinic at Columbia. At first, Freud had thought this was from nerves, but he had become convinced that the man really did believe they would be impressed by New York.

"Wait—just wait until you see this!" had become his constant refrain.

They had just come from a restaurant in the Chinese section of the city, where they sold live crabs and carp on the sidewalk, and where Jung had eaten the most incredible dish of chopped meat smothered in what seemed to be earthworms. So far—besides the earthworms—they had been dragged to see an opera company, a symphony, and a recital at a new, orange-brick concert hall—all very credible, though distinctly inferior to their equivalents in Vienna, or Berlin. There had been a tour of a new art museum, just off the vast, wooded Central Park, which Freud had liked a good deal more, the museum's wealthy, American patrons having bought up an impressive quantity of first-rate pictures—though again, it really couldn't stand up to the great European capitals.

"How could they? After all, they don't have two thousand years of culture behind them," he remarked with what he thought was good-humored condescension to Jung.

"But look at what they've accomplished already! What is the republic—barely a century old?" Jung pointed out. "They are a fresh, young people, with a young psychology. In another hundred years, I predict, they will surpass anything in Europe!"

"Yes, I suppose their rich men will be able to buy up everything by that time," he answered bitterly, wondering if Jung was deliberately trying to be perverse.

He found the thought of such a philistine victory infinitely depressing. New York's greatest triumph, he thought, lay in something Abe Brill didn't try to show off. That was its raw power—from its busy harbor and its dangerous streets to the ugly, overgrown skyscrapers sprouting out of the sidewalk. New York—and America—was all about *size*, overwhelming, indomitable size. The city was dark, and grim, and furious, like some enormous, inscrutable god-machine, and no one was at the controls.

He wondered if it was the city itself that was wrecking his digestion and his sleep, filling his head with nightmares—

In the dream the woman patient who had sent the orchids to his stateroom stood before him in her dressing gown. She was as beautiful as the flowers—much more beautiful than he remembered.

She undid the dressing gown, and let it slide to the floor. Then she climbed up on the bed, and smiled back at him reassuringly—even wantonly. She got on her hands and knees and began to lift up her underwear, revealing her lovely bottom and her sex—bright red as the officers' uniforms.

He eagerly took out his cock, preparing to enter her, when she looked back at him again. Only now her face was the mask, the totem he had held up in front of his father as a disguise. But no—he looked closer and saw that it was transformed, somehow, into the face of the tanned man, from the Bleikeller, still perfectly preserved. The gaping, silently screaming face, inconceivably ancient—

Then the scene changed, and they were in the Aula again, the great ceremonial hall, before all the assembled minds of science, with his penis hanging limply out of his fly. Trying to hide behind the lectern, hoping they wouldn't see it—

They careened on down through the jammed streets, working their way around trucks, and wagon teams, and push-carts laden with all kinds of goods—a sort of gigantic, endless maze, designed to test nothing but one's reflexes and survival instincts. They were making their way through a largely Jewish neighborhood now, the shop signs in Hebrew and Yiddish as often as English—though he noticed that on many streets the Jews seemed to live cheek by jowl with

335

everyone else, Italians next to Bohemians next to Irish next to Germans.

From the street level of the open touring car Freud could look right into the faces of the men and women shuffling along beside them. He caught the eye of one young man without even a pushcart—hauling a huge pile of cloth on his back and head, holding the bundled lawn in place with one hand, using the other to sweep out a space for himself in the never-ending river of people.

The man didn't avert his eyes from Freud's gaze, but stared back with the expressionless, neutral stare he had seen so often in New York—as if he were looking right through him, neither giving ground nor presuming intimacy.

It is the stare of nomadic tribesmen, he thought, *each circling the same water hole.*

It was a Semitic face, swarthy and sharp, unshaven, his eyes dark and hollowed. Not a Viennese or German Jew, he felt sure, but from some point farther east—long, religious curls hanging down from underneath the immense burden of cloth that covered his hat. A face not unlike that of the apparition, the monolith he had seen wandering up the Ringstrasse before he left Vienna, staring around himself like a creature from another age, suddenly transported to modern Europe.

In the Chinese restaurant, there had been a large, rather fiendish-looking Oriental at the front door, standing with his arms crossed, a pair of silver-handled axes and an opium pipe by his feet. Inside, though, all the waiters had been whites, a young black man with incredibly long and elegant fingers playing a piano. What a stew—what an *ongepotchket* collection of peoples!

And then—in the middle of dinner—while Jung was throwing back his chopped meat and earthworms and something that looked like chicken feet, one of the waiters had stepped into the middle of the room and begun to sing.

Another Jew, Freud felt certain—a short, timorous-looking man, with a large nose and dark eyes, who nonetheless stood with his arms by his side, and began to belt out an infectious ragtime number:

> Come on along
> Come on along
> Let me take you by the hand—

His voice was only adequate, but he was accompanied by the elegant-fingered black man, and the other waiters—and then, to Freud's intense embarrassment, most of the other diners joined in, thumping their fingers on the table, keeping time with their knife and fork handles. The song was another meaningless American ditty, attached to a bouncy, simplistic beat, but it proved absolutely irresistible—Freud himself, to his consternation, tapped his feet in time under the table:

> Up to the man
> Up to the man
> Who's the leader of the band—

—going on and on like that. And when it was finished, launching into more jaunty ragtime numbers, and sentimental ballads, and nonsense rhymes. Until Freud was quite unable to eat or even think anymore, rushing off to find the bathroom hidden deep downstairs by the kitchen while Jung kept munching contentedly away on his earthworms.

What was to be done with such a country?

31

BIG TIM

He looked for Herman Rosenthal over at the old Garden Cafe on Seventh Avenue, where he knew Beansy liked to go with his wife. He wasn't there, which Sullivan took for a good sign, at least. Maybe he had gone to ground—though he knew Herman was just as likely to be projecting magic lantern displays of his affidavit off the Times building.

He made the rounds of the old Tenderloin, checking all of Beansy's favorite haunts, but he still could not find the man. His groin was still hurting him, and he felt thirsty. He wasn't much of a man for a glass, but he thought just now a short beer or a whiskey might ease the pain. He pulled his boater down over his eyes and ducked down into a two-cent restaurant for a quick swamp.

One always took a chance going in such places, he knew, no matter who one was. A ponce or an alderman, a judge or a bum—you were just as likely to wake up in the river the next day, drowned for the jinglers in your pocket and the new collar on your shirt.

He was lucky; this one didn't seem so bad. It didn't compare to the cellar beer dives in the Mulberry Bend, where the walls crawled with cockroaches and the drinks were served in old tomato cans. Or the block-and-fall joints on Chatham and Pearl streets that catered to the tramp trade. In the winter, they had a woodstove in the middle of the room, which the tramps were welcome to sit around so long as they could swing at least one foot to show they were still awake. From the street they looked like some kind of great, collective insect, the men's heads bent down by the stove—nothing but a huddle of rags, with dozens of legs swinging back and forth, even as they slept.

He drained a beer, needled to give it any kind of a head, then a finger of whiskey that burned like kerosene, which it might well have been. He walked up to the street again, swaying a little as he walked—the pain in his groin receding all right, all his other faculties blurring as well as the alcohol spread through him. Bad as the whiskey and the beer had been, he already felt a need for more. He could feel other appetites growing in him as well.

Think where this has led you before

And what if it had, where was the harm in it? What had he ever done to anyone? He thought of the soiled doves, lingering beneath the Bowery elevated. The older ones terrible to look at, plainly touched with the Venus curse. But there were always at least some new girls, peering shyly out from behind the steel pylons, faces filled with innocence, and trepidation, and sometimes a tremulous hope.

"Didn't I always treat them right?" he murmured aloud to himself on the street.

Didn't they say you couldn't throw a brick over a workhouse wall without hitting one of the Liberator's brats? And then there was Parnell, and King David in the Bible. A man of his station was due a little license, after all. He always took care of them—took care of his mistakes, too, even when there was ample reason to doubt their pedigree—

• • •

He swung toward the east, walking more rapidly now. If not the Bowery, then he knew of some places on Elizabeth Street. All young girls, all very young and tender. His oldest could be their age now but there was no chance of *that*, they were all out West, or in the convent——

And if he had the curse, that wasn't his fault, was it? In their profession, a case was bound to come along, sooner or later. Besides, he wouldn't have to do anything, just sit on the bed beside them and talk. Just bask in the pleasure of sitting next to a pretty young girl on her bed. How many times in his life did a man get to do that?

He noticed a saloon, and stepped down into it for another quick boilermaker. It was a Bohunk bar, workmen in their tattered jackets and hats and tobacco-brown-stained shirts staring dully at him. When he came out, he wasn't sure where he was.

He stopped on the dark street, still full of people pushing past at that hour of the night. He really had to find Herman. Gyp could be hunting him even as he stood there. The faces of the soiled doves passed before him again, peeking shyly out from under the elevated.

"Just a quick one," he told himself. "Just a quick refreshment. I'll be very careful."

His mother loomed up out of the dark street toward him: a thin, black, spectral figure, wearing a tricornered hat. He took a horrified step back.

"I'm glad I found you," Mrs. Frances Perkins said, walking up to him and offering her hand, straightforward as a Brooklyn pol. "I didn't know if I could get through your entourage at the saloon."

"You know I'm always happy to talk to you, Mrs. Perkins."

He recovered himself as best he could but she smiled knowingly, and held on to his hand——close enough to smell the whiskey on his breath, he realized, and he was ashamed.

For a social worker lady, she was a natural-born politician, able to seize on any weakness.

"You know what I've come about."

"Certainly, certainly," he said bluffly, trying to back away a little.

"Can we count on you with the Hours Bill?"

"Well, now, you know you have me sympathies on that one, ma'am, but the next session's a long way off, an' there's some would say it's an infringement on private property——" he hemmed, driven to unseemly honesty by her uncanny resemblance to his dead ma.

"I'm glad to hear you're on our side, at least in principle," Mrs. Perkins cut through his regrets. "I'm sure you know from experience that fifty-four hours is more than enough for any girl or mother to work in a factory. Your sister was a factory girl, wasn't she, Mr. Sullivan?"

"Well, yes, as a matter of fact——"

He could still see her in that tiny flat on Clinton Street, after his mother had died and she was the sole support of them all. Slumped over the kitchen table, struggling just to get up and make the supper.

"Of course, I don't have to tell you how many votes such a bill would draw in your district. I'm sure you're aware of how many it would siphon off from the Socialists."

"You have a point, you do have a point, Mrs. Perkins," he conceded, starting to smile despite himself. "That last labor bill did get us plenty of votes——"

"Good. Then what could be a happier coincidence of good conscience and good politics, Mr. Sullivan?"

Spoken like a Jesuit father!

"I don't know," he told her, and laughed out loud. "I'm sure I don't know, Mrs. Perkins!"

"Fine then," she said, and gave his hand another hard shake. She looked still more closely at him, studying his blurry, sleepless eyes.

"Take care of yourself, Tim," she said, motherly again.

"I will, Mrs. Perkins. I certainly will."

She gave his hand yet another firm, solicitous squeeze, then walked briskly, only a slight twirl of her umbrella betraying her satisfaction. She was headed down a dark street, in a bad neighborhood, but Sullivan thought she could take of herself.

Even as he watched her leave, though, a figure detached itself from the shadows, silent and smooth as a rat, and moved toward him. Big Tim recognized him right away. It was Arnold, another one of his Jewboys, a dapper little man in an elegant, gray silk suit, and an actor's jaunty fedora.

They're all so small

"Hello, Dry Dollar," the man hailed him quietly, confidently using Big Tim's childhood nickname, even though he hadn't known him for more than a couple years.

"What brings you downtown tonight, Arnold?" Big Tim asked politely, knowing full well there was a good reason.

There always was—Arnold never did anything without a purpose. Of all his boys, Big Tim liked and trusted Arnold the least, but he was sure he would go the furthest.

For one thing, he was the best gambler Sullivan had ever known—unbeatable at pocket billiards, and nearly as good at poker as he was himself. More than that, though, he was unmatched in pulling in the big marks. A few years before, Big Tim had put him in charge of his casino upstairs at the Hotel Metropole, in Times Square. Arnold had promptly quadrupled the profits, luring in millionaire's sons from all over the country and even the Continent—plying them with enough women and enough champagne that they didn't mind being taken.

After that, he could hardly refuse when Arnold had asked for a place of his own up on Forty-Deuce. The other, gentile gamblers had been no more fond of the idea than they had been of Beansy Rosenthal butting in on them, but of course Arnold had made it all right; had charmed and *shmeered* and bullied them until everything was jake. There were never any problems with Arnold.

"I hear there's a certain little sheep gone missing," he told Big Tim now.

"Well, yes, that could be," Big Tim admitted cautiously.

"Mmm. This one didn't stray very far."

"No?"

"I was just lookin' around my old digs, and who should I see?"

"The Metropole? *That's* as far as he's got?"

"Uh-huh."

Arnold's eyes were hidden under the brim of his fedora, but Big Tim thought he saw a small, cruel smile around his lips.

"Only a *shlimazel* believes in *mazel*," he said.

"All right. I'm much indebted to you, I'm sure."

—but Arnold was already fading back into the shadows, waving him off.

"Consider this a little favor from an old friend. Maybe sometime down the road."

He found Herman just where Arnold had said he would—in the cafe of the Hotel Metropole. The Metropole wasn't Big Tim's kind of place, even though he owned it. There were plush carpets, and candles with red shades at each table, and enough palm trees for a tropical forest.

He had invested in it once the Tenderloin had spread up past Times Square, hoping to pull in the toff trade, but the place had been something of a bust once Arnold had moved on. It felt unbearably stuffy in the summer heat, despite the two giant electrical fans, slowly wafting the curtains back and forth; a five-piece chamber orchestra from Hungary sawing away in the cafe. The room was infested with the types sitting at Herman's table now: Boob Walker, and Dan the Dude, and Denny Slyfox—peanut gamblers and confidence men, who preyed on the rubens and scared the more respectable clientele away.

Big Tim stood in the cafe doorway watching Herman for a few minutes—so happy, so childishly confident, gesturing expansively as he told some story, his gold watch and cuff links glinting brightly as he swung his arms about. Then he retreated silently to the lobby desk, where he had the gambler paged. To his overwhelming regret, Herman came right out, eager as a puppy dog, his pudgy flesh rolling loosely beneath a swank new green suit.

"Big Tim!" he said, grasping his hand, his eyes so eager and grateful that Sullivan barely had the heart to tell him what he had to. "I knew you'd back me in my hour of need! You're a true friend and a gentleman, and I won't forget you."

He gave him a wink, and a convivial elbow, until Big Tim finally had to pull him aside, behind one of the Metropole's faux marble pillars.

"Herman, Herman, what'd ya come out for?"

Rosenthal looked baffled.

"Why, because you called was why—"

"*How did you know it was me?*"

"Because you said it was."

"Don'cha see it coulda been anyone? Any brain tickler or hackum in the city, just *sayin'* it was me?"

Herman's face fell.

"I didn't think a that."

"Well you gotta *start* thinkin'. You gotta start thinkin' good an' hard about everything you do, an' everywhere you go. Jesus Christ, man, don'ch you understand? Ever since you started to roll out the velvet, there's a cove on every street corner anxious to see your ground sweat."

"I didn't think about it," Herman said miserably. Then he brightened. "But don't you worry, Tim. Didn't you see it? I told 'em you was behind me a hunerd percent. You got nothin' to worry about."

"*Jay-sus,* Herman," Big Tim sighed. "Forget about that. Whattaya even doin' here, all by yerself? Why don'ch you talk to your friend, the D.A., get some protection?"

"Aw, Tim," Herman smirked. "How would I skin anybody at cards, coupla lousy dicks followin' me everywhere I go?"

"Herman, Herman. Don'cha see this is for keeps, boy? They want your head before they have their supper."

"Who? Who does?"

Herman looked absolutely bewildered at the idea that anyone would want to hurt him.

"You *know* who, Herman. Look, why don'cha just let the whole thing blow away? Tell the D.A. you're sorry, but your memory's shot to hell. Give Charlie Becker his money as a sign of good faith, then get out of town for a while."

"Give Becker *his* money? The way I figure it, he owes *me* money!"

Beansy Rosenthal was more hurt and resentful than ever, and there was a childlike petulance in his voice Big Tim had heard before, and that he knew could bode no good.

"Look, Herman, just whattaya think yer gonna get out of all this, anyway?" he asked softly, trying a new tack.

"Fifteen thousand," Rosenthal told him. "Fifteen grand for shutting me down. That's figurin' lost operating profit, equipment costs—the whole *shmeer.* Fifteen thousand, an' then maybe I'll leave town—"

"C'mon, Herman. Who's gonna come up with that kind of cash for ya? New York is a nine-day town. You lay low somewhere out in Jersey for a while, an' everything'll blow over."

"No! I just want what's comin' to me, is all."

The wobbly, gelatinous face suddenly hard, the chin thrust out obstinately.

"Oh, Jesus, Herman! What's comin' to ya is a quick death an' a nice funeral—if you're lucky. Can't you see that?"

He knew even as he said it that he had gone too far. Herman Rosenthal looked stunned at the bluntness of his words. His mouth wobbled open, and his eyes welled up.

"That's simply the way it is, man," Sullivan said more softly, starting to back out of the Metropole's luxurious lobby.

"But aren't you my friend, Tim? Aren't you behind me?"

"It don't figure whether I am or not. No one can keep you safe from a whole city. Not even me."

He turned and walked away, leaving Herman standing there looking like he was about to cry. There was no hope for it, he knew, so why did he still feel bad? It wasn't his lookout to save fools from themselves. He had warned him, hadn't he? He had warned him, what more could he do?

A little later that night, Big Tim Sullivan finished his latest whiskey and climbed slowly up the steps of the diving bell onto Mott Street. A shadow moved out from behind a lamp-post as he staggered along.

"Fresh girlies!" it hissed, a thin, greenish face staring up at him in the lamplight.

"Fifty cents. Young! Very young!"

He pushed on past, still trying not to think about Herman. He had never hurt anyone but himself. No one but himself, and Nell, and what was his obligation there? There had been no sons, no children at all. She hadn't been comfortable with his normal, manly desires, so what was he to do?

Yet he could still see her on the deck of that excursion boat up to Bear Mountain, just after they were married. Her teeth showing as she laughed, one hand holding on to her hat against the wind. So fresh, so young, her skin so white—

He remembered, too, the disgust on her face as she turned

away from him. The look of sheer loathing.

He stopped in the middle of Mott Street, and looked back to where the dangler was still lurking behind his lamppost, hissing at the passersby.

"Young girlies! Very young!"

He was drunk, he knew, which was not a good state in which to do anything. He could just as easily go home, have another drink, fall into a deep and oblivious sleep. But it was that hour of the night when a man's desires become inextricably entangled. He wanted to do anything, *any*thing at all, no matter what it was.

32

ON THE BOARDWALK

On Sunday, Kid took her over to Wormwood's Monkey
Theatre, to see The Greatest Aggregation of Educated
Animals on Earth. "Educated" was the operative word, used
to pull it over the rubes. There were none of the big lion-
tamer acts, the trained horses, or the diving elephants. Just
hundreds of smaller animals—monkeys and chickens,
anteaters and lemurs—cackling and fluttering madly about
onstage, pecking out addition problems, and juggling milk
bottles.

For the grand finale the animals acted out a drama entitled
"The Pardon Came Too Late." A squad of uniformed monkeys set out to electrocute a chicken, which they strapped
down into a tiny, highly realistic electric chair, with all the
efficiency of real prison guards. Meanwhile, across the stage,
a lemur scribbled timidly at a scrap of paper. He rolled it
quickly up and stuffed it into the long snout of the anteater,
which then slogged its way slowly, agonizingly over toward
the prison scene—the crowd slowly reduced to helpless fits
of laughter.

It looked as if the anteater might finally make it, the monkeys were taking so long in their frenzied, officious monkey
ways: pushing the chicken's head down, strapping its feet
together, then apart, forcing its beak open for the leather

gag. When the anteater was waylaid by a sudden torrent of—*ants*.

The crowd was screaming, raging with laughter, as the anteater scuttled back and forth across the stage, snorting up its meal. Esther was laughing, too, though she didn't know why, though she hated the whole, awful idea of the animal play. She laughed along the way she did in the movie parlors at people being slapped and punched, and falling down—out of sheer tension, and helplessness.

The anteater still dawdled over his meal. The chicken raised a final, futile squawk as the monkeys bore it down. One of them pulled down an enormous, red switch—and for a few, long seconds the stage went dark. Then a bolt of lightning split through the blackness, and the animals let up one long, terrible shriek together. The audience, convulsed with laughter just a moment before, was shrieking now, too, in mindless terror and delight.

Then the lights went on again—to reveal a steaming, fully prepared plate of fried chicken sitting in the electric chair. The crowd laughed and applauded, the house lights went up, and they all made their way to the exits, ignoring the monkeys who bowed and doffed their prison guards' caps behind them on the stage.

"My golden heart," Kid said when he saw she was frowning, as they came out of the theatre into the blinding glare of midafternoon Coney. "My little *kalleh*—what make you?"

"I don't know," Esse told him, shaking her head, taking the arm he offered, unsure herself what was bothering her. "It's just so—stupid, so mindless."

"Ah, that's what's bothering you. Never mind. Come—come with me."

He walked her up past the grand hotels: the Manhattan Beach, and the Hotel Brighton, and the Oriental. Magnificent, matchstick birdcages, with great blue tea tents out on the lawn and green awnings, and pennants flying from each turret.

Kid took her into the Brighton, where you could get a glass of champagne for ten cents—the bar jammed with sunburned men and women, stinking of the sea and the fried-food stands along the boardwalk. The champagne was mostly flat, and it left a burning aftertaste in her mouth, but Esther drank it down anyway, then had another glass when he offered it to her. She stood at the bar and watched the other men, particularly the older men, feeding it to the women bathers as quickly and eagerly as they could. They laughed with their heads thrown back, drunken and red-faced, and let the men put their arms around their shoulders.

Esther put her glass down and left the hotel without another word to him, her head spinning a little.

If she was to do this she would do it under her own power, by God

"Sweetheart, what's wrong?" he clucked, following her solicitously out onto the evening boardwalk.

She didn't answer him, because she couldn't trust herself to say anything. They walked along in silence, back to where he lived in the Tin Elephant. Esther knew it, she had seen the strange little hotel many times, though she had never been in. Now she walked right up the winding metal staircase, still without saying a word—past the whores hanging out over the balcony in their underwear, smoking languidly, waiting for the first customers of the night. They smirked to see her, but she only smiled back at them, feeling a little dazed.

So this is what it's like to be a whore?

Back in the bowels of the Elephant, she could hear one of them strumming a mandolin. It was an old song she had heard before, sung by the Irish girls on Chrystie Street, back when Lazar still lived with them.

> There's a little side street such as
>   often you meet,
> Where the boys of a Sunday
>   night rally;
> Though it's not very wide, and it's
>   dismal beside,
> Yet they call the place Paradise Alley.
> But a maiden so sweet lives in that
>   little street,
> She's the daughter of Widow McNally;
> She has bright golden hair, and the boys
>   all declare,
> She's the sunshine of Paradise Alley—

She climbed up the rest of the stairs and went to his rooms, which looked exactly as he had described them: crammed back in the telltale, scatalogical curve of the Elephant's Arse. When he unlocked the door she went in and sat on the bed, and took off her hat.

Kid stood watching her for a little while, over by the one dresser, warped and scarred by the sea. Then he walked over to where she sat, and Esther lifted up her arms to him, and held him around the neck, and kissed him on the mouth while he was still standing over her.

He pulled her up, and she let him, still kissing him, holding him fast around his neck and his shoulders. He began to undress her, slowly pulling off the green-and-gold mermaid's bathing suit, and she let him do that, too. She let him lower her to the bed again, until she was sitting naked on his bedspread, trembling a little there despite the heat that was like the inside of an oven.

And when he moved to kiss her again, still fully clothed himself, she let him. She let him kiss her anywhere he wanted to, she let him do anything he wanted to do. She made love to him right out there on top of his bed, so unlike their hidden coupling by the pigeon coop, so *blatant*.

And afterwards, when they were lying crammed together on his narrow bed—the sweet saltiness of their underarms and thighs intermingling, tasting of the sea and the sun from the afternoon—it was she who reached for him again, she who led him slowly through it all again, until they were both satisfied.

So this is what it's like to be a whore—

—she thought, lying on her back. Lying naked on a whore's bed, in a hotel for whores, out on Coney Island.

What did it mean? Was she a whore like the women outside in the hall? Like what the men, the cops and goons always called them on the picket lines?

She looked over at him, and he gazed back at her adoringly. She had all she could do to keep from laughing, pleased and triumphant as she was.

So this is all it takes—

"You are an angel—" he started to say.

She giggled—the way she imagined a whore might—and hit him with the pillow. He looked stunned for a moment—then grinned, and pulled the pillow away. They struggled for a little while more on the bed, laughing.

"I have to go," she said finally, subsiding.

"Don't."

"Don't?"

"Stay with me tonight."

"All night?"

"And the next night, an' the night after that."

"What would they say? I got to get back."

She got up from the bed, starting to walk around to retrieve her clothing where it had been strewn in such haste. When she did, she noticed that the door of the dresser was open, and there was a full-length mirror on the inside.

How strange, how unreal it was to see herself naked, in this dull, spotty mirror, in a dilapidated tourist hotel. The glass so marred and scratched up by the sea salt, and by years of uncaring guests, that she could barely make herself out. The light wasn't very good either. It was late in the evening now, the sun was already setting a little earlier, and the only illumination coming into the room was the refracted glow from the amusement parks, shining behind them on the beach.

But she could see herself there—as she had not seen herself since she was a little girl. As she had never expected to see herself, in such a place.

So this is what it's like to be a whore

Her hair, unpinned, flowing straight down her back, the way only actresses or women in the dirty postcards they sold up by Surf Avenue wore it. Her large brown eyes wide, full lips open in surprise, as if she were about to say something. It was her, all right, though she could not have identified the rest of herself before: the sinewy, slightly worn figure; full, spaced breasts; wide thighs and hips, one a little higher than the other.

That was just her, she thought in wonder. That was all she was.

He reached out and pulled her back to the bed in the narrow room.

"Stay," he whispered to her. "Stay. Please."

"I can't," she said again, unconvincingly.

"Whatta you have to go back for? Why not stay out here all the time?"

She could see the smirk on her father's face:

This is what you have, this is what you do instead of a family?

"I can't." She shook her head. "I got——*things* going on."

"*Ach*, what things? Working yourself to death on the machines?"

"Just——*things*."

And if she stayed, how long would she stay? She thought of the job, and the strike, and her parents. But also her friends, the Talkers' Cafe——a whole life. A person, a *real* person, would have a whole life she couldn't just walk away from.

"To hell with 'em," he said suddenly, fiercely.

"With who?" she asked, taken aback.

"With all of 'em, any of 'em——I don't care who they are. To hell with what they want you to do. You don't got to live like anybody else does, you should know that. You're too fine. You just stay——just for tonight. Then we'll see."

Why not? Why not take this, at least?

She smiled at him——and gave in.

"All right. Just for tonight," she said, ashamed of herself and pleased at the same time, just as glad not to be headed back to the city yet.

Monster! Wretch! You really are a whore, an unclean bone, he raved at her, in their continual, one-sided conversation. She dismissed his specter with a toss of her head.

She didn't care, she didn't care what any of them might think: not him, or her mother, or even Clara. At least for this night, she was that woman in the mirror, that stranger, bold and naked in a strange man's room.

She had seen her father in front of the storefront synagogue——once, back when he had still been reb——arguing furiously with a member of his congregation. His eyes flashing, brow knitted ferociously, prematurely white hair rising in tangled curls as he grew more agitated. How frightening, how formidable he had seemed in his anger! Ranting and raving over some point of Talmud no greater than a sesame seed, which he allowed to carve a chasm between himself and a man he had known for years, all the way back to their village in Russia. Ridiculous, still, in his greenie clothes—the baggy shtetl pants, belted with a rope, shoes soft as slippers, the ill-cut coat—but at least like someone of significance. Like someone whom people might follow, even found a synagogue. Like someone's father.

The image of him there returned, sometimes, unbidden—like tonight, blowing in from the sea, through the open window of the Tin Elephant. Yet far from being frightened by it, his rage, his formidable appearance only intrigued her. It made her want to ask him again why he had never adapted to the ways of his new country.

Do you think I couldn't have made a fortune if I wanted to? he would sneer at her, showing his teeth. *I was brilliant! Not a scholar in a hundred miles could compare. All the best houses had me at their table; they thrust their daughters upon me!*

Then why didn't you? Why rely on an old woman and a girl to earn your meat for you?

Ach, you don't understand! How could you? How could you know what it was like?

He would fold his hands into each other—two, three times, the way he did when he was truly confused.

One evening, when I was still a boy, I was coming home from the Bes Midrash. I came over a hill, and there I saw the whole village sleeping before me. Why I had never gone that way before, I don't know, but I came over the hill and there, no bigger than my hand, was the whole village. Just as it had been for three hundred years, sleeping out in the open, as helpless as a tethered lamb.

And? And so what does that have to do with me?

There I saw the whole beauty of our lives, as the Upper One Himself might have seen it. That was His revelation, granted to me. I looked down, and saw it all there——so beautiful, so perfect in its simplicity, and its poverty. Following the same eternal laws, enduring the same outrages, year after year. A whole life dedicated to the Uppermost in its humbleness, its goodness.

And? And you left it?

I had to leave it. He said it matter-of-factly, the way he did all his betrayals. Hoping to numb the pain, she decided——

I had to leave it, we all had to leave it. And yet I will not forget it. To forget it, to repudiate even the least important of our laws, would be to make of it all a cruel joke. Don't you see? To abandon it would be to mock all those years, and all of that suffering. To make of it a sacrifice without meaning.

So instead you continue it. You continue the sacrifice, on and on!

But he would not be listening then, she knew. His eyes would be milky and distant, clouding up to think less of the village than what he himself had been: a young yeshiva bocher, granted his revelation:

I was so lovely then! So lovely, he would remember, wringing his hands together. *So fine!*

She fell asleep, again, in her lover's arms.

Lying on his back, with her snoring gently into his shoulder, he was amazed by how she felt against him. He loved all the little things about her: her full lips, her eyes, the unevenness of her hips that lent a small swagger to her walk. The deep seriousness with which she looked at him sometimes.

She had little dimples at the very edge of her shoulders, he had noticed for the first time tonight. Tiny indentations, barely noticeable, on the back of each shoulder, but completely endearing. He ran a finger over each one as she slept against him; thinking of nothing, listening happily to the waves through the open window.

Everything in the little room was always damp: the bedding and the curtains, and all his clothes. Even the chairs and the floorboards, and the single dresser, with its drawers that wouldn't close all the way: damp and warped, with jagged white silhouettes of salt etched into the wood.

At night, when she wasn't there, Kid would lie in bed and listen to the ocean rolling and hissing up on the sand. It was so close, so much nearer here than it had ever been before, save on the boat over, and there it had been different—a bottomless, gurgling horror on the other side of the rusty hull.

Sometimes, listening to the sea from the Elephant's Arse, it seemed to him that he and Spanish Louie must have been forgotten already. That if they waited long enough, the sea and the sand would cover over everything—the crazy old hotel in the shape of an elephant, and the great parks back on Surf Avenue, and all memory that any of them had ever existed.

But he could hear, too, the drunken shouts and protests of the last stragglers staggering home from the park, or out to sleep on the beach, and he knew it was only a matter of time before they came for him: at night, most likely, without a sound to be heard above the whores' racket. Or in the midway crowds, over in Steeplechase or Luna Park, Gyp and his boys all around him before he even knew it.

He should be away. The day before he had tried to make serious plans, tried to decide on a city at least: San Francisco, perhaps, or Baltimore, but it had all come to nothing. He simply couldn't concentrate on the problem for more than a few minutes at a time. The question that kept coming to mind was more basic:

Why did he do it?

The lack of an answer had begun to gnaw at him. What in the world had ever led him to whack the most dangerous man in the City over the head with a coal shovel?

Was it for the dwarf? Kid had felt bad for him, sure—especially when he thought he was a boy. But he had seen things like that happen before—or even worse—and he had kept his head down, and his mouth shut. He hadn't been drinking, or under the influence of some mab. He had done it without hesitating, without thinking about it, which was probably the trouble.

And now—here he was: stuck out here on this sandbar with Spanish Louie, 'til God only knew when. And all because of the actions of a moment.

Why, then?

He looked over at the woman snoring sweetly beside him. She wouldn't mind, he knew; she would understand. If he told her she would approve of what he had done, and understand that he had to go.

He knew all this—but still he could not leave. It seemed impossible that there was any other life outside this room: the sleeping woman in his bed, the roll of the surf outside, and the sea air, blowing gently in through the window. How could he flee this homey little room, this city, the woman sleeping beside him? This was his love, and he sunk into a blissful sleep despite himself.

33

TRICK THE DWARF

In Bostock's Circus the great cats stalked Captain Jack around the main ring: a flat-haired man with a huge black Kitchener moustache, and a cold, shaming stare. He stopped the beasts with his look, drove them back on their haunches with his one good arm. They crouched behind him, pawing the air, and followed him through slitted eyes, waiting for their chance.

It was the closest thing to legal suicide: a one-armed lion tamer. They packed every performance, waiting for the next disaster. Three years before, Captain Jack had got too close to one of his charges, a great, shaggy, Nubian lion called the Black Prince, and the beast had snapped two of the fingers off his right hand—gulped them down before he could even feel they were missing, much less retrieve them. The hand became infected, then gangrenous, until finally he had to have the whole arm off.

Pushing himself out in his wheelchair every day with his one remaining arm, glaring at his cats, staring them down as they were put through their paces. Until finally he returned to the ring left-handed, relying only upon the whip, with no extra hand to reach for his pistol. He took on nine lions at a time, nine cats stalking and circling him around the ring, his empty sleeve flapping as he moved.

In the grand finale, he held them all at bay and trotted out the Black Prince himself. Forcing the snapping, hissing beast around and around the ring in tighter and tighter circles, until it was too dizzy to stay on its feet. Then he pushed it over on its side, gentle as a pussycat by now, pulled up its head by the mane, and gave the creature a loud, humbling kiss on the nose.

There were other amazing acts in the Dreamland circus: Mademoiselle Aurora, a brisk, matronly woman in a tutu, who forced her half-ton polar bears up into tottering pyramids with only a wooden staff. Madame Morelli and Her Magnificent Leopards. Herman Weedom and His Pulsating Pumas and Laughing Hyenas—

You could hear them all day, shouting and cursing their animals through their routines, working constantly to come up with something new, something better for the crowds. Barking out their commands in German, the international tongue of obedience, until it felt as if we were living next to a permanent camp of mad drill sergeants.

The worst was a strenuous little bald man named Eckleburg, who preceded Herman Weedom. He affected a monocle and a pair of jodhpurs, and screamed so constantly at the pumas and the rather cowed, mangy hyenas that his audiences rooted for the animals.

One day a young, shaggy-eared African elephant named Lucy, who had helped set up the first Dreamland tents, wandered into his area of the animal circus after a stray bushel of carrots, scaring the pumas and interrupting his rehearsal. Eckleburg struck her over and over again across the trunk with his little whip, raging helplessly at the beast—

"*Raus, raus*—can't you leave us alone?!"

—until Lucy had simply picked him up and thrashed him about. Her trunk snaking out too quick for Eckleburg to even cry out, breaking his back and staving his head in before anyone could intervene, finally dropping his lifeless body in the ring and going back to pick up her carrots.

After that there was some talk that she should be destroyed. Instead, they had put her on display, like everything else on Coney—and a few weeks later she killed a man who tried to feed her a lighted cigarette. In some places a rogue elephant that kills two men might be considered an unacceptable menace, but in Dreamland we liked to look at things from the elephant's point of view. They only made up a new sign for her, reading belatedly, STAND BACK! MANKILLER!—and put her in a cage made deliberately too small for her to turn around or lie down in, so that she would bellow, and pace neurotically up and down in place all day long. Looking the way a mad, dangerous elephant *should* look. Until eventually she really was mad, finally slumping against her bars, great yellow eyes staring furiously out at the circling crowds.

34

TRICK THE DWARF

They liked the elephant, and the circus. I took them to see the diving elephants at the Dreamland Lagoon, and the acrobats, and the Flight to the Moon, and Hell's Gate, and the Doge's Palace——anything to keep them occupied and under wraps, after the fiasco at the rat pit.

It was impossible, I knew. Sooner or later, someone would see them. I was hardly an anomaly out on Coney Island, and even in Manhattan I could still pass undetected, in my disguise. So long as I was not standing directly under his own, withering gaze, I knew I was safe.

But it was different for them. Any one of their old pals or rivals could have picked them out——and they liked to come down to Coney, gallivanting up and down our own little Bowery in their stolen motor cars. Banging away at the rifle galleries, and picking up the mabs, and trying to wrench the coins out of the floor of the Silver Dollar Saloon with the rest of the rubes. The big one, the dumb one, was still walking around in broad daylight dressed like a dago nightmare, trying to con the bens and sams out of their folding money. It was only a matter of time before he was spotted——if not by one of his old friends, then by another hack driver, or a cop, or any other active citizen who kept his nose to the ground and knew how to cuddle a telephone.

The other one was different. He was smarter, and quieter——but also more careless in his way. I saw him. He strolled out on the boardwalk on Sunday mornings like a man who was spying on life from a safe distance. Waiting, watching——like he was weighing all the possibilities.

I was intrigued, despite myself. I started going along with him, and he never seemed to mind. He would stride along, one arm looped paternally over my shoulders, explaining all the ways there were to make money.

"Anybody can be gulled," he said, gazing appreciatively at the customers moving up and down the wooden boardwalk. "Cops, pols, gangsters. Anybody. The only question is how big a racket you need to do the job."

"Anyone? Really? For how much?"

"Oh, for anything."

"*Any*thing? Anything at all?"

"Uh-huh. You just have to know how to do the job."

"Really? I bet you couldn't sell someone, say, the Brooklyn Bridge."

"Sure."

"That ain't true," the big dumb one in the sombrero insisted. "You can't do *that* one no more. Not the Brooklyn Bridge. *Never* the Brooklyn Bridge. *Manhattan* Bridge, maybe."

"Sure you could," he said, rubbing his chin and looking over his friend. "You wanna lay a little money on it?"

"You're on. A finiff."

They spit on their palms and made a quick, furtive handshake.

"I wanna see this," I challenged, my voice skeptical——but so desperately hoping he could do it.

He grinned again, set his shoulders, and said the words I most wanted to hear.

"All right. But you gotta help."

I lay snoring in the Bowery gutter, dressed in my best suit, my head soaked in bad gin. Through slitted eyes I could see him leaning down, plucking me over like one of Herman Weedom's scavenging hyenas——Pancho Villa sombrero nearly covering me while he rummaged through my pockets. Finally, he pulled out the stock certificates: the green, cheaply printed shares they had shown me before, and that I was certain no one, not even the most gullible ruben, would buy.

"You! You there! Stop that at once! Where is a police officer?"

The mark came forward, a middle-aged man with his wife, stern and respectable as a dentist. Spanish Louie made to run off——but then *he* was there, grabbing his arm, holding him in place, pulling the cheap, smeared shares out of Louie's hand.

"What's this? What's this?"

That was my cue. I opened my eyes, pushed myself blearily up to my feet. I staggered toward him, carefully slurring my speech, vibrating inside with the excitement of this new acting job.

"He'sh tryink to rob me?"

The dentist intervened, obviously disgusted as much with me as with the pickpocket, his wife averting her head while he clutched her arm as firmly as he would an impacted molar.

"He certainly was!" The dentist could no longer control himself. "Only this gentleman prevented it."

"Julius!"

The dentist's wife was trying to pull him away, red-faced and sweating under the broiling afternoon sun, but old Julius wouldn't budge.

"I'm just trying to see that justice is done here——"

I pretended to focus on the green pieces of paper, still in his hands.

"My shares! Did—did he get them?"

"No, thanks to this gentleman!"

My eyes went back to Kid, peering sympathetically down at me, the drunken freak. *How I loathed that look, even in our play-acting*—

"Julius—"

"*You* saved 'em?" I belched, for good effect. "Well, I owe *you* a reward!"

I pulled the crumpled bills, one by one, from my pockets, as slowly and methodically as I had been instructed. The dentist frowned; his wife looked away again. Kid put up a hand—

"That's not necessary—"

—but I would not be dissuaded.

"No, no! You earned it. These are invaluable!"

I counted out all the money—some twenty dollars, all the ready bills and silver dollars I was able to dig up around my palace. He handed over my shares—and I shoved them hastily back into a breast pocket just as he had instructed, tipsily doffing my hat and staggering off to a saloon around the corner—while Kid steered the dentist off down the midway by his elbow. There in the saloon, with larceny still racing through every inch of my being, I ordered up a whiskey and sat in the exact seat in the back of the room he had stipulated.

I sat down, to wait for the next part—and waited, and waited, slowly sipping through one whiskey, and then another. Until after the better part of two hours I couldn't take it any longer, and hurried back to the Tin Elephant; huffing and puffing up the stairs on my miniature legs, past the lounging whores to the Elephant's Arse.

I burst into their little, curved room—as much as I can burst into anyplace—relieved to find them there, and not in jail or worse. Unable to keep from blurting out my question even as I saw the broad grin plastered over the dumb one's face, and the smaller, subtler one spread slowly over *his,* and knew the answer before I heard it. Though of course I still had to ask.

"Tell me! Tell me—did it come off? What about the mark?"

"Why, you were, kid," he said. "*You* were the mark."

35

KID TWIST

Monk taught him everything, with the quiet seriousness of a father teaching the Talmud to his son. It was Monk who taught him how to run a stuss game, and the banco scam, and the drop scam, and the mysterious art of how to render a man senseless by tapping a cigar ash in his beer.

He taught him all the short skin games: the ones that were new, and the ones that were old, and the ones that were so old they could be used as if they were new again. It seemed to him that Monk made some of them up on the spot, as if he were continuing a good joke, or a story:

"A man walks into a bar with a dog—"

He sat quietly in the back of the bar, cool and dim in the late afternoon, nursing a short beer and a cigarette, idly watching the scene out on the sidewalk—until he saw the man walk in with the dog.

"Hey, Mac, mind de mutt fer me," the man told the bartender, setting the animal down on a stool, pressing a shiny, fresh silver dollar into his palm.

"I got a big deal goin' on. You mind him, dere'll be more in it for ya later."

"Sure," the barman grunted, casting a baleful eye on the animal. The man went out again, and Kid was on.

He drained the glass, took a last drag or two on his cigarette—forcing himself to move slowly, slowly, the way Monk had taught him. Making his way nonchalantly, a little wobbly, toward the barroom door.

He swayed in toward the bar, banged into a stool, almost knocking it over, drawing the bartender's attention. That was when he noticed the dog.

Nothing too dramatic, nothing too obvious. *You're playin' to one man, Kid, not de galleries.* He did a little double take, that was all—and walked on. Just before he reached the door Kid stopped, and looked back at the dog. He started out again, walking backwards this time, and bumped beautifully into a much smaller man—still staring at the dog.

That's when you come back—

"Pardon me, bub, is that, uh, is that your dog?"

"No, it ain't," the bartender told him, vigorously squeaking his towel around a mug. Suspicious but curious already.

He had been all the way across the room, he couldn't possibly have heard their conversation—

"No? Hmm. Well, you know that's a Rhodesian ridgeback, don'cha?"

"Dis?" The barman looked down incredulously at the dog—skinny little black-and-white mutt, picked up from the East River garbage docks, trained just long enough in Monk's inimitable fashion to sit still on a bar stool.

"Sure it is. A genuine, full-blooded Rhodesian ridgeback, unless I miss my guess. In Africa, they train 'em to hunt lions. It's a great hunting dog, friend—can'tcha see the way it's sittin' there?"

The bartender stopped wiping his glass, looked down at the dog again, a glint of disbelief still in his eyes.

Now was the time to whip out the money.

"Say," he half whispered, leaning over the bar. "Say. You *sure* that ain't your dog?"

Kid pulled out the billfold—a Hoboken roll, fat with ones, a couple twenties on the top, held in place with a gaudy, ruby-studded clip. The bartender twisted his neck around uncomfortably.

"I told you——"

"Say it was your dog. What wouldja take for it? Two hunnerd? Five hunnerd?"

"I told you. It ain't my dog," the bartender said firmly now, resisting temptation, thinking of the ferocious mug on the man who had left him——the bull neck and cauliflower ears, the flattened, pugnacious nose that just shouted trouble.

"But just say. Just say it was," Kid persisted. "How much? A thousand? Thousand five?"

"Look, mister." The voice steely now with regret. "It ain't my dog."

"All right. All right for now."

Slowly, ever so slowly, he slipped the billfold back into his pocket. The barkeep's eyes followed it down, trailing over Kid's duded-up clothes, the diamond stickpin in his tie, diamond studs on his shirt and cuff links.

"You say so, mister. But, you know, whose dog is it if his owner don't come back? You read me? Whose dog is it then, huh? Full-bred Rhodesian ridgeback an' all."

He ambled toward the door again, setting his hat carefully on his head. Looking back toward the barkeep once more.

"Maybe I'll be back. You think it over, an' just maybe I'll be back in a couple hours, okay? We'll see whose dog it is then."

He was out and around the corner quickly then, down an alley, and through a back cellar to another bar. The idea was not to give the man time for a second thought——not right away, that was.

Kid slid into his seat at the bare little table, where Monk already had his beer for him.

"So?"

"He's soaked," he told him, and Monk nodded with satisfaction. He sat there, slowly sipping at his drink.

The rule was always to wait through at least one slow beer, maybe two—while they talked and whiled away the hour, letting desire rise and blossom. Wait until it was time for Monk to go back in, and proclaim loudly that his deal had fallen through, and he was left penniless. Wait for the barkeep, with smug and greedy eyes, to ask innocently if he might help Monk out, by taking the dog off his hand for a few dollars. The perfectly ordinary dog, which the bartender had convinced himself by now was a purebred Rhodesian ridgeback, and would fetch thousands of dollars. Whenever Kid returned.

Of course, it didn't do to wait too long.

"Did I ever tell ya da time I waited too long?" Monk asked him.

"No."

"I waited too long, an' I picked de wrong dog. It hadda little cold when I picked it out, but I thought I nursed it right. Turns out it was pneumonia. Mutt drops dead. Falls right off de bar stool while I'm out."

"So what'd you do?"

"Whattaya think I done? I go back in dere, wailin' away, right on schedule: 'Oh, I lost me last dollar, I got squeezed outta me life's savin's, wha'do I got left in dis world to my name?'

"Only dere ain't no dog dere for me to sell. I'm just wailin' an' wailin' away, lookin' for de dog dat ain't dere. I'm noticin' de bartender ain't makin' no move to buy de dog, de way he's supposed to. So I finally gets t'rough an' simmers down, wonderin' what de hell is goin' on. An' all de bartender says is, 'This just ain't your day, fella. Yer dog is dead, too.'"

Kid pulled the tourist aside, into the theatre alley off Fourteenth Street, produced the wondrous machine from its bag.

"Gimme a bill—"

"Oh, no, Mac," the chubby-faced rube smirked. "I know this trick. You use your own bill, if this is so great."

You know nothing

"All right."

He pulled out a tenner, fed it carefully into the top of the miracle machine—rubbed up to a silvery glow, and shaped suspiciously like a meat grinder, if you wanted to look too closely. He cranked the handle—and two more, identical tenners slid slowly out the other end, one after the other. Before the last one was out, the tourist was reaching for his wallet—

He tapped the sailor coming out of a Water Street bar, gave him the story on the up-and-up:

"Look, I can see you been around, I'll play it straight. This is all counterfeit."

He held the weighty bag of money up before the tar's eyes; opened it for him, let him see the bank notes there: tens and twenties so good they might have been, well, *real.*

"Not a bad job, huh? Thing is, the cops got it in for me, an' one more collar I go up to Sing Sing for life. What'll ya gimme for the whole lot?"

He was around the corner like a shot, shoving the gob's money into his vest pocket before he could sort through the top bills and discover the sawdust and torn-up bits of newspaper below—

Of course that was all their recreation, their fun and games, as it were. The rest of the time they went back to the steady drudgery of shaking down peddlers for protection money, of poisoning horses and cheating at stuss and heaving ballot boxes into the East River. All that, and sometimes worse.

"Remember, kid," Monk always told him. "Whatever you do, make sure you do it in the dark. All kinds a t'ings can go on in de dark—an' nobody knows just who did what."

He sat in the cellar of the stuss den on Rivington Street, waiting for the Bottler. The dank, plain little room cleared out of bens and sams for once—just Gyp the Blood and Spanish Louie and the Grabber sitting with him behind the felt cloth with the cards in the deck painted crudely upon it.

The Bottler padded cautiously down the steps, bowler tucked down low over his eyes like a turtle in his shell, his own boys right behind him. Kid stood up to greet him:

"All right, let's see if we can't work this out—"

That was when the lights went out. There was a string of bright flashes, the pistol shots incredibly loud in the close little room, and then they were all racing up the stairs and out into the street. So that when the police finally arrived and turned the lights back on there was only the Bottler, lying over the painted ace, shot through the heart, and who was to say who did anything?

They turned the Bottler's share over to the Grabber, just to make sure that one was pacified, and Kid sent a huge green wreath to the funeral, and wore a black armband to the stuss game for the next two weeks, which everyone agreed was a thoughtful and considerate gesture.

But the Bottler was a Five Pointer, so the price had to be paid. The next week they found Denny Holt dead as a mackerel over on Avenue A, and then Matty Holt swore revenge, and the war was on—

Kid stood under the elevated, sticking his arm out around the pillar, pointing blindly across the street in the general direction of where the Five Pointers were. He squeezed the trigger, felt the pistol jerk—laughed out loud at the joy of firing a gun in the middle of the street.

Bullets pinged all around him like a Bowery shooting gallery—ricocheting off the el pylons, smashing windows, bouncing off the trains above. Citizens coming home from work screamed and tumbled down the elevated stairs, scrambling for cover, the gangs still blazing away.

A flying squad of cops marched determinedly down Allen Street, tapping their nightsticks along the manhole covers. A hail of bullets from all sides sent them running back down the street, their high hats tumbling after them. The shooting went on into the night—the gangs intoxicated with their control of the street, boys from the Hudson Dusters and the Gophers and just plain freelancers joining in, until the darkened street was wreathed in smoke, and the air was pungent with the smell of powder. Bullets whizzing past his ear, knocking birds off the telephone wires, winging off fire escapes and trash cans and trolley cars. The whole neighborhood pinned down in their homes, nobody able to sleep or venture out from under their beds—until finally, well past midnight, another, much larger column of cops came barreling down the street from the Rivington station house, now firing their revolvers as they came.

The gangsters slipped away, quiet as smoke, back down their familiar alleys and courtyards. Leaving a few of their number curled up like old dogs on the pavement for the sanitation men to clear away in the morning.

The trouble was that this one was too big to cover over with a few arrests and a few dollars to the police reporters. The Hearst papers had ahold of it, and too many citizens were outraged. Big Tim and Mr. Murphy himself had felt obliged to call a meeting at the Palm with Monk and Paul Kelly, the elegant little I-tie who led the Five Pointers, and it was agreed that Monk and Kelly would settle their differences in a boxing match, to be held on neutral ground up in the Bronx.

"This'll be a clean fight, by the rules," Big Tim warned.

"You ain't got no worries dere. I done some sparrin' in my day," Monk told him.

"I done some myself," Kelly retorted. "You know I once beat Benny Leonard——"

"Dat's a goddamned lie, because Benny's a Yid, which means a wop like you wouldn't have a tooth left in his mouth if you really fought him, instead a in your dream world——"

"Shut up," Big Tim told them brusquely. "You think I don't know the two a yas can fight? Why d'ya think I chose this? It'll be a draw, by the way. You two're such experts, I expect you to make it look good."

"What da hell!"

"I can take that yegg——"

"That's it!"

Big Tim slammed his hand on the table for silence.

"I want you two bummies to carry each other. Bang away on each udder all you like. But that's the end of it, you got me? I need you both for the election. Somebody wins, this goes on, and if it does I'll come down on both your necks."

The Bronx car barn was pungent with the smell of straw and old leather, motor oil and horse piss. The makeshift bleachers filled with cheering, shouting gangsters and their mabs. Big Tim himself seated down front, with two solid rows of cops—just to make sure everything came off like it was supposed to.

It was a fight they would talk about forever after on the East Side. The two gangsters battering each other back and forth across the ring like a pair of bantam roosters: Kelly a little slimmer, a little swarthier, a slightly more elegant boxer. Monk making up for what he lacked in finesse with ferocious, bull-like rushes across the ring. Both of them splitting lips, knocking out teeth, closing each other's eyes to dark little slits. Until finally, having pummeled each other for more than three hours and convinced all present with the sheer magnificence of their struggle, they collapsed at the exact same moment in a heap—still trying weakly to punch and gouge each other where they lay on the blood-splattered canvas.

Then their men, shouting and weeping openly at their splendid performance, had lifted them both up and carried them out of the car barn, into a pair of beautifully appointed carriages. Releasing the horses and drawing their champions back downtown themselves, all the way to their respective brothels.

Two weeks later, before their wounds were barely healed, Big Tim threw a ball for them all up at the Haymarket, in the no-man's-land of the Tenderloin. Monk and Kelly met at the center of the old hall and shook hands, before their devoted minions, and after that they sat up in their boxes like a pair of pashas, surrounded by their molls and their lieutenants, presiding regally over the grand march of the Eastmans and the Five Pointers.

But it couldn't last. It never had before, and there was no reason it would now, and soon the two gangs were blackjacking each other up blind alleys, cutting themselves up in Water Street dives, and firing pistols down crowded sidewalks.

"We'll wipe up de earth wit' dose guys," Monk boasted. "No mick or wop is ever gonna run de Lower East Side again"—but by then the election was over, and people were fed up with the gangs. The pols removed their protection, and the cops were looking out for anything to run them in on.

They got Monk one night up in Times Square, for trying to roll a drunken young gentleman for his calfskin gloves. He had spotted the gent staggering up Seventh Avenue, with a lushroller already on his tail, and the gloves as fine a piece of goods as he had ever known, soft and yellow as butter. But the bruiser he took for a lushroller was actually a Pinkerton detective, hired by the sport's daddy to look after him, and equipped with a police whistle and a big horse pistol. It was just the mistake they had been looking for, and before it was all over Monk found himself stuck away in the Tombs, with bail denied and every door now shut to him. Kid had gone up to Fourteenth Street with Gyp, to plead for him at Tammany Hall, but even Big Tim wouldn't hear it this time.

"Who's gonna toss your ballots in the East River next time you need help with Mr. Hearst?" Gyp had asked him menacingly.

"Anyone, lads, anyone," Sullivan replied, seemingly unperturbed by Gyp's impertinence—sounding almost sad about it all. "That's just it—I can get anyone what wants a favor from me, or needs my protection. An' I can get 'em to do it wit'out turnin' all of Jewtown into Dodge City, there's the rub."

"What makes you think we'll stand for it?" Kid challenged him.

"Oh, my boys, my loyal *bhoys*. D'ya think any of us is just free to do as we please? I got to answer to Mister Moiphy, an' he's got to answer to the financial interests, and the governor, an' the voice of the people. Even Jesus Christ Hisself only sits on the right hand of God the Father Almighty, an' don' think the Holy Ghost ain't lookin' to take His place."

There was talk about springing Monk before his trial could take place—a big, dramatic breakout from the Tombs, or the courtroom—but that's all it was, was talk. Big Tim saw to it that he was too well guarded for anyone to get ideas, and even if they had sprung him, there was no place to go—not with the big man's protection lifted. The judge gave Monk ten years in Sing Sing, and when the news came down Paul Kelly himself was quoted in the papers as saying it was a great shame, and that he, personally, would pay ten thousand dollars to see Monk free—though somehow the money was never forthcoming.

The day Monk was sent up, all the Eastmans who had stayed loyal to him gathered down by the Chambers Street ferry to see him off—though the booly dogs hustled him out of the wagon and onto the Sing Sing boat too quickly for anyone save for the news photographers to get more than a glimpse. They had waited around anyhow, standing in the rain, until the prison barge was loaded with its sad cargo and shoved off. And that night back in the dance hall, there were many toasts drunk to his health, and the waiters led them through one slow, dirgelike chorus of "The Boston Burglar" after another:

> I was born and raised in Boston
> A town you all know well
> Brought up by honest parents
> The truth to you I tell
> Brought up by honest parents
> And raised most tenderly
> 'Til I became a sporting blade
> At the age of twenty-three—

—until there wasn't a dry eye left in the house, and everyone was having a pretty good time.

Not that *he* forgot Monk. Every week, at least at first, Kid would take the Hudson line up to Ossining, to bring him some smokes and maybe a new fantail pigeon or a pouter he thought he might like. There was a turnkey they could *shmeer* so he let him right into Monk's cell, and they sat on his bunk and jabbered about the boys, and old times, and his chances for parole. But invariably, after a few minutes their conversation would peter out, and both men would find themselves staring at their shoes.

"It ain't so bad, Kid," Monk rasped, sardonic as he had been when Kid first saw him, lying shot in the gutter. "I got me boids t'rough de window, an' dere's even a kit or two down in the kitchen. I lived t'rough worse already."

But Kid noticed every time he came how much lumpier and yellower Monk looked in his baggy prison stripes— how low, and damp, and lightless his cell was. It was depressing, and soon he was going up less frequently, only every few weeks or so, then every few months, then he barely had time to see him at all.

After that, after the big shootout and Monk's arrest, it was the end of the big gangs. Paul Kelly and most of his Five Pointers laid low for a while, and then they turned straight, or went into the real estate business. Kid and Gyp and anyone else divvied up the Eastmans, and fought over their rackets. The last time he saw them was huddled under the East River dump:

Above their heads the leavings of a city spilled down the wooden platforms and into the river, where it wound around Corlears' Hook. They could hear the ragpickers and the bonepickers, the coal dusters and the hair weavers and the dog renderers, methodically digging and scratching their way through the teeming shore.

They had carved out their own space, down below the dump platform, among the piles of beer cans piled up as proudly as skulls: seven or eight men with boys' faces, wear-

"Don' be like that. *Kine hora,* Kid—there's ain't nothin' ever been done that can't be fixed."

"That's where you're wrong, Louie. That's where they lie to ya: nothin' that's been done *can* ever be fixed. Not really."

They went on waiting. They went on rides to the moon, and down to hell, and up to Heaven, and the Matterhorn, and the top of the Steeplechase, and the Ziz. But sooner or later, he knew, Spanish Louie would go, as soon as he had talked up enough courage.

Kid convinced himself it was no less safe to let him go back. It was only a matter of time, anyway, before one of them spotted Louie strolling through the crowds in his Mex outfit, or wandered into the Elephant in search of some gooh. The dwarf was right: he would have to let him go, and take their chances.

"You know enough not to sell me out, don'cha, Louie?" he at least asked him before he left, seeing him off at the rail station.

"Sure, Kid."

"No, I mean it," he said, gripping Spanish Louie by both arms so hard the pigeons fluttered out of their roosts in the beams of the station house. Looking into his face, trying to get him to understand at least this much out of pure altruism.

"You know that Gyp'll *say* you're square with him, but he won't mean it. All it means is he'll have me an' you, too. An' he'll do ya, Louie; he'll do ya sure as a cop'll pick up a stray finiff. You know that much, don'cha, Louie?"

"Sure, Kid. I know that," Spanish Louie swore, as sincerely as he was capable of.

"You see what I'm talkin' about, Louie?" he repeated, still holding his arms. And Louie repeated it dutifully—

"Sure, Kid, I see it; I see it same as you do"—though Kid knew, even as he said it, that he did not see it at all.

Only a shlimazel *believes in* mazel—

381

He put him on the train to the City, with instructions to return no matter what within three days. Yet he was not terribly surprised when there was no sign or word from Spanish Louie after three days, or three weeks, or three weeks after that.

For a while Kid holed up in his room, with a pistol out on the bed and another on the dresser, waiting for them to come for him——though he knew that even these would not be enough. That there was nowhere in Dreamland or all of Coney or the whole City where he could hide for very long, if Gyp the Blood came after him.

He knew he should go, but he did not go. It wasn't the sweaty little room holding him back, he knew, or the rides or the lights or even the ocean rolling outside his window every night. It wasn't any of them, or even the opportunities that presented themselves, but the chance to see her again.

What a hell of a thing!——

——he muttered to himself in the morning, pocketing his change and his handkerchief, his chewing gum and his key, his guns and his blade and his dice. A hell of a thing all right, but it was undeniable: it was the girl.

He smiled to himself, a little embarrassed, just to think of it. To come all that way, from that *ongepotchket* little village——to go through everything and not get caught, avoiding all the snares——only to end up here, at the very edge of the sea. At last, here he was, tied down to something, but he felt curiously free and light, despite all the mess he knew he was now in.

First hitting Gyp with the shovel, and now this. Now the girl. He had looked down and seen her on the beach, and now he was caught.

After that he stopped worrying altogether about Spanish Louie not returning, or selling him out. He stopped worrying about one of the boys running into him, and walked out into the Sunday crowds again, in his best, cream-colored suit. Come what may, he would be ready for them—as ready as he ever could be.

Out in the surf, the bathers leaped and bobbed and squealed their way through the waves. They clutched onto the guidelines, squeezed into little wedges of beachfront partitioned off by hedges of barbed wire rolled right into the water. The happy clamor of the crowd subsumed in the roll of the breakers, the screams from the distant roller coasters. Men making human pyramids, and sticking out their chests. Women bending over and flipping up the skirts of their bathing costumes, grinning audaciously at the camera.

He looked out over the beach for a long time—then he sat down and began to take off his socks and shoes, rolling up his pants legs as quickly as a child. Until he could walk barefoot out on the warm sand, feeling it wriggle through his toes, holding his shoes in one hand, and keeping one eye out, as always, for whatever he might find.

37

GYP THE BLOOD

He had the dream again.

He came out of the jungle, and was suffocated in the black, close space. The bodies of ten or twelve men curled up around him, head-to-knee, like cats. The air heavy with the smell of wet wool, and sweat, and perfumed smoke.

Li Yuen—Fountain of Beauty

It was always the same dream. He was in a jungle, the leaves green and ripe and luxuriant, air thick with decay. In the distance were the towers of a strange city, but all around him he could catch glimpses of beasts moving through the underbrush: the faces of leopards, and of apes, and the gray haunches of elephants. There was the sound of music coming from somewhere, and the sound of water, and he was looking for something.

He didn't feel threatened by any of the animals—but beneath it all was a terrible feeling of dread, of low, lurking menace. He turned, expecting to see a pair of eyes staring at him—ape eyes, or human eyes, cold and bestial—but all he could see were more heads, the shifting, circling shapes and faces, receding slowly through the leaves—

•   •   •

He sat up coughing, reaching automatically for his guns—one in his vest, another one tucked beneath the hard little *chum tow* that cushioned his head. *Still there.* Next he checked for his wallet: everything in order, and he breathed deeply from the heavy, smoke-laden air, and wondered if he should have another bowl.

He picked up his *yen ngow,* and began to scrape the tiny, long-necked spoon through the little *dows* on the *yen gah* before him.

Three bowls—over how long? Was it still night? The same night?

All he remembered was padding down into the low basement room on a miserably hot, rainy afternoon. His anticipation building with each step he took—slipping through the unmarked door and holding up one finger to Mock Duck sitting like a stone ancestor in the vestibule.

One dow, he had said firmly—

When had that been?

It wasn't just the opium. He loved the whole ritual of the vice, so much more refined, so much *purer* than anything in the world above. The porcelain *dows* on their *yen gah* rack, waiting to be filled and screwed onto the pipe. The sponge to clean the pipe, and the thin *yen hock* needle to fill it. The little pair of scissors to trim the lamp wick—its yellow, tremulous flame the only light in the deep and weighty darkness.

Only then did the hop begin to do its work: the blissful, floating transcendence. So clean, so immaculate—so far beyond anything to be had from needled beer, or good whiskey. The lush, brooding dreams—

Li Yuen—Fountain of Beauty. Fook Yuen—Fountain of Happiness.

● ● ●

He could easily go for another, but there wasn't enough of the black, congealed grease left, and an aggregation was picking up around the door—a fiddle, and a singer, and some fool banging out one of the old hop house staples on its untuned piano, trying to get someone to buy them another *dow:*

> Did you ever hear about
>   Willie the Weeper
> Willie the Weeper, yes,
>   the chimney sweeper
> Had the dope habit and he had it bad
> Listen and I'll tell you 'bout the
>   dream he had—

Gyp began to gather up his coat and hat, the hophead musicians annoying him too much to stay. Anyplace else, he would have simply told them to shut up and meant it, but he was leery about trying anything in Chinatown.

> They went to a land called Kankatee
> Bought a million cans of hop
>   and had a jubilee
> Visited the neighbors for
>   miles around
> Presented the King with a bottle
>   of Crown

> He went to Monte Carlo where he
>   played roulette
> Won every penny and he never
>   lost a bet

Played every night till the bank
went broke
Laid himself down and took
another smoke

It went on and on, like all hop songs. Endless verses of dog-
gerel, sung just so the yaps could think they were still alive.
Gyp had no doubts on that score.

He signaled for Sam Kee, Mock Duck's man, who picked
his way swiftly through the hop sleepers laid out on their
bamboo mats, his tight yellow silk robe swishing gently in
the darkness. The Chinaman brought him a hot towel, and
Gyp flipped him a coin and ran it roughly over his face while
Sam Kee quickly set the *yen poon* tray to rights—rearranging all the delicate instruments in their sacred, eternal order.

He looked down at the little rack of *dows*, then glanced
silently up at Gyp.

"Don't worry," Gyp grunted. "I'll be back someday."

The Chinaman shuffled obediently off with his tray. Gyp
stood up and stared into the little mirror on the wall, examining the ragged, dirty patch of bandage along his scalp. At
least his head had stopped hurting for a while—although he
could already feel it beginning to throb again, even as he
fingered it.

He straightened his bow tie, smoothed down his bright
yellow suit as best he could. Even in the faint lamplight, he
could see a matching yellowish tinge around his eyes, a two-
day growth on his face. Things couldn't go on like this, he
thought—but then again, why couldn't they?

He walked through the room, after Sam Kee, toward the
door and the narrow, discreet flight of stairs that led back up
to Mott Street.

Mock Duck sat by the door like a Buddha, an expression-less figure in a mandarin's silken robe, a skullcap crowning his broad, flat face, a coat of chain mail protecting his pot-belly. The chain mail was part of a reputation for craziness he cultivated as head of the Hip Sings, in the impenetrable gang wars of Chinatown. When the wars were on he was also known to simply walk out on the street with a pistol in each hand and begin firing, moving slowly around in a cir-cle with his eyes shut.

Lately, though, Mock Duck had been much less gregarious. There had been a little girl who slept at his feet, Gyp knew, and brought him tea and almond cookies on a tray, but the child welfare agencies had made him give her up. It would have been all right if she had just been one more heathen Chinee, but some socially minded hophead had noticed she was a little white girl—brought from San Francisco, it was said, after her mother had abandoned her in a brothel there. Mock Duck had fattened her up, and doted on her, dressed her in silken Chinese dresses and put ribbons in her hair—until the child welfare people got wind of it, and packed her away to an orphanage where she got to sleep in a wool night-dress, and pray on her knees every night on the hard wood floor, and bathe in freezing cold water every morning.

Well, everybody had their troubles; that was why you went to a hop den. Mock Duck sat silent and unseeing by the door, apparently oblivious to the fools making such a racket.

> But in the morning, where am I at?
> I thought that I was in my sweet
>   baby's flat
> But in the morning I'm right in line
> Mister Hop Sing Toy you're no friend
>   of mine

That was the difference between himself and all the Willies, Gyp knew: he never expected to wind up in some sweet baby's flat. He was satisfied if he could find his pistols and his money and stagger out into the heat.

Up on the street the muddled yellow-brown light was nearly unbearable. It was another steamer, the air like walls of heat he had to break through with every step.

He made his way to Canal, where they sold fish still twitching and flapping in their barrels, and live crabs, and fresh chickens and pickles along the sidewalk. The blue-bloused Chinamen eyed him warily before vanishing down into their basements like rabbits dropping down a hole.

They were a mysterious race, he assured himself. That was why he went down to Chinatown, when there were now hop shops in the Tenderloin, and on the Bowery. He preferred the anonymity, the feeling that he had walked into another world on Mott Street—the sudden openings into rooms where men sat eating with wooden sticks, the smiling, golden idols in their gold and scarlet temples—

Up along Grand Street, Gyp stopped and bought a piece of raw sugarcane from a Chinese boy for a penny, then ran his tongue pensively along the rough, bitter stick. The wound on his head had recommenced to ache, slowly infuriating him all over again.

He stalked blindly off to the east. Already, the bandage had made him a laughingstock with the mabs, and in the saloons. Somehow they would have to be found; it would have to be taken care of right away, before he could complete his father's task, or even the little number Big Tim wanted him to handle—

He stopped in his tracks at the corner of Mulberry Street. There he was, right before him, sauntering through the crowds. At first he didn't trust his own eyes; it seemed incredible that even *he* wouldn't know enough to lay low, at least for a few weeks more.

Yet it was him, all right, big as life. The moustachios were gone, and the ridiculous Mexican get-up, but there was no mistaking him: It was Spanish Louie, all right, ambling along Grand Street as casually if he were out for his Sunday constitutional.

Gyp couldn't believe his luck as he closed in on the long, stoop-shouldered back before him. He made himself go slowly, his eyes darting back and forth through the crowd in case it was somehow a trap—but he didn't believe that Spanish Louie could dissemble this well. More likely he was just being stupid, as usual.

Gyp homed in, sidling inconspicuously through the sidewalk crowd, letting himself be jostled along until he was right behind him.

Steady, steady—

He searched the street ahead for a likely alley, a handy basement doorway. Reminding himself he didn't want to finish the man off—not just yet, not here. Not until he had scared Louie into telling where Kid and that damned dwarf were—

There was a small gap in the walls of tenements just ahead, a little thieves' den the I-ties called Bandits' Roost. It might be trouble if some of them were home, but it was a risk Gyp was willing to take. He couldn't be sure that he'd ever have a setup this plum again.

"There you are, boy-o!"

He felt the wooden stick like a knife under his shoulder blade and whirled around, furiously.

"Big Tim himself'll be needin' a word wit' you, son."

It was Buckley, the squat little cop. Gyp nearly spat with

anger——*to be interrupted so close to the mark!*

"Not now, *tsitser!*" he hissed. "Lose yourself, I got business."

"Oh, you do, you do at that, my boy," Buckley smirked, one hand already reaching for his belt.

Gyp pushed him away, started back through the crowd after Spanish Louie. Too late, from the corner of his eye, he saw the club coming up, felt it crack down on his skull before he could turn around. He felt his knees buckle, and as he fell to the sidewalk he could see Louie strolling on ahead, out of reach——oblivious to what was going on less than half a block behind him.

The last thing Gyp saw, before he blacked out, was Buckley standing over him, grinning smugly.

"How the mighty are fallen," he said, and gave him a vicious kick in the side.

BOOK SEVEN

Then I heard Siegfried's horn sounding over the mountains and I knew that we had to kill him. We were armed with rifles and lay in wait for him on a narrow path over the rocks.

——CARL JUNG

38

THE GREAT HEAD DOCTORS FROM VIENNA

Freud had gone uptown in the morning looking for his old friend Siggy Lustgarten from medical school, but the man had left town on vacation. Afterwards he decided he might as well get it over with and look up his sister's family, but the directions were vague, and he had a hard time finding the address.

It was better here, uptown. The farther he went the wider the streets seemed, the cleaner the air. The apartment houses were immense, gracious structures of granite and brick and marble, instead of the awful, dull brown stone that even the best homes in New York seemed to be made of. Spires of vast new cathedrals going up beside them, at least as big as anything in Europe.

America, carrying the faith forward——

He had almost been forced to bring his own family to this place——and he wondered how different all their lives would have been, if that had come to pass.

Well, it would not have been so bad, really. A few comforts sacrificed, here and there, but one could get along. One could always get along——

It had been right after he married, the same year of his last military reserve duty, up in Olmutz. There had been an incident—one that made him wonder seriously if he could ever make a decent living in Vienna as a Jewish doctor, much less one with his ideas—

"Reservists! If we had been using live ammunition you all would be dead now!"

The voice made him freeze, huddled in the ditch where he was. The huge, braided general had ridden up behind them, just as the officer was handing Freud his list of ghastly wounds. He was an enormous man, in another, spectacular red and yellow uniform, bellowing merrily at his cowed troops: a certain General E. M., master of ordnance on the general staff—one of the bellicose anti-Semitic clique at the imperial court.

Freud knew him. He had recognized him right away. He was fatter now, great gut spilling over his saddle pommel, but the voice, the swagger were still unmistakably the same—

He had run into the General six years before, during his first call-up, at a Vienna military hospital. Freud had been a young officer-cadet then, just starting his medical training, bored and contemptuous of the endless military maneuvering. On his birthday he had slipped away to town, as he so often did, to read the newspapers in the Ringstrasse cafes, and silently toast himself with an *einen kleinen Braunen*.

While he was gone, the General had come into the company clinic—a thinner man then, sleek as a whip, with a wolfish grin. Bellowing just as he was now, demanding a cure for a dose he had picked up in an officers' brothel, complaining that he had urgent business with the emperor. Freud had been caught out, absent without leave, and when he got back that night the general had personally arrested him. He had clapped him into barracks for a week, his big teeth grinning maniacally at him through the barracks window.

"That will teach you to run away, my fine Jew doctor!"

He had never been so humiliated in his life. That week, lying in his barracks bunk day and night, enduring the taunts of the other young reservists, he had felt close to a nervous breakdown. His whole record, his whole career teetered on the edge of ruin. In his despair he had remembered again that time, when he was seven or eight, that he had peed on his parents' bedroom floor. His father railing at him:

The boy will come to nothing!

And now here was his General—back like a bad dream, more inflated than ever. Freud tried not to look at him, keeping his eyes fixed on the list of hideous wounds, and the great man did not seem to notice him. After a few more harangues he had kicked his long-suffering steed into motion, gone on to rebuke another section of the line.

But that night, back in the one decent cafe in Olmutz, the General had appeared again, dominating a boisterous table full of general officers, all in their medals and parakeet uniforms. The waiters had all hovered about them, attending to their every need, and Freud and the other junior reserve officers had not been able to get the slightest attention.

As he watched them Freud grew more and more resentful—not wanting to do anything that might draw the man's attention but seething at the humiliation, the unfairness of it all. Until finally he had reached out and pulled at the apron strings of a waiter as he scurried past with more brandy for the generals.

"Hey! Over here, you! Who knows? Maybe someday *I* will be a general, too!"

The other officers at his table had erupted in laughter, a waiter even reluctantly coming over to serve them at last.

Freud had sat grinning sheepishly, basking in the audacity of his act—until he noticed that the men around his table were no longer laughing, but discreetly lowering their faces into their hands and beer glasses.

"You? A general?"

The great, fat General was standing there, smirking just behind him, a cigar in one hand and his brandy snifter in the other. He had opened his tunic, and undone the top button of his pants to let his immense stomach breathe, and it occurred to Freud despite himself that he looked like nothing so much as an angry father, preparing to undo his belt for a whipping.

"A man who leaves his post could *never* be a general," he said as Freud scrambled to his feet, nearly knocking his chair over in his haste. Behind them, it was the turn of the canary generals to laugh and grin now. Freud stood dumbly at attention, waiting for whatever more might be coming.

When he was a child, he remembered, his father had told him a story about how a gentile had once confronted him on the sidewalk, tossed his new hat in the gutter, and told him to get out of the way.

"What did you do?" Freud asked him.

"Well, I picked up my hat," he said, and Sigmund had burned with shame for his father's cowardice.

Yet now all he could do was stand at attention, waiting for the General's pleasure. To his infinite relief, the man merely flashed his great, toothy grin at him, and began to turn away—making a curt, dismissive gesture with his hand as he did so.

"A deserter could *never* be a general," he repeated—then flung back over his shoulder:

"Besides, you're a Jew!"

The generals at their table roared with laughter. So did the waiters and the civilians at the other tables, and even the other junior officers at his own table were smiling behind their hands. And all Freud could do was bow stiffly, put down a few coins for his drink, and make his way out of the restaurant.

He tried scrupulously to avoid the general throughout the rest of the maneuvers, but as luck would have it he had run into him again in the regiment's indoor pool. It was a cool afternoon, and the general was the only other officer present, wading hippopotamuslike into the water, the ripples spreading out across the entire pool from his immense, hairy white stomach.

Freud had almost decided to leave once he saw that they were alone, but instead he forced himself to stay.

What did you do?

Well, I picked up my hat——

The General looked less intimidating, even ludicrous now, stripped down to his swimming costume, and Freud wondered to himself that he didn't have epaulets sewn on his trunks as well, or something to show at all times that he was a general. The idea almost made him laugh out loud——

Just then the General spotted him; the huge, awful grin spread slowly across his face.

"So there you are, my good Jew!"

Freud said nothing, peeling off his shirt and wooden sandals, placing his towel carefully along a chair. He walked over to the edge of the pool and stood there, peering down into water murky with the steam seeping out from the sauna room.

"What a fine physique you have!" the general called out, grinning wider. "How about pulling them down for a moment and giving us a peek, eh?"

Freud stood frozen where he was.

"Come on—just a peek. I've always been curious to see what a circumcised Jew cock looks like. How about it?"

He looked out at the General, treading water across the pool like some great, white manatee, fat little hands and legs churning away under the surface.

"Huh? Just one peek. Or maybe I'll confine you to barracks again. How would you like that, hmm? Then I can come and take a look whenever I want—"

Still Freud had controlled himself, saying nothing, letting no hint of expression cross his face. Instead, he straightened up and made a low, perfect dive into the pool, the General's meaty laughter still ringing in his ears as he slowly, deliberately swam his laps.

He would not permanently give up the civilized comforts of his native city for some American wilderness. He would make his home in Vienna, and fight for his new science, his Cause, painstakingly building up his practice, winning respect for his theories.

And so he had arrived on the shores of the New World as the conquering hero, to be lauded and honored by the greatest minds of science.

It will be like an incredible, omnipotent daydream—

He had thought about it for months: taking the stage at Clark, up in Worcester, the audience applauding fervently, leaning forward to catch his every word—

Yet somehow he still could not fully picture it. It remained murky, like the pool room water—as if there were still something unexplored, just beneath the surface.

When he finally found his sister's apartment, in another new, well-appointed building in Harlem, it was locked up tight as a drum. They, too, had left on vacation, the landlady informed him, Anna and his two little nieces, Martha and Hella. She thought perhaps Eli was still in town; if he wanted, she could leave a message for him—

"That's quite all right," he thanked her.

The idea of having to spend an evening alone with his brother-in-law, without even Anna and the children to intervene, was too appalling to contemplate.

"I will see them on our way back through the city."

He tipped his hat and walked out into the late-summer sunlight, intending to walk back downtown to the hotel. But he took a wrong turn off Amsterdam Avenue and found himself lost again, wandering through a beautiful, rambling park built ingeniously into a hillside.

When he emerged, he realized that everyone on the street around him was dark-skinned. A whole city of black people, brown people, tan people, larger than any in Africa, he realized—yet still contained easily within the greater City of New York.

He was astonished most of all at how European, how *American* they all seemed: the same clothes, the same foods, the same stores. The same manners or better than the whites downtown—men and women bowing politely, tipping their hats to each other on the street.

Bleach their skin, put them out on the Ringstrasse, and no doubt they would be indistinguishable from the cream of Viennese society. Put them in Berlin and they would be proper little Germans—

Lost in his thoughts, he realized that he had become physically lost as well. Each street seemed to go on forever, and even though they were wide and straight and numbered he could no longer remember which way was downtown, and which was up. There was little shade on the raw new blocks, the white cement sidewalk hurting his eyes. He was very tired, and he needed a toilet, and something to drink, but there didn't seem to be anyplace, any public place at all in this baffling, impenetrable city—

He stopped to rest, leaning heavily on his walking stick, mopping at his face with a handkerchief. The black faces swept by him—staring through him with the same studied disinterest with which that Jewish bundle carrier had looked through him in the car downtown. The perfect, impervious stare, neither unfriendly nor engaged.

Him, too—that Jew downtown. Dress him up right, put a few polite phrases in his head, he could pass for any of Vienna's maskilim—

A sudden shameful memory bobbed up—of the nationalist German student societies he had joined briefly, back in his college days. All that marching and shouting, everyone wearing a cornflower or a white carnation in their lapel. Drunken evenings in the beer gardens, reading endless excited screeds about the true German character, the German soul. The blood of Goethe and Schiller and Beethoven, fairly bubbling with genius!

What foolishness; what utter infantile dreck! All to make ourselves feel like geniuses, too. Now the whole world revolves around such nonsense—

He was beginning to feel faint. If he could only get some quick transportation back to their hotel—but there were no cabs around, none of the hired cars or hansoms that were ubiquitous downtown. The only train he saw was a demonic, elevated railway in the distance, with a breakneck curve around which the engines roared at full speed, spewing black smoke and whistling madly.

His hands trembled a little on his walking stick. This was ridiculous, he thought, lost as if he were himself in the middle of Peary and Cook's Arctic wastes. But if he couldn't find some way out soon he was sure he would urinate in his pants and faint right here on the sidewalk, perhaps worse—

"May I be of assistance?"

An elderly gentleman peered down at him. He wore a clerical collar and a neat, black, tailored suit, and an air of quiet, implacable dignity. He had a high mane of white hair under his bowler, and very fine skin, burnished nearly red along his tight cheekbones.

"May I be of assistance?" he said again, bowing courteously and tipping his bowler, introducing himself as a Dr. Betancourt. His eyes were grave but concerned, and Freud, finally realizing what he was saying, gripped at the man's arm.

"*Ja, Ja,* if you could, I am trying to get back to the hotel . . . . "

"I can help you get anywhere you want to go," the man replied in perfect German, with a Berlin accent. "Unfortunately, the cabs do not come to this part of the city. May I prevail upon you to come to my home first—until you recover yourself?"

"That would be very kind," Freud stammered, letting the older man lead him along the sidewalk by the arm as naturally as if he were his aged father.

The minister helped him up the low stoop of another immense new apartment house, white as a sarcophagus, and filling an entire block. Inside, though, his study was cool and dark, restful as a nap after the hot, white street. The curtains were drawn, letting in only a thin crack of light. It was a cluttered, active room, piled high with books and papers—a couch, a couple of patent leather chairs, the minister's writing desk and chair.

Freud sat in one of his leather chairs, sipping a cold glass of lemonade. It was brought in to him by a handsome young boy who then disappeared into another room, off a long, dark hallway. Like everything else in America, the apartment was huge and mysterious.

"My sister's boy," Dr. Betancourt informed him gravely. "We are all living doubled up these days, but he's a good boy, very respectful. I've sent him to rent a carriage for you."

Freud looked around the room in a new light. He noticed now a small plate and service set in a corner, some bedding hidden back behind the couch. This one room was obviously where the man not only worked, but ate and slept as well.

"Tell me, are you with one of those fine new churches I noticed going up?" Freud asked politely.

"Ah, no," the minister said, looking down at the floor, a faint smile flickering across his face. "We meet in a storefront just now—though we hope to have the money for a church of our own someday."

"Oh, I see!"

Freud looked away, embarrassed—and noticed a little bookcase, where he was surprised to see copies of his own work, in the original German, part of a small but excellent library in sociology, philosophy, the physical sciences.

"You have my books——" he blurted out, immediately ashamed at his own immodesty.

"Oh, yes, I've read all your work. It is a great honor to meet you in the flesh—Dr. *Freund,*" the minister chuckled, and Freud smiled bleakly.

"Let me say, I think your work is brilliant, very brilliant indeed—if a little narrow," he said more seriously

"Really? In what way do you find it narrow?" Freud asked, sighing a little to himself. "Is it the sex?"

"No, no, that was all right"—another smile wrinkling cherubically across the minister's face. "No, that was fine. Only—I think you don't give enough credit to other influences, outside the family."

"Such as?" Freud asked, unable to keep the instant combativeness out of his voice.

Dr. Betancourt wheeled around in his chair to the wall, where a small shaving mirror was hanging. He leapt up spryly, and took it off the wall, bringing it over to Freud.

"Have you ever been in a fun house, Doctor?"

"I don't believe so, no—"

"Oh, you really should someday, Doctor. They have all kinds of mirrors there, you know: big mirrors, little mirrors. Squat mirrors, short mirrors, skinnifying mirrors. All *kinds* of different reflections, staring back at you. *That's* how we see ourselves, Doctor—through *all* those mirrors."

Freud peered down into the shaving mirror the cleric offered him, the face of a stern but sympathetic grandfather peering back—neat white beard, precisely combed hair, the deep, symmetrical grooves along his cheeks and under his eyes.

How old I am getting How old

"But that implies *culture* then, eh?" Freud objected. "A *national* psychology, in which Germans must be analyzed as Germans, Americans as Americans—whatever that means—"

Dr. Betancourt shook his head.

"No, no. I mean the mirrors are *all* kinds. There's the mirror a man looks in when he wants to think of himself as a lover, and another when he wants to think of himself as a husband, or a father, or a great man. And there's the mirror a man looks into when he wants to think of himself as a white man."

"Then what you are saying is that alienation is *inherent*," Freud said slowly. Betancourt smiled again.

"How could it not be?" he said softly. "Look around you—at what we have built. How could we not be alienated, in this modern world? How could we *not* be?"

"All right. Suppose what you say is true. But what about

trying to show the patient—the person—a *true* image of himself? Hmm? What about getting him to face an objective reality?"

"Is that what you do, Doctor? Is it? Do you describe a quantifiable, scientific reality? Or are you really telling stories?"

"Stories?"

"Oh, good stories, likely stories, stories that make sense," Dr. Betancourt said with a booming laugh, leaning forward and tapping Freud's knee to make sure he was not offended.

"Stories that make people think their world makes sense—but *stories* nonetheless."

"Maybe. For now," Freud answered, forcing himself as always to consider another truth. "We don't know enough yet. But eventually, yes: there is no reason we can't measure everything about the mind, right down to neurosis, and paranoia—in scientific, biological quantities."

"Isn't there? What is the true image in a fun house, Doctor? How do you pick it out? You've seen something of our city—what is the true American? What am *I*? A black man, a minister of Christ? Some kind of New Negro? A *nigger*?"

The grin was still there, hard as stone on the minister's face now.

"Yes, yes, I see what you mean," Freud said hastily. "But if it's true, how do we keep any grip on reality? What is to keep men from being taken over completely by some idiotic mysticism?"

Dr. Betancourt put down his mirror and held his hands out, as if he were coming to the punch line of a good joke.

"That's why the only answer is Divine Love, Doctor. Eternal, unreasoning love."

"Do you really think man is a divine creature, sir?" Freud asked, as politely as he could.

"No. I think he is an animal—just as you do, Doctor. If

he *were* divine, reason would suffice. But because he is, at heart, an animal, reason will never be enough."

"That's a very fatalistic belief."

Betancourt gave him a curious look.

"That is the test of a man, as you must know, sir. To look at the world without illusions—and still live with honor and decency."

The handsome, quiet young boy returned; the carriage was waiting downstairs. The minister pumped his hand and sent him on his way, refusing any of the ugly, green-and-black money Freud tried to press on him.

"Oh no, oh no," he protested, gesturing around the small, darkened room. "Our talk has been reward enough. How I envy you—going back to a place like Vienna, where men talk about such things every day!"

"Yes, well," Freud hemmed, thinking of the strutting officers in their comic-opera uniforms, the fat burghers and their ladies, the bully-boy students with their chants and badges.

"How I wish I could see it!"

After some more, effusive good-byes, the minister's young nephew drove him down into town, the streets slowly, steadily narrowing, the ghastly towers and skyscrapers rising on each side, as if all of America were flowing into this single, vast clot of humanity.

How many mirrors could there be in such a place?

Freud shook his head. The courage to live with the truth—yes, he could face that. But to live without *any* truth—to rely on man's love, or God's?

No, that was too much. He shook his head, watching the silent black boy maneuver the carriage expertly through the raucous, roiling city streets. There was *only* truth, he decided, and he would stay faithful to it even if he never got to the promised land.

39

ON THE BOARDWALK

Their gondolier poled them sullenly along the twisting canals of the Doge's Palace. From the balconies of plaster villas, string quartets serenaded them with the latest Broadway show tunes.

Esther sat in the stern, holding a copy of the *Forward* and his straw hat in her lap, while he stretched out in the bow, watching her other hand drifting through the dark, greenish water.

"Whattaya read that stuff for?" he teased her.

"To stay informed," she said, smiling back at him.

"*Eh*. How much do you need to know, anyway?"

"It's important to know if you're going to change things."

"Things change all the time," he shrugged. "What's that got to do with anything?"

Their boat stopped at a small restaurant, nestled under a romantic plywood castle and the romantic Venetian night sky, a few feet above their heads. It was lit by a large electric ball, beneath yards and yards of blue gauze. They stepped carefully up onto the piazza while the gondolier stood by indifferently, smoking a cigarette. They got a table and ate spaghetti, and *tiramisu*, while another of the ubiquitous violinists strolled around, playing favorites for a few coins.

"You know, you can trust me," she told him abruptly,

408

looking very seriously at him across the table with her big brown eyes.

"What?" he asked, startled, trying to sound as innocent as possible.

"You can trust me, is all. I know you're out here for a reason—"

"What? How d'ya know that? Why—"

"C'mon," she said impatiently. "I see you out here, marking time. Living in that place. Even I can figure that one out."

He started to protest again, and she held up her hand.

"Sometimes I think you are my own *dybbuk*, and I just dream you up when I want to," she smiled. "It's all right— I don' need to know what it is. It's just you can trust me."

"*Eh*, well, it's nothing—" he fumfered.

"I think you're hiding out from something, that's what I think."

"You shouldn't get involved," he told her. "It's nothing for you, little dove. I told you I was a very bad man."

"But what is it?"

She reached an arm out across the table, but he looked away.

"It's just things. It's just something that happened in the dark," he muttered.

Nobody can see what happens in the dark

"You can trust me, is all—no matter what it is."

He looked at her, across the little table—so earnest, her eyes big, and moist with emotion—and he thought that he probably could tell her. He could probably tell her anything, now that she had promised. She would even admire him for this, most likely.

So why was he ashamed of it?

It wasn't that, exactly—it was more that he still couldn't figure it out. He didn't care to have her idolizing him over something he still didn't know about himself.

Nobody can see what happens in the dark

40

BIG TIM

"Where to now, Big Tim?" Photo Dave was asking him.

"Oh, the jails, Dave. By all means, the jails."

"What about His Nibs?"

They had another meeting scheduled with the mayor. There was always another meeting with the mayor.

"First the jails, I think. Doesn't our Savior tell us not to let a soul languish in jail?"

They cut back along the *Chasir Mark* on Hester Street, then up to Broome Street, where the new police headquarters floated like a dreadnought above the traffic.

The thing was five stories of solid granite, with marble trimmings and plenty of Grecian flourishes. Its classical grandeur, its sheer ponderousness, were supposed to establish once and for all the authority of the Law——gleaming white and pure. Inside, everything was very modern, very professional. There was a running track and a forensic-sciences laboratory and a Rogues' Gallery and even a chauffeur's waiting room.

It was yet another self-deception of the reformers: if you built something big and new enough, you could make the people to fit it. On the day they had moved over from the old headquarters, on Mulberry Street, Sullivan had watched dozens of cops waddling through the streets in their long, old-fashioned coats, hauling armfuls of all the old junk: spittoons, and framed photos of the old boys. The usual green regimental flag, with a gold harp, from the Fighting Sixty-ninth. Dusty, red-bound arrest books, dating back to Boss Tweed's day. Soon it all looked like any other station house around the City, snug as Paddy's pub.

"Help you there, gints?" one of the jolly cops behind the front desk came sauntering over. He was full of the barely contained exuberance of men who worked all day with other men, and did as they pleased. But even he pulled up a little, once he saw who it was.

"Mr. Sullivan!" he exclaimed, immediately so respectful Big Tim half expected him to pull at his forelock.

"Oh, I know who yer wantin', sir. He's down below. Buckley brought him in last night. Possession of a great old pistol— "

"Ah, now there's fast work for you," Big Tim told Photo Dave, before turning back to the sergeant.

"Very well, then, Sergeant—play Virgil to our Dante, an' lead us down to him."

The basement holding cells stunk of piss, and puke, and unwashed flesh, and down the middle of the stairs there was already a well-worn groove, where the turnkeys walked their charges. The inevitable Paddy legend had it that the place was haunted, but Big Tim tended to doubt it. The cells were depressingly mundane, like every other jail in every other station house in the world: blurred, desperate faces staring out at them from behind the bars. Big Tim tried not to look back, afraid he might see a constituent, or someone he simply pitied. There was no time today—

Before Teddy and Reform there had been fewer cells.

Instead, each station had its own flophouse in the basement: a row of hard, whitewashed slats for beds. Clotheslines hung above a potbellied stove. The ubiquitous sign on the wall, commanding NO SWEARING OR LOUD TALKING AFTER NINE O'CLOCK. On the worst winter nights there might be two hundred, even four hundred sleepers in a precinct, whole families sacked out around the stove.

The stoves smoked something terrible, to be sure, and the sheets and the blankets were a sickly yellow color, and everyone was locked in until the morning——but it still beat the Tombs, or the street grates. Then the Holies had decided that you had to commit a crime to end up in a police station: another arbitrary distinction, separating the poor from the criminal. Now the sheltering cells were filled with drunks, while families froze out on the street——

They came to the last and largest cell in the basement, deep in its shadows.

"Here he is——number 99. Best one in the house, just like you wanted."

The sergeant hesitated before opening the door, and one look made Big Tim understand why. The prisoner sat poised on the edge of his narrow cell bunk, staring back at them. A compact young man, dressed up like a dude, but dangerous and mad as a caged panther.

"All right, you——I don' want no nonsense outta ya now," the police sergeant blustered rather unconvincingly. The young man in the cell said nothing, just stared back out as if he were measuring the distance to their jugulars.

Big Tim cleared his throat gruffly to break the spell, tipping the sergeant like a headwaiter.

"Very good, Liam. Leave us to have a little chat now."

"Certainly, sir," the copper said, snapping into action and moving to unlock the cell door——but not, Big Tim noticed, before he pulled out his truncheon. He didn't blame the cop; the man would clearly have killed any of them as soon as look at them. He felt a little flutter of fear himself—but he squared his shoulders and strode into the cell like a lion-tamer, leaving Photo Dave outside to make sure they were not interrupted.

"Well, well. Lazar Abramowitz," he said, needling the young gangster immediately.

"Gyp's my cap, don't flog me with it," he snapped, angry but also surprised.

Big Tim had never known a gangster, Jewish, Irish, or Italian, who wanted to be known by his real name. They liked their brave, outlandish monickers—but most of all they didn't want their mothers to know.

"Whatever you say, Gyp. Anyhow, possession of a weapon, that's a serious charge."

He sat down on the bunk, as close to Gyp as he could get. When he did, he marveled that the gangster's whole body was trembling, as if enraged by the injustice of it all.

"You know that's a wheezer!" he burst out. "I do my work with a bully, or a neddy. I need a pop, I have the moll carry it. You know that as well as I do!"

"Uh-huh. Well, I can't wait to hear you tell *that* to the jury. I'm sure it'll make a very pretty defense."

Gyp lapsed into a sullen silence, and Big Tim noticed in the dim light of the cell that his thick, handsome head of hair was matted with blood and makeshift bandages.

"My, my, did Buckley do that to you?" Big Tim tsked. "By God, he's an enthusiastic man with a nightstick. You could take a few pointers—"

"That *vitzer*? He didn't do more'n tap me. It was some other lump of horse, with a shovel," Gyp snorted. "But I'm gonna see to him—"

"All right, now," Big Tim snapped, suddenly grabbing Gyp by his red silk cravat with one hand, and resting his other forearm on his head wound, leaning in with just enough pressure to make the gangster wince despite himself. The man's eyes spun with rage—but Sullivan thought he saw just enough caution, just enough sense to hold him back.

"There's a certain t'ing I asked you to do, an' the hour's grown late."

"I know," hissed Gyp. "I'll do it. Just as soon as I take care of—"

"There's no time! Do whatever you like to Kid Twist or any of your other hoodlum pals after you're finished. I don't want to hear any more about you an' your Lenox Avenue boys cavortin' down the Grand Duke's, or getting the sweet Jesus kicked out of you at a rat-baiting, for Christ's sakes. You'll do as you been told, an' do it now, or I'll see to it you do a full stretch up in Ossining."

He flung Gyp roughly back against the cell wall, deliberately banging his head, and jumped up from the bunk—daring the gangster to come after him. Infuriated, Gyp started to push himself up, and for a split second Big Tim thought he had mistook his man and that he might actually go for his throat. Only at the last moment did he manage to restrain himself and settle back into his cot, glaring up at Sullivan with those cold, restless panther's eyes.

"Good," Big Tim told him. "At least you got that much sense left in your idea pot."

Gyp nodded, his face a dour mask now.

"All right, then. Up wit'cha—we can't have an innocent man like you takin' up the taxpayers' cell space. The Simon Pures wouldn't go for it."

They took care of the paperwork at the desk, where Big Tim paid off the sergeant. A small fine, or the bail money for a vagrant, or a bribe—he didn't even bother to ask. It was yet another false distinction, obscuring the central fact of the matter: you paid money to get out of jail.

When they walked out of the station, Gyp scuttled quickly away without another word, lost in the sidewalk crowd within seconds.

"What, no thank you?" Big Tim called mockingly after him.

He got no response, but he was sure he had been heard. Whether he would be obeyed or not was another matter.

"Mind what I said now!"

"Ah, but he's a runt," Photo Dave said, shaking his head as he watched Gyp stride off into the city. "No John Morrisey, or Bill the Butcher, is he?"

"No."

"But then they're all small these days. Little runts. Why, I remember they used to come six feet at least, an' built like a trolley car. They just don't make gangsters like they used to."

"No, they don't."

They descended the police station steps, Photo Dave Altman still reminiscing about the great clubbers and eye-gougers of his youth. It was true enough, though: they were all relatively small, quick men nowadays, adept with a blade, or a pistol. Thoroughly unintimidating at first glance, but more serious and deadly than ever.

When Tim had run with a gang himself they had seemed like mere boys, by contrast—Googy Corcoran and Baboon Connolly and Red Rocks Farrell and all the rest of the Whyos. They'd even had a price list printed up: PUNCHING, TWO DOLLARS; EAR CHAWED OFF, FIFTEEN; DOIN THE BIG JOB, $100 AND UP.

Damned foolishness, all of it, and it was only luck that he had had the good sense to move up to politics, before he ended up in Sing Sing himself, or stretched out in a cold city morgue.

He had been saved, in the end, by another ward heeler, not much different from himself. Tammany always needed the gangs—to provide muscle at the polls, and to squeeze money out of the businessmen. To perform certain unsavory tasks such as this one. But they had to be controlled, to be kept under a few wraps, or they would be of no help at all.

It wouldn't do to have the tail wagging the dog, which was why he had got his gun law passed. He'd made big, weepy speeches for it up in Albany, even got his name attached to it: the Sullivan Law, making it a felony for a citizen to carry a concealed weapon.

It had driven the reformers crazy. They couldn't figure out his angle, though it was simple enough for those who had eyes to see. This way, a cop could plant a pistol on anyone they wanted to bring into line. The gangsters tried sewing up their pockets, or having their women carry the pieces, but as usual they missed the big picture. The point was having the law on the book; they could always be cold-cocked first and the pistols produced later on, down at the station house in the cops' own good time.

That was the way of things. That was the way it had to be, with the Organization in charge. And that was why Handsome Charlie Becker and Beansy would both have to go.

Still, Big Tim couldn't help but shiver, to think of the restless animal he had just let loose on poor Herman. He could just see the wide, handsome, fleshy face: lips full and red as an actor's, small black eyes always moist with emotion. The cleft chin no doubt trembling a little with emotion, as he dictated his story to the district attorney:

It is purely a matter of friendship

41

SADIE MENDELSSOHN

Her mother would say that she was always meant to be a whore, that it was marked on her by that woman on the courtyard, and no matter what Sadie said she would not believe otherwise.

The trouble was that the woman refused to keep her curtains closed. She had her customers right there, on the narrow, white pallet, one story down and directly across from their bedroom window. Sadie and her sisters could see everything, even through the dirt-streaked glass.

The shuffling parade of men, heads down, still wearing their hats. Some of them touching her tentatively, some of them falling on her in one clumsy rush, pushing her down on the pallet. Fast or slow, skinny or fat, as different as each individual snowflake—though all of their things were so much the same.

Sadie and her sisters thought the woman was very beautiful, with her deep black hair and very pale skin—pale enough for the blue veins to show through everywhere but very delicate, very fine. They watched her as she lay sleeping in the morning, the sheets kicked off, lying flat out naked on her back, in a dead sleep. Her arms flung over her head. Her slowly heaving breasts, and the patch of black hair down at her thighs, a little comfortable flesh around her hips, bulging out from her fine, plump bottom the men seemed to like so much.

Her mother forbade them to watch. She was always very careful, alone with three girls, too chary even to take a *roomerkeh*. Yet when she came back from her job at the umbrella factory, pressing the spidery metal frames into their taut canvas sheaths, she would find them all at the window of their bedroom, gazing raptly down into the courtyard.

There was nothing she could do to get them to stop. She tried punishing them. She tried changing her bedroom for theirs, even though it was much too small for three growing girls—but still, whenever she was out, they would sneak across and peer out her window at the whore below.

She finally confronted the woman. From the same window, they could see her—their little mama—arguing agitatedly with the beautiful, dark-haired lady. She implored her to stop, she threatened to tell the police. She even offered to sew up curtains for the *kurveh* herself. But none of it did any good.

"Who are you to tell me my business?" the woman argued. "It's my home, I can do what I want."

"But my daughters. It's my daughters who are seeing such a thing!"

"So? Who are your daughters, that they should live like Rockefellers? Better they should see how life is!"

"But why this, so soon? It's not decent—"

"Better they should see how I have to live!" the woman had persisted madly, obstinately. "Better everybody should see how I have to earn my bread in this world, than to hide behind their curtains!"

She could do nothing with the woman, and the police weren't interested. She tried complaining to their alderman, who sent a member of his staff around to investigate——but the next thing she knew, her daughters saw the alderman's assistant, young and shy as a *yeshiva bocher*, standing with his hat in his hand in her room. And soon he, too, was heaving and bouncing around wildly on her narrow little bed, without even taking his pants off. He was one of the quick ones——

They continued to watch her, every moment they could. It wasn't so much her profession that fascinated them as it was this peek into adulthood.

They studied her avidly for clues. They watched how she dressed, pulling up her stockings and garters, and strange, silky underwear. They watched her brushing her hair in the morning, and eating a piece of chicken, alone at her little table, on a Sunday afternoon. And sometimes, late at night, a sound would wake them——cats fighting, or an ash can ringing on the pavement——and they would look out to see her coming in, gliding around drunkenly as she shucked off her clothes.

When she thought about it, years later, Sadie thought that was probably why she really kept her curtains open. So *somebody*, anybody, could see her there and know she was still alive.

And still——one morning after Mama went out they rushed to the window and saw her sleeping on the floor of her room. At first they thought this was another perverse adult prerogative, but then they had noticed that her skin appeared to be even bluer, even more translucent than ever. She seemed to be in a deeper sleep than they had ever seen before, and in an even stranger position——her back arched up, and her neck twisted to one side, completely naked again, but with her feet curled, and her fingers bent toward her palms, as if she were clutching something.

She slept like that the whole day, and the next day, too—but they said nothing, afraid for Mama to know they were spying again. There didn't seem to be a mark on her, but she was still lying on her back, hands clutching the air. Soon after that, they saw the landlord come in and open the door, accompanied by the same shy young alderman's assistant who had fetched him. And when he opened the door, they could see, both men grabbed their faces with their handkerchiefs, and the landlord hurried out while the *yeshiva bocher* of an aide stood there, hat in one hand, handkerchief in the other. Until finally, after a long time, the crew from the morgue came, and tossed her cold, blue body up on a stretcher, throwing a horse blanket over her nakedness before they carried her down to the street.

Her mama always liked to say that it marked her, but Sadie knew something about life, even then. She had never felt any desire to be like that woman—not even on those achingly tired mornings after she and her sisters had started going to work at the box factory, and they used to envy how late she could sleep in the morning. She never *wanted* to be a whore.

The trouble came later, when Sadie started going up on the roof to hang the laundry. She liked it on the roof; it was airy, and cooler, and there were always people around: Mothers and daughters hanging the wash. Naked little children, running around giggling. Bill collectors and nurses from the Health Department, both with their little black satchel bags, going house to house down the whole block without ever having to set foot in the street.

The young men liked to sit up on the roof, too. They drank beer, and tossed the cans down into the courtyard, and raced the pigeons they kept in narrow, tiered coops behind the water barrel.

She loved watching the birds—the gorgeous jacobins and the fantails, the puffed-up, strutting pouters and the tumblers and rollers, turning their fancy tricks in midair. Soon she was going up every evening to watch them swoop and sail between the tenements, descending in tighter and tighter circles, always returning to the tar roofs and their cramped coops behind the eternal, wooden-staved water barrel.

The boys let her sit by them, and watch the birds for as long as she wanted. One of them, whom they called Crazy Butch, was especially nice to her. He was their leader, and the handsomest one, she thought—tall and big-shouldered, with a sleek moustache and a little scar on his left cheek, and a bowler hat he wore at a rakish angle. He always had an easy grin for her, and he let her hold the pigeons, even his most beautiful fantails, and gently stroke their heads in their cages.

She was still no fool about it. She knew he was older than her, and a *shtarkeh* for some street gang, and probably a thief as well. But sometimes, in the room she shared with her sisters, Sadie couldn't help but dream about him taking her to a show or one of the dancing academies on Norfolk Street.

From when she was a little girl, she had stood in the street before the entrances of the dancing academies. On the nights of competitions, every girl in the neighborhood would stand by the door, just to watch the dancers enter: the women in their beautiful dresses, the men in their best cutaway suits, their feet already barely touching the sidewalk as they floated inside to dance.

Inside, it was really a very different thing—but no less fun. As soon as she was old enough to make any money, Sadie would run right over in her kitchen apron, whenever

Mama was away for a few minutes. She had never been any-where so exciting. The whole room vibrating, the dancers sweating and stomping, cheek to jowl, around the floor. A wild-haired, apoplectic dancing professor standing in the middle, trying to keep time by tapping a cane on the floor. Everyone ignoring him, flirting and eyeing each other around the soda bar, over their celery health tonics—

Sadie smoothed down her skirt, checking her apron at the door with all the other mama's girls—looking about for a partner who might take her swooping and rolling around the room as weightless as the pigeons turning their tricks in the air.

One summer evening, she went up on the roof when it was empty. Usually it was crowded at that time with women tak-ing in their laundry, but it had been raining that afternoon, and none of them had put their wash out. It was risky, she knew, to be up on the roof all alone, but the evening was so beautiful, after the furious late-afternoon shower had died away, that she couldn't resist. Besides, when she got up she saw that the young men were there, removing the oilcloth they had draped protectively over their coops, carefully looking over their delicate birds to make sure none of them had caught cold.

"Hey—c'mere, c'mere!"

She sidled up to them quietly, around the water barrel, not wanting to disturb their solemn inspection of the birds. They looked like little boys, she thought, dressed up in their fathers' clothes—in their cheap, fancy suits and oversized bowlers, so serious and preoccupied with their pigeons.

"C'mere!" Crazy Butch had spotted her, grinning as infectiously as ever.

She had walked on over, shy but pleased they were happy to see her. The rain had stopped completely now, sunshine glinting off the black puddles on the rough tar roof. It was one of those few cool moments of relief after a summer rain, before the muggy air rose again, turning the evening even hotter than it had been before.

"C'mere," he said, holding out a bird to her, and she had taken it in her hands and held it there. It was one of his best fantails, she saw—the broad, blue-and-white tail feathers spreading out between her fingers.

She clutched it there, feeling its small life, its throat and heart throbbing in her hands, and looked up at the roof boys. They stood all around her, grinning, and she grinned shyly back—thinking that she must be holding the beautiful bird wrong, thinking that she must not be able to appreciate just what it was they knew about the pigeon.

"C'mere," said Crazy Butch again—and holding her not ungently by the shoulder, he kissed her on the mouth.

She couldn't quite comprehend it immediately—her mouth hanging limp, unanswering, still grinning foolishly over the pigeon in her hands.

"Whatsa matter, wasn' that good enough for you?" he said, and kissed her again—right in front of all of them, right on the mouth again. Then all down her cheek, and her neck, running his hands roughly, probingly up and down her breasts, her sides, her hips.

She stepped back, stunned, still holding the pigeon. One of the other boys shoved her back, and Crazy Butch kissed her yet again, his teeth tearing at her lips this time. Then another one of the young men stepped up and kissed her, and another.

There was a raucous cry from the pigeon—nothing like the cooing noises she had heard them make before—and she realized dully that she must be squeezing it too hard.

"Leggo a de boid," Crazy Butch said, still grinning that boyish, infectious grin at her.

"What?" she asked.

"Leggo-of-de-boid," he repeated, impatiently this time.

"What?"

She didn't feel like she could understand anything. They were still kissing her, the roof boys, stepping up and groping at her, running their tongues over her face, grabbing at her breasts.

"What? What?"

The grin still on his face, Crazy Butch shook his head and walked up to her, pushing his way past the rest of them. He raised his arm, and she thought *He's not going to hit me He couldn't possibly be going to hit me.* And then he did, slamming the back of his hand across her face.

She fell backwards, her hands opening, releasing the pigeon at last. It shrieked off, gorgeous blue-and-white plumage spreading out behind it. Crazy Butch, still grinning, offered her a hand up. When she just lay there, he yanked her up by one arm, and pulled her back behind the water barrel, squeezing her head under his arm until she could barely breathe.

"C'mere, c'mere. Dat's it. Be a good goil, now, little *kalleh.* Be a good goil—"

—his pals standing back a little now, still leering at her. Sadie realizing in that moment that he didn't even know her real name.

"You just let us do it to ya, or we'll do ya," Crazy Butch promised, starting to tear away her dress and petticoats.

It was then that she started screaming. She didn't think about it, she didn't even realize that she was screaming at first. Before, when the kissing had started, her throat had been too dry for her to do anything, but now she started to scream, and kick, and hit out. They tried to stick their hands in her mouth but she bit them, bit at their fingers until she could taste their blood. She kept yelling and screaming as loud as she could, screaming for Mama, and her sisters, and anyone else who might come to her rescue.

But it had been raining, and there was nobody else on the roof. She herself had often heard screaming, down in their rooms, and she was never sure where it came from, or if it was for real, or just the make-believe of children. That was just the way things were in the City. At most she might look out the back window—but there was only the narrow view of the courtyard, a few windows below and above—

Something was shoved into her mouth—something oily and horrible that made her gag. She was hauled behind the weathered, bulging water barrel, where they pulled off the rest of her dress and her underclothes, tugged down the cheap stockings Mama had bought her in the *Chasir Mark* against her better judgment, and raped her right there on the tar roof, beneath the pigeon coops. Two of them holding her arms down, two more on her ankles; the rest of them joking, and smoking, and drinking beer. Crazy Butch first, then another and another, until her thighs were one numbing mass of pain.

It seemed to go on forever, the yolk-red setting sun blazing in her eyes from just over the edge of the roof. The pigeons cooing just above her head—rustling and fluttering around at first, but then settling down to sleep as the sun set. The boys' grinning, peach-fuzzed faces above her, still wearing their daddies' bowler hats as they sawed back and forth, cutting her slowly in half. Behind them she could see the water barrel and she tried to concentrate on it. She tried willing it to burst its old staves, and flood the roof, so that the water might sweep away everything before it—herself, and the boys stabbing into her, and the indifferent pigeons—all of it, all of them, right off the roof. But it did not.

They didn't let her up until the sun had set, and they knew that people would be coming up soon, to smoke and chat, and sleep outside in the restless, humid night. Down below she could already hear the sounds of supper ending, all throughout the tenement: the plates being scraped and washed, chairs pushing back from the tables, and pipes being lit, and she thought that there would soon have to be an end to it.

Instead they stood her up, threw the oilcloth they used for the birds over her head, and dragged her staggering and stumbling down the stairs. They took her along darkened, subterranean hallways to a windowless basement room, where they pushed her in and locked the door. Leaving her to pass out on a narrow metal cot she found there.

She awakened in the darkness, hours or days later, she was not sure which. Her throat burning with dryness, thighs crusted with her own blood. Thinking of her mother and sisters, far above, and wondering if she was going to live. She had to figure out some way to live, she decided, not like that woman down in the courtyard—

They put her through the lineup. They kept her chained to the cot, with nothing but a single blanket and an old pisspot, and came back to rape her over and over again for weeks. Bringing their friends, pouring cheap whiskey down her throat, making her do more and more disgusting things. Feeding her only a few scraps of old bread and herring, until she lay dizzy and feverish, too weak to do anything but lie on the bed.

When they finally let her out, it was too late. She tried to find Mama and her sisters but they had moved, and no one knew where they had gone to. It took her many more months to locate them, and by then it was too late, she had become a whore, just like they wanted.

They sold her off to one pimp after another, as she

worked her way up from Mott Street to Fourteenth Street and the theater crowd. For a time she was in a house in the Tenderloin where she worked a badger game for young girls—dressing up in short fluffy skirts, with ribbons in her hair, and a corset to hold in her womanly breasts. When she got too old for that she went to another house, one with a madam, where she at least got to keep a little of her money. There was nice carpeting, and a real piano downstairs, and sometimes in the late afternoon, before the evening trade started, she and the other whores would all sit around and sing their favorite, weepy old hymns:

> There is rest for the weary,
> There is rest for you,
> On the other side of Jordan,
> In the sweet fields of Eden,
> Where the Tree of Life is blooming,
> There is rest for you——

Then one night, at the height of the evening, when all the girls were busy and the piano player was taking his break, she had left her room between customers to get some water. Tiptoeing downstairs, she had seen the customers sitting there, calmly smoking and swinging their feet, sitting in the parlor like men awaiting their turn at the barber's.

That was the night she left the house, after prying open the little tin safe she knew the madam kept. She was determined to find her mother and sisters, and this time she succeeded. This time, searching until nearly all her money had run out, refusing to go back to the street even for a night, she finally found her mother and one of her sisters living up in the Bronx, on Jerome Avenue, just off the Grand Concourse. And when she finally did—when her mother opened the door and stared on her like she had returned from the dead—she could not help but burst into tears.

That was when she discovered that Mama believed her to be forever marked by the whore in the courtyard. Mama had heard about her, had even known where she was for months, and now she would not take her back.

"Your sister Deborah is gone, too!" Mama had told her, furious—Sadie's other sister, Rebecca, looming silent and gaunt as a ghost in the hall behind her, a stranger to her.

"Because of you—because of that *nafkeh* downstairs!"

"I just want to help. I brought this——" Sadie offered, holding out the few coins and bills she still had left. Her mother pushed her hand away.

"Bah! Do you think that you can sneeze and blow away the past? It's too late, too late! God help you. May your name and your memory be forever blotted out of this earth!"

She couldn't go back to the good house after that, of course, and she had wound up with another pimp, and lost the rest of her money. Soon she had been reduced to trawling under the elevated on Allen Street, and the Bowery, peeking out from behind the pylons, along with the other soiled doves. Until that night, looking for customers, cold and miserable, scared half to death the next one would mark her or take all her money, she had held out her hand to the man who turned out to be her Lazar:

Gimme a penny, mister?

And he had taken her in hand. He bought her some new clothes, and got her the first good meal she'd had in a week. For a while she had made a good living again, up in the Tenderloin, and the swank new hotels off Times Square. She was still young, and men liked her figure, and she knew from hard experience how to make them laugh and put them at their ease.

Sadie was just grateful to have enough to eat again, a

warm place to sleep, and good clothes. He used her to entertain other gangsters and pols he was especially interested in,
and to do little odd jobs, and he was satisfied as long as she
did what she was told.

She thought for a long time, too, that maybe he liked her.
Love, she told herself, was a thing of ice-cream-soda
dreams, but he must at least like her. Why else, after all,
would he feed her and clothe her in fine new dresses? Why
would he have her put ribbons in her hair and keep herself
up? He had other girls, other business; he *must* like her.
Maybe, she even dared to let herself believe, he was the reason for everything she had been through—the rape on the
roof, and her mother's rejection, and even the dead woman
down in the courtyard apartment.

Slowly, slowly, she had disabused herself of this notion. It
was the hardest thing she had ever done, harder even than
willing herself to live in that unspeakable basement room. He
didn't like her. He was not in love with her. She knew it from
a hundred, a thousand little things over the years: a disgusted
glance, a word, the lack of his touch, his expression in a mirror or a windowpane, when he thought she wasn't looking.

Still, she had put it all aside; blaming it on her graying
hair, her own mistakes. Still walking the streets for him, still
performing the little tasks he told her to do. Afraid of him,
afraid of what she would be without him.

But he did not love her. That was the final, incontrovert-
ible fact. And when she realized that, she let herself go for a
while, not caring, thinking she might as well die from the
curse, or some thug's knife under the Bowery el, than to live
out this life.

And then, that day out on Hester Street, she inveigled the
dress peddler while he poisoned the horse. She stood there,
watching the magnificent animal lying on its side in the
street, and she decided the same thing she knew, back in the
lineup room: she wanted to live.

After that, she started to think, and save for herself again. Yet Sadie still didn't know just how to leave him. It would have to be a clean break, so that he would have no idea of how to find her.

A few weeks after the horse, he came back to the el to give her another job. He only shook his head when she showed him what little she had made that day. She was holding out on him like crazy now, but he didn't even suspect, that was how little he thought of her charms.

"I want you to follow somebody for me," he informed her.

"Follow somebody? I don't know if I can do that so good."

"You're no good out here anymore, you goddamned well better be able to do this," he said, his eyes cold and contemptuous. "Otherwise you're no use to me at all."

He wanted her to follow his sister, Esse. He took her past the tenement on Orchard Street to make sure she knew what she looked like, even though they had met before. Lazar had brought her over to meet her—one of his larks. And afterwards Esse had come down to see *her,* where she worked under the elevated, and tried to talk her into going into a settlement house, or getting a factory job.

At most people, she would have laughed. The only thing Sadie could imagine worse than dying in a Water Street dive, screaming of the curse, was going back to the box factory where she had worked as a girl—folding up cardboard boxes fourteen hours a day.

Yet she was touched by the sister's concern. It wasn't like the Reform women, or the Christian missionaries, who always seemed to be trying to run up their quotas of saved souls, offering her something they knew she didn't really deserve. Besides the guilt and shame she felt over Lazar, she seemed really worried about Sadie.

"But can't you see the risk you're running here? How can this be any life for you?" Esse had finally insisted, and Sadie had let her down gently.

"An' what do you got to offer me instead?" she had pointed out. "A slow death, every day? At least this way, I have a little fun."

The sister had seemed crestfallen.

"I know, I know. But it don' seem right."

"Don' worry about me—"

She had a brief fantasy of them as true sisters-in-law, living down the hall from each other. Sipping tea in the afternoon, in each other's apartments. Making big family dinners together on the holidays, with all their children around the table—and maybe her own sisters, and her mother, too—

It will never be, she told herself, watching as Esse retreated through the elevated's wavering shadows.

That life will never happen for me

And now he wanted her to spy on Esse. This was another new development, and one that seemed to her to have some potential if she played the angles right. She had no idea how yet, but it was obviously something he wanted, and if that were the case she would make what she could out of this, and see how well he liked it.

42

SADIE MENDELSSOHN

The next Sunday, Sadie was waiting when Esse came out of the Orchard Street house, skipping quickly down the stoop, past the German saloon with its golden-horned goat out front. A woman not unlike herself, with long brown hair and large, brown eyes, full lips. A little thinner than Sadie was, with wear and work——though that was changing, too, she reflected a little sadly, her own flesh melting away as she grew older under the el.

Sadie followed her onto the trolley, up to Grand Central, then switched to the train with her inside the new, dazzling white terminal. There Esse got on the New York & Sea Beach line, taking it out through the long flatlands of Brooklyn, all the way to Coney Island, and Sadie followed her——out of the station, and down Surf Avenue.

The sunlight struck her like a sudden slap. Sadie turned her face up to it instinctively, closing her eyes and holding her hands out to either side, like a supplicant. She had worn an old, shapeless black dress——the better to be inconspicuous, but completely inappropriate for the beach. Still, she felt herself now drenched in the clean, dry heat, right down into her bones.

It had been years since she had been out to Coney; the last time had been the summer when she tried working the Brighton Beach hotels and the Steeplechase for a season. But it reminded her now of when she had been a little girl, and their mother had taken them to the beach for the day. Then she had stayed in the water for as long as she could, until she was shivering with cold, and Mama had called her in to have one of the chicken sandwiches she had made. She had snatched her up, dried her with an old blanket and laid her down to warm on the sand, letting the sun soak through her bathing costume, her underwear, her skin, until she was dry and warm like she had never been before.

She could still see Esse's figure up ahead, walking swiftly, purposefully toward some attraction or meeting place. Dazed with sun, she stumbled after her as best she could, passing into Dreamland at the main gate, under the wings of an enormous, naked angel with breasts so magnificent they would have made her the most popular girl on the Bowery.

What she could be here for, other than the rides, and the attractions, Sadie could only guess. Lazar had told her simply to follow his sister, and to keep track of anyone she met, anyone she talked to. Now, to her surprise, she saw her go up to a man—and one she recognized, in a gangster's flashy suit and bowler. He took her tenderly by the arm and greeted her with a kiss on the cheek, genteel as any long-married husband.

Sadie felt a deep pang of jealousy, but she kept following them along the boardwalk. It wasn't hard: they strolled slowly along the boards, gazing out at the sea, leaning a little on each other, oblivious to anyone else. Then, to her further amazement, they turned in at a seedy, tin hotel for prostitutes, shaped like a giant elephant.

• • •

Sadie stood outside, contemplating the hotel for a few minutes, noting where a small, yellow light came on. Then she walked back along the boards, knowing everything she needed to know.

She had met a man. The sister had met a man; it was something Gyp would like to know—especially considering who the man was.

She wandered back along Surf Avenue, wondering just how to play this one. She bought an ice cream cone, then a pink-and-blue cloud of cotton candy, and a beer. She even rented a bathing costume, a pretty little sailor's suit, from one of the bathing pavilions along the beach, and walked down through the sand in her bare feet, basking in the sun and running her toes through the water.

She met a man—

After the beach, Sadie had walked back into the parks, and went to see the diving elephants, and the one-armed lion tamer at Bostock's Circus, and a funny little show made up completely of dwarves and midgets. One of the dwarves gave her a metal flower, and she cut her finger on it, but he had been very nice to her, and had wrapped the cut up in a handkerchief. He was a misshapen little man, with a big head and tiny, sawed-off arms and legs that made her shiver inside.

He gazed up at her meaningfully when he handed her his handkerchief but she was too distracted to figure out what he wanted. She took the flower, and wandered along the boardwalk again, stopping by the Tin Elephant, under the little square of yellow light she had seen go on earlier. It was still on, and she waited patiently, watching the whores wandering in and out with johns they had found on the midway, or the Ziz coaster. Watching them eye her curiously, hostilely, as more competition. For that's what she was, a whore—

She met a man—

Gyp would give a lot to find out these things, she knew. Maybe enough to get herself free, even set up on her own. And wasn't that what the woman on the courtyard had been saying to her mama? That a whore was always justified, for who looked out for a whore but herself?

Then again, it could be risky. Lazar would hate whoever told him, she knew that. And either way, it was still doing his bidding, depending upon his mercy. And she did like the sister, even if she was lucky enough to be in love.

She stood, and thought, and waited for a long time more. Until after dark, when his sister finally came out again, and Sadie trailed her slowly back up the boardwalk. Back to the train and the City, where Gyp was waiting to hear her report. And just what that would be, she hardly knew herself.

43

TRICK THE DWARF

I didn't mind when that big fake Mexican left. I knew it made it all the more likely that *he* would find us, but I didn't care. I was just as glad to have the other one all to myself.

He should have run, too, after that. He should have hopped the first boat around the Horn, a train to California, a steamer down the islands—anywhere he could go, so long as it was far away from that monster.

I told him as much—yet I knew he never would. Only the outlaw can never quite bear to leave home. Instead he stayed around, waiting for—what?

And then, as the days went by, and neither Spanish Louie nor any of Gyp's *boychiks* showed up, we both began to think that they never would. Maybe Louie was smarter than any of us knew, maybe he had lit out for the territories himself without telling any of us. Maybe he had just let us *think* he was going to saunter back into his old haunts and let Gyp the Blood get his balls in a wringer.

I didn't care. I was happy to have him there, telling me stories, showing me new little cons from the big world. It was almost like having a friend—or another father. I pretended that it could go on like this indefinitely, lulled by the succession of sun, and sand, and salt water. And somehow,

I believed, as I had never felt even with my father, that he could keep the worst from happening.

Why should I have been different from anyone else? Everything in Dreamland was as transitory as the sand it was built on, but no one would believe it: not my poor subjects, planning out their gardens and future families, secure in the notion that they would live in the Little City the rest of their days. Not Matty Brinckerhoff, dreaming of tiny model towns that would astound future archaeologists. Most certainly not my exquisite, mad Carlotta, believing she could stay beautiful and mad and innocent forever.

And not the hordes who came to Coney, for a week or an hour: trudging dumbly forward, gazing at all the wonders. Never doubting that things would keep getting better, more incredible. Never doubting that more wonders would be trotted out in perpetuity, for their entertainment, until the old rhetorical question would come to seem like a curse:

Will wonders never cease? Will wonders never cease?

Ours was the most credulous of ages, for everything came true. How could you walk through the hissing, gleaming phantasmagoria that were Dreamland and Luna Park, and Steeplechase—past all the electrical wonders, and the exotic tribesmen, the death-defying rides, and the tiny babies fighting for life in their incubators—and not believe in anything, anything at all?

There was something else to keep him in Dreamland, of course—there always is. He had met her out on the beach: a machine operator from one of the garment factories in town. She was sweet enough, intelligent enough: pale, Semitic features, sharp chin, sharp nose, full lips. Nothing exceptional, really.

He brought her to visit sometimes—balancing nervously on a miniature Louis XV chair, trying not to gape at my Carlotta while she went through her mad spiels. I smiled to see how much he was in love with her, no matter how ordinary she was.

Soon, though, I found myself beginning to envy their ordinariness. She was nothing special, I kept assuring myself. Charming in her reticence, almost graceful. A shy little factory girl, to hold hands with, and make love to, and trace great dreams upon. How common, how sentimental, like something from an O. Henry story.

Yet how far it was beyond me. The old dream reawakened: surely, it couldn't be so impossible, so extraordinary for *me* to find someone like that. There were pretty young girls married to old, fat fools, to simpletons, and cads, to drunks and scoundrels; I know, I saw them every day, in the crowds at the Big Tent.

Why not a dwarf? Why not *me*? All that implacable, irrational longing I had buried under fine carpets and good Madeira came rushing back. To *never* have anything like that. Surely, there would be *someone* for me besides a half-mad sideshow midget—someone *real*.

I saw her at the end of the Grand March. I had just finished slouching around the ring, leading the first parade around the Big Tent before we broke into our nauseating little song, and there she was. Sitting in the front row of the gallery, wearing scarlet ribbons in her curled brown hair. She was wearing a coy little sailor's suit, virginal white and trimmed with blue, ridiculously girlish, really, but it made her look all the sweeter and more vulnerable.

None of the men could keep their eyes, or their hands, off her. I watched them whispering things to her, their rough whiskers brushing her ears, slipping a hand down along her arms, her thighs, trying to pry open her knees. Testing, always testing her, seeing if they could make her laugh—seeing how far they could go.

She let them do as they pleased. She didn't put up a fuss, or do more than vaguely brush their hands off her—large, grey eyes staring off forlornly into space, somewhere through the canvas of the big tent.

Something compelled me to impress her, to play to her, to tell her that I—yes, *I*—understood. That out of all the pawing, leering men who converged on her like flies on an ice cream cone splattered on the boardwalk, that *I* understood what she was going through—

Well, isn't that always the way with men, even normal men, big men, learned and erudite men? To think that they, and they alone, know what a woman wants?

It is incredible how everything else falls away when we fall in love. How beauty, social position, false airs and income, all peel away like the layers of an onion and we see, yes, *we see* how wonderful they are—and how much they need us. To make that astounding presumption—and then the added presumption that if by some stroke of luck rarer than lightning they *do* know—they *do* see how we know them—that somehow they will love us for it in return.

I understood all this—how unlikely it was—but none of it made any difference. Instead, when the song began, I shoved my way to the front, flinging out my arms, bellowing away. Willing to do *anything* in that moment just so she would notice me—in her adorable sailor's suit, sad grey eyes looking away at nothing.

A real girl, just like the one he had—

When it was time for the baritone to kneel and sing at the

end of the song, I sprang forward. I got ahead of him, clamped my hand firmly on his mouth, surprising him so completely that he was still singing when I abruptly pulled my hand off a moment later—then clapped it back on, then off—his *profoundo basso* reverberating like an Indian war cry. And it was funny, it was very funny: the baritone's eyes widening in shock, glowering murderously at me. Me rolling my eyes, smirking, appealing to the heavens—for all the world a cheap, carny dwarf. For all the world like that small, sick creature in the clown's suit who whacked the ladies with his electric cattle prod when they stepped off the Steeplechase.

I got her attention. It was very funny; the whole grandstand shook with laughter, and the men forgot her knees for the moment, holding their sides and belching with laughter.

And best of all, she saw *me*. Her whole face turned up at once as she laughed, her eyes still forlorn, the way a child can laugh just after she's been crying. Looking down at *me* out of all the freakish little people before her.

The band struck up, the crowd began to leave. I followed her with my eyes. As she filed down the steps of the grandstand—the fat lechers still trying to rub up against her, steal a quick feel—I grabbed a painted, wire flower from the hat of a clown, and ran up to present it to her.

She stopped to look at it, truly surprised—and grasping the little metal rose by its petals, cut her finger. Mortified, I whipped out a handkerchief—a huge, endless clown's handkerchief—and dabbed at her finger with it. She looked alarmed at first—wondering if this was one more cruel Coney joke—but then she let me blot up her wound, smiling beatifically while I quietly drew the joke handkerchief back to myself.

"Thank you," she told me, as if nobody in the world had ever offered her such a kindness before.

"Thank you," she repeated, and I was completely smitten, standing there in the circus ring, watching her continue on out with the rest of the crowd, sucking absently at her pierced finger.

I had a love. I was suddenly afraid my feelings were completely, laughably obvious to everyone else and I looked around furtively, but no one else seemed to notice. My fellow performers and citizens were all involved in their regular end-of-the-show hijinks, racing madly about the ring, turning handstands, slugging furiously away at each other.

Carlotta, my queen, was making her speech, giving them a patented royal wave good-bye with her handkerchief. She appeared to be as regally, as sublimely oblivious as ever. Looking at her standing there, I thought she was radiantly beautiful, and that I was certainly, absolutely not in love with *her* anymore. I had a normal woman.

44

HERMAN

Beansy Rosenthal waddled quickly over to his usual table in the Metropole cafe his handsome, ample flesh jiggling excitedly.

"Tonight's the night!" he exulted to the men waiting around his table before he had even sat down.

It was after three A.M., but it was still hot and humid as midday inside the Metropole, the giant electrical ceiling fans doing little more than pushing the hot air around, the candle flames and the curtains fluttering rhythmically in the open windows.

"What's tonight?"

They pushed in reluctantly around the corner booth, Dan the Dude and Boob Walker and Denny Slyfox, making room for Beansy's big seat.

"Tonight's the night I get it!"

Oblivious of the looks they gave each other, Herman pulled a hand fan from his suit pocket and began to fan himself. He swept it back and forth over his triumphant, self-satisfied face, the green, tattered cardboard fan advertising *Henderson's Waterproof Celluloid Collars, Cuffs and Shirt Bosoms—Economical, Durable, Indispensable.* The other gamblers looked down at their drinks, their faces inscrutable.

"'Zat so, Herman?" Dan the Dude asked at last. "An' just what is that you're gettin'?"

The music stopped, and they all shut up out of force of habit. It was the Hungarian orchestra's night off, and here was a ragtime piano player filling in. He had just finished tearing through "The Bunny Hug"—and now he ripped right into "The Oceana Roll." The cafe was nearly empty, and it was too hot for dancing, but an actress sitting near the front got up and joined in, singing the silly, music-hall words in a low, strangely melancholic voice:

> Billy McCoy was a musical boy
> On the cruiser Alabama
> He was there on that pi-an-a
> Like a fish down in the sea
> When he rattled some harmony
> Every night out on the ocean
> He would get that raggy notion
> Start that syncopated motion
> Lovingly—

"Just what is it you got comin'?" Dan the Dude asked again.

"Fifteen thousand dollars!" Beansy proclaimed happily. "Not a dime less."

"They're gonna pay you fifteen grand? For hollerin' your head off to the D.A.?" Denny Slyfox repeated incredulously.

"Sure! How's that for a bargaining tactic? They gimme fifteen thousand, which is what they owe me for shuttin' down my place, after all, an' I get lost for a while. Just for a little while, 'til this blows over."

"Uh-huh. You told the front page of the *World* how you been *shmeering* a police lieutenant. Howzzat gonna blow over?"

"I dunno," Herman shrugged contentedly. "I'll go down,

443

make some money rollin' the rabbit suckers in Atlantic City
for a while, come back an' say I don't remember so good.
Don' worry so much! It's a done deal."

"Uh-huh."

Just see that smoke so black
Sneak from that old smokestack
It's floatin' right to heaven and it
    won't come back
Now here and there you'll see a stool
    and chair
A slippin' 'round the cabin shoutin'
    "I don't care!"
And then the hammock starts a swingin'
And the bell begins a ringin'
While he's sittin' at that pi-an-a
There on the Alabama
Playin' the Oceana Roll

The actress sang on. They were all quiet around the table,
thinking what they would about Herman's good fortune.

"C'mon, c'mon! I'm makin' out fine! Have another
round——"

He seized a passing waiter with one of his thick, fleshy
hands.

"C'mon, what's everybody havin'? Just a horse's neck
for me——I gotta stay sober to count my money!"

The waiter departed with their orders and Herman had
just turned back to the table when Arnold Rothstein materi-
alized at his shoulder, dapper and gray as always. He rested
a hand on Herman's shoulder and spoke quietly next to his
ear.

"Could you come outside a minute, Herman? I got somebody out here wants to see you——"

The other men at the table looked away, or spoke loudly to each other, studiously trying not to hear. Herman Rosenthal's face split into a beatific grin.

"Ah, ya see there, boys? What'd I tell ya?"

No one said anything, and Rothstein disappeared as quickly and unobtrusively as he had appeared. As soon as he was gone, Denny leaned over the table toward Herman.

"Are you really gonna go out there?" he hissed at Beansy.

"Sure, why not?"

"Herman, Herman. They got anything for you, let that lobbygow bring 'em in here."

"Ah, listen, there's nothin' to worry about. I got it on good authority—"

The waiter returned with their drinks, and Herman took a large gulp from his horse's neck—ginger ale with a lemon peel. He started to stand up, and Denny gripped his arm.

"Jesus, Beansy, I'm tellin' ya—don't move out of this room. They got anything for ya, you let 'em come in here—"

> Sailors take care!
> Oh, you sailors beware!
> For Bill will play on 'til you drop!

The actress finished her song, and the piano player took a break. In the abrupt silence they could hear a motorcar idling out on Forty-third Street. Smiling, Herman Rosenthal detached Denny's hand from his coat and stood up.

"Don' worry. Just don' let the waiter take my glass. I'm gonna be back here in five minutes with fifteen thousand dollars to finish my drink."

The big electrical ceiling fans gave another push at the curtains, shoving them out through the open windows, and for a moment they could see the car out there—large and black, with the headlights off and the motor running, three or four faceless heads in the backseat. Then the curtains danced back in, and it was gone.

Beansy Rosenthal was already up and moving to the door of the cafe, still smiling, waving his little green fan advertising Henderson's Celluloid Collars in front of him. He stopped at the hotel desk, grabbed a breath mint, checked his tie in the polished brass counter. Then he walked through the revolving doors, folded back flat against the heat, and stepped out onto West Forty-third Street.

Two men were waiting in front of the car, and as Herman stepped out he could feel the third one come up behind him, out of the shadow of a service door. He frowned, thinking for the first time that he might have made a mistake. He recognized the men in front of him, and he didn't quite care to look around at the third man. None of them, he knew, was Big Tim Sullivan.

"Hello, Herman," said Gyp the Blood, grinning, his hands in his pockets.

Beansy looked over at the car, still fanning himself with the little hand fan. Relieved, he saw there was yet another man still in the backseat of the car.

"Hey, Dry Dollar," he called out softly, in the hot, quiet night. "Hey, Big Tim! You got my money?"

The figure in the backseat leaned forward until his head could just be seen in the light from the street lamp, but it was just Arnold Rothstein again. His face was calm, almost expressionless—his very presence so surprising Herman that he didn't even notice the guns coming up out of Gyp the Blood's and Whitey Lewis's pockets, or hear the hammer being cocked on Dago Frank's pistol behind him:

"Ah, Beansy." Rothstein shook his head just before the shots split the heavy, dank night.

"Ah, Beansy. You never did have the sense God gave a duck."

45

BIG TIM

The annual excursion chowder of the Timothy D. Sullivan Association was held on the last, glorious Sunday in August. It was an airy and cloudless morning, and one which gave no hint of the heat that would crush the afternoon like a day-old carnation.

The grand parade stepped off from Tammany Hall right on schedule, led by three brass bands, and two boxing champions, and every Regular ward leader, and district leader, and alderman and congressman and assemblyman in the City. Big Tim and Mr. Murphy marched at the head of the whole procession like archbishops at the Easter procession, bedecked in sashes and long coats and top hats despite the already rising heat. Marching so grandly and somberly that all the assembled nations of the world, waiting to board the excursion boats, could not help but give one great, spontaneous cheer, even those who didn't have a word of the English yet, or know where they were going, or why.

They had begun to assemble down by the South Street piers before dawn: mothers in their babushkas and fathers in their beards and soup-strainer moustaches, kids still in their stiff, square, wooden shoes. The single young men, digging their hands shyly into their pockets, or the ones in groups, loud and exuberant and menacing, already passing the pint around between them. The factory girls, in their best new hats, laughing and grinning boldly.

It was an overwhelming multitude—but the Wise Ones had done their job faultlessly, and everything went off like clockwork. There were not one but two shiny white new paddle wheelers waiting at the docks, the *Annie LaForge* and the *Flo Murphy,* and when the gates were opened there was everyone marching on two by two, as neat as Noah.

The Jews in *payehs* and phylacteries, and head scarves and broad hats. Bohemians in buttoned-up shirts, still reeking of tobacco. The Italians in bright scarves, with mandolins and hand organs and penny whistles. Irish stuffed into Sunday suits, and a handful of scowling Ukrainians and the last Germans from old *Kleindeutschland* and Syrian Jerusalem-traders up from the Battery and even the occasional guarded black face, quietly taking up a place on the periphery of the crowd.

And on the boat, there was everything for the slow haul up to College Point: ice cream and candies and accordion players and jugglers for the women and children on the excursion deck. And for the men down below there were free cigars and an open bar, and stuss games and roulette wheels, where the house won back in an hour twice what Big Tim had laid out on the festivities. Until everyone was having such a good time eating and drinking and losing money that they broke out into all the old clubhouse favorites:

> Hiawatha was an Indian, so was Navajo
> Paleface organ grinders killed them many
>   moons ago.
> But there is a band of Indians that will
>   never die,
> When they're at the Indian club, this is their
>   battle cry:

> Tammany, Tammany, Big Chief sits in
> his tepee,
> Cheering braves to victory, Tammany,
> Tammany,
> Swamp 'em, swamp 'em, get the wampum,
> Tammany—

—the two boats singing back and forth to each other, resounding with one raucous nonsense verse after another, toothless old men from Russia mumbling along with drunken Irish gangsters and teenage factory girls—

> Chris Colombo sailed from Spain, cross
> the deep blue sea,
> Brought 'long the Dago vote to beat out
> Tammany.
> Tammany found Colombo's crew were
> living on a boat,
> Big Chief said: "They're floaters," and he
> would not let them vote,
> Then to the tribe he wrote:
> Tammany, Tammany, get those Dagos
> jobs at once,
> They can vote in twelve more months.
> Tammany, Tammany, make those floaters
> Tammany voters,
> Tammany.

It was a grand day, and the biggest turnout anyone could remember, but Big Tim felt unaccountably jittery and depressed all the way up to College Point. He sat in one of the private cabins, nursing a lemonade with Mr. Murphy and some of the boys from Albany, letting them cheer him up with some of their constant patter. Dignified, Germanic Bob; Al with his infectious grin and huge schnoz, and a gut jutting out like he'd swallowed a cannonball. Clever little Jimmy, swank as a card sharp, humming his Tin Pan Alley songs, head swinging alertly back and forth like a trained parrot's. All of them trying not to show it but all of them, he knew, just as excited as any of the yoks to be going on a picnic.

How little they require of us—

Still restless, he stood up and paced around, looking out the portholes. He was gripped with a dreadful premonition that something would go wrong. He couldn't even look when they reached the Hell's Gate shallows—though the greatest threat to their safety came when everyone at once rushed to the rails, peering down eagerly to see where the *General Slocum* had foundered, and so many Germans had been lost.

When they docked at College Point, Big Tim felt as if a cloud had passed, and he adjusted his suit and sashes, and went out on deck with Mr. Murphy and the others to greet the crowds. Both boats ran Old Glory up the mainmast, and everyone on board rose as one, and put their hands over their hearts, and sang "The Star-Spangled Banner" with just as much fervor as they had the old Tammany songs.

Endless wooden tables awaited them, laid out end to end down to Flushing Bay, sagging under the enormous platters of chicken and fried clams, pots of clam chowder, countless schooners of beer. Later on there would be whole swamps of ice cream trundled out from the boat ice boxes, and great urns of iced tea, and coffee, and frosted cakes, melting brilliantly in the noon sun. There would be swimming races, and footraces, and diving contests, and pick-up baseball games, played out in the green fields. There would be a greasy pole, and boxing matches and wrestling matches, and more gambling—always more gambling, fleecing his loyal constituents of their last few disposable dollars—

Cousin Florrie and Flat-Nose Dinny scowled and paced about, barking out orders like drill sergeants, while Mr. Murphy sat ensconced among the other district leaders, close-mouthed as the wooden Indians carved along Tammany's portals. Big Tim moved among the people, gladhanding and promising, handling the reporters along for the free feed:

"Big Tim, I noticed Mr. Murphy wasn't singing when they played 'The Star-Spangled Banner,'" said the man from the *Herald*. "Why would that be?"

"I'm sure I can't say, boys. Maybe he didn't want to commit hisself."

He kept walking, while the newspapermen guffawed behind him, shaking more hands, nursing another lemonade in the growing heat.

"Big Tim, if you please, a real question—" asked the serious young man from the *Tribune*.

"Is this for a real newspaper, then?"

More laughter.

"What can you tell us about the murder of Herman Rosenthal?"

The other reporters fell silent, embarrassed as if someone had farted in church. Big Tim only paused to look duly stricken.

"Poor Herman was a good friend of mine—as I think you can see from the affidavit he left with the district attorney. P'rhaps too good for this world."

"Is there any truth to the feeling it was mixed up with politics?"

Big Tim stared at the man as if he hadn't heard right.

"D'ya know anything in this world that's not mixed up with politics, Frank? But if you look around yourselves, gentlemen, you can see that we're in the business of makin' voters, not bumpin' 'em off."

"Does it have anything to do with corruption in the Strong-Arm Squad?" the man from the *Journal* asked more precisely.

Big Tim started walking again.

"Are you implyin' there's corruption on the highest levels of City Hall? Why, by God, I know I've had my own fallings-out with the Little Little Napoleon, but that's a very serious allegation to raise."

There was an immediate little flutter of notebook pages behind him.

"Are you saying the *mayor* has something to do with it?"

"Good God, man, of course not! What'd I just get through tellin' ya? I'm just pointin' out the continuin' wonders of Reform. I mean, here you have a Reform mayor, and a Reform district attorney, and a Reform police commissioner. Various little kiddie reformers chasin' around their skirt tails—and what do you get? A state's witness—a brave, righteous young man—gets shot down right out on Forty-t'ird Street. Well, it makes a body think."

"So you blame them?"

"I don't blame anyone, blamin's not my business. Maybe there was no tipoffs; maybe no money changed hands. Maybe it was just simple incompetence, all around—but isn't that all the more reason why we need a good, capable man like Judge Billy Gaynor to give us *real* reform?"

The man from the *Times* laughed.

"Are *you* a reformer now, Big Tim?"

He stopped again, looking off toward the American flags hanging limply above the *Flo Murphy* and the *Annie LaForge*.

"I'm the people's servant, boys. The day the people truly want reform, that's what they'll get from me. Now—how about somet'in' to drink? This is a chowder, after all."

The reporters surged eagerly over to the free schooners of beer.

Late in the depraved, wilting afternoon, he stood to speak on the makeshift scaffolding the Wise Ones had thrown up with their usual efficiency, the rude boards covered over with red-white-and-blue bunting, until it looked like a veritable throne of democracy. Behind him, in folding chairs, sat all the boys, Bob and Jimmy and Al, and Mr. Murphy, wiggling a straw between his teeth like some rube farmer.

They had all taken their long coats off, stripped down to their shirtsleeves and suspenders during the afternoon, to join in the baseball games, and the seafood, and perhaps even hoist a few, it was that hot. Now, though, the collective soul of propriety, they had rolled their sleeves back down, and put their coats and top hats back on for the speeches. Their bright-red, sunburnt faces looked up expectantly from under the high black hats, sweat rolling copiously down their cheeks—a row of pale, cautious men, dragged out to bake for a few hours in the sun.

"Sullivan! Sullivan! A damned fine Irishman!"

Out in the crowd below him, the faces were merrier, more pixilated, already beaten to a hard bronze by the sun. It was the perfect moment. The bloom was off the day, and the people below him were tipsy and tired and sated, but not so tired yet they wouldn't stand for a speech. Big Tim turned to shake hands with Mr. Murphy, who smiled his polite, parson's smile, then with all the rest of them in turn, the whole firmament of the Democracy. Milking the moment for all it was worth, letting the cheers rise steadily.

Then, when he was ready, he turned to face the people.

The words fluttered through his head again, and he thought he had it now. The beginning of the annual picnic speech:

Here in America——the land, the only land in the world that can truly be called the Land of the People——

And on like that. But what did it mean? It was the land of the people all right; they were as common as the ground underfoot, and as beaten down and uncomplaining.

Land of the people——

He thought of all he could tell them. All he had been thinking about for months now, about poor Herman, and Mrs. Perkins, and even his Nell, laughing on the deck of their excursion boat, years ago. About the street Arabs, and the working girls, and the proud, grim-faced men who stood in the back of his bars to ask him for favors.

He thought of telling them all that——and he knew they would not listen, for they already knew it. They milled about below him, the people, full and contented for once, thinking of little more than the boat ride home. When the men would be singing drunkenly down in the hold, the babes asleep in their mothers' laps up on the deck, and the green lights of the pier glowing like fireflies before them.

And when they had docked at South Street, there would be a whole new procession home. A torchlight parade, winding its leisurely way through the streets of the Lower East Side, up the Bowery to Chatham Square, where there would be fireworks, and one more drunken toot, and then all of them——the sleeping babes, and the drunken men, and their long-suffering wives and mothers——would be carried off to bed, to their suffocating little homes, from which they would rise with the sun the next morning, and go out to work again.

What did he need to tell them, then?

That he had seen that same dark pier of home, just the week before, stacked high with children's coffins from the Charity Commission? They died in droves in the summer, from the measles and the diphtheria, and the whooping cough and the consumption. They died from cholera, and polio, and scarlet fever——and from falling off streetcars, and

454

out of windows, and out-and-out starvation. Worst of all were the floaters—the unclaimed children who came floating up in the East River when the weather got warm, bloated and disfigured. To lie for weeks and months, unclaimed in the city morgue—

There were never enough parents who could pay—for all the seventeen-cent insurance policies the undertakers and the scam artists sold door-to-door. They brought the bodies to the pier, where they could be loaded without delay or ceremony, hauled up to the potter's field on Hart's Island, not far from where they were reveling now. All those tiny coffins, piled up casually there by the longshoremen, awaiting their meager contents.

Oh, but they knew that already. Hadn't he seen them often enough down on the selfsame wharf, wailing as the coffins were loaded? They knew it, but he must not tell them.

Democracy is a lie then. A sweet, mutual, indispensable lie, like the Holy Trinity, or the Catechism, or the life everlasting, but a lie nonetheless.

It was his duty to keep up his end of the mutual lie. To make it so real and vivid that the lovely, roiling, drunken mob out there would make it the truth, would continue to rely on it as they did the confessional, or the Holy Communion.

He stood up straight and grinned out at them. His people. They cheered back, and he tapped his notes on the front rail, even though he had no need of them, the words still running through his head—

Land of the people

"Folks," he began, "I'm a Democrat. I've been a Democrat all my life—"

—and the cheers rolled like thunder across the Flushing Bay.

455

BOOK EIGHT

*The ancient darkness would
outlast the greater light and the lesser
light; the epilogue would be spoken in
the freezing night.*

—CHARLES REZNIKOFF

46

ON THE BOARDWALK

They sat hand in hand, watching the disasters roll by through the years. The wind blew, the waves whipped up— the city of Galveston collapsed before their eyes. Mount Vesuvius belched up flames and deadly ash, the men and women of Pompeii racing around in their sandals and togas.

All the cataclysms of scrim and plywood, dry ice and magnesium powder, built to one-eighth scale, wedged into the plaster-of-paris villas and man-made lakes along Surf Avenue.

THE AUDITORIUM IS EQUIPPED WITH 11 EXITS AND MAY BE EMPTIED WITHIN TWO MINUTES! read the signs, but Esther understood that they were only part of the attraction. It was a vicarious thrill, a sense that, for once in their lives—after all the daily disasters of rent and jobs, sickness and worry— they floated, smugly, above the fray. She was sure it was very much what God Himself must have felt like.

The scale-model sailboats glided through the clouds along the mountain lake, high above the rough mining hills, the miniature railway and houses of Johnstown, Pennsylvania. The dam broke—and torrents of black water roared down upon the town, uprooting cunningly realistic trees, ripping up the railway, tossing whole locomotives in the air.

"I don't know what I would do," she breathed to Kid, beside her, equally fascinated in the dark. "I don't know if I would have the courage."

"What is there to do, little bird?" he shrugged, smiling. "You die or you don't die; that's all there is to it."

"You—you would do fine!" she told him, her eyes shining. "You would always know what to do."

"I dunno," he said, shifting a little uncomfortably in his seat—an uneasiness she interpreted as modesty, and she leaned her head against his shoulder. But he was thinking of the rat pit again.

He just picked up the shovel He didn't even think He just picked up the shovel and all of a sudden it was in his hands and he was bringing it down on Gyp the Blood's fine head.

Was that wise? Was that brave?

After intermission, the great navies of the world sailed into New York harbor, flags flying and anthems playing—and let loose a crushing salvo. Wall Street fell, and the Woolworth Building. The Statue of Liberty, and City Hall; and all the new skyscrapers and the quiet streets and steeples of Brooklyn and even Coney itself—the impeccable miniatures of the three great parks—razed flat by the terrible, miniature bombardment.

The crowd burst into applause, different clumps of people even standing up and singing along with the national anthems as each fleet sailed past—the Japanese and the Russians, the Spanish and the Italians, and the French, and Germans, and British. They roared with delight as the model dreadnoughts and destroyers reduced their city to a rubble.

Then—for the grand finale—the band struck up "The Star-Spangled Banner" and the American fleet, which had apparently been dawdling somewhere up the Hudson, came steaming out to fight. The crowd rose as one, roaring and cheering. Singing along with the national anthem—singing *something*, whatever it was, in a dozen tongues—as the American warships took them on: sinking all the combined navies of the world, one by one, the Japanese and the Russians and the French and the Italians, and yes, even the Germans and the British, the last Union Jack slipping forlornly under the waves.

The American fleet swung around the harbor once more in a victory procession, the crowd standing and cheering so ecstatically that the bleachers shook and wavered beneath their feet.

"Have you ever thought what war would be like?" Esther asked.

"Sure I have," he joked. "Why do you think I left Lithuania? Fourteen years in the Czar's army, dove; you can bet I thought on that!"

But that wasn't it, he knew. It was a greater desire—to separate himself from everything and everyone he had ever known—to be *away*.

So what was it to him if Gyp broke the back of that dwarf— or even a boy, like he'd thought at first? He'd seen worse. What was it to him—to bring him down like this, stuck somewhere again, stuck out in Coney Island, of all places—

The shows were good for an afternoon's entertainment, and afterwards he was happy to let her idolize him, to think how cool-headed and competent he was. He bought her a cone, a great mountain of strawberry ice cream, topped with a cherry and held in a thin waffle wrapper, and she munched at it contentedly as they strolled through the Luna Park midway.

He gazed up, into the clear blue, unruffled sky—and saw the pig's head. It loomed above him, along a wall, one in a row of leering, mocking plaster-of-paris heads, each at least twice the size of a man. A wolf's head, a clown's, a pig's. Huge and pink and hairy—the same head he had shoved away, years ago, that first night in America, as he swam to shore through all the filth and offal of the harbor—only larger and more grotesque than ever.

47

ON THE BOARDWALK

Coming to meet her at Camp's ice cream the next Sunday, Kid thought for the first time that he might love her.

She was supposed to meet him under Camp's ambitious signs promising 21ST CENTURY SPECTACULAR! IT IS TO EAT—— IT IS TO LAUGH——IT IS TO DRINK——where he saw she had been discovered by the parks' roving collection of pantomime freaks: a huge policeman in blackface, round as he was tall; a nine-foot Irishwoman that hid two midgets inside. A race act consisting of a Mick with a battered top hat and an actual harp, an I-tie with a pointed cap, a Hebrew with two thick, curly points of hair sticking out of each side of his head——

They paraded around her, hemming her in, joking and hooting incoherently. He could tell she was intimidated by the way she clutched her bag and edged a step back from the small mob of merrymakers.

Yet for the most part she held her ground, staring stubbornly ahead, her face reddening as the pantomime freaks danced around her. Standing there like any of a hundred thousand other girls on Coney Island, in her one good white summer dress, shapeless, flowered hat on her head. But sticking it out——holding her place, until his heart was pierced to see her there.

Esther watched him walk up the boardwalk toward her, and thought again how fine he was. Hard and wary as any tough, in his gaudy summer suit, until a smile began to leak out around his mouth when he recognized her. She was relieved——to have him rescue her from the huge pantomimes gallivanting around her——but also just to see him again, after the long past week of work.

She had no delusions about what he was, or what he might be: a thief, certainly; maybe a thug, maybe a murderer—— maybe even a pimp. She knew she ran certain risks——that he might take her for her money, her love, or worse. She knew she ran the risk, even, of ending up a whore——and while she could not conceive of any way that would come about, she was aware there were hundreds, probably thousands of women lying in brothels and hotel rooms right now who had thought the same thing. Women who had simply taken a chance for love.

She knew better than to expect anything from him—— beyond this day, strolling the boardwalk with him, her demon lover. Yet it was enough. She considered the most catastrophic possible end of her affair quite calmly.

Whatever it was to be, it could wait——as he strode up to her on the boardwalk, and all the prancing pantomine figures faded away.

"*Nu*, dove, what do you want to do today?"

"I don't know." She considered, chuckling, happy just to be with him again. "What say——I teach you swimming today!"

"Huh? Well, all right," he muttered, not so happy about the idea of going into the water, but an idea forming in his head already.

Down by the beach, on another wedge of sand marked off by barbed wire, he rented a single wooden cabana from the proprietor, pretending they were man and wife. The man smirked, and handed over the key and a black, rented bathing suit for him—not caring if they were man and wife, or King Solomon and the Queen of Sheba.

"In here—"

He led her into the tiny wooden cabin, mounted on short legs in the sand, the only light what snuck in through the cracks on the side, and the little hole on top. There, he sat himself on the changing bench, while she drew her mermaid bathing suit out of her bag, hesitating before him.

"Do it," he whispered, imploring. "Do it, *please*—for me."

"It would be too noisy in here—"

"Just to see—just to *see*."

She smiled, her face above her mouth obscured in the slanted light, and deliberately, casually, began to take off her clothes. Slowly removing one garment at a time, neatly folding and arranging them, giving him time to look. Until when at last she stood easily naked before him—all that she was, smoothed and worn and calloused—he moved off the bench, onto his knees, embracing her around her thighs, and sliding his cheek along the warm, soft flesh of her stomach.

They walked down to the seaside together—Kid feeling more than a little foolish in the long leggings that stretched down over his knees. But he plunged on in, flailing and floundering around, while the children smirked, and she laughed at his efforts. She could not even get him to float without sinking beneath the surf.

"Face it, *hertzalle meine*—Jews don't float," he told her—but she only laughed at him.

"Greenie! Yok! Let's see if you can wade, anyway."

They joined the other bathers along the line. Esther leading, Kid clutching grimly to the guideline behind her, inching his way through the waves.

It was a rough day, and the swells rose suddenly and smacked against the bathers' chests and heads. She took most of the swells for him, trying to get him to bob along with their motion. But even this he did awkwardly, the water repeatedly surging up into his mouth and nostrils. It was full of old wrappers, and bottles, and all kinds of other litter, but still infinitely cleaner than the harbor water he had first jumped into.

She looked back at him, laughing, and he had to laugh, too. He stood up again, and looked out to the horizon, past the breakers and the excursion boats, the buoys and the diving piers. He could see the open sea, and beyond that—nothing, all the way back to where he had come from.

48

ESTHER

The strike broke out one morning at the Triangle factory, over Wenke the *shadchen*, of all people. The union leaders had held more meetings. They had raised more money and made more plans, talking far into the night at the Talkers' Cafe, under the stern tower of the *Forward* building. Yet the moment when they might have any chance against the owners was fast passing them by—and still they talked, and still they waited.

Then Wenke had brought his pathetic line of girls into the shop again. He had gone into the office to argue over the rate with Bernstein, and they could hear all their same violent arguments, even through the closed office door. Yet this time, when he emerged, Wenke was not sunk in his usual, glum acquiescence but still shouting defiantly at the shop manager.

"I'm sick of this slave-driving!" he screamed. "You ask me to do this? Don'cha think I'm a human being, too?"

"That's the offer, bite the feather bed if you don't like it," Bernstein told him, as cool as ever.

"Never! Never! I don' care if you stand one foot on heaven an' t'other on the earth, I won't do it! I won't make my girls do it, I don' care if I starve to death!"

"Fine! Then go, what's stoppin' ya?" Bernstein shouted

back in his face. "Only—the girls stay!"

"My girls?" Wenke stuttered. "*My* girls? I'm the subcontractor, they work for me—"

"They stay here. Go on up to the tenth floor if you don' want to stay, and cash out."

"*Pah!* See if I don't, then!" Wenke spat out, and started toward the elevator. But Kristol and Podhoretz were already making their way across the floor, grinning maliciously, and he began to hedge.

"Wait—are *they* going with me?"

"What about it? You wanted to go, just go."

Bernstein waved a dismissive hand at him. Wenke shuttled back toward where his girls huddled in their usual corner, but the two floor supervisors walked after him, still grinning.

"Wait, wait! I don' want to go with them!" Wenke cried out, appealing to the whole shop. "Can't you see? They're going to give me a slugging, once they got me in the elevator!"

"*Get out!*" Bernstein shouted at him, at the top of his lungs, and now Kristol and Podhoretz seized the *shadchen* by his long, sticklike arms and began towing him toward the yawning elevator.

"They're going to give me a slugging!" Wenke called out hysterically, as they dragged him down the length of the shop floor like a sack of felt scraps. His *yarmulke* dropped off, the long, waxy strands of his hair trailing along the floor.

"People, *please!* Will you stay at your machines and see a fellow worker treated this way?"

The two foremen threw him in the elevator and shut the door—but Esther could still hear Wenke's shouts and screams as the car went down, the dull, terrible sound of blows striking a body.

"All right, everybody back to work," Mr. Bernstein

announced calmly, the captain of his ship once more.

But it was too late. Women were already standing up at their work stations—the shop growing suddenly quiet as they began to shut down their Singers and unscrew them, cradling the machines in their arms as they hop-skipped down the length of the benches toward the stairs. Esther heard herself shouting with the rest.

"Up! Up! Everybody out!"

There were no fiery speeches, no appeals to unity. Nothing more than that simple command, going up and down the benches in a dozen tongues:

"Up! Up! Let's go!"

"Girls! Sit back down!" Bernstein ordered. "Any girl not back in her seat in one minute gets five dollars taken out!"

But this was too much of a threat, it only underscored how serious the situation was. The usually impeccable Bernstein had overshot his mark, and now none of them dared to be left behind. They kept going, shoving past him when he tried to block the stairs—past the goons, Kristol and Podhoretz, who had come back up and stood smirking in front of the elevators, unaware of what was going on.

"Up, up! Everybody out!"

Esther shook with the emotion of it, she could barely see straight as she gathered up her own coat and hat, and unbolted her machine from the bench. Such a simple little gesture, almost like going home in the evening, but how dangerous, how daring it seemed! Afterwards she wasn't even sure why she had done it. None of them were: after all, Wenke wasn't really a worker, he was a boss, and a cockroach boss at that, who brought his pathetic girls in to lower their rates and keep them in line.

Maybe it was simple resentment at being subjected to such a spectacle. Maybe it was their whole, cumulative degradation realized in that moment, but whatever the reason, they kept going: sweeping up to the tenth floor, and down to the

469

eighth; spreading the word to the pressers at their hissing iron coffins, and the cutters at their workbenches, and the pieceworkers and the little girl string pullers, and the floor sweepers. All of them, even Wenke's forlorn line of incompetent girls, coming out with them—nobody wanting to be left behind. Plodding down the stairs and squeezing down in the elevator until the whole shop was out—out on the sidewalk on Washington Place, smiling and shielding their eyes against the unaccustomed midday sun, and wondering what it was they should do now.

After that, though, the strike spread like a conflagration. Before the week was over, all the big factories were on strike, and the little shops, too; at Schwartz's, and Agronick's, and the Marquis and Haskin's and Berlant's. Clara got wind of it at once, where she was working over at Leiserson's, and before the day was out she was leading parades of strikers through the Village and the Lower East Side to any shops that were not out yet, banging broomsticks on the sidewalk grates and yelling up at the shop windows:

"Out! Out! Everybody out! The strike is here!"

The next morning, on her way to the settlement house, Esther saw the *fabrente maydlakh,* the fiery girls, out on every street corner. They spoke in Yiddish, and their stiff, classroom Italian and Portuguese, but the message came through in their hands, and in their faces, and the stirring tremor in their voices.

Little groups of women were gathered before them—some of them no more than children of fourteen or fifteen—talking excitedly over the latest news and rumors. The newspapers were already calling it The Uprising of the Twenty Thousand—then the Thirty Thousand, then *Forty*—and there were rumors that women were walking out of shops down in Philadelphia, and up in Rochester, and even out in Chicago.

Every night the union offices were jammed with more women, bustling about under the glowing yellow balls of light. The strike committee met in continuous session: Clara and Leonora O'Reilly uncompromising and making speeches, Mrs. Perkins and Miss Dreier listening quietly, little Rose Schneiderman careful and reconciling. Clara's friend Pauline Newman staring owlishly out of her large glasses, organizing everything.

The question in everyone's mind was whether they could get the men who headed the garment unions to call a general strike. The women's strike committee wanted to demand recognition from the big shops, but the men weren't willing to risk making it a fight to the death. They preferred to settle for another small rate increase—so they could go back to organizing, and planning, and all the endless talking.

"You got to seize a revolutionary situation when it happens, *bubbeleh*," Clara insisted. "They don' always present themselves right on schedule, like a streetcar. We got everybody out *now*, we have to seize the chance."

"We'll need every help we can get if we go after it," Leonora O'Reilly warned them, looking at Mrs. Perkins, who sat perfectly composed across the table as always, in her black, triangular hat. "This is the time we need our friends to stand by us!"

The ladies *were* out on the street—setting up free coffee stands by the picket lines. The strikers shied away from them for days, embarrassed, afraid to take so much as a cup of coffee or a cruller because they thought of it as charity. It was only later, as the weather changed, and they were wet through and through by the incessant rains, that they yielded, shamefacedly picking up their little cups and pastries from the society matrons. Yet more was required.

"You can be sure of our support," Mrs. Perkins told them, in that firm, cool voice that allowed for no contradiction. "Anything we can do, we will."

They all knew, though, that it didn't change what was coming next.

"Soon they'll start with the arrests: they'll be hauling us in like streetwalkers."

"We can take it," Clara boasted. "There is no sacrifice the women won't make for the union!"

Esther sat beside her in silence, and wondered if Clara really knew what she was talking about.

What does it even mean, any sacrifice? she asked herself. What would *she* be willing to sacrifice?

Esse had busied herself like the others, organizing collections of food and coal for the strikers' families. Selling the *New York Call,* the only English-language paper that was backing the strike, out on the street corners. Helping at the free coffee stands—the wealthy ladies in their fine coats so kind, so maternal toward them but condescending as schoolteachers. As the days and weeks went by Esther put in longer and longer hours, until she was living at the settlement house, not even bothering to go home, but stealing a little sleep when she could on the office couches.

Yet she knew it was nothing. The real work, the real test of herself was still ahead. Out on the picket lines.

"This is when you see what kind of a chicken you are," Clara had only chuckled when Esse confided her fears in her friend. "This is where you see what you are really made of!" Which was exactly what Esther was afraid of.

She gnawed it over, walking back from the hall at night. The summer was rapidly fading away now. Street gangs lit bonfires in empty lots, challenging their enemies to come out and fight. Already the evictions had started up. Families stood begging out on the street among all their possessions, a *Shabbos* candle lit on top of their dresser, a begging saucer beside it.

There was no place for her to go to now, no way she could avoid it. Now, she knew, all of her years of wondering would come to an end. All her days leaning over her machine or staring out the back window, down into the courtyard with its weird gravestone paving blocks—one way or another, all of her wondering about herself would finally be resolved.

Inside the union hall, the women swayed slowly back and forth, vague, bulky shapes in the predawn darkness. They were dressed in their good coats, and their best, wide-brimmed hats, folded with grand ribbons and bows, covered with netting—many bought just for the occasion. They didn't like risking them on the line or in jail, but the press was bent on depicting them already as prostitutes, and street trash, and they were determined to show how respectable they really were.

When they first gathered there was all kinds of speculation about what would happen:

"Do you think they'll give us a slugging?"

"I hear everybody's goin' to jail. That's their tune now—"

"What's it like in there? What's it like? Do you know?"

They sang the "Internationale," and then the "Marseillaise," to keep their spirits up. Yet as the time to go drew near they spoke less and less, each woman and girl silently steeling herself to what lay ahead. Their lines still swaying slowly, unconsciously back and forth, like old men at their Talmud.

• • •

Outside, it was a miserable morning. It had been raining for days, off and on, and they could hear the rain begin again now, cold and relentless, as they waited.

How nice it would be to be at my machine, Esther thought, treading in place, loathing herself for even thinking such a thing—but thinking it nonetheless.

How nice it would be to be inside, in the warm factory, pumping the pedals—

Clara came down the line—no longer one of the *fabrente maydlakh* just now but their gentle commander, giving a kiss or a touch to a woman here, a word to one there. Esther felt immediately embarrassed, as if somehow she might read her thoughts. Clara stopped in front of her, and held her hands in her own, her square, passionate face now kindly and serene.

"Don't worry, little bird, don't worry. We will all be out there. We will help each other be brave."

She kissed her cheek and passed to the head of the line, hoisting herself up on a chair to give them a final talk before they marched.

"All right, you know what to do," she told them, no fire in her mouth for once, only the radiant confidence of a great general.

"Remember: you got to walk in a straight line, keep on the sidewalk. Keep moving. Stop, an' they can arrest you for loitering. Talk, an' they arrest you for soliciting.

"Of course," she said, some of the old mischievousness returning to her eyes, "of course, they may just arrest you anyway. They don't even play by their own rules, the little *yentzers.* Just do what you can, an' don' worry, the union will get you bail."

Esther nodded, and smiled with the rest of them—though she knew that in fact the union's bail fund was already almost exhausted, and that the magistrates could remand them to the Tombs with no bail, for as long as they pleased. She tried not to think of the prison, with its grim gray slanting walls. When she was a child they had still let paying crowds in to see the public hangings. It all seemed impossible—she had been a good girl her whole life. What thing had she done, what harm had she meant, to risk being locked up in such a place?

"All right—if you're ready. Remember: you are people, and you got the right to do this for yourself. If we stick together—and we are going to stick—we will win."

The doors opened, and the strikers filed out along the gray slate sidewalks, their cardboard signs brushing against the leafy tree branches beat low by the rain. They wore white sashes with their union locals, and brave, defiant slogans like WE ARE NOT SLAVES! or DOWN WITH THE MALEFACTORS OF WEALTH! sewn in the same, careful hand with which they had once sewn shirtwaists and fine ladies' cloaks.

They walked quickly, heads down, through the Village streets already filling up with indifferent carters and pushcart vendors and hod carriers, off to their own work, their own city. The rain fell off a bit, a little light beginning to seep through the sky, as they turned the corner on Washington Place to the Triangle, with Clara striding happily at their head.

Up in the Triangle, the young women shuffled and turned awkwardly, in time to the scratchy phonograph set up in the corner. The music filled the eighth floor, echoing off the barren walls and hardwood floors.

They weren't much better at dancing than they were at sewing, being very young, and green, and Mr. Bernstein had all he could do to contain himself. But allowances had to be made, he knew, and he forced himself to be patient, and Kristol and Podhoretz to keep their hands off the new girls.

The scab girls got an hour for lunch, and breaks for tea.

And every morning, they pushed back the long heavy benches, and set up the phonograph, and even gave out little medals for the best dancers. Bernstein supposed the time didn't really matter anyway, their work was so poor and slow, though he was certain that he could find chickens who did a better waltz.

The phonograph began to wobble, the tune suddenly uncertain, needle scratching across the tinny metal record. Podhoretz kicked at the table to get it back in groove, but the needle only skittered all the way across the record and the music went out. In its stead, they could hear the commotion outside, echoing down the canyonlike streets. The scab girls began to drift away from the dance floor, over to the windows.

"Girls, girls! All right, girls! Back to work! Don'ch you wanna see who got the medals?" Mr. Bernstein said loudly, clapping his hands.

They ignored him. All the girls now—and Kristol, and Podhoretz, and the rest of the floor supervisors, too—throwing open the windows and gazing eagerly down at the strike.

There was a crowd waiting for them. Esther could see right away this wasn't one of the crowds of the idly curious, the often sympathetic onlookers who had gathered early on at the picket lines, before it became old hat.

They were cops, mostly, sweating freely in their long coats, and Pinkertons, hands shoved deep in their pockets, hats pulled down menacingly over their eyes. Just to one side was another group they recognized immediately: a bunch of gangsters, with their whores in tow, leering together at the women as they marched into position around the Triangle building.

When the marchers came into view, a shout went up, and

they began to call out all kinds of crude insults. The cops making circles with their thumbs and forefingers, and poking their nightsticks obscenely in and out.

The women swung into a long line, in double file, slowly circumambulating the building. Clara marched defiantly up and down the pickets, exhorting the other strikers.

"Keep going, keep going—they can't bother you so long as you keep moving," she reassured them, glaring over at the cops as if daring them to try it.

"Sing! Sing!"

They broke into a long, solemn chorus of "My Country 'Tis of Thee," but the police and the gangsters only began to jeer at them again.

"Why don'cha go home and wash the dishes?" a man's voice yelled out.

"The dishes were done before I left the house. Are you satisfied now?" Clara yelled back.

"Oh, what beauties! You want more, I'll give you more, all right!"

"We're your sisters and wives and mothers! Have some respect!" ——but this only brought another chorus of catcalls and raspberries.

"If you was my wife you wouldn't be able to sit down for a week!"

She wanted to be as brave, as bold as Clara herself, but she was not. She wanted to say a prayer, or sing along, but her mouth was too dry, and the words would not come. The faces of the cops and the gangsters seemed to her empty of any spark of humanity—like nothing so much as the grotesque, heavy-lidded heads of wolves and clowns and pigs that hung on the walls in Luna Park. But the grim faces of the women marching with her, Clara yelling her defiance, seemed no more real. As she marched around with the rest, Esther knew then that she did not truly believe in anything—in the righteousness of their cause, or the religion of her father, or anything else, anymore.

The morning she had come home, after her night at Coney Island, he had been waiting. Usually at that hour he was already at the Lodz synagogue, debating the great questions of Talmud with some of the few scholars who would still talk to him. But this day he had been waiting, sitting in a chair right out in the kitchen. Her mother beside him, wringing her hands in the kitchen towel.

"Is there any depth to which you will not debase yourself?"

But she saw that there was no ritual cut in his lapel. No sign of mourning—for she was still their servant, and she knew there was nothing she could do, nothing at all, that they would care so much about.

"Your son you declared dead over a pot of stew. But you can still take money from me."

She did not believe in anything, anything at all, save having as much fun as she could out on Coney Island. He was right—her soul was barren, as barren as this cold, wet day, and if she could go back to that ludicrous whore's hotel right now, with her boy, she would go, she was sure of it.

The cops made little beckoning, baby sounds through their teeth.

"Come on, honeys. Come on, sweeties, come to Daddy!"

"*I'll* give youse a raise, all right, long as you do me a favor——"

"Ignore them! Keep marching. Sing!" Clara yelled at them.

My God, Esther thought, watching the eager faces of the

police, tapping their sticks in the palm of their hands.

My God, they really want to do it. They really want to beat us.

One of the gangsters made a gesture, and the brightly dressed whores flounced into the line, each one attaching herself to a striker. They looked like something from nature at first, like mating birds—the picketers in their respectable gray and black marching clothes, the whores in their thick makeup, red and yellow and sky-blue dresses, as bright as if they were in a dance hall. Smiling broadly, scooping up the strikers' hands in their own arms. The strikers were thrown off stride by this approach, still wary, but confused by their friendliness—

Esther saw a prostitute attach herself to the woman in front of her, folding her hand into both of her own like an old friend. Suddenly, the picket sprung back, crying in pain, dropping her sign and clutching at her bleeding hand. The hooker laughed, holding up her hand, where she clutched a mottled piece of glass, jagged on one end and stained with blood.

All along the line, the whores poked savagely at the strikers with hidden needles and hairpins, little knives and pieces of glass—all the tricks of their trade. The strikers faltered. More signs fell to the ground, and the line began to dissolve as they pulled back from their tormentors. They were stronger than the whores; it was easy enough for them to break their holds, but now they had come to a standstill, and everything was chaos.

"Keep moving! Keep moving! Back in line!" Clara implored them. She wrenched a whore away, pushed her into the street, tried to get the line moving again. Other strikers were lashing back now, some of them even hauling off and punching at the hookers. But this was just what the police wanted:

"Lookit the horis, fighting over their corner!"

Esther had been overlooked so far in the melee. She had continued marching, stepping politely around the struggling women, feeling vaguely absurd. But now one of them was moving toward her——mouthing the same lines the rest of them were saying, sticking dutifully to the scenario that they were all whores. She wore red ribbons in her graying brown hair, a tattered red hussar's jacket wrapped around her shoulders.

"Hey, *girlchik*, this is my corner," she said wearily, the voice familiar——and Esther, bracing herself for the assault, looked closely and recognized the woman his brother had once brought around.

"I know you," she said——and to her surprise the woman stopped where she was.

"I know you. Your name is Sadie. It's Sadie, *isn't it?*"

This could only mean that her brother must be here, in that pack of jeering, smirking creatures, baiting them with the foulest insults she had ever heard.

"Listen——" The woman was struggling to say something more, holding up one hand as if to ward off a blow herself.

So this is what she is come to——looking so tired, so wrung out and patched together. That her brother should do such a thing——

But where was he? Where was he? She stood on her toes, looking over the crowd.

"All right, that does it!" a huge, moustachioed sergeant at the front of the police confirmed exultantly. "Let's clear *all* these whores off the street, boys!"

The police charged, gleefully whooping and waving their clubs, smashing at everyone around them, knocking down whores and strikers alike with their sticks until some of the pimps actually felt obliged to run in and rescue the merchandise.

"Oh, come to Papa!"

"Get 'em, get 'em, *get 'em! Filthy* whores!"

Ahead of her, Esther saw the big sergeant grab a small

young striker around the waist and lift her up, pinioning her against him, then rubbing her repeatedly up and down his front like a rag. Lazar's woman was caught now between the police and the strikers—still trying to say something—the cops jostling her as they charged into the line, knocking her off balance.

"Come on, you sluts, we'll give you work!"

"This is not your job, this is not your job!" Clara kept yelling at the cops. One of them charged right up to her, clubbing eagerly at her head. She deflected his blows only with her arms and the high, wide hat she was wearing.

"Tell us *our* job! Dirty *whore*!"

"The law! The law! You're supposed to uphold the *law*!"

Clara backed up, squaring off, and pointed left and right at their badges.

"I see you! Number 457! Pendergast! I see you! 306! Nash!"

Another cop charged at her, and gave her a thwack with his club so hard on her left side that it knocked her down. She rolled over quickly, though, and got back up on her feet, dodging away as he tried to kick at her.

A blue coat suddenly loomed up in front of Esther, its shiny brass buttons right in her face.

They got all dressed up for this, she thought idly, noticing the shine on the brass, his name, KAEHNY, on the little silver plate.

He grasped both her arms and kissed her, right on the mouth, his breath hot and rancid with the smell of his chewing tobacco. He grinned at her, then pulled her to him, nearly folding her in half as he tried to kiss her again. She bit back hard at his lips, forcing him off—and he stepped back and took a full swing at her head with his club. She was only just able to get her arm up, partially deflecting the blow.

"Cut me, will ya, ya *gawd-damned* whore!"

She staggered away, her head ringing, the pain pulsing in

her upper left arm. Out of the corner of her eye she could see him coming after her, lifting his nightstick, and she tried to duck, tried to cover her head again although she could barely get her arms up.

"Try me on, you *yok*!"

Kaehny the cop howled in pain, reaching futilely around, dancing up on his toes. Clara was behind him now, plunging a long hat pin right through his thick winter-duty coat, into his backside. She held it there, laughing openly at him as he swatted desperately, comically behind himself with his club.

"Yah, how's that for a prick, *chachem*?"

"Devil! I'll teach ya——"

Kaehny swung from the hips at Clara, but she just moved out of the way——the swing so hard the cop's hat fell off. Esther thought he looked suddenly so much younger, so much less sinister——his long, homely freckled face and his red stringy hair uncovered. Her only concern was for Clara, though, and she gave the cop a good, swift kick in the back of his knee, folding his leg under him and sending him sprawling into the gutter.

"That's it! Fight, fight, you might as well!" Clara called out wildly, cheerfully, pulling Esse back toward the building. "They're going to give it to you anyway, you might as well get something back from the bastards!"

Everything was frenzied now, nightsticks and blue elbows and fists flying. The sidewalk was littered with huge, flattened hats, lying out on the pavement like great dead moths. One by one, the strikers were being clubbed to the ground, dragged off to the waiting Black Maria the cops had pulled up. The few women who were still up were kicking and punching out ferociously at the whores, and the cops, and the gangsters.

"Come along, you goddamned tramps!"

The big sergeant came at them. His hat was gone, too, dark hair slicked down miserably with sweat on his forehead. All the fun was out of him now. He was huffing and puffing strenuously, and there was nothing in his eyes but low, grim menace.

"You have no right to arrest us! You have no right to arrest *any* of us!" Clara shouted at him—for what new, invisible tribunal, Esther couldn't guess. She put her hand on Clara's forearm, steadying herself, waiting.

The sergeant started for them, one hand gripping his club until his knuckles whitened. He raised it over his head—and Sadie, her brother's woman, came up suddenly at his side, and plunged the sharpened comb she carried into the cop's neck. He gasped in pain, and swung around, chasing after her.

There were too few strikers left by now, though, and too many cops. Three more officers tripped Sadie up, clubbed her to the ground and hauled her off. Esther felt another ringing blow to the back of her head. They were all around her now, and the next thing she knew she was pitching forward on the sidewalk. Two more cops grabbed her arms before she could rise, scraping her along the ground before they picked her up and chucked her into the back of the paddy wagon.

"Here, here—you all right?"

Some of the younger girls in the wagon, mostly Italians, were trying to help her, but she could see that they were badly hurt themselves—most of them bleeding from the mouth, their noses and teeth smashed, one girl's arm hanging limply.

"I'm all right—it's not so bad—"

She lay where she had been thrown—staring out the back of the wagon where she could see Clara, still backed up against the building, all alone now.

"It's not fair! It's not fair!" she was yelling, almost triumphantly, as if she had finally proven her point.

One of the biggest cops, who must have stood at least a foot taller than Clara, ran forward and hit her a quick blow with his nightstick under her arm. She doubled over, but quickly stood up straight again. She had no breath to curse them anymore, but her eyes still shone contemptuously. Another cop ran up, from the other side, and hit her in the ribs, and then they were all over her, slamming shot after shot into her sides, pummeling her face with their fists until she slumped over on the sidewalk, and Esther heard herself screaming Clara's name, over and over again, as she tried to scramble back out of the truck, certain they were killing her.

But they hadn't. Two cops picked her up like a sack of coal and toted her over to the paddy wagon, dropping her roughly on her back. Clara's eyes were closed, and her face was already swollen and covered with blood, but she moaned when they threw her in, and Esther, crawling over, could see she was still breathing. They threw Sadie in on the other side of her—a little less banged up and still conscious, but with her eyes spinning in her head, the red ribbons in her hair now torn and matted with blood.

One of the cops came up to the doors, and began to shove them back, as roughly as if he were reordering cords of firewood. He pushed the doors shut, and bolted them, and chained them from the outside, until they were left in the unbearably overcrowded darkness for the fast, jolting ride over the cobblestones to the Tombs. The only sounds the hard breathing, and groans, and soft crying of some of the girls.

Before they left, before the doors were slammed shut almost in her face, Esther stared out at the jeering crowd of gangsters—most of them by now looking a little bored by the action, a little annoyed at the wailing and weeping of their beat-up whores. She kept searching, until she was sure she had seen what she was looking for: a slim, neat man, decked out in an immaculate, three-piece russet suit. His hands in his pockets, surveying the scene as casually as if he had just wandered upon it.

Then she knew he was there. Then she knew for sure her brother had seen it all.

49

ESTHER

At the Tombs they were hauled back out of the Black
Marias, again like so much firewood, and marched off to the
holding cells. There they were handcuffed to each other and
to the cell bars, and left for hours without anything to eat or
drink. Most of the women could only lean, or crouch down
around the bars of the overcrowded cells, balanced against
one another, careful not to twist the cuffs that held them
together. None of them talking much, trying to conserve
their strength—

Deep in the prison, they could not even hear the distant
church bells Esther had used to mark the passage of time at
the sweatshop. There was only the sound of distant, receding footsteps, the slam of doors and the jangling of keys—
a fun-house echo of noise that sounded like a moan, or a
scream, but was only another door closing. The only way
they could tell time at all was a slow, gradual darkening, as
the light faded from unseen windows, and the night rose
around them like a fog.

Esther stood silently among the restless, softly groaning
mass of women—trying to help Sadie, who was still dizzy,
to keep her cuffs up so they didn't tear her wrists so much.
Trying to help Clara, who was hurt worse than anyone else.
Trying to be brave and quiet, a pillar of strength among

them until she was sure that they had been utterly abandoned, and gave in to her despair.

"Where are we?" she cried out, despite herself. "How
long can they keep us here? What are they going to do to
us?"

"Easy, little pigeon, easy there." Clara soothed her, rocking back and forth on her haunches, whistling through her
teeth in her pain. "Don' worry, they won't forget about *us*."

Yet it was all she could do to keep from crying out again
as the darkness rose—to keep from wailing, and rattling her
cuffs against the bars until she got *somebody* to pay attention.

He is right, she thought of her father, clenching her chat-
tering teeth together, trying anything she could to still herself.

*He is right and I cannot get through this I am nothing on my
own*—

"Easy, easy, this will all pass," Clara was still soothing
her, her voice dreamy and clotted with pain and fatigue, but
Esther still could not keep herself from despairing.

He is right He is right, the unreasoning thought kept
resounding in her brain, until she herself had fallen into a
restless half-sleep, there against the cell bars.

I am nothing myself—

They were unshackled, and hauled out in the middle of the
night, for the state to do its business.

The night court was a low, musty wooden courtroom,
overheated by a potbellied stove, and barely lit by a couple
of dull balls up around the magistrate's bench. Bailiffs sat
sleeping in the corners like fat old toads, and the night court
reporters leaned their chairs back against the wall, feet stuck
up against the benches with practiced cynicism, spewing
long brown jets of tobacco at the cuspidors.

The magistrate was another Tammany ornament, an

impressive old Yankee with a hoary beard and flaming blue eyes. He sat up behind an ancient, whittled bench, flanked by the dull yellow balls of light—the great seal of the City of New York, with its windmill and tulips and beavers, glowing faintly on the wall behind him.

The strikers sat on the Whores' Bench, made to wait while the magistrate set to rights all the disorders of the night: dispatching the drunks and the brawlers, the wife beaters and pickpockets and procurers. At least they got to sit, finally, and many of the women, the younger girls particularly, fell asleep even though their fingers were turning blue from the tightness of their cuffs.

The cops, the reporters—even the other prisoners—all craned their necks to get a good look at them. Sitting next to Esther was a real prostitute, beaten up and hauled in because she had stopped paying protection money to the cop on her street. After her was a young girl who had been seduced and abandoned by her employer, and another one, no older, who was accused of luring a man to her room for the purpose of robbing him. They sat upright and defiant, basking in the attention, staring back at the judge and the idle gawkers, proud as aristocrats.

Finally, at four in the morning, they were arraigned in a long line before the magistrate, who spoke in a rolling, stentorian voice for the benefit of the press, and told them they were on strike against God and nature and sentenced them each to fifteen days in the workhouse:

"If you women are determined to work outside the home, you must show a proper respect for those good enough to employ you. Loyalty to your employer is the first part of learning to love your work."

After the sentencing, they were led out another door of the courtroom, along with the whores, across a dizzying,

latticed metal walkway called the Bridge of Sighs. Below
them, a great chasm spun down into space; crisscrossed by
more metal bridges and walkways, dotted with small, oven-
like cell doors.

They were in jail.

First they were were made to strip and hosed down with
freezing cold water, deloused and crudely cropped of their
hair, until they were left blind and naked and humiliated,
choking and coughing on the thick white powder.

"But where does it all go? What do they do with it all?"
Esther wondered out loud, watching the thick, beautiful,
brown and black curls of their hair pile up in one corner of
the room. A matron came by and hit her so hard and so suddenly on the back of her calves that she dropped to her
knees.

"No talking!"

They were issued heavy wooden shoes and striped tents
of dresses that they had to pin to keep from falling off.
Their cells were no more than seven feet by three and a half,
with barely enough room to stand between their iron cots
and the wall. There was no running water, only one tin pail
to drink from and another to go in. There were no windows,
and the only air came through small chutes built like chimney flues into the ceiling. When it rained, water dripped in
on them, and even when it didn't, the walls of their cells
were always wet, as if the prison were constantly bleeding
from its stones.

Their job was to scrub the stone floors over and over again,
on their hands and knees, with only a hand brush and a few
filthy rags.

"This is a workhouse, so you will work!" the head matron,

a lean, gray, slab-faced woman, smirked at them, as if they had no idea what real work was.

In fact, the scrubbing was almost a relief. Esther found that it used a whole different set of muscles from the sewing.

The Almighty must have given us an infinite number of bones and muscles and sinews to be tortured!

She was more worried about her friends. Sadie wasn't used to this sort of work; her hands blistered and bled copiously into the gray, polluted wash bucket. Clara was still aching from her broken ribs, and coughing up blood. Esther tried to help them, but it was forbidden to talk or to let them lean against her, the matrons stooping over and whacking them with their rubber truncheons when they tried—or just for the fun of it.

At least the three of them got to share a cell together. They would take down their iron beds, and talk in whispers or even sing a little before falling asleep, holding hands. There were large gray rats in the darkness, and enormous cockroaches that ran over their legs, but with the three of them together it wasn't so bad. Once she got over her shame for having panicked in the holding cell, Esther decided that she had to talk to Sadie.

"It was a brave thing what you did," she told her shyly, a little enviously.

"*Ach*, it was just doing what a person would do," Sadie shrugged, turning her head away, even more embarrassed than Esther was.

Sadie's fantasy came flooding back, so strong she could barely speak: *The two of them, living down the hall from each other, visiting during the day. And on the holidays, all of them around the table together—*

"I'm so ashamed of what he has done," Esther muttered—unsure even how to address this woman who was—what, to her? Her brother's woman, almost her sister-in-law, almost her sister.

"He doesn't know how to live like a decent person anymore," she said, as if in explanation.

"I know, I know," Sadie sighed. "I love him more than silk and velvet. But oh! What a bastard!"

Twice a day, they were marched in their heavy Dutch shoes and shapeless, sexless dresses to a room as large as the shop floor—with the same long benches and table laid out end to end. There they ate, instead of sewing. The matron ordered them to say grace, then they were served raw gruel, in the morning; old bread made out of bran and corn, and stale potatoes, and sickly yellow soups, crawling with maggots, for supper. Clara took it only until she had recovered enough to speak clearly and forcefully again.

"No, we won't say grace!" she announced one night, as determined as ever, rapping her tin spoon against her bowl for attention.

"Who are you to force your religion on us? This isn't the Czar's Russia. And we won't eat any more of this filth! We aren't swine, you know. You must feed us real food, like real people!"

The other, more permanent prisoners seized the opportunity to turn over their bowls, and bang gleefully on them with their spoons until the matrons surged in among them, thrashing away with their truncheons. All of a sudden there was a small riot under way, and Esther cringed down below the table, not wanting any more of this, not wanting to get beaten again, but she had no choice. They grabbed hold of Clara under her arms and started to pull her up, but she yelled so loudly that Sadie impulsively grabbed hold of her on one side, and then what could Esther do but to hold on to the other side—trying somehow to pull her back down and away from the vicious matrons.

A bell started clanging insistently somewhere, and more

guards, men and women, came charging in. They pried their fingers off of Clara, clubbing away at them until Esther felt dizzy and sick to her stomach. By now the whole room was in an uproar, the women hurling their bowls at the matrons and overturning the tables, still more guards pouring into the room and beating them back against the walls.

They were half hauled, half marched back over the stone floors and the Bridge of Sighs to the warden's office—a remarkably well-appointed suite of rooms within the grim gray prison. Real drapes, and bookshelves, a thick Persian carpet and an enormous globe—altogether a better apartment than any they knew.

The warden himself leaned back against the front of his desk, his gently rounded gut pushing out his buttoned brown vest. Staring mildly at them as they were dragged in and set in straight-backed chairs before him, their hands cuffed together, feet fastened to the chair legs.

"I understand you won't eat," he informed them, tapping the bowl of a pipe against one palm. "I understand you won't say the blessing."

"It'd be a blessing if we could eat that filth!" Clara retorted.

The warden brought over a felt-bottomed chair of his own, and leaned in toward them, speaking confidentially:

"Why is it you don't want to say the grace?"

"We're not the same faith."

"Is it that—or is it that you're really atheists, without any faith at all?"

Clara laughed at him.

"Sure, I'll proclaim it to the world: I'm an atheist. Though some of the girls are still believing Jews. Not to mention Catholics and Protestants, God help them."

"Enough of your insolence! Come on, now. Tell me: who put you up to this?"

"What?"

"Was it anarchists? Some gangster? Who got you girls to go out?"

"Do you think these heads on our shoulders are made of straw?" Clara snorted. "These women can make up their minds for themselves; *they* don't jump like a puppet when some boss tells them to!"

"All right, you've brought this upon yourself!"

Suddenly the warden was shouting at them, standing up and calling in the matrons again.

"You won't eat? Fine! Then you'll be force-fed!"

"No! We're not on a hunger strike, we just want real food——" Clara started to protest, but she was seized and bent over the back of the chair she had been sitting in a moment earlier. The matrons grabbed Esther and Sadie next, unfastening the cuffs but dragging them forward. Pinning back their arms and stuffing thick rubber gags into their mouths before they could even protest.

Esther found herself pressed cheek down upon the warden's desk, the tattered, green blotter reeking of ink, a collection of miniature good-luck Democratic donkeys right in front of her. One matron held her neck and head down; another one wrapped a tight rubber strap around her elbows, hooking them painfully back behind her.

"Search them! Search them thoroughly first!" the plump little warden cried excitedly.

She felt the billowy, shapeless prison dress being parted, the matron's fingers poking roughly, cruelly up into her.

"——show them what happens to the likes of them! The whores, the whores! The insolent whores!"

Some kind of metallic tube or hose was thrust even more roughly up into her——then a spray of water that churned up her guts until she could not control them. She could not believe anything like this was happening to her. It was as if she had no control over her body any longer, the matrons shoving and opening her up where they would. They flipped her over on the desk, so that she was staring straight up at the ceiling fan now, and the long strips of flypaper hanging down from it. Began to snake another long, thick tube down her throat—

She was sure she would choke to death on the contraption. The small metal nozzle on its end scraped horribly along the roof of her mouth, but still they kept shoving it down. She began to gag, her tongue being pushed roughly back down her throat. She felt like her head would explode, and she wanted to scream at them *Stop it Stop it You are killing me*—but she couldn't get anything out over the horrible, relentless tube.

They kept shoving it down, too hard and fast for her to do anything but try to swallow it. An even more wretched sensation hit her stomach as they pumped down the thick gruel, forcing it down into her until she thought that she would burst.

Oh God, she thought, *how can they do something like this to a person How can they do this*—

The matrons pulled the tube back so abruptly that she thought they were wrenching her throat out with it. They released her, and she staggered up from the desk, clutching at her raw throat, unable to emit so much as a sound, even with the tube gone. Across the room, Sadie lay shuddering on the floor against her chair; Clara leaned over retching dryly above hers.

There was an unbearable stench, which Esther realized came at least in part from her. She was all the more humiliated to know that the weedy little warden had been in the room the whole time. He looked red-faced and flustered, one hand tapping excitedly on a chair arm.

"Take them down to the dark rooms," he ordered crisply now, but refusing to look them in the eye as they were drawn up before him again.

"Show them what their agitation will get them!"

They were led down more endless, stooping, mazelike corridors to three separate cells, even smaller than the one they had shared, and without any window or light of any kind. The matrons shoved Esther inside the first one, strapped her to a rough pole in the corner, sitting upright. She could hear them taking Clara and Sadie on down the hall.

They can't be going to just leave me here They can't be going to just leave and go away——

It was the darkest place she had ever been in, without even a hint of light coming in from under the door. There was only the scuttling sound of the vermin, the inescapable stink of herself to remind her that there was anything else in the world. She strained to hear every hint of a footstep, any movement at all outside the black, stifling box.

Once a day, it seemed, they came with food, and to empty the bucket she defecated in. Each time seemed like a revelation. The heavy steps of the guards suddenly right outside, the bolts peeling back like gunshots, the door flying open. Even the pale gray block of light from the prison corridor made her eyes hurt. The guard would walk across the floor, drop the tin plate by her side with a gloating little smile, and walk back without a word. She couldn't bear their leaving.

"Don't do this, don't leave me here," Esther broke, and pleaded with them at the last moment, though she had sworn she wouldn't.

"You don't have to do this; don'cha know that I'm your sister, don'cha know that our fight is the same——"

They only kissed her, still grinning, and left her in the dark room.

Her mind kept slipping, like a bad piece of cloth that caught and bunched under her hand, and she tried to force herself to concentrate on outdoor things, on the sun and air and trees. She tried to think on the summer she had spent up on the Palisades, with Clara and Gina and the rest, all of her friends, strung out along the cliff ledges like so many mountain goats. But there was no one to help her now, or Clara or Mama here, to offer her any consolation or hope. There was only the blackness.

At first she kept wishing that *he* was there, her *dybbuk*.

He was right, he was right, she thought, and all she wanted was for him to come and rescue her——to take her back to the beach at Coney. *He* would know what to do, with all his cunning little tricks and turns. *He* would always know a way out. All she wanted was to be in his arms, tucked away in their little room at the Tin Elephant, listening to the waves.

But as the hours stretched on, Coney Island seemed further away than the other side of the world and her dybbuk, her boy, just another one of her dreams. There was, instead, only the voice of her father——that father who was always with her.

The worst thing that ever happened to us was to get to reach the promised land.

What did you expect?

He would shift uncomfortably in his big, sagging leather chair, look away from her.

I don' know. Like Poland, maybe. Only with more cows.

So in your disappointment, you make it a misery for everyone.

He would shrug at her, she was sure——a gesture both belligerent and fatalistic.

So——you don' like it so much, why don'ch you leave?

And what would you do without me? What would you and Mama do?

She would watch him smile sardonically, underneath his dirty white beard.

You are afraid. That's what it is. At least be true to yourself, even if you are not true to me, or to the Law. You are afraid to leave.

Her first inclination would be, as always, to shout him down. To tell herself *That's not true!* until she could hear nothing else. But now she did not have to, because she *knew* it was not true. She was no longer afraid to leave them, she was no longer afraid of anything now that she had ended up in the worst place she could possibly imagine. She leaned back against her post, in her pitch-black cell, and he faded before her.

When they let her out of solitary, Esther could barely see. Everything seemed weirdly thin and elongated, etched with a strange burning light even in the dim, buried corridors of the Tombs. When they put her back in the cell with Clara and Sadie, none of them said a thing. They simply sat on the floor in the grimy, ludicrous dresses, trying to keep everything from spinning around them.

"Saturday! Saturday baths!"

The matrons came bustling down the hallway, thunking on the cell doors with their truncheons.

"Out to the bathing rooms!"

Someone yanked open their door, and the three of them helped pull each other up, staggering blindly against each other. They were marched out into the hall, into a long line of their fellow strikers, now all but unrecognizable in their identical, blousy dresses, hair just starting to grow raggedly back in.

They were marched in single file, back over the Bridge of Sighs again. Esther assumed they were being taken back to the rooms where they had first been hosed down and doused with insecticide, but instead they were led to a different section of the endless prison. There they were once again made to strip in the strictest silence, hanging the tent-like dresses carefully on pegs.

They were hustled on in through a low archway, to a dim, moldy room filled with several great vats of water, and decorated with the finest tilework of leaping dolphins and naiads. A room smelling of human dirt and sweat, and echoing with low groans, and grunts and shouts. Even through her blinking, distorted half-blindness, Esther thought that the lugubrious guards now seemed unusually animated and eager to move them into the baths.

When they entered the watery, echoing room she saw why. Before them was a scene of the most wanton depravity. The long troughs of water were filled with embracing women. Women languidly, voluptuously, unmistakably making love to one another as they bathed. Kissing each other right on the mouth, on breasts, on their sex. Lingering in each other's arms, kicking water heedlessly over the sides of the tubs like strange aquatic creatures, like the naiads on the wall, as they rolled pleasurably around.

Nearly all of the lovers were the more permanent inmates of the workhouse. Most of the strikers hung warily back by the entrance—though Esther saw that the matrons were enraptured by the spectacle, standing right up by the tubs and peering in. A few of them even taking part, stripping off their blousy, institutional uniforms to become one with the women reveling in their bath.

Clara and Esther and Sadie stayed rooted with the other strikers, clutching their hands up over their breasts, gazing helplessly at the stunning spectacle—until they began to laugh. It started with Clara, giggling in short, restrained bursts to save her busted ribs, and then the rest of them caught it. They began to laugh uncontrollably, holding their hands up over their mouths—not wanting to offend the other women before them, though they were all past noticing.

They had a good, long laugh, and then they climbed into the mildly dirty, mildly warm water, letting it swirl up and around their tortured bodies. Leaning back against the troughs, their arms around each other's shoulders, still laughing a little—at what they had seen, at the sight of the matrons out of their uniforms. At themselves, for being so shocked at what was, after all——after all the cruelty they had been through——nothing more than the sweet, sad sight of women in a prison, making love to each other on a Saturday night.

50

BIG TIM

Big Tim Sullivan hurried up Broadway, and over to
Washington Place. The rumor going around for days was
that the women were going to march down to City Hall, and
the boys liked to say his ears were so close to the ground he
could hear the third rail humming. The damned thing was,
he still didn't know what he should do about it.

A block from Washington Place and the Triangle, he could
already see the crowd, hear the chanting and the speeches.
The street was covered with shapeless, flattened bundles of
hats and other clothing, busted billy clubs and strike placards,
and even a few startling red slicks of blood. A police horse lay
in the gutter, where it had slipped and broken its leg on the
rain-slicked street. The cop stood over it with tears in his eyes,
and looked away as he lowered his pistol toward its head.

Big Tim hurried on, pushing through the crowd. Just
ahead of him, lining both sides of the street, was a thin line
of women pickets, already roughed up, grimly holding on to
what remained of their placards. Some of the worst thugs in
the City and their whores ran up and down their line, poking
and grabbing at them. The cops looking on, pointing and
grinning, thumping their nightsticks in the palms of their
gloved hands, intervening only to arrest the factory girls if
they struck back.

Even as he watched, two burly officers in their greatcoats grabbed a pretty, frail-looking striker by the arms, making her drop her placard in the street. She could not have been more than seventeen, but they held her there while a third cop stepped forward and, grimacing slightly, punched her once, twice, right in the mouth, first with his left hand and then the right, until the blood ran down the side of her mouth, and she folded up in the street.

"All right! That's enough of that!" Sullivan shouted, but nothing could be heard over the noise of the crowd. Soon a general melee had broken out, fists and clubs flying everywhere.

Big Tim staggered away, walked blindly back the way he had come, sitting down finally on a little park bench, across from where he had seen the crying policeman shoot his horse. The horse was still there, legs jutting stiffly out. A pack of street children already dancing around it, pulling hairs from its tail to wear for finger rings.

He had always liked working with horses, himself. That had been his first job on the up-and-up. He had been in charge of changing the team on the old streetcar line up to Grand Central, back when it was still horse-drawn.

He would stand waiting with the next team, holding their halter in one hand, feeling the power of the six shuffling draft horses in his right arm. The horses waiting patiently while the change was made, steam rising in clouds off their sweating, matted coats in the frigid winter air—

There was another roar from the crowd down the street, and the sound of drums and horns. Big Tim stirred himself, peering up Washington Place.

There was a solid column of women marching down the

street now, arms linked, singing as they came. The gangsters and the whores gave way, herded back by the cops. They itched to get at them, he could see, clubs still at the ready. But marching at the head of the column, and along its sides, was a phalanx of society ladies, easily distinguished by their expensive dresses and their fancy hats. Faced with this obstacle, the cops wavered, then fell back, unsure what to do. On the column came, eight across, the women singing louder with each stride they advanced unmolested, the fickle crowd cheering them now, swept along in their wake.

Mrs. Perkins had come to see him the day before, in that same triangular black hat that was so much like his mother's. She was all business, though, stern and foreboding, and she brought one of the society women, a Miss Dreier, a veritable goddess with her fine silk dress and flashing blue eyes.

"You've got to help the strike," Mrs. Perkins had told him, as flatly as ever. "That's all there is to it. This is too much; you've got to do something."

"Well, now, you know the Organization strives to be impartial in labor disputes," he had tacked miserably. "After all, there are many disparate interests in the City for us to—"

"Tim Sullivan, that's the biggest lie you've ever told in your life, and you know it," she cut him off. "You have the police out on every corner clubbing those women—and pimps and their whores, too."

Big Tim sucked in his breath abruptly, but she went right on, spelling out the reasons again why Tammany should support the strike as objectively and straightforwardly as any district leader.

"I know—you get money from the owners. So where are they going to take it, as long as you control all the votes? If you let the strike down here, you might as well turn fifty thousand votes over to the Socialists."

"I don't know, ma'am——"

"Another thing," she said, brushing off his objections. She stood up, and Miss Dreier rose with her. "One more thing you should know. If you don't see that this strike gets settled and call off the police, the society ladies are going to march. That's right; they'll be right out on the picket line, with the strikers. See if they're not."

And here they were, marching down Broadway, large as life. Big Tim hurried on down to City Hall, where Mr. Murphy was already waiting in the mayor's office. The Little Little Napoleon was there, too, sitting stiffly behind his huge desk, trying to cozy back up to Mr. Murphy—— though Sullivan happened to know it was far too late for that. For the time being they let him stay, since it was, after all, his office.

"Jesus, Charlie, have you seen it out there?" he said, collapsing on the mayor's couch as soon as he came in. "They're cuttin' down women an' babes-in-arms like they was known felons."

"Yes, it is concernful," Mr. Murphy said calmly, swaying back and forth in one of McClellan's impeccable little Windsor chairs.

He gave no indication that anything was amiss, and it occurred to Big Tim that he sat there like the engineer of a highly volatile machine, constantly, imperturbably checking the gears and the gauges.

"They are marchin', you know. They're on their way."

"Yes."

"Marching?!" the Little Little Napoleon barked. "What are they marching for?"

"For right here. To give you a petition, I think."

"What? That's outrageous! Am I some common criminal, to be served their summons?" McClellan fumed. "I won't allow it! Why haven't the police dispersed them already?"

"Oh, only because there's a few dozen women from the society Four Hundred marchin' at the head of the line," Sullivan informed him. "Or do you want yer new, progressive police force clubbin' the wives an' daughters of the richest men in New York?"

The Little Little Napoleon seemed as flummoxed as his old man had been during the Seven Days.

"I'll—I'll do something. Call out the militia, then!"

"You'll do exactly what we tell ya," Big Tim said blackly, fixing the mayor with a look, "if ya ever want to hold so much as an alderman's post in this town again."

"Why not let them present their petition?" Mr. Murphy shrugged. "That way you'll look all the more judicious to the working press."

"Ah, but Jay-sus, we got to do somethin' more about this," Big Tim insisted, shaking his head.

"Why?" Mr. Murphy asked. "Why not just let the strike run its course, and see where we are then?"

"Because it's past all that now," Big Tim told him, thinking again of the grimacing cop punching that young girl in the mouth. "Because if we let it go this time, they won't forgive us."

"Do you really think that's true?" Murphy asked again, actually curious—the man of science, the perfect political engineer. "What are the owners gonna say if we back a settlement?"

"Why don'cha ask their wives? They're right outside there—"

There was a tremendous noise, just beyond the graceful Georgian windows of the City Hall. An enormous throng was pushing its way down Broadway, sweeping aside the last, tentative cops, forcing them back into a thin blue line right under the mayor's office.

"We can always get money," Big Tim said, repeating Mrs. Perkins's arguments. "Where're the owners gonna go with their boodle, anyway? We got to hold on to the Organization."

Mr. Murphy stood up and walked unhurriedly over to the window, where he peered out through the drapes at the mass of strikers and society ladies, singing and shouting up at the mayor's office with one voice. He watched them for a little while, his cold, engineer's eyes unblinking.

"Well, some adjustments may have to be made," he conceded.

51

ESTHER

There was a crowd to greet them at the gates when they got out of the Tombs, a mob of ladies to press garlands of roses and little medals upon them. The Sisters of the Eagle, one of the wealthy women's lodges, sang three choruses of the "Marseillaise" for them, and a long line of undergraduates from Barnard College—bareheaded and clad in austere white shirtwaists—gave them three long, solemn huzzahs.

They stood politely, listening to all the speeches and the tributes. Clutching their flowers, still disoriented to be back in their real clothes and out in the sunlight. Afterwards they marched uptown to a reception at the Colony Club, and a huge dance at the Hippodrome, the vast indoor circus Brinckerhoff and Bet-a-Million Gates had put up on Forty-third and Sixth, with its block-wide promenade and electrified gold-and-silver elephant heads.

They walked in to thunderous applause, the cutters and the other male workers bowing low before them. Each one was paired off at random with a partner—and then they went slowly spinning and turning around under the great vaulted ceiling—still dizzy from the prison, the women and the male cutters alike moving deliberately, conscientiously through all the steps they had learned at the dancing academies on Norfolk Street.

At the Colony Club, they sat stiffly at little round tables
with gilt-edged chairs, the strikers sitting right beside Miss
Morgan and Mrs. Harriman and Mrs. Belmont—the working women distinguished by the little medals that hung
around their necks on red, white, and blue ribbons.

Waiters trucked out trays of chicken and carved roast
beef, bowls of lobster bisque, and glasses of syrupy red and
green tonics. The strikers ate hesitantly at first, afraid it
might still be charity. Glancing over shyly at the rich women
they were seated with, afraid to even try struggling with the
salad lettuce. Then the waiters brought out the cakes—
huge, splendid, chocolate layer cakes, still warm, and moist,
and slathered with icing—and they lost all their inhibitions,
plunging into them as soon as the plates reached them.

It was all a dream—a last-year's lemon pie, Esther thought,
watching them. The wormy bread and raw gruel, her time
in the dark room—everything from the prison was already
impossibly far away. She fingered the medal that hung down
between her breasts: a laurel wreath, inscribed on a shiny
copper surface.

Is this how you forget? she wondered, for she was certain
that she had forgotten nothing in her life, not one of her
woes.

Mrs. Perkins, noting their delight with the chocolate cakes
the same way she quietly observed everything, kept the staff
bringing out more and more of them while the speakers
marched up to the podium. There was Miss Dreier, and
Leonora O'Reilly, who cried on cue, and Mother Jones, who
told them, "This is not play, this is fight"—her eyes glittering, arms outstretched like a martyr as she talked. And
Clara, who let them have it, as usual, "though you might not
want to hear it, about the thousands of girls out there who
can't go on any longer. They're down an' out at present, an'

506

there ain't a bit of fire in their grates nor a piece of bread in their cupboards, while they are out on the streets fighting for dear life."

There was audible sniffling in the room, handkerchiefs fluttering like rousted pigeons among the tables, and Mrs. Perkins returned to the podium, and asked for their attention again.

"Now I would like to turn the floor over to one of the striker women," she said. "A regular girl, someone who has not been a leader previously, but who showed undaunted courage in facing the terrors of the workhouse. I would so like for her to come up here and talk about her experiences."

To her shock, Esther saw that she was looking straight at her and offering her hand. She thought that it must be a mistake, that the moment she presumed to stand up and move toward her it would be discovered, and she would be left standing mortified in front of the entire room.

But no—it was her. Mrs. Perkins stayed there, holding out her hand, a small, sympathetic smile on her sharp, Yankee face, and slowly, haltingly, Esther stood up and walked to the podium. She grasped the hand—surprisingly rough, and stronger than she had expected—and let Mrs. Perkins help lift her up the step to the speaking podium. She stood there, staring down at the room full of her fellow strikers from the shops and the factories, and the society women—all of whom burst into applause.

"I never thought so many things would happen to me," she began, her voice already faltering.

The rich, well-dressed women stared back, their eyes large and wet. The strikers looked up at her, too, but they were more interested in their great, fat pieces of chocolate cake. No more than fourteen or fifteen years old, many of them—just girls still, happily tearing through their cake and their glasses of milk. She looked out at them, and she thought of all she had been through in the prison—of the beatings, and the dark room, and their cruel violation in the warden's office, and she could not go on——the tears streaming freely down her cheeks.

"It's just that——" she began again, but the words would not come. She wanted to tell them all she knew. She wanted to tell them how it was, going in the black of night to a subcontractor's shop on Division Street, or working forty hours of overtime every week at the Triangle, during the rush. She wanted to tell them how terrible the apelike, jabbering faces of the cops had been, and how frightening it was on the picket line. She wanted to tell them that all these young girls digging enthusiastically into their chocolate cake had hearts and minds, too, that they weren't just married to their machines, but dreamed of better things, finer things. She wanted to tell them how much they——how much *she*——longed not only for food, and shelter, and better wages, but also for knowledge, for books and music, and flowers and time to do just as she pleased.

She wanted to tell them all these things, but she could not find the words. She looked over at Mrs. Perkins, her hard face suffused with understanding now, looked back out at the wealthy, weepy women, and the girls plowing through their milk and chocolate cake at the little, golden tables, and she had no words, there were no words for how she loved them, or what they had been through. There were no words for her life.

52

ON THE BOARDWALK

They moved together, in one slow, sinuous motion. Esther scarcely able to believe that they were here, doing this now, after so much wishing and hoping. Feeling him behind her, feeling his hands, playing over her breasts, her hips, her neck and open mouth. Feeling him with her——

She stretched, and shimmied with pleasure, a little fearful, more than a little proud that she could do such a thing. Proud that she could defy her father, defy the cops who had called her a whore, defy them all. Defied and defiled, she didn't care anymore. She was just glad to be back out here, in the strange little elephant hotel. There would be things to settle later.

He ran his hands down her straight, soft back, over her shoulder dimples, holding on to her. Running his hands tenderly over the bruises along her thighs, her jaunty, uneven hips, her ribs——the angry strawberries everywhere she had been beaten. Gently moving together, up and down, easy as the waves on a mild day. Just glad to have hold of her, just glad to have her back, certain now that he loved her.

53

BIG TIM

The woman surprised him one afternoon up in Albany, coming out of the great Romanesque pile that was the capitol. He was thinking about Mrs. Perkins's hours bill, and he didn't notice her until she was right beside him, laying a gloved hand demurely on his arm. She looked smaller than she did in the newspaper photos, and she was wearing a veil, but there was no mistaking her. It was the wife of Charlie Becker, currently fighting for his life in court over the murder of Beansy Rosenthal.

"Pardon me." She had gone up to him, waiting until he was alone. A small, composed woman, modestly dressed, with a warm, sympathetic face just making the turn into middle age.

"Pardon me, Senator Sullivan, I wanted a word," she said softly, and then how could he deny her? A sweet, sad woman like that, her weariness etched in her face. A schoolteacher, no less, who worked overtime teaching the backward children's classes up at P.S. 90.

"The overage children have always appealed to me," she said, smiling shyly under her veil. "You know, Charlie liked them, too. He always took a great interest in my schoolwork. Sometimes, if his hours permitted, he would come to class, and help me collect papers, or write out report cards."

"Ah, did he, ma'am?" Big Tim had murmured like a regular idjiot while Helen Becker went on, quietly, breathlessly making her plea.

"You know, I still do all the housework. The cooking, the cleaning—that doesn't sound like someone who's very rich, does it, Mr. Sullivan? Certainly not someone who made a fortune on graft like they say in the papers."

"No, ma'am."

"I know Charlie's innocent. I spent the whole day of the murder with him. We went out to Coney Island together, and had a picnic, and he never once mentioned the name Rosenthal. Does that sound like someone who would have done such a thing?"

"No, no. I can't say that it does——"

She brushed the veil away, looking into his eyes and trying to smile, the worry coming through instead.

"Any help you can give us would be most gratefully appreciated. We're all each other has in the world, so far."

She dropped her eyes, and looking down Big Tim could detect the slight rise of her belly beneath her black dress, in her otherwise slender body. No doubt she was at least several months along.

"I never regretted it, though," she stammered, her upper lip wobbling. "Despite everything that has happened, I never regretted that we met and married. I never had a woman friend who I confided in. My only friend was my husband. I sometimes wonder why this could not have happened to people who did not love each other so much."

Big Tim had mumbled something about all the help he could provide, and got the hell away as soon as he could. So Charlie Becker was a model husband, who loved his wife, and liked to collect the papers from the backward children's class. So what exactly was he supposed to do with that information now?

54

ESTHER

Out on the streets, the tide was turning now. Every day, more of the bosses crept, humbled, into the union halls, to sign their surrender and agree to recognize the union.

Every day, the society women were out on the line with the striking women and girls, tormenting the cops by their very presence. They tried to sort them out from the strikers, but it wasn't so easy. The wealthy women exulted in dressing up as much as possible like the working girls, like it was some kind of masquerade. Miss Dreier herself was pulled in, grabbed roughly off the street by her hair. The police sergeant who had arrested her discovered his mistake only at the booking, crying out openly in his frustration: "Why didn'cha tell me you was a rich lady before I arrested ya?"

They boycotted the stores that used scab goods, sat up in the dim, stuffy night court long after midnight with their husbands and their chauffeurs and their personal secretaries, to bail out the union women.

The strikers yelled back now at the cops and the goons, and they ran off the scabs and the whores who tried to break the line. Esther herself went back on the lines, and picketing over at Leiserson's one evening she saw a striker chase a particularly nasty forewoman right into the lobby of the shop, knocking her down, covering her with punches and kicks and curses, until she was left huddled on the floor, holding her arms over her head.

The great task that remained now was to get the official union leadership, the men who ran the garment unions, to go along—to hold out for full recognition of the union and their rights, instead of settling for another fleeting raise. Esther worked most of the time in the settlement house office now, and she knew how hard a chore that would be. The men were sympathetic, as always—they were leaning, but they were for the most part cautious, suspicious men, as shortsighted as moles, and they were reluctant to fight the strike out to the end.

The Cooper Union was filled with coughing and sniffling and nose blowing. The women stood in the aisles and the windowsills, still wet and cold from the line. Weak with hunger and pneumonia, clutching to seat backs and railings to keep themselves up, leaning eagerly forward to hear what the men union bosses had to say.

Esther sat up on the stage with twenty more women, each wearing a sash that read WORKHOUSE PRISONER, or ARRESTED, or SENT TO THE DARK ROOM; all beneath one big banner inscribed THE WORKHOUSE IS NO ANSWER TO A DEMAND FOR JUSTICE. Dressed up in the best hats and coats they could salvage from the picket lines, a yellow artificial flower, a net of lace—

First Feigenbaum, the chairman of the meeting, spoke, and then Miss Dreier, and Morris Hillquit, the Socialist politician, and a wiry little lawyer who they cheered to the ceiling when he advised them to stay out.

"That's all right! You're all right!"

"Why should we go back, we got nothin' to lose an' maybe even something to gain!"

"We are starving as we work, we might as well starve while we strike—"

Samuel Gompers himself spoke next, the little, robin-breasted cigar-maker in his skullcap, strutting stuffily on the stage, the women rising to their feet to see him.

"A man would be less than human if he were not impressed with your reception," he proclaimed. "But I don't want you to give all your enthusiasm to any man, no matter who he may be. I would prefer that you put all of your enthusiasm into your union and your cause."

The cheers surged up through the low, crowded, gaslit room, drowning out his next few words—

". . . there comes a time when not to strike is but to rivet the chains of slavery upon our wrists—"

More cheers, until the crowded, basement hall seemed to shake:

"Yes, Mr. Shirtwaist Manufacturer, it may be inconvenient for you if your boys and girls go out on strike, but there are things of more importance than your inconvenience and your profit—"

The hall was in tumult now, Feigenbaum gaveling for order.

"Please, please! We must debate this rationally!"

—but there was another commotion in the back of the room. A small woman, a striker, was literally carried forward, propelled along toward the podium on the backs and shoulders of the men and women in the crowd. Esther saw at once that it was Clara, her face still puffy and bruised from the beating she had taken, still wincing with every brush against her ribs.

"Who is this?" Feigenbaum asked, but the women drowned him out:

"Let her speak! Let her speak!"

They put her down on the platform, and Esther could see that battered as she was, she was still Clara, the most fiery of the *fabrente maydlakh*, eyes flashing, hands gripping the podium while wave after wave of cheers and applause rolled over the auditorium.

"I have listened to all the speeches," she told them, when the room had finally hushed—speaking in Yiddish, in her fervor, the simultaneous translations running quickly through the hall, into Italian, and Portuguese, and Bohemian, and English—

"I have listened to all the speeches, and I am one who thinks and feels the things they describe. Like you, I have worked, and like you I have suffered, and I would not have patience for further talk. I move that we fight the strike out to the end!"

There was pandemonium again, and it took Feigenbaum, with an air of resignation, ten minutes to restore order.

"I take it, then, that you want to hold out for full recognition of the union, for everything? You are aware of what that means?"

"Yes, yes!" thousands of voices shouted back.

"Do you give me your word, then? Will you take the old Jewish oath with me then?"

The whole audience rose—those who were not on their feet already—holding up their right hands, smiling, tears glistening, as he led them in the Jewish oath, adapted for the purpose at hand. All of them, the Italians and the Portuguese, and even the Yankees, reciting it word by word after him:

"If I turn traitor to the cause I now pledge, if ever I forget thee, may my right hand wither—"

55

SADIE MENDELSSOHN

Sadie faded back through the crowd of working women outside the Tombs. She could see Esther looking for her, holding a hand out for her at one point, but she hung back, shuffling off to one side—then turned away down Pearl Street. Other whores who had been caught up in the picket line hurried off around her, heads down, arms clutched across the bright tatters of their street clothes.

She wandered up past Canal Street and over to the Bowery, unable to think of anyplace else to go, trying to decide what to do next. She had just stopped under the el to light a cigarette when she felt a hand on her shoulder— startling her so much she almost dropped the smoke.

"What happened?"

The dead, level voice, genuinely seeking information now, but full of implied menace if he didn't get the answer he wanted. She composed herself before she spoke, fighting down the feelings of guilt and shame he automatically provoked in her, even when she had done nothing wrong.

"What happened out there?" Gyp repeated, already impatient. "You were supposed to get the strikers arrested, not yourself. What the hell were you doin'?"

She turned around deliberately, doing her best to seem indignant.

"Whattaya mean? That fat cop slugged me!"

The hand uncoiled out of the shadows, smacking across her face before she even saw it. It sent her staggering back, but she steadied herself, and stood her ground. Knowing she had to if she was going to survive.

"You don' know what it is to be slugged yet."

"Look, *look* what they done to me!"

She thrust her face recklessly toward him, showing the deep, purple bruises fortuitously provided by the matrons, her cropped, disheveled hair—counting on his deep disgust to make him believe her.

Now my disgustingness is my greatest asset—

It worked. He turned his face away, to her bitter satisfaction, too repelled to even look at her.

"Never mind," he told her. "I got somethin' else for you to do anyway."

"What?" she demanded—then more subserviently, when he looked suspicious: "What else can I do?"

"Follow her. Follow her again. You sure you didn't see nothin' the last time?"

"No, no—she just went to that *farshtinkener* little cafe of hers," she said, almost too quickly.

"You sure?"

The hand dug into her shoulder, working its way around her collarbone as if measuring how much force it would take to snap it in half.

"You *sure?*"

"Yes, yes," she gasped in pain, his one hand more painful than anything the matrons had done. "I told you—just talkin' with all the *fonfers* there."

"All right, then," he told her, letting her off for now. "All right. Follow her. An' this time—let me know everything."

"I did!" she made sure to protest, a quick shiver of fear running through her—but he was already walking away, melding with the shadows of the Bowery el.

Out on Coney, Sadie wandered through the grand, chandeliered entrance of Luna Park, the big red heart over its arch, pierced with two leaning crosses like some bizarre Catholic icon—gratuitously labeled THE HEART OF CONEY ISLAND.

Inside, everything glowed orange and white and gold, even in the daytime. A forest of towers and minarets, and flowing arches. And all around her, sticking out of the walls on every side, were the grotesque, leering, heavy-lidded heads: wolves and clowns, apes and pigs and hyenas, sneering down at the passing customers.

She wandered over, through the titillating Dreamland arch; over to the circus tent where she had seen that show that had been so funny, with all the parts played by dwarves and midgets. She walked in again, trying to buy herself time, seating herself in the bleachers. She remembered how all the men had bothered her that day. How she had worn a rented sailor's suit, and they hadn't been able to keep their hands off her, grabbing at her knees, her ass, her breasts—

She had looked good that day, she thought, assessing herself professionally—as good as she was capable of looking anymore. They would not find her so appealing today, all bruised and thinned out from prison, even though she had worn a wide, netted hat to hide her mutilated hair.

Sure enough, as the show went on, they kept their distance, no doubt thinking she was one more bit of trash washed up at the Tin Elephant down the beach. She was just as glad—relieved to be let alone for once, to sit watching the shenanigans of the circus freaks down below her while she figured out what she had to do.

It was the same show, the exact same performance, no doubt repeated over and over again, every day: the miniature fire wagon and mounted police, the doll-like midget queen, trotted out to make her same speech—all making their same dutiful efforts to seem just like real people.

It's ridiculous, she decided. Not funny or hysterical, but all just ridiculous.

The show was just ending, in the same exact way: all the sad, misshapen little people singing at the top of their lungs, in their high, shrill voices. Until one of them stepped forward, stooped to one knee, and sang in a deep, croaking bass. Another dwarf, the particularly ugly one who had given her a flower, ran frantically up to him—again—and stuck his hand over his mouth—again—making the singer's bass reverberate like a trumpet.

Everyone laughed, and she stood up, moving just ahead of the crowd to the exit. Out of the corner of her eye, she could still see the dwarf, with his big bubble head and his tiny arms and legs, running up to her. He held up a flower—just like before, just like the one she had cut her finger on.

She had learned her lesson now. She gave him a small smile, and kept moving toward the exit.

"Wait! Wait, you don't understand!" he called breathlessly, still running alongside her in the ring on his stumpy, inadequate legs.

"I understand," she muttered. "It's the end of the show."

"Wait!"

The dwarf kept running, kept squawking in his high, funny voice.

"I'm in love—" he said, and stopped, gawking up at her. The rose, she saw, was a real one this time.

"What?" she said, looking down at him, wondering why he had not finished what he was saying. People were staring, and she ran a hand up along the side of her head, embarrassed, pushing her hair back under her hat. Her fingers brushed along the butchered ends of her hair and she stopped, grasping what had happened.

"Oh, I see." Sadie smiled ruefully, remembering now how

hideous she looked with her bruised face and chopped-off hair, hideous even under the wide hat; her deteriorating wardrobe. The dwarf just kept staring at her, open-mouthed, big head tilted all the way back on his shoulders.

So that is what I have come to. So grotesque even a circus freak is repelled.

In that moment, she realized she had come to the end of her career. Only the Water Street bars could possibly remain for her.

That was when she made up her mind. She hadn't told him anything the first time, but now she was decided. *Follow her*, Gyp had said, and she hadn't disobeyed him. She already knew where Esther was: out in the Tin Elephant, with him.

Sadie walked out there along the boardwalk after she left the midgets' show. It was nearly dark now, the first hints of fall beginning to spread their shadow over the beach. The boards stretched out endlessly over the desolate, sandy plain, toward an apocalyptic sunset, and only a few dark, slightly sinister figures broke the flat landscape. Most of the vacationing couples were gone now, leaving the whores and their customers to trawl the boardwalk.

She hurried out to the dilapidated tin hotel, where she stood under the light she had marked before. She waited for what seemed like a long time there, until it was completely dark and even the piercing white beacons of the park seemed very far away.

Sadie waited so long she wondered if they were there now after all, but she had noted the window well, and finally she saw her, coming out of the lobby, looking around herself a little furtively. She walked up to Esther—relieved to see her again, staring solemnly, uncomprehendingly back at her. Getting a certain pleasure out of seeing her face change.

"Well, chick," Sadie said to her, "it looks like it's time to start on my reform——"

56

ON THE BOARDWALK

Esther sat on the worn bedspread back in the Tin Elephant, where she had retreated as soon as Sadie had given her the news. Kid beside her, looking sheepishly at the floor.

"You could have told me, you know."

"Ach!" He waved one hand in the air. "It's my *tsouris*. Why should you worry about it?"

"You might have told me."

"I didn't know he was your brother, you know. I swear to the Highest—"

"I know, I know."

She sat on the edge of the bed, swinging her feet, trying to think what to do now.

"He'll never let it go, you know."

"I know."

"He'll never give it up. You got to get out of here."

He only looked at her.

"You should have been gone already. And you stayed—"

"I stayed for you," he said fervently. "That's why I did it."

521

"Enough! That's nonsense talk. You got to go, and soon."

"What about her? Will she tell?"

"No," Esther said slowly, considering it. "No. Sadie won't tell."

"Unless he gets it out of her . . ."

They were quiet again, trying to ignore the whores cavorting in the hallways.

"He's such a bastard," she sighed.

57

TRICK THE DWARF

I saw her. I saw her again at the show, after looking out for her for days and weeks, and then I was sure it was fated. She had come back, and I would not let her go this time.

I did the same trick I had performed for her before, leaping forward to stop up the baritone's mouth. It was a signal to her—but this time she didn't seem to appreciate it, didn't laugh the way she had before.

She left her seat before the grand finale was even quite over. I didn't care; I ran after her, plucking up another rose—a real, red rose, this time, which I had kept on hand in case she should ever return. Repeating myself, I knew, but wanting to do anything to get her attention, hoping she would take it as another lover's signal.

And then—I saw her. I saw her up close now, instead of across the ring, and even as I started to mouth those infinitely unoriginal words—*I love you*—I stopped myself.

She was different. She had been put through the wringer by God only knew who—some beast of a pimp, a boyfriend, a husband. Her face was mottled and bruised, her hair chopped short. She looked like she had aged ten years since I'd seen her last, even under the hat she used to hide it. She looked like, well, like a common street whore.

She saw me staring. She saw the disappointment in my face, I know——unable even to complete my trite love sentiments, the real rose still in my hand. She saw me and the lips of her mouth turned up, as if she knew exactly what I was thinking.

"Oh, I see," was all she said, but I could see the wound; I could see the proud and bitter resignation on her face, just before she turned away.

What had I done? After all, I had seen into her soul. The bruises and the hair were just superficial marks. What had I done? In the crucial moment of my life, I had hesitated, and now she was lost to me.

She was already out of the Big Tent, but I couldn't let her go. I had to follow her, explain myself to her somehow.

I looked back at the rest of my people, now finished with their act: jumping up and down, turning pratfalls and somersaults to entertain the crowd as it filed out. No one had noticed me, across the ring with my flower. Carlotta, my queen, was gazing placidly into the emptying stands, obviously pleased with how her speech had gone over.

I climbed the wooden barrier of the ring, crept out after the paying customers, smearing my showman's makeup off on my sleeve. I followed them——followed *her*——out of The Little City, as my true self——leaving all the freaks behind. Out on the boardwalk there was no sign of her, but I couldn't let that stop me. I would find her if I had to search the whole City——

58

THE GREAT HEAD DOCTORS FROM VIENNA

They stood before the rampaging fossils, gazing up at their terrible teeth and claws, spikes and horns.

"Look at all the old monsters," Jung murmured. "God's anxiety dreams of Creation."

Freud shot him a look—but Jung seemed to actually be referring to the museum displays. They were arranged in a powerful, almost sensational manner: head-to-head, rising up on their back legs—as if their skeletal remains were complete creatures unto themselves, still locked in mortal combat.

There was room after staggering room of them: brontosauruses and pterodactyls, woolly mammoths, and a *Tyrannosaurus rex,* all jumbled together. One particularly vivid tableau featured the fossil of a great sloth, stuck in a tar pit. A saber-toothed tiger had rushed in after it but now it, too, was stuck, snarling back over its shoulder at a pair of wolves. Already, the wolves, distracted by their own bloodlust, were padding obliviously into the tar trap, and their own demise—

The whole thing was a Pleistocene morality play. It was also a fake, of course. All the real fossils—sloth, tiger, wolves—would have been hopelessly jumbled and crushed by the weight of ages. Yet how evocative!

"How bungled our own reproductions are by comparison, how wretchedly we dissect the great artworks of psychic nature," he muttered to himself. He thought particularly of the Rat Man case, thinking that somehow he had bungled it, had reduced its meaning in how he wrote it up.

Still, there must be a way—

He looked over at Jung, engrossed in an exhibit on Ancient Man. If he could not do it himself it would have to be passed on, perfected, through his protégés. He, Freud, was just a conduit. The Cause must continue.

From the outside, the museum was another vast new American creation, ringed with fairy-tale turrets of soft pink granite. It fronted on the Central Park and there, on the museum stairs, a large, equestrian statue of Roosevelt, the former president, had been erected. He was dressed up like a cowboy, with an Indian chief and an African bearer at either side of his horse—a boy's storybook idea of a hero.

Freud felt more at home in the park. He suggested they all go for a walk, but Ferenczi lingered at the museum with Brill to play with his latest toy, a new American camera, so he had Jung all to himself. They strolled along winding paths that opened out onto charming vistas of man-made lakes and meadows, little gingerbread bridges and fountains. The woods were filled with birds, and bold gray squirrels that seemed almost tame, hopping up to beg for tidbits.

"Still no porcupine," he joked, and Jung smiled politely.

He was being most attentive, hanging on his every word, and Freud thought how good it was to be with him again, how like a brilliant, doting son he could be. Why he had been so suspicious of him, Freud could not imagine now. Some unruly bit of homosexuality, no doubt; he would have to root it out completely before it destroyed their relationship—

He was just trying to say something about it to his crown prince—when, abruptly, Jung pulled him off down another, lesser path, his face suddenly so troubled that Freud leaned over him in concern.

"What—what is it?"

"*Mir hat getraumt,*" Jung said anxiously. "A dream came to me. If I could ask you . . . ?"

"Certainly, certainly!" Freud urged, surprised and delighted by this new offering.

"It's not much, really, but it was extremely vivid. It started in a house—my house. I was on the upper story, in a salon full of fine old pieces of rococo furniture, old masters on the walls—"

"*Your* house?"

"*Ja, ja*—I wondered at it myself, that I should have some place so grand," Jung said, very sincerely. "I said to myself, 'Not bad.'"

"Not bad at all, Doctor," Freud said dryly.

"But then, you know, I realized that I did not know what the bottom floor looked like, even though it was my house. I went downstairs—where I saw that everything was much older."

"Older?"

"All the furnishings, the paintings—everything dated from at least the fifteenth or sixteenth century—perhaps even medieval! The floors were made out of simple red brick. Everything dark and murky."

He paused—fine, stolid, Swiss head peering closely at Freud through his pince-nez, obviously trying to gauge his reaction so far.

"Please go on, Doctor. Unless that's all—"

"No, no—there's more! I decided, well, 'Now I must really explore the whole house.' Immediately, I came to a heavy door—"

"You opened it—"

"I opened it—and found a stone stairway leading down into a cellar. Naturally, I descended the staircase—and found myself in another beautiful, vaulted room. I could tell at once it was very ancient! There were layers of bricks between the stones, and chips of brick in the mortar—like classical layers of archaeology. I knew the walls dated back to Roman times—perhaps before!"

They had stopped in the path now. Jung's manner had become quite agitated, Freud noticed. He gestured excitedly as he told his story, little flecks of spit flying from his lips. Somehow, Freud felt light-headed, almost faint himself.

"Was that all?"

"*No!* There's more. My interest in this house was now intense. I looked around on the floor—and discovered a ring, sticking out of one of the stone slabs. I pulled on it—and the slab lifted. There was another stone stairway."

"Another one!"

"This one made out of narrower, cruder steps. I followed them down to another level, into a low cave, cut into the rock."

"And then?"

"The floor of the cave was covered with dust and broken pottery. Scattered bones—human and nonhuman, I think. And there—on the floor of the cave, as if I had been intended to find them all along—there lay a pair of primitive human skulls. Obviously very old, and half-disintegrated."

"And then?"

"Then I woke up."

"*Ancient* skulls?" Freud pondered, his eyes narrowing. "It sounds as if we are back to your peat-bog men, Doctor. Your lead roofer."

"No, no, not like that, I don't think! Believe me, it's nothing to do with your death—" he said hastily, but Freud cut him off.

"You said you had some ideas about them. What were they?"

"Oh, they're still very formative," Jung fumbled, even reddening a little. He paused, the quick little eyes behind the pince-nez studying Freud's face.

"It's just, well, I thought perhaps the skulls might be my wife—and perhaps my sister-in-law," he blurted out.

"Really?"

Jung nodded rapidly, turning away, and Freud felt relief wash over him.

Of course that's it, Freud assured himself, remembering a bad bit of business Jung had got into with a female patient a couple years before—one that had threatened to wreck his marriage and his career, before he had begged Freud to intervene.

This is just more of the same—another domestic crisis. He's fallen in love with his sister-in-law, that's all. How touching of him to confide in me!

They resumed walking, in silence now. Freud slid his arm reassuringly through his old pupil's, and was rewarded with a boyish smile. Yet as he did, he couldn't help thinking how closely Jung's situation resembled Freud's own intellectual love for Minna, his sister-in-law.

Could it be he is trying to flatter me? Or just dissemble?

They stopped again, at the end of their path. They had come out at another cunningly manufactured pond, still being constructed beneath a high rock. Atop the cliff was a decorative overlook, a lovely castle turret, right out of the Rhineland, or certain bluffs above the Danube where it wandered through Austria—

Just then the children came running up the path toward them, pumping their short, chubby legs. Freud smiled to see them: a whole nursery of well-dressed, upper-middle-class children, boys and girls, no more than four or five years old. They ran off the cinder path and onto a park green, squealing happily, their governesses laboring to keep up with them.

"How delightful they are!" Freud laughed. "You know, for a moment I even took two of them for my nieces. Of course, that was from the last time I saw them; they would be much bigger by now——"

"Yes, there are all kinds here," Jung smiled back, nodding toward the children.

A park officer hove up imperiously, identifiable by his arm badge, and brown shirt and black tie.

"Children! Who's in charge of you? Off the lawn at once! Even you should know better——look at the signs!" he barked, waving them off the grass with a curt, imperious gesture. He pointed dramatically to one of the little signs, posted low to the ground, that read KEEP OFF THE GRASS! not only in English but also German, Italian, Yiddish.

"Look at that oaf!" Freud scoffed.

The children only squealed some more and ran off, their broad faces beaming——the park official repeating his curt, impatient wave. Freud would have walked after them, just to watch, but at that moment his gaze swung back to the little cliff overlook. The pond before it had not yet been filled up, he noticed, but there was a thin layer of stagnant black rainwater; a few dead pigeons floating on top. He stared at it all for a long moment——the miniature Rhineland castle, the dead birds, and the black muck in the pond——and felt his stomach lurch. He made that his excuse to turn back.

"It's terrible over here, you ask for a bathroom, and they escort you along miles of echoing stone corridors, down to the very basement," he rambled on to Jung, dissembling as he went. "And when you finally get there——a veritable marble palace! only just in time. The sign of a society still in its anal stage, all this primness about toilets!"

——though in fact there was something else bothering him. Something loitering just below the surfaces of conscious memory, though he still could not quite retrieve it——

59

BIG TIM

The night before the election was like Christmas Eve throughout the East Side. Children tied brooms to their stoop railings in hopes of a Tammany sweep, and Florrie and Christy had the boys out hammering up the bleachers in Chatham Square and hanging red-white-and-blue crepe paper over everything that moved slower than a brewer's wagon.

By the evening, all the Wise Ones were back in Big Tim's saloon across from the Tombs. Later on, as the first tabulations started to come in, the place would be mobbed with all those who had ever loved him, but for right now he had the doors bolted and the shades drawn. Inside, it was the tightest possible circle: just himself and the family.

"Has everything been done that could be done?" he asked—his grave, ritual question.

"Yessir, Dry Dollar!"

"All of it, Tim!"

They sounded off, one after another, with military precision, eyes gleaming with pride, eager for his approval. They looked shiny and buffed for the occasion, though he knew they'd been out since before dawn, passing out palm cards and minding the ballot boxes; voting the bathhouse bums and the firemen's widows and the foreign sailors.

No matter how many times he had been through it, Election Day made his blood run. It was when everything boiled down to its simple primordial struggle: to win. To get the vote out, get back in office, or there was no use talking about the right and wrong of anything else.

Outside, the streets were mobbed with their supporters, bellowing and hoisting their brooms, marching up and down Broadway like madmen. All through the day—and all the night before, and the day before that—the gangs had been out, heckling and throwing things at the Socialist soapbox orators or the rare independent. As soon as they were driven off, Sullivan's own speakers took their place, trying to drum up any last-minute votes through the sheer silver of their tongues.

Of course, the speeches didn't make much difference at this point, for all their fire and eloquence. Not that they ever did. Only a fool voted on "the issues," or because someone could really roll the velvet. Votes were won through a lifetime of service. And when they could not be secured that way, there were other methods.

The whole miserable rabble of ward leaders and precinct captains and gangsters that they called the Organization had been set to with that purpose, and it worked with a magnificent efficiency and singlemindedness. They had become The Machine.

"All right then," Big Tim said, standing up, the men around the table standing with him: all dark, well-cut long coats, dignified as undertakers. Bowlers and gloves, and clean white collars, and a bright red carnation in each man's lapel. Big Tim solemnly looked over each one, pretending to inspect them but in fact just stealing another moment to look at them, as pleased and proud as any father.

"All right then, lads."

He turned to Mr. Feeley behind the bar, and Photo Dave and Sarsaparilla Reilly hastened to attend to him——although this one day the ritual was different. Feeley held out the bar mirror to him, same as ever——but now instead of filling his pockets with coins and bills, they carefully brushed down his coat and hat. Peering into the glass, Sullivan saw the same, broad slab of face, hard and expressionless, with only a hint of cloudiness around the eyes.

"It'll do," he said, to himself as much as the boys, but they immediately backed off. The Wise Ones stood in a row by the door, hats in their hands, waiting for him. He placed his silver dollar on the bar for Mr. Feeley.

"Let's go then, lads——"

——and they plunged out into the carnival streets of an election evening.

"Sullivan! Sullivan! A damned fine Irishman!"

Outside there was a writhing, shoving mass of brass bands and flags and confetti. Huge posters of names and slogans were pasted to the sides of every building, and up on an equestrian statue of the Revolution someone was waving the old regimental banner of the Fighting Sixty-ninth, from the great slaughter at Fredericksburg: a gold harp on a green field, the ends tattered by Confederate bullets from half a century before.

We are a long-remembering race

"Big Tim!"

The street children were pushed aside now, mobs of men and women filling the streets, laughing and shouting gleefully, raucously. This once they asked nothing of him. They simply wanted to touch him, to be around him, shoving past the phalanx of the Wise Ones to shake his hand, pummel his back—to be with a winner.

As though I am their champion

He let himself be propelled up and down the Bowery, and Allen Street, and Canal, in a vast torchlight parade that wound its way all through Lower Manhattan until they wound up in Chatham Square, following the results as they were projected by magic lantern against the front of the graceful white tower of the *Jewish Daily Forward* building. Taking it right into the heart of the Socialists' territory— little clumps of earnest men standing off in the shadows, in their beards and shabby suits, looking glumly at their shoes as the Tammany votes poured in.

Yet even some of the Socialists seemed to be celebrating, caught up in the sheer exhilaration of it all. When the result of each new Tammany triumph flashed up on the sheet, the crowd waved their torches and gave a wild, drunken cheer. Their faces sharp and greedy, as they chanted for victory in the flickering orange light:

"Well, well, well! Reform has gone to hell!"

Later on there were speeches with the whole of the Organization up in Union Square. Mr. Murphy was there to pump Sullivan's hand on the speakers' platform, looking genuinely pleased for a change, and Big Tim made his usual speech about how he was a Democrat, and always had been, and always would be.

It was a good night for the Tiger, not quite so good as the night, so long ago, when they had last elected Grover Cleveland president, but a good night, nevertheless. Big Tim had won his old state senate seat back easily, not that there had ever been much doubt. The Little Little Napoleon was finished, and his men had been soundly thrashed in the council, and the alderman races, and even for the assembly and the Congress. The same went for the Republicans and the Simon Pures.

Mr. Murphy had put over his replacement for mayor: another reformer, an odd little judge named Gaynor, who liked to quote Frederick the Great and Cato and Epictetus, and who was so blunt and sarcastic he didn't really seem to care *who* backed him.

Big Tim suspected already that they were playing too fine a game in trying to ape Reform, and that Gaynor would eventually prove more trouble than he was worth, just as McClellan had. Not that it much mattered. They would just get rid of him later, if they had to—same as they had with the Little Little Napoleon. Reform came and Reform went; only the Organization was forever.

Down below him in the Union Square park the crowd was still ecstatic with victory, breaking into more of the endless Tammany songs:

> Fifteen thousand Irishmen from Erin
>   came across
> Tammany put these Irish Indians on the
>   police force
> I asked one cop if he wanted three platoons
>   or four,
> He said: "Keep your old platoons, I've got
>   a cuspidor,
> What would I want with more?"
> Tammany, Tammany, your policemen
>   can't be beat,
> They can sleep on any street.
> Tammany, Tammany, dusk is creeping,
>   they're all sleeping,
> Tammany—

—each chorus more nonsensical than the last, the mobs bellowing them out faithfully at the top of their lungs.

The cheering went on and on, and the men tossed their hats in the air, and Big Tim snuck away with Sarsaparilla and Photo Dave. He would be careful to make appearances at all his saloons, then have a celebratory seltzer water with Mr. Murphy, up at his place, and start planning the next campaign—there was *always* a next campaign. Then it would be off to bed, before the cheering faded away, and the crowds went home, and he would have to face the fact that Election Day was over.

BOOK NINE

*When the work of interpretation
has been completed,
we perceive that a dream is
the fulfillment of a wish.*

——SIGMUND FREUD

60

TRICK THE DWARF

The greatest roller coaster ride of all time took place on a balmy Sunday afternoon on Coney Island on September 6, 1901, at 4:07 P.M.

It was on a new coaster, called The Rough Rider, where each train was run by its own motorman. Done up in full San Juan Hill regalia. Instructed to make 'em scream, the louder the better—*that's what brings in the paying customers*. Until that afternoon when one of the ersatz Teddies, pushing his train at full speed, snapped off the rear two cars and sent them soaring out, sixty feet into the air above Surf Avenue.

After the accident they didn't close The Rough Rider, or even change it. The crowds were greater than ever for the roller coasters—*thanatos* and *eros*, the death wish and the pleasure principle, all at the same time. You could see them in the long line, staring avidly at the twisted track, the hole in the guard rail where it had smashed through. Wondering what it was like—

The cars rising slowly along the impossibly steep track, jerking and grating on their chains. The dread growing steadily in the pit of the stomach, until that last, awful moment, when you pause for a moment at the peak, and look down over the impossibly narrow, curving track, face-to-face with what you have done. Yet always sure that at the very end, you will be pulled back from the brink—

Did they understand it? That's what all the gawkers, the rubberneckers in line wanted to know. After the impossible happened, and the chain broke, and they crashed through the last barrier—did they understand in those last, suspended moments above Surf Avenue, before they hit the ground, that theirs was the greatest thrill of all?

61

THE GREAT HEAD DOCTORS FROM VIENNA

On their next-to-last day in New York, Dr. Brill finally took
them up to his clinic at Columbia. It was a small, red-brick
building that stood out in its unpretentiousness on the raw,
rambling campus. Like everything else in New York the university was still under construction, though there was
already an impressive, colonnaded library with a great dome
in place, white as a tomb.

The tiny clinic, however, was no more impressive inside
than out. The remaining patients were mostly neurotic
cases of minor interest, though Freud didn't tell dear old
Brill that. The doctor hung on his every word. The night
before, he had had them over to his own home, where they
had met Mrs. Brill—a tall, slender woman, charming and
uncomplicated. She had served them by far the best meal
he'd had since landing in this dyspeptic city. For the first
time in America, Freud felt at something approaching
peace.

Brill was called away for a moment, and Freud wandered out
into the garden of the little brick clinic, unwrapping a new
cigar. Ferenczi was off somewhere perusing his guidebook,
but Jung was sitting in the garden under a copy of Rodin's

Thinker, looking over one of his sooty American newspapers.

"So, Doctor—any word on your race?" he called to him. "Who got to the North Pole first?"

Jung looked up, smiling and blinking in the hazy sunlight, squinting at him through his pince-nez.

"*Neine, neine,* nothing yet. It's a treacherous region."

"It is indeed," Freud remarked.

He peered down the height upon which the university was planted, past another splendid English park to a wide, slow-moving river.

"I remember reading about old ships that got caught in the ice floes up there," he remarked idly.

"Really?"

On the other side of the river was a magnificent range of bluffs, plunging dramatically down to the water—covered with ferns, and other trees, all very picturesque. Freud stared out at the cliffs, while he talked on absently about the Arctic wastes:

"It seems the seasons change very rapidly, and they miscalculated, and were caught by the ice. Whole ships hemmed in for the winter. Sometimes, the pressure of the ice would start to crush the hull, and the sailors would have to make out across the ice for civilization."

Freud stopped, lost in his own reverie—listening to the ice slowly bending and cracking the great ship beams in the endless Arctic nights. Like something from the savage dawn of the world: striking out by sled or foot in the twilight—so remote from the beautiful, tranquil bluffs across the river. Like the bluffs of the Wachau, along the Danube, or the Rhine. Or the little outlook in the park the day before, above the black water and its dead pigeons—

There was a gesture: the man in the park raising his hand, chasing the children away—

*In the dream he was standing in the Aula again, the great cere-
monial hall of the university. Surrounded by all the great minds
of science he would speak before, up at Clark.*

*On a table before him crouched the woman patient who had put
the orchids in his ship cabin—younger and more shapely than ever.
He looked over at Jung—who was now the General from his military maneuvers, wearing a cape and his ubiquitous pince-nez. The
General made a small, curt gesture with his hand—and the woman
wiggled seductively under her bright-red dressing gown, lifted up
the back of it to reveal her bottom, as red as the gown itself—*

*He felt himself becoming aroused, and held his penis in his
hand, moving toward her. She looked back over her shoulder at
him—and he saw she was wearing a disguise. Her face was now
the face of the tanned man, the man in the Bleikeller, screaming silently across the ages—*

*His penis hung limp in his hand, and the General peered in at
him through his pince-nez. He made another small, curt gesture
for him to go on, to perform, but Freud could not. He had to urinate, and he dashed off the stage, back through the beautiful
apartments—until he was standing outside on the train platform again. He was standing next to the sick old man, he was
standing next to his father, blind in one eye, holding up his glass
urinal, and a conductor was working his way down the platform,
but they didn't have a ticket.*

*He held up the mask in front of his father—the mask of the
tanned man, from the lead cellar. He held up another mask in
front of his own face. Thinking that would fool the conductor,
thinking now he would have to let them on.*

*But looking down, he saw that his father had his penis out—
had it out, and was already beginning to use the glass urinal.*

Freud staggered, and looked around. He felt an urgent need
to urinate himself—and looking down he saw to his shame
and his horror that he already *had*. That in fact he still was

micturating, the fine brown fabric of his trousers darkening even as he watched. Jung's mouth was open in shock, his pince-nez dropping from his nose.

"Let me help you," he said, and Freud shook his head, backing up around the *Thinker*.

"Let me help you," Jung said again, touching his elbow, and Freud let him guide him in out of the sun, into the shade of a bench next to the red-brick clinic, his newspaper with its headlines about Peary and Cook held up chastely over the shameful pants.

"*Zeeser Gottenyu*, how humiliating," Freud muttered, leaning his head back against the wall of the clinic, as Jung fanned his face with his hand.

"What am I going to do, what am I going to do?" he murmured, helpless as a fainting opera diva. "What happens if I do this up at Clark? What will they think of me? Oh, I could just die!"

"Let me help you," Jung repeated, his glasses firmly back in place now, staring down firmly into Freud's eyes.

"Can you? Can you help me?"

"I can—if you let me."

He knew what he wanted. Freud looked up at him for a long moment—then quickly nodded his head.

"*Ja*, all right, anything—if that's what it takes."

He lay on a couch in the little clinic, wearing a pair of old trousers provided by Brill. Jung sat in a chair, just behind his head. He had taken care of everything—sending Ferenczi back downtown for another pair of pants. Making sure they would not be interrupted—

"The urinating is simple enough," Freud began, running through it a little desperately. "That's ambition—the god-like ability to put out fire by *pishing* on it."

"The lectures, the honorary degree—they will be the climax of your ambitions," Jung agreed. "But by trying to disgrace yourself, you are also trying to undermine everything you have accomplished. Clearly, this is a conflict."

"But why? I have some misgivings, of course—whether I can answer my audience's expectations," Freud pondered. "Yet they are at *our* mercy. They must applaud, no matter what we bring them."

"Doesn't it strike you that you have reversed the paternal position?" Jung pointed out. "Your father discovers you wetting yourself, at seven or eight, and despairs: 'The boy will amount to *nothing*!'"

"Yes, yes—the traces of my old neurosis," Freud said impatiently. "And then I dreamed that *my father* had become incontinent, and that I was his nurse, carrying around a glass urine vial. So now you are saying I am in my father's place."

He twisted around on the couch, craning his neck to look at Jung.

"So then *you* are in my place, taking care of *me*."

"Is that what you think?" Jung asked.

"I don't know," Freud hesitated, genuinely unsure.

"There was something else," he went on slowly. "Some dreams."

"Tell me," Jung commanded.

The overlook in Central Park, the dead birds floating in the black water. There was something else—the gesture that man had made toward the children—

In the dream, the General made a curt, dismissive gesture with his hand. So like the gesture he had made in the cafe in Olmutz years before, dismissing Freud. But why did it remind him?

"Tell me your dream."

"First—there was something you said. In the park."

"Something *I* said?"

Freud put his feet down on the floor again, and swung around to face him.

"Just after we had been to the museum—with all those bones, and the Neanderthals."

"Yes—you mean about *my* dream?" Jung asked suspiciously. "The two ancient skulls, in the cave?"

"There was that, but something else. Something about the children we saw."

The man had made that gesture toward the children—and Jung had said something. Something about the children—

"The children? I don't think I remember. Tell me about your dream."

"You said there were *all kinds,*" Freud reminded him, speaking quickly now, the memory pouring back. "You remember: the children were playing on the lawn, and I said I thought two of them looked like my nieces. And you said, 'Yes, there are all kinds.' What did you mean by that?"

"I don't know," Jung half shrugged.

"You meant *Jews,* didn't you? You meant some of the children were Jewish."

"I suppose," Jung shrugged again, looking away. "That, and all other kinds of nationalities."

It was beginning to fall into place, the way it always did when he was finally picking the lock on a difficult case—

"The skulls—they represent two different *kinds* of people."

"Well, I suppose that's possible—"

"Gentiles, perhaps—and Jews?" Freud pressed.

"You're taking over the analysis," Jung accused him. "Tell me about your dream."

"I don't think so."

It all made sense now. The pince-nez that the Cruel Captain had worn. His own military tormentor, the anti-Semitic General. The same gesture that the General and Jung had made. Then there was the little Germanic castle in the park—and below it, the dark water, the black muck of occultism.

It all came down to Jung, who was one and the same with the

Cruel Captain, and the General. He wished to overthrow Freud, of course, that was perfectly natural, but there was something more. Jung knew he was relying on him to rebut all the usual notions about race and culture—to keep his psychology from being pigeonholed as "the Jewish science."

Yet now Jung was insinuating that racial differences were real, and predominant—that he and Freud were somehow different kinds.

"Tell me something first," Freud maneuvered. "The house—that was *your* house?"

"Yes."

"Meaning, yours, personally? *Or your race's?*"

"Well, both, I suppose," Jung blinked.

"Ah, yes. The House of 'Europe,' with its Roman walls and medieval furnishings. The House of 'Germany,' perhaps? Or maybe the 'Aryan' house?"

"Well, what of it?" Jung said impatiently, suddenly defiant, like a schoolboy caught in some petty lie. "Why not? Why not accept that different peoples have different psychologies?"

"No."

"Can't you see the difference?" Jung asked, almost pleading. "The Jews or, say, the Chinese, with their ancient cultures, their old books—they must have a different psychology from newer, younger races, such as us of German blood. Surely you can't deny that, if you have any belief in culture—"

"That same mystical nonsense," Freud said flatly. "We are scientists. We are dealing with what we can test, and perceive, and measure."

"But surely you can perceive culture!"

"Oh? What is the difference, then? Explain it to me. Let us forget about the Chinese for right now. Explain to me— how are Jews different from gentiles? Is it just the old books?"

"No," Jung said slowly. "There's, well, there's just what you are arguing now, with your refusal to acknowledge the mystical."

"And that is?"

"There's a certain *materialism*, say, in Jewish culture. As opposed to the higher, *spiritual* belief of the gentile, the German."

Freud felt his mind filming over with anger, but he forced himself to think rationally, logically. He leaned over the edge of the couch, his cold, clear eyes boring down into Jung.

"So. The two of us, born a few years, a few hundred miles away from each other, wearing the same clothes, speaking the same language—raised in the same *bourgeois* culture— we are fundamentally different beings? Different species? I am the materialist—and you are not?"

Jung stared at him, his eyes wide and angry, but saying nothing. His silence told Freud all that he needed to know.

So that was it: Jung was to be the analyst to the gentiles. Freud would be relegated to a corner for the "Jewish" science, after all. Like an old grandfather confined to the attic—like a half-blind, incontinent old gentleman, carrying his own urinal around.

In Jung's dream—if it really *was* a dream, and not some dissembling invention—Jung had used Freud's own symbols, his own dream against him. Of course he had read in the *Interpretation* of Freud's dream in the Aula—escaping through one, beautifully finished room after another. Now Jung was claiming them for himself—particularly the ornate, rococo, upper story of the "Aryan" house.

The reception hall, crowded with scientists, was the upcoming lecture at Clark. Jung—as the General, as the Cruel Captain—was gesturing for him to accept the "differences" between the children, between all Jews and gentiles. The woman on the table, in her ancient mask, represented all that occult, racial dreck—*Nirdvanda,* and *numinosum,* and the higher, spiritual genius of the German race. All the sloppy, excited mysticism he wanted Freud to join him in. Not to mention the rich female patients he had always planned to pick up in America—

"The dreams. Your dreams," Jung was pressing him. "You won't tell me?"

"I cannot risk my authority," Freud replied, getting up and pulling his jacket as close as he could around the baggy, borrowed pants.

"Oh? You may have just lost it!" Jung said peevishly. "You are putting that authority above the truth!"

"We shall see, Doctor."

He felt sick at heart, yet relieved, in command of himself again—the way he always did when he had solved a problem. There was a commotion in the hallway—Ferenczi returning with more pants from their hotel—and Freud walked over and opened the door.

"The session is over," he told his former protégé, with a faint smile. "I must change my trousers."

him in. Not to mention the rich female patients he had
always planned to pick up in America—

"The dreams, Your dreams," Jung was pressing him—

62

BIG TIM

Big Tim Sullivan stood by the waters of the Hudson, waiting for the boat home. From the dock he could see the lights
in the great pile of the capitol, up on the top of State Street.
Soon he would see them begin to flicker out, one by one. It
was the last night of the session, and once the last light was
out he would not see them again until it was time to take the
train back up to Albany in the fall.

It had been a good session, run like clockwork. Bob and Al
had everything wrapped up so well that he had decided to
leave early, instead of waiting for the last, midnight boat. That
ship was like the hell-bound train, with every state senator and
assemblyman from Kinderhook to Coney Island on board.
There would be a band going, and plenty of liquor, and the last,
cutthroat card games of the session. The solons singing endless
choruses of "Goodnight Ladies," as they dropped each upstate
legislator off at some rotting, deserted little pier along the river,
sneaking in endless hotfoots and other great practical jokes.
Until at last the City delegation churned, bleary with drink,
into the grim, gray piers of the West Side, amidst the mighty
ocean liners and the other sagging river ferries.

This night, it was the early boat. There were just Little
Tim and Cousin Florrie, his legislative aides, with him.
They stood together on the dock, smoking cigars. Big Tim

had even sent Photo Dave and Sarsaparilla on ahead. Tonight he wanted no more company than his brooding kinsmen, to lift at most one glass, and ponder the dark water, and try to get some sleep before he returned to Manhattan, the Place of the Whirlpool.

The boat was running late. Sullivan looked behind him, up the hill, even though he didn't think he should. The lights were still on in the capitol, which surprised him a little. The session should have been wrapped up by now, so that his fellow legislators would have time to make their final arrangements, time to say their fond farewells, and make a last stop at their favorite saloon or whorehouse. Burn any last incriminating papers or receipts—

But the lights were still not out—and now, as if in a bad dream, two men were hurrying down the hill toward him, half walking, half running, as fast as they could go without tumbling down the slope. Big Tim felt a premonitory twinge in his groin.

"Here's trouble," Cousin Florrie grumbled as the messengers descended.

The two men recognized the waiting figures on the end of the dock, and began windmilling their arms. Just then the grand steamer *Annie Moore* hove into view, moving leisurely down the slow current of the Hudson.

"There's trouble wit' the hours bill!" one of the men was hallooing. "They need you up the hill! Mrs. Perkins says—"

"Not that old crow again," Florrie moaned.

Big Tim glanced at the elegant white boat finally pulling up to the dockside. Inside, he knew, was light and warmth and rest. Inside was a cushioned seat, and a bed if he needed it, and a quiet glass of beer and a good book. He looked back up the hill at the capitol.

"You got to come now!" one of the messengers was shouting, still running toward him. "They're callin' a quick vote, an' we're at least three shy. They need you!"

The settlement in the garment strike had gone over well, and Mr. Murphy had given Big Tim the nod to go ahead and pass the hours bill. It wasn't much, just a limit on how many hours the employers could force defenseless women and children to work every week. But it was something, it was something the people who lived and worked in his district might actually feel every day, and Big Tim had actually felt good when he had locked up its passage just before his departure.

Or so he'd thought. Obviously, something had gone wrong, that was just the way it happened sometimes, despite the most careful work. There was always some dog in the manger, some venerable senator or assemblyman who could be bought back for the price of a beer or a quick cozy. It didn't much matter, they could always ram it through again next session, or next year. That was just the way these things went, and he had a boat to catch.

Except. Except. Sullivan could picture the skinny, rail-backed Yankee lady, with her black tricornered hat so like his old Ma's, standing stoical and expressionless as her beloved hours bill went down to defeat. And he thought on his sister in Clinton Street, leaning over the table so tired she could not rise to make supper.

"Now, boys, it looks like we'll be on the hell-bound boat after all," he told the relations.

Big Tim Sullivan huffed into the assembly chambers, his breath coming in short, rusty stabs. Little Tim and Cousin Florrie held him up under the arms, their own breath reverberating raggedly. Mrs. Perkins strode across the assembly to them, stern Yankee face melting in relief.

"I knew you'd come," she said, in a fond, maternal whisper. "I knew you wouldn't let us down."

"Now, Mrs. Perkins, don'ch you worry about a t'ing," he

puffed benignly, charmed despite himself. "It's all in the bag. I won't let you down on this one."

Al and Bob came up, looks of anxiety and professional embarrassment on their faces. In the chamber behind them there was near chaos, the representatives of the people shouting and pointing and standing up in their chairs as Al's men tried to stall the vote, demanding roll call after roll call.

"I dunno what happened, Tim," Al said miserably. "We had two to spare, dead square, but then the wheels came off it."

"In the senate, it's the upstaters," Bob told him. "The City stayed firm, but they got to the damned farmers——"

"Ah, but they always do," Big Tim assessed, rubbing his hands at the thought of doing what he did best. Cousin Florrie and Little Tim began stripping him down for action, peeling off his hat and coat and scarf.

"They played us for flats, ran the boodle caravan by right under our noses, an' waited for the last minute to play their hand. Smart, smart! But they can't win, don'ch you worry, Mrs. Perkins. We've got truth an' joostice an' good Christian morality on our side," he told her——already figuring who owed him favors, and who he could blackmail, and who he could out-and-out intimidate into doing the right thing.

"We'll get yer fifty-four hours for you and the poor workin' girls!"

Down to his vest and shirtsleeves, Big Tim Sullivan waded eagerly into the tumult on the assembly floor, looking for votes.

63

ESTHER

She met Sadie at the settlement house on the Day of Rejoicing in the Law, when even the *goyishe* politicians were allowed into the synagogues, and there was a carnival air throughout the East Side. Sadie stood by the door of the settlement, brazenly smoking a cigarette, one hand on her hip. She wore a grand, volcanic black-and-white hat, the tattered red hussar's jacket flung over one arm, a single, rattan suitcase by her feet.

She smiled broadly when she saw Esther, and waved to her, fingers sticking out of a lacy black half-glove.

"So here I am, like one more penniless greenie," she joked, though Esther could see she was nervous.

"You'll be all right here. No one would dare try anything with you."

"*Ach,* but to be reformed! My soul bleached white. I should have let the Lutheran missionaries have the work, they take such pleasure in it."

"It won't be so bad. You can learn things——"

"Oh, yes. Like what?"

She dropped the cigarette and ground it out beneath one boot heel, a little stream of smoke trickling out ruefully between her bow lips.

"Well, to cook, and to sew——"

"I already know *that*. Even whores know such things."

"But there're other things."

"Like what?"

"Well—"

"Yes, yes, I know," she told Esther, a brittle smile on her face. "I can learn about the Constitution, and how to keep my teeth clean, and serve tea, and write a good English sentence. And all so I can sew shirts in a shop."

"It isn't so bad—now."

"Oh?" Sadie laughed, still teasing her but serious, too. "Isn't it?"

The strike had been all but settled. The Triangle was one of the few shops still holding out, but Clara was sure it would soon have to give in, too. Everywhere else, they had won recognition of the union, and better pay and better hours, and a fair division of the work during the slack season. And all of it still meant working fifty-four hours a week, bending over the machine until her back ached, the needle pulsing through her finger.

Esther had liked working in the union office—organizing things, arranging speakers, filing papers, writing up grievances. She had even come to enjoy speaking to the other strikers, and at the rich women's clubs, once she found her voice. It had seemed like a real life—how a person worked, instead of being one more part of a sewing machine.

And this was what she was wishing on Sadie—if she was lucky, and could get steady work as an operator. How different it would be—from the dangerous, drifting hours out on the streets, from saloons, and midnights huddled under the elevated, and strange men with whiskey breath. What would *she* take, Esther wondered, to let strange men put their hands on her and take her to bed? Even with all of it— the syph, and the pimps, and the fear of having your throat cut one night in a lonely room—even with all of it, how much worse would it be to be a real whore?

"That's all right. Don'ch you think I never thought about this before? That's all whores do, is wonder where they're going," Sadie told her, touching Esther's face with one of her half-gloved hands.

"At least this will be mine, my decision, such as it is. At least I got away from *him*, that has to count for somet'ing."

"Yes, it does. Of course it does."

Esther wanted to leave her with some consoling words—something inspiring, like she used at the union meetings, or the society teas. She wanted to tell her that it didn't need to last forever. That there was a new day coming, and maybe soon she would be able to get a real education, or start a family, or at least work in a decent place, where she was respected and paid a living wage. Sometimes, when she started on these spiels for the union, her old vision for Orchard Street would come spinning back to her—the broad new streets, and the clean, expansive tenements, the happy people walking out to work in the morning—and the hope and the dream would come shining through in her face and her words.

That was all right for the rich women and the factory girls. But Sadie, she knew, would know better.

"Good-bye, good-bye, dear! Don' be a stranger!"

Sadie kissed her impulsively on both cheeks, and Esther smiled and kissed her back

"No, never!"

She left her at the settlement house with her one bag, walking backwards and waving to her until she was far down the street. Sadie waving back from the doorway, still joking, her gray eyes still smiling, sweeping her arm over her head:

"Good-bye! Good-bye! Don't forget me! When you see me next I will be as clean as the driven snow!"

Her mother's eyes, always so fearful and evasive, now stared unseeing at the stained gray ceiling above the kitchen table where she lay. A fly crawled unmolested along her forehead. Esse's father sat in a chair beside the table, rocking slowly back and forth while he said Kaddish, but nothing broke her awful concentration.

From the sidewalk Esther had spotted the black smudge, planted like a giant thumbprint across the front of the tenement. The boarded-up windows—nuggets of smashed glass glittering in the street, crunching under the feet of the hurrying, oblivious pedestrians—all the usual signs of a small, passing disaster in the City. Esther spit through her fingers and looked away when she passed such things on other streets—but now she could not.

"They said it started in the walls," her father told her. "In the electric wiring, but I know it was those Irisher cows across the hall. Why they didn't succeed in killink all of us, I don' know. There was smoke all over, an' I wanted to go upstairs—get up on the roof, the quickest way."

"That was smart thinking," Esther said, noting that his *luftmensch*'s genius for survival was still intact. Of course he would know the quickest way out of any trap.

"She didn't know if the fire ladders would reach so far. She said we had to stay an' fight it, we had to fight for our things."

The old reb snorted.

"Fight for what? A bowl, a pan? A sewing machine? I went up on the roof. When it was over and I came back down, she was like this. They said her heart gave out."

Hanging off one of the kitchen chairs, Esther saw a small, singed towel, embroidered with one of her mother's cheerful *ongepotchket* sayings: *Happy sunshine!* She turned away from him, dismayed as ever at how much more cynical, how much more callous he was in reality than even the cantakerous old fool of her daydreams.

She looked down at her mother's face—so gray and hollowed out that she thought if she were to apply just the slightest pressure, it might crumble under her touch.

A life lived for others

She straightened up, faced the old man.

"So. What will you do now?"

"What should I do, with a son who is dead to me and a daughter who will not do her duty?" he said, with his routine bitterness. "What can I do, where can I go, when every hand is turned against me?"

"That's up to you," Esther told him. She turned to Kapsch the *roomerkeh*, who was loyally sitting *shivah* next to her father in a three-legged chair—the only other surviving piece of furniture in the charred apartment.

"The place is yours, so far as I'm concerned," she told him. "*He* won't be able to afford it, not even a piece of it."

"You are an unnatural woman," the reb hissed at her. "Where will you go now? Back to your pimp, wherever he's keepink you?"

His words gave her a certain epiphany—not that it much mattered anymore.

"Was it you who put him up to it? Was he doing your dirty work, spying on me?"

The old man said nothing, swallowing his anger and looking down at the floor.

"Ah, but how can that be, since after all he's dead to you?" she asked him. "How can a dead son do such things?"

"I must have done some great sin to be cursed by the Upper One with such children," he spat out. "One of them a monster, an' the other with a lump of coal for a heart!"

"Yes, it's all from God, isn't it?"

Esther leaned down so he had to look at her, holding his chin in her hand and gazing into his eyes.

"You know, Poppa, if God lived on the earth, people would break all his windows."

"More blasphemy from you! At such a time!"

Ignoring him, she bent over her mother and touched her, once, on her decayed cheek, then straightened up to go.

"And what about me? What about me, then?" he demanded, tears running down his bearded cheeks. He looked like a little old man seated there, suddenly not ferocious at all.

"You? You'll have to get acquainted with the face of a coin."

She walked out of the apartment and shut the door gently behind her. She paused in the hallway, and noticed the *mezuzah* there that she had always sternly neglected. It had been blackened by the fire, along with the whole length of the doorway, and was hanging loosely from the ashy wood. She moved to touch it—whether to salvage it or tear it off, she wasn't sure—but again she could not.

No, she thought. *Let it stay. I won't be a hypocrite. For all the good it will do, let it stay.*

She walked back outside. It was the beginning of Purim now, and the streets were filled with children wearing long, bent noses and princess crowns, tricornered hats and wizards' robes festooned with stars and moons, gleefully scaring the *goyishe* kids.

She looked back up at the narrow slat of a tenement, and thought coldly enough that a few more fires, and maybe her dream would come true—that they could level the whole thing, and put up modern, shiny buildings. And yet, she wondered, if such a thing should ever happen, if they ever found themselves in such a bright and shining place, would there be any place for the costumed, cavorting children all around her? Would there be any place for them at all?

64

GYP THE BLOOD

Gyp waited until she came out of the settlement house: wearing her black tricornered widow's hat, an umbrella clutched primly in one hand. Rigid, straight-backed figure striding on obliviously through the dark, littered streets. He followed her—staying just far enough behind, feeling the hot rage roiling within him.

He didn't know what he would do to her yet. He had just traced Sadie to the settlement house the day before. He had waited and waited for her, and he hadn't seen her come out yet, but he had seen *her*—the social worker lady who ran the place—walking out fearlessly in the evening, even after midnight.

She turned toward the west, cutting across the Bowery on Hester Street, then back down toward the Mulberry Bend. She stopped at another settlement house, then one of Big Tim's saloons. He stuck back in the shadows—the streets growing steadily more deserted, the *Chasir Mark* all closed up for the night now.

In the Bend, there were no streetlights, no one to stop him. All the myriad Italian storefronts, in every front hall-way, all closed up now, it was so late. Nobody left on the street, just a few mothers rocking their fussing babies. He moved in, gripping a knife in his pants pocket, but still unsure of what he was going to do. Scare her into producing Sadie? Cut her? Do her right here on Mulberry Street?

All he knew was that it was time for people to stop interfering with him. He gripped the knife in his pocket. Coming up swiftly behind her now, letting his feet flap loudly on the pavement——hoping to terrify her, freeze her with the sudden noise.

Instead she whipped around, brandishing her umbrella at him like a sword. He pulled up just before he impaled his stomach on its end, his fists still clenched in the air.

"I know you! I know who you are!" she shouted at him——in a voice impossibly large, and louder than a fishwife's. Already, the women rocking their babies were stepping forward, men with hands in their pockets walking out of the shadows where they had been sucking on their dry clay pipes.

"I know who you are: *Lazar Abramowitz!*"

She yelled out his name like a curse, like an alarm——still shaking the umbrella at him, keeping it on him as he tried to get around her. Lights were going on all over the tenements now, in the rows and rows of crooked little window squares. More people were coming out, moving toward them, sleepy Italian voices rising mellifluously through the night.

"Lazar Abramowitz! Lazar Abramowitz!" She kept yelling his name—his damned name.

"I know who you are!"

——still suspended there, at the end of her umbrella. Wanting to do anything, to shut her up——

No that is not my name That is not who I am at all Not at all——

"Lazar Abramowitz! Don't you come threatening me—trying to keep that poor girl whoring for you!"

He retreated back up the street——while she kept bellowing absurdly:

"Lazar Abramowitz is menacing me out here on the street!"

He backed up a few more steps, then turned and began to hurry away in the night——then to run, racing down the sidewalk, his name chasing after him.

He walked most of the night, not even sure where he was going——trying to think what to do next. At the end of it, he found himself back across the street from the settlement house with its scrubbed brick walls and neat little window planters. He stared up at it, thinking about Sadie inside, and wondering why he really wanted her back at all.

What he really wanted, he knew, was another *dow* over at Mock Duck's. To float away, into that lush, immaculate world. That was all he really cared for, not some Bowery whore, not even getting revenge for his broken head anymore. Just that blissful spot down in a Chinatown basement, reeking of damp wool——where *she* might be, pure and sweet and girlish, looking at him with such kindness, as he put his hand on her hip——

He turned away, staggering blindly back toward something——Mock Duck's, or some Tenderloin dance hall, or a stuss game. Back to the next bit of business. He was through with her, and with that fool Kid Twist.

Why did he hit me Why did he hit me like that, anyway? What a thing to do!

It was time——now that he could be humiliated by a whore and a lady social worker. Time to go back to Mock Duck's and sink into a new *dow* full of the greasy black hop, and maybe never come back. It was time——and looking back toward the settlement house one last time, back toward the mottled, dawn skyline, he saw the dwarf.

It was the same one, he was sure of it——the one who had posed as a newsie at the rat pit. Lingering by the settlement house himself, right outside the windows. Looking up for something, or someone, a single rose held ridiculously in his fat, tiny hands. He put it down, among the other flowers in the window planter, and scurried off, his little legs moving with surprising quickness.

Gyp was too startled to move for a moment—and then he followed, his big strides catching up quickly as the dwarf scrambled, unawares, back toward the subway station. Concealing himself easily among the milk wagons, and the produce trucks, and the pushcart vendors, all trundling their goods out for the start of a shiny new day—until he saw just where the little man was headed.

65

ON THE BOARDWALK

They stood in the Hall of Life, staring down into the incubator at the baby girl—almost up to full size now, squirming and struggling with normal, blind, infant energy. Esther resolutely ignoring the breathless, rustling commotion behind them.

The incubators were piled one on top of another—an impossibly small, red infant in each one. Pink diapers for girls, blue for boys. Their eyes no more than slits, waving arms and legs toward the single, wan lightbulb in each of their glass boxes. Tiny tubes running to their arms, and mouths, and noses.

The hall, dim as twilight, housed all the premature babies in New York. All the babies—blue with anemia, yellow with jaundice, wracked with pleurisy—that the hospitals, not believing in incubators, had handed over to Brinckerhoff and his mad doctors. All the babes pushed out onto the beds of dazed and uncomprehending prostitutes, or lifeless tenement women, or hapless middle-class girls in secret boardinghouses. Addicted from the first moment of life to laudanum or alcohol or benzene, scooped up and trundled over to a hospital mostly for form's sake, and then on to Dreamland. Yet still to *live,* somehow to *live*—in the warm, glowing glass boxes.

Up at the front a barker cried out over and over again:

"Come see the struggle for life! Come see the eternal struggle of Man! Five cents!"

There was no need for him. Already, they smeared the glass with their fingers and their cheeks and noses: straining to see the babes, their tiny chests heaving up and down, the tiny eyes even blinking open, staring at the single, warming lightbulbs bright as the sun.

The miracle of life—but that wasn't the attraction. The City was lousy with life, teeming with life. It pushed its way up through every sidewalk crack, swarmed in every basement, scuttled inside each tenement wall.

Instead, the crowd kept running back and forth across the room, pants and skirts rustling obscenely as they rushed to catch the climactic struggle.

"Hey, I got one over here!" a pimply-faced teenage boy called out, and they all hurried over, bobbing and ducking around each other to see the little red infant. Its tiny heart, clearly discernible in the emaciated chest, gave one more heave, then lay still.

"It's dead! It's dead!"

Some of the women screamed or affected to faint, but more people pushed in, taking their place. Somehow, the infant raised its left arm—and the heart started again, for one beat, then another, and another. It stopped—then started—then stopped, the child's left leg kicking spasmodically a few times before it lay still.

"Over here! Over here!"

The doctor and nurses, who had been busy across the room, now hurried over. They pulled the incubator out of the viewing gallery—though everyone could still see the doctor in the room just behind it, trying to massage the heart back into beating with a single finger, half as long as the child's whole chest. Working gently over it until at last the boy's skin had turned as blue as the diaper he was wearing, and he stayed motionless on the little operating table.

The tiny corpse was covered with a handkerchief-sized white towel, its incubator pulled out of line to be examined, sterilized—a new one, complete with another, struggling child inserted into the wall.

"She'll be going home soon. She's almost ready."

Esther stayed where she was across the room, adamantly ignoring the spectacle. Its outcome easy enough to discern from the crowd's low moans—as if they were surprised at themselves, to be so disappointed by the boy's death.

"Oh, look at her!"

She leaned in, smiling at the large, healthy baby girl, identifiable only by a number above her incubator. Kid leaned over watching *her*—watching her small, bent shoulders that only he knew were dimpled—and he loved her.

All his experiences, even the things he had reveled in, back in the City—his midnight Bowery walks, and the theater galleries, and the sawdust barrooms and tattoo parlors and the rat-baitings; all the can rackets, and the trimmer balls and the nights with shy and large-eyed factory girls, picked up in cafeterias—all the *savory* of his previous life— seemed to him nothing now but a strange and meaningless existence. All of his life—even from its beginning, living among the corpses back in Old Zagare—now seemed dim and distorted and unreal, compared to being with her now.

That was why he had picked up the shovel, back at the rat-baiting. This was where it had led—no matter that he had done it without thinking, or that he had saved some weird carny dwarf instead of a newsie. Pushing forward in the endless, blind crawl of life. That must be it, or what would it be? It had led him here—all of it had led here—and he would not go back, he would not move on. He would stick.

He reached down, held her hand surreptitiously in the twilight hall, whispered, "I love you," close to her ear.

"What?"

"I love you," he insisted, as earnestly as he could say anything—and she laughed and clutched his hand as they stood there, watching the red infants struggling for life.

"What is this—my *dybbuk* getting sentimental?"

"I love you and I only want you, I don' care."

"Yes," she murmured, teasing him. "Yes, yes, my Rockefeller prince. You just want me 'cause you're stuck out here, an' I'm the only girl you got for now."

"No, no—it's not that. I love you—"

"Uh-huh. If my brother doesn't kill you or me or the both of us first."

"Esse, you don' understand," he swung her around, looking her sternly in the face—trying to force her to take him seriously.

"I love you. Stay with me—marry me. Like the eye in my head I will treasure you."

"You're just saying that because you saw the kids," she smiled. "Such notions. Besides, maybe I want to live, just all on my own. Maybe I want to live, just for me. What do you say to that?"

"Whatever you want to do," he told her, very gravely. "I mean it. You live any way you want to live, just so long as you live with me."

"So? We will live together then like nobody has ever lived before?"

"Why not?" he told her earnestly. "Why not? Doesn't everybody? Doesn't everybody we know? There is nothing now like it was before!"

"Ah, my birdie boy," she sighed, still smiling. "What a dreamer you are."

She thought of all those smiling faces in the Gallery of Disappearing Men—all those ebullient, confident men—and she wondered what they had told their wives and sweethearts. Believing it, no doubt, with all their soul—at the time.

"My *dybbuk*—my dreaming devil," she told him, touching his face. "Well, tell me more, you may seduce me after all. It's been known to happen."

They strolled outside, the late-afternoon sunshine slanting down in their eyes, making them squint as they walked out of the twilight world of infants.

66

BIG TIM

He heard the news about Charlie Becker in his saloon. Mr. Murphy had Little Jimmy bring it down——looking splendid as a cardinal, careless as a spring day.

"The jury convicted him," Jimmy announced in his suave, slightly amused voice, as if he had been reading the rhymes to one of the songs he liked to write.

"I see, I see. Well, that's no surprise," Big Tim thought out loud, which was not at all like him. "After all, Whitman threw everybody else into the Tombs, an' threatened to warm up the chair if they didn't finger him. Tell me, is he plannin' to go after anybody else?"

Jimmy shrugged, thin shoulders barely stirring the shoulders of his immaculate pin-striped suit.

"You would know better'n me, chief. Word is it's Becker an' Becker alone's gonna take the splash."

So Murphy had gone ahead and let the strong-arm lieutenant drop. Whitman, the idjiot Reform D.A., was already busy drumming up a campaign for governor in the papers:

> We will prove that the real murderer, the most desperate criminal of all, was the cool, calculating, scheming, grafting police officer!

Of course the Holies had already taken up the cry. They were practically rubbing their hands over the idea of special investigators, and blue-ribbon commissions, and indignant public hearings. Stretching on and on until they had exhausted even the public's appetite for scandal.

"Silk hats and silk socks, and nothing in between," Tim muttered.

At most, all they would accomplish was marching poor old Handsome Charlie Becker off to the chair. One moderately corrupt, moderately stupid police lieutenant. It seemed a poor catch, for all their sound and fury, and Mr. Murphy would be glad to let them have it. Reform would be sated for the moment, and everyone could get back to business as usual.

It had been very courteous of Murphy to let him know, Sullivan reflected, before he heard it blurted from the newsies peddling the afternoon extras. It was the sort of consideration he had never had from old Croker. He was a deft man, Murphy, making all the right moves. No doubt he would raise Tammany to new heights—though for what purpose, Big Tim wasn't exactly sure.

Whatever it was, Sullivan knew he should go up to Murphy's place and consult on it. He rose up from his table and moved out into the street—so preoccupied that he neglected his usual ritual of checking himself in the barman's glass, and leaving Feeley's silver dollar on the counter.

Big Tim walked slowly up Centre Street, and then Lafayette. He could go only so fast, even if he wanted to; his groin was a perpetual mass of fire now. Nothing worked. He'd tried the mercury cure, and the fire cure, and the arsenic cure, but it still hurt worse than ever, and they only seemed to make him more absent-minded.

At Canal Street there was a road gang of Italians, tearing up paving stones in the middle of the street. Gaunt men, stripped to the waist, skin burned nearly black, wielding pickaxes in great, slow arcs. They worked under the supervision of a padrone with a big paunch and a shotgun tucked under one arm, who actually touched his cap to Big Tim as he went by.

"Just like the old country," Sullivan wondered out loud.

He didn't know the Italians so well, except that they worked sixteen hours a day when they could get it, and slept in alleyways or the back of stores, and sent half their pay home. They took the worst jobs in the City, except for the darkies, working the road gangs, sorting over the garbage scows for anything, anything at all they could salvage for the ragpickers' market in Bottle Alley.

Land of the people—

He cheered up a little when the street children spotted him, as always, and swelled up around him—spilling out into the street, oblivious to the fast-moving traffic.

We must pass some kind of street regulations, he thought vaguely. Other cities had them, after all; fine, progressive towns like Cleveland, or Portland, Orgeon. Something to slow the speed of the wagons, and the onrushing automobiles, some way to prevent the interminable tie-ups at every intersection.

"Big Tim! Big Tim!" the children were screaming delightedly. He had forgotten to load up, but there was still enough jake, enough old candies in his pockets for them to be satisfied. He smiled benevolently down at their gaptoothed grins, their matted hair, the boys and girls skipping along barefoot on the paving stones. They gathered around him until he was finally forced to stop altogether in the middle of the street, standing with his arms extended like some failed scarecrow, while all the little birds picked through his pockets.

They scrambled off when they had what they wanted. He left most of them at the corner of Broome and Centre, under the shadow of the great white police headquarters. One of them had found a rusty iron ring off a streetcar wheel, and soon they were all busy, clattering it back and forth across the granite paving stones. The policeman standing guard at the front entrance looked on disapprovingly but he didn't dare run them as long as they were with Big Tim.

"I'll be comin' back this way presently," he made sure to call out to the cop, "an' I don' want to see 'em disturbed."

The man nodded as gravely as any salute, and Big Tim left them still playing happily, under the aegis of the ponderous white dreadnought.

"What do we owe this man?" Mr. Murphy said mildly, sipping his tea. "After all, he pushed the thing, right from the start."

"To be sure," Big Tim agreed. "God and the people hate a chesty man."

"He was the one who insisted on saving his press agent. He was the one who insisted on all the rest of it."

"What's to keep him from talkin', though?"

"What if he does? Who could he finger?"

Mr. Murphy's logic was infallible, as always. After all, it had been Becker who had gone to *him*—not the other way around. Sullivan had kept him carefully separated from any of the actual shooters. Besides, Beansy's own words, so carefully leaked by the D.A., indicted only Becker.

A ghost of a laugh played itself out along Murphy's lips.

"Rosenthal already exonerated you before he died. You were his best friend, remember."

"I'm sure Whitman wishes he'd kept that affidavit secret now," Big Tim remarked dryly.

"Oh, I don't think so," Murphy said mildly, right as always. "This way, it's all tied up neatly. He can take his little police lieutenant and run for Albany. Otherwise he'd have to raise a whole new row, and who knows where that would lead? Takin' on the whole Organization—turning over stones he don't want to look under."

Mr. Murphy shook his head.

"These people. They think they're pious, when in fact they're only bilious."

On his way back from Mr. Murphy's he found himself thinking of poor Helen Becker, pleading her husband's case to him. He had read in the paper that she had lost the baby. It had been a difficult delivery, and when the doctors had asked if they should choose her or the child, there had been no husband around to answer on his wife's behalf. They'd had to put the question to the mother herself, and she had chosen to live, God help her. When that got out in the papers there was no stopping the invective and the death threats that poured down upon her. She had tried explaining that if she died, Charlie would have no one else in the world in his greatest hour of need, but of course that appeased no one.

That warm, sad-eyed woman, trying to smile at him. She brushed at the veil with her hand, and her face flitted before him like a moving picture image, merging with Herman Rosenthal's.

I wonder why this could not have happened to two people who did not love each other so much.

He headed back down Centre Street, back toward the police headquarters. The children were still there, Sullivan saw, still rolling the hoop and playing any number of new games around it, spun off into their dreamy child's world of visions and nonsense songs—before it was time to go search out a warm grate to sleep on again, a discarded crust of bread to eat.

He wondered if *they* played such games—down in the convent in New Jersey, or out West. No doubt they had better ones, more toys, and real lawns and fields. And always enough to eat, a warm place to sleep, good clothes. He was a good provider. He was a good father.

An automobile came wheeling fast around the corner from Spring Street, a big yellow touring car. It picked up speed, then seemed to swerve toward the clot of playing children—the driver struggling to keep all four wheels on the road.

"Fools!" Big Tim shouted in warning, and he broke into a bandy-legged run for the children, but he was still a block away, too far to do anything. The other pedestrians jamming the sidewalks just stared as he ran past.

"Fools!" he yelled again, hoping somehow that would get the cop on picket duty to do something—but the street kids had seen the touring car as soon as he had. Most of them scrambled easily out of the way with their youthful, street-trained reflexes—but a small knot of children remained frozen in the street, unsure of which way to jump. There was a little girl in a ragged dress, and two boys in bare feet and overalls, one of them wearing an oversized cap tucked down low over his eyes. The car bore down upon them so quickly that Big Tim could see the other boy was still smiling, blinking up from his game, not sure yet what was going on.

"Jump out!" he yelled, staggering down the street now, smashing into people on the sidewalk—but that was all there was time for.

The car's horn sounded wildly, but it kept moving, careening toward the little knot of children like they were a gaggle of pigeons in the road. Perhaps the driver was still fighting with his gears, trying to find the brake—not many of them really knew how to operate the big, murderous machines they drove—but he didn't slow down. Not then, not even after he had run straight through the children— still harooging and speeding down the street, anonymous behind his driving goggles, his only identifying marks a yellow hat and flowing scarf that perfectly matched the color of his car.

"Goddamned *fools!*"

Sullivan cursed after him, scanning the street in the car's wake. Two of the children—the little girl, and the boy with the oversized cap—had miraculously jumped out of the way at the last possible moment, guided by whatever instinct for life had kept them alive on the streets this far. They sat in the gutter looking very scared, the other children gathering slowly around, staring at them with religious awe.

The third child—the boy who had been smiling—was still in the street, lying crushed and quiet along the cobblestones. One of his legs was flattened and bleeding, a dark tire track across the bare skin just above his knee. He lay on his face—and when Big Tim got to him and turned him over, he saw there was another mark, branded on his forehead by the car's grill. The dirty pair of overalls that did not reach his knees were all he wore. His eyes were closed now, but his lips were open, and still smiling—like one of the street kids in the pictures Sullivan remembered—pretending to be asleep.

"Get his parents!" he cried at the frightened, uncomprehending children around him.

"Get someone to help!"

He looked up toward the enormous police headquarters, but all was quiet. Even the one cop on guard duty was no longer at his post. There was no one to help but him, and Big Tim slid one arm under the child's limp neck, another under his knees, and torturously lifted the boy up himself.

"Whose child is this?" he demanded sternly of the children again. "Whose child is this, I must get him back to his home!"

There was no answer from any of the children. Most of them had already begun to melt away again, down their familiar alleys and cellars, but others followed from a safe distance as Big Tim walked slowly down Lafayette Street with the dead child, repeating his question to anyone he passed:

"Whose child is this?"

The crowds of people walking past gave them quick, surreptitious glances and kept walking, without breaking stride. Big Tim turned down Broome Street and lurched aimlessly toward the East Side, no longer repeating his question out loud but mumbling and humming a little to himself, holding the boy out before him in his arms, so that maybe whomever he belonged to could see he was there.

67

ON THE BOARDWALK

The ships glided through the brilliant fall sky: zeppelins and aeroplanes, Spanish galleons and battle cruisers and rocket ships, all making long, lazy loops above the oblivious crowds.

Esther sat with Kid in the front seat of a red airplane with big black crosses on the wings, leaning into him, clutching the safety bar in front of her. It was the next-to-last weekend of the season. The long Indian summer had finally ended, and the air had turned fine, and crisp, and clean. One more week of the rides and the shows and the dancing halls—and then on the unbearably sad and wistful last weekend there would be an *Oktoberfest*—a last excuse to lure the crowds out.

She would be back at work by then. The Triangle still stood, a scab shop, all but alone among the bigger shops and factories. The Triangle women who had gone out were blackballed, but she had arranged with Clara to go back in under another name, a different hairstyle—to start all over again, organizing the scabs and the new girls.

She was sure she could do it. Mr. Bernstein never looked too closely, and the foremen would be too busy squeezing and fondling the girls to notice. She would be on her own, depending on no one this time, not even Clara. And if she succeeded——who knew? Clara's friend Pauline was not even twenty——a good seven years younger than Esther herself——but she had already been made a traveling delegate for the union. Leaving her machine behind, riding the rails from city to city to spread the cause.

And what about him?

Where would he go, when the summer ended? The Tin Elephant was nearly deserted now. It would be closing for the winter soon, the whores moving on already to more seasonal resorts. Her brother was persistent, she knew. It was only a matter of time before he found Kid——even if she never had anything to do with him again.

The night before, listening to the tide in bed, she had tried to persuade him to go away——become one of the Disappearing Men.

"Don' worry, moon, I can take care a myself," he had insisted, smiling at her. "There's no need to go anywhere."

They had talked on into the night about what to do. Until their words had started to slur and slow to the lapping pace of the waves, and they had fallen asleep in the mercifully cooler arse of the Elephant. He awakened her in the middle of the night, pulling up her nightgown——a small, insistent tugging——and they had made love still only half awake, drifting in and out of dreams, the only sound the bells from the buoys in the harbor.

It was really a *farpotshket* situation. Everyone talked about going, but no one did. He should leave, and she should leave him; this ice-cream-soda romance was over, despite all his fine words about marriage. Soon the birdcage hotels along Brighton Beach with their dancing pavilions and their champagne bars would be shutting down. The cool, healthful breezes off the ocean would blow harder and colder, until the island was inhabited only by the gulls and the sandpipers, and the midgets in The Little City, shivering in the darkness of their medieval streets.

But still he did not go, and she could not leave him. Instead, she came back out, to Coney Island and one more weekend together. She leaned in closer, hooking an arm through his as their airplane sailed through the immaculate autumn air.

He got off the train, and lifted his face instinctively to the sea air—a slender, inconspicuous man now, in a conservative black suit and black bowler. Out of the corner of his eye he could see Whitey and Louie the Lump, waiting for him. He waved them on with a small, impatient gesture, and strode with the crowd into the Pavilion of Fun.

He stood there in the middle of the park, taking everything in—the booths, the rides, the endless, winding line for the Steeplechase under the beaming idiot's face: STEEPLECHASE—FUNNY PLACE—STEEPLECHASE—FUNNY PLACE. He dropped his hand into his coat; fingering the rubber-handled Iver-Johnson .32 hidden deep in the inner pocket. Looking over every face, making sure that nothing got by him.

Sigmund Freud was jostled rudely forward by the big holiday crowd. All around him were the lowest types imaginable, waiting impatiently for their turn on the horses. Sailors with their tarts, seedy clerks with women still in bathing suits. Already pawing and groping at each other, unable to contain themselves before they got to the ride.

The park was astonishing in its sheer, unabashed vulgarity. The constant, nauseating smell of fried food, putrid shellfish and beef on a spit, and corn cobs. An incessant racket of bands, and reedy organ music.

"A magnified Prater," he sniffed to Ferenczi and Brill, referring to the cheesy midway in the Vienna park—but the Prater was like a summer garden party compared to *this*. Everything louder, bigger, more hysterical—more *American*.

At least it gave him some time to think, away from Jung—now zealously swimming his hundred laps, back and forth between the guideposts out in the surf. Since their aborted analysis at the Columbia clinic they had patched things up, at least on the surface. Jung had renewed his vow of fealty. He had offered again to go first at Clark, with the case of his daughter, and so introduce the delicate notion of child sexuality.

Freud had accepted all this with a show of equanimity. It wouldn't do to break things up now—not over here, on the verge of their greatest triumph. They both understood that. Yet how real was any reconciliation? How long would it last back in Europe, with its incessant cant about national culture? Just how loyal could he expect Jung to be—under such mystical influences?

The reedy noise from the organ pipes swelled up again, making any further, coherent thought an impossibility. Freud tried to say something to Brill and Ferenczi—then held his hands up over his ears.

"I must have been mad to think I could make myself heard in this place——"

Big Tim Sullivan reached the park by sunrise and let his arms hang down to laugh. He had been walking all night, after they had eased the body of the boy away from him, and his shoes and clothes were covered with the dust of Brooklyn, but he didn't mind. He stood waiting patiently for the park to open beneath the Angel of Creation, idly admiring her huge, perfect breasts.

A guard with a great white handlebar moustache marched up officiously to open the gate, blinking to see him in the early morning sunlight.

"Well, little fella, can't wait to get in for the roly-coasters, can you?"

"It looks like a great day for it," Big Tim beamed.

"Well, sure!" the guard laughed, taking him for a bum. "Sure it is—if you got two pennies to rub together!"

Inside, a long line of cash girls marched past him to work in their immaculate white academic gowns. A tall, serious-looking Negro strode by to the powerhouse, wearing a wizard's robe and a hat decorated with little crescent moons and stars and planets.

There was so much to see, but for now he just wanted to get to the ocean. He walked out through the park—stooping to carefully remove his dust-covered shoes and silk socks, before he stepped onto the pristine sand.

I spotted him over at Steeplechase. It was just luck I saw him at all, I was only over there looking for her and there *he* was: Gyp the Blood, large as life. Standing in the middle of the pavilion, turning in a slow watchful circle—looking over everything with the confidence of a man setting up his shot from a duck blind. His goons hanging back just behind him, obviously chafing for action—

A few more seconds and he would have had me. He was already looking over the crowd just to my left, taking in absolutely everything, the way he did. His eyes slowly, inexorably turning my way.

I jumped behind a sausage stand, sunk as low to the ground as I could get.

All I thought of was escape. I could have tried to warn him—warn *them*. But all I thought about under that relentless gaze, searching the crowd like a spotlight, was getting back to The Little City. It would be like a house of straw before him, I knew—yet where else for this little piggy to hide? There was safety in numbers—or at least hostages. Besides, he could never get past Carlotta. She simply wouldn't let it happen—wouldn't let even him disrupt her dream, her kingdom.

I crept away—out through the bungholes and the crawl spaces only we know about, back to The Little City as fast as my pathetic little legs would carry me. I went home to my queen. I needed her—needed her to protect me, needed her blind, unyielding madness to save me.

Freud was mounted on the mechanical horse, arms thrown around its neck like a little boy, barely able to get his buttocks down on the saddle. It lurched off at a terrific speed and he clutched desperately at his hat and walking stick, stomach churning with each dip, up and down the serpentine course.

The park spun dizzily by below him. He looked away—to see the sailor openly fondling the woman sitting in front of him. Unbuttoning the front of her dress, squeezing and sliding his large hands up and down over her soft, malleable breasts. She wriggled back against him, thrusting her bum up off the horse.

All around him, couples on the other horses rubbed and bumped against each other, all but copulating publicly, oblivious to anything else. Behind him, he could see Ferenczi watching them, too, his mouth hanging open. They rode like satyrs on the mechanical horses—wild as the steeds in his nightmare painting, teeth bared, nostrils flaring. All around them the coarsest, most abandoned public behavior he had ever seen, even in the army brothels, when he had done his reserve duty.

At the finish, he dismounted with trembling legs, pulling

down his jacket, brushing the filth of the ride off him. He hurried off, not even waiting for Ferenczi or Dr. Brill—mortified to even be seen in such a place. He pulled his straw boater down over his head—looking up only just in time to see a dwarf in a harlequin's outfit blocking his way, the little man's hands hidden behind his back.

"Excuse me."

He tipped his hat, moved around the grinning dwarf—and promptly felt a paralyzing pain in his buttocks. He spun around to see the dwarf dancing around him, waving the cattle prod madly around above his head.

He leapt desperately forward—anywhere, away from the mad little man—and landed on a grate that emitted a sudden blast of air that sent his hat flying. He went scrambling after it, but it evaded him now as if it were pulled along by a string, skipping from one blowhole to another. He dropped his walking stick, picked it up, dropped it again, groping forward to grab at the elusive hat where it lay along the boards.

Scrambling along on his knees, he heard a burst of harsh, convulsive laughter—and looked up to see a whole arena full of people, bleacher after bleacher of them, pointing and laughing at *him*. Somehow, he was all alone before them on a stage—on his knees, scrambling for his hat—the laughter growing louder and louder around him.

He straightened up, then leaned down with as much dignity as he could muster to retrieve his hat—carefully keeping his *derriere* turned away from the audience—and instantly felt another, agonizing pain. The demented dwarf bringing the cattle prod this time right up through his legs and along his genitals—Freud skipping and hopping wildly forward like one of the policemen they had seen in the movie on the rooftop garden, swatting vainly at the little man behind him while the crowd went wild.

●   ●   ●

Gyp stopped at the rows of animal cages in Dreamland, to mop his brow and take his bearings. At least Louie and Whitey were keeping back, as ordered. They were still conspicuous as canaries in their gaudy red and yellow gangster suits—but then he only needed them for insurance. Anything important, Gyp intended to take care of himself.

He rolled a cigarette and lit it, watching the animals in their cages. The crowds pushed right up to the bars, spitting and poking at the animals with the ends of their walking sticks and umbrellas, forcing the creatures back. The big cats, the panthers and lions and tigers, padded back and forth in the shallow recesses of their cages, growling fearsomely, muscles rippling in the bar-striped sunlight. And at the end of the row was an impossibly small cage that held a great gray elephant. The beast had no room to do anything more than march obsessively up and down in place—its eyes huge and yellow, and filled with a fathomless, mad fury.

Here the crowd was particularly thick, a couple of boys amusing themselves by sticking things in the elephant's trunk—old cotton candy sticks, dropped ice cream cones, anything at all they found on the ground; seeing if it would eat them. A sign over the elephant's cage read dramatically, STAND BACK! MANKILLER!—but they seemed to have no fear. They planted them in the palpitating, nostrillike openings right at the tip of the trunk, then dodged back, giggling.

Gyp remembered his last dream, down in Mock Duck's basement, reeking of damp wool and sweat, and perfumed smoke. How he would prefer to be down there now! Floating in that clean, clear place instead of performing this chore, satisfying as it would be.

Fook Yuen—Fountain of Happiness. Li Yuen—Fountain of Beauty

"We found the place," Whitey said, coming up to him.

"We found it—The Little City."

Gyp shook off his daydreams, dropped the half-finished cigarette to the ground, grinding it under his heel. Down by the elephant's cage the boys were still dodging back and forth, the beast trumpeting madly at something they had fed it.

"All right, then. Let's go see about our little friend."

The psychoanalysts limped back over to the bathing pavilion to meet Jung, who looked fit as a seal in his sleek black bathing costume.

"Physical activity—there's nothing like it, doctors!" he crowed, pumping his arms vigorously, showing his big, gravestone teeth, the eyes that were mere slits behind his pince-nez. "It's as important to the mind as anything else! Strength through health, you know."

"Yes, we've just been riding ourselves," Freud said dryly.

"Oh, Carl, you should have seen what we've been through!" Ferenczi started, but Freud quickly suggested they get lunch, unable to bear the idea of Jung picturing him in such a humiliating, infantile position.

"There's a likely-looking place—"

Brill ushered them over toward a large, elegant sign marked only "To the Roof Gardens." A long line of dignified men and women were making their way to an elevator in a glass pavilion. More of the same vulgar crowd he had seen at the horse ride stood around gawking, but they made no move to join the line—which Freud took as a good sign.

"This must be a decent place, at least."

They entered the glass elevator, crowding in with a dozen others, all politely silent. The door closed automatically, the elevator rose halfway to the roof—then came crashing back to the ground so hard Freud could feel his teeth rattle. They were all thrown together, the elevator listing halfway over on one side; the other passengers falling on Freud and Jung,

Ferenczi and Brill at the back of the car, nearly crushing them.

The side panel of the elevator had at least lurched open, and they scrambled out on their hands and knees—Freud amazed they hadn't all been killed.

So they are fallible, after all, this race of mechanical giants! For a moment he felt oddly triumphant, even as he dragged his body out of the elevator, stepped over the side to the floor, at last—and promptly went skidding onto his ass.

He tried to rise—only to feel his legs go out from under him again, sliding helplessly in opposite directions. He put a hand on the floor to try and steady himself—and brought it up covered with grease. The whole floor, greased, save for the little path directly in front of the elevator.

On purpose!

All around him, Jung, and Ferenczi, and the other passengers were slipping and sliding, windmilling their arms wildly; Dr. Brill apologizing profusely even as he floundered and fell on his face. Outside, beyond the glass, he could see the vulgar crowds, laughing and pointing, already looking ahead to the next elevator.

I knew there was something wrong as soon as I got back. The streets were all empty, the whole city deserted as a graveyard—but that was to be expected. It was a Saturday, and everyone would be working the extra matinee, over at the Big Tent.

The Town Hall—*my* Town Hall—was wide open, though—the windows and shutters open, doors flapping slightly in the breeze as if someone had just turned the whole house out for a spring cleaning. I bolted upstairs, calling for my queen. Calling her name—

I couldn't find her. Every *trace* of her was gone: the trunks packed full of elegant little doll's dresses. The immaculate, miniature hairbrushes and the tiny, delicate vanity. Even the royal bedsheets and quilts, with their imperial, embroidered *CR*.

All gone. The music was starting up at the Big Tent, and it occurred to me she might be over there, already warming up for her daily identical performance. I pushed open one of the fine, tiny windows in the upstairs window, looking out toward the tent, in the square of the immaculate model town.

That was when I saw the coach: a large black carriage by the back door, big as a hearse——a pair of coachmen loading it up with those exquisite child's trunks. I raced back down the stairs, already knowing what I would find. I was just in time to see him whisking her out, behind his phony black magician's cape.

"Wait!" I squealed, and she turned her head just a little for me to see——her face, hard and imperious as a queen, staring off beyond me.

She knew

"Wait!" I cried, but she turned and was gone, vanishing behind the cape, into the big black carriage.

"Too late!"

The phony Marconi grinned at me, above his huge cape. A foot shot out, kicking me backward as casually as an old football.

"Too late! You lost her!"

Then they were gone, the horses pulling the big black carriage away from The Little City at a gallop.

I ran after it——even though I knew I had no hope in the world of catching it. I ran after it, right out of the park, as far as my shrunken legs would carry me down Surf Avenue, yelling after it in my ridiculous, ineffectual dwarf's voice:

"Wait! I'll give you anything!"——until it was long gone, only a black speck slowly disappearing through the new flat lots of Brooklyn.

The elephants stood at the top of the Shoot-the-Chutes in their jeweled blankets and bridles, a long gray line winding up the towering water slide. Each one detached itself carefully, wobbling for a moment on top of the Chutes—then dropped, impossibly, into the great central lagoon of Dreamland.

Sitting up on their tails, holding up their forelegs like begging dogs. Hitting the water with a splash that left the whole crowd squealing and clapping and ducking, soaked by the tidal waves of water.

Big Tim watched closely, beaming and clapping with delight as each magnificent pachyderm came down. The beasts emerged, trumpeting and shaking themselves, spraying the delighted onlookers with water all over again.

The children around the lagoon watched it all wide-eyed, screaming with pleasure as the waves of elephant water hit them. In no time, Big Tim had emptied his pockets to them, buying great plumes of cotton candy, boxes of Cracker Jack, Red Hots™. Soon he had nothing at all, not even carfare back to the City, but he didn't think about it.

Instead he now felt free to keep wandering, hands in his pockets, staring amiably at everything around him—at everything he owned. The midway with its tattoo parlors, and its shooting galleries, and camel rides and con men and hootchy-kootchy dancers. The great rotating Ferris wheels, and the darting, zizzing roller coasters, and the black pantomime policeman, and the delicatessen with everything made out of candy.

How the children he saw every day on the street would have loved this How they all would have loved it—

The gangsters stormed through the miniature city, tearing up the Big Tent, smashing the windows of the perfect little houses, the stained-glass windows in the church, until the glass covered the streets and crunched underfoot. Punching in doors, lifting roofs right off the tiny homes.

The dwarves screamed and fought and grabbed at them. A squad of midget cops bravely formed a phalanx and charged them, truncheons drawn.

The gangsters kicked them aside, flung them away by the scruff of their necks, stomped them like bugs. They looked everywhere, even crashing through the beautiful Town Hall and palace—but he was nowhere to be found. Whitey thought it might be worthwhile to wring a few of the midgets for information, but by now there were real police whistles blowing in the distance.

"Don' worry, I'll find the little bastard," Gyp promised them. "They can go ahead an' run, I'll find 'em. I'll find all the little bastards."

Up on the sixth floor, the mother and daughter stood begging for their lives. Flames licking out through the windows behind them, black smoke trailing up into the brilliant, blue, indifferent sky. There was the clanging of fire bells somewhere off in the distance, but it was clear the engines would never reach them in time. They stretched their hands out toward the helpless crowd below.

Esther and Kid stood watching from the street, arguing about their future.

"How can you do it? How can we do anything with *him* still around?"

"I'll go with you then," Kid told her. "We'll both go away."

"But I don't want to go," she insisted. "Not yet."

"Sure you do."

Before them stood a perfect replica of a city tenement, exactly like the ones most of the crowd had come from. And there in the windows were themselves: men and women and children, dressed like anyone else. A peaceful evening scene: the families settling in for dinner, the mother laying out the table, father reading his paper, the children playing quietly. The crowd sighing to see how tranquil, how serene it looked, how much more peaceful than real life.

"We can't get married. How could we ever afford it?"

"Sure we could. We could live like real people. With a place of our own, maybe children."

"I dunno," she said slowly. "I gotta go back."

"Why? Whatta you owe them anymore? Is that the kind of life you want?"

Did she? The stale, dingy hotel rooms, nights in smoky traveling car parlors. All the far-off cities she had never seen. Coming into a new town in the dead of night, negotiating head-to-head with the sneering men bosses and local union presidents. Standing up to the goons, and the leering, taunting cops.

She wanted it more than anything she had ever wanted in her whole life, including the love of her father.

The afternoon fire started slowly, creeping up between the walls, but easily visible to the crowd below. They shouted up warnings, but the tenants went about their lives, oblivious to it all. But they—they could see the flames, could smell the gasoline.

Suddenly it was everywhere, shooting right up to the top floors. Real flames and smoke, exploding through the windows, showering the street below with glass; sending the crowd reeling backwards. Now the tenants were edging out on their window ledges, looking petrified, clutching tightly to each other for support.

"Wait, wait! Wait for the engines—don't jump!"

"We'll save you, don't jump!"

The crowd shrieked with fear, clutching and clawing unconsciously at each other. A black trellis fire escape ran down the middle of the building—but as soon as a few of the tenants put a foot on it the whole structure fell away with a terrible, ripping sound, leaving the people, men and women both, swinging in air, clutching on to the narrow ledges by their fingers.

"Save them! Save them! *Oh, for the love of God, save them!*"

A fire engine raced up to the front of the building, the crew rushing a single, round life net to the foot of the building. It looked too flimsy to hold anything. Yet up on the sixth floor the flames were licking right up the broad, black skirts of the women, the vests and pants legs of the men.

It was soon obvious they would have to jump. The firemen flung up a ladder—but it only reached partway, only up to the third floor, still much too low—

"Save them!"

Even as they watched, a couple on the top floor picked up their young son—gave him a boost up on their hands—then propelled him downwards, head first.

The crowd gasped, and swayed, trying to will him on to the life net. At first the boy seemed to be on target—but soon it became obvious that he was headed well to the right of the net.

The crowd cried out in horror, wondering if this was some kind of stunt gone wrong—the firemen scrambling desperately toward the falling boy with their net.

"You're missing him!"

He tumbled head over heels now—once, twice, three times—then landed feet first on the net, did another, neat backwards tumble, and came out on his feet, arms extended in triumph.

The crowd burst into applause. Next the boy's mother jumped, then his father. Soon they all began to leap from the windows and the ledges, with superb, clockwork preci-

591

sion—each jump more spectacular than the last. Tearing away the burning clothes they wore to reveal the black leotards, the sleek, muscled acrobats' bodies underneath.

More trucks pulled up, the firemen stepping deftly around each other, smartly flipping out more life nets. The jumpers coming down now two, three, sometimes four at a time, grasping each other's arms, forming human pyramids. The ones from the lower floors not even using the nets but tumbling out to safety on their own, right onto the street. The men and women who had survived the fire escape letting go of their window ledges, falling in effortless, breathtaking pirouettes. Some of them plunging on down right through the street—only to jump up, unscathed, through the cunningly hidden trapdoors.

The crowd cheered and clapped wildly for each one, the acrobats still swooping down, graceful as birds out of the clear blue sky. These were not easy or risk-free stunts, performed without a real net—yet all of them reached ground safely, landing without a scratch, taking their bows.

Esther and Kid limped away, still weak in the knees at the shock of such a spectacle, clutching to each other's arms.

"Whatever you want, my golden heart, my angel—don't you see?" he crooned to her. "Anything we can dream up, we can have it. Anything! Only—us together."

She smiled weakly, put her hand on his arm, still thinking of the spectacle of the fire.

"Tell me about the children again, and a place of our own, like real people."

"You'll do it, then?"

"No. But tell me it again, it's so nice."

He smiled at her, and started to speak—when he noticed something up ahead. Just what it was, he wasn't sure, but he put his face to the wind.

They stalked them past the Barrel of Fun, and the Razzle Dazzle. Past the Venetian Gondolas and the Golden Stairs and the Chanticleer, past the Barrel of Love and the Human Roulette and the Cave of Winds and Human Pool Table and the Down and Out. They stalked them all through the parks, past the diving elephants, and the Fall of Pompeii, and the Hall of Life.

Then Gyp smelled the smoke. The same smell from when he had gone to see *him,* up in the charred little apartment—a ruin, empty save for *him,* and Kapsch the *roomerkeh,* who sat silent and loyal as some old family retainer.

"My repentant son returns," the old man had said, joyously caustic as ever.

Their mother lay on the table, eyes staring upward. He rocked slowly back and forth, the ritual mourning cut in his coat reopened—as if for one more old combatant from the Lodz synagogue.

"I know who he is. I know where they are."

"Too late!" his father snapped. "Do you think it matters *now?* Do you think all this would have happened if you had done what I asked you?"

He stood in the doorway, sizing up the old man. Thinking that if he killed him now, he'd have to kill Kapsch as well, and that might make too much noise.

"I don't know."

"No, no, of course you don't!" the reb laughed bitterly, then wiped his hand across his mouth. "It's just another mistake—you didn't *mean* it. Like losink the money for the *cholent*—like your whole worthless pimp's life. Just a mistake."

He waved him closer, and Lazar walked reluctantly into the apartment, within arm's reach of his father.

"C'mere, c'mere," he urged, still waving, until Lazar bent over, his ear to his father's mouth—his beard and clothes, and even his flesh, still reeking of smoke.

"C'mere, I want to tell you somethink."

He waited, listening.

"It's all your fault," he breathed into his ear.

The old man reached his arms out around him, grasping for him.

"It's all your fault, everything that happened. All of it." He laughed again, as if it were a great joke. "It's your fault I am reduced to ashes—but I forgive you! Come to me."

Lazar stepped back so fast he almost knocked over a chair.

"I forgive you, my son!"

"Get away from me. Get away, get away," he chanted, even as he ran out into the hall, away from that house and his father, stinking of smoke.

Now he smelled it again: the same burning smell, the smell of death in the tenements. He moved toward it—Whitey and Louie trailing behind, mystified. *She* would be there, he was certain.

Freud lay nearly prone on his bench on the boardwalk, soaked handkerchief pasted over his forehead like a plaster, waiting fearfully for when he would be disturbed again. Where the rest of his party had got to, Jung and Ferenczi and Brill, he didn't know, and frankly he didn't care anymore just so long as they left him in peace.

Already, he had been rousted from one bench after another by an electrical shock, a marching band, and a roving band of gigantic, pantomime grotesques: an Indian chief, a nine-foot Irishwoman, a huge, obese policeman in blackface. A gang of maniacal caricatures, gleefully exhorting him to move on, have fun, spend money—enjoy himself!

He mopped at his brow and took his own pulse, wondering that he had not yet had a stroke. They had been around all the parks, buffeted here and there like so much flotsam by the great waves of people. They had been on a staircase that divided in half—one side suddenly plunging down, the other yanking you up. They had been on the sidewalk that sent them plummeting into a giggling heap of clerks and salesgirls, and a roller coaster that left his stomach curdling, and a set of spinning teacups that knocked their heads together.

He had been bashed and jerked and spun about until every part of his body ached: Blasted by the marauding bands and the relentless organ music. Bombarded by the frying grease, and the great, droopy-lidded heads of wolves and clowns and devils, leering from the walls above their head as if suspended there in midair.

A large, well-dressed man with a solid slab of a face plopped down on the bench next to him, whistling a little through his teeth. He braced himself for some further interference, but the man seemed harmless enough—another patron, or victim.

"Madness," Freud muttered, looking furtively around himself. "Utter madness."

"Yes. Yes, it is," the man said, smiling as if he had just remarked upon the weather.

"How can one make any progress against it?" Freud asked, as much to himself as to his newfound companion.

"You can't," the slab-faced man said. "People want what they want, and all you can do is give it to them."

"But how can anything go forward then?"

"We won't," the man said, dreamy as a child—and Freud noticed that despite the richness of his suit his pants pockets hung out emptily, like two white flags.

"We won't go forward at all. Things don't *go* forward," he continued, as if by way of explanation. "The best you can hope is to sell people a good story about themselves, and try to get them to live up to it."

"What about truth?" Freud insisted on arguing, even though he was beginning to think the man on the bench might well be mad. "What about science and logic, and understanding the human mind?"

"What about it?"

A young couple hurried past them, down along the boardwalk. The young man in a gaudy suit the color of a pastry glaze, holding hands with a pretty girl, in a more modest blue dress. They half ran, half walked through the crowds, glancing back over their shoulders as if fleeing invisible demons that seemed to pursue everyone in this land of hurry-up.

Freud leaned over, distracted from his hopeless conversation by the couple's haste, trying to see what they could be running away from. The young man's face, he thought, was almost indistinguishable from the face of the Jew he had seen down in the City's ghetto, hauling along his huge load of garments on his head. Which, come to think of it, did not look that different from the face of the monolith, the apparition he had seen from the Cafe Landtman, staggering up the Vienna Ringstrasse—

Were they Jews, then—this young couple, hurrying along? From the clothes they looked as if they might be almost anything. A gangster and his moll? Workers in the new factory hives that could be seen all over the City, spewing clouds of steam and smoke out into its alleyways? Or both, or neither, or anything they wanted to be in this brand-new cement mixer of a country?

Freud stood up, as he had that day at the Landtman, that day the monolith had first appeared; pointing down at the fleeing couple, appealing to the big, slightly mad man beside him on the bench:

"Look! Do you see?"

—but the man was already gone, strolling off down the promenade, disappearing into the endless, shuffling crowd.

In their ranks, Freud could make out a hundred, a thousand versions of that same face from the Asian steppes. A thousand former peasants, a thousand Jews—now transplanted from their ancient, slumbering villages in Poland, and the Ukraine, and Romania and Latvia and Lithuania. Taken out of their rag-tag clothes, their Old World beards and curls and wigs, and dressed up in bathing costumes and gaudy suits. And right beside them, he had no doubt, a thousand more peasants from their own savage pasts, and their own torpid villages. From Ireland and Sicily, and Africa and China, and all the other lands past human memory and knowledge.

What were they fleeing from, in such a hurry? From the past? From what they were?

And yet, it all continued. The same carnival of superstition. America should have been a new start; by its very nature, it should have put the lie to the old nationalities, the old myth of blood. Yet here it was—the same old nonsense, already starting up again. They flew their new flag everywhere, played endless martial airs and patriotic anthems—strutted about as proudly as any ancient nation. Soon, no doubt, they would have their own new "culture." The idiot god-machine, with no one in charge.

Freud sat down on the bench again, his back rigid. It was no good, he saw that now. No matter their reconciliation, he would not be able to count on his anointed gentile. The future was here, in this park full of mindless, sensational entertainments. Jung's poltergeists in the bookcase, his ancient skulls, and his new race would fit right in. The Cause—*his* cause, his psychology—would struggle on, backed by a few dedicated adherents, wherever they might be found—like all science, still no more than a tenuous breakwater against an ocean of mysticism and ignorance.

"Herr Doktor."

They had discovered him again, on his last bench. Jung's smiling face swam before him, his eyes slits behind the pince-nez.

"Herr Doktor, are you all right?" he asked solicitously.

"America is a mistake," Freud said slowly, looking at him meaningfully. "A gigantic mistake, it is true, but a mistake nonetheless."

He spotted her outside The Fighting Flames. Walking along quickly, purposefully, preoccupied—the way he remembered from when she was a little girl, as if she had somewhere important to go.

This time, he was sure, she did. He followed closely, invisibly, in his citizen's black suit, waving the goons back. Following her right up to Carroll Terry's dance hall, on Surf Avenue.

So this is what the great Socialist is come to

When last he had seen her she was wrestling with a whore, being hauled away in a Black Maria. Now she was hanging around cheap dance halls, waiting for gangsters. He told himself he wanted to see her face one more time when the deed was done—just to see that she knew, once and for all, that she was as bad as he was.

She went into the dance hall, and he waited for a few minutes outside, to make sure she wasn't coming right out again. When she didn't emerge he walked back to Whitey and Louie the Lump, and sent them around to keep an eye on the back entrance.

"When do we come in?" Whitey wanted to know.

"You don't. Just shoot the son of a bitch if you see him come out the back. But you won't. This will only take a minute."

He walked on into the dance hall. The first floor was dark, and nearly deserted, the table and stage empty. There was just a bar with a couple of midday drunks slouched over their short beers. He peered back into the interior—and caught a glimpse of a woman's dress and boot, ascending the stairs to the second floor.

Gyp followed deliberately, gripping the handle of his Iver-Johnson, moving it to his outside coat pocket. He reached the top of the stairs and looked around the second-floor dining room, which was nearly as deserted, nearly as dark as the bar downstairs. He took his time, working his finger around the trigger as he stared calmly into the gloomy room.

There she was: his sister. She sat at a table for two in the far corner of the room—all by herself. He relaxed, loosening his grip around the Iver-Johnson. So she was still waiting for him. He only wondered what he should do next. Go over to her? Just for the pleasure of watching her face, maybe seeing her beg for his life? Or just do the simplest thing: Walk back downstairs and wait at the bar, pick him off when he came in as easily as knocking off one of the bobbing tin ducks in the shooting galleries.

He looked over at Esse, thinking over his choices—and as he did he noticed that she seemed to be looking right back at him and smiling. He frowned, thinking he must be seeing wrong, it must be a trick of the shadows across the immense dining room, for even if she did see him, why would she be smiling? He was trying to figure this out when he heard a small click, just behind his right ear, and he was truly surprised for the first time since that shovel had come down on his scalp.

"Hello, Kid," he said slowly—fingers digging frantically into his coat pocket. But the Kid was quicker—one hand plunging confidently into the right-hand pocket where he always kept his gun, while the other kept the pistol leveled just behind his ear.

" 'Zat it? That better be the only one."

The voice behind him trying to sound tough, and ruthless, but falling a little short.

" 'Fraid so," he admitted—which happened to be the truth, but Gyp let it sound as unconvincing as possible.

"It better be," Kid said, giving him a rough little shove forward—confirming that he was afraid to really frisk him.

His sister had got up from her chair in the corner and came toward them now, a small grim smile on her face. Behind her, Gyp could see the waiters and the tourists scrambling for the stairs, trying to take refuge under the tables. Kid kept walking him toward the windows, holding both guns steady, not giving him any opening yet.

"Hello, Esse," he said as she approached—then he executed a neat little pirouette, facing Kid but still moving back, away from the gun, before Kid could pull the trigger.

If he'd had another iron, even a knife, he might have gone for him, or tried using his sister for a shield. But as it was, Gyp kept backing up, ascertaining that there were no other doors, no other stairs, moving toward the large bank of windows that fronted along Surf Avenue.

"Whatsa matter?" he goaded Kid. "Hard to kill somebody when the lights are on?"

Kid kept walking after him, holding both guns steady on him, his face uncertain.

"Or is it *her*? That bitch—that *whore*!" he spat out. "Did she make you that weak in the head?"

"Do it," Esse said, her voice sudden and loud in the still room.

"What?"

"Go ahead an' do it. Go ahead and give him what he wants."

"God, Esse," Lazar laughed, his back against the window now. "Some Socialist you turned out to be."

"Go ahead. If you won't do it, I will," she said—grabbing the Iver-Johnson out of Kid's left hand, pointing it at her brother. She steadied it with both hands, but he saw there was no fear in her face, only a steady determination.

"You're no better than me, you know that?" he told her, goading her, trying to get her to do it—to do *something,* as

600

the red rage foamed up before him.

"You're no goddamned better than I am!" he yelled.

The windows behind him dissolved in a shower of glass. Gyp dived out after them, backwards, deafened by the report from the Iver-Johnson, wriggling like a hooked fish as he careened down the two stories to the ground. He struggled up to his feet just in time to see them running out the front door, dodging into the startled crowds. Cursing, he hurried around to the back of the dance hall—and met Whitey and Louie coming toward him, abandoning their post.

"Gimme an iron!" he barked at them, his ears still ringing.

Gyp ran down Surf Avenue in the direction Kid and Esse had gone, the others close behind. One of his legs had been twisted in the fall, but he ignored it, moving as fast as he could now, scanning the crowd for any sign of them.

"There they go!"

Louie pointed toward the Hall of Mirrors—just in time for him to see a flash of them, a leg of Kid's ridiculous green-checkered suit disappearing into the fun house, down by the animal cages. Now he had them. It would be dark in there, Gyp knew, but there was light enough to shoot by, and it would be easy to slip out afterwards. Now he had them.

"Whitey, you go around the other side," he ordered, pointing at the Hall of Mirrors. "And *stay* there, this time."

Whitey ran off, and he turned to Louie.

"You come with me," he told him, pulling him back by the elephant's cage, behind the animal's huge, gray bulk, his eyes glued to the fun-house entrance.

"You gonna do him in there?" Louie the Lump stared at him.

"What's it look like?"

"An' her, too?"

He looked away, rolling a cigarette while he waited for

Whitey to get in place. A few more seconds, and he would go in. He took a deep, bracing puff, and glanced through the cage bars at the maddened elephant, its great yellow eye glaring out at him, feeling for the world through the end of its massive trunk—those obscene, grasping nostrils.

He checked the replacement gun Whitey had handed him, making sure everything was in order. That was just one more insult, he thought. One more interference. He would not be interfered with again.

The only thing he regretted, the only thing he regretted at all was that he wouldn't be able to see her face

"I don' know," Louie the Lump shook his head. "You sure you should do 'em right out here like dat? You could get fifteen months for it, easy."

"Fifteen months," Gyp snorted.

Now, he thought. *Now Whitey would be in place*

The long, inquiring trunk snaked out through the cage bars, out into the crisp, afternoon air. Gyp watched it idly at first—then was disgusted by its blind, hungry groping, the wet, yawning mouth he could just glimpse back in the shadows of the cage. He took another deep drag on his cigarette, then placed it carefully, mouth-end down, in one of the trunk's grasping nostrils.

Let him take a bite outta that

"Fifteen months—" Gyp turned back to Louie. There was an enraged trumpeting behind him, but he didn't bother to look back. He didn't see the trunk come whipping back after him faster than a snake, faster than he could have imagined—much too fast for Louie even to get out a warning but not so fast that Gyp couldn't finish his boast:

"—I can do that standin' on my head!"

68

ON THE BOARDWALK

This is how you kill an elephant.

They tried the carrots first. Buckets of carrots. Whole bushelfuls of carrots, and each one loaded with enough strychnine to kill a man but only intended to make her stand still.

She ate them. She ladled them into her great, pointed maw by the dozen, and after an hour of carrots she was still standing—still looking as mad and dangerous as ever, and the big holiday crowd was growing restless.

Next they tried sending in the trainers—one-armed Captain Jack, and Herman Weedom, and even Mademoiselle Aurora, to smooth her huge, rough shoulders with their hands, and whisper into her enormous ears. She only stomped her feet, and waved her trunk around their heads until they turned and ran for cover. After that they tried the police, wading in with their new blue coats and their nightsticks to clap the chains around her legs like they would slap cuffs on a pickpocket. She knocked them down like ninepins, slapped and tumbled them around the ring like vaudeville mayhem players.

Finally they sent in the pygmies—figuring, hell, that even if they weren't in the same weight class, at least it was their game. No one was sure if they had ever seen an elephant before, but they were troupers: racing around the beast, hooting and gesticulating, yelling at it in their strange heathen tongues until she was so distracted the roustabouts could slip in and knot a chain around one of her immense legs.

She broke it off like a thread, but there was another one. Then another, and another, until the thick black coils of iron held each of her legs in place. Another one weighing down that deadly trunk and even her tail, until she was as completely immobilized as her tin image, the hotel down the beach. They soaked her with fire hoses, and wrapped the cables around her hide—smooth black rubber lines, bright copper wires sticking out of the ends like a bagful of eels.

Then they stepped back to see the show.

The Wizard of Menlo Park himself stood on the platform above the impatient crowd, tolerating the photographers' flashes all around him.

"This will prove again that Westinghouse's alternating current is too lethal for household use," he told the ladies and gentlemen of the press in his loud, odd, deaf man's voice, wispy white hair blowing in the crisp fall breeze.

—the old man still fighting that fight, even though it had been lost years ago. He shook hands with his former apprentice for the cameras: Dr. Poole, drawn away from his egg-white enamel engines and his gold oil cups for the occasion. Smiling sheepishly under his necromancer's cap, with the stars and crescent moons that Brinckerhoff had insisted that he wear—smiling for the Wizard despite the smell of Kemmler's roasting flesh still in his nostrils, the dogs and cats of West Orange frying on a tin sheet, while little boys bobbed up and down outside the windows.

"This will prove that I was right—"

The cameras clicked wildly.

"Professah, can we get one a you wit' de elephant?"

She must have known it was coming: The crowd gone still with anticipation. The workmen stepping back as quickly and gingerly as cats. For all they denied it later—claiming she was just a dumb beast who never knew what hit her.

You could see it in the great, unblinking eyes, yellow with hatred and bile. Knowing, and hating, and staring at me as the moving picture cameras began to roll, and the Wizard's hand went up, and I pranced out in front of the crowd.

Someone noticed a battered, dog-eared book sticking out of the great man's coat pocket: *Ragged Dick*.

"Great stuff for boys," he quacked at the reporters. "It happened like that for me, you know——"

——though they knew every detail of his life; every schoolchild in America knew the story of the penniless boy, selling notions and candies and newspapers car to car on the train——

"I saved the stationmaster's son from getting run over by the express. Gave me a job, and a car to work on my experiments, and that was all I needed to rise——"

The band struck up the overture from *Aïda*, the favorite opera of the ghetto—the opera of elephants—and the crowd grew quiet. The Wizard went over the controls, setting the last fuses. All that remained was for someone to go out and pull the gigantic, ornamental prop switch, set up for the benefit of the restive holiday crowd.

"I can't watch it. What a horrible thing to do!"

Out on the periphery of the crowd, Esther strolled arm-in-arm with Kid—now wearing a respectable, somber, citizen's suit. She put a hand on his shoulder, and they walked away, out along the boardwalk in the clean fall air—even though he was dying with curiosity.

The rides kept running in the three vast parks, all of them filled with customers, still humming and spinning and whirring like so many mechanical gears. The bathers still staggering out into the surf, clutching onto the guidelines, braving the chilly, late-season water. More crowds still coming, all the dry-goods clerks, and the ladies' maids, and the cigar rollers and the factory girls and the day laborers and the streetcar conductors—still pouring into the park with each train, and trolley, and excursion boat.

There was something for everybody at Coney Island.

All it required was a fool, a freak—a dwarf in a harlequin's suit, to trip the switch and set off the spark.

I danced out before the big, eager holiday crowd, my face painted harlequin white.

I danced out—grinning evilly, watching the furious yellow eye of the elephant watching me, and knowing what was going to happen next.

Not knowing everything, of course: Not knowing that when the big, fake switch was pulled it would seem to the crowd like nothing had happened at first, even with ten thousand volts now pulsing through her body. Nor that eventually she would begin to twitch, ever so slightly, within the chains wound round and round her ankles. Or that the smoke would then begin to trickle out of her ears, and the great, moist yaw of her mouth, and the groping nostrils of her trunk. Or that finally, like an expertly cut tree, she would fall over suddenly, even quietly—as quietly as an elephant can fall—the great trunks of her legs toppling over, her convulsive, splitting muscles snapping every last layer of chain and cable, thick as they were, so that in her death throes she would be, at last, completely unchained. If only she could rise—

No, she did not know everything. After all, she was only an elephant.

She knew enough.

> Meet me tonight in Dreamland
> Under the silvery moon . . .
> Meet me tonight in Dreamland
> Sweet dreamy Dreamland
> There let my dreams come true

69

BIG TIM

He heard the nightingales in their silver birches, calling to each other across the moonlit backyard. It was the first warm night of spring, and that restless hour toward morning, when he found himself lying fully awake, unsure of where, or who, or what he was.

He had been up late playing cards with his keepers. Sullivan would play only for matchsticks—they were good fellows and he didn't want to take their money. Instead he had heaped up a great pyramid of the little wooden matchboxes before him.

"Jay-sus, Tim, but they said you was off yer head," Tommy Condon teased him, shaking his head in mock amazement.

"Any man who can play poker like that can at least be mayor," the other *bhoy*, whose name was Jack McGrath, snorted.

"Ah, yer flatterin' me, boys," he told them. "But any man who couldn't take you two right down to yer drawers in a rubber has not only lost his mind but his vital signs as well."

They were good boys, he liked them both. It had been like that throughout the winter, the three of them joshing gently back and forth, living quietly in the little house up in Eastchester. Brother Paddy and the rest had done all right by him; he had no complaints. There were plenty of books, and the food was good, and these two fine lads were always on hand, to see to his every need and entertain him when he wanted company.

"He's comin' along just fine," he'd heard Tommy Condon tell Paddy at the door when he left that afternoon. "I wouldn't be surprised if he wasn't back and about an' in his old place before the summer."

"Well, I don't know about that, but it's a comfort, after Florrie and Little Tim," Paddy had told him, shuffling a little uncomfortably in the doorway. "Sure, that's been tragedy enough for everyone, them both goin' stark ravin'. I don't know as there's any remedy for the curse, though."

Big Tim had heard all of it, sitting in the little nook under the stairs, and he thought it a balanced assessment of the situation. So Cousin Florrie and Little Tim had finally cracked up. That still left Paddy, though, and maybe with a little seasoning he and Dinny and Larry Mulligan could run the district, at least while he was away.

He had been away for a while. First there had been the asylum, then another house in the country; then Paddy had taken him to Europe for the cure.

That had been a time. He hadn't been over since he'd taken Nell, nearly twenty years before, but to his surprise and immense pleasure, he had found that he was known in all the great capitals of the Continent. Everywhere they went, sightseeing around the great cathedrals and the historical staircases, some of his countrymen had recognized Big Tim Sullivan. It had been just like the Bowery, they'd come up to shake his hand and tell him how often they had voted for him, and what good Democrats they were.

And so what if they all claimed to be down on their luck—when in fact he knew most of them for broken-down rummies and ne'er-do-wells, who would never have known luck in the first place long enough to hit it up for an Indian nickel. He had gathered them up as he had gone, carted them with him from spa to spa, and ancient site to ancient site, and finally crated them home, all at his own expense.

That was when the Wise Ones had started to really get frightened, the way he was passing out the boodle. He could hear them talking: it was one thing to grease the wheels, but he was handing out bills like they were calling cards.

He knew they didn't like it, but he couldn't help himself anymore, he *had* to give it away. And not just to the old boys from home, but to the beggars, the down-and-outs, the street musicians and the flower girls and the children, everywhere he went.

So what if they weren't from the Old Fourth Ward—so what if they weren't even Americans. They still needed it, didn't they? It was still up to him to look out for them, for if he didn't, after all, who would——

They hauled him back on the next boat—and ever since then Paddy had had him up at the little house with Tom and Jack. They were good boys, it was a good arrangement, nice and peaceful. They got him all the city papers, and kept him informed of the doings in town.

"Didja see about the plate Mrs. Becker put on Charlie's coffin?" Tommy asked him, his exuberant face betraying the flush he held in his hand.

"Yes."

"'*Here Lies Charles Becker—Murdered By Governor Whitman.*' Now ain't that a thing?"

"Yes." Big Tim smiled benignly, and drew to an inside straight.

"They're sayin' the governor's gonna make her take it off," Jack put in. "They're sayin' it's libel, an' the D.A.'ll put her in the Tombs unless it comes down."

"Libel? On her own husband's coffin?" Tommy scoffed. "Put a widow in jail for tellin' the truth?"

Why indeed? They had all ridden far enough on poor Charlie Becker. Whitman, the idjiot D.A., had indeed been elected governor, for his unflinching, incorruptible zeal in sticking every gangster in town in the Tombs until, one by one, they had "confessed" that it was Charlie Becker who had fingered poor Beansy. There was even talk of Whitman being nominated for president, God help the poor Republicans.

Mr. Murphy, meanwhile, had played the whole thing six ways to Sunday, as usual. He had pumped just enough money into Becker's defense fund to see that he kept clammed up—but not enough, as it were, to see that he was acquitted. When Roosevelt had come back from Europe and split the forces of Reform, both in the City and all across the country, the Grand Sachem's triumph was complete. Everything was confused, and the balance of power, once again, lay neatly in Tammany's paw—at least for the time being.

Sullivan liked hearing the stories, the stories from the City—as far away now as if they were from Vienna, or Madrid, or one of the other great capitals he had visited on the Continent. He tried to pump them for more, but Tommy and Jack had fallen asleep at their places, their mediocre cards still in their hands. They had been pulling slowly at a whiskey jug all evening, and now they snored contentedly in their chairs.

Big Tim pushed his own chair quietly away from the table, leaving his great pot of matchsticks where it was. He had only had tea himself. He felt quite awake, but he headed upstairs anyway, to his little room under the eaves. He had even fallen into a light, pleasant sleep—when he heard the nightingales calling from across the yard.

He found himself walking out in the bright moonlight, toward the birch grove. He didn't quite remember how he had got there, but then he often lost minutes, or hours, even whole days, now. They said it was natural, they said it was to be expected. He had gone out through the kitchen door, he remembered, leaving Tommy and Jack still dozing at the table.

Like Pilate's guards at the Tomb—

He wondered if they, too, would miss a resurrection, and tramped on into the little grove of trees.

For some reason, he realized, he had put on his good coat and top hat. Well, it was just as well, he figured. Too bad he could not come up with a sash to boot.

All around him now, in the trees, he could still hear the little birds and their soft, insistent call, though he could not see them. His eyesight wasn't what it used to be—though the moon was so bright tonight that he could see well enough to read a newspaper by it—if that were what he wanted, if he had not already wasted enough hours of his life scanning the columns of tiny newsprint, with their meaningless words scattered like horse manure.

It was such a fine night, he decided to go on with his stroll. There was a path that led out the backyard, down through the woods to something shiny—a river, he thought. He walked placidly on down. His groin didn't hurt so much anymore, not since the surgery, though it was still all bandaged up, and sore to the touch, and they said it didn't satisfy.

It was a fine night, an incomparable night, the moon

seeming to warm up everything in its path. It had been a night like this the first time he had ever won an election. Not a general election, or a primary, but something even more important: a clubhouse nomination to the state senate, from the Organization.

It had been touch-and-go. Even with Croker's backing, there had been plenty of competition for such a plum spot, and plenty of money on the table, and it wasn't clear right to the end who was going to take the day.

The night before, Sullivan had looked up some of the old folks, and got a little of the tongue. The election was to take place in the lavish new Wigwam on Fourteenth Street, with the voters passing between the candidates to put their ballots in the box. To make it fair, the candidates were supposed to wait back behind the rail, and refrain from making any last pitch for themselves.

But Big Tim had watched and waited, and whenever he spotted one of the old boys, the old braves, he would use the broken bit of the old tongue he had picked up.

"Remember the boy from home," he would call out to them in the Gaelic. *"Nach cuimhin leat an buachill on bhaile!"*

They couldn't stop him because they didn't even know what he was saying. And meanwhile the faces of the oldest voters glazed over with empathy, just to hear the words— just to hear the language they had not heard for a generation and had banished from their hearts.

It had been a walkover. The first of many. The first of so many good times.

He sat in his box at the Hesper Club, surrounded by judges and captains of industry. The Wise Ones were there, and Big Tom Foley, and Charlie Solomon, and Mr. Murphy. Watching the grand march of the Annual Timothy D. Sullivan Association Ball, down on the floor. Watching all the gangsters and gam-

blers, the cutthroats and the pickpockets and the confidence men and the ponces and the whores—all of his people, saluting him; parading happily through the bands, and the confetti, the wild, frenzied racket:

"Sullivan! Sullivan! A damned fine Irishman!"

He reached the bottom of the small ravine the path led to, and found it was not a river at all, but a rail bed. It was a very narrow gauge, an old branch of the Harlem line, the trees crowded so closely around that it barely seemed to make a disturbance in the thick underbrush. He walked along it like it was an old friend, recalling other good nights, other glorious victories.

Out in the snow, the line stretched for ten blocks. Eight thousand pairs of shoes they gave away that Christmas, right after the Panic, and eight thousand turkey dinners. And afterwards, after presiding over the whole thing, nodding and solemnly shaking their hands like some papal nuncio, he had walked around the corner and found them all squatting in the snow, swapping the new shoes back and forth. He hadn't even thought about sizes—and they hadn't asked. They had simply taken what was given, and gone around the corner to wriggle around in the snow, trying them on and swapping with each other. His people—American women, and children, and old men—squatting in the snow like peasants, not wishing to give offense to the mighty lord.

There had been all the Election Days, and all the grand, torchlight parades, and the brooms strapped to front stoops

in hopes of a Tammany sweep. There had been all the platforms in their red-white-and-blue bunting, and all the mindless speeches, and the great cheers.

He remembered the Sleeping Italians, during the year of the
great blizzard. They hired Italian road crews to dig out the rail
lines, so food and coal could get through to the city, and some
genius had hit upon the idea that they would work faster if they
had their native cuisine. Wheelbarrows full of lasagna and
spaghetti, Italian bread and chianti, had been carted down to
the Grand Central station. And of course after eating all that
the work crews had fallen into a deep and imperturbable sleep.
Frantic officials of the New York and Erie lines ran about, try-
ing to wake them up, but nothing could rouse them.

He remembered that night, his footsteps echoing through the
station. The yellow gas lamps burning low, the waiting room
silent save for the snoring and a stray man here or there, gently
strumming on a mandolin.

And when they awakened, after a couple of hours, they had
worked like piledrivers, clearing the ten-foot drifts off the rails
in no time. How little they required, and how hard they had
worked. A little food, a little rest. He had always wondered why
it couldn't be arranged, somehow, to do at least that little for
them, for all of them. He was sure there was a reason, though
he could not remember what it was.

Then there was the night they had found him, still wandering aimlessly around the East Side with the dead boy in his
arms. He just didn't know where to put the boy down once
he had picked him up, until they had taken him out of his
arms, and he had wandered away, walking all through the
night, out to Brooklyn, and Coney Island, where they finally rounded him up the next day.

After the asylum, and the hospital, they had traveled all over the Continent, and everywhere they went, in every one of the ancient capitals, there was someone who knew Big Tim. He took them all home, sailing into the great harbor, with all the boys hallooing from the rail, backs to the Green Lady, straining to see the Bowery.

He had taken Nell on the Grand Tour, too, years before, to see if they could make it up. He could still see her, smiling on deck, holding one hand on her broad hat—*No, no*, he realized, that was just after they were married, and took the excursion boat up the Hudson to Bear Mountain. She didn't smile much at all by the time he took her to Europe. It was to make it up to her, but she didn't care much for a man's things, she didn't much care for a man's thing, and what was he to do? He had scattered his seed; all through this great land of the people it would rise, and multiply——

Something rustled in the old leaves and the stickers near his feet, and he bent down to see what it was: some small rabbit, gone to ground, perhaps. But it was too subtle a disturbance to be that, he thought, and on bending down for closer inspection he saw that it was the rail—the narrow, steel rail, hard as a dagger, vibrating gently in the underbrush.

He got down on his knees, and put his ear against it, the way he'd read the Indians did, in the dime novels. Sure enough, he seemed to hear something coming. He squinted far down the track and spotted a single, round headlight moving briskly through the woods—though the moon was so bright any experienced engineer could have driven by its light alone.

He got down all the way, and laid across the track, his head resting against one rail, knees propped up over the other. How easy that skinny boy's knees had been to maneuver, even in death. He could have walked with him all night. He laid his head back against the rail, and took his hat off his head, and held it over his abdomen.

Well, I was going to bed I'll just bed down here

He wondered idly if it was a mortal sin, since there was no active hand involved. The rails vibrated more quickly under his head and knees. Out in the middle of the woods here, the train would not even blow its whistle; there was no need for it. Chances were they wouldn't see him, even with the moonlight. He had just laid down for a sleep, and the train had just come along, and there was no one the wiser.

It was a question best left for the theologians. All he knew was he wasn't going to get to the screaming, like Florrie and Little Tim. It was best left this way, out of sight and mind.

The rails began to gyrate madly.

Remember the boy from home!

70

TRICK THE DWARF

They sent Charlie Becker to the chair, and later that same fall the Grabber finally got to Spanish Louie. They found him lying on the sidewalk one morning in Twelfth Street, near Avenue A. There wasn't a mark on him, but nobody had any doubt it was the Grabber.

Just who the next of kin was, no one knew, and some of the boys thought they should inquire through the Mexican consulate or the Arizona Territory. But then, more or less to everyone's surprise, the body was claimed by an elderly Jewish haberdasher from Flatbush Avenue. He gave his son an Orthodox burial, in a storefront synagogue on Hester Street, while the young men lounged around smoking on the steps, and their fathers sat inside, fingering the ceremonial slits in their lapels.

The old reb stood out in the street, contemptuously watching the funeral scene:

What a sacrilege to honor such a momzer! Well, what can you expect? Anything's possible in America

He shuffled into the synagogue, to scrounge at the remnants of the funeral feast: the platters of sour cream and pot cheese, the plum brandy, and the herring and black bread.

Every day, he made the rounds of the storefront synagogues with his begging board, and he always picked up enough to get by: an apple, a piece of dried fish, a chunk of old bread. Even his old enemies from the controversy over the Grand Reb from Cracow gave something, to see him reduced to such a state.

Inside now, in the close, musty interior of the synagogue, he forgot for a moment the pot cheese and the thick chunks of black bread waiting in the back room. Instead, he sat down on a front bench and began to recite a prayer from his childhood, rocking slowly back and forth. He had spent his life in such close, darkened places, trying to comprehend the mind of God, and soon he forgot where he was. He kept rocking, as if in prayer, but singing instead an old song from Russia to himself:

> By the little brook
> By the little bridge
> Grass was growing . . .

The fire started in Hell Gate, while they were getting ready for the opening day of the season, on Easter weekend. Even that churlish Russian scribbler could not have written a better ending for it: Two workmen were trying to fix a short in the wiring, in the early morning hours of Black Saturday. There was a spark, some idiot knocked over a bucket of pitch, and then it was all over.

Before half an hour was up, Brinckerhoff's tower was a pillar of fire, visible all the way to the Bronx. Tired old Satan was finally consumed by his flames, toppling back into the wreckage with a grateful sigh and the fire went on, leaping swiftly over to Venice, and the Doge's Palace. It swept up Pike's Peak and the Oriental Scenic Railway, raced down the trellises of the Whirlwind roller coaster, gobbled up The Rough Rider in one great wave of fire.

Soon all of Dreamland was burning. The fire commissioner pulled the only double-nine alarm in the history of Brooklyn, but it was already too late. The pumpers and the hook-and-ladders responded from ten miles around, whole companies clanging across the Brooklyn Bridge, galloping down lonely Long Island roads—too late, too late.

The fire spread to Wormwood's Theater, where the educated chickens and anteaters, the monkeys and lemurs and trained pigs scampered for cover. The parrots and birds of paradise sailed screeching through the park, their tail feathers ablaze, tracing a brilliant path through the night before they, too, were consumed by the fire.

In Bostock's Circus, the great cats screamed and clawed at each other in their terror, biting and tearing at their bars. Captain Jack and his helpers wrestled most of them into their traveling cages, but the Black Prince—the beautiful black Nubian lion who had cost him his arm—bounded away down Surf Avenue and was lost. He ran after it, begging it to come back with tears in his voice, but it clambered up the parapets of Dublin Castle, and there it roared against the night, singed and terrified by the burning splinters that fell out of the sky, until a Brooklyn cop finally put it out of its misery with his revolver.

The fire rolled up to the gingerbread walls of The Little City. The alarm bells rang, the sirens sounded—just as they did every afternoon and evening, six shows a day—and our miniature fire department, the best-drilled fire department in the entire world—came racing out.

They worked with a cool and quiet grace, I had to give them

620

that much—hitching their horses, hooking up the hoses as swiftly and efficiently as any real fire company on the scene. They made a stand right under the wall of heat and flame, pouring water into the blaze that crested high above them. While behind them their wives and their children and all the other little citizens of The Little City worked with equally grim courage to wet down rooftops, and put out cinders, refusing to abandon their perfect, miniature town.

"My God, look at them!" a voice said behind me. "How they love the place!"

I turned to see Brinckerhoff, a salvaged bottle of gin gripped by the neck in one hand. I had wondered if he'd gone down with his tower, but here he was—his lemon-yellow linen suit singed a little 'round the edges, but otherwise none the worse for wear. I could see that he was still thinking, the gears of that relentless entrepreneur's mind still whirring as he watched the little firefighters:

"What courage! What tenacity! If only we could show them this—it's better than any show we ever put on! If we could bottle it, somehow."

"Bottle what?" I yelled back at him, my words all but lost in the roar of the fire that seemed to tower higher above them the more water they pumped into it. "Bottle what? Sheer desperation? Pure, pig-blind foolishness?"

The wind whipped up from the sea, showering the sparks down now on our tiny dream city faster than they could put them out. It devoured The Little City as I watched—slowly at first, step by step, then in one lunging, triumphant gulp, like some Feltman's diner wolfing down a plate of steamers. The people—*my* people—leaping and dashing out ahead of it, as fast as their little bodies would carry them. Left with absolutely nothing, now, not even the single trunks or traveling bags they had before, moving from town to town, sideshow to sideshow. Everything lost now, because they had chosen to try and make a stand.

Not me.

I was not about to contest anything with the City of Fire. I was going to get a few portables, at least—anything I could sell, or pawn, for cash money. I stuffed what I could from the doomed palace into a carpet bag—candleholders, gilt-edged china, a bottle of the best Madeira—and ran. At least I had something, and if it was not enough to last a lifetime, well then what was?

Just after three in the morning the great eagle tower of Dreamland caved in on itself, nothing more by then than an ashen hulk. The fire rampaged up and down the beach like a mad giant, stomping all the splendid plywood and plaster confections along the boardwalk—the flames, for once, released from their fixed and frozen courses. Cannibalizing the Fighting Flames—then, with one gigantic, orgiastic roar, taking Dr. Poole's enamel, egg-white powerhouse, with its gold oil cups and its gorgeous mosaic table.

It looked then as if the fire might consume everything on the island. Not only Dreamland, but also Luna Park and Steeplechase, and Feltman's and Stauch's, and the Tin Elephant, and the Centennial Tower, and all the shooting galleries, and the whorehouses and the flophouses, and the tattoo parlors and the clip joints and the oyster bars, all sheltering under their skirts like shanties against a castle wall. Until the whole island would be razed as flat as when the first Dutch sailors found it, a pestilential sandbar, overrun with mosquitoes and skittish brown rabbits.

The surf began to fill up with steamers and pleasure boats, yachts and trawlers and garbage barges—a motley flotilla of anything that could float, preparing to try and evacuate all of Coney if it came to that. It would have been something—a grand Götterdämmerung. Think of the movies they could have made! The postcards they could have printed up, the reenactments they could have produced on Coney itself, once it was rebuilt: the pleasure-loving masses, and the firemen, and animal trainers, and the freaks and the showmen—all wading out into the churning, boiling water, fighting past the barbed wire and the rain of burning splinters, under the hellish and unnatural light—

Reality is rarely so obliging. Instead, the winds shifted, the flames ran out of fodder. The fire puttered out at the edge of the Great Galveston Flood Exposition, peeling the paint, the picture of the tidal wave, right off the walls—but that last cosmic irony was the best it could manage. It expired there—saving Luna Park, and Steeplechase, and all the rest of the midway for their own inevitable infernos at some later date.

After it was all over—after the fire had burned itself out and Dreamland was safely leveled, and no longer any box-office threat—the great Tilyou, and Feltman, and all the other owners came over, one by one, and silently shook Brinckerhoff's hand.

"Don't worry," he told them—he told all the reporters, and the politicians, and the money men, with his usual, boozy self-confidence.

"Don't worry—Dreamland will rise again from the ashes, more brilliant and wonderful than ever."

The very next day he had a booth out, ten cents admission to see the smoking ruins—and I believe that given the chance he *would* have built it again. He would have built it over and over again, and let it burn down every five years or so, and built it still again—always bigger, and grander, and stuffed full of greater and greater marvels.

But after Big Tim was put away he couldn't get the money, and then the war came, and the movie palaces. The old Dreamland, the old Coney, seemed to recede further and further into the past, like a dream you had just the night before but can't quite remember by breakfast. They never put up anything like it again; they never put up anything more than another big sideshow hut, which they *called* Dreamland, and filled with freaks, and fakes, and vaudeville acts.

They replaced the diving elephants with pigs, and the incubator babies with cockroach races, and every year, everything seemed to get a little more tired, a little more seedy and dilapidated, as the public moved on to new wonders, and the parks slowly retreated under the gentle, relentless breezes of the sea. Until we came to live wholly in this world, where all the miracles, all the real spectacles, are locked safely away on a two-dimensional screen.

And as for the rest of it, who knows? You want an epilogue, but who knows where people go? They get swallowed up in the crowds, and all that is left is speculation.

Maybe Esther did get married, and settled down to churning out children in spite of herself. While he got a good position with the City, or made his fortune bottling celery tonic that tasted like old socks but which they always loved in the kosher dairy restaurants and the teahouses. Until they all got nice and fat, and moved into the apartment of their dreams, along the fine and spacious new streets of Brooklyn, or the Grand Concourse, up in the Bronx.

Or maybe they didn't. Maybe she went back to the Triangle, along with Sadie, to try to organize the scabs, and the green girls, and all the other yoks and fools and half-wits who didn't know how to do for themselves. The two of them working side by side on the long benches that ran all the way across the shop floor. Helping Sadie steady her lawn until she learned, the two of them exchanging a smile from time to time when they looked up, to see each other there—a little more worn, a little grayer every year. Sharing a cup of tea together during the fifteen-minute lunch break—

Like something from a movie—something she might see at the nickelodeon at Union Square: a heroic biography of an ordinary life, where the prince, or the big break, or the moment of truth never did quite arrive.

Or maybe she did become a traveling delegate: going town to town in the smoky Pullman parlors, a little sliver of excitement going through her, no matter how many times she had done it before. Inspiring the machine girls, and facing down the cheap goons, and the cockroach bosses. Speaking before the wealthy, concerned women at their teas and their literary societies—always half envying, half smiling at their limousines and their drawing rooms, their fine vases, and books, and silver tea services, their easy way around a salad plate—until finally, even that sliver of excitement was gone. Sitting on the edge of a worn quilt, bone-tired, alone in a dingy YWCA room. Not exactly the ending she had envisioned, perhaps, but still keeping that faith—keeping the faith of *one day,* one shining future, when she could sit out on the stoop of her porch on Orchard Street and see that decent world she had always craved.

Or maybe it was something in between. Maybe she stayed on. Maybe she married Kid, or moved in with him, and they lived as no one had ever lived before—a love based upon mutual respect, and understanding, and friendship. Maybe he respected her right to live any way she chose, but maybe the traveling delegate's job never did quite materialize, and she had to stay up in the Triangle.

Still trying to do the good work, to get the girls to listen, and care, and sign up with the union——until one early spring afternoon on the eighth floor, when the ash from some cutter's cigarette caught in one of the big scrap bins, full of cutouts that didn't quite fit into one pattern or another, waiting to be hauled away by the felt dealer.

The fine, thin lawn catching at once. The fire leaping up out of the bins, catching on to the little wisps of patterns. Skipping quicker than a thought across the room, from one pattern to another, strung above the cutters' desks. The men swatting at them too late, sending the burning lawn floating like fireflies across the room——until the whole burning line collapsed into the bins.

The machine girls already putting on their coats at the end of the half-day Saturday, not even aware of it yet. Just a few more minutes and they would have been out. Already making their way toward the stairs, singing one of the popular new dance-hall tunes:

> Every little movement has a meaning
>   all its own
> Every thought and feeling by some
>   posture can be shown

Mr. Bernstein, still cool and calm in his shirtsleeves, barking out orders to contain the blaze, trying to keep everyone moving toward the doors. But then the fire reached the barrel of machine oil kept right by the stairs door. Then the first women discovered that the fire doors were locked, just in case they were trying to steal a few pennies worth of lawn. Then——as if in a dream——one of the errand boys went to grab a fire hose and it fell apart in his hands.

Then some idiot, hurrying up with a bucket of water, opened the elevator doors and let the new air billow across the open shop floor—

And after that, of course, there was no stopping it: the men and women trampling each other to get to the stairs, beating on the elevator doors as they closed. The lines of women calmly making their way out onto the fire escape— only to have it tear away from the building with an awful noise, pitching them down into the alleyway below, pitching them through a greenhouse roof, impaling them on a cast-iron fence—

All across the Village they heard it. Mrs. Perkins, having tea with some friends, paused with the cup in her hand to hear the fire alarms going off, the running in the streets. Hurried to the scene with the rest of the neighborhood—all of Little Italy, and the Lower East Side, running over to see what was happening. The fire trucks rolling up—their ladders too short to reach beyond the sixth floor, their nets too weak to hold the leapers. The cops holding the crowds back—watching open-mouthed as the girls they had beaten just months before plunged to the ground.

One hundred forty-six people in fifteen minutes they counted it—that's all they could do—

One hundred forty-six women and girls and men in fifteen minutes. Impaled on the steel fence crashing through the green-house glass

Leaping from the windows At first they thought below they were burning piles of lawn being thrown from above Leaping from the windows, and the ledges, as the flames licked up at their legs falling with dull, awful plops along the sidewalk Falling right through the fire nets right through sidewalk through the basement deadlights Falling but not rising Falling but not som-

*ersaulting Falling, only, and laying still save for one woman—
one woman, the papers all reported, who fell right through a fire
net but then bounced up and walked Walked as if there were
nothing wrong with her, maybe weaving a little bit as if she'd
just come out of a saloon but walking like anyone else five, ten,
fifteen paces before she fell down, dead, just like that*

And maybe they panicked and fled with the rest. Maybe they
died huddled under a bench, a machine; or maybe they made
it up to the roof and safety, or down in one of the elevators
before they stopped running.

Or—maybe—Esther stood by the benches, calming the
younger girls, guiding them toward the door. Stopping their
panicky sobs, telling them to breathe. Putting out the cinders on their billowing dresses with her hands. Guiding
them out until there was no one left, save for the utterly hysterical and hopeless, sobbing quietly under the benches.
Staying at her post, guiding them all out until it was too late,
the fire had cut her off, and it was impossible even to see the
stairs for all the smoke.

It happened so quickly

She wasn't intending to be a martyr. That's not what she
was, after all; that's not what Clara would have wanted from
her. She was a person among people, there were people she
loved, and wanted to return to. It happened so quickly—*one
hundred forty-six in fifteen minutes*—so that by the time she
had the last one out and looked around to save herself it was
too late.

And did she turn then, toward the windows? Did she smile
with a small, bitter pride, thinking *Now I know At least now I
know that I could do it*—

Did she turn then to the window, thinking there might
still be a way out? After all, she was no martyr. After all,
who would have thought that the fire department could be

so idiotic as to not have a ladder that went over six stories in a city of skyscrapers? Who would have assumed that the City fathers would have been so busy gorging themselves that they could not have given even a passing thought to the public safety?

No one ever gives up, not completely. Would she have stepped to the windows, thinking there still might be hope—and looked down then, to see the crying, gaping crowds, looked down to see the insufficient ladders flailing futilely below, and the women ripping right through the nets. Looked down then—and known there was no chance?

Or would she still have held on to some hope?

The papers said at least one young woman, in final, democratic, socialist irony, pulled what money she had out of her pocket before jumping and scattered it to the crowds below—thereby ensuring that others besides the single stealthy thief would share in her misfortune. The papers said that a young man out on one of the ledges—obviously a real man—helped the girls jump to their deaths—that he held and steadied them, then lifted them out, and let them fall. And that then he held the last woman to him, and kissed her, before he let her fall, then jumped right after, so everyone assumed she was his fiancée.

An *unlikely* story, an all-too-perfect story, typical of the public press. And shouldn't the women have gotten to make this last choice, after all, to jump or not to jump—having had no other choices to make in the entirety of their short and miserable existences?

(How like a man, to drop a woman off a ledge and make it look like a romantic gesture!)

But just *say* he was there, when she stepped out of the window—

Stepping out on the ledge on an early spring day. Stepping out on the ledge on a perfect, early spring evening, with the trees just beginning to bloom, their green and pink buds covering the full ugliness of the tenements below. Looking down over the crooked streets of Little Italy, and the green of Washington Square, and the handsome Florentine clock tower across the park.

Looking all the way uptown, all the way up to the Palisades—the rest of the City stretching out so vast, so indifferent. Street after street full of people beyond the immediate commotion, striding along calmly, obliviously, walking on toward their own errands, their own lives, their own troubles.

Imagining *him* out there, Kid out there, somewhere, striding along the streets, savoring the City the way he did, eating up every moment. Did she think of him out there, enjoying himself, oblivious to what was going on even though he might have been only a few blocks away in the Village? Hearing the fire engines again, annoyed at their constant wail—another passing annoyance in a city full of them. Hearing the fire engines as he stopped by the open-air markets, stooping down to sniff at the pears and the apples. Stooping down to buy a fish, a piece of meat, a cabbage for their dinner. Stooping down, maybe to buy a flower for her—a real flower—from a passing girl. His head spinning with schemes to make them rich, to get them a better apartment—

Did she think of him, out there, and wish him well?

And did she notice *the real man*, there on the ledge—if he *was* there—when she stepped out on the ledge herself, at four o'clock in the afternoon of a perfect spring day? The man who was obviously a superior man, the newspapers said—his superior face pale and tear-stained. Did she smile to see him, and lift his face up to hers and kiss him—just a panic-stricken boy, not at all her *dybbuk* from Coney Island—

Oh, how she would have loved to have him there, her dream lover!

Did she kiss him once, as a poor substitute, with the flames already billowing out the window behind her, already licking up the folds of her long, black dress? Did she kiss him—on the late afternoon of a perfect spring day, and then step off the ledge of the ninth floor of the Triangle Shirtwaist Company?

Still not giving up completely, still trying to aim as best she could for the net, for the firemen scurrying hopelessly back and forth below like circus clowns. Still not giving up, even when she hit the net, and tore right through. Bouncing back up, just like the acrobats at Fighting Flames, and thinking *I did it Somehow I did it*—and actually walking five, ten, fifteen paces along the street before the gasping, open-mouthed cops and firemen, a little drunken smile playing across her face. Before she fell down.

Maybe. Maybe she did. And maybe Sadie, separated from her in the smoke, in the confusion—maybe Sadie banged and banged on the elevator doors until her fists ached. The stairs already jammed, the smoke cutting off everything and nobody coming back for her. Screaming for the elevator, *demanding* the elevator, refusing to accept that it would not be back. Refusing to die trapped up in some sweatshop fire-trap, the whole idea of it too stupid for words—too much of a dirty joke, to die for some cockroach garment boss after whoring herself on the streets all these years.

And when the elevator did not return, did she scream even louder—tugging and scratching at the metal doors, getting the other screaming, trapped women waiting there with her to pull, too? Until by sheer force they managed to pry them back—revealing only the open shaft, gaping below them. And when the others hesitated and wobbled on the brink, did she jump in—grabbing hold of the elevator cable, scraps of the company's precious lawn wound round and round her hands to cushion the burn, the electric shock she knew would come?

Did she jump right in, taking her best chance? Sliding down the cable until it burned right through the lawn. Holding on until she lost consciousness from the pain, and fell the rest of the way to the tin roof of the elevator, denting it with the impact of her body. Reviving hours later, half-drowned in the runoff from the fire hoses. Still on top of the broken elevator car where it was lodged in the basement, which was where the firemen found her late that night, soaked and freezing, with deep red creases across both her palms, looking mean and crazed as a wet cat but *alive* still *alive*——

And whether it made any difference at all——after all the special editions, with their shocking pictures of the flattened, dead bundles of women lying out on the sidewalk, and the drop-jawed cops and the burnt-out factory floors, and whether these sufficiently horrified the good citizens of the City——

——and whether it made any difference, after all the incensed speeches, and the inquests, and the futile lawsuits, and the hearings, and the inspections, and the careful new legislation arranged by Mrs. Perkins, and rammed through by Big Tim's boys, Bob and Al, up in the state legislature——

——and whether it made any difference, after the days of endless funerals through the Lower East Side, the hearses crossing at the intersections on Avenue C and Avenue A and Broome and Hester and Delancey and Division, so many that the mourners followed the wrong hearse sometimes in the confusion. After the final grand funeral procession, winding its way through the City streets on a freezing, rainy April day with the smell of smoke still in the air——the day when the City morgue gave up the last of its dead, the last seven coffins, containing bodies of the women no one could identify and no one would claim plus an eighth, grisly box containing all the dismembered, charred pieces scooped up at the site. The enormous, silent, gloomy crowds, huddled under umbrellas along the sidewalk the working girls walking shivering bareheaded behind the hearses the working girls looking up from their machines staring down from their firetrap lofts the families in their home sweatshops waving handkerchiefs out the windows of their tenements as the solemn mourners passed.

Converging finally before the burnt-out factory soon to be reopened under the same management. Converging on the park at Washington Square, the men the women the mothers with babes in arms—wearing the little white badges reading WE MOURN OUR LOSS carrying the long banners reading WE DEMAND FIRE PROTECTION—converging on the little green swath of trees littered with monuments to great men. Where, when the sinuous, black streams of humanity finally merged, there arose spontaneously a long, piercing, inchoate, feminine cry of grief like nothing ever heard before or since in the entire City, not even when all the Germans drowned—

—and whether all that finally made a difference, and led to Reform, and the whole, marvelous, bountiful present we enjoy right now as opposed to the dismal and long-ago past—whether all that came to pass—well, that, as they say, is another story.

71

TRICK THE DWARF

"And that's all?" Yolanda, the Amazon Queen asked.

"That's all."

She nodded, satisfied, working on a lump of betel nut in her cheek, skin the color and texture of a well-used saddle.

"Time to get back."

It was fully dark on the ruined pier. Below them, along the sea, the City of Fire had come to life, and they could make out the inevitable evening crowds, beginning to pour out of the subway and the express trains and the trolleys.

They drifted back toward their booths, and their sideshows: Yolanda, and Nanook the Esquimau who was really a woman, and Ota Benga the Pygmy, who was not really a pygmy at all but an out-of-work piano player from St. Louis—not that it mattered in this City, where even the names of the freaks and the gangsters were repeated over and over again.

Trick the Dwarf trailed after them, beginning to hurry as he heard the music start to rise, the murmur of the crowds increase. Not quite so many people, perhaps, as in the old days; they had other entertainments now, all the movie palaces, all the new cars, and their gin flasks.

He had a longer walk now, all the way back to Steeplechase—and then there was his costume to get into, and his face to put on: the mad harlequin's face, leering and jeering as he chased the customers across the blowholes, swatting at all the tall legs with his cattle prod. Chasing them all across the stage with as little dignity as he could provide—while in the stands, everyone was laughing.

I know a story.

THE GREAT HEAD DOCTORS FROM VIENNA

The evening after their visit to Coney they left the City, and
took the night boat up to Fall River—beginning the long haul
to Worcester, and Clark University, pulling slowly out into the
Hudson, past the looming Palisades that reminded Freud so
much of the Danube—and then down to the sea.

After they made port it was still more long hours on the
train through this infuriatingly endless country. Past all
the neat little towns and farms of Massachusetts, until by
the time they reached Worcester they were thoroughly
exhausted.

They revived somewhat when they met President Hall at
the railroad station—an austere, white-bearded man, who
greeted them with an air of deep and solemn reverence. He
had a comfortable home, full of books and cigars, and a
jolly, plump, extraordinarily ugly wife, who called them her
boys and saw to their every need. She plied them with good
wine, and the best supper they had had in America, served
by two grave Negro servants in dinner jackets.

The following day the lectures began. The university was
new but well-endowed, its facilities simple and dignified,
and Freud thought it was a fitting platform. Everything
went off without a hitch. All the local papers covered the
lectures, and the Boston *Evening Transcript* even sent a

reporter out to interview Freud, and Jung kept his promise, introducing the shocking notion of childhood sexuality with the case of his own daughter, Agathli.

And when it was time for him to speak, when he walked out to the lectern, it was indeed the realization of an incredible, omnipotent daydream. All the terrible anxiety and turmoil of the preceding weeks fell away. Not even the presence of that little *ekel* Stern could spoil it. Looking out over the room, he saw there before him the best minds in all the fields of science and education, and history and anthropology, and mathematics and philosophy and—psychology. All of them, dressed up in their regal academic robes and mortarboards, applauding thunderously for him—for *the Cause*.

And afterwards, when he received his honorary degree, the applause was even greater. One particular woman, short and plump and voluptuous, even stayed the whole week. She sat in the front row, listening avidly—dressed in a white dress with a dramatic rose at the belt, a pair of startlingly intelligent eyes behind her rimless glasses. She jumped up after every lecture, applauding ferociously and peppering him with questions. These, too, were quite intelligent, and Freud would have been intrigued to meet her, but his American colleagues assured him that she was a dangerous anarchist, and after each lecture they formed a protective cordon around him—a phalanx of the stately, learned men in their academic robes, slowly shuffling him away from the inquisitive little woman.

By the end of the week he was exhausted again—sustained as he had been on the ongoing exhilaration of the lectures, the long, invigorating talks afterwards with so many great men of science. After their work was done, he was glad to let Brill lead them on a further excursion, off to Niagara Falls, and then into Canada, where he filled out a postcard for his daughter Sophie, and Brill wrote one to Mrs. Brill, which they all signed: BEST FROM ABE, FREUD, FERENCZI, JUNG.

They traveled on, to a little camp near Lake Placid that one of his new American admirers had loaned them. It was just a rough set of converted farm buildings on a rocky, barely cleared patch of ground, but Freud found it idyllic. There were walking trails through the woods, and all around them loomed the majestic, tree-covered peaks of the Adirondacks, and he and Ferenczi made a great joke out of the fact that the house where all the psychoanalysts were lodged was named *The Chatterbox*.

Jung professed not to be amused. A certain, permanent coolness had settled over their relations. Things had stayed patched up in Worcester—thanks to Jung's sacrifice of his daughter—yet even this had backfired. Jung was hinting now that he had gone against his own principles to support him—that there might be certain other nonsexual, *spiritual* aspects of childhood development.

Freud had refrained, for the moment, from asking if Jung really meant *cultural* aspects. That boil would have to be lanced once and for all when they got back across the other side. He was not looking forward to it, but if it had to be, it had to be, he resigned himself. Another gentile—a real man of science—could always be found to lead the Cause forward.

For now, he tried to put it all out of his mind and simply relax, the way he always liked to after such sustained periods of work. In the absence of any civilized cafe, he took up his other main hobby—scouring the woods for new and unfamiliar species of local mushrooms. The air was clean and invigorating, and Freud tried not to think too hard of anything at all—not the strife to come, or the long journey home with Jung, or his anxieties over the Rat Man case—nothing at all but the beautiful daydream just behind him.

He had largely succeeded, when one day he came upon a small creature lying right across his trail. There was no blood, no visible marks of what might have caused its demise. It was as if it had just *stopped,* and right away, Freud knew what it must be. He whistled for his friends, and poked gently at the creature with his stick, but it was unmistakable:

A porcupine.

GLOSSARY

blood, no visible marks of what might have caused its

To live in New York a hundred years ago was to hear a dozen
different tongues every day on the street. I have tried to depict
one small corner of that experience. The following are words
and phrases with which the contemporary reader may be
unfamiliar. They are, as indicated, drawn mostly from either
Yiddish or Bowery gangland slang. The Yiddish spellings
tend to be rather subjective. This is inevitable, as Yiddish is,
after all, a language drawn from both German and Hebrew,
transliterated from the Hebrew, and spoken with different
inflections and accents in cities from Moscow to Los Angeles.
I have tried to use those spellings that seemed closest to their
usual, New York pronunciations. For the definitions, I am
deeply indebted to many sources but especially to Herbert
Asbury's *Gangs of New York* and Luc Sante's *Low Life* (as
regards the Bowery), and above all to Leo Rosten's *The Joys
of Yiddish*. I am also very grateful to David Rakoff for being
good enough to vet the following list.

A GOY BLEIBT A GOY: *Yiddish.* "A goy is still a goy," or
   "What can you expect from a gentile?"
AMERIKANERIN: *Yiddish.* An American, or in this case, a
   daughter of America. Often used as an admonishment.
APPOKOROS: *Yiddish.* An agnostic, atheist, or skeptic; one
   who has fallen away from the Jewish faith. More pre-
   cisely, it referred to a non-observant, highly
   Americanized Jew.

ARBEITER ZEITUNG: *Yiddish.* The leading radical Yiddish-language rival to *The Jewish Daily Forward*—for a while.

AUS: *Yiddish.* Out.

BABA: *Yiddish.* The neighborhood witch. A folk healer.

BALEBOOST(EH): *Yiddish.* An excellent homemaker, or bossy woman

BEGGERIN: *Yiddish.* Beggars, or layabouts.

BES MIDRASH: *Yiddish.* The "house of study," attached to the synagogue, where boys study for their *bar mitzvah*, and where Jewish men of all ages go to learn *Torah* and *Talmud.*

BHOYS: *Irish.* Boys, or more accurately, good old boys. The old gang.

BLIND PIG: *Bowery.* A back-alley bar, usually illegal. Also known as a *blind tiger.*

BLINTZ: *Yiddish.* A rolled-up pancake, rather like a crepe, usually filled with cottage cheese and smothered in sour cream.

BLOCK-AND-FALL JOINT: *Bowery.* A bar featuring bad or doctored liquor, where patrons will "get a shock, walk a block, and fall down."

BOOLY DOGS: *Bowery.* The police.

BOYCHIK: *Yiddish.* A boy. Used both affectionately and derisively.

BRAIN TICKLER: *Bowery.* An assassin.

BUBELEH: *Yiddish.* Literally, "little grandma," it is a term of affection used for "darling," "honey," "sweetheart," or "dear child," between family members or close friends.

BUBKES: *Yiddish.* Beans, and also "A whole lot of nothing!"

BULLY: *Bowery.* A homemade blackjack, usually consisting of a lump of lead tied up in a kerchief.

BUMMERKEHS: *Yiddish.* Bums, tramps. Also slatternly women.

BUNCO: *Bowery.* To scam one into something, the occupation of a "bunco artist," or con man.

CAP: *Bowery*. One's name.

CHACHEM: *Yiddish*. Literally a clever or wise person, but usually used sarcastically. Its closest equivalents might be "wiseguy" or "bub."

CHALLAH: *Yiddish*. A soft, braided egg bread, with a glazed crust.

CHASIR MARK: *Yiddish*. The "pig market" on Hester Street. So called because it was said that one could buy anything *but* a pig there.

CHUM TOW: *Chinese*. The small headrest on which opium users recline.

COCKROACH BOSS: *Bowery*. Usually the owner of a small garment shop, or a subcontractor.

COVE: *Bowery*. A man.

DOW: *Chinese*. In this context, an opium pipe bowl.

DOWNSTAIRSIKEHS: *Yiddish*. The downstairs neighbors.

DRECK: *Yiddish*. Garbage, crap.

DRESSKE: *Yiddish*. A dress.

DYBBUK: *Yiddish*. A demon, or demonically possessed person.

EKEL: *Yiddish*. A stinker; a repulsive person.

FABRENTE MAYDLAKH: *Yiddish*. The "fiery girls," who led The Uprising of the Twenty Thousand with their passionate speeches and undaunted courage.

FARPOTSHKET: *Yiddish*. Messed-up, sloppy. All bollixed up.

FARSHTINKENER: *Yiddish*. Stinking.

FINIFF: *Bowery*. A five-dollar bill.

FLATS: *Bowery*. A sucker—or, as Asbury puts it, "A man not acquainted with the tricks of rogues."

FLOG: *Bowery*. To malign.

FONFER: *Yiddish*. Literally, one who talks through his nose. A double-talker, a fake or braggart. A cheat.

FOOK YUEN: *Chinese*. "Fountain of Happiness." One of the most popular types of opium in New York at the turn of the century.

GAONIM: *Yiddish.* Refers to learned rabbis or heads of Talmudic academies. Literally (from the Hebrew), it means "geniuses," and is sometimes used sarcastically.

GEMARA: *Aramaic.* Literally, "to learn." One of the two main parts of the *Talmud,* it is a learned commentary on the other part, the *Mishnah*—and thereby an interpretation of the interpretation of the first five books of the Bible. Compiled in Palestinian and Babylonian academies between the second and fifth centuries A.D., it is largely in Aramaic, although it also contains considerable amounts of Hebrew.

GEVALT: *Yiddish.* An exclamation of disbelief or exaggeration, usually "*Oy gevalt!*"

GIRLCHIKS: *Yiddish.* Girls—used either sarcastically or as an endearment.

GOLD MEINE: *Yiddish.* "My gold," or "my golden one."

GOLD PLATED HOLIES: Political reformers.

GOLDINEH MEDINA: *Yiddish.* Literally, the "golden country," and widely used as a euphemism for America. Its alternative meaning, though, is "a fool's paradise."

GOLEM: *Yiddish.* A sort of Frankenstein's monster, invented by learned rabbis—according to legend—to shield the Jewish community from anti-Semitic onslaughts. As such, it also means a simpleton, a clod, or a slow-moving person.

GOO-GOOS: Political reformers—a derisive contraction of "good government" types.

GOOHS: *Bowery.* Prostitutes.

GONIFF: *Yiddish.* A thief.

GORNISHT MIT GORNISHT: *Yiddish.* "Nothing with nothing." Worthless.

GOTTENYU: *Yiddish.* "Dear God!"

GOYIM: *Yiddish.* Gentiles, or all non-Jews.

GOYISHE: *Yiddish.* Refers to gentile things, and also to alleged attributes of *goyim.* These could be both good and bad, as in *"goyishe kop"* or "gentile brains" (poor) and *"goyishe mazel"* or "gentile luck" (good)—and as opposed to *"yiddishe kop"* (good) and *"yiddishe mazel"* (bad).

GREENIE: Short for "greenhorn"—new, unassimilated American.

GROUND SWEAT: *Bowery.* A grave.

HACKUM: *Bowery.* A slasher, a bravado.

HAIMISHE: *Yiddish.* Homey, warm, unpretentious.

HERTZALLE MEINE: *Yiddish.* "My heart."

HIGHBINDERS: *Bowery.* Chinese.

HOKKING YOUR CHAINIK: *Yiddish.* Literally "striking a teakettle," it means to "pull your chain" or otherwise annoy one.

HOLIES: Political reformers.

HORSE'S NECK: A ginger ale with a lemon peel.

IDEA POT: *Bowery.* Head, or brain.

JINGLERS: *Bowery.* Money, particularly coins.

JURY-CHECKER: *Bowery.* A typical, Tammany make-work job. Jury-checkers were hired by the city to check up on citizens who had got out of jury duty, and make sure their excuses were valid. Al Smith worked for a time as a jury-checker.

KALLEH: *Yiddish.* A young bride, or married woman. Also a daughter-in-law.

KEROSENE CIRCUIT: A circuit of cheap theaters showing popular plays and vaudeville-like variety shows.

KIBBITZ: *Yiddish.* To interfere in, or give one's uninvited, expert commentary on a subject.

KINDERLE: *Yiddish.* Child, kid.

KNAYDL: *Yiddish.* "Dumpling." Usually an affectionate term for children, though sometimes used derisively.

KNISH: *Yiddish.* A dumpling, usually filled with groats (*kasha*), cheese, potatoes, or other treats.

KOCHLEFFL: *Yiddish.* Literally, the long wooden cooking spoon used to stir a pot, but also a live wire; an activist and organizer.

KOLYIKA: *Yiddish.* A crippled, sickly, or stupid person——but in this case, a misfit; in Leo Rosten's words, "An inept performer: a singer off-key, a pianist who hits wrong notes, a waiter who spills the soup." Also written as *kalikeh.*

KRAAL: *Afrikaans.* An enclosure for livestock, or a rural village with a stockade.

KURVEH: *Yiddish.* A prostitute.

LANDSMAN: *Yiddish.* A countryman. Or more specifically, someone from the same province, region, city, or *shtetl* back home. Jewish immigrants to America often formed *landsman*'s clubs, to provide members with insurance, financial aid, burial sites——and a social life.

LATKE: *Yiddish.* A potato pancake; served anytime, but especially to commemorate the *Chanukkah* holiday.

LI YUEN: *Chinese.* "Fountain of Beauty." A leading type of opium in New York at the turn of the century.

LOAFERIN: *Yiddish.* Loafers, no-accounts.

LOBBYGOW: *Bowery.* Someone who hangs around hotel lobbies, looking for the chance to run errands, procure women or liquor, and the like.

LOCH IN KOP: *Yiddish.* Hole in the head.

LOMDIM: *Yiddish.* "Learned men"——sometimes used sarcastically.

LUFTMENSCH: *Yiddish.* Literally, "air man." Can refer to a dreamer or an impractical person, a man with his head in the clouds——but in the late-nineteenth and early twentieth-century ghetto and *shtetl*, meant a man without an occupation; one who could not or would not make a living.

LUSHROLLER: *Bowery.* A thug who specializes in robbing drunks.

MABS: *Bowery.* Prostitutes.

MACHER: *Yiddish*. A powerful person, a big man—and usually one who throws his weight around. Known to be used derisively.

MAMA GAB: *Yiddish*. From *momme loschen*, or "mother tongue." That is to say, "Yiddish."

MAMALEH: *Yiddish*. Literally, "little mother," this is used as an endearment for female friends and family members of all ages and positions.

MASKILIM: *Yiddish*. Literally, "the enlightened ones." Originally applied to adherents of the eighteenth-century Jewish enlightment, the *Haskala*—but often used sarcastically.

MAZEL: *Yiddish*. Luck.

MEIN BEN YOCHID: *Yiddish*. My only son.

METSIEH: *Yiddish*. A bargain or find. Often used ironically.

MEZUZAH: *Hebrew*. A small, usually oblong container, fastened to the right of the doorjamb, on the front of Jewish homes. Inside are printed verses from Deuteronomy 6:4–9, 11:13–21, beginning with "Hear, O Israel, the Lord our God is one." It consecrates the home, and observant Jews touch their fingers to their lips and then to the *mezuzah* when they enter or leave.

MIESSE MESHINAH: *Yiddish*. A bad fate.

MIKVAH: *Yiddish*. A ritual bathhouse for women.

MINCHA: *Yiddish*. The daily late-afternoon prayer service in Judaism.

MIR HAT GETRAUMT: *German*. "A dream came to me."

MISHNAH: *Hebrew*. Literally "to study, to teach," it is the "Oral Law," the first part of the *Talmud*, the collective interpretation of the *Torah*, or "Written Law." Compiled over seven hundred years by the sages, scribes, and rabbis of Israel beginning in the fifth century B.C., it is a grand collection of ethical teachings, opinions, court decisions and, in Leo Rosten's description, "anecdotes, aphorisms, thumbnail biographies, philosophical treatises, and tiresome hair-splittings."

MITZVAH: *Yiddish*. A good deed; a divine command.

MIZRACH: *Yiddish*. A framed religious picture placed on the wall of a synagogue, religious school, or private home, to indicate the direction of Jerusalem——and hence in which direction one should pray. Literally, from the Hebrew for "east."

MOLLIES: *Bowery*. Women, and usually the friends of gangsters, as in "molls."

MOMZER: *Yiddish*. A literal and figurative bastard. An untrustworthy, impertinent, difficult——and usually very clever——individual.

NAFKEH: *Yiddish*. A prostitute.

NAYFISH: *Yiddish*. An innocent, a weakling——or a coward.

NEBACH: *Yiddish*. "The poor thing." A victim, or sad sack.

NEDDY: *Bowery*. A slung shot, or blackjack.

NER TAMID: *Yiddish*. The "everlasting light" of God—— represented in synagogues by oil lamps hung by the altar.

NU: *Yiddish*. An interrogative, as in "So?" or "What's up?"

ONGEPOTCHKET: *Yiddish*. All mixed up, slapped together.

OY: *Yiddish*. An exclamation, often expanded to *oy vay iz mir* (roughly, "Oh, woe!") or *oy gevalt!* (more or less, "Oh, good God!")

PAYEHS: *Yiddish*. The long side curls and sideburns worn by very Orthodox Jewish men and boys.

PEANUT POLITICIANS: *Bowery*. Small-time politicians, usually associated with Tammany Hall——though not as closely as they would like.

PHYLACTERIES: Two small leather boxes filled with strips of parchment containing bits of Old Testament scripture and worn strapped to the forehead and left arm by Conservative and Orthodox Jewish men during morning worship, save on the Sabbath and religious holidays. The straps are tied in seven knots.

PISH: *Yiddish*. Literally, to urinate. Hence, a *pisher* refers to a bed-wetter—or more generally, a "nobody," or a young whippersnapper.

PITSEL: *Yiddish*. A little piece, a morsel—often used to refer to a pregnancy, or an infant.

POP: *Bowery*. A pistol.

RABBIT SUCKERS: *Bowery*. Young, drunken sports, out on a toot—and thereby ripe for the taking.

REFORM: A term used to describe any and all of the myriad crusaders, from all lengths of the political spectrum, Socialist to Republican, who tried to reform Tammany Hall's own particular brand of city government. Often the reformers would try to work together in grand coalitions, which, until the advent of Fiorello La Guardia, enjoyed only fleeting success.

ROLL OUT THE VELVET: *Bowery*. To blab, or inform, "velvet" meaning "tongue."

ROOMERKEH: *Yiddish*. Roomer, or boarder.

SACHEM: *Bowery*. An Indian wise man or chief, it was adopted by Tammany Hall in its elaborate aping of Native American ceremony and titles. Tammany's foot soldiers were commonly referred to as its braves, the leaders as its sachems. Mr. Charles Murphy, the head of the entire organization, was officially the Grand Sachem.

SHABBOS: *Yiddish*. The Jewish sabbath, observed, from sundown Friday to sundown Saturday, with prayers.

SHABBOS GOY: *Yiddish*. A gentile recruited to perform certain chores around a Jewish home or synagogue forbidden to the observant on the Sabbath. These might include starting a fire, putting out candles, turning on a light switch, or ringing a doorbell.

SHADCHEN: *Yiddish*. Literally a marriage broker, it was used in the garment trades to indicate a subcontractor, or anyone else who "makes a match" between an employer and a worker.

SHAMMES: *Yiddish*. Literally the "servant" of a congregation—the sexton or caretaker of a synagogue. More colloquially, though, it refers to a flunky, a sycophant, or a stool pigeon.

SHANDE FOR THE GOYIM: *Yiddish*. "A shame before the gentiles." Someone who discredits all fellow Jews through his or her actions.

SHAYGETS: *Yiddish*. A male gentile. Usually derisive.

SHEYNE YIDN: *Yiddish*. Literally, "beautiful Jews," and used to describe dutiful and pious Jews. Also used sarcastically, though, to refer to the richest and most pretentious residents of the ghetto.

SHIVAH: *Yiddish*. The traditional seven days of intense mourning following a Jewish funeral. Friends and relatives "sit *shivah*" in the deceased's home, where they pray, mourn, and eulogize the dead.

SHLIMAZEL: *Yiddish*. An unlucky person, or born loser.

SHMATTE: *Yiddish*. A rag. Often used self-deprecatingly, to refer to an old dress or other garment.

SHMEER: *Yiddish*. To smear, or paint—but also to bribe, as in "greasing a palm."

SHOFAR: *Hebrew*. The ceremonial ram's horn, blown in the synagogue during the high holidays of Rosh Hashanah and Yom Kippur.

SHOHETIM: *Yiddish*. A ritual, kosher slaughtering house.

SHPREKL: *Yiddish*. A little sprinkle, or in this instance, a little nothing.

SHTARKEH: *Yiddish*. An enforcer, or strong-arm type. A tough guy.

SHTETL: *Yiddish*. The poor, isolated, rural villages and towns where most Eastern European Jews were forced to live up to the Holocaust.

SIMON PURES: Political reformers.

SKIN: *Bowery*. In this context, to cheat or con.

SLUNGSHOT: *Bowery*. A type of blackjack.

TALMUD: *Hebrew*. The massive, 63-book commentary and

interpretation of the first five books of the Bible—or the "Five Books of Moses"—compiled over a thousand years by a wide range of Jewish scholars. One of the world's great religious works, the *Talmud,* in Leo Rosten's words, "embraces everything from theology to contracts, cosmology to cosmetics, jurisprudence to etiquette, criminal law to diet, delusions, and drinking."

TEN-TWENTY-THIRTIES: Large popular theaters in cities and towns around the United States at the turn of the century, showing plays and variety shows. The name reflected the price of the seats, ranging from the cheapest, dime seats in the balconies, down to the best, thirty-cent seats by the stage.

TOCHIS: *Yiddish.* Bottom, or buttocks.

TOCHISES AFN TISH: *Yiddish.* Literally, "buttocks on the table," it is used to mean "Let's get down to business," or "Put up or shut up."

TOKHTER: *Yiddish.* Daughter.

TREIFE: *Yiddish.* From the Hebrew for "torn to pieces," it refers to any nonkosher food—and also to an untrustworthy or nonkosher person or enterprise.

TRIMMERS: *Bowery.* Thieving prostitutes.

TSITSER: *Yiddish.* A habitual kibbitzer.

UBERMENSCHEN: *German.* Supermen.

VENUS CURSE: *Bowery.* Venereal disease.

VITZER: *Yiddish.* A joker, a wiseguy. A smart-ass.

WHEEZER: *Bowery.* A joke, particularly an old joke.

YAHRTZEIT: *Yiddish.* The anniversary of someone's death, commemorated in Judaism with prayers and fasting, and with the burning of memorial lamps and candles.

YARMULKE: *Yiddish.* The skullcap worn by observant Jewish men as a way of showing respect by always covering one's head before God.

YEN GAH: *Chinese.* The little rack on which the opium pipe bowl is placed before and after it is smoked.

YEN HOCK: *Chinese.* An opium dipping needle.

YEN NGOW: *Chinese.* The tiny spoon used to scrape opium bowls.

YENTA: *Yiddish.* A gossipy, interfering woman, often a shrew or a vulgarian.

YENTZER: *Yiddish.* Literally, "one who copulates," and often used to describe a slut or a Lothario—but in this instance refers to its alternative definition of a crook or swindler.

YESHIVA BOCHER: *Yiddish.* A scholar from the *yeshiva,* or religious school. Beyond that, it means a shy, inexperienced, innocent young man.

YIDDISHE: *Yiddish.* Refers to all things Jewish. See *goyishe.*

YOK: *Yiddish.* An ox, a clumsy fool. Usually a new arrival from the old country.

ZEESER GOTTENYU: *Yiddish.* "Sweet God!"

ACKNOWLEDGMENTS,
AND A NOTE ON SOURCES

I have found that, as a rule, you can't beat reality; the best you can do is try to rearrange it. I have found this to be generally true as a writer, and particularly true in writing about the American past, where the facts often sound so novelistic that I was often at pains to make the reality sound even vaguely plausible.

The first obligation of historical fiction, like any other fiction, is to tell a good story—a real story, one that engages the reader. Its characters should walk and talk, lust and crave, disappoint and surprise. But this leads to another, inevitable question: What obligation does a writer of historical fiction have to the truth, that is, to the historical record? To me, this obligation is the same for any writer, whether the setting is historical or contemporary. That obligation is to what I would call an essential core of truth.

For the most part I have stuck close to the historical record, as best I could determine it. I have tried to depict as accurately as possible how one part of the world in America, circa 1910, looked and smelled and sounded. I have tried to show, as best as I understand it myself, how people of that world lived and died, what they dreamed of and aspired to, what they loathed and feared.

What I have felt bound above all to get right is human nature. That is, how people—actual historical personages and fictional characters alike—really thought and behaved, and not just how I would have wished them to act and think.

In some instances I have changed names and places, constructed composite characters and altered chronologies. The visit of Freud, Jung, and Ferenczi to America, for instance, actually took place in the summer of 1909, while both the Triangle Fire and the Dreamland fire occurred in the spring of 1911. I have, as well, changed the order in which certain events in the life of Freud—such as the tribute he received in the Prater, and his descent upon the psychoanalysts' congress—took place.

George McClellan had already passed from City Hall in favor of William Gaynor when the Herman Rosenthal affair reached its crescendo, and the resulting trials and execution of Rosenthal's killers, real and otherwise, took a few years more—by which time Big Tim Sullivan had also passed on. I have also (slightly) altered the timing of several cultural events in American history, such as the advent of Chaplin's Little Tramp and Mack Sennett's Keystone Kops, and the construction of New York's Municipal Building.

Readers who notice these—and others—are to be commended for their knowledge of American and New York history, but they should realize that such choices have been made intentionally. I hope that they will further amuse themselves sniffing out the real, unnamed, historical personages I have snuck into the narrative.

Of course, many of the characters in *Dreamland*, great and small—Freud and Jung, Kid Twist and Gyp the Blood—are real people. Others are purely fictional creations. And then there is Matthew Brinckerhoff, an amalgam of the great Coney Island entrepreneurs George Tilyou, Fred Thompson, Elmer Dundy, and Capt. Paul Boynton—all under the noble rubric of my brother-in-law.

Again, though, I have tried to explore essential, vital truths. The account of the Rosenthal murder herein, and the beginnings of Freud's break with Jung are, as far as I can determine, both accurate and not widely known. Much of the dialogue between the fathers of modern psychology, and the particulars of Freud's time in America, are verbatim as it has come down to us.

I have tried as well to capture the spirit of the age. Hence there are some passing homages to the coming of the modern in American life and letters—to Whitman, Melville, Eliot, Fitzgerald, Kafka, and others. I have also tried to put into words some of the more striking visual images of the time and place, to incorporate the photographs of Alfred Stieglitz and Edward Steichen and others, and the paintings of George Bellows and Edward Hopper and the Ashcan School.

In this endeavor, I have benefited from so many historical sources that it is hard to know where to begin. A few of the most outstanding in regard to Coney Island and a general overview of entertainment at the time include Richard Snow's fabulous collection of hand-colored picture postcards and text, *Coney Island Postcards*, and his wonderful narrative poem, *Funny Place*; Maxim Gorky's journalistic accounts of his visit to Coney; John F. Kasson's *Amusing the Million*, and David Nasaw's *Going Out*.

In depicting life in the Lower East Side and the needle trades, I relied primarily upon Annelise Orleck's *Common Sense and a Little Fire*; Leon Stein's *The Triangle Fire* and the fine collection he edited, *Out of the Sweatshop*; the Milton Hindus anthology, *The Old East Side* (particularly for its passage from Thomas Davidson's writings); Hutchins Hapgood's study, *The Spirit of the Ghetto*; Theresa Malkiel's *The Diary of a Shirtwaist Striker: A Story of the Shirtwaist Makers' Strike in New York*; the letters and papers of Pauline Newman; Dorothy Day's writings about prison life; Ronald Sandor's *The Downtown Jews*; Naomi Shepherd's *A Price Below Rubies*; Steven Fraser's *Labor Will*

Rule: Sidney Hillman and the Rise of American Labor; Rose Cohen's memoir, *Out of the Shadows*; and Jacob Riis's classic, *How the Other Half Lives*.

For gangland and the Bowery life, my primary sources were Luc Sante's *Low Life*; Herbert Asbury's *Gangs of New York*; Robert Lacey's *Little Man: Meyer Lansky and the Gangster Life*; and Albert Fried's *The Rise and Fall of the Jewish Gangster in America*. Andy Logan's meticulous research in *Against the Evidence* established what I believe to be the real circumstances behind the death of Herman Rosenthal—though few are aware of the truth to this day.

For Irish political life, I used Jack Beatty's superb biography *The Rascal King*; Olive E. Allen's *The Tiger: The Rise and Fall of Tammany Hall*; William V. Shannon's *The American Irish*; and William L. Riordon's immortal *Plunkitt of Tammany Hall*.

In regard to Freud and Jung, I have relied heavily on the many writings and biographies of the two great psychoanalysts, and also upon Dr. Saul Rosenzweig's eye-opening *Freud, Jung and Hall the King-Maker*, and on Frederic Morton's panorama of pre-World War I Vienna, *Thunder at Twilight*.

Three reference works have been invaluable: Kenneth T. Jackson's *The Encyclopedia of New York City*; Eric Homberger's *The Historical Atlas of New York City*; and, as noted in the glossary, Leo Rosten's *The Joys of Yiddish*.

Outstanding as all these works—and others—are, it was a source in an entirely different medium that was one of this work's chief inspirations. Ric Burns's incandescent documentary *Coney Island* is a masterpiece; a riveting history of the place, and a trove of astonishing pictures and films of its all-too-brief heyday. I was struck at once by such real-life incidents as the execution of an elephant – and the fact that men and women who lived in constant fear of seeing their tenements burn down around their heads would travel to

Coney Island to see the same thing as an entertainment. Burns's images combine with outstanding text by Richard Snow to provide a vibrant portrait of Coney, the people who went there, and the three great parks that rose along its sands.

Apart from all these works of nonfiction, I am deeply indebted to the many outstanding writers of novels and short stories from the time and place I am writing about. They provided me with an incomparable insight into the hearts and minds, the idioms and folkways of the Lower East Side. Their great contributions to American literature has been too long overlooked, and I have tried to pay small tributes to them throughout this book.

The works I have in mind are Abraham Cahan's *The Rise of David Levinsky* and *Yekl*; the many writings of Anzia Yezierska, including *Hungry Hearts, Red Ribbon on a White Horse, Bread Givers,* and *How I Found America*; Samuel Ornitz's *Allrightniks Row (Haunch, Paunch and Jowl)*; Charles Reznikoff's *By the Waters of Manhattan*; Michael Gold's *Jews Without Money*; and Henry Roth's *Call It Sleep*.

No matter how large his library, every writer is inspired and restored primarily by the people around him. With that in mind, I would like to thank first and foremost my wonderful wife, Ellen Abrams, for her unstinting support and encouragement. She has always believed in me, and has been my constant star.

Henry Dunow, of the Henry Dunow Literary Agency, is a rock in the best and the worst of times, and I cherish him with all my heart as both an agent and a friend. His assistant, Jennifer Carlson, was always cheerful and helpful in the face of mountains of photocopying, frantic phone calls, and general disaster.

My editor, Daniel Conaway, deserves much of the credit for the final shape which *Dreamland* assumed. His insights and ideas improved the book immeasurably, and I value him dearly as a friend. My publisher Marjorie Braman, believed in *Dreamland* from the beginning, and was instrumental in getting it published. Dan's assistant, Constance Chang, was also a tremendous help in both providing editorial comment and coordinating some of the production work.

I am very grateful for David Rakoff's enthusiastic support of *Dreamland* in HarperCollins, and for his vetting of my Yiddish, which saved me from several embarrassing mistakes. Leo Sorel had the patience and fortitude to trek all the way out to the current Coney Island, where he snapped a wonderful array of photography.

Melanie Thernstrom did me the great and typically generous service of introducing me to Henry. Richard Zacks and Christa Santangelo provided me with helpful information on Coney Island and Jung, respectively. Mary Deady of the Irish Consulate in New York got me through my complete ignorance of the Gaelic tongue.

Finally, I would like to thank my family, and all those who have given me their love, help, and support over the years, including Sharon Abrams, Matthew Brinckerhoff, Ann LaForge, Chris Spelman, Jack Hitt, Joan Greco, Richard Feeley, Marcie Weisberg, Gail Buckland, Susan and Dennis Holt, Steve Hubbell, Steve Sherrill, Paul Tough, Julie Just, Nathan Ward, Katie Calhoun, and Allen Barra.

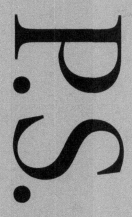

P.S.

Insights,
Interviews
& More...

About the author

About the book

Read on

Meet **Kevin Baker**

© Ellen Abrams

KEVIN BAKER was born in 1958 in Englewood, New Jersey. He grew up mainly in Rockport, Massachusetts. His career in writing began early: his first professional job (at age 13) was as a stringer covering school sports for the *Gloucester Daily Times.* After graduating from Rockport High School and from Columbia University with a degree in political science, Baker worked at a number of freelance and writing jobs, including writing political position papers for the Public Securities Association and answering letters for the Office of the Mayor of the City of New York. He then signed on as the chief historical researcher for Harold Evans's celebrated history of the twentieth century, *The American Century* (Knopf), which was a 1998 *New York Times* bestseller. In 1993 Baker published his first novel, *Sometimes You See It Coming,* based loosely on the legend of baseball great Ty Cobb. *Dreamland* is the first volume in his trilogy of historical novels set in New York. The second volume, *Paradise Alley,* was a *New York Times* Notable Book in 2002. The third volume, *Strivers Row,* will be published in February 2006. He is married and lives in New York City. ∾

Kevin Baker Leads a Tour of Coney Island

LET US BEGIN at the beginning. That is, the corner of Surf and Stillwell avenues, on Coney Island, the very tip of Brooklyn, New York. Just down the beach to the west was where, in 1609, Fitzgerald's Dutch sailors first touched "the fresh, green breast of the new world," and man came "face to face for the last time in history with something commensurate to his capacity for wonder." It was those sailors who gave the place its name, "Coney," coming from *konijn,* Dutch for the wild rabbits that once roamed through the dunes and sea grasses of the island (back when it really was an island, instead of a peninsula attached to Brooklyn and the rest of America by years of landfill).

But here is Nathan's Famous, which is not merely the only place in the known world where you can order chow mein on a bun but a New York institution, with an indissoluble tie to the world's first hot dog. Nathan's was founded in 1916, by Nathan Handwerker, who learned his trade down at Feltman's fabulous restaurant (which was a few blocks down the beach to the east). It is Coney's most inviolable article of faith that sometime between 1867 and 1874, Charles Feltman, a German immigrant who sold pies on the beach, got a wheelwright named Donovan to fix up a stove on his wagon, and the two men ate the world's very first red hots, at the corner of East New York and Howard avenues.

Now, if you actually believe that nobody thought to wrap a sausage in a piece of bread before Mr. Feltman, there is another piece of real estate here in Brooklyn that I would like to sell to you. But then, on Coney Island, the most accepted truths are usually fantasies, and the fantastic is usually true.

Let us retrace Mr. Feltman's steps on ▶

> 66 **It was those seventeenth-century Dutch sailors who gave the place its name, 'Coney,' coming from *konijn,* Dutch for the wild rabbits that once roamed through the dunes and sea grasses of the island.** 99

3

down toward the water. To the left, just across the street from Nathan's, was Henderson's Dance Hall and Restaurant—an enormous theatre that staged grand, Broadway-style spectaculars and musical reviews. The lot to the right, across the Bowery and behind Nathan's, was where Stauch's used to be—an even grander emporium, featuring four separate bars and a dance floor that could accommodate 3,000 couples. Louis Stauch, "a sharp, slight nervous man who dressed like a country deacon," came to Coney as a teenager in 1870, and never left the island for the next 25 years—not even to buy new suits or go on his honeymoon. "People gad about too much," he liked to say when anyone suggested he go on vacation, and after all, why should he have left the completely self-sufficient world he had created for himself at the center of America's most popular resort?

On to the boardwalk. It seems all but synonymous with Coney Island now, but in fact the boardwalk was not even built until 1923, after the golden age of Coney had already subsided. Before its advent, savvy entrepreneurs bought up plots of the beach and actually rolled barbed wire all the way out into the surf. They drove light towers and guidelines into the shallows, too, and charged for "Electric Bathing" at night.

Of course, Coney Island's first great attraction was the ocean and the relief it provided. The first hotel, the Coney Island House, was built in 1824. The island was connected to the mainland then by a shell road and celebrities such as P.T. Barnum and Daniel Webster summered here. After the Civil War, the New York & Sea Beach Line and the Iron Steamship Company carried rising middle-class families to huge new "Stick Style" hotels along Brighton and Manhattan and Oriental beaches (to the east), and there were hopes of making the whole area another Newport.

Instead, as Richard Snow wrote, Coney Island remained "a place of windy desolation." The popular entertainments included drinking and dancing around raging bonfires set on the beach. In 1870, a reporter stumbled upon a sign in the sand that read "Bathers Without Full Suits Positively Prohibited by Law"—a sign propped up over the rotting carcasses of a dog and a horse. Newport it wasn't.

The battle over just who Coney was for and who would be welcomed here was about to begin. It was a battle that would be fought primarily with weapons of mass entertainment, and is one that still goes on today.

At first, the new, respectable entertainments of Coney concentrated on sheer height, like the Parachute Jump (just a half-block or so on the left). One of the most familiar landmarks of Coney Island, it actually began life as part of the fabled 1939–40 World's Fair over in Flushing Meadows, and was moved only when the fair closed.

If you walk down the boardwalk a little more to the west, just past the

4

Parachute Jump, you will find yourself looking at the very pleasant minor-league ballpark built for the Brooklyn Cyclones (a Mets' farm team). A hundred years ago this was the site of the first real amusement park in America: the first, and last, of the three great parks from Coney Island's golden age—Steeplechase Park.

It was built by the greatest and most indigenous of the Coney showmen, George C. Tilyou, who got his start selling souvenir bottles of salt water and cigar boxes full of sand on the Coney beaches. In 1894 he tried to buy the gigantic new Ferris Wheel from the Chicago Exposition and have it moved here. His offer refused, he procured a wheel half the size, planted it out here in 1897, and, in a typical Coney ruse, put up a sign calling *it* the largest Ferris Wheel in the world.

Whatever its size, Tilyou's new wheel (and his new park) could be seen from 38 miles out to sea. And by the turn of the century, Coney Island in all its electrified splendor was the first thing that millions of immigrants pouring into Ellis Island would see (at least between May and October). They did not first glimpse the Statue of Liberty, so much farther up New York Harbor, but the glittering, spinning "City of Fire" that Coney was already fast becoming.

Tilyou, indefatigable and endlessly resourceful, was the new Coney's guiding spirit. When the first Steeplechase Park burned down in 1907 he built a new one—and wrapped it in a great glass trellis that shielded it against the elements (his rivals claimed that Tilyou went to church every Sunday to pray for rain). Presiding over it all was a grinning, endlessly repeated lunatic head. It would become the symbol of manic American fun for a century—the obvious archetype of *Mad* magazine's Alfred E. Newman, among many others. Under its tufted, devilish hair, its rows of immaculate, even teeth, and vacant, staring eyes was the perfect, soul-of-brevity advertising phrase: "STEEPLECHASE—FUNNY PLACE."

We will now head back the way we came, while you consider such an entertainment—but stop for just a moment and take in the empty, weed-strewn lot just to the right of the Cyclones' ballpark. Until a few years ago, it contained the remnants of the Thunderbolt roller coaster. Remember the scene from Woody Allen's movie *Annie Hall,* where the young Alvy Singer is living with his family in a house under a roller coaster? That was shot right here. The house was a real hotel, the Kensington, built in 1900. The coaster was built right over it in 1926, and incredibly enough coexisted with the hotel until the ride was shut down in 1983. It would go on to make perhaps the most beautiful ruin in the history of New York, enveloped in creeper vines, until Rudy Giuliani in typical authoritarian fashion had it peremptorily torn down one night. On Coney Island, even the ruins are ephemeral. ▶

Kevin Baker Leads a Tour of Coney Island *(continued)*

We will leave the boardwalk now to walk up Twelfth Street to Surf Avenue. On your left is Dick Zigun's "Sideshows by the Seashore" and Coney Island Museum. It was Zigun who started the Mermaid Parade— the good-natured debauch held here every year around the summer solstice. In the museum, you can still see some of the mechanical horses used on the Steeplechase ride. And then there are the sideshows. . . .

Just what is a sideshow? Or, more pressingly, what is entertainment? Here we arrive at another of the central questions that Coney has always posed and never really resolved: a battle between high and low culture.

At Zigun's you can find most of what we would find unobjectionable diversions today—sword swallowers, flame swallowers, and nail sitters. On the old Coney, you would have seen other things that we no longer tolerate at all as entertainment—freak shows, displays of aboriginal peoples, or worse. A popular game at Coney, as at most carnivals at the turn of the century, was a "Son of Ham" show in which contestants tried to hit the head of a black man with a baseball to win a Kewpie doll.

But let us consider a harder choice: the Infantorium, an exhibit at Luna Park put up by Martin A. Couney—the doctor who invented the incubator for premature babies. Dr. Couney could not get an established hospital to take a chance on his device for saving the lives of "preemies," so he set up shop here at Coney and at world's fairs around the country. He was no quack. The vast majority of the thousands of babies in his incubators were saved, and Dr. Couney never charged parents for their care. Instead, the public paid—a few cents to see a literal life-and-death struggle. (They also paid one of the barkers calling their attention to the Infantorium: a struggling, young immigrant from England named Archibald Leach, who would go on to make a bigger splash in show business under the name of Cary Grant.)

What is a freak show? What is cruelty in another time? At Dreamland park, you could find Midget City, a miniature town modeled after the medieval German city of Nuremberg. It was the actual home of three hundred midgets and dwarves. They lived there all year round with their own circus, music hall, police force, and fire department. The inhabitants of Midget City endured a fishbowl existence for the gawking, laughing crowds that was still better than how most of their compatriots lived at the time: in lesser circus sideshows or stuffed away in the attics and cellars of their shamed families.

What is cruelty—or what is cruelest? Samuel Gumpertz, the manager of Dreamland, specialized in live displays. At various times he brought some 3,800 indigenous people over to Coney—Africans and Eskimos, Hawaiians and (East) Indians, Bantoc tribesmen from the Philippines. Not that Coney Island wasn't an equal opportunity employer when it came to displaying human flesh. Another showman, soon after the conclusion of the Boer War, brought a pack of British and Boer veterans over to Coney. They would act out in pantomime the battles they had just fought for real. When public interest waned and the show went broke, many of the play soldiers decamped to become real-life mercenaries down in Latin America. Reality became fantasy, fantasy became reality. On Coney Island they kept looping back into each other like some cosmic carnival ride.

Time to take a breather from all these questions of human turpitude. Let us walk back on up to Surf Avenue and cross over to the north side of the street. Here you can see the lovingly restored Bishoff & Brienstein Carousell, complete with brass ring. Built in 1910 and imported to Coney in 1939, it is the last of the sumptuous, hand-painted German carousels that used to proliferate on the island. Take a ride, if you like, but then continue up Twelfth Street on the east (right-hand) side of the street.

Here on the site of this innocuous housing development was where it all began. This was once Sea Lion Park—the very first enclosed amusement park of any kind in the United States. It was opened in 1895 by Paul Boyton, an eccentric adventurer who became famous for crossing the Irish Sea in an inflatable wet suit. His park featured trained seals and sea lions, and that Ur-amusement park ride "Shoot-the-Chutes," a straight flume ride down into a man-made lake that you can still ride in most amusement parks today.

Right next to Boyton's park, at least when it first opened, was "Coney's Colossus"—a wooden, tin-roofed hotel built in the shape of an elephant. It was 150 feet high and contained 34 rooms, along with a cigar shop in one of the legs and an observatory in its howdah. The height of fashion at first, it eventually came to be filled with prostitutes before burning down in 1896.

"At night its eyes glowed yellow above the bathhouses and band shells and carousels," writes Richard Snow. "Complex, facetious, and a little sinister, it was an augury."

A park full of sea lions run by a man in a wet suit; an elephant-shaped hotel filled with whores—it was still nothing compared to what would rise on this same site: Luna Park.

Luna was the second and most spectacular of the three great amusement parks from Coney Island's golden age. Indeed, it was the most beautiful amusement park ever built anywhere—22 acres of spinning half-moons, giant wheels, and fantastic architecture. It was, as described by Alfred Bigelow Paine, ". . . an enchanted story-book land of trellises, columns, domes, minarets, lagoons, and lofty aerial flights. ▶

Kevin Baker Leads a Tour of Coney Island *(continued)*

And everywhere was life—a pageant of happy people; and everywhere was color—a wide harmony of orange and white and gold, under the cloudless blue."

It was built by Elmer "Skip" Dundy and Frederic Thompson. Despite all the moon imagery throughout the park, it was named for Dundy's sister. Dundy was the money man and Thompson the dreamy, alcoholic creator of enormous entertainments, multitudinous stage shows, and huge theatres (such as Manhattan's long-departed Hippodrome). Luna may have cost as much as $1 million, and before it opened on the night of May 16, 1903, its proprietors were so tapped that they spent the day running up and down the island borrowing $22 in change for the customers.

That first evening 43,000 customers poured through the gates. The change ran out and many of them were admitted for free, but it didn't matter. Luna Park was already a smash, and by the end of the season it had cleared $600,000 over the partners' original investment. Many of their employees were paid on a percentage basis—one of them netted a whopping $116,000 and promptly retired.

But the real triumph was Thompson's. He had set out to build a city fit for a perpetual charivari—to "depart from all set rules of architecture except those which have to do with proportion and good taste"—and he had succeeded brilliantly.

"A spirit of frolic must be manufactured, and it cannot dwell where straight lines, dignified columns, and conventional forms dominate," he insisted.

Manufactured fun—what an innately American concept! Indeed, part of Luna's appeal was a tale of mass production. The park had 1,500 workers, 200 horses, and 25 trained elephants. There were 1,214 separate towers, minarets, and spires, 70,000 palms and plants, and 10,000 flags. It would take $400,000 just to prepare Luna to reopen each season—along with eight boxcars full of paint and 720,000 linear feet of lumber.

But most of all there was light. Some 1.2 million separate lightbulbs, to be precise, in that pre-neon age—enough electricity to light up a contemporary city of 500,000. Luna Park specialized in technological marvels both real and fanciful. A typical ride was the "Trip to the Moon," during which (they were told) customers would "skim the cream from the Milky Way." The "flight" took place in a great green airship, featured recorded thunder and lightning, and ended with a show of more midgets and dwarves waving pieces of green cheese and singing popular songs with the word "moon" in the title.

But the big show was the electricity. The powerhouses at both Luna Park and Dreamland were exhibitions unto themselves—the one at Dreamland featured gorgeous gold and enamel instruments and murals that traced the history of science and electricity. At night the great parks became frozen necklaces of fire, turning the whole island into something that had never been seen before.

"The view of Luna Park . . . suggests a cemetery of fire, the tombs, turrets, and towers illuminated, and mortuary shafts of flame," wrote James Huneker. "Dreamland . . . stands a dazzling apparition for men on ships and steamers out at sea. Everything is fretted with fire. Fire delicately etches some fairy structure; fire outlines an Oriental gateway; fire runs like a musical scale through many octaves."

Even a visiting Maxim Gorky, who despised much of Coney, was awed: "Thousands of ruddy sparks glimmer in the darkness, limning in fine, sensitive outline on the black background of the sky, shapely towers of miraculous castles, palaces, and temples. Golden gossamer threads tremble in the air. They intertwine in transparent, flaming patterns, which flutter and melt away in love with their own beauty mirrored in the waters. Fabulous and beyond conceiving, ineffably beautiful, is this fiery scintillation."

What could be better? Aesthetically speaking, the makers of amusement parks should have stopped back in 1903, for they would never outdo Frederic Thompson. But this is America. More is always more and more is always possible. Let us zigzag back across Surf Avenue, toward Astroland, a rusting but doughty successor to Luna erected in 1963 during Coney Island's hard times. One cannot blame it too much for being a survivor—a latecomer that by today has lasted longer than most of Coney's earlier parks. In the spirit of Coney Island it features "Deno's Wonder Wheel," which claims to be the world's only combination Ferris Wheel and roller coaster (for the unnerving way the gondola cars slide forward at certain times). There is even a John Glenn "skyride" to the moon.

The reigning king of the Coney coasters, a few blocks on to the east along Surf Avenue, is the Cyclone. The Cyclone was built in 1927—an old-style, wooden coaster so famous that it lent its name to the ballclub that currently plays on the ruins of Steeplechase Park. Go have a ride on it, if you dare, and then continue east on Surf Avenue to the New York Aquarium.

Welcome to Dreamland. The aquarium has been here since the 1940s, when Robert Moses pushed it off the tip of Manhattan island, and today Coney's feral cats stalk its poor penguins. But it was on this site in 1904 that Dreamland, the last and the most grandiose of the three great Coney amusement parks, was erected.

Dreamland was a spectacle of both respectable, family entertainments and the more sordid public tastes. The park was expressly designed to ▶

9

provide instructional moral entertainment for customers of all ages, but it protested too much—starting with the huge marble frieze of a female "Creation" draped over its main entrance. Men used to come to stare at its gigantic, shapely, and unclad stone breasts.

Inside it was more of the same. Dreamland was huge, white, and overbearing. It cost $3.5 million to build and never really returned a profit on the investment, no doubt in part because of the ceaseless priggishness that characterized many of its exhibitions. There was an extremely treacly "Trip to Heaven," and a "Hellgate" in which a girl was plunged down into Hades for the sin of admiring herself in a new hat. ("Hell is very badly done," wrote Gorky, smirking over the emaciated, tubercular-looking performers who played the demons.)

But elsewhere there was plenty of life and real entertainment. Dreamland's central white tower, 375 feet high and festooned with golden eagles, did look very beautiful—particularly at twilight. It presided over a lagoon into which sitting trained elephants would go sliding down a water chute each day—a bizarre, hilarious sight.

There were many other animal acts at Dreamland, some of them nearly as strange. Consider "Wormwood's Animal Theatre—The Greatest Aggregation of Educated Animals on Earth," in which 125 trained chickens, monkeys, lemurs, and even anteaters performed a play called "The Pardon Came Too Late."

There was Bostock's circus, which featured a British lion tamer named Captain Jack Bonavita. A lion's swipe took off two of Captain Jack's fingers during one performance. His right arm subsequently became infected and had to be amputated. But in true stiff-upper-lip British fashion, each day while he was convalescing the captain would wheel his chair up to the offending lion's cage and stare down his nemesis. As soon as he was well enough, he returned to the ring with one arm—and ten lions.

And there was cruelty. In one of the last (and undoubtedly the worst and most crassly commercial) acts of Coney's gaudy age an elephant was electrocuted here at Dreamland in 1910. Topsy, the offending beast, had helped to build the park, but she had killed two men (one of whom had fed her a lighted cigarette). She was condemned to die before a large Sunday crowd and a moving picture camera. Her trainer refused to help the police and park guards chain the electrodes around her enormous feet, and a bushel of strychnine-laced carrots failed to calm her, but they finally pulled the switch anyway. There, on the surviving blurry black-and-white film, the animal still stands, begins to smoke, then falls over all at once like a great tree. So much for moral instruction.

Elsewhere Dreamland did feature many instructive tableaux on history, current events, and all sorts of disasters. There was a very good replica of the Doge's Palace from Venice—although inside, gondoliers pushed one along canals past rather cheesy Italian restaurants and bands. There were reenactments of the Fall of Pompeii, the Great Deep Rift Coal Mine, the Russo-Japanese War, the Battle of Manila Bay, the Galveston Flood, the earthquake in Messina, the explosion of Mont Pelee, and the Johnstown Flood.

In the era before television, before radio, or even newsreels, these recreations served as the closest experience to being there. The most popular tableau of all was a speculative one: Luna Park's "Great Naval Spectatorium"—later cynically relabeled "War Is Hell." Fulfilling the odd masochistic desire of New Yorkers even then to see their city struck down by catastrophe, ships from the combined model navies of Britain, France, Germany, and Spain sailed up the Hudson and reduced Manhattan to rubble. Then, to great applause, the American fleet would tardily emerge and sink all of the enemy dreadnoughts in turn.

Here was the immigrant experience in action—the customers of this now multiethnic nation vicariously displaying loyalty to their new home. An even more intriguing exhibition at Dreamland, "Fighting Flames," featured a perfect reproduction of a typical New York City tenement. The six-storey building was set afire several times a day. As many as three hundred performers took part in the show, leaping from the upper floors, balancing on window ledges, or crying piteously for help. Other actors came to the rescue with real fire engines and hoses and put out the fire as the crowd wildly applauded.

Who were the people who would come to see such an entertainment? Many of them lived with the constant danger of fire themselves in their own very real tenements and workplaces. The *General Slocum* fire and sinking, the deadliest disaster in New York history before 9/11, took place on the East River in 1904—the same year that "Fighting Flames" opened. The city's second worst disaster—the Triangle Shirtwaist Factory Fire— took place in 1911 (Dreamland's last year), and in the years between there was no shortage of deadly house, theatre, and sweatshop conflagrations in the real City of Fire. Why would people who might at any moment become victims of similar disasters themselves come to see such things?

The answer for many of the new Americans, I think, was that Coney Island and its manifold entertainments served as a vast screen on which they projected their best hopes and worst fears for the modern world that was rapidly emerging all around them. "If Paris is France," George Tilyou had prophesied, "then Coney Island, between June and September, is the world." Here they could come to see the world—in all of its technological wonders and inventions, its natural and manmade disasters, and its sheer, sordid, magnificent humanity. ▶

One last stop. A coda. Walk on back to the amusement park and the funhouse just beyond the Cyclone. Sometimes, somehow, the most unlikely trace of something beautiful remains when the rest of it has been expunged even from living memory. Finding such traces is another of the small urban joys that are fast vanishing from our society. But here it is. The lurid front of the funhouse before you now is much more vulgar, much flimsier, and much less grand and menacing than the facade of the old Dreamland "Hellgate." But the basic concept, that of a vast Satanic figure enfolding the building itself, remains.

It was at Hellgate, appropriately enough, that workmen preparing Dreamland for opening day in the spring of 1911 accidentally kicked a bucket of hot tar into the circuitry. Lightbulbs exploded, sparks flew, and within half an hour the mighty Dreamland tower was a pillar of fire visible all the way to Manhattan in the night sky. Some 33 fire companies from all over Brooklyn responded to the double-nine alarm—as did the fire brigade from Midget City, which fought the flames as valiantly as any of the other companies—but it was too late. As burning parrots dove through the air Captain Jack Bonavita and the other trainers rushed to save the panicked animals. They managed to rescue nine of the crazed lions but the tenth (a three-year-old called Black Prince) was too badly singed and terrified to heed their efforts. The police were forced to shoot it to death on top of a scenic railway called the "Rocky Road to Dublin."

By morning the park was gone—despite the best efforts of four hundred firefighters. There was immediate talk of rebuilding Dreamland and the other great parks with more permanent fire-resistant materials, but it was only talk. The park was an estimated $2.1-million-dollar loss and carried just $400,000 in insurance. It would reopen only as a small, rather shabby sideshow.

The great decline of Coney had begun and soon none of its founding geniuses would be left to halt it. Tilyou would be dead by 1914. Dundy had died in 1907 and Thompson was lost to his fantasies without his financial guidance. By 1919 he had lost his park, turned a fortune of $1.5 million into $664,000 in debt, and died in bankruptcy.

The biggest crowds were actually yet to come to Coney, carried by the subway. The very biggest was the estimated two million who descended on the beach on July 4, 1947, captured in a memorable Weegee photo. Coney Island became a homier place for a while, honeycombed with beach bungalows—a Riviera for the urban masses. But after World War II the masses had more money than they had ever seen before, and they began to go farther afield for their fun—to Jones Beach, Cape Cod, Hawaii, and Europe (and to those vast, dreary Coney imitations that Walt Disney would open in Florida and California).

An Excerpt from Kevin
Baker's Strivers Row

Coney, meanwhile, kept growing ever more squalid, dirtier, and more melancholy. Luna Park, damaged by a series of fires, was finally finished off in 1946. Steeplechase, the first of the great parks, tried to hang on a little longer. The proprietors even brought out stacks of television sets to try to lure the masses through their latest idol, remembering that tent movie theaters had once thrived on Coney. But TV was a very different thing altogether from an outdoor movie show, and the very presence of the sets meant only that the intruder was already within the gates. The televisions attracted only a few poor old ladies eager to watch the afternoon soaps, and one fall evening in 1964 Steeplechase's house calliope played a last rendition of the island's theme song, "After the Ball Is Over," and the park closed for good.

Over the years since, rumors of a new, rebuilt Coney have proliferated. Disney would come, or the city, or Donald Trump. But it was not to be and it will never be. The best (and the worst) that can be expected is a certain very mediated, corporate idea of fun—which might well be no improvement at all on the amiable honky-tonk ambience that now prevails. The idea of the amusement park—that of a place where everyone could go just to have fun—went out to everywhere from Coney Island, so that to this day in the most obscure corners of the country or the world you can still stumble across some local carnival called Steeplechase, or Luna Park, or Dreamland. But in the century of the videogame it is likely that the days of the amusement park are numbered. Enjoy what remains in the present and those reminders of the past that still reverberate around you. ❧

An Excerpt from Kevin Baker's *Strivers Row*

IN THIS FINAL INSTALLMENT to his bestselling and critically acclaimed *City of Fire* Trilogy, Kevin Baker tells the story of two young men (one a young Malcolm X) trying to find their way through the temptations and pitfalls of life in World War-II era Harlem. *Strivers Row* will be available in hardcover from HarperCollins in Winter 2006.

MALCOLM

He had his bag on before they hit the station. Ripping off the still soggy sandwich uniform, forcing his long legs through the gorgeous reet pleats as they pounded down the tracks along the Hudson. Barely noticing the wide, slow-moving river, the elegant silver bridge shimmering in the late-afternoon haze as they flashed by.

"Pe-ennnsylvania Station! *Pennsylvania* Station!" the conductor was hollering, in words that even he couldn't help make sound like a song.

Then they were bolting up into a world of vast steel spiderwebs, and large black-and-white clocks floating in the late afternoon sunlight pouring through the roof. Below the towering metal trellises the platform waiting benches were filled with young men, in uniform or without. Packed around the railing above them were girlfriends and wives and mothers, staring wistfully down, so close to the objects of their affection but separated by the closed train gates, not daring to call out lest they break their hearts or their own. The soldiers and soon-to-be soldiers sitting in their own glum silence, avoided their gaze, smoking or pacing around.

Then they were out in the cavernous main hall. The crowds there even thicker, their

> " They were bolting up into a world of vast steel spiderwebs, and large black-and-white clocks floating in the late afternoon sunlight pouring through the roof. "

quietest murmurs echoing off the marble walls, sitting or sleeping on their duffel bags and suitcases. Thousands of people, waiting alone together. They ran past a mother—a large, white woman with gray hair, and a simple, worn smock of a housedress. Her face was twisted up in undisguised agony, the tears running freely down her face, while her rough, thick hands twisted violently at the handle of her pocketbook. But Malcolm noticed that no one stopped to talk or console her, those men and women who walked by her looking annoyed, even angry, as they might pass someone with a contagious cough.

There was the sound of singing then, a beautiful woman's voice with a light Irish brogue descending from above. So beautiful and startling that he slid to a stop, his flat, sweet-potato shoes skidding on the smooth marble floor. He peered into the ropes of cigarette smoke, twisting up to the reaches of the vaulted, honeycombed ceiling far above him, trying to discern where the voice was coming from. Dizzied by the sheer scale and beauty of it, the vertiginous, marble columns and the lustrous amber walls—realizing only dimly that the lovely, Irish voice was not singing at all, merely reading out endless lists of departing trains, and their destinations.

"What you gawkin' at boy? Those Harlem frails ain't gonna wait forever!"

Sandy Thorne thumped him on the back, pushing him on.

"Oh, man, this *is* the place!" Malcolm exclaimed. "Just like I thought!"

"Mr. High Pockets, out on a bat!"

Piling into the cavernous backseat of a Checker, the others forcing Malcolm to sit facing them, like a little boy, on the lower, foldable jump seat.

"Ho, ho—stay there, Square! We got to look you over!"

"Got to make sure you're ready for the chippies uptown!"

The rest of the crew were giggling like schoolboys, shrugging off their kitchen uniforms in the cab. Struggling into suits that were more conservatively cut than Malcolm's but still sharp—light blues and greens, and creamy whites, with bright, skinny ties that gave him a pang of consternation.

"I thought you said this was a righteous town," he scoffed at them. "How'm I gonna be gunnin' the hens with you three togged like that?"

"Listen to Mr. Samuel D. Home," Paddy scoffed at him. "Son, you should latch onto the fact that this is the *Apple*."

"You gonna get conked up good, you don't mind us!"

Malcolm grinned back at them, feeling as if he would burst out of the cab.

"Hey, I'm mello as a cello, rippin' an' rompin', trippin' an' stompin'."

"Uh-huh. This is *Harlem,* son."

"*So where is it?!*" ▶

An Excerpt from Kevin Baker's *Strivers Row* *(continued)*

"Well, you watch now. Keep an eye out here, when we reach the Main Stem."

"Huh?"

"One-hunnert-twenny-fifth street, *son*."

"What for, what for?"

He peered avidly out the cab window, wondering if it had anything to do with women.

"Keep lookin'."

"For *what*?"

Suddenly there was color everywhere, as if someone had just switched the screen to Technicolor, like in *The Wizard of Oz,* which he had seen six times back in Michigan. Men wearing green, and yellow, and red sports shirts. Men wearing porkpie hats, and Panamas, and fedoras, men in white and lemon-lime and peach ice cream suits—even men wearing sharper zoots, he had to admit, than what he had on himself.

And *women.* He was sure that he had never seen so many beautiful women in his entire life. There were women everywhere, at least two for every man, not counting the clusters of soldiers and sailors gaping and gesturing at them on every street corner. Women wearing gold and ruby-red glass in their ears, and open-toed platform heels that made them sway with every step. Women in tight violet and red and blue print dresses, held up only by the thinnest of shoulder straps over their smooth, brown backs. Women striding up from the subways, stepping regally down from the trolleys and the trains, and women, everywhere he looked, strolling out of smoking storefronts, as if their smoldering presence had touched them off.

"What—they on fire?" Malcolm asked in bewilderment, squinting at the smoky little shops, the mysterious lettering in their windows that boasted *WE OFFER: The Apex—Poro—Nu Life—Hawaiian Beauty Systems—*

"Mm-hmm, you bet they are," the cabbie laughed up front. "Those Thursday girls, they always on fire! Even when they ain't gettin' their hair straightened—"

"You in luck, Nome," Lionel told him. "It's *Thursday.* Kitchen Mechanics' Night. All those maids an' mammies, an' calkeener broads—Friday's they one day off. They be gunnin' for *you* tonight."

"For real?"

" 'Course for real, Samuel D.!"

"Where you think we should take him first?" Willard asked the others. "Up the Savoy, beat out a few hoof rifts? Braddock's? The Elks? Take him to a buffet flat an' have a good laugh?"

"Nah, man. We gotta take him by Small's first."

"Yeah, *Small's. That's* the place to get him his first drink in Harlem!" ∾

16

Have You Read?

At the height of the Civil War, word spreads through the poorest quarters of New York City that a military draft is about to be implemented—a draft from which any rich man's son can buy an exemption. The outrage this inspires escalates into the worst urban conflagration in American history.

Down in the waterfront slum of Paradise Alley, three women—Deirdre Dolan O'Kane, Ruth Dove, and Maddy Boyle—struggle with their private fears as they wait for the storm to descend upon them. Deirdre, devastated by news that her husband Tom has been wounded at Gettysburg, must turn for comfort and aid to two women she has always judged as morally depraved—Ruth, married to an ex-slave, and Maddy, a hard-living prostitute.

Paradise Alley is an unforgettable portrait of three women who come together to protect their homes and families from the brutality of a city—and a nation—gone mad.

"Extraordinary. . . . A triumph."

—Geoffrey C. Ward,
New York Times Book Review

PARADISE ALLEY (unabridged audio cassette)

Listen to *Paradise Alley* in its entirety, as narrated by the author.

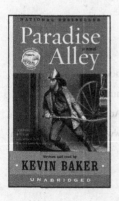

SOMETIMES YOU SEE IT COMING

John Barr is the kind of baseball player who isn't supposed to exist anymore. An all-around superstar, he makes his New York Mets team all but invincible. Yet Barr is a mystery, with no past, no friends, no women, and no interests outside of hitting a baseball. Not even Rapid Ricky Falls, a.k.a. "the Old Swizzlehead," his streetwise teammate, can get a handle on him. Neither can Ellie Jay, the sportswriter who wants to think she admires Barr's skill on the field but who also might be in love with a man who isn't really there.

Barr leads the Mets to one championship after another. Then chaos arrives in the form of new manager Charli Stanzi—a well-known psychopath—and the team falls apart. When Barr starts to unravel after receiving a note found in his dead mother's papers, Falls and Ellie Jay rush in to help . . . but only if he will let them. Hanging in the balance are his sanity, the World Series, and true love.

"A winner. . . . Put this one on the shelf with Bernard Malamud's The Natural." **—Time**